THE DINOSAUR FOUR

GEOFF JONES

Editorial Services by Sandstone Editing
www.SandStoneEditing.com

Cover Illustration by Dave Kang
www.DaveKang.4ormat.com

Marketing Support
www.IonogenMedia.com

ISBN-13: 978-1499677010
ISBN-10: 1499677014

For Mom and Dad

*Thank you for teaching me the love of stories
and for believing in me.*

THE DINOSAUR FOUR

I

THE CAFÉ

ONE

The ticking sound began while Lisa Danser counted out change at the register. *Dammit, what now?* Strange noises usually meant something was about to break. She had sunk every last dollar into The Daily Edition Café and could not afford any serious repairs. The sound made her think of a pilot light, but she couldn't remember anything in the store that used gas. *If it's a gas problem, won't the city take care of it?* Considering all the fees and taxes she paid, they better.

Tick Tick Tick.

She remembered the cases of wine in the back closet. If the city sent someone out, would they care about the alcohol on the premises? Lisa had recently applied for a liquor license, hoping to sell wine and cheese in the afternoon, when business was slow. She didn't think anyone would mind that she had alcohol in the building as long as she wasn't selling it, but she was not certain.

Tick Tick Tick Tick Tick.

Lisa looked over at her barista, Beth, who chatted away with a tall man in a UPS uniform while she tamped grounds in an espresso filter. The law said that Beth was old enough to sell wine, even though she was still a year away from being able to buy it.

The delivery man smiled at Beth. Attractive baristas sold more coffee and earned better tips. Lisa knew it was discriminatory, but she only hired cute young women. Beth fit the bill. She was thin, flirtatious, and bubbly.

"Good day today?" Beth asked as the espresso brewed.

"Good enough. Almost done with my route." The delivery man had a friendly face.

"Lotta boxes?"

"Not too many, but I still have one that's pretty large and has to go up three flights of stairs."

"Sorry." Beth turned off the espresso machine. "But it sounds to me like you are complaining that your *package* is too large." She shook her head and made a *tsk tsk* sound in mock contempt.

His eyes grew wide and his brown skin darkened as he blushed. Lisa froze for a moment, wondering if the girl had crossed a line, but the man broke out in warm laughter. Lisa's current customer, the woman waiting for her change, gave the UPS man a sidelong glance and pressed her lips together.

Lisa really wanted a classier establishment, where the staff did not sass the customers. She wanted to charge a little more and begin paying off her debts. Once the liquor license came through, Beth would need to act more professionally.

TICK TICK TICK TICK TICK.

Two men standing in line craned their heads, also looking for the source of the sound. At least she wasn't imagining things. This made Lisa feel better until she recognized one of them, a regular who always seemed on the verge of asking her out. If he ever actually did, she owed Beth ten dollars. She hoped he wouldn't. She did not know how she would answer him. The guy was decent looking and seemed nice enough, but he repeated the same conversation day after day.

The UPS man stopped chatting with Beth and looked from side to side as the noise grew louder.

Distracted, Lisa lost count of the bills in her hand. She began again. This earned a loud exhale from the woman waiting for her change. She wore a tailored blazer and designer jeans. Lisa could tell she would not be leaving a tip.

TICK TICK TICK TICK TICK TICK TICK.

The sound seemed to come from all around. No matter how she turned, Lisa could not pinpoint the source. "Ok, what *is* that?" She threw the money down in the register and looked out the windows on the front and left side of her café, hoping to spot something that might be causing the noise. As usual, she saw only the intersection of two streets right near the edge of downtown Denver. Bright light from the low morning sun reflected off the windows on the building across the street.

The woman in the blazer looked down at the register and up at Lisa. Her mouth formed a small round circle and she looked as if this was the first time in her life she had ever been ignored.

The hair on Lisa's neck stood on end as the ticking grew louder. Suddenly the noise ended with a pop. It felt as if all sound had been sucked out of the air.

Outside the plate glass windows, the city vanished.

TWO

The lights went out, plunging the room in darkness. Lisa screamed, emitting a small squeaky sound. Battery-powered emergency halogens came to life above the front door, providing enough light to see around the room, but not nearly enough to make up for what they had cost her. One of the men in line gasped, a high hitching sound. It was the regular, Lisa realized.

The building lurched to the left. Lisa had never been in an earthquake before, but this had to be what it felt like. Several people screamed now and Lisa wondered if her insurance covered earthquakes.

A chunk of plaster fell from the ceiling and hit Lisa's shoulder, ripping her sleeve and slicing shallow grooves in the skin of her arm. She sucked air through clenched teeth and rubbed the cut.

The building shifted again and a gust of air hit Lisa in the back as something large collapsed behind her. Two joggers sitting near the front of the store stood and moved toward the door. *Don't go out there*, Lisa thought. That was wrong, though, wasn't it? You were supposed to get outside during an earthquake. Yet for some reason it seemed like a terrible idea. Before the couple reached the door, one of the six-foot tall windows exploded in a crinkling blast. They threw up their arms to shield their heads, but most of the glass shattered outward.

"Shit!" shouted the older jogger. He dragged his girlfriend back to the center of the room.

The door flew open, slamming into the empty window frame, and a young man stumbled in. "I can't believe it. Everything is gone! Denver is *gone!*"

The man ran all the way to the back of the room and moved behind the counter next to Beth. She put her hands on her hips and gawked at him. "What the hell, dude? You want a job?"

He turned toward the front of the store and the emergency light shone on his face, revealing dozens of small cuts, each a red line of blood.

"What do you mean, gone?" asked the UPS man. "How is it *gone?*"

It dawned on Lisa why going outside seemed like bad idea. It wasn't just dark inside; it was dark out there as well. That made no sense. The sun had been up for half an hour.

Lisa stepped out from behind the counter, careful to close the register first. The bitch in the blazer seemed to have forgotten about her change and now clung to the back of the orange couch which separated the counter from the seating area up front.

Beth followed Lisa, grabbing her arm with two hands "Lisa, what's happening?" She was such a toucher. Lisa shrugged her off and walked to the wide window along the left wall. The view normally showed the hotel across the street, with the Starbucks in the lobby. A Starbucks, Lisa often noted, that did a fraction of the business her store brought in.

"Is everyone okay?" demanded the jogger. He wore running shorts that were too small for him and an angry expression. "Is anyone hurt?" No one answered.

Outside the window, Lisa saw only darkness.

She moved her head around to shift her perspective and realized it was not completely black out there. In the sky above, she saw stars. *Was there supposed to be an eclipse?* Below the window, she detected starlight reflecting off of something. Something moving.

"That looks like water," the delivery man said.

Somehow, in addition to an earthquake and an eclipse, they were also experiencing a flood. This was impossible. The only water nearby, Cherry Creek, was barely more than a trickle and flowed along the bottom of a canal fifteen feet below street level and two blocks away.

The room shifted again. It only moved a few inches, but it canted at the same time, spilling mugs from the shelves and more plaster from the ceiling. Lisa turned to see a large box containing an expensive espresso machine slide from a high shelf and land on the knee of an old woman sitting alone. The woman moaned, long and low, as she doubled over her leg. *That's going to be an insurance claim*, Lisa thought. She turned back to the window, her stomach rolling.

"Would somebody please tell me what the fuck is happening?" demanded the running shorts man. Again, he was ignored, but this time he huffed to express his disappointment. The other jogger, the young woman with the red pony-tail, cowered against him.

Lisa studied the dark shapes outside. She shielded her eyes from the glare of the emergency lights. Below the starry sky, she saw a jagged line that looked like the tops of trees. She wanted to ask, *is that a jungle out there?* but she didn't want to sound stupid. Instead, she let her jaw hang open and reached for the window, pointing.

Just before her finger touched the glass, a twenty-foot section of wall separated from the building and fell outward. The window exploded in a spider web of cracks as it hit the water and disappeared into the rushing current. The room filled with the sound of the flowing river.

The floor running along the now-missing wall cracked and dropped, as if on a hinge, leaving Lisa on a thirty-degree slope, a slide that led right down to the water. The ceiling above fell at the same time and a large chunk from upstairs slid past, landing with a splash. Water sprayed into the café and slickened the slanted floor.

Lisa slid down the slope, twisting and turning and reaching back for anything that could stop her. She felt like she was falling out of the world. Just as she opened her mouth to scream, she hit the water and went under.

THREE

Tim MacGregor watched as the woman washed away downstream. A wide river flowed from left to right where Chestnut Street had been moments earlier. Warm, humid air flooded the room. He couldn't understand how this was possible.

Another man who had been standing in line shouted "Lisa!" and fumbled off his black suit jacket.

How did he know her name? Tim wondered. It was easier to ponder their relationship than whatever was happening. Someone else had shouted that downtown Denver disappeared. That didn't seem right, though. The café had moved. It had *gone* somewhere. Tim had felt the shifting. *But how? Where?*

The man threw his jacket onto an empty table and backed up into the room, bumping the old woman who sat under the bookshelves. She whimpered and held her leg. Blood glistened between her fingers. Tim wondered what the man was doing and then realized that he was trying to get a running start.

The younger barista walked up to the crack in the floor and stared down at the river.

"Move it," ordered the man. He sprinted forward, straight toward the missing wall. Tim grabbed the barista's arm and pulled her clear. The man sprung off of the sloping floor and flew out over the water. He landed on his side and swam downstream.

Tim had never been in this café before. His new girlfriend, Julie, had told him to meet her here. He had just walked in, hoping to see her, when the ticking started. He felt paralyzed. He wanted someone to tell him what to do.

The man disappeared into the night as he swam off after Lisa. *What if that had been Julie?* Tim felt guilty, both for his inaction and for his inability to swim. Colorado was a thousand miles from the nearest ocean, he remembered defensively. If he jumped in after them, he would just be one more person in need of rescue. *That doesn't mean you can't do something. You aren't injured. Do something.*

"This is nuts," said another customer, a man wearing a UPS uniform. "Where did they go?" Tim shoved past him and hurried toward the entrance. Blinded by the emergency lights above the door, he stumbled over a fallen chair and kicked it out of his way without stopping.

"Hey! Watch it, buddy," barked an older guy wearing jogging shorts.

Tim ignored him and stepped through the now-empty window frame by the door. He stood on a portion of sidewalk covered with broken glass. To the left, the concrete jutted out over the river. To the right, it stopped above a muddy bank. Straight ahead, the sidewalk simply came to an end.

He saw the man floating downstream. Tim took several steps out over the river, but the man was too far away to reach. He looked around. Beyond the sidewalk, he saw no sign of Denver. The sky above held more stars than Tim had ever seen in his life, even camping in the mountains.

He hurried to his right and stepped down onto the muddy ground. The café sat on the edge of a river in a wide clearing, surrounded by a wall of trees.

"Hey, wait," called someone behind him. It sounded like the UPS guy.

Tim did not look back. The two people in the water were washing away. Tim caught sight of the swimming man, illuminated by starlight. Further downstream, he saw a frantic splash that must be the woman. She disappeared around a bend. Tim ran after them, slipping in the mud despite the thick tread on his work boots. He stopped watching the river and focused on his footing. As the woods closed in, he pulled out his mobile phone and shined the light ahead of him.

The heavy humid air reminded him of summer vacations at his grandfather's house in Minnesota. It felt nothing like Colorado. Thin stems slapped at his arms and legs. Tim paused, realizing that the café must be nearly out of sight. He turned to look back, wondering if it would still be there.

The Daily Edition Café had occupied the bottom corner of an old, eight-story building. A ragged ruin two stories high now hung halfway out over a river. The café itself looked mostly intact, but the suite next door was nowhere to be seen. Half of the second floor remained, with uneven walls and no ceiling.

Denver hadn't disappeared, they had. The café had been scooped out of the building and deposited on this riverbank. Tim wondered briefly what had happened to the rest of the structure, back in Denver. Did it collapse? Had anything happened to Julie?

He pushed the thought aside and pressed on. Tim lost sight of the river when he took a wide arc past a thicket of thorny brambles. He began to feel lost in the dark and wondered if he could find his way back to the café. He stopped and tried to slow his breathing so that he could listen for the sound of rushing water.

FOUR

William Crockett stood on the sidewalk and peered into the dark woods, searching for the young man who had run off. His long-sleeved UPS uniform felt sticky in the warm, humid air. At three inches over six feet, William had a good vantage point, but after forty-two years, his eyesight was not so sharp. He saw no signs of life. *What in the hell is going on?* He worried about his sons. Had whatever happened here also happened at their school?

William walked to the left end of the sidewalk, where it jutted out over the river. He squinted, searching for anything else that looked like a building, but he saw only dark shadows. He turned around and walked to the other end, where the sidewalk stopped above the muddy shore.

Holding on to the bricks, William leaned around the corner and looked at the side of the building. More shadows. He studied the wall, which belonged to the suite next door to the café. A real estate office, he remembered. Little of that room remained. The wall was blank except for a light switch and a framed photo of the Rocky Mountains. William followed the wall upward. The ceiling of the realty office jutted out only a few inches. Above, the wall continued past the second floor, where it ended with a jagged edge. It looked like one of the buildings in the World War II video games his sons played. William wondered what was in the suite above the café.

He looked down. Pieces of wall had fallen and stuck in the mud along the edge of the building. The ground looked solid enough, but the café was the only thing that remained of Denver. It was the only thing that felt real. He was afraid to step down. William returned to the center of the sidewalk and steadied himself on a parking meter, looking downstream again. The sky looked lighter over the tree tops.

Someone took his arm. He jumped and turned to see the young woman who had been flirting with him while she made his latte. "What's happening?" she whispered. She sounded close to tears.

"I don't know." He looked at the girl, wishing he could think of something to say that might make her feel better.

"Where the hell are we? Are we even on Earth? Look at the stars. They don't look right."

William looked up. "They're brighter, that's for sure. All I know is the big dipper, and I can't find it." He put his arm around her. "But it still feels like Earth. It feels like the Florida panhandle to me. The humidity, the insect noises."

"What happened to Lisa?" she asked. "My boss."

"The guy who jumped in the water was catching up to her, right before they disappeared around that bend." William pointed. "The other guy ran off in the woods, in the same direction. I think he went looking for them. I been kicking myself for not going after him, to help."

The young woman blew out a long, slow breath. "He has a crush on her. The one who jumped in the river, I mean. He comes in almost every day. He'll save her." She sounded like she was trying to convince herself.

"What about the other guy?"

She shook her head. "Never seen him before." She paused. "I'm Beth, by the way."

"William."

William nodded toward the woods. "I think the sun is coming up. Once it gets a little brighter, we can go looking for them. If they aren't back by then."

"They'll be back." Tears welled in Beth's eyes. She walked along the sidewalk toward the shore. Like William, she stopped right at the edge.

They were joined by a woman wearing a tailored blazer. Her boots crunched the broken glass on the sidewalk. "Have you figured out what happened to us?" It sounded more like a demand than a question.

Beth spun to look at the woman, who stood with her hands on her hips, as if she was posing for something. "Well," Beth began, "While you were inside, a television crew planted a forest around us. It's all a big prank." She put a finger to her lips. "You can't see them, but there are cameras watching right now. Don't do anything embarrassing."

The woman gave Beth a curt smile and looked around. She bent over and picked up a piece of broken glass. "This must be how that young man's face got cut up, when the window broke."

Beth gasped. "Are you a detective?" The woman did not respond.

"How is everyone doing inside?" William asked.

The woman in the blazer met him eye to eye. She had to look up, but she managed it without seeming small. "I think everyone will be okay. The redhead is patching up the old woman. She's a bit of a bleeder."

"What about the guy with the cuts on his face?"

"She tried to look at him too, but he wouldn't have it. He's pacing back and forth and freaking out. I think he's okay, though. The cuts aren't very deep." She dropped the glass shard and stuck out her hand. "I'm Patricia Hayman."

William gripped her hand with a firm shake. "William Crockett. And this is Beth." Beth kept her arms folded but offered a small smile.

Patricia walked out to the end of the jutting sidewalk and crouched, looking down at something. "Come see what I found over here."

FIVE

Al Stevens had been hoping the café might be quiet today, that he might spend a few extra minutes chatting with Lisa after she made his coffee. He kicked his feet and swam downstream in the dark, trying to catch up to her.

Ahead, Lisa flailed and flapped like an injured bird. Al kicked harder, closing in on her. He couldn't understand what was happening. His mind jumped to terrorism, but that didn't explain why it was dark out. Or why he was swimming in a *fucking river*. A small voice whispered in the back of Al's mind. *This is perfect.* He didn't need to think of something clever to say. He didn't need to worry about his hair or his teeth or his breath. He just needed to save Lisa.

The river swept them along. Al caught up to Lisa and hooked an arm around her. She shrieked. He tried to tell her to calm down but sucked in a mouthful of river water instead.

Al coughed and paddled toward the shore. Lisa slapped at the water with both hands, hindering more than helping. As they moved from the center, the current slackened into small eddies. "It's okay," Al said. Lisa gripped his arm.

A voice came from the dark shore. "Over here! I gotcha."

Al saw the dim shape of a man and swam toward him. When he felt the gritty bottom, he pushed Lisa out ahead of him and she stumbled to her feet.

The man held onto a sapling with one hand and lifted Lisa onto the peaty bank. He turned back to Al. "Hey, look! What is that?"

Al spun around. "What? Where?" The river rushed by endlessly in the dark.

"Something slid down the bank on the other side."

Al squinted but saw only frothy bubbles swirling in the starlight. "It's pretty dark, buddy." He coughed and spat as the young man helped him onto solid ground.

"It's Tim."

"I'm Al. How did you find us, Tim? We were in a coffee house. Where did you come from?" He pulled at his wet shirt, trying to stop it from clinging to his body.

"Same place. I was standing right behind you in line.

"Great."

Al moved over to Lisa, who leaned forward on both hands and spat on the ground. He knelt and patted her back as she coughed. "It's okay. You're okay now."

Tim held his phone overhead for light. Lisa's dark hair hung down the sides of her face in sloppy wet strings. She wrapped her arms around her wet blouse and shivered, despite the muggy heat. "Why are we…? Where did we…? Wh- what's happening?"

Al pulled her to her feet. One hand landed on the side of her breast and he awkwardly slid it up under her armpit. "Are you okay?" When she didn't answer, Al gave her a gentle shake and repeated, "Lisa, are you okay?" She finally responded with a small nod.

Al looked at Tim. "She might be in shock. Can you get us back to the coffee house?"

"Yeah. I think so." Tim started off through the brush. Al moved his arm around Lisa's waist and they followed him back upriver.

Al had visited The Daily Edition Café almost every day for three years, and now, because of some kind of crazy-ass disaster, he had his arm around Lisa Danser. He normally considered himself lucky if his hand brushed hers when she gave him his change. He could feel her inhale and exhale in sharp, hitching breaths. He felt the hard bone at the top of her hip and the soft flesh on the side of her belly.

He tried to look at her face, but she stared down at her feet as she walked across the uneven ground. She had lost one of her shoes in the river. Al wanted to say something clever, but he couldn't think of anything. He pulled her close, trying to stop the shivers.

As they followed the light from Tim's phone back through the woods, Lisa put her arm around Al to steady herself. He smiled. He didn't know where he was, or how he had gotten here, but he knew one thing. This was a good day.

SIX

Inside the café, Callie Grey tended to the old woman's shin while her fiancé held his phone overhead to provide extra light. Callie knew that Hank wanted to be outside with the others, trying to figure out what was going on, but she needed him. The sight of blood made her want to vomit.

While cleaning the wound, Callie had asked her normal set of introductory questions. They helped distract her from all the blood.

"What is your name?"

"Helen. Helen Davies."

"And where are you from, Helen?"

"I was born on the island of Crete, in Greece, seventy-six years ago."

The questions came automatically to Callie, who practiced psychiatry in a downtown office. She earned twice what Hank made as a prosecutor, thanks to the medical degree which allowed her to write prescriptions for all the anxieties brought on by affluence. The medical degree also meant that Callie was the most qualified to patch up the old lady.

"Greece. How did you find your way to the United States?"

"An Englishman named Lawrence Davies met me on holiday and brought me over here when I was nineteen. My mother was so angry about that."

From the tone, Callie detected that Helen wasn't too sure about it either. She noted that discussions about this subject could probably be drawn out over several months of sessions.

The young man with the cuts on his face paced to the front door and then back to the side wall. He leaned over the sloped floor where one of the baristas had fallen into the river. "I don't believe it."

Hank took a slow, deep breath. Callie sensed that his fuse had run out. The irony never failed to amuse her. *She* was the redhead. She was supposed to be the one with the temper.

The man with the cuts on his face had repeated "I don't believe it" non-stop since coming inside.

"Hey kid, come over here," Hank said. The young man looked up with a vacant expression. Hank nodded. "Yeah, you." He walked over and looked down at the operation.

The falling espresso machine had peeled away an inch-wide strip of skin from the front of the woman's shin, starting just below her knee and running all the way down to the top of her foot, where it was still connected. Blood flowed freely from the exposed flesh. Callie held the tissue-thin flap between her finger and thumb. It looked like a piece of used packing tape. Callie reached for a fresh napkin and dabbed at the skin flap to remove the last few bits of dirt. Then she stretched it across the front of the woman's leg, hoping it would help stop the bleeding.

"What's your name, son?" Hank asked the young man, who stared with his mouth hanging open.

"Morgan." A dozen shallow slices covered his face.

"Morgan, I know you don't believe it. None of us can." Hank said. *He is so proud of himself for not losing his cool*, Callie thought. She almost always knew what Hank was thinking.

Hank continued, "But when you repeat yourself over and over again, it just makes a bad situation worse. You're freaking people out."

Morgan showed an expression of disbelief. "Dude, shut the fuck up! This is some kind of end-of-the-world catastrophic shit. I'll say whatever the hell I want."

Hank's face turned red and Callie thought for a minute that he was going to hurl his cell phone at Morgan. "God-dammit, don't you speak that way in front of -"

Before Hank could finish, Morgan turned and wandered out the door to join the group outside.

"Count your blessings, honey," Callie said. "At least he's gone." She had finally aligned the flap of skin with its original location on Helen's shin.

Hank grunted and glared toward the front.

Callie dabbed the edges of the cut with a paper towel, soaking up fresh blood. She dropped the towel into a trash can Hank had found for her. It landed with a splat. She forced herself to stop and look outside, through the missing wall. It had grown bright enough to see the clearing on the opposite riverbank, with a dark forest beyond.

Hank checked the screen on his mobile device.

"Still nothing?" she asked him.

He shook his head. "No bars, no service. The map says, 'Satellites not found'."

Callie dabbed up the remaining blood. Helen winced and moaned. "Why did this happen?" Her voice sounded almost childlike with fear.

Callie stopped. "I don't think anybody knows yet." She gave the woman a sympathetic smile. "I don't suppose you have any Advil or Tylenol?"

Helen clutched her purse, which looked large enough to hold a pharmacy. "I always carry a bottle of aspirin. They say it's good for the heart, you know. Larry died of a heart attack."

"Aspirin is a blood thinner. We need yours to thicken right now." Callie tried to press the napkins against Helen's leg more gently. Blood seeped out the sides of the skin flap. "How bad does it hurt?"

"I can barely feel it. I don't see why you're making such a fuss." She smiled, showing teeth that were too perfect to be the originals.

"I just wanted to stop the bleeding. You were making quite a mess in here." She turned to her fiancé. "Hank, let's see if we can prop up this nice lady's leg."

Hank pulled a small table over to the orange couch and they got Helen to sit back with her leg across the tabletop, higher than her head. Callie swapped the bloody napkins for a fresh set and nodded, satisfied that the bleeding had finally begun to slow down. She stood by the table, holding the napkins in place and allowed herself to look around.

The café looked like the scene of an explosion. The emergency lights made a pair of bright cones as they shone through the concrete dust hanging in the air. *We probably shouldn't be breathing that.* All of the other lights were off and the back corner of the room had caved in. The river rushing by below the missing wall created the sensation of movement. After looking at all of the blood, the continuous motion was almost too much. Callie sat down on the couch next to Helen and closed her eyes.

"It's real, babe," Hank said. "We have been teleported into a goddamn forest."

Teleported. Callie rattled off other possibilities in her mind: a dream, a hallucination, a drug. Someone might have drugged her at a night club. Hank had told her about a case like that once. Maybe she was lying unconscious and defenseless somewhere. The idea seemed almost preferable. At least it made sense. Teleportation did not make sense.

A pair of large bugs flew in the open wall and spiraled around in the light cones in the front of the building. They looked like wasps and buzzed like toy helicopters.

"Hey gramps," called Morgan from the front of the building. "We found something."

Callie looked up at her fiancé. Even in the lousy light, she could see in his eyes that he needed to go out there.

Hank held up his hand as if swearing an oath. "I promise not to murder that dumbass. I just want to go outside and scope things out."

She gave him a small grin. Hank always knew what she was thinking, too. It helped make up for the age difference. "Don't go out of sight, okay?"

Hank responded with his biggest courtroom smile, showing wide rows of perfect teeth that *were* still the originals. "You got it, babe. I'll be right over there."

SEVEN

Hank stepped out onto the front sidewalk. Four parking meters stood in a row and a green metal trash can sat bolted to the concrete. The executive lady hunched down in her designer jeans and held her own mobile device over an object near the end of the sidewalk.

Hank wasn't sure who he disliked more, Morgan or the woman in the slick business casual outfit. She had come around poking her nose in everyone's business, as if it was her job to check on them all. She probably thought her blazer and jeans ensemble looked hip and cool. He thought she looked lazy. Nobody dressed up any more, especially in a cowboy town like Denver.

Not that you look any better yourself right now, counselor, he thought, looking down at his flimsy jogging shorts and art museum t-shirt. He squatted next to the woman.

The light shone on a severed hand, with a few inches of forearm still attached. It looked like a woman's hand. The diagonal slice was perfectly smooth. Two grey circles of bone were visible in the center. A small puddle of blood pooled on the concrete.

"Morgan here thinks he saw her earlier on the sidewalk," explained the business woman. "He was right outside when all this began."

On some days, Hank and Callie stopped at the café after their morning run. Callie would enjoy her latte and gossip about her patients. She would eventually notice the time and they would run back to their tiny penthouse and scramble to get ready for work. On other days, when they ran straight home, they usually had time for a hot wet fuck in the shower. *Why couldn't today have been one of those days?* Hank thought.

He pointed at the hand on the sidewalk. "Did she fall in the river too? Whoever this was?"

"I didn't actually see her when it happened," Morgan said. "I was looking in the window." He pointed to his slashed face and grinned. "That was lucky, huh?"

"So what happened to her?"

"Think about it, man. She was right at the edge. Most of her was on the outside, but her arm was on the inside. She was walking along, perfectly fine, when all of a sudden, whammo!" Morgan brought his hand down in an axe-chopping motion. "No arm!"

Hank pressed his lips together and breathed through his nose. Callie called this his "bull snort." He looked around and realized that he was still as clueless as when he first stepped outside. He had learned nothing. *That's not completely true,* Hank thought. He had been able to conclude beyond a reasonable doubt that he disliked Morgan even more than Ms. Business Casual.

"Is this a goddamn adventure to you? That woman might be bleeding to death in the street back in Denver."

"At least she's still in Denver."

EIGHT

Patricia Hayman stepped down from the sidewalk onto the riverbank mud and studied the lone footsteps of the man who had run off downstream. She noticed with annoyance that thick mud clung to the sides of her Lucchese boots.

Whatever was happening required a plan of action. The first step toward taking action was assessing the situation. Assessing was one of Patricia's strong points.

She walked out onto the mudflat, deliberately not looking down at her boots, and turned back to the building. The coffee shop sat on the inside curve of a wide bend in the river. It appeared alien, out of place and alone. More than half of the building sat on solid ground, but a decent chunk extended out over the water's surface. The river itself stretched about thirty feet across. On each side, the tree line pushed back a hundred feet from the water.

Patricia remembered her son going through a phase where he was obsessed with books that showed cutaway views of buildings, vehicles, and even made-up things like movie spaceships. The café looked like it belonged in one of those books. She squinted and thought about it. *No.* The café really looked like the part that was *missing* from those pictures. Back in downtown Denver, the rest of the eight-story building must look like it belonged in a cutaway book.

The building scoop on the riverbank consisted of the café, most of the floor above, and part of the sidewalk out front, which jutted out over the water at an angle. Patricia saw nothing to explain how it had gotten there.

This situation needed leadership. The two women inside were not up to the job. The old one was injured. It was just a scrape, but she was having difficulties with the simple act of clotting.

Callie, the jogger who was patching her up, seemed dazed, almost in shock. She had not even come outside yet. She did know a little medicine, Patricia noted. That might come in handy.

Hank, Callie's cradle-robber boyfriend wearing the silly short-shorts, was the last person Patricia would put in charge. He stood at the edge of the sidewalk and looked down at the surrounding clearing. Patricia wondered if he was afraid to step off the building. She herself had thought twice before stepping down. What if the café returned to Denver and left her behind? Then she remembered the ticking sound. If the event was to happen again, the ticking sound would give her the warning she needed to get back inside. She tried to cut the guy some slack. Not everyone could be as observant as her, especially in the middle of a disaster.

Beth, the young girl with the smart mouth, pushed past Hank and hopped down. She began to wander around the building. The move struck Patricia as more careless than brave. The girl's sarcastic attitude ruled out any sort of leadership possibilities.

William hopped down and caught up to Beth, taking her arm. "Hey, don't get too far away, okay?" She nodded in reply.

Patricia noted the exchange and gave William a check in the plus column. His close-cut hair showed grey at the temples, which indicated maturity. Another plus. Yet for some reason, he had never risen beyond a manual labor job. He wore a uniform with his name stitched on the front. It was a strike against him. The fact that he was black and everyone else here was white meant strike two. Patricia did not care herself, but most people wanted a leader who looked like them, someone with the same sort of background. She decided not to make a call about William quite yet.

Three candidates remained: the woman who had fallen into the river, the guy who had jumped in after her, and the

man who had run off into the woods after both of them.
Falling into the river ruled out the barista. *Her name is Lisa,*
Patricia remembered. The man who jumped in had shouted
it. Patricia never forgot a name. Remembering names helped
put people at ease and demonstrated your own authority.

The younger man who had gone into the woods to help
them was worth considering. He hadn't done anything quite
so foolhardy as jumping into a strange river that appeared
out of nowhere, but he had shown bravery and initiative.

Patricia had been in Denver to shut down a hard disk
manufacturing plant that was losing money and showed no
promise of turning around. Patricia herself had made the
decision. It was the right choice, even if it meant putting fifty
people out of work. Her boss had wanted to wait until the
end of the quarter, to give the plant one last chance, but she
had fought him on it and won. She knew the move made her
seem like a hard-ass and she was glad for the reputation. At
the same time, shutting down the plant six weeks early had
allowed her to divert costs and provide a little extra
severance. This would make the company seem more caring,
and she had already talked to the marketing department
about spinning the story in that direction. Not *spinning*, she
reminded herself, *positioning*. The vice president of
marketing hated the word "spin."

Patricia watched the downstream woods for Lisa or her
would-be rescuers. Above the trees, the sky had brightened
to a dull grey.

William joined her on the mudflat, followed closely
behind by Morgan. The edges of Patricia's mouth curled up.
You completely forgot about this fellow, she chided herself. Of
course she had. Morgan was a shiftless punk who probably
never held a job for more than six months and considered
drinking in a parked car the height of leisure. One of
Patricia's greatest fears was that her son might grow up to be
like Morgan.

"I can't believe it," Morgan said, looking around.

Patricia ignored him and gestured downstream. "That direction is clearly east." The time change must be important, she thought. The sun had been up in Denver, but they had arrived here before sunrise. That meant they must have moved a few hours to the west. Considering this, plus the humidity, Patricia deduced that they were somehow in the Pacific Northwest, probably near the coast. She doubted anyone else had figured this out.

The bouncing light of a cell phone appeared in the woods downstream and three figures emerged from the jungle. Lisa had her arm around the man who had jumped into the river after her. He had rescued her, which certainly counted for something. The trio stopped at the edge of the clearing and gaped at the building. The younger man put away his cell phone.

They looked just as confused as everyone else. Patricia waved them over. When they grew close, she stuck out her hand and said, "I'm Patricia Hayman, and these gentlemen are William and Morgan."

Tim and Al gave their names but Lisa merely stared at the building with an empty look until she noticed the other barista. "Beth!" They ran to one another and embraced tightly.

Patricia continued watching the other two. Al, the hero of the day, was unable to hold eye contact. His light blue dress shirt looked beige from the muddy water and his sleeveless undershirt stood out in stark relief, hugging his body. His wet hair clung to his forehead in a jagged pattern. He fidgeted around and kept looking over toward Lisa.

Tim crossed his arms. "Any idea what happened?" He seemed to want someone to take charge.

Patricia was happy to oblige. On her office wall, a framed print showed a foaming Rottweiler with the caption: *If you want a job done right, do it yourself.* Patricia concluded that she was the best and therefore only person to take charge of this group.

She told the others, "We need to stay together, make sure everyone is okay, and collect all of the information we have."

Morgan gawked at her. "What are you, the principal or something? We don't *have* any fucking information."

William put a hand on his shoulder. "Easy. She's trying to help."

Patricia turned to Al and Tim. "Nice work, you two." Providing positive feedback would help establish her leadership. "You saved that woman's life." Al nodded at this.

Tim lifted his chin in the direction of the café. "Is everyone else all right? How many of us are there?" Patricia gave the young man a second look. He was asking the right questions. Tim was the only one in their group who did not seem completely out of place on the riverbank. He looked like a modern cowboy, wearing a blue chambray shirt, jeans with a belt, and yellow leather work boots that belonged in the mud. He only needed to swap his baseball cap for a cowboy hat. He looked strong, too. Patricia decided that Tim was someone to keep close by.

"There are ten of us," she answered. "The older woman skinned her shin pretty badly, but everyone else is okay."

Al asked, "Lady, do we know anything? Anything at all?" Patricia detected desperation in his voice.

They were looking to her for answers. "Call me Patricia, please." She spoke crisply. "I don't know how we got here, but there is something you had better come and see." She led them up onto the sidewalk over the rushing brown water. She squatted to remove a dishrag that someone had placed over the severed hand.

Morgan said, "I saw her right out front just before this happened. I got a face full of glass, but she lost her damn hand."

When the dishrag came off, Tim dropped to his knees.

"What's the matter?" asked William.

"My girlfriend, she -" Tim leaned over the hand, examining it from all angles. "She was supposed to meet me here."

After a moment, Tim pulled away and shook his head. "The fingernails are too long. Julie's are cut short."

Al crossed his arms. "So back in Denver, there's a woman who lost her hand and a big empty hole where this place used to be. I get it. But where are we?"

Patricia replaced the dishrag and stood up. "I have a theory about that." She waited, wanting their full attention. Now was the perfect time to explain how she had deduced their new location, Oregon or possibly Washington State.

Before she could begin, William stated, "Not where, my friend, *when*. We have gone back in time."

"What in the world would make you say that?" asked Patricia.

The delivery man's eyes held wide as he slowly raised his hand to point. "Them dinosaurs coming out of the forest."

NINE

Nine giants stood at the tree line on the other side of the river. The sound of the water rushing below the sidewalk had masked the noise of their approach. The dinosaurs stood on four legs, with two shorter ones in the front and massive tree trunks in the back, which supported thick tails extending out into the air behind them. The largest were bigger than elephants. They stared across a thin layer of ground fog at the giant foreign block. *This is their watering hole*, Tim realized.

"That is one fugly duckface," said Beth. She hurried back toward the building, pulling Lisa with her.

The long face of the lead dinosaur flattened out toward its mouth. Bulbous mounds of red, blistery flesh grew around its eyes and nose, giving it a diseased appearance. Strands of thick mucus hung from its nostrils and a cloud of flies buzzed around its head.

"They're duckbills," said William. "Duckbilled dinosaurs! My boys could tell you exactly what kind they are."

"Are they dangerous?" asked Patricia, shaking her head slowly back and forth.

"They're plant eaters," William answered. "But look at them. They're huge."

"They're amazing, is what they are," said Patricia. She climbed down from the sidewalk and sidestepped along the bank, staring at the herd across the river. Thirty feet of rushing water, plus at least thirty yards of mud on the far shore separated her from the creatures.

- - - - -

The lead dinosaur, a hadrosaur species known as *Edmontosaurus Regalis,* walked a few steps down from the trees. It rose up on its back legs and angled its face toward the foreign object, sniffing. It did not like the large, strange-smelling structure on the river bank. One instinct demanded flight. The herd should leave before any trouble occurred. Another instinct said that territory could not be yielded. The rest of the herd remained at the forest's edge, motionless except for the gentle oscillations of their tails.

- - - - -

"Ma'am, do you really think it's smart to get so close?" Tim asked. Behind him, Beth stepped up onto the sidewalk, still pulling Lisa by the hand.

Patricia waved her off. "Look at them. They're harmless. They're plant eaters, like the man said." She stepped forward until the tips of her expensive boots extended over the edge of the bank. "Someone take my picture. Is there enough light to get a picture?"

The dinosaur in front bobbed its head a half dozen times, scattering the swarm of flies. Bobbed *his* head, Tim noticed. A pink fire hose hung between the creature's back legs. "*Patricia!*" he whisper-shouted. The animal turned at the noise.

William had seen the same thing. "Lady. That's a bull. Like a bull moose."

"Guys, I appreciate your concern, but they are on the other side of the river." She spoke slowly, as if explaining things to children.

The hadrosaur dropped back onto all fours. As its front legs landed on the ground, a clump of dead skin sloughed off the side of its neck.

It charged, accelerating into a full-out gallop. At forty feet in length, it covered the distance across the mudflat in five bounding steps.

Lisa let out a small squeal as Beth pulled her into the café. Al followed them inside, shoving Morgan and Hank into the building simply because they were in the way.

Tim and William stood alone on the sidewalk. *It's a feint,* Tim thought as he watched the dinosaur run down to the edge of the water. Animals made false charges to scare away threats. A rutting elk had charged him once on a hunting trip, and then stopped some fifteen feet away.

William hopped down onto the muddy shore and started toward Patricia.

Inside the café, Hank watched through the front wall. *"Are you stupid?"* he roared. "Get the hell in here!" Tim wasn't sure if he was shouting at William, Patricia, or both of them.

Callie grabbed her fiancé's arm. *"Hank."* She tried to pull him deeper inside the café, but he shook her off.

On the river bank, Patricia held up one hand. *"There, there,"* she said as the bull reached the opposite shoreline. "Mustn't show fear," she muttered out the side of her mouth. The color had drained from her face.

The animal did not slow down as it plowed into the river. A wake of water sprayed high into the air and rained down on the sidewalk. Even half-submerged, the dinosaur towered above Patricia as it closed the gap. The bull's eyes, on either side of its massive head, were unable to see directly forward. It slowed slightly and twisted its neck so that it could look down at the woman. Its right eye glared at her over the red bulbous wattle growing across its face.

William, wet from the spray kicked up by the animal, reached out for Patricia, though he was still a good six feet away from her. He clawed at empty air.

Patricia began to backpedal. One boot stuck in the mud and her foot came out of it. She caught herself and kept her balance, but grimaced as the wet sticky mud soaked into her sock.

With an effortless lunge, the animal burst onshore in front of her.

Patricia held out both hands as the hadrosaur reared up on eight-foot hind legs. Its front feet came down together. One slid off of Patricia's shoulder, separating her arm from her body as it passed, while the other struck her chest. Both feet connected with the ground an instant later, crushing the woman beneath. She died immediately, but the dinosaur continued to stomp, drumming Patricia's corpse into the ground. Its foot connected with her head and disappeared shin-deep into the mud. Blood splayed up on the underside of its chest and neck.

Screams came from inside the building.

"What the shit!" shouted Morgan.

Hank pushed his head through the open window frame and bellowed at Tim, "Kid, do something! Don't just stand there like a fucking idiot!"

Tim gave Hank a sidelong glance. *Do what? If you've got any great ideas, come on out here.*

William fell backwards onto the ground, unable to look away as the dinosaur continued to drill the woman into the mud. His mouth hung open in a soundless gasp.

The hadrosaur finally stopped and grew still, its feet firmly planted where moments earlier Patricia Hayman had stood. It slowly turned its head toward William and the café behind him, blinking absently whenever a fly buzzed too close.

William crab-crawled backwards across the ground.

The hadrosaur lifted a bloody forefoot out of the mud and rotated toward William. It blew out air in a long, slow hoot and charged.

Tim climbed halfway off the sidewalk and grabbed William under the arms. Ten years of working as a carpenter had made him strong. He hefted the man up onto the concrete just before the hadrosaur reached the building. They backpedaled together toward the front entrance until they felt hands grab them and pull them inside.

The bull stopped by the sidewalk and let out a low, coughing honk. Across the river, the rest of the herd lumbered down to the opposite shore. Half of them waded across.

Lisa wailed. Al took her in his arms and held her. Everyone shifted deeper inside, trying to disappear into the darkest recesses. The wall containing the bookshelves blocked their view of the bull hadrosaur just a few feet away, but they could see several of the others across the water.

The herd seemed to relax now that there were no longer any people visible. The other dinosaurs waited while the alpha took a long drink from the river, and then they all took their turns, two or three at a time. A pair of juveniles, each the size of a camel, stood close by their mothers.

The dinosaurs spread out around the mud flats, most of them keeping their distance from the structure in the middle. The bull hadrosaur walked alongside the building and sprayed three gallons of urine against the outside wall as he passed.

TEN

Callie squatted with the others on the black rubber mat behind the counter. She felt light headed.

"Will someone please explain to me what is going on?" pleaded Helen. Callie realized that the woman had not seen the attack.

Beth, breathing hard, said, "There's a herd of duckbilled dinosaurs outside and one of them went on a rampage and charged that Patricia lady and it trampled her, and -"

"Sweetie, you can talk faster than I can listen."

"We are in the past," explained Callie. Saying it out loud made it sound silly. She had to be dreaming. She needed to pee and any minute now she would wake up and walk to the bathroom. She would tell Hank about her dream in the morning and they sure as hell would not stop at the café after their jog. She took Helen's hand. "We are in the time of the dinosaurs, and one of them just killed a woman."

"Killed her?" said Morgan, trembling. "It pounded that bitch into the *ground!*" He somehow whispered and shouted at the same time.

"Hey," said Hank. "Call her a bitch again and I will throw you out there."

Morgan rolled his eyes. "It's just a word, pops. It doesn't mean I actually think she's a bitch."

Callie wished Morgan would stop pressing Hank's buttons. If he lost his temper here it wouldn't help anything. Her bladder groaned at her. She really did need to pee. Just a quiet moan for now, but she knew it would get louder.

"I'm supposed to meet my grandson," Helen said. "He works downtown and he meets me here every week." She looked from face to face. "He must be wondering where I am."

"Lady, your grandson is lucky he isn't here," snapped Hank. "We are in some serious goddamn trouble right now." Helen hugged her purse close against her chest.

Callie put a hand on her fiancé's arm. "I'm not sure that's helping, sweetie."

"What's your name, ma'am," asked Tim, who sat across from her.

"I'm Helen. Helen Davies."

"Nice to meet you. I'm Tim MacGregor. I was supposed to meet someone here this morning too." He gave her a sympathetic nod. "A woman named Julie. We just started going out. I was looking forward to seeing her again."

Callie smiled. Tim's friendly drawl seemed calming. "I'm Calista Grey and this is my fiancé, Hank Atherton." Before anyone could comment on their age difference, she turned to her right. "And you must be William." She pointed to the embroidered name on his UPS uniform.

"That's right. William Crockett."

Al said simply, "Al Stevens. Stevens Information Systems."

"I'm Beth. I work here. *Worked* here anyway." She gestured toward her boss. "Lisa owns the place."

Lisa nodded. "How is your leg doing, Helen?"

"Oh, it's better. The bleeding has stopped. I'm so sorry I created such a fuss."

"That's nothing! Look at my face," said Morgan. He twisted his head back and forth to show off his cuts, which had dried in thin dark lines. "I'm Morgan Baker."

"Looks like an improvement to me," said Beth. Morgan cackled.

"So now we know we're in the past," William said. "Why did this happen to us? Did you all hear that ticking sound?" Heads nodded in the dim light. "Does anybody know where it came from?" This question was met with silence.

Callie felt her bladder swelling at the base of her belly.

Beth asked the group, "Do you think this happened anywhere else? Maybe it wasn't just us. Maybe it happened all over the world."

"I've been wondering that myself," William said. "I have two teenage boys in school. At least I hope they are in school, and not someplace like this."

"I don't care if there's anyone else here," said Morgan. "I just want to know how we get home."

"Maybe we could leave a message for the future," Beth suggested. "We could carve a note on stone. Millions of years from now, they'll find it and know what happened to us."

Morgan shook his head. "No way. That could wreck things. That could screw up the timeline. All of us might never be born. We can't leave any trace."

Hank huffed. *That was stupid*, Callie translated mentally. Hank had shamed more than one defendant on the witness stand with that sound.

Hank stared at Morgan. "Don't you think this two-story building is a bit of a trace?"

"Well I don't hear you coming up with any fantastic ideas," Morgan said.

"As long as those animals are out there," Hank gestured with his thumb, "We don't have any choice but to sit here and hide."

Callie shook her head. "I gotta pee," she announced. "I drank a lot of water during my run this morning." She felt the need to explain herself. "And then after that, I had a large latte."

"I already checked," Lisa said. "My bathroom didn't make it. That part of the building collapsed." She leaned over and indicated the back corner, where the ceiling had caved in. Thin hints of sunlight broke through in a few places.

Morgan reached up on the counter and grabbed a paper coffee cup. He extended it in Callie's direction. "Here. We can all turn around."

Callie put her hand on Hank's arm before he could respond. "Sorry, but I don't think so, Morgan. I can barely go when someone is in the stall next to me. I'm not peeing in here."

Morgan shrugged and tossed the cup over his shoulder.

"Well you can't go outside," Al said. "Those things are still out there. Most of them are probably on this side of the river now."

Hank puffed up. "Hey buddy, she'll go wherever she wants to go."

Callie felt her face grow warm. Her freckles were probably flaring, but at least in the dim light no one would see. She hated being told what she could and could not do almost as much as she hated Hank defending her. "They have ignored us ever since we got out of sight." She stood and snatched a handful of napkins from the counter.

"Cal, are you sure?" Hank asked.

"I'm just gonna go on the sidewalk. The part overhanging the river. I'll be fine." She gave him a half-serious look. "Can you make sure no one peeks?" She crept out from behind the counter and into the seating area.

The open wall on her left showed the far bank across the river. The closest hadrosaur had dropped to the ground and lay with its belly in the mud. Its mottled, grey-green backside faced the building and its long, muscular tail wagged back and forth, making a fan-shaped pattern in the mud. Another hadrosaur nibbled at a clump of ferns near the woods.

Callie crept forward and stepped through the window by the front door. She looked to the right and saw Patricia's empty boot stuck in the mud at the edge of the river. For a moment, the need to pee disappeared and she felt dizzy again. She made herself take deep breaths. Beyond the boot, four dinosaurs grazed on more ferns. Callie turned left and went out over the water. She squatted in front of a brick column at the corner of the building, where no one inside could see her. Relief hissed out onto the concrete.

A moment later, she was back indoors. She leaned over the counter. "Put me in the record books. I dropped the napkins in the river. I'm the first person in the world to litter."

Hank smiled at her. His deep-set eyes and jutting, bushy brow normally gave him an angry expression. But when he smiled, he changed from Neanderthal to teddy bear. Callie loved to watch the transformation. She felt almost magical when she triggered it.

"Come on back here, babe," Hank said.

"I don't think we need to hide behind the counter. They aren't doing anything. They're ignoring us."

Hank gave her a look. She could tell he wanted to call the shots, but she was sick of sitting in the dark. She walked around and helped Helen up off the ground. "Come have a look." She pointed out the dinosaurs on the far bank.

Morgan walked past. "Who would have thought, huh? Goddamn dinosaurs!" A hadrosaur crossed the mudflat and looked in their direction. Helen stepped back.

"It's okay," Callie whispered. "I don't think they can see inside here, because it's so dark and all."

Helen studied the creature, staring silently for a long while. "It looks like a cross between an elephant and a cow and a lizard."

"So what now?" Morgan asked the room. He walked back to the counter, reached into the glass display case, and took out a bear claw.

Lisa crossed her arms. "Hey, what do you think you're doing?"

Through a mouthful of dough, Morgan said, "I'll pay you back later."

William placed a hand on Lisa's shoulder. "We'll need to share whatever supplies we have here, don't you think?" She looked down and her scowl faded. William continued, "Since we don't have any power, why don't you and Beth see if you can figure out what will spoil? We'll eat those things first."

Callie's mouth dropped. Barely an hour had passed and William was suggesting they might be trapped here long enough for food to spoil. She shuddered.

Beth took Lisa by the arm. "That will mostly be the milk. Come on boss, let's take inventory."

Helen remained at the open side wall and watched the giant creatures on the far bank. They made little noise as they milled about. Their hides were various shades of green, one so dark it looked iridescent. A short layer of furry down covered its back and shimmered in the breeze. Every so often, it rose up on its hind legs to look around, like a meerkat on the savannah.

"Dinosaurs," the old woman said after a long while. "Goddamn dinosaurs."

ELEVEN

Beth joined William and Tim near the front windows. Until the herd wandered away, they were trapped. From inside the café, they could not see out onto their side of the river. Both walls facing in that direction were windowless. They took turns leaning out the front and craning to the right so they could watch the closest dinosaurs.

Their size astounded Beth. One of the larger ones rolled in the mud not too far from the building. Its motion shook the earth. When it rose, a thick layer of brown mud coated its back and flanks. "It's taking a mudbath," Beth whispered over her shoulder.

"That probably keeps the insects off," William said.

"Some of them maybe," Beth noted. A swarm still buzzed around the creature's head.

William put his hand on Tim's shoulder. "Hey, man. I think you saved my life out there. Thank you."

Tim nodded. "You were just trying to do the same for Patricia."

Beth divided her attention between the conversations inside and the giants outside. Of all the people in the café, William seemed the most real. Free of bullshit. He was probably a good father, she thought with a pang of jealousy. He seemed like the sort of guy you would want watching out for you.

A racket came from inside and Beth pulled her head back in the window. Hank stood in the center of the seating area, picking up fallen chairs and trying to put the room back in order. "What the hell was that woman thinking? That's what I want to know. That was stupid."

Beth looked over at Callie. Hank seemed like a bully. He made Beth nervous. Callie looked annoyed, but kept quiet about it. Beth didn't blame her.

Morgan had finished his bear claw and moved on to a slice of coffee cake. "Why does he get to call her stupid? Stupid is way worse than bitch."

Callie held up a hand. "Morgan, shut up."

Beth leaned back out the window for one last look around the corner. The muddy hadrosaur walked over to the river near Patricia's lone boot and took a long drink. It relieved itself at the same time, spraying a stream of wet feces onto the ground behind it.

Beth stepped away from the corner. "Hey Tim. Your turn, man."

"I never saw anyone die before," William said quietly. "That was rough."

Tim moved over to the window. "When I was a kid, my dad used to take me to the rodeo every January. We stopped going after a rider got gored by a bull right in front of us. It ran around in circles with the poor bastard impaled on its head." He leaned outside and peered around the wall.

Lisa spoke up. "At least the rodeo guy knew what he was getting into. Patricia was just a woman buying a cup of coffee." She looked ashen, even in the dim light.

She feels responsible for what's happening, Beth thought. *It's her store.*

Lisa glared at Hank. "And she may not have been very smart, but that doesn't mean she deserved to die." She shivered and rubbed her arms. Al picked up his jacket and draped it over her shoulders.

"What are we going to do about her body?" asked Helen. She had returned to her seat on the orange couch. "We can't leave her out there. Rats will get at her."

"Have rats even been invented yet?" asked Morgan.

"Evolved," corrected Hank. "And what do you propose we do with her, Ma'am?"

Helen frowned. "Well, don't you think she needs a proper burial?"

Hank counted off on his fingers. "One, I don't have a shovel. Two, those things out there don't respond so well to the sight of people. Three, they don't look like they are going anywhere any time soon. And four, she's half buried already. I know you didn't see what happened, but that woman was stomped so deep into the mud I don't think we could move her if we tried."

Beth nudged William and mouthed quietly, "So angry." William winked at her.

"What about the smell?" asked Al. "If we leave that body out there, it might attract something worse."

"I don't know how it could be much worse," Morgan said. "That bastard was fast."

William nodded. "Hippos are the same way. They look slow and fat, but they are actually the most dangerous animals in Africa. Not the lions or tigers, like everyone thinks."

Beth looked at him with wide eyes. "Wow, that's a helpful piece of information, mister. Do you go to the zoo a lot or do you watch the nature channels?" She peeled open a chocolate almond biscotti she had swiped earlier from the back counter.

William smiled. "You *are* a sassy one." She gave him a wink and he went on to explain, "My boys used to love going to the zoo."

"You sound like a good dad," Beth said, chewing.

"Didn't your old man ever take you to the zoo?"

"Nah. My asshat father went to prison for insurance fraud. That's why I'm working now instead of college. But I'm saving up. In a couple of years I'm going to film school."

"Oh, you want to be a movie star?" William smiled.

"Screw that. I want to be a director. I want to make blockbus-"

"Shhh!" Tim hissed. He shoved William and Beth away from the front. "One of them is coming."

TWELVE

Al pulled Lisa close. They were once again huddled in a circle on the floor behind the counter. Al's heart raced. He snaked his arm further around her, feeling the weight of her breast against his wrist. Sitting with his arm around Lisa Danser was more unbelievable than finding himself millions of years in the past. He shifted as he felt himself growing aroused and hoped she did not notice. She rested her head against his shoulder and Al lowered his face into her hair, breathing in the scent of her. *Unbelievable.*

"What's happening?" Hank whispered.

William leaned around the counter, looking out front. He spoke softly back toward the others. "It's sniffing around. Its head is just inside the room."

The animal snorted. The sound filled the space and Al felt the air move all the way in the back of the café.

"Somebody do something," whispered Helen.

"What the hell are we supposed to do?" Hank answered.

William turned to face the group. "I think it's leaving. It pulled back outside."

The building rumbled. Lisa let out a scream and Al squeezed her. The vibration continued, as if someone was operating a jackhammer in the room upstairs. Plaster dust fell from the ceiling.

"What's going on?" demanded Hank.

William took another peek and then put his hands up. "It's okay," he told the group. She's just scratching herself."

"She? What, did you get a look at her titties?" Morgan craned his neck.

The building continued to shake. "She's rubbing her belly on the front corner," William said.

Al rose to look for himself. He peered over the counter. Several others joined him, including Lisa. The wall of bookshelves on the right blocked most of their view. At the end of the wall, one muddy paw hung in front of the window as the hadrosaur scratched against the corner.

The shaking stopped and suddenly the building was jolted to the left. Al steadied Lisa.

The dinosaur out front dropped back down to all fours, her head visible through the window again. The wattled face of the alpha appeared, nipping the back of the female's muddy neck. She jerked away and they both disappeared from view. The alpha bleated a low, stuttery warning.

"I think that's the only male," William said. "That's why I called the other one a 'she.' He's got a harem."

The alpha reappeared at the front window.

"Down!" William whispered. They all dropped back behind the counter again. "He's looking for us. Keep your voices down."

"Why is this happening?" asked Helen.

"Maybe the world was about to end," Beth said. "You know, back in the present. We all got saved by aliens. They sent us back in time so someone would survive."

Lisa rolled her eyes. "Beth, you have made up a lot of weird stuff, but that might be the winner."

"Hey, now," said William. "Maybe it's true and maybe it isn't. Right now we don't know anything. Any ideas could be helpful. Even if they are wrong. They might spark other ideas."

Hank leaned in to the group. "Here's an idea. I think that as soon as those dinos are gone, we should get the hell out of here. Remember what the girl said earlier? There might be other groups like us. This may not be an isolated event. It could have happened everywhere, for all we know. We have to look for others and try to group up."

Al wondered what would happen if they joined another group. "This is our only shelter. There's food here, and tools." In the back of his mind, he wasn't sure he wanted to find anyone else. He knew where he stood with everyone in the café.

"This shelter is going to get knocked into the river if it takes many more hits like that," Hank said.

Helen squeezed the handles on her purse. "Do you know how long it took me to walk two blocks from the parking lot? You can't really expect me to go traipsing off through the jungle with you."

Callie prodded. "You said Lawrence used to take you hiking all over the place on his hunting trips."

"Young woman, my days of hiking died with Lawrence a long time ago." She pursed her lips and shook her head at Hank. "I am not leaving this café. Whoever sent us here will surely try to bring us back. I intend to be right here when that happens."

Al wondered if the old woman might be on to something. If the group wandered away, they might miss out on a chance to get back home. Back to their normal lives.

Hank looked at Helen. "Those things don't seem to be going anywhere. At this rate, we might be trapped in here for a while, no matter what we want to do." He turned to Lisa. "How many more muffins do you have stashed away?"

"Not enough."

"That's great," Morgan said. "You can add starvation to our list of problems."

Beth chuckled. "Morgan, you don't need to worry about starving. You're gonna piss off someone and get thrown into the river long before that point."

"I might jump in the river myself if I have to sit huddled back here with all of you much longer. Is it still out there?" They had not heard anything for several minutes.

William leaned around the counter. "Let me have a look." He stood and crept out into the room. A moment later, he told them the coast was clear.

As Al rose to his feet, Beth placed her hand on his arm. "Hey. That was a pretty cool thing you did earlier, saving my boss."

Al felt his heart speed up. Normally, Beth would not give him the time of day. She was out of his league. To be fair, Lisa was out of his league as well. But Beth was far too cute to even talk with someone like him. Now she was holding onto his arm, right in front of everyone.

"Um, thanks," Al said. He wondered how old Beth was. Her face was perfectly smooth, without a hint of a wrinkle.

Beth smiled, gave his arm a squeeze, and let go.

Al felt scared, but he also felt excited. *Attention from two babes in one day.* He wondered how much he really wanted to go back to his normal life.

THIRTEEN

Thick chunks of white skin hung from the bricks where the hadrosaur cow had scratched herself. The stink of vinegar and rotten vegetation filled the room. Lisa felt a gag in her throat. Morgan walked over and pulled a piece of skin from the bricks.

"Don't touch that," Lisa said. "It's disgusting." Downy tufts clumped on the skin. "It looks mangy."

Morgan held it up in the air. "I'm touching actual dinosaur skin. No other human being in the history of time has ever done that." He leered at Callie. "Now you can put me in the record books too." The others crowded around and examined the skin, but no one else felt the need to touch it.

Outside, the sun had climbed above the treetops and now shone on their building. Most of the hadrosaurs settled into the cool mud halfway between the river and the tree line.

Lisa retreated to the back corner. She felt more comfortable there, partly because it was where she normally worked and partly because it was as far from the water and windows as she could get. She sat on the station that held sugar, creamer, and wooden stirrers.

William sat down at a table near the front corner. Beth took a seat next to him. Tim stood nearby, watching out the windows. The three of them had formed a tidy little group, Lisa realized.

Al wandered back and sat next to her. Lisa leaned into him and he put his arm around her.

Hank paced back and forth through the room. "There must be something special about this location. Most of us don't even know each other. We all just happened to be here at the same time. It's the only thing we have in common." He stopped next to Helen. She had produced a ball of yarn and knitted away at one end of a short red scarf. Lisa found the noise of the clicking needles comforting.

Hank put a hand on Helen's shoulder. "I think you might be right. We need to stay close by, in case someone comes looking for us."

Al spoke up. "A few minutes ago, you wanted to leave."

Hank looked up, nostrils wide. "I don't know what we should do. I just don't like being trapped in here." He resumed his pacing.

Lisa reached across her body and found Al's other hand. "Thank you for fishing me out of the river," she said quietly. Al flexed, hugging her tightly. His arm felt solid. Right now she needed solid. She closed her eyes and listened to the conversations in her café.

"That noise reminds me of the forests in Florida," William said. A cacophony of strange buzzes came from the woods around them.

"You're from there," Tim commented more than asked. "I've never seen the ocean."

"It's beautiful. I miss it. Being transferred to Colorado was supposed to be a punishment, I think. But it turned out for the best."

"Punishment for what?" Beth asked.

"A few years back, I blew the whistle on my boss's boss for phony billings. In hindsight, I think my boss was in on it too. My career went nowhere. I always got the worst routes and the holiday shifts."

He sat back and looked at the jungle, his long legs stretched out under the table. "The transfer to Colorado ended up being a fresh start. I got off my high horse and just did my job." He smiled. "The thing of it was, once I stopped being a crusader, things started going my way. I even got a good raise two months ago. Started allowing myself a morning beverage at this place. Maybe that was unlucky, after all, huh?"

"What do you think is happening back in Denver?" Beth asked. "Do you think they've figured out where we are?"

"I've been wondering about that," Tim said. "We've been here more than an hour now. I keep picturing this gaping hole in the corner of the building, with yellow police tape around it. I don't know what Julie's thinking. It's a hell of a way to get stood up."

William looked over at Tim. "You just met this girl?"

He nodded. "Get this; she took me flying on our third date. How's that for cool? We went up in a little Cessna that belongs to one of her pilot friends. Flew south and circled over the Garden of the Gods."

"So she's a pilot?"

"She only has a basic license. She really wants to be a commercial pilot for the airlines. Right now she works as a flight attendant."

Hank stopped pacing and stood next to Tim. "That's a nice story and I'm sure she's a real sweetheart, but do you think maybe we could focus on figuring out how to get the fuck out of here?"

William turned around in his chair. "Listen Hank, I'm as scared as you are. I want to get home to my boys. But until those duckbilled dinosaurs leave, we are stuck here. If you've got some new ideas – *hey!*"

William pushed back in his chair and looked down at his leg.

"I thought something bit me. Ow!" He pulled up his pants leg.

"What is it?" Lisa jumped off the counter and ran to the front.

A pale tick the size of a small pancake clung to William's sock. Eight legs as thick as pencils dug into his skin. The tick's face was buried in the flesh of William's calf.

"Aaaahhh! Aaaahhh!! Get him offa me! Aaaahhh!"

Morgan danced around, squirming. "What the shit!" A second tick crawled across the floor under the table.

"Get him offa me! Aaaahhh! Aaaahhh!"

Helen stepped forward, grabbed the tick behind its head, and pulled. An inch-long needle-like proboscis came out of

William's skin, dripping clear fluid. William's blood pumped visibly inside its translucent body.

"Aaaaaaaahhh!"

Helen dropped the tick and Tim stomped on it. A mixture of blood and white guts squirted onto the café floor. Helen pointed to the other tick, which scurried toward her like a crab. Tim crunched it under his heel.

William finally stopped screaming and pulled his knee up against his chest, rubbing his leg rapidly.

Several giggles came from the group. Tall, stoic William had been reduced to jelly. Nevertheless, Lisa was sure as hell glad there weren't any giant ticks crawling on her legs. She checked again and again and noticed that the rest of the group did the same.

William seemed not to care. He turned to Helen and embraced her. Tears spilled down his cheeks. "Damn bugs."

Lisa noticed Morgan standing halfway through the front window. He stopped with one foot out on the sidewalk. "Yo, everyone, check it out." A juvenile hadrosaur peeked its head around the corner of the building.

FOURTEEN

As big as a stallion, the hadrosaur calf stood on long toe-tips and sniffed at the same wall the female had used as a scratching post. A blue-gray blaze on its face contrasted the flecks of orange in its eyes. It lacked the red blistery wattle found on the older members of the herd.

Morgan peered around the clearing. The nearest adult stood by the edge of the forest, a good distance away. He turned back to the dinosaur. Morgan thought it looked cute. He had once agreed to watch his sister's puppy. After the animal pissed all over his bed, he had taken it out to the park. Never before and never since had he received so much female attention. The juvenile hadrosaur was far cooler than a puppy. "Hey ladies, come have a look at this guy." Beth and Callie walked over and stood along the front wall where they could crane their heads to the right and see most of the animal. Morgan pointed to a series of pale, uneven gashes on the back of the animal's neck. "Look, this little bastard got bit once."

Lisa winced. "I think it's nasty."

Morgan studied the animal. Mud and feces caked its hide. The folds of its skin were speckled with more of the saucer-sized ticks. "He just needs a bath."

Hank, crouched over the smashed body of the tick that had bit William, looked up. "Hey! Get away from there, you dumbass. What the hell are you doing?" The calf wailed softly and stretched its neck, sniffing.

Morgan reached out for it, feeling its hot breath on his hand. "I don't think the little ones are quite so bad, dude," he called over his shoulder. And he imagined that he looked pretty brave in front of the women, standing so close. The duckbill dinosaur was cool. Not as cool as a Triceratops, maybe, but still pretty impressive.

"Yeah, and Patricia didn't think the big ones were quite so bad," snapped Hank. "Get away from there, *NOW!*"

The commotion seemed to interest the juvenile hadrosaur. It had wandered over after all of William's screams about the ticks. Now it stepped up onto the sidewalk with one webbed foot. As it shifted its weight forward, a square block of concrete cracked off and fell into the mud with a thud.

The rest of the sidewalk moved an inch toward the river, rotating the building a few degrees. Morgan teetered forward, now fully outside. He caught himself on one of the parking meters. "Shit, you might be right, Hank." He hurried back into the building.

The juvenile followed him with its gaze, craning its neck around the corner and into the front of the room.

"Go on, now, shoo!" said Morgan, waving his hand.

The hadrosaur bleated and pulled away. It mewled pathetically as it disappeared around the side of the building.

Morgan beamed. "Ha, it minded me!"

The bookshelf wall shuddered as if hit by a truck. Morgan yelped and tumbled out of the way. All of the remaining boxes and mugs flew onto the floor. Helen jumped up from the couch and hurried to the back of the room, taking her knitting and her purse with her.

The wall took another hit. Several shelves broke off and fell to the floor. A hole appeared up near the ceiling and the flattened mouth of the bull's face poked through.

The bull hadrosaur pulled away and reared back to paw at the opening. Patricia Hayman's blood darkened its forelegs. The creature's smell filled the room: shit, mud, blood, and a horrible vinegary musk.

The bull had protected its harem for three years since challenging the previous alpha. It kept the herd small by casting out young males at an early age. A small herd traveled quietly and attracted less attention. Now the watering hole at the center of its territory had been invaded and the bull felt threatened. It pounded the wall again.

Helen stumbled and fell behind the counter. Callie moved to help her.

"You idiot!" Hank screamed at Morgan. "Look what you've done!"

The bull slapped at the building like a child kicking a cardboard fort. Chunks of plaster fell away as the hole widened.

Morgan stammered. "I didn't think -"

"God-*damn* right you didn't!" Hank shouted. "We're gonna die in here because you *can't* think!" He slapped his hand down on a display table near the counter, knocking a stack of coffee grinders to the floor.

Morgan froze, wanting to retreat to the back but unwilling to move past Hank.

The building lurched a few inches and another chunk of plaster fell inward from the top of the wall. The dinosaur stumbled forward, its head fully inside the room. Beth screamed. The creature snorted and moved its neck back and forth, slowly widening the hole.

The hadrosaur blocked their only exit. William called to Helen and Callie. "Come on, ladies. We may be going for a swim. He's going to tear this place apart."

Hank grabbed an aluminum kettle from the display table, "No shit, thanks to that asshole Morgan!" He slammed the kettle down on the table, cracking the cheap particle board. A clanging noise rang through the room.

The animal froze.

Hank brought his kettle down again on the remains of the table, shattering it with a loud CLAAANNNG!

The bull hadrosaur bleated and pulled its head out of the café.

"The noise!" Tim shouted. He grabbed a pair of metal carafes and brought them together with a metallic bang.

"HEY!" he shouted. He slammed the carafes together again and again. The clangs echoed inside the room.

Tim ran to the front and stepped through the window, still banging the metal containers together. The bull hadrosaur twisted away and actually stumbled backwards as it fled from the sound. Morgan burst into delighted laughter as he watched the giant creature run. He grabbed the door handle and began to slam it against the frame. The sound echoed in the clearing.

Hank followed Tim outside, still holding the kettle. Tim held up one container in Hank's direction and they high-fived each other with their instruments, producing a loud *BRONNNG*.

Callie, Lisa, and Al picked up utensils of their own and joined in while Tim and Hank moved down onto the mudflat and continued their discordant symphony.

The bull hadrosaur fled with shit pouring from the vent under its tail. It disappeared into the forest in long bounding steps. The other hadrosaurs followed, crashing away through the trees. One, still lying in the soft mud, floundered to its feet and fell over on one side in a panic before finally getting traction.

Morgan banged the door continuously, laughing out loud as the rest of the group joined him, most of them clanging away on whatever they could find. Lisa held a pair of metal espresso filters by their handles. William clapped two ceramic saucers together until they shattered.

"Run you fuckers!" Morgan shouted, watching the last dinosaur disappear into the forest. He turned to the rest of the group with a wide grin. "That was awesome!"

Hank raised the kettle and slammed it down into the mud. He stood in a wide stance and balled his hands in tight fists.

"Listen, dude, I'm sorry about that earlier."

"Sorry doesn't begin to cover it. You almost got us all killed."

Callie moved to her fiancé's side and wrapped herself around one of his arms. "Leave him be, Hank. He's not worth it. He's just a dumb little prick."

Morgan nodded. He had been called worse.

"Prick?" said Hank. "He's not a prick. He's an asshole. Because nothing but shit comes out of him."

William called down from the sidewalk. "Hank, if he hadn't pissed you off enough to make that racket, we'd still be stuck inside, you know."

Hank looked up, noticing his audience. He relaxed and opened his hands. "Our actions here affect one another," he told Morgan, jabbing his chest with a pointed finger. "Do not do anything like that again."

Morgan nodded. "You got it, bro."

FIFTEEN

The morning sun felt good on William's face, even in the muggy heat. He squinted and examined the scene around the café. The area looked and smelled like a stockyard. Most of the mud had been trampled flat and was land-mined with wet piles of dung.

"Everyone stay within sight of the building," William directed. They all carried their pots and pans, ready to restart the racket at a moment's notice.

"We should keep together," Beth suggested. "In horror movies, the people who wander off alone always get killed."

William nodded. "Sounds like a good idea to me. What other advice do you have?"

"Usually, the biggest danger isn't the monster. It's the other people."

Hank spun around. "Please tell me that was not directed at me."

Callie took his arm. "Hank, it's ok. You don't need to prove anything."

"I do. Right now, we need to be able to trust each other." He looked around at the group. "Do you all know where I was supposed to be this morning?"

"Anger management training?" Beth had her arms crossed, but William thought he saw her tremble. She looked defiant and frightened at the same time.

Morgan snickered.

"Very funny. I was supposed to be at a domestic abuse hearing. A guy with a rolling pin pulverized his girlfriend's face. A fucking rolling pin. You should see the photos from the emergency room." He pressed his lips together and breathed through his nose. "I'm lead prosecutor. I'm the guy that was going to make sure that cocksucker never hurt anyone again. That's what I do. I keep people safe. I'm not the bad guy."

William thought that Hank might be protesting a bit much, but there wasn't any point in arguing about it. "We hear you, Hank. It's all good."

Hank crossed his own arms and breathed heavily through his nose, nostrils flaring.

William walked over and met Helen at the end of the sidewalk. She had finally come outside. He offered her a hand and helped her down. Helen peered across the clearing.

"They're all gone," he assured her.

"I'd like to build a fire. Lawrence taught me how." She wrung her hands together. "Oh, he used to take me on some cold, dreary trips. I never could get warm. I made him teach me how to build a fire quickly, even in the rain. The trick is to leave plenty of room for air."

Callie took Hank's hand. "Come on. Let's get the lady some firewood."

"Hey, maybe I can put my mad barista skills to work," Beth said. "I'll get some water and brew us some coffee." She disappeared inside.

Callie and Hank returned with several dead branches from the tree line and within minutes, Helen had a small blaze going on the ground near the café. The wet wood produced thick smoke as it burned.

Helen sat on the square of sidewalk that had broken off under the juvenile hadrosaur's weight. She beamed at the flames. "A fire always made us feel safe, no matter where we were. I guess those trips were good for something after all." She looked up at the sky. "Thank you, Larry."

"He ain't up there," Morgan said.

Helen looked confused. "What do you mean?"

"Your old man. He ain't died yet, so he ain't up there. He won't be up there for a million years."

Helen frowned and looked down at her fire.

"That was helpful Morgan," William said. "Come on, let's have a look around." He gave Morgan a shove.

"I'd like to come too," Tim said.

The three of them began walking downstream. As they approached the lone boot on the bank, William saw something that looked like road kill which had been passed over again and again until the animal could no longer be identified. He decided he didn't want to see any more and cut inland. He wondered what had happened to Patricia's soul. Would she be alone in heaven for millions of years? He decided he did not really want to find out the answer to that question.

When they reached the tree line, they stopped and looked back. White smoke rose from the front of the building chunk. Broken beams and concrete jutted from each edge of the café, as if all of the other parts of the building had been knocked away by a wrecking ball.

"What is that on the roof?" Morgan asked. "Is that air conditioning equipment or something?"

"That's not the roof," Tim explained. "We were in an eight-story building. That's whatever was in the room upstairs. We should see if there's some way to get up there."

William pointed upstream, "First, let's go have a look from over there and see if we can tell how much of our little building is still on solid ground." The bank jutted out into the water near the upstream edge of the clearing.

As they started walking, Morgan pulled out a cigarette and lit it with a flip-top lighter. The metallic chirp of the wheel scratching the flint triggered an old yearning William felt right behind his eyes.

Morgan offered up the smoke. Tim shook his head. William accepted. "I haven't had a cigarette in sixteen years, since my first son was born." He drew in a long drag and let out a small giggle. "And I have missed them every single day since."

Morgan took back the cigarette. "I gotta be stingy with these. I've only got two more after this one. Then I guess I'll have to quit whether I want to or not."

- - - - -

Al extended an empty coffee cup over the camp fire. "What's the charge?" he said, trying to sound clever.

Beth poured from a French press. Water bubbled in a stainless steel carafe at the edge of the fire. She gave Al a coy smile. "Well, since you saved the owner's life, I think maybe it will be on the house."

Beth's smile was beautiful. He had seen that smile directed at other customers and yearned for it. Never mind the fact that he was twice her age. Not sure what to say, he took a long sip of coffee. It was strong and bitter. Perfect.

"You'd jump in and save me if I fell in the river, wouldn't you?"

Al nodded. "Of course I would." He felt his heartbeat race and his face flushed. He hoped it wasn't noticeable.

Helen coughed and poked at the fire with a stick. "We're going to need more firewood."

Al looked up at the café. Lisa had disappeared inside and he had been hoping to go in and check on her.

Beth winked at him. "Don't worry. I'll get the firewood."

Al nodded again. It felt as if she could tell what he had been thinking. It made him uncomfortable and excited at the same time. "Thanks for the coffee." He stepped past Helen and climbed up onto the sidewalk.

Inside, Lisa worked in the back corner, in the collapsed hallway that led to the restroom. She crouched by the light of several small votive candles. A few thin slivers of sunlight bled through from where the ceiling had fallen in.

"Candles, huh? I've never seen candles in here before."

"Well, I was hoping to class up the joint." Lisa hefted a fist-sized chunk of concrete off to one side. "I'm trying reach a storage pantry right over there." She pointed to a door. Debris blocked all but the top edge. "It's mostly sugar and coffee beans, but there are two other items I wanted to find."

"Is one of them a hunting rifle? 'Cause I'd be in favor of that."

She laughed. "Afraid not. The first is oatmeal. I usually add it to the menu in the fall, and I'm pretty sure I've still got a few cases left. The other is wine." She turned around and looked at Al. "It dawned on me with singular clarity that I could use a glass of wine right now. Or four."

"You running a speakeasy back here?"

"Ha. Hardly. I spent far too many afternoons sitting alone in the café waiting for a customer to walk in. Waiting and wishing I had a glass of wine at hand. Wine always makes waiting easier. When I realized I could operate a wine bar in the afternoons, it felt like a light bulb going off overhead. I submitted the application for a liquor license several weeks ago."

Al wondered if drinking something that dulled the senses was really a good idea, but decided not to bring it up. It looked like she had a long way to go before she would reach the pantry anyway. "How much do you have?"

"Two cases from a trip to Napa Valley with my sisters last year and a few samples from one of my vendors."

Lisa looked back at the pile. "Oh, hey. Come have a look at this." She picked up a silver box the size of a toaster oven and held it in the candlelight. "I found this in the rubble. It must have fallen through from the floor upstairs." Heavy wires sheathed in thick metal bands protruded from one edge. "You were in computers. Stevens Information Systems, right? Can you tell me what this is?"

Al studied the box, moving close to her. "It's not anything I've ever seen." Circuit boards were visible through a crack on one side, but there wasn't any sign of a keyboard or monitor, and the cables coming out of it were nearly two inches in diameter. "That isn't your normal office computer. I wonder if much of the second floor came back in time with us. How do you get up there?"

"I don't know. They have their own entrance in the other side of the building. There must have been an elevator back there." Lisa put the box back on the floor. "There were some strange people working upstairs," she explained. "They were very secretive. They would always stop talking any time you got too close. I usually saw them out in the alley smoking cigarettes." She studied Al. "You don't smoke, do you?"

He smiled. The answer to this one was easy and he could see that it would earn him some points. "Never touch them. Barely drink, either."

"Yeah, well, if we find the wine, you gotta have a drink with me, ok?"

Al took a risk. He reached out and touched her chin with his thumb. He wanted to move in for a kiss, but he was terrified she would pull away. After the smile from Beth, he already felt aroused. Was that clouding his judgment? The candlelight added to the mood, but it was too dark to read her expression. She *owed* him a kiss, didn't she? He had saved her life and risked his own in the process. She owed him a hell of a lot more, when it came right down to it, but for now he would settle for a kiss. Al looked at her lips, wondering if he should move quickly or slowly.

Before he could take a chance with either approach, Helen clambered inside through the front window. "One of them is coming back," she called across the room.

Lisa pulled away. "Come on, let's go show him who's boss." She picked up a pair of metal travel mugs.

Al wrenched his jaw in frustration. As Lisa pushed past, she seemed to notice. "Hey." She tilted her head down while looking up at him. "Why don't we continue this conversation later?"

Al swallowed her promise and followed her out of the building.

"Be careful out there," Helen called as they passed by.

Outside, Beth stood at the far edge of the jungle, holding a half-dozen sticks under one arm and her serving tray under the other. She leaned this way and that, peering into the depths of the forest. Something big moved around in the trees.

Beth dropped the firewood and pulled a long serving spoon from her back pocket. She raised the spoon and banged on her tray like a gong.

At the upstream edge of the clearing, William and Tim crouched and looked back at the chunk of building. William rose to his feet as the young barista clanged away. Each crash reverberated with a musical twang.

Callie and Hank held hands in the center of the clearing. Callie's red hair gleamed in the sunlight, almost as bright as Hank's running shorts. Al and Lisa joined them. Lisa took Al's hand and gave him a wink. He smiled at her like a kid in a toy store.

"Beth, that might not be a good idea," Hank called out.

The rustling in the jungle grew louder and closer. Al finally saw movement and realized he was looking too low. A shape grew in the shadows, towering over Beth. She stopped swinging her spoon.

A forty-five foot long *Tyrannosaurus rex* shouldered through the last few rows of trees.

SIXTEEN

Beth dropped her instruments, turned on her heels, and ran, all in one fluid motion. She made it ten feet before the platter and spoon hit the ground. The tyrannosaur stepped onto the mud flat and lowered its jaws toward the girl.

Beth continued to scream as she ran. Her blood-curdling cry pierced the jungle, louder than any of the ruckus they had made with the pots and pans. She screamed like someone in pain, even though she had not been hurt yet. She did not realize she was screaming. She only knew that the monster coming out of the trees looked far more dangerous than the hadrosaurs and did not care one bit about her little clang-clanging.

As Beth ran, one thought went through her mind over and over: *Don't slip, don't slip, don't slip.* The mud was thick, but she wore a decent pair of shoes. Her job required her to stand on her feet for hours, after all.

She felt the ground shake with each step of the giant dinosaur behind her. Beth pushed herself faster. The café was within reach, but she meant to run past it, around the back, and then leap into the river. The current would sweep her right behind the building and out of sight. She pictured her escape as a scene in a movie, both clever and thrilling. Hollywood producers would line up to buy her story once she got home. She wouldn't need to save for film school. She wouldn't need to work her way up the ladder.

Beth closed in on the building, only a few steps from the corner.

The tyrannosaur snaked its head forward. Beth felt pressure on the sides of her body. For a fraction of a second, she thought someone had grabbed her to shove her out of the way. Probably William. William had come to save her.

The pressure tightened and Beth knew she was wrong. The ground dropped away as the tyrannosaur lifted her. She looked down on the café and the open floor above it. Then the jaws ground together, separating her hips from her body. Beth felt a horrible incontinence as organs slipped from her abdominal cavity. The tyrannosaur bit down again. Nine-inch teeth frayed Beth's spine in three places and she ceased to feel anything at all.

- - - - -

Hank grabbed Callie and Lisa by the shoulders and started backing away slowly. "Don't run from a predator," he hissed. "You'll trigger a pursuit instinct." They weren't quite in the center of the clearing, but they were close enough. There was no cover nearby.

The tyrannosaur raised its head upward and pulled Beth's mangled body deep into its mouth with its pale tongue. Her legs, arms, and head all disappeared down its gullet at the same time.

Without pausing, the tyrannosaur turned toward the two couples out in the open. It normally ate two thousand pounds before it felt full. Beth Caldecott barely broke one hundred.

Hank, Callie, Al and Lisa had been backing away steadily. Now Lisa froze, hyperventilating. Hank gave Callie a firm shove toward the forest. Al began to run also, holding onto Lisa's hand and yanking her along. The tyrannosaur took two steps in their direction, blood dripping from its lips.

Not my wife, Hank thought, even though Callie was still only a fiancé. He stuck two filthy fingers in his mouth and whistled, a high-pitched screech that he used at parties and weddings to silence a noisy crowd.

The giant dinosaur stopped and tilted its head. *That's it*, Hank thought. He dug in his heels and sprinted downstream along the riverbank.

The tyrannosaur raised its tail high in the air and kicked forward after Hank, ignoring the others. Prey that ran in a group often scattered in different directions, causing it to lose focus. It preferred a single target.

Hank knew instinctively that he had no chance. He could feel the dinosaur gaining on him. He lowered his head and ran harder, pushing himself. His foot slipped in a wet patch of hadrosaur shit and he tumbled forward, arms spinning. Miraculously, he somehow brought his leg up under him and caught his balance, banging his knee into his chest.

Closing the gap, the tyrannosaur turned its enormous head to one side and started to swing it forward for an easy strike. As the motion began, it caught a strong whiff of the smell that had attracted it to the river in the first place, before it had heard the banging pots and pans.

Even more than a lone target, the tyrannosaur favored carrion. Dead prey didn't fight back. It circled to a stop next to the river.

Hank threw himself into a clump of tall fern-like bushes, gasping for air and wondering how he was still alive. A quick glance over his shoulder showed that the dinosaur was no longer directly behind him. He crawled forward through the foliage and deeper into the trees by the downstream shoreline.

Pawing at the ground near the bank, the tyrannosaur bent over the mud and began pulling with its mouth and tongue.

- - - - -

Callie, Lisa, and Al had reached the forest as well, straight out from the river. They stopped to look back. On the right, Callie saw Hank flit through the trees by the shore, circling in their direction.

The tyrannosaur continued to bite at the ground. The animal stood with its legs wide apart as it bent over. Short, matted tufts grew from its body, giving its skin a moldy appearance. Its naked head and legs looked pale and sickly.

"What's it doing?" Callie asked, breathing heavily. "It's eating the mud. Why is it eating the mud?"

"That isn't mud," Al said, holding Lisa tightly, trying to quiet her sobs against his chest.

With a small tug, the beast pulled a knotted strand of Patricia Hayman's ruined torso out of the ground and gulped it down. Another bite followed, equal parts leg and mud.

"Let's get out of here," Al said. He took Lisa's hand and began to pull her again as the dinosaur sniffed the ground, looking for anything it might have missed.

They ran deeper into the woods, directly away from the river. Callie wanted to call out to Hank, so that he could find them, but she could not force herself to make a sound. The realization shamed her. He had lured that monster away with a whistle, yet she was too afraid to shout out his name.

SEVENTEEN

"Shit shit shit," Tim muttered. He stepped forward. He wanted to do something, but there was nothing to do. Beth no longer existed. "Shit."

"Let's go," William whispered. "We got to stay together, like that girl said." William and Morgan walked quietly upstream. They entered the forest right where it crept down to the river.

Tim looked back one last time. *Oh crap! Helen.* They had left a seventy-something year-old woman alone inside the café. He saw no sign of her.

The tyrannosaur wandered around the clearing, sniffing at everything like a dog. It paused and lifted its nose as it walked around the back side of the structure. With its thick neck extended, its chin reached the top of the building. It sniffed and moved on.

As it passed, Tim saw a woman's face above the broken wall on the second floor, just above the dinosaur's head. Tim wondered if Helen had somehow found a way upstairs. It seemed impossible, but someone was up there.

The tyrannosaur grunted, snorted, and turned to look in Tim's direction. Both eyes focused forward on him. It snorted and lumbered directly toward him.

Oh, shit shit shit! Tim turned and took off into the woods.

Somewhere ahead, he heard William shouting, "*Stay Close!*" and "*Stay together!*" Tim followed the sound. A thick layer of dead needles carpeted the ground and small boulders dotted the forest floor. The light grey rocks were easy enough to see in the morning light, but Tim felt a pervasive paranoia that he would slam into an unseen branch at any moment. As he ran, he searched for a boulder that might be big enough to hide behind or crawl under, but he saw only smooth low shapes. The feeling of exposure ran up his spine like nails on a chalk board.

The crashing sound of breaking tree trunks came from behind. The tyrannosaur was gaining.

Tim found himself planning his route carefully as the rocks grew more numerous. Ahead, through the trees, he saw William and Morgan catch up to Al and Lisa. Lisa stumbled to the ground with a shriek. Al pulled her to her feet without stopping. She kept running, but favored one foot, the one without a shoe. The four of them moved to the right, where the ground rose slightly. Out in front, Tim caught a glimpse of Callie, farther ahead and alone.

A new shape came out of the woods next to Tim. His heart skipped and he flinched away before he realized it was Hank. "It's coming," Hank said between breaths. They could hear branches crack as the tyrannosaur followed them through the woods.

Hank, twenty years Tim's senior, pulled ahead and passed him by. Tim remembered the old joke about outrunning a bear in the woods. *You don't need to outrun the dinosaur,* he thought. *You only need to outrun the slowest guy in the group.* Right now, Tim was the slowest guy.

Ahead, the forest grew brighter as the trees grew thinner, exposing another clearing. The ground sloped down and away to the left. As Tim ran through the last few trees, he saw a rock wall on the right side of the clearing. Above the cliff, the forest sloped up and away.

Al shouted, *"Here, here!"* He wove around a jumble of boulders where the cliff first began. The whole clearing looked as if giant hands had grabbed the ground and pulled up on one side while pressing down on the other side at the same time. Al, Lisa, William, and Morgan raced up the slope on the right.

Below them, Callie and Hank had already passed the split where the cliff began. They saw the others up above and veered toward the wall. It rose up only ten feet high where they met it. William stopped and reached down to help them scramble up. Using their hands to climb, they quickly reached the top and continued forward along the cliff's edge.

If the Tyrannosaurus takes the high path, then what? Tim thought. There was ample room along the top of the cliff for the dinosaur. Tim stayed to the left, on the lower ground. He passed the spot where Callie and Hank climbed up, hoping the tyrannosaur would follow him. The wall grew taller and steeper next to him as he ran.

He looked back to see the dinosaur enter the clearing behind him. Tim tried to speed up, but couldn't. His legs burned. He picked a spot along the cliff about twenty feet high and ran up the scree of loose rocks at the base. He hit the wall and began to climb. In seconds he was halfway up.

"Tim! Hurry! *Hurry!*" William shouted from above. Tim found a diagonal ledge that allowed him to scramble a bit higher. "HURRY!"

The snorting of the dinosaur behind him grew louder. Tim's lungs ached. The top was just out of reach and there was nothing he could grab, no way to get any leverage on the smooth rock surface.

William appeared above, reaching down. "I gotcha boy, *jump!*" He looked at Tim, glanced off beyond him, and then looked back. "JUMP NOW!"

It was a one shot deal. He could jump and he could easily reach William's hand, but if the man did not hold onto him, there was no way he could keep from sliding back down the wall.

He pushed off and reached, his right hand grabbing William's wrist just as William clasped his own. Tim waited for the Tyrannosaurus to bite his legs and pull him back down.

William held tight and hoisted him up over the top of the cliff. Tim rolled away from the edge and lay on the ground.

Panting, Tim swung around and looked back, face to face with the largest predator to ever walk the Earth.

EIGHTEEN

Al couldn't stop smiling. They were safe. The tyrannosaur was only a few feet away, but it could not reach them. "Look at him!"

The tyrannosaur stood in the clearing below, its face even with the edge of the cliff. It clawed at the rocky ground with its feet, but couldn't get enough traction to move any closer. The seven-ton dinosaur sidestepped back and forth along the base of the cliff. It bobbed its head rhythmically as it moved.

"Take this!" Al picked up a stout branch and poked it in the creature's face, trying to get at its eye. He laughed gleefully.

"You're pissing it off," Callie warned. "Leave it alone." She gripped her arms across her chest. Tears ran down her face.

The tyrannosaur turned its head sideways and closed its jaws on the branch. Al released it a split second before being pulled forward. Callie yelped, but Al only laughed again.

Morgan giggled and slapped Al on the back. "Hah! Just look at that fucker!"

Al nodded. The adrenaline rush from the chase through the woods had pumped him up. *We can survive this*, he realized. Their situation did not have to be a death sentence. The cliff itself showed promise. If they could find a cave or a tall rock formation, they could have permanent shelter.

The tyrannosaur's head looked bald, a pale, yellowish pink. The end of its muzzle was covered with mud. Downy grey-green fluff grew on its hide, starting at its thick neck and continuing across its body to the end of its tail. Its eyes were large black globes with no discernible pupils. Its nostrils flared as it breathed.

The dinosaur snapped at the group again, scraping its chin on the edge of the cliff. Al noticed bits of pink flesh caught between its teeth and suddenly remembered. *Beth.* She had finally begun to take notice of him and now she was gone. *Don't be foolish*, Al thought. *Don't be cocky either. It's not like you're going to hook up with more than one girl all of a sudden.* Beth had always been cold to him back home, anyway. He knew he should focus on… "Lisa!" Al turned to look for her.

Lisa sat trembling against a tree trunk, a few yards back from the drop-off. She pressed her fists tightly against her temples. "Oh my God, Lisa!" He ran to her and put his arms around her. She buried her face in his chest and wailed. Al held her tightly and said "I know, I know," over and over again.

William pulled Tim to his feet and held onto his hand for a moment. Tim broke free and wrapped both arms around the tall man. "Thank you."

"Hey, you might'a made all the difference there, staying down at the bottom. If that thing had taken the uphill track, we'd still be running. Besides, I owed you one."

"It could still get up here, you know," Callie pointed out. The tyrannosaur could simply walk back to the beginning of the cliff, make a u-turn, and come right up after them.

"He's not smart enough to figure that out," Morgan said. "Are you, you dumbass?"

Hank pulled his phone from his pocket and took a picture. "Smile, you son of a bitch." The tyrannosaur snarled at the flash.

Al tried to pull Lisa to her feet, but she felt like dead weight. He leaned back to get a better look at her. The bottom of her foot was bright red. "Lisa's hurt."

Callie and Hank came over. Callie's face was still wet. "Christ, Lisa, I'm so sorry." Lisa sobbed harder.

Al held up Lisa's foot so that Callie could get a look. Lisa had landed on a pointed rock or a branch or something during their run through the jungle. Blood oozed from a dime-sized hole in the center of her arch.

The tyrannosaur dropped away and turned its head. Hank jumped up and fanned his arms wildly. "Oh no, you don't." The movement reignited the creature's attention. It lurched back in their direction, scrambling against the base of the cliff with its massive feet. Hank hollered and danced around. The tyrannosaur stretched its thick neck to reach for him. It flexed the black claws on its pale yellow arms, like the talons of a hawk reaching for prey.

Al snickered. "Looks like Captain Angry is happy for a change."

Callie looked over at her fiancé. "That's how he gets when he's watching the Broncos." She tugged at Al's sleeve. "Help me tear this off."

Al extended his right arm and together they ripped off the sleeve of his dress shirt. Callie folded the cloth flat and wrapped it around Lisa's foot. She tied the ends together like oversize shoelaces. "That'll have to do for now. Is everyone else okay?

William scanned the group. "Helen! She's still back at the building."

"That's not all," Tim said. "I think there was someone else back there."

"What do you mean?"

"I saw a woman on the roof. Or upstairs, really, I guess. Right before this thing chased us away."

"Are you sure it wasn't Helen?"

"This woman was on the second floor, up above the café. Helen had trouble climbing in and out on the ground floor. Besides, the woman I saw, she looked younger."

Al studied Tim's long, tan face. "We were in the café the whole time. If there was really someone upstairs, why didn't she call for help?"

Tim shrugged. "I'm just telling you what I saw."

Al leaned in close to Lisa. "Come on, you gotta get up now." He helped her to her feet. Her sobs turned into quiet gasps.

"Well, we have to get back to the café," William said. "We can't leave Helen by herself, and if there is someone else there, they might know something about all this."

"That's suicide," Al said. He walked Lisa forward. She hopped along, clinging to Al and holding her shoeless foot off the ground. The tyrannosaur snapped at the group. Lisa flinched. Al pulled her close and turned to the others. "Going back down to the river means going back to where this guy can reach us. Back to a spot where two people have died already. I say we follow this cliff. If we can find a cave that's out of reach, we'll be safe."

He looked around. The cliff curved away in the distance as far as he could see. Jagged rocks jutted from the edge here and there.

"It does make sense to go on a little farther," Tim said. "And the farther we lure him from the river, the better. But we gotta get back to that café. What if the building suddenly goes home while we're not there?"

Al shook his head. "If you want to die, that sounds great. This thing showed up after all that noise we made with the pots and pans. So we know it has good hearing. Then, it went straight to Patricia's remains, even though it practically had Frank there in its mouth."

"*Hank*," said Hank. He stopped taunting the tyrannosaur and began paying attention to the debate.

Al went on. "Despite the fact that it *had* him. So its sense of smell is spot-on too. And most importantly, it knows now that the river is a place it can find food."

Morgan took on the job of distracting the dinosaur. He clucked like a chicken and strutted back and forth, flapping his arms.

"Hey, what's that?" Callie pointed. "Is that water?" She gazed over the tops of the trees that grew on the opposite side of the clearing below.

Al shielded his eyes from the sun, which shone directly on his face from straight ahead. He saw pink light on a few thin clouds in the distance. Finally, in between the lowest sections of the canopy, he saw sparkling glints on the horizon.

"That sure is water," William exclaimed. "That looks like the ocean."

"Ocean?" Hank stammered. "What the hell does that mean? Are we not even in Colorado any more?"

"There was an inland sea here," William said. "The heartland of America was covered with water at one point in time. *This* point in time."

Tim wandered further down the cliff, craning his head for a better view. The tyrannosaur followed along below him, enticed by a single individual breaking from the pack.

Al marveled at the side view of the creature. Its neck looked too big for its body, like the neck of a hyena. The downy tufts growing on its back and flanks were thicker, matted, and ragged.

Lisa looked up at Al. "So what happens if we do find a cave? We had food and water back at the café."

"We hunker down until that monster loses interest and wanders off." Al pointed over at the tyrannosaur, which continued to follow Tim along the cliff. "The important thing is to keep you safe. Once we're sure the coast is clear, some of us can go back for supplies. And for Helen."

Hank shook his head. "And just leave her alone until then? I don't think so."

Al answered carefully and slowly. "We have to find a stronghold. Some kind of high ground. Like this, but protected on all sides. Once we find that, we can send someone back for her. We've been away for less than half an hour. She's fine. Besides, Tim says she *isn't* alone."

"All the more reason to go back there," Hank said.

"Hey, it's coming back." Morgan pointed. The tyrannosaur was following Tim back to the group.

"I've got a better idea," Tim said when he reached the others. "I say we kill this dinosaur."

NINETEEN

"You've got my attention," William said. He was glad for another option. This group argued more than his teenage sons.

Tim waved them further down the cliff. "Come this way." He walked near the edge, where he could get a good view of the clearing. The tyrannosaur followed along below.

William sucked in a sharp breath. "Easy son. Don't get so close." William stayed back from the drop off, along with everyone else.

Tim looked over his shoulder. "I work as a carpenter, framing houses mostly. I'm up on half-built rooftops all day. This is nothing."

He stopped the group at an outcropping that split off from the cliff face. A finger of rock the size of a car stuck straight up, with a four-foot wide crevice between it and the cliff. It looked like a chunk of ice ready to calve off from the end of a glacier.

"We lure him over here and then apply a little leverage to that boulder," Tim proposed.

The luring part did not seem to be an issue. The tyrannosaur stood below the fractured rock, sniffing around. William imagined the boulder falling onto the dinosaur and breaking its leg or possibly killing it outright.

Morgan tittered. "Now you're talking. I want to find out what T-rex tastes like!"

"I'm betting chicken," said Hank.

Tim walked away from the cliff. "Let me find a branch or something we can use." He disappeared into the woods.

The tyrannosaur tested the wall below in search of a foothold. The cliff here was taller and the dinosaur's head no longer reached the top. The clearing widened a bit, giving the creature more room to pace around. Any time it started to wander off, Morgan drew it back with his clucking chicken imitation. He laughed and occasionally threw softball-sized rocks at its head. The dinosaur snapped at the air each time it was hit, like a dog biting at a bee.

William looked down at the tyrannosaur. Before they became teenagers too cool for the zoo, William's sons had loved the raised walkway above the giraffe exhibit. They always made him purchase a bag of "giraffe biscuits," which looked suspiciously like wheat crackers. The giraffes' massive heads came right over the railing and their long purple tongues took the biscuits from the boys' hands. As William looked down at the tyrannosaur below, he thought of the giraffe exhibit. This was terrifying, but it was also awesome. *I don't care how old you boys are, you would love this.* At the same time, he was glad they weren't there.

Tim returned, dragging a fallen sapling about eighteen feet long and as thick as his calf. "Come on. Let's give this a shot."

The group gathered around and together they extended the tree over the edge. They fed it into the crevice between the outcropping and the cliff face. Tim moved to the front and carefully positioned the far end of the trunk against the boulder, as low as possible. The tyrannosaur snapped at dangling branches. It stripped off dead leaves that hung from the sides but it could not reach the trunk itself.

Tim braced the midpoint against the edge of the cliff. The other end rose into the air, creating a perfect lever. Everyone moved alongside to grab hold of it, with the tallest, Al and William, in the back. William counted to three and they all pulled down.

Instead of prying off the rock, the sapling simply bent to the ground in a wide arc.

The tyrannosaur snapped at the crevice, trying to get at the branches inside, but could not fit its mouth into the gap between the cliff and the jutting boulder.

"Let's try a battering ram," Tim suggested. They brought the tree back up and positioned it straight out, this time against the high part of the boulder. William counted again and they all heaved forward.

The rock shifted slightly on their third stroke. On the fourth heave, the tree trunk bowed out to the side, pushing Al close to the edge. The tyrannosaur snapped in his direction. He screamed, exciting it even more. The inside of its mouth was an ugly blank white.

"Pull!" Al shouted, still holding onto the tree. The others yanked the tree back, tugging Al away from the edge.

"This tree is worthless," he spat. "It's going to get us killed." He shoved it over the cliff. The dinosaur bent and sniffed it in the clearing below.

"It moved," Tim said. "That rock moved a little. We can still kill this bastard. There's got to be a way."

"There's a way," Hank said. "If one of us got down in that crevice, there should be enough leverage to push it loose."

William looked over the edge and then at Hank. "Are you volunteering?"

Callie took him by the arm. "Hank, no."

"Don't worry, babe. I would, but my rotator cuff isn't up to it. But Tim could manage. He climbs around on half-finished rooftops all day, right?"

Tim chewed absently on his lip and nodded slowly. He looked to William. "What do you think?"

William looked over the edge. The thought of climbing down the cliff wall made his stomach tumble. But the tyrannosaur's mouth clearly could not fit in the crevice. Tim would be safe as long as he stayed in the gap. William wanted the creature to die. It had killed Beth and there was no way to know how long it would stick around. He looked up at Tim. "Can you do it?"

Tim nodded.

"I think it's worth a shot."

Tim turned and sat down on the edge of the cliff with his feet dangling into the crevice. Twisting around, he anchored his hands in a crack and reached below with one leg.

Morgan squirmed away. "Whoa, dude. That's insane."

The dinosaur scrambled forward and mouthed the crevice with renewed interest, but its oversized jaws could not fit into the gap.

Tim stretched with his other leg, touching the boulder behind him. The distance was too far to get any real leverage. "I've got to get lower." Tim walked himself down into the crevice with his hands on the cliff and his feet on the jutting rock behind him. As the gap narrowed, the going seemed to become easier.

"Tim, you don't have to do this," Lisa called. "We can figure out something else."

"He's already down there," Hank said. "Let him try."

"Yeah, but how is he going to get back up?"

William felt his stomach tumble again. Lisa was right. If Tim did somehow knock the rock free, he wouldn't be able to use it to climb back up. He would need to scale the cliff in front of him. William leaned forward to look over the edge.

Tim dug his fingers into a crack on the wall. He braced his elbows against the cliff and walked his legs up on the rock behind him. Tim's arms trembled as he held himself horizontal and pushed the rock with his feet.

"It's moving!" Callie shouted.

The rock shifted and widened the gap. The tyrannosaur noticed this and nosed forward. The crevice was still too small for its oversized jaws, but not by much. Spittle from the tyrannosaur's breath landed on Tim as the dinosaur snapped at him.

Tim let his legs drop from the rock behind him. His knees slammed against the wall below and he grunted.

"That's enough," William said. He realized that if the rock broke away and *didn't* land on the tyrannosaur, Tim would be exposed on the cliff at exactly the height of its jaws. "Get out of there, Tim. This isn't working."

"What's that noise?" Callie said. A high-pitched shriek came from the woods across the clearing.

Down below, Tim let go with one hand and flexed his fingers, stretching them. William's heart pounded in his chest. He couldn't tell if Tim's feet were on some sort of ledge below, or if he was supporting his entire weight with his other hand.

The tyrannosaur grew still and quiet.

"I need some help here, guys," Tim called up.

The yelping sound repeated over and over as it grew closer.

A small dog burst into the clearing below. It stopped right behind the tyrannosaur and yelped louder, then turned and ran in the direction of the river. Its short, scruffy tail curled pathetically under its belly. The remains of a leash bounced along on the ground behind it.

"Oh my God!" Lisa gasped. "Is that a dog?"

"What's happening?" Tim called out, "William, I need a hand."

The dog's pursuer emerged from the forest. *Triceratops horridus.*

Morgan's face froze in an enormous grin. "Fuckin' A!"

The animal was huge, nearly as tall as the tyrannosaur, and three tons heavier. It knocked over a thirty-foot tree as it shouldered into the clearing and then came to a stop facing the tyrannosaur.

TWENTY

The two dinosaurs focused on one another, both motionless. After more than a hundred thousand years of coexistence, tyrannosaurs had developed an instinctive fear of the horned dinosaurs. Triceratops traveled in large groups and worked together to run down predators that ventured too close. They did more than just chase away intruders. They pursued them in groups of five or six, sometimes for hours, until they exhausted their enemy. They attacked as a team, surrounding the predator and striking from all sides. They did not stop until the intruder was gored to death by dozens of strikes with their horns.

The Triceratops in the clearing stood alone, however. It had wandered away from its herd. The tyrannosaur sensed a rare opportunity. With its eyes locked on the horned animal's face, it stepped slowly away from the cliff wall.

The Triceratops charged. Its massive head lolled from side to side as it ran. The tips of its meter-long horns swished audibly through the air.

The tyrannosaur opened its mouth and let out an earth-shaking bellow.

TWENTY-ONE

Tim heard and felt the roar, but could not see anything other than the cliff wall. It was the first time the tyrannosaur had made more than a few gasps or grunts. The angry sound pounded Tim's chest. Pebbles rolled down the cliff wall into his hair. He shouted up at the sky, "Can you guys lower a branch or something?"

He heard no reply.

Tim looked down and saw a wider ledge to his right. He had to lower himself further to stand on it, but at least he was able to take some of the weight off of his hands. It also brought him closer to the opening between the rock and the wall. He looked out over his right shoulder.

In the clearing below, the Triceratops barreled forward like a locomotive. The tyrannosaur lifted its foot high in the air and brought it down just before the Triceratops made contact. The foot landed on the giant frill that grew back and away from the horned animal's face. Three massive claws clenched through leathery skin below one of the long horns, piercing bone. The tyrannosaur kicked downward at the same moment, rotating the charging animal's head and slamming it to the ground. A victim of its own momentum, the Triceratops slid forward on its front shoulder. The tyrannosaur sidestepped, lowered its head, and sunk nine-inch teeth into the Triceratops' hip.

Rubble and dust rolled down the cliff into Tim's face as the twenty-thousand pound Triceratops came to a stop below. The boulder behind him shifted away several more inches, widening the gap. He looked up again. *"Hello? Is anyone there?"*

The tyrannosaur leaned forward over its enemy, raising its tail high in the air. Its jaws were splayed so wide around the Triceratops' flank that it could not close its mouth.

Lying on its side, the Triceratops dug its legs into the ground and pivoted toward its attacker. Once it gained traction with its feet, it snapped its head upward and one of the three-foot spikes lacerated the side of the tyrannosaur's belly.

Yes. Please. Kill it, Tim thought.

The tyrannosaur released its grip, roared, and backed away a few steps.

The four-legged battering ram bounded onto its feet and pressed the attack. It charged ruthlessly, aiming its horns for the tyrannosaur's gut. This time the charge connected. The short, wide horn on its nose plunged deep.

The Triceratops pushed forward, backing the tyrannosaur into the cliff. Tim gripped the handhold tightly in front of him and closed his eyes as the tyrannosaur slammed against the crevice. The predator's neck blocked out the light and the boulder shifted inward now, leaving Tim with only a few inches of clearance. As he shifted his grip, he felt the rock scrape his back.

This is it, Tim thought. The group up top had probably used the distraction to flee back to the river or maybe to Al's mythical cave. Whatever happened next was out of his control. Remembering how Morgan had touched the hadrosaur skin in the café, Tim let go with one hand and reached out to touch the tyrannosaur's hide. The downy layer felt as soft as goose feathers, but underneath it was like living rock. Hard, rough, and flexing.

The tyrannosaur lifted its knee, dislodging the horn from its gut and knocking away the Triceratops' face. As it stepped clear from the wall, the giant boulder broke free. It tumbled back and off to Tim's left, away from the two dinosaurs battling on the right. Tim felt a shake when the rock hit the ground below. He was now completely exposed on the side of the cliff.

Oh shit, oh shit. He inhaled and discovered that he was about to scream without even meaning to. He stopped himself, realizing that it might draw their attention.

Tim watched the Triceratops dig in with its hind legs and snort. It pawed the ground with one of its front feet. Tim looked for a crevice or handhold he could use to pull himself up. As long as the tyrannosaur stayed focused on the battle, it might not notice him. The rock wall at the local gym had little plastic knobs every ten inches. *Where the hell are the goddamn plastic knobs?* Above him, the wall was smooth and flat. Without the boulder behind him for leverage, there was no way to climb up.

The Triceratops stopped snorting and lunged, head lowered and horns horizontal.

With the boulder gone, Tim realized that the trajectory of the next charge would drive the tyrannosaur right into him. If he wasn't crushed, he would be knocked from the wall. He looked down. He considered dropping twenty feet onto the jagged rocks below, but could not make himself let go.

The tyrannosaur did not allow the Triceratops to drive it backwards. The predator repeated its earlier move, lifting a leg and kicking downward on the charging animal's face. This time it caught the horned beast on the snout. It kicked hard, turning the Triceratops' head away from its body. The tyrannosaur swooped down and buried its teeth behind the creature's large frill. Tim heard a series of pops as ten thousand pounds of jaw pressure separated the Triceratops' neck vertebrae. The animal screamed, emitting a series of high-pitched screeches. The tyrannosaur squeezed harder and the screaming stopped.

A branch from above hit Tim's hand, almost knocking him off the cliff. "Yes!" He grabbed it. "Pull me up, now!"

As the others hoisted Tim up the rock wall, the tyrannosaur turned. The beast clearly saw him, but did not care. It leaned forward and opened the Triceratops' gut. Mounds of intestines filled with fermenting plant matter spilled out. The predator sunk its head into the chest cavity and fed.

"Get me the fuck away from here," Tim said through hitching breaths as he came over the top of the cliff.

TWENTY-TWO

Callie held Hank's hand as they walked through the woods. The ground sloped gently upwards. No one had said anything since they had pulled Tim over the wall and quietly disappeared into the trees above the cliff. Hank led the group, and he seemed to be steering them slowly to the right, back toward the river. Callie wondered if the café was still there.

"Guys, look over that way," Al said. Everyone stopped. He pointed at a cluster of mossy stones among the trees off to the left. "I think we should head in that direction." In the distance, larger formations of rock loomed in the shadows.

Hank took one look and said, "Nope." He started walking again.

Callie stayed right beside him. It made sense to get back to the café and she wasn't about to leave Hank.

Al called after them, "This is the perfect time to search for shelter. That tyrannosaur has all the food it needs."

"No shit!" said Morgan. "It totally worked that Triceratops. Poor guy. Triceratops is my favorite, you know."

Hank responded without looking back. "We're going to help the old woman. She needs us. You keep searching for your Fort Knox as long as you want."

Callie gave his hand a squeeze. "What about the rest of them?" she asked quietly. "We shouldn't split up." Hank stopped and they both looked back.

"There's also the woman on the second floor," Tim said.

Al rolled his head around, looking at the canopy above. "If she even exists. Are you sure you didn't imagine her?"

"I saw something."

William turned to Al. "We need to get back to Helen. And we all need to stay together."

Lisa pulled Al close and looked up at him. "I want to get back to my store. If something else shows up, I won't be able to run very fast."

"How is your foot?" Callie asked.

"It hurts."

So far, Lisa had limped along without complaining. As a runner, Callie had experienced blisters that felt like gaping holes on the bottom of her feet. When she actually looked at them, they were always smaller than she expected and only skin deep. Lisa had an actual hole. Callie had seen muscle fibers inside the wound when wrapping it up.

Al took a deep breath and looked around, swinging his head from one person to the next. Callie thought he looked like a cornered animal. "Okay," he said.

Hank gave a snort through his nose and they all started up again. Callie took his arm. "Thank you for the whistle," she said quietly. "Back by the river. I thought I was a goner."

Hank pulled his lips wide. He made the shape of a smile, but he wasn't smiling. "I thought I was a goner too. We gotta be careful, babe. After what happened to that girl, we gotta really look out for each other. We should make some ground rules when we get back to the river. For all of us."

"Like what?" Morgan asked. Callie guessed that Morgan was not a big fan of rules.

"Like how far away from the building people should go. Maybe some kind of watch duty. And we clearly should not make any more loud noises."

"Loud noises did chase away those duck-bill dinosaurs," William pointed out.

Hank nodded. "But it was obviously a mistake to assume that trick would work with the other kinds. The noise brought that T-rex right to us."

Morgan had been picking at the dried blood on his face. He flicked a scab off into the air. "You said it, man. Beth was practically asking to be eaten."

"Beth said that nobody should go off alone. We all agreed. And where was she? Right at the edge of the woods by herself. If we're going to come up with rules, we have to stick to them."

Callie put her hand over her face. She could see where this was going. She was used to Hank's matter-of-fact pronouncements. For him, it was simply about learning from mistakes. He didn't realize how it made him sound sometimes.

Morgan nodded. "Yeah. It's a good thing, too. We're all a lot safer now that she's gone." Morgan reached up to scratch the back of his head. "Wait. I think I'm mistaken. I think maybe you're actually an old jackass for suggesting that what happened to Beth was her own fault."

Hank puffed air out his nostrils. "I'm trying, Morgan, to come up with ideas to keep us alive." His voice rose as he spoke.

"No. I'm still mistaken. You're not an old jackass. You're a shit-brained, girly-pants-wearing son of a bitch."

Hank stopped walking and yelled, "I don't have to take this from you, you goddamn punk!"

"Punk?" Morgan blurted. "Is that the best you can do?"

William stood with his arms crossed. "Hank? What were you saying about making loud noises?"

Hank pressed his lips together and tromped off in front of the group. Callie followed a few steps behind, hoping he would calm down on his own. Most of the time, people looked to him for leadership. If he were wearing one of his nine-hundred dollar suits today instead of his silly jogging outfit, he would probably be in charge here.

The group walked on. Morgan finally broke the silence. "So that was a dog back there, right? A real, normal dog? Please tell me I wasn't high."

William chuckled. "Never mind the dinosaurs. You see a brown mutt and that's what makes you think you're high?"

"Maybe Beth was right," Lisa said. It was the first time she had spoken the girl's name since she died. "Maybe what happened to us happened all over. Maybe the dog came from another group somewhere."

"No, no, wait a minute," Morgan said. "I think I saw that dog before. Was it on the sidewalk earlier?"

Hank clenched his fists and spoke in a low voice to Callie. "He's the quintessential unreliable witness. Half of my job is keeping assholes like him off the witness stand."

Callie unfolded one of the fists and laced her fingers between his. She gave him a look that said, *let it go.* If Hank stayed angry, he would not be able to think straight. He nodded, understanding. She felt a rush from their simple exchange. It amazed her that two people could understand each other so well.

"Hey, listen," Tim said. The sound of rushing water came through the trees. They caught a few glimpses of the river ahead. Turning to the right, they followed it downstream. Soon they arrived at the clearing.

William stopped the group at the tree line. The café was still there, sitting on the edge of the river. They saw no dinosaurs on either side. A thin grey wisp rose from Helen's fire.

Callie studied the jagged walls above the café, looking for Tim's mystery woman, but she saw no signs of life. Three dark shapes circled in the sky high above. "Are those buzzards?"

"Pterodactyls maybe," said William. "Come on. The coast is clear."

Halfway across the mudflat, they were greeted with a bark. The dog ran to meet them, wagging his tail.

Helen stood on the sidewalk. One hand held onto a parking meter and the other formed a fist on her hip. "So, can I expect you people to abandon me again at the next sign of trouble?"

Callie climbed up and gave her a hug. "I am so sorry. We had to run. Are you ok?" Helen accepted the embrace and the attention, which Callie assumed was all she really wanted.

"I'm fine," Helen said. "I hid inside until this dog showed up. His name is Buddy. It says so right on his tags." She seemed to have endured her isolation without incident.

Buddy's short coat showed a dozen shades of brown. His fur faded to a sandy tan color around his face and thin muzzle. His ears flopped asymmetrically.

William kneeled and rubbed the mutt's shoulders. "Hey Buddy. I was going to name you 'Rex'."

Helen had removed the remains of the leash from his collar. "I fed him milk and a croissant." Buddy wagged his tail spastically as everyone took turns petting him.

Lisa asked, "Do you know where he came from?" She sat on the edge of the sidewalk and held her injured foot.

Helen nodded. "I'm afraid so. He went right to that woman's hand out on the sidewalk. He sniffed it and he started whimpering." She looked down. "I feel so terrible. I kicked the hand into the river. He sounded like he was crying and I just could not bear it."

"Why is he wet?" Morgan asked, smelling his fingers.

Helen wiped her eyes. "He jumped in and fetched the hand. He brought it right back to me. I had to kick it into the river a second time, and then hold him until it floated away."

Hank put the pieces together. "So that woman was walking down the street with him when all this happened. He must have run off when we first arrived."

"That's right!" Morgan said. "The lady was walking a dog. I remember that now."

"That means there isn't another group here," Lisa said. "We're all alone."

Helen turned to the group. "What about you all? Tell me what happened."

Callie looked at the others, wondering where to start, and realized that Tim was gone. Before she could ask about him, he appeared around the back corner of the building.

"Hey everyone. You'll want to get over here. I found the woman upstairs."

II

THE FOOTBALL

TWENTY-THREE

The woman lay in a pile of rubble with both legs pinned under a slab of concrete. A chunk of iron beam lay next to her. Blood on the beam matched the ugly black stain on her lab coat. Her eyes were dull and Callie thought the woman was dead until she saw her blink. Fresh tears streamed down her cheeks.

"Do you have any painkillers?" she asked.

Tim had led the group to the back corner of the building, where jagged beams of rebar stuck out from the wall, forming a makeshift ladder. Everyone except Helen and Buddy had climbed up and crowded around. Fallen walls and broken equipment filled most of the space. It felt more like a rooftop patio than a room. The broken remains of the exterior walls rose less than two feet in most places.

The corner directly above the café's back hallway had collapsed, which explained the rubble blocking Lisa's storage closet and bathroom. The edge of the wall hanging out over the river had dropped away as well, directly above the spot where Lisa had fallen in.

Callie knelt and began to examine the woman. "How bad are you hurt?"

She grimaced. "I don't think it could be much worse." She pulled up the side of her shirt.

Callie fought off a gag reflex. *This is why I'm in psychiatry and not a practicing physician.* She forced herself to take slow, deep breaths. The right side of the woman's torso had been peeled open. She had apparently pulled it closed again. Blood congealed along the edges. Vulgar blue bruises ran across her belly and jagged ridges under the skin could only be broken ribs. Red stains darkened one cup of her bra. Callie focused on the woman's face to try to calm down, but what she saw there hurt just as much to look at. Row after row of tear streaks ran from her eyes.

"That's sick," Morgan said, loudly enough for the woman to hear.

"You're an asshole," Hank said.

"But look at her. How is she even –"

"Morgan!" barked Callie. "Climb back down and get the aspirin bottle from Helen's purse. Now."

Morgan left for his errand.

The woman looked up. "Was that a T-rex?" Her voice trembled, barely above a whisper.

"Sure was," William answered. He took the woman's hand.

She managed a thin smile. "That's pretty cool." Each word came slowly, dragged out with a terrible effort.

The others all stood back, Callie noticed, horrified and unsure how to respond. The woman's eyes were sunken and she smelled of urine and something else foul and rotten. *That's the contents of her stomach, exposed to outside air,* Callie thought. She stood for a moment to get away from the smell.

Hank sometimes told her about courtroom photos of dead bodies. Some of the descriptions were grisly. This was worse. Courtroom photos did not include the fetid odor rising from this woman's belly.

"We got to get this off you," William said, gesturing at the slab of concrete pinning her legs. He turned to the others. "Listen up. See if you can find something we can use as a lever." They all climbed over the collapsed walls and tumbled equipment. "Be careful," William added.

Morgan returned with the aspirin. "Hey Hank, catch." He tossed the bottle across the room, keeping his distance from the dying woman.

Hank unscrewed the cap and passed the bottle to Callie. "Didn't you say earlier that aspirin is bad for clotting?"

Callie nodded slowly. "I just want to help her with the pain right now." She raised her eyebrows, hoping Hank could read her mind. *It doesn't matter if her blood clots.* The woman under the concrete slab was not going to get better and all they could do was ease her suffering.

She hoped he could tell what she was thinking. He was seventeen years older with an ex-wife and three children. Callie never believed in soul mates, or fate, or even true love, but she had never met anyone who understood her the way he did. Sometimes it felt like they could read each other's minds.

Hank seemed to get it. "Come on, Morgan, let's see what we can find up here. Maybe there are some spare clothes." Callie smiled. She knew that he was sick of his t-shirt and running shorts. Hank always felt more comfortable in a suit and tie.

Callie knelt by the woman with a handful of aspirin and a plastic water bottle.

"Just give me a small sip," the woman said. Callie dribbled water onto her lips and tongue. "Shit, that's good."

"There's plenty."

"No. My stomach's not up for it." She spoke in gasps, each sentence coming out in one long exhale.

"What about the aspirin?"

"Put 'em in my mouth. I can absorb them through the skin in my mouth."

Callie placed five aspirin in the woman's mouth. She hesitated and added two more.

"Thank you." The woman began to crunch. "Anderson would have loved the T-rex." Her mouth looked like it was full of chalk.

Callie could almost taste the bitterness. She gulped from the water bottle and asked, "Who was Anderson?" Questions were good. Questions would distract this woman from the pain and they might learn something useful.

"Anderson was a boy genius. Twenty-two years old. PhD in Quantum Mechanics."

"Was he in here when this happened?"

The woman nodded almost imperceptibly. "Right over there."

Callie scanned the room and it dawned on her that she was looking at the ruins of a lab. "You caused this didn't you? What were you doing up here?"

The woman squeezed her eyes shut. "It wasn't supposed to go off today. We were running a... test. The first trial was next week. Three in the morning. Just in case. When no one is around." She stopped and winced for several seconds as a round of pain wracked her body. Callie put her hand on the woman's forehead. It felt hot.

Morgan glared from across a pile of rubble. "I got news for you, bitch. We were around. Right downstairs, as a matter of fact."

Lisa nodded. "You set off a time machine in the middle of downtown Denver. What the hell were you thinking?"

William held up both hands, palms out. "Easy there. That won't help."

The woman focused on William. "It wasn't time travel when we started. It was invisibility." Her lips formed a wry smile. "Anderson thought he could make you invisible."

Lisa pushed aside a broken machine made out of several polished spheres. "Invisibility. This building wasn't zoned for anything like that. You wouldn't believe the hoops I've been jumping through just for a license to sell a few stupid glasses of wine." Lisa's mouth clenched up and she looked like she wanted to cry. She stared out into the jungle.

Square white tiles two feet on each side covered much of the room. Morgan began to fling them over the side of the building. "What are these, anyway?"

"Ceiling tiles," Tim said, looking up. He squatted by a network of cables that met in a junction on the floor.

"Yeah, but there's no ceiling. Where did they come from?" Morgan flicked one of the tiles like a Frisbee and watched it fly across the river and land on the other side.

"This room had a high drop ceiling," Tim said. "The rest of it is still in Denver."

Morgan grabbed two tiles, one in each hand and flung them up and backwards over his head. Underneath, he exposed a body. *"Gaahh!"* Morgan danced away with a high-pitched squeal and fell on his ass.

Hank and Al came over and examined the corpse. It belonged to a man with light brown skin. His face had been split apart by falling machinery.

Morgan scrambled to his feet and backed away. "What the shit. I think I just found Professor Anderson."

"Morgan, shut up," Hank said.

The woman under the rubble scrunched her mouth and shook her head. "Anderson was a genius, but... zero patience. We could not get him to slow down."

"So this was an accident?" William asked her. "It wasn't supposed to happen?" She nodded in response, allowing her eyelids to fall.

"Is there someone in Denver who can bring us back? Someone who knows what happened?"

She mouthed the word "No" without actually saying it and lay motionless. Callie leaned over her and felt shallow breathing on her ear.

"Keep looking folks," William ordered. "We need a lever."

They found two other bodies, or rather one and a half. The corpse with the split face looked good compared to the others. The second man had been burned or electrocuted before a heavy, floor-to-ceiling cabinet had toppled onto him. Every inch of skin was covered with black flakes. Foul fluids oozed between cracks in the char.

The last body had been sliced in half near the edge of the room. The slice looked like the cut on the hand they had found out front on the sidewalk. All three corpses wore white lab coats like the woman. None of them wore pants that Hank was willing to trade for his jogging shorts.

The room contained desks, computer banks, hundreds of fallen ceiling tiles, and all sorts of heavy wiring, but nothing they could use as a lever. Tim explored the edge of the building, and finally found a length of metal pipe running inside the wall. A twelve-foot section had bent outwards when the wall crumbled into the river. Tim grabbed it with both hands, put his boot on the wall below and pulled. The pipe broke free and several rows of cinderblocks fell with a splash.

They positioned the pipe under the slab, near the woman's pinned legs. William and Hank dragged the iron beam into place to act as a fulcrum.

Al, William, and Tim lined up along the pipe, just as they had with the tree trunk on the cliff top, while Hank squatted at the woman's shoulders, ready to drag her out. William gave a nod and they all pulled downward. As the slab of concrete began to move, barely a fraction of an inch, the woman awoke, hissing and squealing. Her eyes squeezed shut and her lips pulled back from her teeth.

"Down, down, down," William said and they released the pressure.

Hank stood, breathing heavily through his nose. He moved away from the woman, almost out of earshot, but not quite. "She was up here the whole fucking time. Why didn't she scream for help?"

Callie bit the insides of her cheeks to keep from snapping at him. She wished she could explain to the others why her fiancé sounded like such an asshole sometimes. Hank always wanted to save everyone, to be the hero. When he couldn't, it made him angry. Asshole angry. "I think one of her lungs is collapsed," she said finally. "I don't think she could scream if she wanted to."

William moved back to the woman's side. Fresh tears streamed across her cheeks. "Please. Wait until the aspirin kicks in. Or maybe not. I might be better off staying like this... until we get back."

"Get back?" William asked. "You said there was no one to bring us home. We're stuck here."

The woman looked more and more exhausted. She inhaled a long, slow breath and said, "No. Not as long as you stay close to the football." Her eyes fell shut again.

TWENTY-FOUR

William's face grew frantic. "Wait, wait, what? What football? What are you talking about?" The woman lay silent. Her chest rose and fell in slow, uneven breaths.

"Tim, go get some food. Sugar or chocolate or something. Hurry!"

Tim nodded and set off. William realized the young man could be counted on to do just about anything he asked. He didn't complain like the rest of them.

William stood. "Look around everyone. We got to find something that looks like a football." The room grew quiet as the others spread out again. They were just like his sons, William noticed. As long as they had jobs to do, they didn't bicker quite so much. He gazed around at the roofless room and tried to imagine how it looked before everything had fallen apart. A large metal structure filled one corner, with wire-wrapped tubes jutting out in all directions. It looked like a ten-cylinder engine on steroids.

"It isn't up here," Morgan whined. "It's gone." He paced back and forth along a row of shelves that leaned against one another like oversized dominoes. Each shelf was lined with bracket-mounted computer hardware and every piece was connected to the next by short, curved cables.

Tim returned with a bag of dark chocolate covered espresso beans and a tablecloth. William nodded. "Perfect." He put one of the beans inside the woman's lip. "Come on."

"This is to keep the sun off," Tim said, unfolding the tablecloth.

Callie and Hank stood in another corner next to a stack of monitors, most of which bore spider-web cracks across the front. They had found nothing resembling a football.

"Hey," said Morgan. "What about that cabinet on top of Mister Slushy? Maybe the football is in there."

Al moved close to give it a look, carefully stepping around the pink fluid that pooled under the body. The cabinet's doors were face-down on the burned corpse. Al grabbed a corner and tried to lift it, but it would not budge. "I don't think their science experiment was in a supply cabinet," he said finally. "But if you want to come over and help me lift it, maybe we can get our hands on some extra notepads and toner."

Morgan took one look at the charred body and shook his head.

Callie pointed to a spot near the center of the room. "Look how all those wires and cables are hanging over the edge. The experiment was there, in the middle. It must have slid into the river when the floor broke." She returned to the unconscious woman. "Am I right? Was it by those wires? Did your football thing slide over the edge?" The woman did not respond.

Hank asked, "Is she dead?"

"No, not yet," Callie whispered. "But I honestly do not know why not."

Morgan picked up a keyboard. "Yeah, well that bitch needs to stay alive long enough to tell us how to get out of here. This is her fault." He threw the keyboard over the side of the building.

Tim and William finished suspending the tablecloth above the woman. They created a canopy that blocked the sun, which had climbed over the trees and shone directly onto the building.

"Hey, look at this," Lisa called, pulling a folder from a desk drawer. "They had a contract with the Department of Defense." She flipped through a few pages. "This is insane. Right here in my building." Al looked over her shoulder while Lisa read. "There's a ton of stuff about 'observational deflection,' whatever the hell that means."

"It sounds like that invisibility business," Hank noted.

Al nodded and read an excerpt. "Yeah. It says here, 'Bending light will render the target virtually invisible.' There isn't any mention of Denver. This contract is with some Silicon Valley company called 'The Alto Group'."

"Who the hell are they?"

"I don't know. Venture capitalists maybe?" Al offered.

"That sounds about right," Hank said. "A group of hot-shot scientists with easy funding and no oversight. They get sub-contracted to do research for the military. They tried bending light but they accidentally bent the space-time fabric or some crazy shit like that instead. And they didn't bother to tell anyone. We are going to have a hell of a case against them when we get back."

"We got to get back first," William said. He sat in the shade next to the woman and held her hand while he spoke quietly to Tim. "You said you saw her, when we all ran from the Tyrannosaurus?"

Tim nodded.

William tried to picture how she had propped herself up high enough to be seen. "I can't imagine how much that hurt, for her to rise up like that."

"It did," she whispered, without opening her eyes. "It... opened me back up. But I had to see it. A T-rex."

Her teeth were black from the chocolate bean. William offered her another, but she refused. "I'm not going to be eating... for a while." Fresh tears rolled down her face. "Things aren't hooked up right inside me," she explained, moving her hand in a circular motion over her stomach.

"Can you tell us about the football?" William asked quietly. "We can't find it and we don't know what to do with it." Everyone froze and waited for her response.

"Yes," she answered and then lay silent again. William wanted to grab her by both shoulders and shake her, but he knew better.

Tim reached over with a raised hand, just for a gentle tap, but William stopped him.

"Give her time," William whispered.

"Time?" said Morgan. "That bitch has had all the time in the world." He walked over and reached for her.

William sprung to his feet, grabbed Morgan's outstretched arm and shoved it against his face, splitting open two of the scratches on his cheek. "Do not touch this woman!"

Morgan backed away. "It's her fault."

William stood facing him until the young man sat down on the side of an overturned desk.

"He's right," said the woman under the concrete. She spoke slowly and deliberately, her eyes still closed. "We did it. We made a time machine. The device is... ellipsoidal. It's shaped like a football, but bigger. It will take us back." More tears fell as she spoke.

Hank whispered, "Going back is not going to do her any good, is it?" Callie shook her head.

"It's over there, just beyond that pile. It was sitting on a little stand. A tripod." She gestured across the room to the spot Callie had identified earlier. "Dig it out or leave it. Either way, it will work. It's tough. You don't have to do anything. Just be close."

Lisa and Al moved to the area she indicated. The floor sloped downward toward the river just like the section of floor directly below, in the café. Al peered over the edge into the water. "Whatever was here slid down into that river. It's gone."

"Nice," said Morgan. "Good job lady."

William thought for a moment, his eyes bright. "We can get it. We can dam the river, or divert it. Even if it takes us months." He regretted the words as they left his mouth. The woman lying in front of him clearly did not have months. Nevertheless, he would not stop until he found it.

She shook her head slightly. The action triggered a coughing sputter. Blood welled in her mouth, changing the outline on her teeth from black to crimson. "You don't have time. It will go off automatically after... fifteen hours." She opened her eyes. "But it didn't sink. It floats. We made it float because there was an inland sea back then. Back *now*. We didn't want it to show up... here and sink straight to the bottom."

"The sea," exclaimed Callie. "We saw the sea from the cliff. If that thing fell into the river, it must have floated down to the sea. It's probably washed up on the beach or something."

"Fifteen hours," repeated William, looking at his watch. He guessed that three hours had passed already.

"That isn't much time to find it," Lisa said. "For all we know, it's stuck against a rock somewhere along the river. Or if it reached the sea, it could be halfway to Africa by now."

"We've got to try," William said. "We've got time, and we've got a chance to get home now." He wanted to hug his sons. They never hugged him anymore, not since they became teenagers, but they sure as hell were going to give him a hug when he got back. If he could survive fifteen hours in the Cretaceous, he could make his sons hug him. He leaned over the wounded woman. "Assuming we can find your machine, how close do we have to be to it?"

She closed her eyes again, but kept talking. "Not sure." She gave a ghastly grin full of blood-outlined teeth. "Our test was only supposed to have... a four-foot radius. It wasn't supposed to take the whole room."

"What the shit," Morgan spat. "You took the whole room, the room downstairs, and some of the sidewalk out front too!"

If the woman heard him, she gave no sign of it. "Tell me about the T-rex."

"It killed a Triceratops in the jungle," William answered. "A short hike from here. We're hoping it fills up and leaves us alone."

Morgan was unable to remain seated. "I'll tell you about the T-rex, Doctor Dumbass. The t-rex ate a girl. A cool girl who was nice as fuck."

William turned and looked at him but didn't say anything.

"He's got a point," Al said.

Tim waved his hand. "Everybody shut up for a minute. We're talking about a time machine here." He crouched close. "Listen, ma'am, we lost two people. One got trampled and the T-rex killed the other. Can we reuse this thing, this football? The time machine?"

William's mind raced as he considered the possibilities. "That's right. We can set it to take us back earlier, before everything happened. We could save the people who died, and even stop you from... from even being here."

The woman lay quiet for a moment. "Maybe."

"Tell us what to do."

"You can't reset it. It has to be recharged in the lab." She gestured weakly at the ruined machinery in the corner. "But it has a power reserve. A fail-safe. It will take you back twenty minutes." She began another fit of hitching coughs. Fresh blood leaked from the gash on her side.

"Twenty minutes," Morgan said. "What the hell good will that do?"

The coughing ended on a wet note and the woman explained slowly. "We added the fail-safe in case we... screwed up the past. If we got home and things were not right."

"This is insane," Al said.

The woman went on. "Use it after you get home. Go back twenty minutes and get everyone out of the building. Get *me* out of the building." She turned her head to one side and let thick blood pour from her mouth.

"Jesus, give her more aspirin," Al said. He lowered his voice. "Give her all the aspirin and put her out of her misery."

William put one hand on the woman's shoulder and gave it the slightest squeeze. He wanted to be sure he understood everything. "So we go find the machine, wait fifteen hours, and it will take us back to Denver? Then we use the fail-safe, go back twenty minutes earlier and clear out the building. That's it? Nothing else?"

"You need to be here," she said. A bubble of blood formed at her lips. It popped as she talked. "Bring it here. It's a swap. If you're here, it will take you back to our building. If you're ten miles away, you'll show up ten miles away."

"A swap," said Callie. "Does that mean there's a chunk of dinosaur land back in Denver right now?"

"Sounds like it," Hank answered.

Morgan's mouth dropped. "What the shit! There could be dinosaurs loose, running around."

Hank dismissed him with the wave of a hand. "Only if they were right here, in this exact spot. The chances of that are pretty slim. William, ask her how to trigger the fail-safe."

William nodded and looked back down at the woman. Her lips pulled away from her bloody teeth in a wide grimace. "Do you want more aspirin? It might help with the pain."

"No." She rolled her head back and forth in a slow, wide arc. "It doesn't hurt anymore." Her head stopped rolling and she fell silent. Everyone stared at her.

"Is she dead?" asked Morgan.

William put his hand on the woman's chest, just below her neck. He held it there for a long time. Her skin was warm and he felt movement under his fingers, but after a moment he realized that it was his own pulse. "Yeah. I think she is."

He stood, stretched his tall frame, and looked around the rubble, double-checking that they had not missed the device. *Fifteen hours.* He corrected himself, *Twelve.* Still, there was hope. "We've got about twelve hours to find that device and get back here. We should leave immediately."

"Are we sure?" asked Al. "That machine killed three people." He looked at the woman. "Make that four. It clearly did not work how they wanted it to. What if it takes us back another hundred million years instead of forward? What if it blows us up? Are we positive we even want to mess with it?"

William said, "We don't have a choice. My kids need me and I'm going to do everything I can to get back to them. Even if I die trying."

Al looked around the group. Everyone else nodded. "Well then, we better get going."

TWENTY-FIVE

Lisa stood behind her counter, packing pastries into a canvas shopping bag. It would take hours to find the device and they would need something to eat along the way. "The Daily Edition" was printed on one side of the bag in old-fashioned newsy typeface. For reasons she never understood, people happily paid her twelve dollars for the bags. They liked her café. It had been a newsstand once and people still felt nostalgic about newsstands. But twelve dollars for a *bag?*

She wondered if she should stay at the store while the others went to look for the device. Her foot still throbbed where the rock had pierced it and she did not want to be in a situation where she had to run from something. Her café was the only place on the planet that felt safe. Also, it felt wrong to leave Helen alone again.

Helen had listened patiently as everyone explained what they learned upstairs. "So this machine creates a bubble around it when it goes off?"

"Yeah," Morgan said. "A big invisible bubble that makes a ticking noise."

"And everything inside the bubble goes back to Denver?"

William nodded. "That's right. It goes off automatically in about twelve hours."

"And you think the machine got washed down the river?" Another nod. Helen had clammed up after that. Lisa thought she knew why. Helen could not go searching through the jungle with the rest of them, even if she wanted to. She would hold the group back. She was terrified of being left behind.

Lisa understood. If the others failed to return before the device went off, anyone who was not with them would be stuck forever. Of course, there was still the small matter of actually finding the thing.

Al came around the counter and collected an armful of water bottles, also printed with The Daily Edition logo on the side. It felt strange having customers behind the counter, especially Al. For three years, he had come into her café almost every day. Of course, so had a lot of customers. She realized early on that repeat business went up if she opened an extra button on her blouse and took the time to get her makeup right. It meant getting hassled and flirted with, but most of her customers were well-meaning. Most were professionals.

Al gave her an awkward smile as he filled the water bottles from the cooler next to the sugar counter.

Al normally had trouble making eye contact and fidgeted during small talk. She usually smiled politely, served him his drink, always a large black coffee, and moved on to the next customer. Recently, Lisa had read a book called *Tech Lords*, about seven of the most successful entrepreneurs in the world. Most of them didn't have very good social skills either. Al wasn't a multi-millionaire, but he did run his own business, just like her. Besides, her ex-husband had been slick, cool, and popular. And a total jerk. Their marriage had lasted a whopping thirteen months.

The water cooler ran dry and Al swapped out the bottle for a full one. Lisa hated changing the heavy blue bottles and usually had to get Beth to help her. Al lifted the five-gallon container effortlessly from the ground by its neck.

Maybe he wasn't slick, cool, and popular, but Al had been there when she needed him. If not for Al, she would have washed right down the river, just like the time device. Lisa stopped what she was doing and called out to the room. "Hey. We should make a raft."

William looked up from his seat at one of the tables, where he had been poring over papers from upstairs, hoping to find some clue about the device. "You are brilliant."

Lisa blushed. She knew she was determined and she knew that she was a hard worker. But she couldn't remember the last time anyone had called her brilliant.

Al screwed the cap on the last water bottle. "Do we have time to build a raft? And what if there are waterfalls or rapids along the way?"

Lisa drooped, deflated. "Thanks for the support."

Al froze, holding his face perfectly still and emotionless. He looked guilty. Lisa almost felt sorry for him. He didn't seem to know how to navigate around women.

Hank walked over. "We can't afford *not* to take the time. Rafting down the river will be much faster than walking through the jungle."

"Hold on," Tim said. "I thought I saw something this morning when I pulled Lisa and Al out of the water. It looked like an alligator. A big one."

Hank whipped around. "You *thought* you saw something? Because I *know* I saw a Tyrannosaurus-fucking-rex out there in the jungle. I'll take my chances on the water."

"At least on land, we can run," Tim said. "I can't swim. And even if I could, I couldn't out-swim an alligator."

Hank shook his head. "I'd still take my chances with a raft. If we hike all the way to the ocean and that time machine is snagged on a branch halfway down the river, we're screwed."

"And how do you propose we build a raft?" Al asked. "Should we push the whole café into the water and see if it floats?"

Hank walked to one of the small wooden tables in the middle of the room. He lifted it up and set it on its side. "We use the wood from these tables. We empty out those plastic water jugs and use them for pontoons."

"Those jugs are our only source of fresh water." Al's voice rose an octave. He sounded desperate. "Are you out of your mind?"

Buddy let out a low growl under one of the remaining tables. Lisa empathized. She didn't like the arguing either.

Hank slowed his own voice and spoke deliberately, enunciating and projecting. "I believe that if we work together, we can build a solid raft out of the materials at hand in thirty minutes." He looked from face to face. "We will not need the water in those jugs if we return home in twelve hours. And if somehow we fail, I'd like to point out that we are standing next to a river."

"That river is *brown*," Al said. "I am not going to let you dump out those jugs."

"That isn't your call to make. We have to do whatever benefits the group. Whatever gives us the greatest chance of getting home."

"What about the greatest chance staying alive? It isn't your decision either. It isn't even your water. It's Lisa's."

Lisa's eyes went wide. "You know, rafting was my idea, but maybe we should – "

Morgan entered the room, throwing open the front door even though he could have walked through the empty window next to it. "Hey, hey, hey-hey-hey! Morgan is here to save the day!"

"Shut up, Morgan," William said without looking. He was studying one of the wooden tables. He turned it over and tugged on a leg. Lisa hoped he would make a decision before Hank and Al came to blows. "The idea of building a boat makes sense," William said. "We would follow the same path taken by the football. I'm just not sure we could build anything that would actually hold us." He looked around the room. "And any time we spend trying to build a raft is time we could spend walking toward the sea. We could cover a lot of ground in thirty minutes."

Callie looked over at Morgan. "What the hell are you wearing?"

Morgan hooked his thumbs under the thick straps that ran down each side of his chest. He turned from side to side, showing off his discovery. It looked like a backpack without the pack. A small red handle hung from the strap near his waist.

"This here is a two hundred and thirty dollar, type-five, quick-inflate personal floatation device," Morgan said proudly. "And there are three more just like it upstairs."

"So what?" Al said. "You found a life jacket to wear on our imaginary boat."

"Personal flotation device, bitch. And this is only the start. Come outside and I will show you our imaginary boat."

TWENTY-SIX

A bright yellow box the size of a suitcase sat in the mud near the remains of Helen's fire.

Hank looked at it and thought that Christmas had come early. "Is that what I think it is?"

Morgan nodded and spread his arms with a flourish. "It's a five-person inflatable emergency life raft. United States Coast Guard certified."

"Morgan, I love you," Hank said.

Al leaned over and studied the box. "It'll take more than half an hour to blow that up."

Morgan pulled open the Velcro top. "Try half a minute. It uses a CO2 cartridge." He looked around to make sure everyone was watching. Even Helen had come outside. Morgan reached down and grabbed a red strap. "Check this out!" He gave the strap a firm tug and the yellow bag emitted a high-pitched hiss. Buddy whimpered.

The hissing bag began to erupt out of itself. Buddy tucked his tail between his legs and bounded up the broken concrete. He almost knocked Helen over as he disappeared inside.

Morgan beamed. The yellow bag turned inside out and an outer ring took shape. Thirty seconds later the hiss died down, leaving a twelve-foot-wide octagonal raft. Black nylon straps ringed its perimeter.

Hank studied the raft. It was certified to hold five people, but he thought they might be able to squeeze in six. He didn't think it would hold eight.

"I don't understand," Helen said. "Why would they have a raft if they were going back in time?"

Hank considered for a moment. "They knew there was an ocean here, but they must not have known exactly where it was. It's the same reason they made the time device float." He turned to Morgan. "What else did you find up there?"

"Come on," he said, and led them around the building to the rebar ladder. "It was that cabinet, man. I really wanted to make sure the time machine wasn't in there. I mean, how stupid would we feel if we all went down to the sea and it was in the cabinet the whole time?"

As they pulled themselves up onto the second floor, they saw the cabinet standing upright, both doors open.

"How did you lift it?" William asked.

"The lever. That piece of pipe you tried to use to lift the concrete off that lady." Several layers of ceiling tiles had been laid across the body Morgan had named Mister Slushy. Morgan stepped up on this makeshift platform and stood in front of the cabinet. The bottom tile soaked up pink fluid like a sponge.

"It's like, everything we could possibly need." Morgan showed off his find. He picked up a box of fishing tackle in one hand and a small camping stove, complete with a propane tank, in the other. "Tarps, PFDs, matches, sunscreen, bug spray, hunting knives, first aid stuff, flashlights. There's even a short shovel."

"Is there a gun?" asked Hank. Morgan shook his head. "Then there isn't *everything* we could possibly need."

Al took a knife and unscrewed the end of the hilt, revealing a compass. "This is awesome."

Lisa huffed. "These people were planning an expedition from right here in my building."

William reached over and took out the short-handled shovel. "This might make a decent paddle," he said. "It's decided. We're taking the raft and we leave in five minutes."

The others started to get ready. Tim took out the remaining life jackets. "I'm not at my best in the water. Hope ya'll don't mind if I take one of these."

Hank, Al and Callie formed a bucket brigade to move the supplies downstairs. Al collected each item from the cabinet and carried it to the edge of the building, where Callie tossed it down to Hank. Lisa and Morgan stacked the gear inside.

When the last item had been thrown down, Hank approached William by the raft. "So you're calling the shots here." It was a question in the form of a statement. Hank wanted to see how William would respond.

"Folks seem to be listening to what I have to say." William was tying the shovel to one of the black nylon straps that ran along the circumference of the raft.

"I'm glad we're going down the river. It's the right call."

William smiled. "I don't know if it really is the right call. If there is something in the water, we'll be sittin' ducks."

Hank shook his head. "I don't understand. If it's not the right call, why did you make it? What kind of leadership is that?"

William cinched the knot and stood. "I never managed anyone. I never had anyone report to me. But I learned from raising my boys that making decisions and sticking to them helps get everyone on the same page. Even when the decisions are not perfect. Having folks on the same page can go a long way toward turning an okay decision into the right one."

"You know that raft will only hold five or six people, don't you? What's your plan for that?"

William made a chewing motion with his mouth. "I don't have one yet. I'm hoping it works itself out. Helen could ride down with us, but there's no way she'd make it back here."

"What if we find the device but it goes off before we get back?"

"We have to get back. We don't want to return to Denver in the middle of a freeway, or have a building collapse on us. We have to get back here."

Tim walked up and offered the last two life jackets. William and Hank both refused. "Give them to the women," Hank said. "See that Callie gets one." He didn't know if she would find it sexist or valiant, but he was going to make damn sure she wore one.

Lisa stepped out front. Tim extended a life vest. "Want to wear this?"

Helen spoke up before Lisa could answer. "You aren't really going, are you hon? Even if the raft makes it to the ocean, you still have to hike back here. You'll slow them down with that hurt foot."

Lisa took the life vest by one strap and examined it. "I haven't made up my mind yet."

"Well, don't stay here on my account. Whatever happens, I will be fine. But you can't burden the others like that. You'll slow them down." Helen hobbled slowly back inside.

Lisa handed the life jacket back to Tim. "Hurry back, dammit."

Hank watched Lisa disappear around the side of the building. The decision about who would go and who would stay had worked itself out, just as William had predicted. Hank took the last life jacket for himself and vowed to make sure they returned with the device in time.

TWENTY-SEVEN

Al climbed down from the second floor using the makeshift ladder of rebar and broken concrete. All of the supplies had been removed from the cabinet and transferred downstairs. He still couldn't believe their good fortune. They had enough gear to conquer this world if they wanted to.

Lisa met him as he stepped down onto the mud. "Hey Al Stevens, how about we pick up that conversation from earlier?" She took his hand and led him behind the café. He wanted to share his excitement about the supplies. The look on her face told him to keep quiet.

She held on to his hands and turned to face him. "Listen, I have decided to stay here at the store." Al furrowed his brows but did not say anything. "I can't leave Helen here by herself and I can't run. I think I will be safer here. Besides, it's a five-person raft."

"That's ridiculous. We can make seven fit. And if not, we can shove Morgan overboard. I think everybody would be fine with that."

Lisa smiled. "We can't make eight fit, and I'm not leaving Helen here alone. I'll be safe. You just gotta make sure to find the device and bring it back here."

Al felt dizzy. He wasn't sure what to do. He wasn't sure what he *wanted* to do. He didn't want to leave Lisa behind, but he really wanted to be there if they found the time machine. He didn't trust the others not to screw something up. "I don't know..."

She smiled at him. It was different from the smile she gave him each day when he collected his morning coffee. "I will be fine."

"I could stay with you," he said.

He saw fear on her face. "No. You have to go with them. You have to make sure they come back in time. For me."

Al swelled. "I promise." She was sending him on a quest.

"I want to thank you for saving me in the river this morning." She looked up at him, one hand on his arm. "Nobody ever saved my life before."

He knew that if he kept his mouth shut, he wouldn't say the wrong thing. He tensed up, flexing his bicep.

Lisa reached up on her tiptoes and kissed him full on. Her lips pried at his mouth. Al kissed back, wondering if he was doing it the way she liked. He held onto her lips with his own. Her eyes were closed, so he closed his too, until she broke away.

"You're welcome," he said. They both smiled. She pulled him close again and held him tightly.

Al panicked as he felt his erection pressing against her, embarrassed about what she might think. He remembered his mother's disgust when she saw him with an erection at the age of eleven. She had put him in the shower with cold water on full blast. At the time, he didn't even know why it happened.

He tried to pull away, but Lisa reached to the small of his back and brought him closer with a wink. Was she actually pleased? They heard someone approaching and separated.

Around the corner, Morgan climbed down from the second floor. "It's getting *nasty* up there," he said.

"Oh crap, the smell," Al remembered. He and Lisa followed Morgan around to the sidewalk. "We've got to do something about those bodies. They'll draw every predator in the area."

William shook his head. "There's no time. We have to get going. We gotta find that thing and get back here before it goes off."

"We can't leave Helen and Lisa here with those bodies upstairs. They will ripen in this heat. They'll be like a beacon."

Hank tossed a few bags of supplies into the raft. "You stay if you want, Al. I'm going to find that device."

Buddy watched from a distance. He had come back outside and circled the raft, sniffing it from all sides. He seemed less afraid of it now that the hissing had ceased.

Al looked back at Lisa, unsure what to do. "It's okay," she told him. "I'll take care of the bodies. I've scrubbed enough puke and shit from the café's toilet over the years." She looked like she was trying to convince herself as much as Al. "At least Morgan got the cabinet off of Mister Slushy for me."

"So you're staying behind?" Callie asked. Lisa nodded, looking both exhausted and sad. Callie gave her a hug.

"There was nothing you could do," Callie said.

Lisa smiled and took a deep breath. Al thought she looked close to tears. He tried to figure out what Callie was talking about and then realized she was referring to Beth. Lisa was still distraught over the death of her employee. *Her friend*, he corrected himself. He made a mental note to comment on it when they returned.

William directed Hank and Tim to slide the raft into the water. "We've got a little more than eleven hours, by my guess." He scanned the edge of the jungle. "That dead Triceratops should sustain the tyrannosaur for days, and I can't imagine there are many other predators in its territory. We'll be back in modern times before it grows hungry again." He looked over at Helen and Lisa. "All of us."

"We'll see what we can do with that fishing tackle," said Helen. "Get back here early and maybe we'll have dinner for you. We can have a cook-out while we wait for the time to run out."

William nodded. "You do that and I will take you out to the fanciest restaurant in Denver when we get home."

Helen moved close to Lisa and put her arm around her.

William held the raft steady from the shore while Tim, Morgan, Callie, and Hank all climbed aboard. The raft sank lower and lower, but it remained watertight and afloat. It wobbled as they took their seats and stabilized once they spread out.

Al wanted to give Lisa another hug, but felt embarrassed with everyone watching. He smiled at her instead and climbed aboard. He felt the water rushing below through his shoes. The bottom was a simple piece of neoprene-coated nylon stretched from side to side.

Callie and Hank kneeled at the front, wearing the last two life jackets. William climbed aboard in the back near Al.

Tim sat on his knees close to the center. Morgan stood behind him, holding his hands out for balance like a surfer. He wobbled and grabbed Tim's head to keep from falling. "Sit down Morgan," Tim snapped.

Hank picked up a pair of long sticks and gave one to Al. "That's to push us off any rocks we encounter along the way."

William took the shovel, tied to the end of a nylon strap, and pressed it against the riverbank to shove them away.

As they drifted out from the shore, Buddy came running and leaped across the gap. The mutt's legs stretched out in front and behind as he flew. He landed next to Tim and slid across the nylon decking.

"Buddy!" cried Lisa.

Tim reached down to pet the scruffy brown mutt. Buddy wagged appreciatively.

"Keep him off the sides," Hank warned. "He might pop them with his claws."

Lisa looked on as the raft floated away. Her lower lip trembled. "You take care of him," she called, her voice hitching. "And make sure to get back here in time."

Al watched her standing on the shore as they floated away. Lisa was filthy, her clothes were torn, and her hair was in shambles. He had never seen anything so beautiful. She actually seemed to *want* him. She had felt him hard against her and didn't shudder or turn away. *You are not going to lose that woman*, he told himself.

As they moved into the middle of the river, the current picked up and carried them along.

"We will come back for you," Al said. "Don't worry." He hoped he sounded heroic.

TWENTY-EIGHT

Lisa bandaged her foot using sterile pads and surgical tape from the first aid kit Morgan had found in the supply cabinet. The wound didn't show any signs of infection, but only a few hours had passed. She wondered if there were different types of bacteria to worry about in the prehistoric world.

"I can show you how to make a pair of moccasins," Helen told her. "You know, in case they don't find the machine in time." Helen hopped up and scurried behind the counter, where she grabbed one of the twelve-dollar canvas shopping bags. "We could use the material from these. Look, we could cut out a section with words on it and use that for the sole. It will give you a little traction, sweetie."

Lisa imagined Helen tracing around her foot to get the right size and shape, like an arts and crafts teacher. Helen probably made a terrific grandmother. Lisa also noticed how quickly the woman moved around in her excitement. "Are you feeling better? You seem a little more spry than you were before."

Helen looked like a child caught with her hand in the cookie jar.

"You were playing up your weakness, weren't you? So that I would stay behind with you."

Helen grew serious. "I may be old, but I don't want to die any more than you do."

"I don't blame you. I applaud you. But you gotta keep up your act better than that."

"I got excited," Helen said. "Sewing is my weakness." They shared a smile. Lisa's sewing abilities began and ended with loose buttons, but she understood.

"Well, let's you and I stick together. Maybe we'll get back home soon." She rose. "I need to go upstairs and clean up. Those bodies are starting to smell, and we don't want to attract any attention."

"What are you going to do with them?"

"I don't know yet."

Lisa went outside and circled around to the rebar ladder on the back of the building. She climbed carefully, stepping on the ball of her foot to avoid putting pressure on the cut. She smelled the bodies as soon as she pulled herself over the wall. If she could smell them, the locals could too. The temperature on the second floor felt ten degrees hotter than down below, but she noticed a small breeze. *That can't be good.* The breeze could carry the scent away for miles.

She walked over to the corpse of the woman who had told them about the time device. Someone, probably William, had lowered the tablecloth onto her. Lisa seemed to have her own personal protector in Al, but William took care of the whole group. Pink stains dotted the cloth.

Lisa considered her options. Burying the bodies was out. William had taken their only shovel. She could stack rocks on them and build some sort of cairn, but that would not cover up the smell. A funeral pyre would dispose of them. Of course, fire would also spread the smell of cooked meat. Did dinosaurs like cooked meat? She looked out onto the mudflats below. If she was going to burn the bodies, she would have to drop them off the side of the building and drag them to the edge of the woods, as far away as possible.

Because of the collapsed corner above her bathroom and the jagged wall that ran above her bookshelves, there was really only one good spot to drop the corpses onto the mudflat below. She would need to climb down and move each body out of the way before she dropped the next one. Otherwise, they would land in a pile on top of each other. The thought brought up half-remembered images of war crimes from the news. She shuddered and wiped her brow. This job would take all day. By the time she finished, the others would be back. It would be so much easier to just dump them... *into the river.* It would be like a burial at sea. That was appropriate, wasn't it? Honorable, even.

Lisa thought about going downstairs to run it by Helen. The old woman probably knew more about these sorts of things. When she first opened The Daily Edition Café, Lisa phoned her father every time she had to make a decision, even about the smallest thing. As she talked through each option, she ended up making the choice on her own. It took several months before she realized this and stopped calling so often.

She needed to dispose of the bodies before they attracted attention. The river would do it. Decision made.

Lisa pulled back the table cloth. The woman's head lolled to one side and her mouth hung open, revealing a bloated, bloody tongue. Up close, the stench was stronger.

"What the hell were you thinking?" Lisa felt her lip tremble. Beth had died because of their stupid experiment, or accident, or whatever. She wanted to cry. The look on Beth's face as she ran from the tyrannosaur was burned in her memory. Lisa wanted to drop to her knees and bawl.

The moment passed. A good cry would be a waste of time. Lisa got to work. She had learned long ago that the best way to approach a job, especially a job she did not want to do, was to confront it head on and finish it. *That doesn't mean you have to start with the most difficult part.* She replaced the sheet on the body. It was going to take some work to get the concrete off of the woman's legs.

She walked around, careful to avoid the two areas where the floor had collapsed, one over her bathroom and one overhanging the river. *This is where the device was,* she realized as she looked at the second spot. The floor here sloped down toward the water, just like the floor in her café below. *It probably fell in at the same time I did.* She tried to remember if she had seen anything, but all she could remember was flailing around in a river where Chestnut Street should have been.

Lisa moved to the scientist with the bisected face. "Doctor Anderson, I presume." He had filled his pants with a foul load upon dying. "Serves you right, asshole." Staying angry at them made the job easier.

She grabbed the corpse's hands and started pulling. Doctor Anderson's split face hung back and his Adam's apple thrust up at the open sky. As Lisa got moving, the two halves of his face smacked together, making the sound of a sloppy eater.

Lisa's shirt was wet with sweat by the time she had pulled the body to the sloped floor over the river. She kept her distance from the edge and retrieved the metal pipe Morgan had used to raise the supply cabinet.

Placing the pipe against the body's midsection, she pushed Doctor Anderson like a chef pushing a pizza into a brick oven. "Rest in peace, Doctor." When the corpse reached the edge, it rolled slowly over and disappeared. She heard a splash a split second later.

"Ok, who's next?" Lisa turned back to look at the shattered room.

A hissing growl came from behind the leaning shelves of computer servers.

TWENTY-NINE

As they rounded the first bend, Al found the spot where he had helped Lisa out of the river. Tim rose up on his knees and looked in the other direction. Al followed his gaze. "Do you see your alligator?"

"No." Tim gestured to a steep bank on the opposite side. "I saw something slide into the water right over there. Or at least, I thought I did."

"Well, it's gone now," Hank said. "If there really was something there. I sure as hell wasn't thinking straight when all of this first went down."

Tim hadn't imagined the woman on the roof. Al thought that he probably hadn't imagined the alligator either. He looked at the brown, swollen water rushing by the sides of the raft. If anything was below them, they would never see it coming.

They drifted along and soon the muddy slope was out of sight. Tim sat back down.

William put one hand on his shoulder. "Hopefully it's long gone, whatever it was."

The raft moved fast enough to produce a slight breeze, but the heat and humidity still felt stifling. William used the shovel as a rudder, keeping them in the stronger currents near the center. Multi-winged flies the size of songbirds flitted along the shore. Long segmented legs dangled from their bodies.

Morgan dangled his hand into the cool, coffee-colored water. Al thought that probably wasn't the smartest thing to do, but didn't say anything.

The river widened after they passed the first few turns and the trees grew close on both sides. A pterodactyl swooped from a branch and snatched one of the flies from the air with a loud crunch. Soon, the crunching surrounded them as pterodactyls crisscrossed the river.

"Why can't you hear it when a pterodactyl goes to the bathroom?" Morgan blurted, sitting up. Without waiting for an answer, he exclaimed, "Because its pee is silent!"

William chuckled. "That's good, Morgan. My boys would have loved that one back in grade school."

Morgan smiled and leaned back against the side of the raft. He put one of his two remaining cigarettes into his mouth and brought out his lighter.

"Nope," said Hank.

Morgan looked like he wanted to protest, but then he simply put it away.

They drifted on, watching the shoreline for any sign of the football. Al tried to remember how far away the sea had been from their glimpse of it atop the cliff. He guessed the trip downriver would take at least a couple of hours. He wished that Lisa could have come along somehow. The ride was almost relaxing.

Tim did not appear to be enjoying himself. He remained hunkered on the floor in the center.

Callie seemed to notice as well. "Tell us about your girl, Tim," she prompted.

Tim chewed on his lip. "Her name is Julie. We were supposed to meet up this morning. She just got back from flying up and down the coast of California." He gave a small grin and his shoulders dropped a little. "She's a flight attendant. I met her playing softball."

"That's pretty cool. She sounds like a keeper."

"Yeah. Julie is different."

"What makes you say that?" Callie asked.

Tim tilted his head. "Oh, I'm on your couch now, is that it? What will this session cost me?"

"It depends on your insurance," she said with a chuckle.

Al squeezed the stick in his hand. Their small talk came so natural. Tim was clearly terrified of being out on the water, yet he was slick and charming.

Tim thought for a moment. "Julie is someone to live up to. All the girls I went out with before... They were, I dunno, they were just dates. I had fun, they had fun, but I honestly never wanted to spend any real time with them. Julie, she's not like that."

Morgan raised his hand for a high-five. "*Score.*"

Tim left the hand unanswered. "Nah. Believe me, I know a score. But Julie... I want to impress her because I sincerely want to impress her." He shrugged. "I don't know if that makes any sense."

Morgan lowered his hand.

William gave Tim a wide smile. "Makes perfect sense to me, brother."

Bullshit, thought Al. *If she isn't a score, she will be soon enough.* Some men treated women well and some did not, but they all wanted the same thing. His mother had pounded that simple fact into him. And as he grew into puberty, he found it to be true. Sometimes it was all he could think about. You only had to look at the nearest screen to know how the world worked. Television, movies, the internet. It was all the same. Men wanted sex. Women controlled access. Once you understood that, life made sense. It certainly explained why Al's father had run away with his smoking hot secretary.

"She must be quite a girl," Callie noted.

Tim nodded. "Yeah, we've only been out three times, but she's pretty amazing."

"Three dates and she still isn't putting out?" Al blurted. He wasn't sure how many dates it should take, but he wanted to sound like he knew. He wanted to sound like one of the guys.

Callie glared. "Al, don't be a jackass."

He felt his stomach drop. *Good job, Stevens. Way to let 'em know what an idiot you are.*

Tim said, "Right now, I just want to see her again."

Al felt his face grow red. The rest of the world never had trouble getting laid. He turned to watch the river behind them and bit the inside of his cheek. *It isn't too late. Apologize. Tell them it was a stupid comment and you're sorry.* Apologizing always worked, even when you didn't do anything wrong. *Especially* when you didn't do anything wrong.

"Listen, Tim," he began.

Morgan stood up and pointed. "What the shit!"

A clearing opened on the right. More than twenty Triceratops stood along the curved shore. The raft drifted straight toward them.

Buddy's hackles rose and he began to bark. *Arp Arp Arp Arp Arp Arp!*

William scooped water with the shovel, trying to move them back out to the middle. Morgan plopped down on his seat.

A large male sporting a half-broken horn above his right eye lifted his head and squawked like a tropical bird. He stood with his shorter front feet in the water and his back legs on solid ground. Spiked quills grew along the top of his tail. Buddy continued barking, a non-stop *Arp Arp Arp!* All of the Triceratops turned to look at them.

The half-horned male charged, kicking up spray. Everyone scrambled to the far side of the raft.

William shouted, "Spread out or we'll tip over!" He moved back to the empty side, facing the dinosaurs, and pushed at the water with the shovel. For a moment, Al thought William was trying to splash the animals, then he realized he was trying to push the raft away from them. Al raised his stick, ready to shove off of the animal's face if it got close enough.

Six other Triceratops followed the half-horn, charging into the water in a great phalanx. "They'll pop the raft," Tim said. Each animal sported long javelin horns and a parrot beak.

A surge of water from the rushing dinosaurs reached the raft and pushed it farther from the shore. Al grabbed one of the nylon straps on the edge of the raft and held tight.

Callie pointed. "Look, they're stopping." The seven dinosaurs glared, standing in water up to their chins. Their faces formed a wall of horns. Their massive heads turned as one, the horns slowly tracking the passing raft.

William stopped paddling. "They can't come in." He laughed. "Their heads are too heavy." The wide frills growing out of the backs of their skulls looked like solid bone. "Those frills must weigh three hundred pounds. If they go in any deeper, they'll drown."

"Look at them all," Callie pointed. Beyond the shoreline, the forest opened up to reveal a great open slope. A series of rolling hillsides covered with thousands of animals stretched off in the distance as far as they could see. "It's like those paintings of bison on the prairie."

Hank pulled his cell phone out of a plastic baggie. "Cameras!" He held the phone steady to record a video while several others raised their phones.

The raft floated away from the clearing and the trees closed in again along the shore. The seven Triceratops slowly retreated from the water. A pair of short-horned juveniles wandered down to the bank and lapped with fat tongues.

When the Triceratops were no longer visible, Buddy finally stop barking.

Morgan sealed up his camera in a plastic bag. "We are going to be so famous when we get back. I wonder what they will call us on the news." He counted on his fingers. "*The Prehistoric Eight.*"

"Hey," said Callie. "You forgot about Buddy." She gave the dog a scratch on his chin.

"I don't think they would count the dog, babe," Hank said. "Besides, I've been thinking. There may not be any publicity about us at all. We may get money just to keep quiet."

"What?" said Morgan. "No way. We've got the best story ever."

Al thought Hank might be onto something. If they did somehow make it back, the government would cover this up before word got out that time travel was possible. There was a good chance all eight of them would quietly disappear. Al wondered if they should be in such a big hurry to get home.

Hank crossed his arms. "Between the liability suits and the hush money, we could all become millionaires."

Callie said, "I could keep quiet for a few million bucks. I'd quit my job. Hearing other people complain all day gets old."

"Europe," said Hank. "We could honeymoon in Europe for a year."

Callie grinned. "Sounds like fun."

"I would buy the biggest party house and never work again," said Morgan, rocking back and forth. "Sweet!"

"You'd burn through it in less than a year." Callie chuckled. "What about you, Tim? What would you do with a million dollars?"

"I'd help Julie pay for the hours and training she needs to get her professional license. Then I'd have my own personal pilot. We could go anywhere."

"Funding her pilot's license would seal the deal, huh, bro?" Morgan said with a dirty grin.

Callie shook her head and rolled her eyes. "Boys!"

Boys? Al thought. *Morgan can say whatever the hell he wants, but I'm the one who gets called a jackass?*

Tim smiled. "You know Morgan, I would help her out regardless."

"You would, wouldn't you," Callie said. "*That* little fact, Morgan, is what will get him laid." Tim's smile grew wider.

"Hey, whatever it takes." Morgan winked at her. "Not everyone can rely on the formidable reputation of *Morgan's organ.*" This brought a round of laughter.

Al turned away from the group and scanned the sides of the river for the so-called football. He forced himself to breathe slowly and thought about what he would do if he became a millionaire. He could make the trip to Nevada a lot more often. His year revolved around the annual vacation, which his friends thought was a gambling trip. He claimed he went to Reno because the odds were better than in Vegas, but in fact, it was easier to get to brothels in northern Nevada.

Each year, for four days, Al Stevens knew love. The release came after twelve months of building, pent-up frustration and those last few weeks were both unbearable and delicious with anticipation. He thought about that first moment, when the girl would reach down into his pants and grasp him. He cherished that first grab almost as much as the climaxes that came later. A multi-million dollar windfall from the government would buy a lot of grabbing.

You don't need that anymore, he told himself. He actually had a chance with someone. Lisa Danser had felt his erection and smiled. The girls at the brothels smiled, but they were paid to smile.

Al wondered if there was some way he and Lisa might stay behind when the others returned to the present. Here was an entire world to conquer, without all of the bullshit of modern life. They could be Tarzan and Jane. She would never go for it. She would hate him forever if she knew he was even thinking about it.

As they rounded a bend, a smaller river joined theirs from the right. The swirling currents spun them around in circles. Morgan held his hands overhead like a kid on a roller coaster. Beyond the junction, the river slowed again and William used the shovel to straighten them out.

Dizzy from the spinning, Al turned to face forward once more, just missing a swarm of bubbles that surfaced behind the raft.

- - - - -

The bubbles rose from the nostrils of a forty-foot crocodile which had followed them from the ruined building. It had feasted a day earlier on the carcass of a drowned ankylosaurus and would not be hungry again for more than a month. But the raft had piqued its curiosity, so it followed. The great reptile had lived for eighty years but had never smelled anything like it. Submerged, the crocodile allowed the current to push it along, adjusting its course with the occasional swish of its fifteen-foot tail.

At first, the strange yellow shape seemed like flotsam, speeding up or slowing down with the currents. But every so often, it wriggled and splashed like an injured animal. There was some kind of life to it. Life meant food.

At the Triceratops shore, the object had really come to life, but the crocodile had steered clear, wary of the old guardians along the shore. Their horns posed no threat to an animal that struck from below, but their sharp beaks could slice through hide and bone.

After the yellow object floundered and flailed out to the middle of the river, it grew motionless again. The crocodile drifted and watched. Finally, it decided to attack. The reptile exhaled and sank to the bottom, where it began to swing its tail back and forth in larger and larger motions, increasing speed. It angled upward; poised to open wide just before it reached the surface.

THIRTY

Lisa held the length of pipe like a sword as she crept across the laboratory. She heard small angry hisses and a wet smacking sound. She was trapped on the upper floor. The only way back to the café was to climb down the outside of the building and run past whatever was down there. *It can't reach you up here, whatever it is,* she thought. Then she pictured the dinosaurs with the long necks. If one of those came along, there wasn't anywhere to hide.

She had to see what was making the noise. She crept to the end of the leaning shelves and looked over the jagged wall. Nothing.

Uck! Uckawk! A barking screech came from the back side of the shelves. The pipe felt heavy in Lisa's hands. She jumped around the corner.

Three small winged creatures pecked at the open side of the dead man who had been sliced in half. They looked like oversized bats with stork-like beaks. Blue veins ran across pale blotches on their piebald skin. The largest pulled a length of entrails from the body.

"Hey! Get away from that!" Lisa burst forward, waving the pipe. The reptiles took flight, screaming a guttural *Uck Uck Uck* at her. The pterosaurs flew to the tops of the surrounding canopy, where they landed gracefully and perched in a row.

"Yuck." The sliced man lay by a doorway that led out of the lab and into whatever room or hallway had existed next to it. The body had been cut in a diagonal line that ran from one side of his head to the middle of his thigh. He had probably been trying to flee from the room when the accident occurred. Organs lay on the floor, spilling out of his abdominal cavity like some kind of mortician's cornucopia.

Lisa grabbed the man by his wrist and began to drag him. *At least he's light.* Only a thin strip of his head remained, with an ear attached to a slice of skin. The side of the man's torso folded together as she pulled, and a burgundy knot fell out. She would have to come back for it. She dragged the body around the domino shelves and over to the section of floor that sloped down to the river.

She released the half-body and pushed it down the slope with the pole. It soon floated away in the river below.

"You gotta go back for the guts, Lisa." She thought she might be able to spear the loose organs that had fallen from the bisected body. She did not want to have to pick them up.

As she returned around the shelves, Lisa saw that one of the pterosaurs had beat her to it. It snatched the last two round globs. They filled a pelican-like pouch under its chin. Lisa raised the pole and the pterosaur departed to the trees.

"Thanks, partner," she said, giving a sarcastic thumbs-up as it flew away.

Lisa moved on to Mister Slushy, ready to get the worst over with. She used the pole to push the ceiling tiles off of his body. His left foot had somehow escaped the charring or electrocution that had turned the rest of him into a soggy, blackened mess. She grabbed the foot and pulled. He was heavier, but he created his own slug-like trail as she dragged him. He moved along easily on the slick fluid and black flakes. "Bye-bye, Mister Slushy," Lisa said as he disappeared over the wall.

Finally she turned to the woman who had told them about the time device. Lisa repositioned the metal pipe under the concrete slab. It took several tries, but she finally levered the concrete high enough to drag out the body. The woman's legs bent unnaturally in multiple places, all the way down to her... *her shoes!* Lisa dropped the woman's shoulders and stooped next to her feet, pulling off a pair of patent leather flats. *Size seven! Forget about moccasins.* She wondered if she should have stripped the other bodies, or at least looked for anything useful in their pockets.

Lisa sat down and put on the shoes. *It's not like these even matter,* she told herself. *The others will be back soon and we'll all be heading home.* Her bedroom closet was full of shoes. Lisa flexed her toes. It felt good to have shoes on both feet again and it would be easier to climb back downstairs. She realized that if she had found the shoes earlier, she could have gone down the river with the others. With Al.

Lisa rummaged through the woman's pockets, but found only a parking stub. Her belongings must be in her purse, probably stashed in some other part of the building. Lisa pictured an employee break room just outside the radius of the device. She laughed. *Probably the same room where they kept the gun locker.* She took the woman by the arms and dragged her to the slope. Lisa felt something separate inside the woman's shirt along the way, but the body held together long enough to make it to the slide.

After the woman disappeared under the muddy current, Lisa inhaled deeply through her nose, testing the air. The first smell she noticed was her own stench, much worse after working in the heat. That was a good sign. She wiped her hands on her pants, determined to use an entire bottle of antibacterial lotion down in the café, and climbed downstairs.

Helen wore a kind face. "That must have been unpleasant."

Lisa smiled. "You don't know the half of it," she said, exhausted. "There were bird dinosaurs picking at one of the bodies." She was alone in the café now with Helen. If the others never came back, what then? Tears started to well in her eyes. She wondered if she had made a horrible mistake.

Helen wrapped her in a lavender-scented hug. "Let's get your mind off it, sweetie. Let's see if we can do something with all that equipment they found upstairs."

THIRTY-ONE

Four feet below the raft, the giant crocodile detected a new smell. It changed its trajectory at the last moment, descending back to the cooler depths. It tasted blood in the water, faint but unmistakable. Blood almost always meant easy prey. The crocodile turned upstream to follow the scent, scattering a school of small silver fish.

The blood led straight to the split-faced body of Doctor Anderson. The crocodile felt satiated as it gulped the corpse into its gullet. The reptile would not need to eat for a month thanks to yesterday's Ankylosaurus, but it might not find anything else for twice that long. A stuffed belly insured against lean times. The smell of blood continued to waft by, and so the crocodile swam further upstream, engorging on the buffet that wafted along on the currents.

As the crocodile fed, the raft drifted farther away behind it, forgotten.

- - - - -

Beyond the junction, the river grew wider and the current slowed to a crawl. William paddled with the shovel to keep them moving. Callie pointed at his hand. "You mentioned a couple of boys, but I don't see a ring."

"Nope. Never married. You are looking at an honest-to-goodness single black father." He chuckled and continued, "Their mother was a lot of fun. Probably not too unlike the girls Tim used to go out with. She never quite grew up, though. So I raised the boys myself. Those boys helped *me* grow up."

"How old are they?" Callie asked.

"Eleven and thirteen."

"Oh, that must be fun."

William sighed. "Yep. You can see why I need to get back to them. They are in that giant sorting machine called middle school. I got to make sure they get sorted onto the right path. The one that doesn't mean working in fast food and living paycheck-to-paycheck for the rest of their lives. Or worse. I need to be back."

"Julie has a nine-year-old son," Tim said. "I have no idea how to act around him."

"Damn, son," said William, "You are serious about this woman."

"Yeah, well getting stranded millions of years in the past puts things in perspective."

Al kept a blank face as he listened. They were supposed to be looking for a time machine, but the raft ride had turned into a fucking social hour. They should be discussing survival tactics. How do you navigate without GPS? How do you predict the weather without an app? The idea of living without technology sounded glorious. He would never have to look at another screen. Al provided technical support for small companies that had no IT departments of their own. Most were too inept to look up simple solutions on the internet, especially the realtors.

Al had discovered that if he actually solved problems, he lost business. They didn't need him any more. But if he fixed things *just enough*, he would get another call six months later. The customers didn't mind. They saw him as the hero.

Now he was a hero for real. If they made it home, would Lisa still see him that way? Or would they go back to café small talk? Hell, the café was totaled, so there wouldn't even be that. She would be a celebrity. Everyone in the world would want to meet her. Here, there were exactly four other men on the planet to compete with. One of them was already paired up and one of them was Morgan. Al thought his odds seemed pretty good.

The secret was to find shelter. If they could find a secure cave, they could live long happy lives here. Lives of freedom and adventure. Here, it didn't matter if you never knew the right thing to say. All that mattered was that you could take care of things. Al had proven that to Lisa. He took a deep, invigorating breath. The air held more oxygen than in modern Denver. Al felt great. All he had to do was go along on this silly treasure hunt and hope they never found the time machine.

As they grew close to the sea, the raft began to scrape across the shallow bottom and even came to a complete stop several times. Hank and Al used their sticks to push the raft forward. The midday sun bore down on them and Callie's pale skin began to redden. When they rounded the final bend and finally caught sight of the ocean, everyone cheered. Al forced himself to emit a hearty, "Yeah!"

After twenty minutes, though, they seemed no closer. An onshore breeze held them in place, possibly aided by in incoming tide. *Tides in Colorado*, Al thought. This world was amazing.

"We aren't getting anywhere," Morgan complained.

"I think we should walk from here," William said. There was no bank on the left hand side, only an endless maze of reedy marshes, so they poled over to the right, where they found a sandy shoreline.

Buddy bolted as soon as the raft was close enough, performing another epic leap across a three-foot gap.

"Buddy, *wait!*" Callie shouted. The dog zig-zagged away, disappearing into clumps of sea grasses.

Hank put a firm hand on her shoulder. "Easy with the shouting, babe. That might attract attention."

"But he's *gone.*" She glared unhappily.

"He'll come back, I betcha," William said. Al thought he was just trying to make her feel better.

Al climbed off of the raft and onto the sandy bank. He scanned the river ahead. There was no sign of the football. He wondered if they had missed it somewhere along the way? Did the thing even exist? They were relying on the delusional words of a dying stranger. A stranger who was responsible for their very situation.

The woman had claimed the device floated. Anything could have happened to it though. Maybe it had been weighed down by rubble that had fallen on top of it. For all they knew, it was sitting on the bottom of the river right below the café, pinned under a pile of concrete, just like the woman herself had been. His heart pounded as a new possibility occurred to him. *What if the device is back at the café and Lisa finds it?* She and Helen might end up going home before the rest of them got back.

William unfastened one of the black nylon straps from the side of the raft and wrapped it around the trunk of a short shrub. Callie, Hank, Tim, and Morgan all took off their personal floatation devices and tossed them into the raft. None of the vests had been inflated.

Morgan watched William tie up their boat with a look of dismay. "You're wasting your time, man. We can't use it to go back upriver." Just in case the condescending tone wasn't clear enough, he added, "Duh."

"We might need it later," William explained. "Maybe the machine is way out in the ocean and there are jellyfish everywhere. Or who knows what?"

"Jellyfish." Morgan cringed.

Yeah, Al thought. *Or maybe we're stuck here for the rest of our lives and we might wish we had a raft at some point along the way.* He appreciated William's forethought.

William finished hitching up the raft and collected the shovel. "Ya'll know I'm from Florida," he said, starting off toward the sea. "It'll be good to see the beach again."

Tim reached into the raft to retrieve his life jacket. Un-inflated, it amounted to little more than a collection of straps. He put it back on, just in case.

The hike to the coast took them another hour. The ground alternated between boggy and sandy and they were forced to backtrack several times around wide, stagnant marshes. William left the group more than once to hike back to the river, in case the device was stuck along the shore somewhere. Each time, he returned empty-handed.

Mosquitoes attacked them in great clouds.

"Maybe one of these will get trapped in amber," Callie said, smacking her neck and cringing at the bloody splotch on her palm. "Someone will find it someday, extract the blood from its belly, and make a clone of me." Hank laughed and put his arm around her. Al felt a jealous itch crawling up his back. Hank probably bent her over every single night.

Finally, they crested the last row of dunes. They stood at the top, looking down at a wide beach of dull brown sand. To their left, the mouth of the river widened to cover a half mile.

The sea itself was apparently quite shallow. Several hundred yards out, they saw dozens of the largest animals to ever walk the planet.

THIRTY-TWO

A herd of four dozen titanosaurs grazed offshore in knee-deep water. They munched on seaweed, slowly reeling long strands into their mouths like children slurping spaghetti. Their necks stretched eighty feet out. As they lumbered along, they kicked up small waves which rolled back and forth between them.

Tim looked in awe at the ocean spread out before him. All that water. He had never seen the ocean before. It looked like dull slate, not the brilliant blue-green he expected.

"They aren't real," Callie said. "They can't be. Someone put something in my drink and I'm hallucinating." Hank put his arm around her.

Morgan snapped his fingers. "I know those. Those are Brontosauruses."

William shook his head. "I don't think so. They're in the sauropod family, but these are bigger. And besides, they don't use the name 'brontosaurus' any more. It's 'Apatosaurus' now."

"*Pat o'saurus?*" Morgan snickered. "What are they, fucking Irish?"

William squinted at the offshore giants. "These look more like diplodocus. See how long their tails are?"

Morgan clapped William on the back. "I am so glad I got stuck in the land of the lost with the world's only black dinosaur nerd."

William smiled. "Someday, Morgan, you will have children of your own and you will become an expert on dinosaurs, or insects, or Japanese fighting robots, or something."

"I'm already an expert on Japanese fighting robots, bro."

Callie looked over. "Maybe he'll have a little girl and become an expert on princesses."

William chuckled and studied the great beasts in the distance. "Diplodocus wasn't so big though. Those look enormous."

"Hey!" Callie pointed. "Forget about the damn dinosaurs. Look what I see!" Off to the left, about a quarter mile out from the surf, an orange light blinked, like a buoy marking the mouth of the river. "That's got to be it!"

They all gazed at the object bobbing in the water.

"Fuckin' A," Morgan said. "I'm going to get so wasted when we get home." He lit his second-to-last cigarette.

Tim focused on the device. It glinted in the sunlight. *I have got to take swimming lessons.* He had a few thousand dollars saved up in the bank. *Maybe I could take Julie on a vacation to Hawaii.* He wondered if it was too early to invite her on a vacation. "How far out do you think that is?" he asked.

"Less than two thousand feet," Hank said. "You all stay here. Build a sandcastle or something. I'll go get it."

"We gotta be careful now," Al cautioned. "So far, the plant eaters have been just as bad as the meat eaters. Maybe we should wait until they clear out."

Hank looked across the water at the wading giants. "Those things are so big, how can they even notice us? We're like ants." Most of the herd grazed beyond the time machine and nearly a hundred feet separated the device from the closest dinosaur. They moved slowly to the right, following the coast southward. "Besides, it doesn't look very deep." The water appeared to be three or four feet high where it met the dinosaurs' legs, even the ones farthest out. Hank turned to Al. "I'm going to just walk out there and get that damn thing."

"Wait," Callie began. "I've been thinking. Remember what Beth said about horror movies? Don't split up." She paused. "Let's all wade out there as a group. Let's stick together."

William nodded. "It sounds like a good idea to me. If something happens, we can help each other out."

Hank stared at his fiancé and gave a shrug. "Alright, but I'm not waiting on anyone." He started down the dune, sliding on loose sand.

Tim considered offering to stay behind and watch their backs. The water *did* look shallow enough to walk in. He decided he could handle it and started after the others.

"Hey, look who's here," said William, pointing up the beach. Buddy walked toward them dragging the dried remains of a three-foot fish.

Callie smacked her lips. "Mmmm, that looks delicious." The dog dropped to the sand and stripped bits of flesh from the bones, holding the fish between his front paws.

William let out a chuckle. "Let's do this." He followed Hank down to the high tide line. Bits of shells littered the beach, along with an uneven band of withered seaweed. William jammed the shovel into the sand and knelt to remove his shoes. The others followed suit. They all dropped their mobile devices into their shoes. Even though most were sealed up in baggies, they didn't want to risk carrying them out into the ocean. They contained the pictures they had taken, pictures that could be worth thousands. Hank snapped a few shots of the herd at the last minute.

Buddy watched Hank lead the group down to the surf and then returned his attention to his seafood snack.

As they drew close to the water, they picked up the smell of the dinosaurs lumbering offshore. "That's um, that's something." Callie commented. The titanosaurs smelled far worse than the hadrosaurs, even at this distance.

Tim's stomach already felt queasy at the thought of going out into the water. The smell of goat cheese vomit added to his nausea. He opened his mouth to breathe.

The water felt warm, almost spa-like, and the surf amounted to little more than a ripple. Tiny minnows scattered about their feet as they sloshed along. Hank led the way, setting a steady pace.

"This isn't so bad," Callie remarked. "A walk on the beach." Hank smiled and took her hand.

At twenty yards out, they encountered the seaweed which had attracted the titanosaurs to the area. Thick, ropey strands tangled and tugged at their feet as they walked, slowing their progress. "Ok, I take it back," Callie said. "This *is* bad. I hope nothing is living in this stuff."

"You got that right," Tim agreed. He imagined tentacles wrapping around his bare feet and eels slithering along his ankles.

"I doubt there is anything too big nearby," Hank offered. "Not with those things lumbering around."

Tim wasn't so sure. He positioned himself in the middle of the group and shuffled his feet along the sandy bottom as he walked, hoping to scare off any prehistoric stingrays or crabs that might be sheltering under the seaweed.

Morgan stumbled and he fell forward into the water. He came up soaked and sputtering. "What the shit!" The others laughed.

"What does that mean, exactly?" William asked.

Morgan flapped his arms, trying to shake them dry. "It's like 'what the fuck'," he said, as if that explained everything.

Callie pressed him. "Yeah, but everyone else says 'what the fuck.' Why do you say 'what the shit'?"

Morgan pulled a strand of seaweed from his hair. "Because a fuck is a good thing. People always say 'what the fuck' when they are upset about something. Why would you take such a wonderful thing as a fuck and use it to talk about something bad?"

"You've spent a lot of time thinking about this, haven't you?"

"Fuck yeah."

As they moved past the steady whisper of small waves breaking on the shore, they heard a brittle screeching sound from the direction of the herd.

"That's a weird noise," Morgan said. "You'd think creatures that big would sound a little more bad-ass."

"It isn't the dinosaurs making the noise," William said. "It's the creatures flying around them." A cloud of pterosaurs buzzed around each giant titanosaur. The flying reptiles flitted about, landed on the sides of the sauropods, squawked at each other and then flew off again, only to reposition themselves somewhere else. "They must feed on parasites living on the dinosaurs' skin."

Methodically, each titanosaur lowered its head and swung it sideways through the water. When it rose back to the sky, it pulled up strands of seaweed and then chewed the mass into its mouth. They never seemed to drop any.

Their tails extended straight out behind them, ending in impossibly thin wisps that rotated in tight spirals, like little flagellate propellers slowly pushing the giants forward. Every so often, Tim thought he heard the sound of a tail slicing the air, like the swish made by swinging a thin branch.

Hank and Callie led the group by a good ten yards. They seemed to have an easier time wading in their running shorts than the others in their long pants. Hank released Callie's hand and forged ahead. Tim thought that he seemed determined to reach the device first, almost as if it was a race. Tim did not object. There was no reason for everyone to come all the way out and the sooner they got the time machine, the sooner they could head back.

The football-shaped object bobbed gently in the water, its yellow-orange light blinking on and off every few seconds. It looked alien and out of place in this otherwise natural world.

When he finally reached it, Hank spoke out loud. "Gotcha!" He took it into his hands. The device was more than three times as large as a real football and encased in shiny metal. Hank lifted it triumphantly over his head and turned to face the others following behind. Water dripped onto his hair and a smile broke out on his face. The object was covered by eight panels, four on each hemisphere, alternating between orange paint and polished aluminum.

Enough, Tim thought. He turned to look back at the shore. A few yards behind the group, he saw the forty-foot crocodile. Its upper jaw and snout broke the surface, creating a low wake as it swam silently toward them.

THIRTY-THREE

"Fishing is all about patience," Helen said, watching the bobber dance in the current. Four lines extended off the sidewalk pier. Two lines ended with lures from the tackle box and two others ended with hooks holding small white worms Lisa found under a log near the tree line.

"That's why I never fished," Lisa told her. "No patience."

"You got this store up and running. That must have taken some patience." Helen had never worked outside the home. Lawrence Davies believed a family needed a wife and a mother. Helen believed it too, when it came down to it. She couldn't imagine what it would take to run a business by herself.

"I think my lack of patience helped me," Lisa said. "I never sat still. I always had to find an improvement."

"You did the right thing, dumping them in the river," Helen said. She didn't actually believe that, but she thought Lisa needed to hear it. Helen thought that bodies should be buried. She didn't believe in cremation and she certainly did not believe in river dumping.

The first body had startled her. She had been sorting through the fishing supplies when it landed in the water. A few drops from the splash hit her. She had watched in horror as the remaining three corpses fell from above and then floated away. *That's going to be you, Helen Davies, if you aren't careful now.*

Still, what's done is done. Chastising the woman wouldn't help and it wasn't as if the two of them could dig four graves by themselves.

"It was starting to get pretty nasty up there." Lisa had washed her hands three times with antibiotic soap after climbing back down.

"I suppose there wasn't any other choice," Helen admitted. "Still, sweetie, when my turn comes, I'd really prefer to be buried."

"I promise not to dump you in the river."

Helen wasn't sure if she was being patronized, but it did not matter. She had made her wishes known. "Look! There was a nibble." She pointed a bony finger at one of the white and red bobbers.

Helen had seen nibbles about every five minutes, and she pointed out each and every one, hoping to keep Lisa distracted now that she had run out of things to do. The remaining "Daily Edition" canvas bags were all stuffed with supplies. Everything that they might need had been carefully packed. She had divided up all of the camping and survival gear from the cabinet upstairs, along with what remained of their food. If they found themselves needing to depart, they could grab at least two bags each on the way out. Of course, if they needed to leave, there might not be time to grab anything. Helen was not sure she would leave the building at all, no matter what happened.

She felt hopeful about the fishing. It had all come back to her. With fingers stiff from arthritis, she had carefully threaded each of the lures and fish hooks on the first try. Every few minutes she adjusted one of the lines and checked to make sure the bait had not disappeared.

"Do you think they'll even find it?" Lisa asked. They had not talked about the others since they left.

Helen looked up at her. She did not like to sugarcoat things. As a mother, and now as a grandmother, she had a reputation for being blunt. Her children's spouses found her a little off-putting. She didn't care. People needed to hear the truth. The world had grown far too sensitive. "Lisa, sweetie, we should work under the assumption that you and I are the only two people left alive on this planet and that we will be here until the day we die. Anything else that happens is a bonus."

"You don't even think they will make it back empty-handed?"

"I'm not saying that. But there's a lot that can go wrong. Even if they don't get gobbled up by Lord knows what, they may never find that time machine. Or they may find it and it won't work. Or they may find it and use it without us."

"No way. William wouldn't do that." She frowned at the woman for even suggesting such a thing. "And I don't think Al would let them."

"Isn't the machine going to go off automatically when time is up?" Helen didn't begin to understand how the time machine was supposed to work, but she remembered hearing about that part. "If they don't make it back here in time, they won't be able to stop it." She scoffed, "Do you honestly think they would step aside and let it go back without them?"

Helen saw the despair dawning on Lisa's face. *It hurts to feel like you're going to be left behind, doesn't it?* She didn't enjoy Lisa's pain, but was glad the young woman finally knew how she felt.

Helen adjusted one of the lines. "We'll know by the end of the day, won't we? And if we are stuck here, we've got a lot of things we can use to get by."

"They'll be back," Lisa said. "Al will make sure of it."

"Oh, looky!" Helen squealed. One of the bobbers disappeared under the surface and the line zig-zagged toward deeper water.

THIRTY-FOUR

The crocodile had drifted along leisurely after eating the bodies that floated down the river. The four easy bites had left it feeling full and lethargic, but its curiosity drove it onward.

It found the raft floating quietly at the edge of the water. The reptile approached from the surface, watching carefully for any reaction. Motionless, like a log floating in the current, it waited until it was three feet from the yellow inflatable. In a violent burst of energy, it threw open its six-foot jaws, rolled its head, and grabbed the side of the boat with its teeth.

The crocodile was rewarded with a foul hissing as the raft collapsed between its jaws. Nothing in its mouth suggested the taste of food. It shook the yellow rubber free and turned away.

Having made the journey almost all the way to the sea, it decided to swim the final stretch. Females could sometimes be found near the mouth of the river and it was never one to turn down a visit with a female.

The crocodile almost gave up when it reached the seaweed, which caused as much trouble for it as it did for the six small creatures ahead. But their irregular splashes tantalized the reptile and their scent matched the smell of the four morsels it had eaten earlier, so it carried on.

As it clawed through the tangled strands, the crocodile focused on its prey, but it also watched the giant sauropods further out. Millions of years of evolution had taught it to avoid anything that large. It grew increasingly uncomfortable as it moved away from the mouth of the river, but one of the small creatures stopped just a short distance ahead and off to one side.

The small creature that captivated the crocodile's attention was Morgan Baker.

Back on the beach, Buddy abandoned the remains of his fish and rose to his feet. Staying above the high tide line, he began to bark.

- - - - -

Hank Atherton had played soccer every year of his life since the age of eight. It helped him stay fit. It helped him make and maintain important connections in Denver's political scene. Most of all, though, it provided an hour each week where his mind was distracted from the troubles of his job. When he played, Hank focused entirely on the game and nothing else. Few things in life occupied him so fully.

Holding the time device over his head, Hank made the throw-in toss of his life. He reared back and flung the device forward with all of his might. The motion tore three of the tendons in his rotator cuff, though he did not notice.

The device arced high over the water, its orange light blinking on and off like the beacon on a passing airplane. The rest of the group watched with dismay and wondered what he was doing. The time device landed at the exact spot Hank Atherton had aimed for, behind Morgan and alongside the head of the giant crocodile.

As soon as the device left his hands, Hank sucked in a lungful of air and shouted, *"RUN!"*

Morgan followed the arc of the football until it splashed into the water next to the creature behind him. He saw the beast, screamed, and sloshed frantically toward the others. The seaweed and water caught him in a slow-motion nightmare.

Run, dammit, Hank thought. Morgan looked like the stupid teenager in a horror movie unable to get away as the monster closed in.

When the football splash-landed next to the crocodile, the reptile whip-snapped its head and clamped its jaws on the orange metal.

As the creature spun its forty-foot body, it created a wave that washed across the shallow water and into Tim, whirling him under the surface.

"*Goddammit, run!*" Hank shouted again. He waded back to meet Callie, caught her hand, and yanked her forward, pulling her out to sea. It was the only place to go. The crocodile was between them and the shore. Hank laced his fingers around hers and vowed that he would not let go until they were back at the damn café. The crocodile had been within striking distance of Morgan and not all that far from Callie. He wondered briefly if it would swallow the device and leave them stranded forever. Then it occurred to him that it might still go off inside the animal and transport the monster to downtown Denver.

- - - - -

Tim spun around underwater until he found the sandy bottom with his hands and righted himself. He tried to rise, remembering not to breathe until his head was above the surface. Other people did that automatically. He realized that his life vest was not inflated and groped for the red handle hanging near his waist. *A sharp tug should trigger it,* he thought. Then he remembered the high-pitched *whoosh* of the inflating raft and wondered if the life jacket would make the same noise. The last thing he wanted was to draw the crocodile's attention.

When he finally surfaced, he found himself only a few feet behind the reptile. It closed its jaws repeatedly on the football. Several eight-inch teeth snapped off in the process.

Tim froze, afraid to make any sound or vibration. He remained in a crouched position with his head just out of the water and tried to catch sight of the others.

"It's coming," William warned, looking back over his shoulder. He started running again, still at least ten yards behind Hank and Callie. "Get closer to the dinosaurs. Hide around their legs."

Tim questioned William's judgment but didn't have any better ideas. Still afraid to move, he let the waves bob him slightly, hoping he would continue to go unnoticed.

The crocodile released the football and turned toward William and the others. A swish of its tail propelled it forward, creating a new wave that washed Tim away and upended him a second time.

- - - - -

The titanosaurs generally did not pay attention to other creatures. Once they survived their first four years, nothing threatened them, simply because of their size. Every now and then, however, some intruding creature needed to be taught a lesson.

The seventy year-old matriarch of the herd swung her head toward the noise of the shouting humans. Her neck travelled a slow, wide arc as her eyes scanned the sea below. She did not notice the six small creatures running in her direction. They amounted to little more than white-caps on the water. She focused on the giant crocodile. Crocodiles rarely came out into the sea, but when they did, they sometimes attacked the juveniles. The titanosaur lowered herself forward on her front legs and cocked her long muscular tail up into the sky. The end of the tail, a strand of sinews and bones no wider than a child's wrist, rose up to a height of one hundred and fifty feet above the surface of the sea.

Most of the other adults in the herd assumed the same defensive position. Thirty whip-like tails rose high in the air.

- - - - -

The crocodile had been watching for exactly this posture. It flipped around without hesitation. At ten tons, the reptile outweighed most of the animals it encountered from day to day, but not the titanosaurs. They were more than triple its size. Instinct told the crocodile that the tail-up posture was something to flee immediately.

- - - - -

"It's leaving!" William called out. "Hank, slow down."

Hank looked around. He and Callie were the farthest out, still some fifty feet from the nearest titanosaur.

Al and Morgan stood near William, both breathing heavily. "Hey, where is Tim?"

"Dammit, I don't know where he is!" Hank couldn't be responsible for everyone. Anyway, the more important question was, "Where is the goddamn time device?"

- - - - -

The old titanosaur matriarch saw that the crocodile was moving away, but decision-making did not come quickly to her. Once she began a course of action, she usually finished it. She turned her hips and swung her tail downward in the general direction of the commotion.

The very tip of her tail, a thin series of bony scutes connected by sinewy ligaments, reached the speed of sound as it swung toward the water. It maxed out at sixteen hundred feet per second just above the surf. The end of the tail swept an arc in the general direction of the threat and then curled back inward and upward. The thunderous crack it produced, like the sound of a giant tree splitting in two, spurred the crocodile faster, exactly as the old titanosaur intended. The swimming reptile kicked off the bottom of the sea in a clumsy run back toward the mouth of the river.

The other titanosaurs snapped their tails within the next several seconds. The ocean boomed like a fireworks finale as the thin, whip-like ends of each tail broke the sound barrier. Several tails skipped across the surface, cutting through the spray. The tail of a titanosaur was strong enough to split the hide of a dinosaur. Years before, the matriarch had hobbled a desperate tyrannosaur that had come after her offspring.

- - - - -

The very end of the tail of the nearest titanosaur passed through Hank's neck at just over one thousand miles per hour. Hank's blood, enriched by the dense oxygen of the Cretaceous air, fed his brain and kept him alive for three full seconds as his head fell from his body.

Hank looked back up at his chest as he felt himself tumble forward and splash into the water. In shock, unaware that he had been decapitated, he tried desperately to raise himself up, but found that he had no control over any motion. Finally his neurons stopped firing and he died, just as his headless body pulled free from Callie's hand and collapsed in the opposite direction.

- - - - -

Callie was scanning the water behind her, still trying to find Tim, when the tip of the dinosaur's tail cut through her fiancé's neck, missing her own head by inches. She heard what she thought was machine-gun fire and felt a misty breeze. Callie wondered if the military had shown up to save them and reclaim the time device.

Then she heard a splash and Hank started pulling her hand again. She wanted to tell him to stop, that they were safe, or at least that they could quit running. The giant crocodile was swimming away. She doubted she would ever really feel safe again. Before she could get the words out, Hank pulled free and fell into the water.

"Hank?" She started forward. "Guys, Hank fainted! Get up here." Reaching into the sea, Callie grabbed her fiancé's shoulders and pulled him up, trying to get his mouth above the surface. For several seconds she watched blood spurt from his empty neck.

Understanding slowly came to her. *No. Not us. We were the fast ones. We were going to make it.* These thoughts cycled again and again in her head as her mouth opened with a wailing cry that she had no ability to stop.

THIRTY-FIVE

Helen untied the fishing line from the parking meter. The tension felt right. She gave it a quick, gentle tug. "He's hooked!"

"What do I do, what do I do?"

"Get the bucket and bring it over. Just hold it underneath so he doesn't flop away." Lisa grabbed the bucket, which was actually a five-gallon plastic trash can that had been used to collect coffee grounds behind the counter.

"Look at him go!" Helen said. She wrapped the line around her hand and felt it squeeze tight.

Lisa danced behind Helen as she pulled in several arm-lengths of fishing line. The bobber splashed back and forth across the surface.

"Get over here. Get ready!"

Lisa held out the trash can with her head turned back as far away as possible.

Helen reached down over the edge of the sidewalk, grabbed the line just above the bobber, and wrapped another length around her fist. It cinched against a blue ridge of veins. Holding tightly to the parking meter, she rose in one swift motion, lifting her arm high into the air.

A four-inch fish flew from the water, thrashing at the end of the hook.

Lisa exhaled. "They really better find that device."

Helen lowered the tiny fish into the trash can, where it knocked against the plastic walls.

Within a half hour, the trash can held eight fish. The largest was just over five inches long. All eight put together would barely feed one person. Lisa had filled the trash can with river water and left it in the shade on the front sidewalk to keep them fresh.

Helen had changed out all the fishhooks for larger ones and they had not caught anything since. The two women sat at a table near the front of the café. Helen knitted, but she had trouble concentrating. The plastic needles clacked slowly together and she stopped frequently to make corrections.

She felt discouraged. Larry always caught a big fat walleye or trout on their camping trips. What she had caught didn't even qualify as fish. They were minnows. She began to doubt that she and Lisa could survive here alone.

Helen had also begun to worry about her pills. Her purse held a plastic container with little compartments for each day of the week. Today was Wednesday, so the first three compartments were already empty. The remaining four compartments each contained eight pills. She thought she could live without the diuretic and anti-depressant, but she was not so sure what would happened when she stopped taking medication for her thyroid, blood pressure, potassium, osteoporosis, and glaucoma. Worst of all, she could not remember what the eighth pill was supposed to treat. *Maybe it's for my memory.*

Helen put down her knitting needles. "Sweetie, would you explain to me again how the machine is supposed to work." Their only chance, she thought, was for William and the others to come back and save them.

"It goes off automatically fifteen hours after it brought us here."

"And how much time do we have left?"

Lisa pulled out her phone and checked the clock. "A little less than seven hours, I think. That's assuming William's estimate was right. And assuming the machine actually works. And assuming they find the damn thing."

A pterosaur landed on one of the parking meters outside.

"Look," whispered Lisa.

The pterosaur held its pale bat-wings wide and turned its head from side to side, surveying the scene. Perched upright, the creature stood about two feet tall. It cocked its head as if asking a question. Lisa cocked her own head in response. "What do you want, little guy?"

The reptile hopped off the meter and landed on the sidewalk next to the trash can. It held its head perfectly motionless as it stared into the water. In a flash, it stabbed, jack-hammering into the bucket with its beak.

Lisa jumped up, knocking over her chair, and ran out the front window.

The pterosaur turned, leapt off of the sidewalk, and flapped away.

"Great."

"How many are left?"

"Two." Lisa picked up the bucket and moved it inside.

Helen sucked air, making a hissing sound. They still had plenty of muffins and scones, but at some point they would run out. Two tiny fish would not sustain them. They needed something bigger. "That flying fella had some real meat on him," Helen commented. "If we could catch one of those, we would have a meal."

"I was okay with the idea of eating prehistoric fish." Lisa scrunched up her nose. "I'm not so sure about bird dinosaurs."

"Sweetie, if we're stuck here, you might need to move outside your culinary comfort zone. If you're hungry enough, you'll eat it."

"How do we even know it's safe to eat? Could it be poisonous?"

"I'm sure it's fine. Probably tastes like squirrel."

"Yuck. What the hell does squirrel taste like?"

"Chicken."

"Well, why didn't you say it probably tastes like chicken?"

Helen smiled and resumed knitting. "So what happens if the others find the machine and it goes off before they get back here?"

Lisa gave a small shrug. "Well, I guess they will go back to some other part of Denver. Someplace east of the city, since that's the direction they went." She dropped her hands on the table. "If that happens, we might find out eventually, because whatever was *there* will show up *here*."

Helen stared. "I don't understand."

"You swap places. Whenever the machine goes through time, it swaps out whatever is there. If the machine goes off in the jungle three miles east of here, they will arrive… I dunno, maybe in the Denver Zoo, because that's three miles east of my café. And then the lions or zebras or whatever would be transferred here."

"Ok, I get it," Helen nodded. "Whatever is in the same spot in Denver will get swapped here." She made a clucking laugh. "Imagine being trapped in dinosaur times and getting eaten by a lion."

"Beth would have loved the irony," Lisa said, staring into space. She patted the table repeatedly. "But they really need to get back here before time runs out in order to do anything with the fail-safe."

"Explain that part again. What does the fail-safe do?"

Lisa took one of Helen's knitting needles and placed it in the middle of the table. "This is time. The needle's point is where we were when we left Denver, ok?" She took a scrap of yarn and laid it on the table so that one end touched the point. "This is the path we took, back to here." She traced the yarn along the needle and touched it to the knob at the other end.

"That's where we are now," Helen said. "Dinosaur time."

Helen realized that Lisa was explaining it to herself as much as to her. "After fifteen hours, the machine follows the same path back." She traced the yarn again.

Helen nodded for her to go on.

Lisa placed a much shorter piece of yarn at the point and curved it to touch the shaft of the needle an inch back. "This is what the fail-safe does. It takes us back twenty minutes. When we get back to Denver, we're supposed to go back in time twenty minutes and stop the experiment from ever happening. We go to the café and tell ourselves to get out of there, so that we never go back in time at all." She removed the longer piece of yarn. "If we succeed, this never happens."

"Why would they make the time machine do something like that?"

"Beth..." Lisa took a deep breath. "Beth was always telling stories when business was slow. Some that she read, some that she saw at the movies, and some that she made up. She loved to make up stories about the customers. Anyway, she told me a couple of time travel stories where people went back in time and accidentally erased themselves or made some change to human evolution. Everyone had gills or green skin when they came home. I think maybe the researchers upstairs were afraid of something like that happening."

Helen thought it all sounded insane. "How could you possibly use the fail-safe if you got erased?"

Lisa crossed her arms. "I don't know, Helen. I don't know if any of this will work. I'll be surprised if they make it back here with the device, much less figure out how to use the failsafe."

"You think we're stuck here?"

Lisa nodded. "I want you to teach me how to catch one of those bird-dinosaurs."

THIRTY-SIX

Callie sat on the beach, cold and clammy and still sobbing. Someone sitting next to her picked bits of seaweed from the tangles in her hair. She wasn't even sure who it was. She didn't care. Occasionally, he rubbed her arms. A distant part of her realized that she was shivering and he was trying to warm her up. It did not work.

Callie stared at the sand in front of her, hating herself. Somehow, beyond comprehension, she was not thinking of Hank. She thought instead of Andrew. Andrew, the guy she had slept with just two weeks before Hank proposed to her. *No. You didn't sleep with him, did you Callie? You fucked him.* This brought a fresh round of wracking sobs.

It wasn't really cheating, was it? She and Hank were only dating at the time. Of course, they had been *only dating* for a year and a half. Fucking Andrew had been the best sex ever. She had not regretted it for a moment, because somehow it had brought her closer to Hank and then sure enough, two weeks later he had proposed. Down on one knee and everything. It was more than she deserved.

The tears flowed and the sobs came with each breath. She wanted to take it back. She never should have let Andrew buy her that drink.

She looked up as William, Morgan, and Tim walked out of the surf. Tim stopped at the high tide line and took off his personal floatation device, still uninflated. He threw it down on the ground. Morgan held something in his hands and Callie wondered for a moment if it was Hank's head. Callie made herself look and saw that it was the time device. She saw a few shallow dents from the crocodile's teeth, but it seemed otherwise undamaged. The orange light blinked on and off.

Callie remembered standing in the ocean, unable to move and screaming hysterically with her hands splayed and shaking at the side of her face. William had splashed over to her, shouting her name. Hank's head bobbed into his knee.

She had wanted William to bring Hank's body ashore, but she couldn't form the words to tell him. It would have meant picking up the head. How do you tell someone to pick up a head? William had dragged Callie, quite literally kicking and screaming, back to the beach.

William walked up to her. *This will be good,* she thought, still crying. *William has never had any training in grief counseling. He won't know what to say.* It didn't matter. There wasn't anything he could say.

He crouched and put a hand on her knee. "Callie, we got to move on now, girl," William told her. "We got the device. It will go off soon. We have to get back, and you've got to come with us."

He brushed the sand off of her feet and put on her socks, slowly rolling them up and adjusting the toes so that the stitch ran across the top. "My boys used to make me fix them this way," he explained. Then he put on her running shoes and tied them tight with double knots. When he finished, William took her hand.

Callie looked at him. *Go with you?* She looked out to the sea. The herd had moved south, where they were slowly disappearing into the haze. Many of the pterosaurs remained behind, splashing and playing out in the water. They screeched as they dropped to the surface and then climbed back up to circle overhead, like buzzards. *That's where we were,* she realized. The pterosaurs were fighting over Hank's remains.

She couldn't stop crying and she didn't know what she wanted to do. She wanted it to be over. She turned and noticed Al, sitting beside her with his arm on her shoulder. How long had he been holding her? She suddenly knew one thing she wanted. She wanted to be away from Al. She shrugged free and allowed William to pull her to her feet.

Al glared. He walked away and yanked the shovel out of the sand.

William squeezed her hand. "That's it, girl. We got to get back now."

Forcing herself to not look out to sea again, Callie turned toward the dunes and started walking, not sure exactly which way to go, but wanting to get as far from this horrible beach as possible.

She walked alone in front of the group with her arms folded across her chest, hugging herself tightly. She forced herself to stop crying. Her throat was raw and her eyes had dried out. As she wandered around the dunes, she focused on a single question: *What am I supposed to do now?*

That's a stupid thing to ask, came a response, surprising her.

She didn't look around. It was clearly Hank's voice, and since Hank had been beheaded, it was clearly in her mind. Callie gave a small nod. *Okay. I get it.* She was a psychiatrist after all. This was obviously her mind's way of coping with the fact that she was in shock. As soon as she got back home, she would write herself a prescription for Lorazepam and try to sleep for a year.

You're supposed to keep going. You're supposed to get back home, said the Hank-in-her-head. *You know that's what you need to do.*

Callie gave another almost imperceptible nod.

A few moments later, William walked over and took Callie's hand again. They walked hand-in-hand without saying anything.

THIRTY-SEVEN

Tim walked behind Callie and William and tried to picture how he would react if something happened to Julie. Even though he had only known her for a few weeks, the thought unnerved him and he had been unnerved enough already today. The crocodile had swum right by him when it turned to flee. Tim had frozen as it approached, crouched with his legs bent, ready to propel himself away at the last minute and knowing damn well that it wouldn't work.

The reptile had raced past though, correcting its course and aiming for the mouth of the river. It seemed to take forever to go by. Then the sound of gunfire had erupted across the sea, adding to Tim's fear and confusion. The crocodile had leaped forward and its tail actually connected with Tim. He saw stars as he was knocked yet again into the water.

As he came back up, gasping, he heard Callie's screams and knew something had happened to Hank.

Tim thought back to his father's funeral. At the service, Tim had tried to console his mother, a stoic Minnesotan. "Happens to all of us," she had told him.

Maybe, he thought. *But it shouldn't happen to your fiancé.* He wanted to console Callie. No one had ever told him what sorts of things to say at a time like this. Everything that came to mind seemed trite.

As they moved away from the sea, the ground became less sandy, making it easier to walk, until finally they entered a dense forest. The trees slowed them, occasionally blocking their passage and forcing them to circle around. Overhead, the canopy filtered most of the sunlight. They walked through a mixture of conifers and strange palm trees with fronds that sprouted at regular intervals along their trunks, instead of just at the top.

William tried to keep the group close enough to hear the river on their right, but the thick foliage often drove them deeper into the woods. For several long stretches they left the sound of rushing water.

Tim trusted William and the dense forest made him feel secure. It was difficult to imagine a dinosaur coming at them when the trees were only a few feet apart. At least, not a very big one.

Buddy came and went, sometimes darting ahead and sometimes lagging behind, always sniffing furiously at whatever strange smells he encountered.

They entered a stretch where low plants covered the forest floor about two feet off the ground. Flat, horizontal leaves grew closely together, creating the illusion of a floating surface. As they walked through these plants, they disturbed several small unseen creatures underneath. Buddy ran after one of the scurrying sounds, barking furiously, with only his tail visible above the leaves.

"Buddy! *Shhhh!*" William snapped at the dog. To Tim's surprise, Buddy quieted immediately. The dog raised his head above the leaves and looked back, ears lowered. William smiled. "I vowed I would never get another dog after what my boys went through when Max died. This little guy might change my mind."

William, Al, Morgan, and Tim each took turns carrying the football. At forty pounds, it was not too heavy, but its size and shape made it awkward to hold. Except for the blinking light on one side, the device was completely smooth.

William walked over and spoke quietly to Tim, so that none of the others could hear. "Have you noticed what I noticed?"

Tim looked around. "No. What?"

"No fail-safe." William patted the device in Tim's arms. "That woman was lying to us."

Tim rolled the device over, revealing a panel the size of a dollar bill and held in place by four flat-headed screws. "Did you see this? I'm hoping it's under here."

"I'll be damned." A broad smile broke on William's face.

"I'm just hoping," Tim went on, "that we aren't supposed to plug it into something back at the café. I never finished my degree in quantum mechanics."

William chuckled. "This thing had better work, considering what it cost us."

"He wanted to be a hero," Callie said, turning to the others. "That's what he told me. He wanted to save us all." It was the first time she had spoken since the sea. "That's why he was the farthest out in the water. That's why he was… where he was when it happened."

Morgan looked at her. "He saved my life, Callie, when he threw the time machine. That croc would have snapped me up if he hadn't. He really was a hero."

Tim smiled. Morgan of all people had found the right thing to say.

Callie's mouth clenched as she fought off fresh tears. She reached for Morgan and embraced him.

- - - - -

Al watched them from behind. He had tried to console Callie on the beach. He had been there for her, hugging her as she sobbed and mewled. And she had practically shoved him away from her.

Then the damn delivery man had been holding hands with her, and now she had herself wrapped around Morgan. Fucking Morgan. It didn't make any goddamn sense. But then again, it never did.

THIRTY-EIGHT

Helen carefully pulled the branch down and tied it to a sapling. Lisa stood back, trying to memorize exactly how the snare was laid out without getting in the way. They stood at the edge of the forest, downstream from the building and about twenty feet from the river.

"This wire will loop around his neck when he reaches for the fish, see?" Helen pulled gently on the wire.

Lisa pictured one of the flying dinosaurs sticking its neck through the loop. "That isn't going to be enough to kill it, though, is it?"

"Probably not. It might choke itself if it struggles, but you'll probably have to come over and kill it yourself. For that, you'll want to build a catch pole."

"What's that?"

"It's a long stick with a circle of rope hanging from one end. The rope runs down the stick. You reach out and loop it around the animal's neck. Then you pull the rope tight."

Lisa nodded.

Helen placed loose leaves and debris around her snare. "We'll want to cook it straight away, so the meat doesn't spoil."

"Oh no," Lisa said. "I just thought of something. Those bird dinos were pecking at one of the bodies upstairs. We can't eat them. That would be like cannibalism."

Helen considered this for a moment. "We'll gut them, just like we would a fish. We won't eat what's in their stomachs. Just the meat on the bones. Think of them as drumsticks and chicken wings."

"Chicken wings," Lisa repeated. She looked at the lone fingerling fish that swam in her trash can, which she had carried over from the café. "I hope none of this matters and the others get back here soon."

"Al will be back for you, I expect," Helen said. She augured a pointed branch through the gills of the other fish.

Lisa nodded. "He doesn't think we're going to get home. He wants to find permanent shelter here."

"He seems pretty interested in you."

"Yeah. I'm still trying to figure out how I feel about him. My first husband cheated on me. I need someone faithful. Someone I can trust."

"My Larry was a jealous one. He never trusted me. He claimed that he took me on all of his hunting trips just so we could do something together and he wasn't about to take up knitting or play bridge." She huffed. "I think he took me hunting to keep me close, so that I couldn't be seduced by the mailman or the deacon while he was away."

"Did you ever fool around on him?"

"Me? Aw, no. I didn't have time for that nonsense. Put your finger here." Lisa did as instructed and Helen tied a knot in the string she had tied to the fish.

Lisa pulled her finger away and stood back up. "Most guys I've dated in the last year or so seem to expect dinner on the table every night and breakfast every morning. That doesn't work for me. I need to run my business. It's everything to me."

"Your business isn't in very good shape. Maybe it's time to try something else."

"Tell me about it." Lisa sighed and turned to look back at the café.

A seven-foot tall dinosaur stared at her from halfway across the mud plain.

"Helen," Lisa whispered.

Helen looked up and inhaled sharply. "What kind is that? It looks like an oster-ich." She pronounced the word with an extra syllable.

The dinosaur, a Struthiomimus, stood on two long, naked legs. Its head bobbed at the end of a tube-like neck.

Bright yellow eyes blinked as it studied the two women. Fuzzy blue down covered its body, except for the rust-colored feathers that hung from its arms.

Lisa shifted her weight, getting ready to run.

The dinosaur puffed up its neck and boomed, *Woo Woo Wooooooooo!*

"Make some noise," Helen said. "Scare it away."

"The noise is what brought the T-rex," Lisa answered.

Lisa felt like a cornered cat. She looked toward the jungle. She thought she could probably reach the closest tree before Helen even got to her feet.

The Struthiomimus strutted forward until it stood less than twenty feet away. It flexed the claws on its hands.

"Don't leave me," Helen said.

Lisa reached down for Helen's arm and whispered, "Get up."

Helen clamped onto the crook of Lisa's elbow, gripping it hard enough to hurt.

THIRTY-NINE

William stopped the group in a small clearing. "Let's take a few minutes to rest and eat." A lone tree stood near the top of a rounded hill. Callie sat against the trunk and watched everyone break out the pastries Lisa had packed in plastic zipper bags for them.

William wolfed down his bear-claw, licking the sweet almond paste from his fingertips. Callie realized that lunchtime had long since passed, but she did not feel hungry. She shoved pieces of a muffin into her mouth mechanically and wondered how soon the device would go off. She guessed they had a little more than five hours, but did not feel like asking the others.

Morgan unwrapped a chocolate-filled croissant and stuffed it into his mouth. He chomped noisily.

Al, sitting next to him, said quietly, "You know, my mother told me it was good manners to chew with my mouth closed."

Morgan brought his lips together. His cheeks bulged. He chewed slowly for a minute and then leaned over in Al's direction. With his mouth wide open, Morgan moaned, "Gaaaahhh!" A thick brown croissant paste bulged between his teeth.

Al looked aghast. "What the fuck is the matter with you?"

Morgan bent over, laughing and snorting.

Al rose to his feet and stood in front of the young man. "Why don't you stand up, asshole?"

Morgan looked up at him, tears in his eyes, and opened his mouth again. "Gaaaahhh!"

Callie thought that Hank would have pulled Morgan to his feet and knocked out his lights.

Al looked like he wanted to kick Morgan where he sat. "William, any advice here? Were either of your boys ever this fucked up?"

"My boys showed more sense than both of you."

Al raised his hands. "What the hell did I do?"

"With all that's going on right now, you're gonna complain about that idiot's manners?"

Morgan tried to swallow his croissant as he giggled.

"Hey everyone, come have a look at this," Tim called from a patch of ground on the other side of the tree. Callie rose and walked over. The others followed. Tim had found a small stone with a flat edge and had removed three of the four screws holding the panel on the side of the time device. He finished twisting the final screw out with his fingers and lifted off the metal plate.

Underneath, an LED readout displayed a line of red digits. It showed 00:04:52:23 when Tim first opened it. The seconds counted down relentlessly. "Just under five hours," William said. "Less than I thought. Still, it's good to see a number. It confirms the story from the woman in the lab and it gives us concrete information." William looked at his wristwatch and set a timer to match.

"This must be the fail-safe," Tim noted, pointing to the only other component under the panel. A hard plastic shield protected a rectangular red button. "There's nothing to it. It's just a button."

Callie thought it looked like the sort of button used to launch nuclear missiles in movies.

What does that do again?" Morgan asked.

"It takes us back in time twenty minutes, if that woman upstairs was right," Al explained.

"Everything she told us has been right so far," William pointed out.

The Hank-voice in Callie's head returned: *Babe, the fail-safe! Why didn't you think of that sooner? Seriously Callie, I wonder about you sometimes.* His tone was light-hearted, but she hated the idea of him questioning her.

Tim looked up. "After we get home, we're supposed to go back twenty minutes and clear everyone out the café."

"That's the plan," William said.

"What happens if we press it now?" asked Al. "Will it take us back twenty minutes ago, here?"

Callie looked up at this. More than twenty minutes had passed since Hank died. *Could we have used that on the beach?* If they had tried, Hank might still be alive.

William gave Al his best smile. "I don't have any idea, but I'll tell you one thing. We are not going to find out. We are going to stick to the plan."

Callie put her hand on William's arm. "So when we go back to the café, we can get *everyone* out of there, right?"

William nodded. "That's what I'm hoping, Callie. That's what I'm hoping." He picked up the football. "We just have to survive another five hours here. Let's get going again." He led the group onward, setting a faster pace than before their break.

About a half hour after their rest in the clearing, they encountered a river cutting directly across their path. They followed it to the right until it joined the larger river, the one that led back to the café. They looked out at the swirling junction that had spun them around on their raft ride a few hours earlier.

William wiped sweat from the back of his neck. "Normally I'd suggest we swim across. It would feel pretty good, I reckon."

"But we don't know if our friend the crocodile or one of his little brothers is around," observed Al.

"Yep." William turned and headed left. "We'll have to follow this river upstream until we can find a fallen tree or some other way to cross." He looked at his watch and shook his head. "Damn. This is going to take us out of our way." They started off again, keeping close to the smaller river.

A few minutes later, a raucous call stopped them in their tracks. It seemed like a series of vowels strung together and shouted at top volume. It was answered by another shout in the distance, somewhere behind them.

"What the hell was that?" Callie whispered. Even Buddy froze in his tracks.

"Probably something small," William answered quietly. "Something way up in the treetops. It wouldn't make that much noise unless it was safe up there, right?" He sounded as if he was attempting to convince himself. As the forest grew silent, they slowly started forward again.

Have you thought everything through, Calista? Hank asked. *That fail-safe only works one time. Don't fuck it up.*

She did not want to think about it. She wanted to curl up and sleep. It was only mid-afternoon here, but it felt much later. *Of course it does.* They had gone back millions of years *and* a handful of hours. *I'm time-lagged*, she thought, inventing a new term.

That's cute, babe, Head Hank said. *I love it.* Callie allowed herself a small smile, her first since the beach. She had always liked it when he called her "babe." Tears welled in her eyes and she wiped them away with the back of her hand.

"What will happen to us if we succeed?" she asked the group. "Help me think it through. What will be going on when we arrive back in Denver?"

William described the scene. "They'll have a police perimeter, with news vans all around. Maybe they haven't figured out that we went back in time yet, but sooner or later they will. They'll analyze the dirt and river water that got swapped out where the café was. I bet my boys are worried sick."

Callie shook her head. "That's not right, though, is it?" She had insisted on a turn carrying the device and held it awkwardly against her stomach with both arms. The scientists upstairs were smart enough to build a time machine, but apparently they weren't smart enough to put handles on the damn thing. "No time will have passed.

When this machine goes off again, it will return us to the moment we left."

"What makes you think that?" Tim asked.

"The fail-safe. The fail-safe button is a twenty-minute jump back. That's what the woman said. We're here for fifteen hours, right? The fail-safe is meant to help you in case…" She paused while Hank finished the thought for her. *In case your fiancé gets his head lopped off.* "In case something goes wrong. Twenty minutes won't help if fifteen hours have also passed by in modern Denver. So for the fail-safe to actually do any good, this thing must be rigged to take us back to the exact moment when we left."

"You're assuming a lot on the part of the inventors," Al said as he maneuvered around a cluster of boulders. "They obviously got a few things wrong, considering how all this went down. I'm not sure how smart those people really were."

William gave him a patronizing look. "They invented an honest-to-God time machine, Al. I think they were smart enough."

Callie went on, "Let's keep going. We arrive back in the café right at the moment we left. Then what?"

William answered, "We get outside and push the button to go back twenty minutes. This all started at about eight a.m. When we use the failsafe, it'll take us back to around 7:40. We run into the café and tell ourselves to get out of the building."

"Why do we have to go outside first?" Tim asked.

Callie answered for William. "Because most of us were already in the café at 7:40. We don't want to swap them forward; we want to get them out of the building."

William nodded. "She's right. We can find an empty parking lot or something, hit the button there, and then go inside and tell ourselves to clear out."

"This is crazy," Morgan said. "I hope you all understand what you are talking about."

Hank's voice urged Callie to keep going. "So then what?" she asked.

"Then we're good to go," William answered. "None of us will ever go back in time. No one has to die."

Callie shook her head. "There's more. We can't just stay there. The seven of us have to return to our empty parking lot and jump back forward twenty minutes. Or else there will be duplicates of us. Two of us, living in the same time."

"Hell yeah!" Morgan said. "I want to party with another me."

The hike grew steeper. The small river flowed down a slope next to them in a series of small rapids. William broke away from the group to look for a section where the boulders were close enough to rock hop across. He returned shaking his head. "The river is still impassable."

Al let his shoulders sag. Callie thought the movement seemed forced, theatrical.

"Do you think we will remember this?" Tim asked the others as they continued on. "When we jump forward twenty minutes again, what will we remember? I mean, if we successfully convince our other selves to get out of the building, *they* will never go back in time. So what will *we* remember?"

Morgan laughed. "This is so fucking nuts."

"I guess we'll find out when we find out," William said. "Here's another question: When we trigger the fail-safe and go back twenty minutes, how much time will we have there? Here, it's set to last fifteen hours. When it goes back twenty minutes, how long will we have before it goes forward again?"

FORTY

The two-legged Struthiomimus took a step closer. Helen squeezed Lisa's arm so hard she cried out in pain.

The dinosaur cocked its head and held open its long beak. It tasted the air with a pointed pink tongue.

"It's got no teeth," Helen said.

Lisa pulled a kitchen knife from her belt. She pointed the blade toward the animal. "Yeah, but look at its hands and feet." Dirty black claws protruded from its scaly fingers and toes.

The dinosaur took a step closer. Lisa waved her knife. "Shoo!" The dinosaur curled its long neck and snapped at the shiny blade. Lisa jerked it back, out of reach.

"Don't leave me," Helen said.

The Struthiomimus took two quick steps forward, pecked Lisa's forehead with its beak, and stepped back.

Stars swirled in Lisa's vision. They looked like the small sparks that sometimes erupted at the end of a fireworks explosion. *I got pecked.* She wanted to laugh, but she couldn't find the air to make the noise. She teetered backwards and landed in the mud on her ass. Everything went blurry.

Helen dumped the trash-can holding their last fish and threw it at the dinosaur. It bounced off the creature's chest and landed in the mud. The dinosaur lowered its long neck and studied the black plastic. It reached down and brought both hands together to pick it up. The dinosaur held the trash can and sniffed it from all angles.

"Holy shit," Helen said.

It looked up at her, dropped the trash can, and stepped forward. With another quick snap of its neck, it pecked Helen, grazing the side of her temple. It arched back for a second strike but Helen had already fallen out of the way.

The animal leaned over her and reached down with its claws.

The fog slowly began to wear off. Lisa saw the dinosaur grabbing at Helen's sweater with three sharp fingers. It shredded the fabric as it tried to find something to grip.

The kitchen knife stuck from the mud a few inches from Lisa's hand. Just beyond it, the dinosaur finally found purchase on Helen's arm and began to pull her up.

Lisa grabbed the handle and rose in one smooth motion. She felt dizzy but made herself keep going. She swung the knife up, striking the dinosaur's neck halfway between its head and its body. The blade bit into flesh, struck bone, and slid free.

The Struthiomimus screamed. The sound wheezed from the slit in its neck like air escaping from an inner tube. *PSSSHHHUUU! PSSSSHHUUUU! PSSSSHHHHUUU!*

It released Helen and rose. It lifted its head into the air, but its neck flopped at an obtuse angle. Blood geysered from the sliced opening in cadence with its screams. The head flopped back into place, pinching the cut closed. Blood misted straight outwards, covering Lisa in a cloud of wet red vapor.

PSSSSHHUUU! PSSSSHHHUUUU!

Lisa took a step toward it, brandishing the blade. The animal ran in a circle, flapping its winged arms. Its neck teetered back and forth, like a bent reed in the wind. Several times, it looked like its head would snap clean off, but it always bowed back in the other direction at the last minute.

That dinosaur is food for a week, Lisa thought. She needed to finish it off before it got away. The Struthiomimus began to zigzag across the mud flat.

Helen moaned. Lisa looked back at the old woman, who lay motionless on the ground near her unfinished snare.

Before she could decide what to do, the dinosaur reached the opposite side of the mudflat. Its screams grew louder as it disappeared into the jungle.

Lisa turned and knelt over Helen. Blood shone through her silver hair.

"I'm okay," Helen said. She pulled back her sleeve to reveal purple and brown bruises where the dinosaur had grabbed her. Lisa hefted her to her feet. They could still hear the shrieks of the Struthiomimus in the woods.

"We've got to get inside, quick."

"Why? It's gone now. I'm okay."

"The noise." Lisa's ears still rang from the dinosaur's screams. "That's what brought the T-rex last time." Helen stumbled and Lisa pulled the woman's arm over her shoulder.

"Come on, Helen, help me out." They trekked slowly across the mud.

FORTY-ONE

Tim used the trunk of a small tree to pull himself up the incline. A fast moving cascade flowed by on his right. Lush green moss covered the rocks close to the falls and dappled sunlight filtered through the treetops. A pure, earthy smell filled his nose. It did not feel like Colorado. It felt like some exotic location. Hawaii, maybe, or New Zealand.

William stopped to catch his breath at the top. The ground flattened out as far ahead as they could see. Above the cascade, the river pooled lazily. "This is getting us nowhere. We're only moving farther and farther from the café."

"At least we've got the device," Morgan said. He placed one foot on a boulder and rested the football on his thigh.

William shook his head. "We can't let it go off here. We're still way more than twenty minutes from the café. We aren't close enough to go warn ourselves."

"I'll give you another reason," said Al. "Lisa and the old lady ain't here."

William smiled. "You've got a thing for Lisa, don't you?"

"Is there a problem with that?"

"Of course not. I think she likes you, too."

Al circled past William, glaring at him. Tim thought that Al was the sort of guy who would punch you for looking at his girlfriend the wrong way. Lisa wasn't even his girlfriend though, as far as Tim could tell.

"The clock is ticking," Callie said. "All this yammering is a waste of time. Guys, we should swim across." The opposite shore was a little less than thirty feet away and the water had flattened out above the falls. "The current here doesn't look too strong."

"What about crocodiles?" asked Al. "Don't you think we should search a little farther?"

William walked over to the river. "This pool does look like the perfect home for a crocodile. A normal-sized one, anyway."

"Or maybe something else," Al prompted.

William nodded. "When I was a kid, I had a friend who walked with a limp after losing his big toe to a snapping turtle. It happened in a pool just like this one."

Al took a step upstream and looked back. "If we keep going, we'll find a safer place to cross."

Callie looked at the others. Morgan shrugged. She turned to Tim, "What do you think?"

"I'm not so comfortable in the water," he answered, chewing on his lower lip. "But I'll do whatever William says. If he thinks we should cross here, I'll get across."

Al blew out a breath of air. "What a follower. If William told you to jump off of a bridge... no, wait. If William told you to jump into a crocodile-infested river, would you do it? Sure looks that way."

Tim's eyelids narrowed. "William has gotten us this far. Fighting him over every single decision doesn't help." He turned to look at the river. Inside, he felt sick. He would be in over his head. Nevertheless, William had not steered them wrong yet. All that mattered was getting back to Julie. "I can cross that river."

William raised his eyebrows. "Are you sure?"

Tim smiled. "Hell no. But I'm sick of wandering and I'm sick of debating everything." He turned to Al. "I want to get home."

"What about the crocodiles?" Morgan asked.

William stepped closer to the water. "You know, there shouldn't be any crocodiles above those falls. We haven't seen any this whole time." Since leaving the sea, they had not encountered any wildlife except for the small creatures Buddy had chased under the plants, and they had not actually seen those. "Tim's offer settles it. The man can't even swim, but he's willing to cross here. Let's do it."

"I suppose you're an expert swimmer, William?" Al challenged.

"Sir, I was a teenage lifeguard at the neighborhood pool. Best job I ever had. Girls love lifeguards. Girls in bikinis." Al bristled at this but William did not seem to notice. "I taught both of my boys to swim as soon as they could walk."

"I want a lesson when we get back," Tim said.

Al stepped over to Morgan and gestured at the football resting on his knee. "Okay then. If we're crossing, we're crossing. Why don't you let me take a turn with that?"

"No." Tim put his palm on the orange metal. "I need it."

Al looked at him, either threatened or confused. Tim wasn't sure which.

"It floats," Tim explained. "I need it to get across, unless you want to wait a couple of hours for me to run back to the beach and get my life jacket."

"Personal floatation device," Morgan corrected. He handed the football to Tim.

They took off their shoes and threw them across the river, along with their mobile devices. William lobbed the shovel across as well. It tumbled end over end as it flew and landed upright with the blade impaled on the opposite bank.

William went first. He waded in until the water was up to his hips and then kicked off, performing an expert breast stroke. The current pushed him along, but soon he pulled himself out on the opposite shore, only a few yards downstream.

Callie moved further to her left around a clump of trees. "I don't think I can quite match up to an expert lifeguard." She pointed to the end of the pool, where the water disappeared in a straight edge. "And I want to keep clear of those falls." The others followed her lead and moved further upstream as well.

William gave Callie a big thumbs-up from the opposite side. "I gotcha." He stood thigh-deep in the water, with one hand on a low branch.

Callie dog-paddled sloppily, making Tim feel a little less self-conscious. She reached the opposite bank right where William waited for her. He helped her out of the water.

Morgan followed close behind, showing slightly better form. He climbed out on his own.

Al looked at Tim. "You gonna make it?"

Tim smiled. "I think so." He remembered attending a party in the second grade. A boy named Carl celebrated his ninth birthday at an elaborate indoor pool in the dead of winter while a blizzard howled outside. The other kids swam, rode the water slides, and jumped off the diving board. The rec center even had a zip line that carried them out over the pool for a six-foot drop into the water.

Each child was required to demonstrate that he could swim one complete lap before performing the activities. Tim spent the entire party sitting on the side.

"Come fish me out if I start to sink," he said to Al.

Holding the football out in front of him, Tim stepped into the river. It felt cool and refreshing. He clenched his toes in the mud, hoping they didn't look like little snacks for whatever primeval reptiles lived in the pool.

When he lowered the device, it floated, but it also tugged downstream as the current caught it. The orange light blinked on and off, calling to all crocodiles in the vicinity. Tim rotated the device until the light was directly on top.

He thought about Al calling him a "follower" and gave a strong kick out toward the middle of the river, hugging the device tightly. He imagined teeth clamping onto his toes. He kicked harder.

The football started to roll on him. Tim flailed with his feet. He overcompensated and the football rolled in the other direction. The current tugged it, almost tearing it from Tim's hands. His face went under. He pictured a snapping turtle the size of a car, rising from the depths and latching onto his legs with a giant beak.

Tim kicked hard and broke the surface. He pulled himself up onto the football and rode it like a sled. Somehow he managed to stay upright. He scissored his legs as fast as he could, with short powerful strokes.

Before he knew it, Tim bumped into the opposite shore, several feet upstream of William, who waded toward him, laughing. "I never seen anyone swim like that." He took the football under his arm and helped Tim out of the water.

Breathing heavily and nodding, Tim turned to look back at the river.

Al emerged close behind. "Good job, kid," he said.

"Buddy!" Callie called out. The dog appeared on the far bank and gave out a quiet yip. "Come on, boy!" Buddy cocked his head to one side and wagged his tail. "I'm not leaving him here," she informed the group. "I'll swim back across and get him if I have to."

"Now just hold on," William instructed. He stood up straight, held perfectly still and spoke firmly. "Buddy, come!" He jabbed his finger down, pointing at the ground next to his foot.

The dog stopped wagging. He gave another small yip and made one of his flying leaps, directly out over the water. Buddy landed with a splash but kept his head above the surface. William let out a quiet cheer. The dog crossed the pool, climbed out, and moved next to him, where he shook vigorously and then sat down.

"That's a good boy," he said, leaning over to rub Buddy's head. The dog's tail wagged back and forth.

Tim looked off into the jungle. "The café can't be more than a couple of hours away, can it?"

William pointed back to the right. "Let's angle off that way and see if we can find the main river again." He started into the woods and Buddy heeled next to him.

Tim nodded. "We might actually make it back in time." The Triceratops hillside changed his mind.

FORTY-TWO

"Shit, that's a lot of dinosaurs," Al said. An open slope stretched out before them, covered by thousands of Triceratops. Blackened stumps and fallen tree trunks dotted the hill, showing evidence of a forest fire some years earlier. The Triceratops herd spread out as far as Al could see in either direction, grazing on the short green plants that had sprung up in the aftermath of the fire. It would take hours to go around. Al did not think they had any chance of getting back to the café before the device went off.

"Those are my favorite," Morgan said as he looked at the herd. Buddy clearly felt differently. His tail curled under his belly and one of his back legs trembled.

"What now?" Tim asked.

"We could make some noise," Morgan said. "Drive them off like we did with the duck-face ones."

William shook his head. "That noise attracted the Tyrannosaurus. We don't know if these guys frighten so easily. Also, there were about ten of those duckbills. There must be thousands of Triceratops."

Buddy emitted a high-pitched whimper. Callie knelt next to him. "You were here before, weren't you boy?" She looked at the others. "That means we're close. Buddy must have come here earlier from the top of the hill. One of these guys chased him back to the cliff." She pointed to the right. "The river can't be far in that direction."

"We can't go that way." William said.

"Why the hell not?" asked Morgan.

"Because this herd goes all the way down to the shore. This is the same hillside we saw from the raft."

Morgan nodded slowly. "What the shit."

"Well, if we can't go forward up the hill and we can't go right, that only leaves one choice," Al said. "We head left, until we find a way around." The hillside stretched for at least a mile, if not more. There was no way to see how far it really went.

Al thought that the hillside would block them even more effectively than the tributary river, which had added an hour to their trip. The device would go off before they reached the café. It would still take them back, but it would return them someplace farther east. Maybe they would end up inside a hollowed-out chunk of a different building, and another group would be sent here. Of course, they would not have a time machine with them.

I will not go back, Al thought. He had a woman waiting for him here. Al had never had that before. *If we go back, she's history.*

He had begun composing a short speech he would give when the time machine began to tick. He would get clear of the device and then return to the café alone. All he had to do was step aside. The others would go home without him. They would understand. In fact, he would be a hero; both back home and when he returned to the café. Al Stevens, the man who stayed behind for his woman. Lisa would be his.

William looked left. "Let's get going." He started off, skirting along the thin growth of trees at the bottom of the slope. The others filed along behind him.

"Do you know why Triceratops is my favorite?"

"No, Morgan," William said.

"Because they're so horny!"

"That's nice, Morgan," William said.

They moved in a single-file line, weaving in and out of the trees that grew along the base of the barren hillside. Most of the Triceratops kept away from the forest's edge. Al wondered if there was a good reason for that. Out in the open, they could not be ambushed.

After hiking for fifteen minutes, they encountered a lone animal feeding on thick vegetation near the bottom of the hill. William led the group in a wide circle deeper into the woods to steer clear of the creature. After putting it safely behind them, William moved back to the bottom of the slope and gazed ahead, his hands on his hips. "This detour is costing us too much time." There was still no end in sight.

Callie pointed to a cleft in the hillside just a short distance ahead. "William, what about that gulch up there?" The group continued forward until they reached the bottom of the ravine, which ran straight up the hill. It looked like it had been carved by rainfall that washed down the barren slope, but now stood dry as a bone. The Triceratops herd kept its distance from the gulch on both sides.

At the base of the slope, the gully flattened out in a wide fan of smaller crevices, but for most of its length, the sides of the gulch formed a trough with ten-foot walls. In three different spots, the gulch was worn down where game trails crossed it.

A large blackened tree trunk stood next to the gulch at the top of the hillside, where the ground flattened out again. The ravine fanned out in a web of smaller cracks near the tree, just as it did at the bottom of the slope. Al thought the tree looked like it had been struck by lightning. He pictured the crown exploding and burning branches raining across the once-forested hillside Beyond the stump, the unburned forest began again.

William looked at his watch. "The device will go off in less than four hours."

"How far do you think we are from the café?" Callie asked.

"Less than an hour, I think. But there's really no way to be sure. If we stay in the ravine and keep quiet, they might leave us alone."

"Might?" Al said.

"Yes," William replied. "And I'm not going to argue about it. Let's do it."

Callie nodded. She looked around and then walked up the slope to enter the gulch.

Tim took the time machine from Morgan. "I'll carry it for a bit now, if you don't mind."

"No problemo." Morgan started up behind Callie.

"You just had a turn, right before Morgan," Al said. "Why don't you let me take it?" The shortcut up the ravine meant they might make it to the café before the timer went off. He would never convince Lisa to stay behind with him. But if he carried the device, he might find the opportunity to accidentally drop it somewhere near the top. With a little luck, it would roll all the way down the hill.

Tim shook his head. "I got it." He turned and started up the ravine.

"Have it your way." Al said. "I'm just trying to help."

William and Buddy followed Tim. The dog walked close to the delivery man, its tail still tucked between its legs.

Al thought back to their discussion about returning to the café. He tried to imagine meeting himself. It seemed ludicrous. He wondered how the people in the café would react when duplicate versions of themselves suddenly showed up and started yelling at them to clear out. *There won't be duplicates of all of us*, Al thought. Hank, Beth, and Patricia would be missing. He wondered what the original Hank, Beth and Patricia would think about that.

Al used the shovel as a walking stick as he climbed. The sides of the ravine slowly closed in and rose to the height of his shoulders. Loose rocks filled the cleft and he had to step carefully to avoid tripping.

As they hiked up the gully, the walls on their sides rose and fell, sometimes hiding them entirely, and sometimes dropping low enough for them to see out. The herd was spread out on this part of the hill and the animals seemed to take no notice of them. The afternoon sun shone down on their faces from directly ahead.

Every so often, Buddy let out a low whimper. William murmured quiet reassurances. Any time Buddy tried to move past him, William whispered, "*Heel,*" and the dog dropped back. Fortunately, Al realized, Buddy could not see out of the gully at all. Hundreds of Triceratops covered the hillside around them in every direction except for straight ahead and straight behind.

At the first game crossing, Callie crouched by a large rock. She raised her hand behind her and patted the air downward, signaling the others to stop. A few feet ahead, the gulch had been trampled flat where it was intersected by a trail that crossed the hillside along the contour of the slope.

Al craned his neck. Three small Triceratops nibbled on spiky succulents to the right, about forty feet away. The distance felt safe, but he remembered how deceptively fast the duck-billed dinosaur had moved.

On the left, a larger Triceratops marched along the game trail straight toward the ravine. Al hunkered back down, trying to hide.

William squatted above him in the crevice with one hand on Buddy's collar. While the Triceratops crossed above, William used his other hand to stroke the dog's muzzle. He looked ready to squeeze it shut if Buddy began to bark.

The animal passing above them was not as large as the one that had battled the tyrannosaur under the cliff, but it shook the ground as it walked and small pebbles rolled into the gully. For a moment it blocked out the sun. *Any one of these animals has enough meat on it to feed us for months*, Al thought. The dinosaur wandered over by the trio of adolescents and nibbled on the same spiky plants. Its body blocked their view of the ravine.

William exhaled after the animal passed and gave Buddy a gentle pat on the head. Callie rose from behind the rock and climbed upward. The four animals grazing off to the right ignored her. Morgan, Tim, William, and Al followed one at a time.

They continued to climb. Halfway up the hillside, they passed the second game crossing without incident. None of the animals were close to the second crossing, so they just continued onward and upward, stepping around massive footprints in the dirt.

The ravine cut deeper into the hillside as they climbed. Soon they were in a channel that rose well over their heads on either side. "This ain't so bad," Morgan said. A moment later, a Triceratops skidded to a stop on the wall above. Dirt slid down onto Morgan as the animal backed up a step to keep from falling in. Its neck frill changed color, flaring from a dull brown to a deep rusty red. The creature bleated at Morgan, a stuttery, neighing noise that sounded angry.

Morgan yelped and dropped to the ground with his hands over his head.

Al watched from further down the gully, frozen. He thought once again that Morgan was the biggest idiot he had ever met. If the Triceratops were to fall into the ravine, it would slide down on all of them, like a piston plunging through a valve.

The animal turned and looked slowly from one person to the next. It pawed the ground and a chunk of dirt broke free, creating a small avalanche on the side of the ravine. The Triceratops stepped back. It would become trapped and injured if it fell in, Al realized. He hoped the animal realized this as well.

"Just keep walking," William ordered in a low voice behind Morgan. He held Buddy in his arms with one hand firmly clamped on the dog's muzzle.

Morgan rose and stepped forward. The Triceratops snorted and turned its massive head to track his movement up the gully. Morgan stumbled in the loose dirt as he watched the beast above him. The animal snorted.

"Don't watch it. Just watch your feet, Morgan." The back of William's neck was soaked with sweat. Morgan got to his feet and continued. William started up after him, and soon he was directly under the Triceratops. He stopped watching it and followed his own advice, looking down at the ground ahead of him. Buddy's eyes locked on the dinosaur above and he let out a continuous whimper-whine, but William passed uneventfully.

Al brought up the rear. The Triceratops watched him but still did not move from its spot up on the lip of the gully. Al stopped and looked at it. Pale green drool dripped from its beaked mouth. Al continued up the slope. When he turned to look back, the creature had ambled out of sight.

Ahead, William called quietly. "Hey Morgan, are they still your favorite?"

Morgan flipped him a middle finger without looking back.

FORTY-THREE

Morgan crouched behind Callie just below the third and final crossing. He pictured hundreds of animals marching back and forth, wearing down the sides of the ravine. He wondered if the rainy season would come and wash their path away.

On the right, just beyond the third game crossing, stood the great splintered tree trunk. The remaining shards of wood looked like a charred, grasping hand, reaching toward the sky.

The upper tributaries of the ravine dissipated in a series of smaller cracks that branched out in several directions beyond the tree. Morgan pointed at the largest of the cracks and whispered, "That won't provide much cover."

Callie leaned out and craned her neck. Beyond the tree, the hill flattened and the woods grew close. "The forest isn't far, though. We could make it there in two minutes, easy. Faster if we run."

"Don't you think running will attract their attention?" Morgan said loudly.

"Shhh!" Callie whacked him on the chest. She shuffled backwards into the ravine, forcing Morgan to back up behind her. "*You* are going to attract their attention."

Five Triceratops stood off to the right, huddled in a circle and facing one another as if carrying on a conversation. One raised its head and sniffed.

"How close do you think those guys are?" Callie whispered.

William rose up slightly and peered over the edge. "It's hard to tell. They are so huge, I can't get a sense of scale. Maybe two hundred feet?"

He looked over to the left side. Morgan followed his gaze. In that direction the nearest animal was at least three times as far away.

"What's the plan?" Tim whisper-shouted from below them, further down the gully.

"It's not like we have any choices here," Al muttered. He stood and shouldered past the others.

"Be my guest, bro," Morgan said as he fell onto his ass.

Al crouch-walked quickly over the crossing. When he entered the largest crevice on the far side, he slowed down again. Little more than a gutter, the walls only rose as high as Al's waist. He stopped next to the lightning tree. It shielded him from the view of the Triceratops quintet on the right. Al leaned on the shovel and glanced back, as if to say, *What are you waiting for?*

Callie began forward across the game trail. Morgan scrambled to his feet and followed close behind. Ahead, Al turned and continued onward.

Piece of cake, Morgan thought. The phrase quickly turned to *piece of ass.* He liked climbing up the hill behind Callie. The view of her tight running shorts kept him moving, like a carrot on a stick. Normally, he would have mentioned this, just for the reaction, but the girl had lost her man today. Morgan's father killed himself shortly after Morgan turned sixteen. You don't mess with someone when they're facing that kind of hurt, Morgan knew. You just don't do it.

He stopped next to the blackened tree trunk, just as Al had moments earlier and pulled out his last cigarette. The ground no longer sloped. It would be easy going from here on out.

Morgan rolled the cigarette between his thumb and forefinger. He could buy all the smokes he wanted once they got back. He looked down the hill to check on William and Tim, mostly to make sure Tim still had that time machine. The view caught his breath. Thousands of Triceratops dotted the hillside below them. Some wandered back and forth.

Many huddled together, facing each other in small groups. A hint of the river sparkled off to the side.

Morgan smiled. They really were his favorite, dumb jokes aside. They were like giant jousting machines. He flicked open his metal lighter, lit the smoke, and flicked it shut with a metallic *shink*. Morgan drew in a long drag.

On the hillside above, Callie froze. She stood halfway between the lightning tree and the edge of the forest, completely exposed. At the top of the hill, the gully had faded down to nothing. She turned and glared back at him.

The largest animal broke away from the circle of five and sauntered over to investigate the strange noise and the smell of smoke. At the edge of the forest, Al disappeared into the cover of the trees.

"It's all good," Morgan whispered. He dropped to one knee in the middle of the ravine and froze. "Just hold still."

"It is not all good," Callie mouthed back at Morgan. She looked angry.

The animal marched directly toward her. She was out in the open and the Triceratops showed no sign of stopping.

Callie turned toward the trees and sprinted across the flat ground. Her fluorescent green running shirt, which made her stand out to drivers along the streets of Denver, caught the attention of the Triceratops. It picked up its pace, loping along like a rhinoceros.

She's not going to make it, Morgan realized. It would be close, but the Triceratops was too fast and the jungle might not slow it down. Morgan examined the giant blackened tree trunk standing nearby. It was fifteen feet wide, with jagged fragments that rose twice that far into the sky.

"HEY!" Morgan shouted. He stepped into view and raised both arms. "Hey you horny cockface!"

The Triceratops wheeled in a great arc toward Morgan.

He laughed out loud, a maniacal titter, and ran back to the stump. Within seconds, he was behind the tree, completely out of the dinosaur's line of sight.

On the hillside above, Callie slipped into the woods.

- - - - -

In the ravine, just below the third crossing, William and Tim crouched together against the side wall. Tim put down the football and wedged it against a rock to prevent it from rolling back down the gully.

The Triceratops stopped close to the tree, unable to see Morgan. It sniffed for a moment and sidestepped a quarter of the way around. Morgan matched its motion, keeping himself on the opposite side of the tree. He giggled.

The dinosaur stopped and circled back in the other direction. Morgan shifted as well, until he was directly below the tree, standing on the game trail.

"It's a standoff," William whispered. "It can't get around the tree fast enough to get him. He's safe."

"Yeah, but they could be at this for hours," Tim answered. "We're stuck here until it gets bored."

- - - - -

The Triceratops swung its massive head left and right, looking for any sign of the small creature that had run behind the stump. The four companions it had left behind stood watch around a nest full of eggs. Small dinosaurs often snuck up for an easy meal this time of year. The Triceratops believed that the creature on the other side of the tree stump was an egg thief. It knew from experience that an egg thief would not leave on its own. It would hide behind the stump for as long as it took and then come after the nest. The tree stump was the problem.

The Triceratops lifted both of its front feet off the ground and lunged, driving itself forward with its eight-foot hind legs. It ran straight downhill, ramming the tree.

The trunk exploded. Splinters of charred wood flew in every direction. A dried cluster of roots sailed over Tim and William and landed on the opposite side of the gully.

Morgan was knocked off his feet and onto the middle of the game path. Dozens of tiny splinters embedded themselves in his chest and face. As with the glass that had struck him eleven hours earlier, he barely noticed. His attention remained on the Triceratops, which swung its head back and forth in diagonal slices, knocking away what remained of the tree trunk. It stomped forward.

What the shit, Morgan thought. The only place to go now was the ravine he had come up through. William and Tim had better get the hell out of the way, because Morgan intended to barrel down that gully like a bobsled.

The Triceratops shuffled forward a few steps. Morgan rose to his feet. He felt something hot running down the inside of his leg and wondered if it was blood or piss. He hoped it was piss, because there was an awful lot of it. The animal stood less than twenty feet away.

Morgan slowly turned his head down and to the right, trying to gauge the distance to the gully. He turned on his heels just as a second Triceratops arrived behind him.

It had come over to investigate the commotion and help chase down any egg thieves. Egg thieves were far too small to attack with horns, so it turned its head sideways and scissored its great beak open and shut as it charged. The lower half of its beak disappeared again and again under the upper jaw with a sound like huge hedge shears. It stretched forward, reaching as it ran.

Morgan brought up his arms in front of his face. The beak caught him in the chest and sliced him in half. His head and arms flew through the air as the beak closed completely. The animal continued its charge, kicking Morgan's legs along the ground. It shook its head and spat out the bite it had clipped into its mouth.

Sand and small rocks spilled down into the gully onto William and Tim.

FORTY-FOUR

In the woods above the clearing, Al held Callie in his arms. *Finally*. She had broken down in tears after watching Morgan get sliced apart. "It's okay. You're safe," Al whispered, his chin resting on her auburn hair.

He was finally making inroads with Callie. Two girls in his arms in one day, and one of them had kissed him. Three years ago, after a particularly good year for Stevens Information Systems, Al had splurged on his trip to Nevada. He had paid for two girls at once. One of them had been a redhead. Probably not a real redhead like Callie, but close enough. It had been a fantasy come true, the sort of thing that never happened in the real world. At least not in the modern world. In the age of the dinosaurs, who knew what could be possible? Callie would get over Hank eventually. Al could wait.

"None of us are safe," Callie cried. "Hank died saving that stupid kid's life and it was all for nothing."

"That stupid kid almost got you killed. We have to be smarter than he was. It sucks, but it's the truth." Al knew he couldn't express how he actually felt about Morgan's death, but he didn't have to go overboard with bereavement either. He stroked Callie's hair. She had suffered terribly today, but he was there for her now. He squeezed her tight, feeling her breasts heave against him as she sobbed. "It's going to be okay."

- - - - -

Callie quieted as Al held her. Sure, Morgan had screwed up. He never should have lit that cigarette or made so much noise. But he also drew the Triceratops away from her. He had been killed saving her life. He didn't deserve to die. People make mistakes. Usually, they learned from th– *Is that what I think it is?* Callie noticed a knot of pressure against her belly. Did Al have a hard-on? She tensed up but stopped herself from pulling away.

No babe, he's got a carrot in his pocket, mocked Head Hank. She was surprised at his nonchalance.

"You're right," she said to Al, not looking up. "We have to be smarter than Morgan was." She needed to get away from him, to stop touching him. "We should probably find cover in case one of them comes sniffing around up here."

Al gave her one more squeeze and released her. She let out a long breath.

"Yeah, let's have a look around," he said. "That's smart." He picked up the short shovel and led her further into the woods.

- - - - -

Tim sat with William in a deeper section of the ravine, where they had hunkered down after Morgan's death. The two Triceratops faced off silently for a few minutes until the one that killed Morgan turned around and lumbered back across the gully. The other animal, the one that had demolished the tree trunk, waited a few minutes longer and then disappeared out of sight to the right. Tim stood and peeked over the edge of the ravine. The trunk smasher had returned to its group of five. Tim surveyed the other side. None of the Triceratops on the left were very close. The one that had killed Morgan had disappeared into the herd.

He felt the seconds ticking away. "How much time do we have?"

William looked at his watch. "Three hours and forty minutes."

Tim felt trapped. He hated waiting. "What do we do?"

William looked down the ravine. "We could try to backtrack to the bottom of the hill and circle around."

Tim followed his gaze. "How long do you think that will take?"

"Hours. But it's just the two of us. We could probably make good time. We could jog."

"Let's get going then," Tim said.

"Hold on. We still don't know how far this hillside goes."

"Then what should we do?"

"We could wait a bit longer and see what happens." William pursed his lips. "We've got some time. Things might change when dusk sets in. Those Triceratops on the right might move farther away."

Tim took of his cap and wiped his forehead. "You think so?"

"I don't know, Tim. Dammit, what do you think?"

Tim froze. Why couldn't William just make the call, the way he had done all day? "I don't like waiting," he said finally.

"Well I'm not too thrilled with the idea of walking across all that empty space up there. You saw how fast they were." William spoke quietly, but there was an angry edge to his voice. "Remember, one of those things followed Buddy all the way to the cliff. If they start after us, they won't let up."

"Whatever you say, man. I'm game to go around, and I'm game to go forward."

William's wide eyes narrowed. "You can't always wait for someone else to make all your decisions for you." He rose to a crouch. "Come on."

Tim felt like he had been scolded by his father.

William shuffled a few feet up the gully. Tim followed. "Wait." He put his hand on William's shoulder. "Drop that dog if anything happens. He'll stand a better chance on his own and might make a distraction."

William nodded and looked over at the football. "You just make sure you don't drop that thing." He clamped his hand around Buddy's muzzle.

William started up the hill. Tim waited until he was halfway to the tree line before leaving the ravine. He clutched the time device close against his chest and cupped one hand over the blinking light to keep it from attracting attention.

One of Morgan's arms lay on the path, with the shoulder blade still attached. A swarm of black flies crawled on exposed muscle.

Beyond the arm, the cluster of five Triceratops stood facing one another. With their heads in the center of the circle and their giant frills extending out from their necks, none had a clear view of Tim. He circled around a cluster of branches from the exploded tree, not wanting them to snap under his work boots. As he got closer to the forest, the hill flattened out and the going became easier. Tim heard shuffles and grunts from the animals behind him. He looked back to his right. The group of five remained in place. He remembered Morgan and looked back to the left.

A gristled old male climbed the hill beside the ravine. The quills growing from its back were worn and withered. It stopped near the crossing and stared up at Tim. Cool sweat dripped down Tim's sides. He stood and stared back, motionless. The Triceratops watched for a minute and then dropped its head to nibble on a clump of plants. Tim began to walk slowly backwards toward the woods. His boot landed on a small rock and he started to stumble. He caught himself and froze again.

The Triceratops paused, but did not raise its head.

You got to watch where you're going. Tim forced himself to slowly turn around. With his back to the dinosaur, he walked toward the forest, convinced the Triceratops would run him down as he crossed the final stretch. He would be impaled like the rodeo cowboy.

When he reached the trees and looked back, the old male was nowhere to be seen.

FORTY-FIVE

Callie and Al sat in the branches of a large tree. When Tim and William finally arrived, Callie climbed down and embraced them both. *See, that's what normal hugs feel like,* Hank said. *No boners.*

She told the voice in her head to shut up. Al might have actually had something in his pocket. Or maybe he was just worked up over the intensity of the moment. Erections were an autonomic response, after all. Maybe it wasn't his fault. *Bullshit,* responded a voice in her head. This voice didn't belong to Hank though. This voice was Callie's own.

William looked grim. "You two saw what happened?"

"Did we see the dumbass get himself killed?" Al climbed down from the tree. "Yeah, we saw."

Callie glared at him. "Al."

"Yeah, yeah, yeah. He didn't deserve to die. But he almost got *you* killed too, you know." Callie did know. Al had pointed it out several times now. "It's a different world here," Al went on. "There's no room for mistakes."

"You don't ever make mistakes?" William asked.

"I'm still alive," Al said, as if that proved it. He started off into the woods.

They hiked for twenty minutes before arriving at another clearing. A great grey shape loomed on the far side of the open field.

"Is this the same cliff?" Callie asked, looking up at the rock wall directly before them. "It can't be the same cliff, can it?" The wall extended in both directions as far as they could see. *You know it's the same cliff, honey,* Hank said. *And you know what that means.* She liked "babe." She didn't like "honey."

Al shielded his eyes and scanned the escarpment. "It's a lot taller. There has to be a cave up there somewhere. If our plan fails, we should come back here. We'd be out of reach from even the tallest dinosaurs."

"And how would we get up there?" Tim asked.

"Just think about it. A rope ladder hanging down the top, and another one from the cave leading down to the bottom. There would always be two different escape routes."

Callie looked up, but saw no sign of any cave. The sun shone down from just above the top edge, leaving the face of the wall a blur of shadows.

"I think it's the same cliff," William said. "But I can't believe we're still so far to the left. We should have come to the river by now."

"Don't look at me," Callie said. "I have no idea where we are. Do you think we're lost?"

"No," William barked. "I have a great sense of direction. I've driven a delivery truck for twenty years and never once used GPS." He looked around. "That raft ride threw me off, though. Too many twists and turns. I really thought we were further to the right."

Al stopped looking for a cave. "Maybe this is a different cliff. Do you think we passed the café somehow?"

"It's got to be the same cliff. Come on." William started to the right, straight down the middle of the clearing.

"Hold on," Al said. He remained motionless. "If this is the same cliff, that means there's an angry Tyrannosaurus up ahead."

Figured that out on your own, genius? mocked the voice in Callie's head.

Al pointed back in the other direction. "Let's head that way and look for a way around to the top."

"We don't have *time*," William said. "For Christ's sake, Al, we have to get back before the device goes off. I want to get back to my sons. We're not going to wander off exploring."

"It doesn't matter how long it takes us," Al countered, "if we are all dead."

"How much time do we have left?" Callie asked.

Tim looked at the readout on the device. "Three hours and two minutes."

"If it's the same cliff," Al countered, "The café should only be a half hour or so away, depending upon how far out we are. We still have time to try to go around."

William looked angry. "We don't have any idea where we are right now. We could be miles away. The only thing we know is that the river is in *that* direction."

"And the Tyrannosaurus?"

"With any luck, the Tyrannosaurus ate his fill and he's long gone. And there could be ten Tyrannosauruses in the other direction. We have to head toward the river."

Al stared.

Tim broke the silence. "I'm with you, William. You've gotten us this far."

Callie thought about it. "Me too," she said. Anything to stop the arguing. She moved closer to Tim and William and instantly regretted it. She didn't want to alienate Al any further. They needed to work together.

Al held his hands open and shrugged.

William's face softened. "Let's go," he said. "And let's all be a bit more quiet from here on."

Al gestured at the football. "Tim, give me a turn."

Callie saw hesitation on Tim's face. "Come on. Let him help out," she nudged.

Al took the device and held it under one arm.

They proceeded silently along the base of the cliff for another half hour before they found their answer. Callie pointed out the giant boulder they had once hoped to pry off the wall and onto the tyrannosaur. It had tumbled to a stop in the center of the clearing.

William stopped the group next to a large evergreen that had been upended by the Triceratops when it chased Buddy into the clearing. The roots of the tree were pried up from the ground at a forty-five degree angle. Underneath, dozens of large black beetles scurried about. They made a clicking sound, like the noise made by insects in the movies. William shuddered and kept his distance.

Beyond the boulder, halfway to the end of the clearing, lay the Triceratops corpse. A row of meatless ribs curved up into the air. The group huddled near the upended tree, trying to stay close to the shadows. The smell hit them after a moment.

"That could be a source of meat for us," Al noted.

"Who wants to eat *that*?" William asked, grimacing.

"It won't smell so bad once it's been cooked. Have you ever smelled a cow?"

"Do you think he's still nearby?" Callie whispered. Then she heard the noise. Her heart raced. "Quiet. Listen." A raspy rumble came from up ahead. "There." Callie pointed. "He's asleep."

The tyrannosaur slumbered in the trees at the lower edge of the clearing, near the Triceratops corpse. Lying motionless on its belly, it looked like another boulder.

William laid out their options: "Ok, we can sneak along the bottom of the cliff and stay in the shadows or we can circle down through the woods below him. Or I suppose we could backtrack and try to find a way up top."

"We should have done that in the first place," Al pointed out.

Callie looked around the upended tree roots. Once they reached the far end of the clearing, it would be an easy ten-minute hike to the café. She wanted to collapse behind the counter until the timer expired. She didn't even want to look at this world any longer. "I want to take the straight route," she said. "The way the sun is right now, you can't see anything in those shadows at the base of the cliff."

"Oh my God," Al said, as if it was the dumbest idea he had ever heard. "Walking across this clearing will leave us completely exposed if that thing wakes up. Do you remember how easily it grabbed Beth?"

"Then let's go through the woods," Tim said. "At least we'll have some cover."

"What cover?" Al spat. "The tyrannosaur chased us through the woods before. The trees didn't slow it down at all."

William made a chewing motion with his mouth. "Why don't we split up, Al? You go around your way and meet us back at the café."

"Will you let me carry the time machine?"

"Not a chance."

"I didn't think so."

Tim held up his hands, clearly annoyed by their bickering. He gave Al a sidelong glance and turned to William. "What do you think we should do?"

Callie wondered what would have to happen before Tim would start taking action on his own.

William stepped away from the stump and looked around. "Let's go down through the woods. If we don't go too far out of our way, it won't take all that much longer. And let's be quiet about it."

"Fine by me," Callie said. "As long as we get moving."

Before they could start, Buddy walked up behind them. Callie gave the dog a quick pat on his head. He sniffed at the beetles under the tree roots and then started off, straight across the clearing, following the same route he had taken earlier, when the Triceratops had chased him here.

"Buddy!" Callie whispered. "No!"

The dog ignored her, but lurched to a stop when it noticed the sleeping tyrannosaur. He hung his head low and sniffed. The fur at the base of his neck stood on end. Buddy started up again, walking just as steadily as before, but now he moved to the left. He disappeared in the shadows along the bottom of the cliff wall.

"Would you look at that," William whispered.

The dog trotted daintily at the base of the cliff. They heard a few rocks roll under his feet, but the tyrannosaur did not wake up.

Finally, the dog reached the point where the cliff tapered down to a low ledge. Buddy turned and looked back at the others, as if to say, *what are you waiting for,* and then continued on in the direction of the café.

FORTY-SIX

William watched Buddy disappear into the woods at the end of the clearing. "Okay then, if he can do it, we can do it." The dog proved they didn't need to loop around through the woods. The café was close. His sons were close.

Tim said, "Are you sure?" He looked pale. "I'm as eager to get back as you are, but this will take us less than fifty feet from that sleeping Tyrannosaurus."

"If we keep quiet, he won't hear us. If we stay in the shadows right at the base of the cliff like Buddy, he won't be able to see us." William inhaled deeply. "And the stink of the rotting Triceratops will mask our smell."

"Speak for yourself," Callie said, sniffing her armpits. "I could really use a shower."

William wondered what would happen if their plan worked and they prevented themselves from going back in time in the first place. Would they all suddenly smell better? He rubbed a scratch on the back of his hand. He wasn't sure when or where he had gotten it, but he knew it had not been there in Denver. If they prevented all of this from happening, would the scratch disappear? He vowed to check the back of his hand as soon as they got home.

William looked at Tim. "Listen to him snore. He's fast asleep. That thing is in a food coma. Look how much of the Triceratops is gone. It has to have eaten several thousand pounds. And honestly, there's no telling what we'll run into if we circle through the woods. Are you up for it, Tim?"

Tim nodded. "I guess so. Buddy made it look easy."

"We should go one at a time," Al suggested. "We'll be less likely to wake it up."

"I'll go first," Callie said. "I want to get it over with."

William saw that she was trembling. He put his hand on her shoulder and looked her straight in the eyes. "You'll be fine. Step on the larger rocks. They'll be more stable. They won't move on you. And take your time."

- - - - -

Callie walked over to the base of the cliff, stepping across large gashes where the earth had been torn open by the two giants in their earlier battle. She listened for the snoring of the tyrannosaur, but could not hear it over the sound of her heartbeat pounding in her ears.

When she passed out of the late afternoon sunlight and into the shadow below the rock wall, her skin still felt hot. She realized that she was sunburned. Her shoulders would be screaming at her in a few hours, and then after a day or so the itching would start.

Callie put her left hand up on the wall as she walked. The cold rock helped her stay steady. She felt a sneeze coming on and froze in her tracks. She grabbed her nose with her free hand and wiggled it until the need passed.

The sleeping tyrannosaur was about forty feet away at the closest point. Callie stared at it as she grew closer. Hank returned from wherever he had disappeared to and yelled at her. *Pay attention, babe. Watch your step, not that fucking thing.*

I know you mean well, Callie thought back at him, *but could you please be quiet?*

After she passed the tyrannosaur, she could no longer see it without turning her head over her shoulder and she knew if she did that, she would trip. So she listened instead. She listened for the sound of it waking and rising and coming after her. A creature that large could not get up quietly, could it? Her body tensed, ready to sprint. If she heard anything at all, she would bolt for the woods. She would zig and zag around the widest trees. She would weave in and out until she lost it in the underbrush.

At the far end of the clearing, Callie allowed herself to turn and look back. The tyrannosaur lay in the same spot, a motionless gray-brown hump. A wide grin formed on her face and she wanted to break into giggles. Callie clamped one hand over her mouth.

They hadn't discussed what she should do once she reached the woods. Should she wait or move on? Looking around and feeling unprotected, she decided to continue the short distance to the café. She held up her hand and gave a brief wave, even though she could not see the others. Then she turned and disappeared quickly into the trees.

- - - - -

William turned to Al. "You wanna go next? Be good to see Lisa again, right?"

Al stared. "Tim should go. I can wait."

Tim's eyes darted down to the football in Al's hands and William understood immediately. Tim did not trust Al with the football. William gave him a very small nod.

"Fine by me." Tim said. He started off.

Al did not seem to notice the exchange. William thought that something was definitely strange about Al, but he was willing to chalk it up to the situation. He wondered how each of these people acted in their normal lives. Al was probably ordinary and boring.

They watched in silence as Tim chose a route a little farther out from the wall, just barely in the shadows. *Careful*, William thought. Tim struck him as someone he would like to be friends with once they got home. He would be a good influence for his sons.

When Tim came even with the Triceratops carcass, he dislodged a rock. It shifted a half turn against another rock, which fell over with a slap.

The tyrannosaur let out a long nasal snort.

William stopped breathing.

Tim scampered over to the wall, dislodging more pebbles along the way, and tucked himself into a shallow depression. He disappeared in the shadows.

FORTY-SEVEN

"Why didn't you finish college?" Julie had asked over a plate of scattered pizza crusts. She locked her gaze on Tim, her turquoise eyes never glancing down or away.

"I didn't see any reason to, I guess. I took a summer job in construction, building houses. When fall came and school started back up, I just didn't see the point." The answer was true, but it wasn't the whole truth. The construction work came easy to Tim. College, on the other hand, was difficult. He could spend lots of money doing something difficult, or earn lots of money doing something easy. At the time, the choice had been pretty simple and Tim had often bragged about it. Now he felt embarrassed.

They sat in the pizzeria that Tim's softball team, cleverly named "The Runs," patronized after every game. The rest of the team had departed more than an hour earlier.

"What were you studying? Had you picked a major?" She twirled her straw absently, but she did not look down at it. Those eyes stayed locked on target. They were the color of the ocean from a tropical resort on a travel photo.

"Architecture. I took a drafting class in high school that I really liked." He shrugged with a sigh. "But the outdoors, the sun... I learned so much on the job. Stuff I could put to use." He looked around the near-empty restaurant. It wasn't often that a girl put him off his guard and Julie had him on the ropes. To his surprise, he loved it.

Julie had shown up as a substitute player at that night's game, filling in for her friend who was out with a cold. They barely spoke during the game. Julie coached first base each inning, aggressively sending runners to second if they had even a remote chance of making it. They always did. Tim watched her from the bench, captivated. He caught her stealing a glance in his direction more than once. Somehow, for reasons he couldn't explain, she wasn't a score. He wanted her, sure. But first he wanted to find out all about her. He wanted to know her.

They stayed at the restaurant long into the night and everything he learned made him want to learn more. She told him about her job as a flight attendant and her goal to move up to the cockpit. She had a son named Joe from a fling nine years earlier. She regretted the fling, but not Joe. She lived with her younger sister Stacie, who took care of Joe while she was away for work, sometimes for several days in a row.

Everything about her seemed interesting, but that wasn't what truly captivated Tim. It was the way she challenged him with probing questions. "What country would you visit if you could go anywhere in the world?" *Argentina.* "What language would you like to learn?" *Spanish.* "What's stopping you?"

Tim went to the library the very next day and checked out an audio book called *Learn on the Run: Spanish.* It was marketed as something to listen to while jogging, but he listened to it on his commute. He quickly found that he knew more Spanish than he realized, from years of working alongside immigrant laborers.

On their second date, Tim took Julie to a Rockies game. Midway through the fourth inning, he took her hand. *Holding hands on the second date!* For Tim, the second date usually meant a few shots in a bar and then a rowdy one-night-stand back at his condo. Now his big move was holding her hand. She smiled and gazed at him. It brought a rush he had never felt before, certainly not from the weekend scores.

"Tienes los ojos mas bonitos del mundo." He had memorized the phrase from his audio book. It was cheesy as hell, but it was also real. How could anyone argue with real? She laughed, impressed by his follow-through. He could not tell if she understood what it meant.

You have the most beautiful eyes in the world. Tim repeated the phrase in his mind as he huddled in the crevice on the side of the cliff. He could hear flies buzzing above the ruined body of the Triceratops. Only one full haunch remained. Round shapes nestled in the folds of its skin and Tim realized that they were more of those giant ticks.

The tyrannosaur did not move.

After another breathless minute, Tim heard the snoring resume. He stepped out of the hollow and moved on, choosing a path closer to the wall and deep in the shadows.

When he reached the woods and looked back, Tim noticed how heavy the air had grown. He looked to where William and Al should have been, but couldn't make them out. The haze and humidity obscured the view. Tim took off his cap and ran his hand through his choppy blond hair which was soaked with sweat. He was ready to get back to the high desert air of modern day Denver.

We split up, he thought, remembering Beth's comment about horror movies. We should have agreed to regroup here at the edge of the forest. He thought about going on. Callie had probably reached the café by now. It was only five or ten minutes from the clearing. He started to follow, but then realized that getting back to the café wouldn't do him any good if the football wasn't there. He decided to wait and crouched down behind the trunk of a large tree.

FORTY-EIGHT

In the shadow of the overturned tree roots, William studied Al's face. The stocky man's square jaw clenched and unclenched as he watched Tim disappear in the distance. *What is your problem, Al?* Was it the race thing all over again? William's boys scolded him for blaming racism on everything. He was glad they didn't see it as much as he did. He wondered if Al took issue with having a black man in charge.

"You know," William began, "I never really wanted to be the leader here."

Al turned to face him, but did not respond.

"It just sorta happened." He paused, waiting for an answer.

Finally Al said, "You're doing a good job. This whole thing is just pretty fucked up. I haven't given you enough credit. You got us this far." Al inhaled. "And I really believe you can get us home."

William could see that Al meant it. "I appreciate that." He looked at the device in Al's hands. There was no way on God's green Earth, and this *was* still God's green Earth as far as William was concerned, that he was going to leave the time device with Al Stevens. "Here. Let me carry that for a spell." William took the football and handed Al the shovel without waiting for an answer.

- - - - -

Al squeezed the handle of the shovel as William walked off with the device. He thought about Lisa's kiss, right before they had left on the raft. Once before, in the eighth grade, a girl had kissed him in the school library. He had gotten in trouble for it. Every kiss after that had been paid for. Until today. Today, Lisa had kissed him because she wanted to.

Al put down the shovel and picked up a round rock the size of a grapefruit.

In his mind he imagined two different Lisas. He saw one who was polite to him every day in her café. He pictured her safe at home after all of this was over, surrounded by the press. She smiled at him as lights flashed from all of the cameras. But that was it.

The second Lisa was the one he had pulled from the river, her wet blouse clinging to her body. The one holding his hand. The one who kissed him behind the building and pulled his crotch against hers. She was his. He imagined exploring this exotic world with her. Learning what plants were safe to eat and when to harvest them. Learning to hunt. They would be conquerors. He pictured her safe in a cave, cooking a haunch of meat over an open fire. They would feast and fuck every single night.

William reached the cliff wall and began to make his way along the base. He walked slowly.

Lisa would sleep with him, Al knew, for comfort if nothing else. Callie would too, eventually. If he was the only living man on the planet, he could have both of them.

Al chucked the rock as hard as he could in the direction of the snoring monster. Branches hung over the edge of the clearing. *Don't hit a branch, don't hit a branch.* They were spread out thinly and Al knew he couldn't hit one if he actually tried to, but with his luck-

The rock flew just below the canopy before landing squarely on the back of the sleeping tyrannosaur. It thumped and bounced off.

The snoring stopped.

William, a third of the way across, did not notice.

You think I have issues with your leadership? Al picked up a second rock and threw it, placing this one out in the open, halfway between William and the tyrannosaur. It landed on stone and split in two with a loud clap.

William froze, staring at the dinosaur. Then he turned to look back at Al. Four hundred feet separated them, but Al could see the disbelief in William's wide eyes.

He knows what I did. A cold chill ran down Al's spine and he felt his bowels begin to loosen. *The others will know what I did. Lisa will know.* He clenched, starting with his sphincter, and then moving up through every muscle in his body.

A slow rumble came from the belly of the beast. It shifted its weight, extending its long tail up into the air. It used its tiny forearms to push up from the ground.

Al shouted as loudly as he could, *"William, FREEZE!"* He ducked into the cavity left by the roots of the fallen tree. *You just woke up a Tyrannosaurus rex.* He knew he should stay hidden, but he couldn't help himself. He leaned to the side and peered through the upturned roots.

William pressed himself against the base of the cliff, holding the football against his hip. He disappeared against the rocks.

The predator stood and looked around. Dried blood from the Triceratops caked its muzzle. The downy fluff on its hide looked almost golden in the late afternoon light that shone down over the edge of the cliff. Al wondered if he had made a terrible mistake.

- - - - -

At the end of the clearing, Tim rose to his feet. *How the hell had William made such a racket?* He felt an urge to distract the dinosaur, to draw its attention. Then he wondered how attracting the attention of a *Tyrannosaurus rex* could possibly be a good idea. Al shouting for William to freeze had been insane. Brave and selfless maybe, but insane. Looking straight down the cliff wall, Tim could not actually see William. The delivery man had found a cavity deeper than the one he had been in. He hoped William was hidden from the dinosaur as well.

The tyrannosaur looked over at the Triceratops carcass and gave a series of deep sniffs before scanning the area.

Just sit tight, William, Tim thought, watching from the trees. *It's got a perfectly good meal right there. Let it start feeding.*

- - - - -

William tried to hold every muscle completely still. Droplets of sweat trickled down his back and sides. He was wedged deep in the shadows. He wore his dark UPS uniform. Even his skin was dark. He should be invisible. The football in his arms was metallic, but in the shadows, it was just another rock. Without moving his head, William turned his eyes down to be sure.

He noticed something strange on the rock wall to the side. The wall lit up, then went dark, over and over again. Bright, dark. Bright, dark. The orange beacon light blinked on and off.

William's breathing picked up. He moved a hand across the surface of the football until he found the light near the bottom of the device. He cupped his fingers over it. *Why didn't I think of that before?*

The tyrannosaur took a step toward the cliff.

Very slowly, William turned his head to the left. The forest was too far. He would never make it. *But the cliff.* The wall directly behind him rose only twenty feet or so and it dropped quickly between him and the end of the clearing. Just a few short yards away, it was low enough to climb.

The tyrannosaur took another step closer. Its head was still in the sunlight coming over the forest above the cliff. It lowered its face. The tip of its nose stuck through the edge of the shadow.

Clutching the time machine tightly against his side, William turned and pushed off the wall. He sprinted along the base of the cliff.

The tyrannosaur's nostrils flared wide as it sucked air to power its two-hundred-pound heart. It leapt forward, thrilled by the chase.

The cliff wall descended next to William as he ran. Soon it was even with his head. Then his shoulders. *Just a little farther.* He made himself wait until he was sure it was low enough, knowing he would only get one chance.

He saw Tim directly ahead, pressed against a tree trunk. The look of horror on Tim's face told William that the tyrannosaur was right behind him.

Watch this, William thought. He found the perfect spot and vaulted up onto the higher ground. He spun on his heels, making a tight u-turn, and ran back up the cliff where the group had fled some twelve hours earlier.

The tyrannosaur reached the cliff right as William passed by, even with its mouth. The dinosaur turned its head and snapped forward. The end of its snout shoved into William. He teetered, but kept his balance. *"Yaah Haaa!"* William kept running up the edge of the cliff.

- - - - -

The tyrannosaur turned toward the end of the clearing. Tim had smiled and pumped his fist at William's escape. Now his smile died and he sank into the tree trunk. It was coming straight at him. It took three steps in his direction. *Oh shit...* Tim's knees locked.

Before it reached the forest, the giant beast made the same u-turn William had taken, stepping up onto the low cliff ledge. It had not spotted Tim. The tyrannosaur plodded along the top of the cliff, sending an avalanche of rocks over the edge with each footstep.

- - - - -

A stitch in William's side stopped him, along with the certainty that he was now safe. The tyrannosaur could snap at him all it wanted from the clearing below, just as it had that morning. William gasped for air, holding the time device against his thighs. He looked down, trying to find Al. *Why?* It seemed as if Al had thrown a rock at him. Or at the dinosaur. *Why did you do that?* He was equally confused and angry.

His heavy breathing masked the sound of the tyrannosaur behind him.

- - - - -

Tim's stomach lurched. William kept them together. When they started bickering, William calmed them down. When they weren't sure what to do, William decided. William was the one who would take Tim home to Julie.

He stepped out into the clearing and screamed, *"WILLIAM, RUN!"*

William turned around as the tyrannosaur loomed over him. He raised the football above his head like a shield.

The time device.

Tim felt as if he was drowning, sucking for air, but unable to breathe.

The massive jaws of the tyrannosaur came down over the football and clamped on William's chest. Nine-inch teeth closed together through William's torso until they touched. The dinosaur opened its mouth back up and slurped in the delivery man's hips and legs before they could fall away, leaving no trace of the man or the machine.

FORTY-NINE

I just killed a man, Al thought.

Atop the cliff, the tyrannosaur looked at the drop-off below and suddenly seemed uncomfortable. A fall from that height would be a death sentence. It turned, shouldered through the saplings, and disappeared into the woods above.

Al had fantasized about killing people plenty of times before. Who hadn't? Most recently, he had wanted to strangle his sister, Deborah, who nagged him endlessly about finding a girl and settling down. *As if it was that goddamn easy.*

Al knew better. Very few people got away with murder. He was quite sure that if he ever actually hurt anyone, he would be caught, prosecuted by some prick like Hank, and then sent to prison for the rest of his life. Even if it was justified. At least, that was true in modern times. Here, there wasn't a single cop or prison on the face of the planet. And now, thanks to that big dinosaur in the ocean, there wasn't even a single prosecutor.

He picked up the shovel and stepped out from behind the upturned roots and strode straight across the clearing. He felt a warm feeling of satisfaction. The time machine was gone. He and Lisa would stay here forever.

There was no longer any need to skirt along the rock wall. The sun had moved beyond the top of the cliff, leaving the entire clearing in shadow. Al took note of the Triceratops as he passed it. A huge hunk of meat remained on its back right leg. It could provide food for weeks, if properly cleaned and cooked. Smoked, maybe. Al wasn't sure how to preserve meat, but if primitive humans could figure it out, he thought he could, too.

For now, though, he needed to focus on the next few minutes. What had Tim MacGregor seen? He had surely heard Al shout at William to freeze, but Tim himself had shouted for William to run, just a few minutes later. Al's shout had been intended to make sure the dinosaur was fully awake, but there was no way Tim could know that. He needed to find out if Tim had seen him throw the rocks.

He found Tim sitting on a small boulder in the woods. Al gripped the shovel in both hands as he approached. *If he suspects anything, you've only got one chance here, Stevens.* Tim was leaner and quicker, but Al outweighed him by at least fifty pounds and Al had the shovel.

He stopped and stood before Tim. "What the hell happened? I couldn't see." Then, hoping he wasn't pushing it, "Where is William?"

Tim looked up, shaking his head slowly. His eyelids closed together, forming narrow slits. He was either furious or devastated. Al couldn't tell which.

Squeezing the handle of the shovel, Al wondered what would work better, a wide swing or a straight jab with the end of the blade. He wondered if he could bring himself to actually do it, up close and personal. *If he knows, I don't have any choice. I have to do it.* He would hide Tim's body in the Triceratops carcass. None of the women would ever go near that thing. Al wrung his hands around the handle, waiting for a reply.

Finally Tim spoke. "He's gone. And so is the time machine. Gone."

"Shit. What happened?"

"It woke up. It chased him up the cliff." Tim glared with anger. Al still couldn't tell what he knew.

Al nodded and pretended to slowly understand. "*That's* what it was doing. I hid under the roots of that tree when it woke up. When I finally looked out, it was walking off into the woods up there."

Tim stared up at Al without saying anything.

Al offered a hand. He would plunge the shovel blade into Tim's neck as he pulled him up. *You've only got one shot here.* If Tim got away and ran back to Lisa, he would be doomed.

Tim looked at the silent woods around them. He seemed to compose himself. "So what do we do now?"

"We survive," Al said. "That's all we can do."

Tim nodded and took Al's hand. "We should have listened to you." Al pulled him to his feet.

"Come on, Tim. Let's get back to the girls."

FIFTY

Lisa rushed into Al's arms when he stepped into the café. He pulled her close and hid his face in her hair. He felt like picking her up and twirling her around. He always sneered when men did that in the movies, but right now he wanted to. Instead, he buried his growing smile against her neck.

"Callie told us what happened," Lisa whispered. "She told us about Hank and Morgan, but you guys found the football. We can undo everything. You did it!"

Al tensed up.

"What is it, Al?"

What is it? The woman he had loved for three years just ran into his arms. He had never been happier in his life. The smell of the sweat on her neck was delicious. He felt an urge to open his mouth and taste it. Instead, he shook his head slowly and kept his mouth closed.

"William is dead," Tim announced. "The Tyrannosaurus killed him."

"Oh my God," Lisa cried. She squeezed Al even tighter.

Al trembled against her. She would interpret it as despair. He steeled his face so that no emotion showed and finally pulled away.

Helen sat on the orange couch where Callie tended to a new bandage on her arm. Callie froze, her lower lip quivering. "No. No. No." She looked from Tim to Al. Her breaths came short and quick. "Where's the time machine? *Where is it?*"

Now they all looked to Tim, eyes wide and mouths gaping.

"It's gone. William was holding it when he died. It ate the device."

Helen covered her lips with her fingers. Callie brought her fists up to her face and shook. Buddy let out a low whimper at Callie's feet.

Al looked out the open window. Late day sunlight touched the tops of the trees along the river. It would be night soon. Their first night.

"What are we supposed to do now?" Lisa asked, looking from one person to the next.

"We survive," Al said. Now that the device was gone, it was that simple. Surely they could understand that much.

Helen grunted, "Our track record for surviving hasn't been so great, young man. We lost half our group in less than a day."

"Hank is *gone*," Callie cried.

She looked comatose, the way she had looked on the beach. Al supposed that to her, she had lost Hank all over again, now that the fail-safe was gone. Which was total bullshit, when you thought about it. They all needed to get beyond that nonsense if they were going to stay alive. "Listen, Callie, the plan was never going to work. I mean, if you think it through, it falls apart."

Everyone gave him the same harsh glare. Lisa backed away.

He realized he had to spell it out. "Okay, look. Let's say we made it home. Then we were supposed to use the fail-safe to go back in time twenty minutes."

"Yeah. That was the plan," Tim said. "Why are we even talking about this?" Al thought he looked ready for a fight.

Al went on. "Right. That was the plan. So we go back twenty minutes and then walk into the café and tell ourselves to clear out of there. Then what?"

Tim circled closer as he answered. "The café would have gone back in time, but it would be empty. None of us would be inside. We were also going to try to stop the researchers upstairs from using the device at all." He faced Al straight on. "What's the problem?"

Al fought to keep himself from rolling his eyes. "Telling them not to use the device has its own set of problems, but forget about that for now. *Who* would have been in the café when we got there?"

Callie answered this one. "All of us. All ten of us. Hank is in the café. And Beth and William. Everyone."

"And where are you in this scenario?"

"In the café. I just told you that. I was in the café too, dumbass."

Now Al did roll his eyes. "Not *that* you." He waggled his finger at her. "This you. *You* you." Al continued, speaking slowly. "There's the Callie in the café, running out into the street so that she doesn't go back in time and a second Callie, *you*, standing there telling her to get out."

Callie nodded. "That's right. So what?" She jabbed at her chest. "This me will go back forward twenty minutes with the device."

Al nodded. He looked around to be sure everyone was with him before he continued. "When the device takes us back forward twenty minutes, where does that land us? Back in a world where we all just arrived from dinosaur time. A world where Hank is still dead."

"You don't know that," Callie spat. "You don't know how any of this works."

"Yeah, that's for sure," Al said. "But think about it. What other possibility is there? Are the timelines going to merge back together? Is the Callie who just spent fifteen hours in the land of the lost going to be reunited with the Hank who avoided the trip? No, because that Hank has a different Callie right next to him, who also avoided the trip."

Callie looked ready to burst into sobs.

"Why would you say this?" Helen asked. "I don't even understand what you are saying, but all you're doing is hurting that poor girl."

"I'm trying to *help* her." His voice grew louder and faster. "We lost the device. It's gone. But the fact of the matter is that the time machine never would have saved her boyfriend. I thought it would make her feel better, knowing that it didn't matter. It wouldn't have worked anyway."

Al stared at Tim, who still stood directly in front him. *You want to hit me, don't you?* He almost hoped it would happen. Tim would look like the asshole for a change and Al would be the victim. Maybe that would at least earn him some sympathy.

"You took away her hope," Helen said quietly.

Al rubbed the back of his neck. "There's *still* hope. We aren't doomed to die here." How they could not see that was beyond him. "We still have a chance here."

Tim glared at him. "A chance? What kind of chance do you really think we have? It's been less than a day and we've already lost five people." He clenched his fists. "At this rate, we'll all be dead tomorrow." He jabbed a finger at Al, connecting with the top of his chest. Al flinched.

"Tim," Lisa called. "We aren't going to survive if we beat each other up."

"Thank you." Al nodded eagerly. Lisa had just come to his rescue. She was on his side. He squared his jaw and looked at Tim. "Listen, we've been scared, rushed and confused. If we stay focused and work together, we can survive here. We can even have a life here."

"A life?" Callie sputtered. "Like, what? Raise some kids and teach them about the good old days back in the future when we had cars and doctors and supermarkets? And then watch them get eaten alive or trampled to death? No thanks."

"You won't have any kids with me," Al blurted. "I got snipped." It was an honest fact, but he regretted the words the moment they left his mouth. A chill ran down his spine and he felt his sphincter tighten. The conversation was not going the way he had hoped.

"Are you *serious?*" Callie sneered. "Is this some kind of prehistoric orgy fantasy for you?"

A bead of sweat rolled from Al's forehead into one eye. He blinked it away. "I'm only trying to keep the group safe," he said quietly. He looked at the angry faces around the room. They frightened him more than any of the dinosaurs.

Tim shifted his weight, as if winding up to throw a punch. Al suddenly realized where he was standing. If Tim hit him, he might knock him back into the river.

Helen rapped the tabletop with her knuckles. "There are going to be some surprised folks back in Denver when that dinosaur shows up."

Tim froze. "What?" He turned to her. "What are you talking about?"

"I don't understand all of that timeline nonsense, but the idea of the swap is pretty clear in my head. The time machine will still go off on schedule, won't it? That woman upstairs told you it was tough."

Tim nodded. "That's right."

Helen continued. "It already floated down to the ocean. Sitting in the belly of a dinosaur for a few hours isn't going to hurt it. So when time runs out, won't it take the dinosaur right back to Denver?"

Lisa nodded slowly. "And if it arrives in a spot where there are people, they'll be swapped too. They'll show up here, wherever the Tyrannosaurus was."

Al had not considered this. "We might get lucky. Something useful might be swapped back."

"How long until that happens?" Callie asked. "How long until the device goes off?" She stared down at the table.

Tim chewed on his lip. "I don't know. William was keeping track. A little more than two hours, I think." He stepped away from Al. "When the device was eaten, I thought it was gone."

Tim looked uncertain. *He's still waiting for William to make a decision*, Al realized. Tim was too much of a follower to take charge of the situation. "Okay then," Al said. "We wait around another two hours and see what shows up. After that, we focus on surviving. I'm going to find a cave, or high ground, or some sort of place we can fortify." He spoke to the room, but he looked at Lisa. "I hope you will come with me."

"How long before the dinosaur moves its bowels?" Helen asked.

Callie jumped up. "We can't wait for that T-rex to take a shit. We're wasting valuable time right now." She looked at Tim, who stared off into space chewing on his lower lip. "Tim, we have two hours." The words came out slow, loud, and clear. "What are we going to do?" Al thought she sounded like Hank.

Tim looked at Callie. "We're going to find that rex and slice open the son of a bitch."

Callie nodded. Her eyes glistened.

"Are you insane?" Al started toward Tim, but backed off when he saw the look in the younger man's eyes.

"Al, we've got to try," Lisa said.

He looked at her, suddenly exhausted. He had been so close. "We don't even know where it went. It could be miles from here."

"That Tyrannosaurus has been staying nearby," Tim said. "He's still got a meal back there. I don't think he's gone very far." He echoed Lisa's words. "We've got to try."

Helen rose and walked over to Lisa. "Sweetie, let's show them what we were up to while they were gone on their little boat ride." The old woman smiled. "I've got an idea."

FIFTY-ONE

Lisa went behind the counter and returned with one of her twelve-dollar canvas bags. Thin points poked against the sides, as if it held a jumble of sticks. "After you left on the raft," Lisa explained, "Helen taught me how to fish. We caught eight."

"We didn't even have to leave the building," Helen explained. She pointed out the front door. "We just dropped in our lines from the sidewalk."

"Is that them in the bag?" Al asked. He looked impressed. Lisa felt proud.

"Nope. Most of them were stolen from us, by this guy." Lisa reached into the bag and pulled out the body of a dead pterosaur. She held the animal by its snake-like neck. Its wings flopped to the ground. The tail of a small fish hung from the pterosaur's mouth.

Lisa explained, "Helen's husband used to take her hunting. She hated it, but she sure learned a thing or two. Like how to tie a snare, for instance. Have a look out there on the shore." She led them over to the front windows and pointed to a trap rigged near the edge of the mudflat. Their last fish sat on the ground, encircled by a loop of wire. The end of the line was tied to a nearby branch, which curved over it in a tight arc.

Helen raised her forearm, showing off her new bandage. "That little bastard pecked me, but I wrung his neck!" She held her fists next to one another and twisted them in opposite directions.

"Is that also what happened to your head?" Callie pointed at the bloody spot in Helen's hair.

"No, that was an oster-rich-a-saurus. He came after us while we were setting the first trap and pecked us both in the head. Lisa cut his head off."

"Not all the way off."

"Oh, whatever. It was hanging by a thread as he ran away. But one thing is for sure. You killed him." Lisa felt proud of this. No one else had ever killed a dinosaur.

Al smiled at her and examined the pterosaur. "That has more meat on it than a Thanksgiving turkey." He turned to Helen. "You'll have to teach me how to rig one of those traps."

Helen looked back out at the snare. "We almost caught a second one right before you all returned, but Buddy showed up and scared it off."

Callie pounded one of the tables. "I don't understand. How does any of this help us?"

Tim raised his eyebrows. "Helen means for us to snare the Tyrannosaurus."

Al turned to him. "That's insane."

Callie held up her hand in Al's direction. "Shush." She looked back and forth between Tim and Helen. "How? How do you snare something that big?"

"The heavy cables in the lab upstairs," said Tim. "There are lots. Some in the walls and some loose in the room." He nodded, working it out in his head. "It's a long shot, but we might be able to bring it back here by banging the pots and pans again."

"Yeah, that'll bring it back here," Al spat. "But how are you going to get it to put its neck through a snare? This bat-thing would barely be a crumb to it. Besides, it's got plenty of meat waiting for it back on the dead Triceratops by the cliff."

"That's right," Tim said. "The Triceratops is our source. We cut some meat from the carcass and use that. It's only ten minutes from here." He looked at the others. "We've got one last shot to get home. That device will go off in less than two hours." He stared directly at Al. "I won't stop trying as long as there is still a chance."

Lisa took Al's hands and looked up at him with wide, hopeful eyes. "Come on, Al. We can go home together. We can get our lives back." She did not understand the tension between Al and Tim, but she knew they needed to all work together if there was any hope.

Al squared his jaw and said, "Let's do it. What are we waiting for?"

FIFTY-TWO

On the second floor, which felt more like a rooftop, Al and Lisa gathered cable for the snares. Al looked over the edge of the building as Tim and Callie disappeared into the woods. They were going to collect bait for their half-baked plan. Al did not like the two of them going off alone. He felt a pang of jealous suspicion. What were they talking about? Were Tim and Callie forming some sort of alliance against him?

Sweat soaked Al's shirt. The sun had disappeared beyond the trees and the sky overhead had grown pale but the temperature had not dropped. *Just two more hours. Maybe less.* Soon it would be dark and all the talk about getting home would have to stop. Along with any thought about wanting to attract a Tyrannosaurus.

"We're going to be famous when we get home," Lisa said as Al pulled on a heavy black cord. Electrical cables ran through an eight-inch gap in the walls. They had pulled out several hundred feet so far.

Pulling the cable was exhausting. It weighed more than it looked like it should. Lisa had offered to help, but Al insisted on doing the heavy lifting. He wanted to show her that he could be counted on to get a job done. He paused to pull his shirt over his head.

His barrel chest wasn't exactly lean, but he was strong. He caught Lisa stealing a glance, just as he sometimes caught the women at the gym.

Al took hold of the cable again with both hands and pulled another three or four yards up through the gap in the wall. *She really thinks this plan has a chance.* Al knew that he had to go along with it. "Maybe we could go on tour together," he said. "You know, go around to all the news shows and talk shows and whatever."

"Sounds like fun."

He looked over at her, trying to detect any hints of sarcasm or mockery on her face. She smiled and raised her eyebrows. It seemed like an honest smile, but he could not tell what it meant. Did she picture them meeting at a television studio, doing an interview, and then going out for lunch? Or did she picture them returning to their hotel room together?

The cable stopped moving. Al gripped it tightly and pulled with all of his strength, but it wouldn't budge. "Time to cut it." Lisa came over and began to saw through the cord with a serrated knife from the survival cabinet.

The second floor was slightly higher than the tyrannosaur's head. The plan was to lure the creature into position by hanging bait from the side of the building. Helen's pterosaur was already in place at the first snare, putrefying in the heat. Such a waste. The body held enough meat to feed all five of them for two or three meals.

In order to eat the pterosaur, the tyrannosaur would have to step inside a circle of thick cable lying on the ground. The loop of cable had been tied in a noose and the end of it ran up the side of the building and across the second floor. On the opposite side, above the river, the line was anchored to a heavy object, ready to be shoved over the wall.

Tim had helped Al set the first snare. They tied it to one of the computer shelves leaning precariously on the far side of the building. The shelf held dozens of racks of hard drives and had to weigh more than three hundred pounds. Satisfied that the snare was secure, Tim and Callie had rushed off to collect bait. The irony amused Al. Just a few hours earlier, the second floor had been littered with bait.

Lisa and Al were responsible for setting three more snares, which required collecting hundreds of feet of heavy cable. Al twisted the current section of wire so that Lisa could cut the opposite side. She was through the plastic sheath and sawing away on the tightly wound copper coils inside. He looked across the rubble-strewn room, trying not to stare at her while she worked. Women did not like to be stared at. A black smear on the floor caught his eye. He followed it to the survival cabinet and realized it marked the path Mister Slushy had made when Lisa dragged him to the edge and dumped him into the river. "Too bad you got rid of the bodies. Who knew we would actually want to *attract* the T-rex back here."

Lisa frowned. "We couldn't use them as bait. That's horrible."

"Sorry. Bad joke."

Her frown disappeared, but her mouth twisted off to one side in a sneer. *She thinks I'm a sicko.* He had to make it right, and quick. *Complement her.* "In all seriousness, you did the right thing, Lisa. Clearing out those bodies was smart." He wanted to call her brilliant. He remembered how her face lit up when William called her brilliant, but somehow the idea of disposing of corpses didn't seem quite up to the word. "You cleared our shelter of something that would attract the attention of a predator. Smart decisions like that will keep us alive."

"It wasn't exactly a lot of fun," she noted.

"That's one of the things I like about you. You don't shy away from hard work." Her smile returned, but her face did not exactly light up.

"I hope they get back soon," she said. "We don't have much time." Sweat beads rolled off her forehead.

Al wanted to point out that the plan was crazy. He wanted to prepare her for the disappointment that would come when time ran out and they were still here. The tyrannosaur was probably miles away, slowly digesting William. Instead, he said, "I just hope Tim and Callie don't run into any trouble."

"I know. It's dangerous, them going off alone."

"They'll be ok. Tim has the shovel." Other than a few small knives, it was the closest thing they had to a weapon. Al imagined Tim trying to fight off a dinosaur with a short-handled shovel. He fought to keep the smile off of his face.

Just another couple of hours, he told himself. After that, everyone would forget about trying to get home and they could focus on real survival. Their ridiculous plan would never work. First, they had to get the tyrannosaur to return to the café by banging pots and pans again. Then they had to hope it would stand still on a snare while they shoved a piece of rubble off the far side of the building. The falling weight would pull the loop tight around its leg and maybe even yank the creature off its feet. If they were lucky, Helen explained, its leg might break.

Once the dinosaur was snared, the plan was to lower a second loop of cable over its head. Then, they would shove another heavy object off the far side of the building to either snap its neck or strangle it. After the creature was dead, they could cut open its belly and retrieve the device. This, Al thought, was the most foolish thing he had ever heard.

With any luck, Tim would run into the tyrannosaur on his hunt for bait and Callie would come back alone. He did not want to compete with Tim, neither for leadership nor for the women. He should have killed him in the woods when he had the chance. He vowed not to pass up another opportunity like that.

Once Tim was out of the picture, Al Stevens would be the only human male on the face of the Earth. It would be him and Lisa and Callie. A beautiful brunette and a stunning redhead. And old Helen to teach them about hunting and fishing, at least for as long as she lasted.

FIFTY-THREE

Tim and Callie jogged through the trees, back toward the cliff and the dead Triceratops. The light in the forest had grown dim, but it was still easy enough to see.

"So much for us not splitting up," she said.

Tim nodded. "Yeah, I know. But we don't have much time."

Buddy passed them, chasing after a foot-long dragonfly.

At first, Tim had considered sending the dog back to the café, but then he decided that having him along might be a good idea. Buddy's senses of hearing and smell might give them an early warning if anything dangerous showed up. Just as before, the dog came and went as he pleased.

"What do you think about what Al said?" Callie asked. "About not being able to save Hank?"

"I don't know. Nobody's ever done this before."

"I've been going over it in my mind. I think there might be some truth to it."

"Don't listen to Al. He's an asshole."

Callie laughed. "You were ready to hit him back there, weren't you?"

"I was ready to knock him into the river." He laughed with her, but then grew serious. "I feel bad about it. Beth said that the second biggest threat in a horror movie was *the other guy*. I don't want to be that person."

Small gliding reptiles leapt from branch to branch in front of them, floating on membranes of skin between their legs. One snatched Buddy's dragonfly out of the air. Buddy chased the creature to a tree and pawed furiously at the bark below it. Another glider swooped by, seeming to taunt him.

"I don't think you are that person," Callie said. "I think Al is dangerous. I don't think he wants us to get back."

Tim looked at her sideways but kept jogging. "That's crazy. Why would anyone want to stay here?"

"Did you see the look on his face when I made that comment about an orgy?"

"You embarrassed him."

"Tim, he has been ogling all of us ever since we got here. Especially Lisa."

Tim agreed that Al was strange, but the idea that anyone would want to stay here was ridiculous. Callie had lost her fiancé. She wasn't thinking straight. "This is a crazy-ass situation. I don't think any of us are really at our best."

Callie stopped, breathing hard. She put her hands on her hips. "What do you do for a living again?"

"I'm a carpenter. I build the wood framing for new houses mostly."

"Well, my job is to observe people. And I'm telling you, there's something not right about that guy." She started running again.

Ahead, the forest brightened slightly as they approached the clearing. Buddy stood perfectly still next to the last few trees, staring forward with one paw lifted. Tim slowed to a stop and held the shovel before him in two hands. Buddy growled quietly, a low rumble from deep in his chest. Tim was panting too hard to hear anything up ahead.

"What is it?" whispered Callie. They saw movement in the clearing, low to the ground.

"It isn't the T-rex. Whatever it is, it looks small. Let's find out."

He stepped forward tentatively, trying to get close enough to see. Buddy launched himself through the trees, his legs splayed wide with each bound. When he reached the clearing, he began to bark wildly.

"Buddy!" Tim dashed after him. Callie ran close behind, also calling his name.

In the clearing, Buddy threw himself into a pack of seven bird-like Deinonychus, which scattered from the remains of the Triceratops.

The Deinonychus were less than three feet long from head to tail, but their emerald plumage made them seem larger. Long wispy feathers sprouted from their heads and ran in a row down their backs.

The two-legged dinosaurs fled in all directions, screeching and hissing. Their mouths were filled with more than sixty sharp points, lined up like the teeth on a saw.

"They look like birds," Callie observed.

"Yeah, birds with arms and hands instead of wings," Tim said. "They're acting more like a pack of dogs, though. Coyotes maybe."

Buddy ran to the right, chasing the three closest Deinonychus toward the cliff. Two leapt up the rock wall, but the third fell short and slid back down. Buddy pounced, grasping the creature by its neck. The dog shook his head vigorously back and forth.

The screeching Deinonychus swung its foot, hooking Buddy's shoulder with a large, terrible claw, but then fell limp as its neck snapped. Buddy dropped the animal and turned back toward the Triceratops, oblivious to his wound.

The four remaining Deinonychus stood silently in the trees just beyond the remains of the horned animal. Tim and Callie approached the carcass.

"Buddy, come," Tim commanded. The dog moved close.

Callie gave a dry, retching cough as she approached the gutted body of the Triceratops.

Tim circled the carcass, searching for a section of flesh he could slice off with the shovel blade. He raised the shovel and struck the dinosaur near the middle of its remaining leg. The steel blade bounced off the thick hide.

"Shit. This isn't working." He pulled out a small hunting knife. "This is going to take forever."

Buddy growled a low warning.

"They're coming back," Callie said.

Two of the larger Deinonychus, showing flecks of gold in their feathers, stepped into the clearing and hissed.

Tim lifted the shovel in one hand and shouted, *"YAAAAH!"* as he took an exaggerated step toward the nearest dinosaur. The two-foot tall Deinonychus turned, ran into the woods, but looped back, this time coming farther into the clearing.

Callie suddenly squealed and jumped back. A baseball-sized tick clung to her running shoe with its long, crab-like legs. She screamed again and kicked, sending the tick flying.

Several other ticks, swollen with blood, moved across the weedy ground in search of their next host.

A rustling sound came from behind. The two Deinonychus that had fled up the cliff had returned. They watched from a distance.

"Look at them. They've got us surrounded," Tim said. "We don't have time for this."

"Tim, there are *lots* of these ticks."

"I'm a little more worried about the bird dinosaurs," Tim said. "The ticks won't hurt us." To prove his point, he stepped forward and stomped on the closest one. It exploded with a satisfying burst, like an overripe tomato, but the fluid that splattered outwards was almost black.

"Yeah, I know," Callie said. "But these ticks are full of Triceratops blood. We can use them to attract the T-rex." She found another tick slowly marching from the carcass. Mustering every last bit of emotional fortitude, Callie reached down and used two hands to pick up the tick, grabbing it by the back of its bloated abdomen. Its black legs wiggled and clicked in the air, reaching for her. "Hold open your bag."

Tim planted the shovel in the soil and spread open one of the heavy duty trash bags Lisa had given them. The nearest Deinonychus took a few steps closer, but Buddy ran at it, barking. The dinosaur retreated to the trees.

"Behind us," noted Callie. The two dinosaurs from the cliff came closer. At the same time, one of the others jumped up onto the remains of the Triceratops and held its feathery arms wide, as if offering a hug.

"Okay, the ticks will have to do," Tim said. He had been hoping to have Triceratops meat they could try to cook in case the plan failed, but he didn't mention that to Callie.

He feinted toward the dinosaurs behind them. They retreated halfway back to the cliff.

Callie picked up three more ticks and stuffed them into the bag. Now that it was partially filled, Tim propped it upright on the ground and began to help her. Together they quickly filled the first bag. Tim tied off the opening when he thought it was too heavy to risk adding any more.

"They're getting closer," Callie warned.

Three Deinonychus surrounded Buddy, holding their arms wide. Sharp talons flexed on their hands. The hair along Buddy's back stood straight up and his tail was tucked between his legs. He growled, but a whining whimper crept into the sound.

Tim pulled the shovel out of the ground and jabbed it at the dinosaurs.

This time they did not retreat. They hissed at him and turned back to the dog.

Buddy's lips were pulled away from his muzzle and he snapped his head left and right toward each of the three dinosaurs around him. The one in the center extended its arms straight out to both sides and shook them. The feathers hanging from its arms danced like a waterfall. Tim realized the center animal was distracting Buddy so that its companions could attack from the sides.

The Deinonychus flanking Buddy on the left crouched, bending its legs for the killing leap.

Callie pulled a plastic garbage bag from her belt and snapped it open in the wind. It crackled as it filled with air, forming a shiny black balloon. The Deinonychus screamed, fell backwards, and retreated into the woods.

Callie chuckled. She pulled another empty bag from her belt and handed it to Tim. "Try this." Together, they opened the bags wide and flapped them in the air. The five remaining Deinonychus scattered. Even Buddy sidestepped away from the snapping plastic, his tail still tucked. Tim and Callie laughed.

They filled two more bags with ticks, aware that the pack continued to watch them from the shadows. They pulled the last few parasites from the folds of skin behind the Triceratops' remaining knee. Tim also collected the Deinonychus that Buddy had killed at the base of the cliff. It weighed surprisingly little.

"Let's get back, shall we?" Callie said, shouldering a full bag. She did her best to ignore the constant wiggling motion of the ticks inside. "C'mon, Buddy!"

The dog bristled as the Deinonychus pack moved in to reclaim the carcass. Buddy gave three sharp barks and then turned to follow Tim and Callie back toward the river.

FIFTY-FOUR

The trip back to the café went quickly. Tim set a steady pace. The sky had turned a bruise-colored purple and the woods were now darker than when they first fled from the tyrannosaur that morning. Callie wasn't exactly sure how long they had left, but figured it was around an hour. Their chances of getting home were thin. *Don't give up,* she told herself. If they didn't try, their chances dropped to nothing.

She believed her chances of seeing Hank again were even slimmer. *Al may be right,* she thought. The realization hurt, but she couldn't hide from it any longer. If she made it to the present and used the fail-safe to jump back and forth, Hank still wouldn't be with her. She would see him briefly in the café and then return to her own timeline without him.

And you're a goddamn expert on time travel now? Head Hank did not seem happy about this line of thought. "Head Hank" struck her as a hell of a name for someone who had been decapitated.

Ha. Ha. Ha. Go ahead and make your little jokes.

I'm sorry, Callie thought back. *I understand that you're angry. You've got a pretty good reason.*

Angry doesn't begin to cover it, babe. We had something.

Callie couldn't argue with that. They did have something. She missed him terribly and she would miss him for the rest of her life. *Whatever that's worth,* she thought. *We're going to be stuck here.*

I don't want to hear any of that now, babe. You need to get your ass back to modern times.

Ahead, she saw the river crossing with their ruined chunk of building plopped in the middle. They had bait now, but she doubted they could lure the tyrannosaur before time ran out. It could be miles away. *What the hell are we thinking?*

We're actually trying to bring that monster back here? She wondered if they would be better off looking for shelter, the way Al wanted.

She felt a chill and the Hank-voice returned. *Babe, I've only got one more thing to say on that matter. I think you already know this, but listen up. Al is trouble.* In her mind, he emphasized the last point by jabbing with his finger. As she approached the building, she saw Al up on the second floor tending to one of the snares.

Callie dropped her bag of blood-filled ticks by the back corner and went to the sidewalk around front. Helen's campfire had died. If the plan didn't work, they would need to build up a good blaze for the night. She shivered at the thought.

Buddy ran past her into the building and coaxed a half-eaten muffin from Helen. The room was lit by votive candles.

"We got some bait," she announced. "I take it there has been no sign of the T-rex?"

Helen shook her head.

Lisa stood back behind her counter again, where she seemed the most comfortable. She looked pale, but maybe it was just the light. Callie walked over and spoke quietly. "Listen. I don't know if you want to hear this or not, but I gotta talk to you about Al."

She expected a rebuttal. Callie had never known a woman to sit by and listen to hard truths about the men they were involved with. From her experience, she thought that the only way Lisa might accept criticism about her man was if Callie coaxed it out of her own mouth. That usually took a month's worth of weekly sessions. More time than she had right now.

For some reason Lisa did not object, so Callie continued. "He's nutso for you. That much is obvious. But I think the key term here is 'nutso.' I think he has been trying to keep us from getting home." Lisa stared silently while Callie went on. "Tell me truthfully, would you have ever given him the time of day before all of this happened?" Callie waited, but

Lisa did not answer. "You wouldn't, and he knows that. I think he wants to keep you here."

Helen watched from her seat at the table, but Lisa still said nothing.

Is she losing it? Callie wondered. She had treated dozens of women for posttraumatic stress disorder, usually following some kind of abuse. Lisa showed classic signs of detachment and avoidance. "Just be watchful, will you?"

Lisa answered her with a very small nod.

Callie couldn't hope for much more than that. She picked up a pair of metal coffee pots. "Let's get ready to make some noise."

FIFTY-FIVE

On the second floor, Al checked the snares to make sure everything appeared in order. Callie and Tim had apparently been successful, he saw, for they had each returned with full plastic bags over their shoulders. Tim carried two of them.

How long had they been out in the woods together? Al and Lisa had finished preparing the snares almost twenty minutes earlier, and then Al sent her back downstairs to check on Helen. Were Tim and Callie gone long enough to form a relationship? Long enough for Tim to impress her with his charm?

All four snares were now set. Each cable ran up the side of the building and across the room to the opposite wall. The first cable was tied to the shelf full of computer hardware and the other three were looped around large chunks of loose concrete. All four counterweights were ready to be shoved over the side, where they would fall straight into the river.

All four snares were also rigged to fail.

Down below, Tim dropped one bag at the base of the building and climbed awkwardly up the wall with the other. Al put his shirt back on. Even though he was in decent shape, he was nowhere near as lean as Tim.

"How did it go?" Al asked as Tim pulled himself onto the second floor.

"There was a pack of small dinosaurs. They were kinda like turkeys, but with more attitude. We have a dead one in one of the bags."

Al nodded. If scavenger dinosaurs had moved in, that meant the Tyrannosaurus was long gone. With any luck, they would never see it again.

Tim looked at the four cables that ran across the building. "How about here? Are things in good shape? We don't have much time."

"See for yourself," Al invited. He felt the hair on the back of his neck stand on end as Tim inspected the wires.

Each cable had been cut. Once Lisa climbed down, Al had sawed halfway through all four of the heavy wires. He had watched the edge of the woods as he worked, terrified that Tim and Callie would return and catch him in the act. He had finished just in time. As they approached, he had been adjusting the final knot to hide the cut on the back side of the anchor object. His sabotage could only be seen from the side of the building that faced out over the water.

If by some slim chance the tyrannosaur did return, Al was not about to stand there and watch their plan succeed.

Tim checked the knot on the closest wire, making sure it was tied securely. He leaned over the side of the building. "It looks good," he said after a brief glance. "I hope it works."

"It has to work, man."

Tim nodded and climbed down to get a second bag of bait. Al wondered if Tim had seen the scoring on the cable when he leaned over. He resisted the urge to run to it and check to see if anything was visible.

As Tim came back up, he extended the trash bag to Al. *One quick shove,* Al thought. He could easily push Tim off and tell the others that he had slipped. *No.* The fall wasn't high enough. The soft mud below might prevent him from even breaking a bone. Al took the bag with one hand and helped Tim up with the other.

The contents shifted and he realized with revulsion that the bag was moving. He threw it down on the floor.

With a chuckle, Tim reached in and pulled out a giant tick, its body distended with blood. "We gathered up a bunch of these little guys. Some were still feeding on the carcass, but most were beginning to crawl away." He dropped the tick and impaled it behind the head with a short spear of rebar. The tick's legs clacked desperately at the floor.

"We got at least two dozen of them," he explained. Tim held it up like a giant marshmallow on a stick.

"Do you really think the rex will be attracted by that?"

Tim leaned over the side of the building. "No, not the tick itself. Watch this." He held the impaled parasite against the outer wall, directly above the first snare. With his free hand, he used the back side of the shovel to smash the tick against the concrete. A pint of blood spurted out onto the side of the building. Thick black clots rolled down the wall. Tim winced. "If that smell doesn't attract him over here, nothing will."

A second tick had escaped the bag and crawled toward Al. He took the rebar and speared it, wincing at the smell of salty rust. Al held the dying bloodsucker over the side of the building for Tim to smash.

III

DAY OF THE DINOSAUR

FIFTY-SIX

The tyrannosaur had fed generously on the Triceratops, eating most of the nutrient-rich organs as well as several hundred pounds of high-protein muscle. A few gallons of blood would not attract it to the café this evening, nor would any pot-banging or clanging.

What attracted it to the café was the river itself.

After eating William at the top of the cliff, the tyrannosaur wandered in a wide circle, marking its territory in several spots, until finally it turned back toward the river, where it could quench its thirst. It would drink its fill and then return to the Triceratops carcass to protect what remained of its kill.

When the tyrannosaur arrived at the clearing and saw the strange object still sitting on the edge of the river, it paused. It felt no hunger, but the instinct to make an ambush kill stopped it just out of sight in the trees.

Buddy began to bark inside the café.

The smell of fresh blood, the noise of the dog, and the sight of the small, strange creatures moving around on top of the structure triggered the tyrannosaur's killing instinct. Any kills, especially easy ones, helped to reinforce ownership of its territory. Twice today, the small, strange creatures had proven to be easy kills.

- - - - -

On the open second floor, Tim reached into the bag and stabbed another tick.

Al said, "Somebody should shut that dog up." He smashed his own tick against the wall below and returned to the bag.

"Let him bark," Tim said. "In fact, we should tell the ladies to go ahead and start beating on the pots and pans now. We don't have much time." As Tim leaned over the wall to smash the next tick, the tyrannosaur charged from the woods. Tim noticed it right away, but the dinosaur covered half the distance to the building before he could pull himself up from the edge of the wall.

Tim tried to dodge out of the way, but stumbled backwards over a pile of ceiling tiles. "Shit!" The dinosaur snapped at the wall. It thrust its muzzle up, sniffing and eyeing him. Tim scrambled to his feet. He swung the rebar to fling away the tick and then made a stabbing motion at the tyrannosaur's nose. It struck like a cobra, snapping its teeth together inches from Tim's hand. His heart skipped. *Do not try that again*. He dropped the rebar and backed away.

Callie shouted from below, "*Tim!* Its foot is in the snare!"

He called out over the edge of the building. "Which one? Which snare?"

"The second one back from the sidewalk!"

Tim scrambled across the room to the second block of concrete and gave it a shove. It teetered and dropped, almost taking Tim with it. He pin-wheeled his arms to keep from falling over the edge along with it.

- - - - -

The falling block lurched to a stop and hung in the air. To Al's dismay, the cable did not break. The copper wire was too strong. He hadn't cut through enough of it.

Al moved to the corner and leaned over the wall to look down at the tyrannosaur. The snare looped tightly around the dinosaur's right leg, just below the calf. Amazingly, their trap was working. However, the concrete hanging off the opposite side of the building did not weigh enough to lift the dinosaur's foot.

"It's caught," Al called out. "But it doesn't seem to give a shit."

The tyrannosaur sidestepped in Al's direction. Tim shouted out, "Is it close to the next one?"

"Yeah, it's right on it," Al moved quickly away from the edge.

Tim shoved the next chunk of rubble over the side.

This concrete block fell, pulled the rope tight, and snapped free as the cable broke right where Al had scored it. They heard a solid splash as the rubble landed in the river below. Al smiled, in spite of himself.

"What the hell happened?" Tim shouted across the building.

Al gave an exaggerated shrug.

- - - - -

The first cable, still holding the tyrannosaur's leg, moved across the room as the dinosaur walked beside the building. Tim ducked as bits of debris snapped loose and bulleted off in all directions.

The beast finally noticed the snare around its foot. It lifted its leg and wiggled it in the air.

"That's right, you bastard! We got you!" Tim shouted.

As if in response, the dinosaur kicked sharply down and back. The block of concrete at the other end of the line rocketed up the outside wall and crashed into the room, shattering free from the cable that held it.

Released from its tether, the tyrannosaur lifted its leg again. It reached halfway up the building and dug in. Grasping with the massive claws on its toes, it pulled down a section of wall as easily as a child stepping on the edge of a sandcastle. Concrete dust rose like smoke. Screams came from the café below.

"This isn't working," Tim hissed.

Al glared. "Are you fucking surprised?"

The building shuddered from another attack and shifted a few inches toward the river.

It's right there, Tim thought. The time device was only a few feet away from them, inside the creature.

The tyrannosaur noticed Tim again, raising its head to peer onto the second floor. Its nostrils flared. A trash bag full of ticks sat just a few feet from the tip of the dinosaur's nose.

What the hell am I supposed to do now? Tim thought. He had been foolish to think they could catch, much less kill, such an enormous creature. Their only source of shelter was about to be demolished. It was growing dark. How far could they flee into the woods in the dark? And what about Helen? Tim reached for the bag of ticks. Maybe he could throw it over the side and buy them a few minutes.

Before he had a chance, the tyrannosaur lifted its chin and brought it down on the edge of the building. A larger section of the wall collapsed, taking down the floor around it.

Almost playfully, the dinosaur raised its foot again, grasping the edge of the hole it had created. It pulled outward. The floor under Tim bent downward, no longer supported by anything. He grasped fruitlessly for something to hold onto as he slid into the coffee shop. A wooden table broke his fall and collapsed under his weight. Dust and darkness filled the room.

FIFTY-SEVEN

Despite herself, Lisa screamed as Tim fell through the ceiling. She stood with Callie and Helen in the back, next to the counter. "What's happening? Where is Al?"

"Still up there, I think."

"What's the Tyrannosaurus doing? Did you snare it?"

"The snare is worthless."

"Well what are we going to do?"

"I don't know," Tim shouted.

Lisa looked at the new opening on the side of the room. The wall of bookshelves was gone. The snout of the tyrannosaur appeared in the hole, sniffing. It backed out, rooted around in the rubble below, and came up with the bag of ticks. It crunched and blood poured from between its teeth.

The shovel lay on the floor just below the missing wall. Tim darted forward, grabbed it, and backed away quickly. The dinosaur's snout reappeared, its chin soaked with blood. Tim held the shovel up like a softball bat. He took a lunging step forward and swung for the fences.

The edge of the shovel blade caught the tyrannosaur's face, slicing the skin just above its nostril. The beast rumbled and withdrew.

Al lowered himself down through a newly-formed hole in the ceiling. He landed on the pastry counter, cracking the glass in a spider-web pattern. "I told you this was a bad idea." He jumped down off the counter.

Lisa gave Callie a long hard look. Then she moved to wrap her arms around Al. "You were right. You were right all along." Her voice hitched as she spoke.

"You're goddamn right I was." He squeezed her tightly. "It's going to be ok, though. Just stay close." Lisa nodded.

Holding the shovel before him, Tim turned. "Al, I need your help here!"

"Forget it." Al looked at the women. "Any second now and that thing will be inside. We have to get out of here."

Lisa nodded. "Whatever you say. Lead the way, Al. I'll do whatever you say."

Al pulled her across the room.

Tim's mouth hung open in disbelief. "Al? Lisa? What are you doing?"

The couple moved behind Tim, near the opening over the river that Lisa had fallen through almost fifteen hours earlier.

The tyrannosaur leaned into the building again. Its face filled the side of the room and it sniffed greedily.

Tim took another swing with the shovel, hitting the gash on the dinosaur's nose. "I'm hurting it, guys."

Al cheered him on. "Good job! You've almost got it!"

Lisa pulled at Al's arm, getting his attention. She looked up at his face, eyes wide. "You'll keep me safe if I stay here with you, right?"

He looked down at her, his face flush. "Yes."

"I want that. Keep me safe and I will give you everything." She waited a beat and then smiled. "I want that too. Don't you?"

Al inhaled deeply. "You have no idea."

The tyrannosaur backed out. The pile of collapsed rubble from upstairs blocked it from entering the café. It dug methodically at the debris with its foot. Another chunk fell from what was left of the ceiling. Al and Lisa flinched, moving closer to the river.

"Tim, what are we going to do?" Callie called out. She held Buddy tightly as the dog barked itself hoarse. Helen cowered next to her.

Tim lifted the shovel, ready to take another swing as soon as the snout reappeared.

Tick. The sound came from nowhere and everywhere at the same time.

Lisa put her hands on Al's arms. "I saw you earlier," she said, still giving him the puppy-dog eyes. She had to be sure. Despite what Callie had told her and despite what she had seen with her own eyes, she had to be one hundred percent sure.

He looked at her, clearly confused. "What are you talking about? What did you see?"

Tick Tick

"I saw you cut the lines, on the backside, where Tim wouldn't find them." She said this simply and pleasantly, as if they were discussing the weather.

TICK TICK TICK

Al looked confused. "You were downstairs... How did you..?"

It was a question, not a denial. It was the confirmation Lisa needed. "I was taking a piss on the sidewalk. I looked up and I saw you do it, you sick son-of-a-bitch."

She gave him a hard shove high in the chest and Al Stevens fell backwards, arms flailing, into the river.

Tim grabbed Lisa and shoved her back behind the counter. He held the shovel up before him, ready to fend off the mouth of the monster.

TICK TICK TICK TICK TICK TICK

The tyrannosaur, having cleared away enough of the rubble, pushed into the café. The front sidewalk broke off from the building and dropped into the river.

- - - - -

Al surfaced a few feet out and shouted, *"You cunt!"* The river swept him along. The first stars appeared overhead, but there was still enough light to see the tyrannosaur stand up inside the building. Two of the remaining walls fell away completely.

TICK TICK TICK TICK TICK TICK TICK TICK TICK TICK

A loud pop filled the clearing as most of the building disappeared.

Because the time machine was not in the exact same position it had been in fifteen hours earlier, the swap was imperfect. A hollowed shell of bricks and mortar remained behind, and new portions of the building arrived, swapped out from the future. They seemed to float in the air for a moment, but then collapsed into a pile of worthless blocks as the current pushed Al Stevens around the bend in the river.

FIFTY-EIGHT

At 8:05 A.M., Mountain Daylight Time, Carmen Madera walked her dog Buddy toward The Daily Edition Café at the edge of downtown Denver. Mixed into the normal cacophony of morning noises, she noticed a ticking sound that increased steadily in frequency. Buddy seemed to notice too. He pulled at his leash with a growl.

A young man walking ahead of her glanced back at the dog. "What the shit, lady? Control your pooch!"

The trainer had told her to stop walking when Buddy pulled. The trick, he explained, was to only move forward when the dog walked politely. It wasn't easy. Carmen did not like to slow down. She liked to get where she was going. Still, she made herself stop and stood her ground, her arm outstretched. As the ticking grew louder, Buddy dug in and pulled harder. Carmen reached out with her free hand to hold onto a parking meter.

The arm holding the leash disappeared just below the elbow, as did Buddy, the young man, and a large, hollowed-out portion of the building next to her. The ground was replaced with a mixture of mud and water, which sloshed out onto the street. Lights flickered and went out on the high ceiling of the second-floor room above. The café, like her hand, was gone.

Carmen held her arm out in front of her. Blood squirted from the end like water from a hose. She realized that her hand was gone just as the pain from two thousand severed nerves reached her brain.

Carmen collapsed to the sidewalk.

- - - - -

The time device was programmed to return at exactly the same moment it departed. However, over the course of sixty-seven million years, a tiny error crept in. For a little more than forty-one seconds, the space previously occupied by the café sat empty, save for the mud and water that had taken its place. A few loose cinder blocks fell from the walls above, but the top eight floors remained intact, supported by the copy center and mortgage company that also occupied the ground floor.

After forty-one seconds, most of the café returned. The football, inside the tyrannosaur's stomach, was offset some thirty feet off from its original position within the lab. A slightly different chunk of building was displaced, and the chunk that returned from the late Cretaceous did not align with the space it had originally occupied. As a result, what was left of the café fell apart in a pile of rubble, with a twenty-five foot tall dinosaur standing in the middle of it.

Breathing became difficult for tyrannosaur. It inhaled and exhaled rapidly to compensate. The mile-high modern air contained half as much oxygen as the air in the late Cretaceous. It turned and poked its head out of the crumbling building and looked around the city streets of downtown Denver. In every direction, it saw blocky canyon walls and shiny, boxy shapes that stank and rumbled like thunder.

Cars screeched to a halt. Pedestrians froze in their tracks.

- - - - -

Tim, lying in the back of the café, rose and looked out the front of the building. The mudflats had been replaced by city streets. Dusk had turned to daylight. He saw metal, concrete and glass in every direction. "Yes! We did it!"

His mobile device buzzed in his pocket. *That's Julie, wondering where I am.* He began to reach for his phone. Then he saw her across the street.

Julie Moss stood at the corner, her blond hair spilling onto the shoulders of a bright blue pea coat. She was every bit as radiant as he remembered. Despite everything, he had somehow made it home and *there she was.* A euphoric smile grew on his face. He realized he was just as excited to be home as he was to learn that she had actually shown up for their date.

Tim grabbed the counter and pulled himself forward, ignoring the shouts from Callie and Lisa behind him. His phone continued to buzz, but he ignored that as well.

- - - - -

The tyrannosaur knew it had to find better air. It also knew that when things went bad, the best reaction was an aggressive reaction. It stepped into the intersection, snapping power lines with its neck. The stinging bite of electricity enraged it further.

Julie stared in disbelief as the dinosaur emerged from the hollowed-out café where she was supposed to meet her new boyfriend. In the back of her mind, she wondered if it was too early to think of him as a boyfriend. Maybe not. She had spent the last three days talking about him with the other flight attendants, after all.

The tyrannosaur stepped forward and Julie started to think that Tim MacGregor really should not be the most immediate focus of her attention. Of course, that was silly because there could not possibly be a dinosaur standing in front of her. She tried pulling her hands out of her coat pockets. The material bunched up each time she pulled, causing her to flap her elbows like a bird. She wondered why she even cared about her arms. Why wasn't she simply running? She looked toward the café, or rather, to the spot where the café had been two minutes earlier. It looked like a bomb had gone off. But that couldn't be true either, because she saw Tim emerge from the side of the building. *Thank God.* He would explain what was going on. After her coffee. What she really wanted right now was an espresso. Maybe a triple.

The tyrannosaur bent down and snapped Julie up in its jaws, destroying her between its teeth. It shook its head violently. Pieces flew from the sides of its mouth as it tore the young woman apart.

Then it started up the street.

FIFTY-NINE

Tim fell to his knees, unable to breath. His lungs constricted. He was trying to inhale and scream at the same time. His mouth hung open and his vision blurred with tears.

He stared at a small clump in the middle of the street. A clump that had fallen from the tyrannosaur's mouth as it shook Julie apart. A piece of her. He had brought this monster here. His breath hitched and he vomited into the gutter. It was his fault. He wanted to go back. He would go back and stay in the past forever if he could. He would get the time machine and use it to –

"The fail-safe."

Tim struggled to his feet, dizzy. A hand grabbed his shoulder. "Tim, the fail-safe!" It sounded like Callie.

His breath returned in quick hitches. The fail-safe was inside the goddamn dinosaur, walking down the street.

Callie thrust the shovel into his hand. "*Tim, go get the fail-safe now!*" Callie sounded commanding. She sounded like Hank.

Tim started moving. Across the street, an oversized white pickup truck sat half on the curb. It was exactly the sort of truck driven by the crews at Tim's construction jobs. He had owned one himself for a few years. The driver of the pickup craned his head out the window, watching the tyrannosaur stomp away. Tim ran to the truck, forcing himself to not look at the clumps he passed in the street.

The driver was more than six feet tall and covered with tattoos. The ends of his mustache drooped below his chin.

Tim ran toward the pickup, a Dodge Ram, holding the shovel low to his side. He ripped open the door and shouted, "*Get out of that truck!*" Hank would have been proud.

Two gashes ran down Tim's face. His clothes were filthy and ragged. Dark blood covered the shovel in his hands. The driver scrambled across the cab and flung himself out the passenger door.

Tim tossed the shovel onto the seat next to him, slammed the truck into gear and fishtailed around a hundred and eighty degrees. He ignored the flapping passenger door and scanned the dashboard for a clock. 8:08 A.M.

How much time did he have? The time machine would only take him back twenty minutes. If he didn't use the fail-safe before twenty minutes passed it would not do any good. It would take him back to a point in time *after* the café returned. After the tyrannosaur killed Julie.

In order to stop all of this from happening, he had to get the device, trigger it, and get everyone out of the café before they went back in time. He really only had seventeen or eighteen minutes. Two or three had already gone by.

Tim swerved to avoid a pedestrian coming out of an alley and accelerated after the dinosaur.

- - - - -

On a parallel street to the north, Lieutenant Harold Daniels of the Denver Police Department received a report of an explosion at the corner of Chestnut and 15th. Lieutenant Daniels, a mounted patrol officer, guided his chestnut mare Hadley away from the 16th Street pedestrian mall to investigate. He expected to find a blown transformer or possibly a backfiring car.

As he approached 15th Street, still several blocks east of Chestnut, the forty-five foot long tyrannosaur passed by. Lieutenant Daniels saw the blood-stained teeth of the beast and determined immediately that the creature was both real and dangerous. He dug into Hadley's flanks. The brown horse galloped forward alongside the dinosaur.

In one continuous move, Lieutenant Daniels unclipped his holster, drew his pistol, flipped off the safety, and fired ten rounds into the tyrannosaur's left shoulder, close to where he thought its heart should be. Hadley continued to gallop, neither slowing nor swerving. She had trained for many hours with Daniels, including live fire exercises, and she performed masterfully.

The bullet stings annoyed the beast. It lurched to a stop, clenching into the asphalt with its claws. It twisted around and roared, mouth wide. None of Hadley's training had included anything like this. She reared up and whinnied, but Lieutenant Daniels held on. He decided to get clear and call for backup. Hadley's front hooves hit the ground and Daniels spurred her like a jockey, hunkering down as low in the saddle as he could get. The tyrannosaur took one step and grabbed the horse and rider between its jaws. It bit down until the neck and flanks of the horse fell away to either side. It swallowed the rest, including most of Lieutenant Daniels.

The tyrannosaur ignored the pieces that dropped and pressed forward. Its heart pumped with adrenaline as it looked left and right, trying to find a way out of this foul, rocky ravine it had somehow ended up in.

Suddenly it felt a new stinging across its chest. It had wandered into the power lines over one of Denver's light rail train tracks. The stinging persisted and the dinosaur backed away, enraged. The street behind it was nearly empty, so it started back in that direction.

- - - - -

Tim drove straight toward it, only a block away now. He pulled on his seatbelt. He would slam into it, breaking both of its legs. Tim floored the gas pedal.

Ahead, the tyrannosaur entered an intersection and looked down the side street, where it saw something friendly and familiar in this world of concrete and asphalt. It spotted the Cherry Creek greenway, a canal-like chasm which ran along the edge of the downtown district. A small creek bordered by grass on both sides ran down the middle, one story below street level. The greenway was a lush oasis in a desert of concrete and asphalt.

The tyrannosaur turned the corner seconds before the white pickup reached it.

Tim screeched through the intersection, locking the brakes and frantically spinning the steering wheel to turn the truck around. He looped back and started down the street in time to see the tyrannosaur stop at the edge of the canal. It roared and stepped down onto the grass below.

Tim sped up again. The dinosaur's head stuck up out of the canal at the end of the block. He grabbed the shovel and crammed its blade deep into the crevice at the back of the passenger seat. Again, he pressed the gas pedal against the floor. The eight-cylinder engine roared forward.

The truck crashed through a short iron railing at the edge of the greenway, ripping it from its concrete footings. The impact barely slowed the vehicle, but it was enough to trigger the airbags. White balloons exploded in Tim's face, blocking his view and saving his life.

The Dodge Ram sailed through the air and collided with the tyrannosaur's shoulder. Five thousand pounds of Detroit steel shoved the animal into the opposite wall of the canal.

The tyrannosaur's body crumpled under the impact. Eleven ribs broke clean through. Three of them punctured one of the dinosaur's lungs, causing it to collapse. The truck held in the air for an instant before falling backwards. Its rear wheels splashed in the creek. Tim waved the white nylon airbag free from his face and tugged the shovel out of the passenger seat. As he jumped down from the cab, his right shin screamed at him. His tibia had sustained a hairline fracture in the crash.

Tim hurried around the front of the vehicle as the stunned dinosaur started to regain its senses. Its head lay before him, one eye looking up. Fresh blood oozed from the gash in its nose where Tim had struck it inside the café, sixty-seven million years earlier.

The tyrannosaur pulled a leg underneath its body and shifted its weight. The dinosaur grunted and pulled the second leg under its body. The truck rolled a few feet away as the tyrannosaur lifted its torso from the ground.

It now focused on Tim. Its head, still low, ratcheted back. The thick muscles in its neck coiled. One quick snap would eliminate this annoyance that had just brought so much pain. It opened its mouth and inhaled.

Tim lifted the shovel overhead and used all of his strength to plunge it directly into the dinosaur's left eye. The blade split the three-inch eyeball like a water balloon. He pushed deeper and felt the snap of the thin bones surrounding the eye socket.

The head of the shovel disappeared into the dinosaur's skull. The tip of the steel blade penetrated the tyrannosaur's brain. The beast reared up, pulling Tim three feet off the ground, and then collapsed in a heap.

Still holding on to the shovel, Tim put one foot on the dinosaur's cheek, just below the eye socket. Time was running out. He yanked the shovel free, splattering his shirt with white bits of sclera from the eyeball. He turned to the monster's belly.

A bicyclist approached on one of the pathways running alongside the creek. "What the hell? Do you need some-?"

"Get away from here!" Tim growled. He didn't have time to explain and he sure didn't want anyone close by.

He heaved the shovel into the dinosaur's underbelly. It felt like striking solid rock. The blade bounced off of its thick hide. "*Shit!*" He didn't have time for this.

Tim reared back, ready to try another strike, and noticed scabbed blood around one of the holes created by the Triceratops' horn in the battle by the cliff. He shifted his stance and rammed the shovel at the hole. It penetrated the wound, widening it. After four more heaves, Tim knew he had found the stomach. Blood, mixed with an oily yellow fluid, burst from the opening and onto his hands. The acrid stench of stomach acid, bile, and decomposition poured over him as he dug into the dinosaur's gut. Every passing second felt like an eternity.

Foul, partly digested hunks of meat spilled out onto the bike path. Tim tried to ignore them, to avoid noticing which were Triceratops and which were human. *Dear God, don't let me find Julie.* He rammed the shovel deep into the body cavity, testing different areas. Finally, the head of the shovel clanged against something metal.

"Ah Ha HA!" Tim shouted. He threw down the shovel and reached into the hole with both hands, covering himself in gore. Out came the football. Its light blinked on and off through a sheen of blood.

SIXTY

Cradling the blood-slicked time device in two hands, Tim spun around. He would run to the café and trigger the fail-safe. He would clear everyone out. He would stop it all from happening.

No, wait.

This was the perfect spot. If he triggered the device near the café, it might swap out someone standing nearby. It might cut someone in half. The path on the Cherry Creek greenway was deserted, though Tim noticed a crowd beginning to gather on the street above.

He dropped to his knees and rolled the device over in front of him. The LED screen had gone blank. Tim lifted the plastic lid from the fail-safe button.

"Please work."

He slid his finger under the lid and pressed the button. The ticking began immediately.

Tick. Tick-Tick. Tick-Tick-Tick-Tick TICK TICK TICK TICKTICKTICK-

The dead tyrannosaur and the Dodge pickup disappeared, but everything else looked the same. Of course. He had only traveled back in time twenty minutes. He glanced around for body parts, to see if anyone had been split in half at the edge. Thankfully, there were none.

He looked down at the device. The LED now read 0:00:09:54 and counting down. *That answers that.* The device had gone twenty minutes into the past and would stay here for half that time. Then it would automatically jump back forward, returning to the moment he had just left.

The timer was now down to 0:00:09:42. He had less than ten minutes to get back to the café.

Tim ran up the pedestrian ramp. *Next question- How long before the café disappears?* He held the football tightly as he ran, each step sending pain up his leg. Had he been fast enough? He tried to remember how much time had passed since the café had returned. The chase to the creek had taken at least five minutes. Maybe more. Probably more. It had felt like an eternity digging the stupid machine out of the tyrannosaur's guts.

Tim reached street level and ran down the sidewalk, drenched in blood and cradling the metallic ball in his arms. The morning crowd, that slow-moving sea of suits, parted around him.

Rounding the corner, he saw the café, two blocks away and still intact. It had not gone back yet. He still had a chance to save everyone. Tim sped up, ignoring the pain in his leg.

A woman approached the café from the opposite direction, pulled along by a brown mutt that looked familiar. Morgan Jackson walked a few steps ahead of her.

Buddy! Morgan! Recognition, followed by realization. "*NO!*"

Tim was still a block and a half away when the café disappeared. The pop echoed down the street. Cinderblocks fell from the walls above. Prehistoric river water splashed onto the street. The woman on the sidewalk, Buddy's owner, held up her handless arm.

He was too late. *William. Hank. Patricia. Beth. Morgan.* They were all on their way to their deaths, and there was nothing he could do to save them.

In front of the empty cavity where the café had been, the woman collapsed to the ground, clutching her arm. Tim stood and watched, wondering what he should do now. Blood from the tyrannosaur slowly dripped from his clothes onto the sidewalk. There was no way to prevent the trip. The café would return with the tyrannosaur in any moment.

A woman in a blue coat passed by. She made a wide circle around him and headed in the direction of the café.

SIXTY-ONE

"JULIE!"

She turned at her name, but her smile quickly disappeared. "Oh my God, Tim? What happened to you?"

Before he could answer, a loud pop came from the café down the street. They both turned and saw dust rolling away from the building. Tim realized he was witnessing the moment he had lived through just over twenty minutes ago. The café had returned with Tim, Callie, Lisa, and Helen inside. And the tyrannosaur.

Tim's heart jack-hammered in his chest. The tyrannosaur would come out any second now. He grabbed Julie and pulled her into an alley. He laughed hysterically. "You're alive, you're alive, you're alive!" He backed into a wall behind a dumpster.

"What -"

"I love you," he told her. He put the time device down on the ground and kissed her on the lips. She gave him a half-smile, half-grimace.

"Please tell me what's going on."

A crash came from outside the alley and they heard screeching cars.

"Don't worry, you're safe. You're safe! Just *stay down*. Take cover." He started to kiss her again but he froze, his mind racing.

I'm back. A second Tim had just arrived in the café. He knew he needed to let the football jump him forward to a world where there was only one of him, but he felt a strange urge to go into the café and tell the other Tim what he had done. He wanted to march Julie over and show him that she was alive. He had saved her life.

Any second now, the T-rex would come out of the café and *it would not kill her.*

Tim stopped breathing. What will happen to Julie then?

The Tim in the café would have no reason to chase down the dinosaur. No reason to go back in time and save her. If he didn't go back in time to save her, how would she end up in the alley? Tim squeezed his eyes shut. Time travel didn't make any fucking sense. It felt like an endless loop.

A roar came from the street outside the alley.

"Tim, what was that?"

He ignored her. *If the Tim in the café doesn't see her die, he won't come back and save her. He won't be here to pull her into the alley. I won't be here to pull her into the alley.* He had to decide quickly. The football would go off soon. The timer showed 0:00:05:52.

Tim pulled out his phone. He would call himself. He would call the Tim that just returned in the café and tell him what to do. No matter what, Julie needed to be pulled into the alley. It dawned on him that he would be calling with the exact same phone, with the exact same number. "I can't use this."

He looked up at Julie, knowing how crazy he must seem. "Give me your phone. Call my number and hand it to me. Hurry!"

Julie fished her phone out of her pocket, only snagging her hand once this time. She pressed a few buttons.

Oh no. He was holding his phone in his hand. Which phone would she connect to? Tim dropped his phone on the asphalt and smashed it with the football.

Julie looked at him with disbelief. He grabbed her phone and held it to his ear. There was no answer, only an electronic ringing every few seconds. Just as he started to hang up and try again, he finally heard a voice, *his voice,* from inside the café. "Hello? Julie, you are not going to believe what-"

"Tim, this is you, from the future."

"Huh?"

Tim froze as the tyrannosaur passed by the alley.

"What the hell was that?" Julie asked.

He ignored her and continued into the phone, giving instructions to the Tim who had just arrived but had *not* seen Julie get eaten. "Take the shovel and grab the white truck across the street. Drive it into the T-rex and kill it. Cut the football out of it and use the fail-safe. Go back and find Julie. Keep her away from the café or *she will die!* Then call yourself."

"Is this some kind of -"

Tim screamed into the phone: *"Shut up and do what I said or JULIE WILL DIE!"* He heard a click on the other end. "Please," he whispered.

Julie backed away. "I don't like this. It isn't funny. Why did you say I would die?"

"You won't," he said, hoping it was true. He handed her the phone and kissed her on the forehead. "Please just stay here, out of sight, until this is all over."

She grabbed for his arm, but he pulled free. "I've got to get out of here. I don't have much time."

He picked up the device. 0:00:03:25 flashed on the display. He looked at her one last time. She was alive. Would she still be alive when he jumped forward? He wanted to stay here, but he could not. There was another Tim here.

He took a deep breath and stepped out of the alley. A white pickup truck swerved to avoid him. "Yes!" he shouted. "Go get him!"

He ran straight toward the creek as the truck raced in the other direction, pursuing the dinosaur. All the way, he silently urged the counter in his hands to slow down, to give him enough time to get back. His leg screamed at him as he ran.

He reached the pedestrian ramp. The greenway at the bottom was empty. Tim ran down the gentle slope. At the bottom of the ramp he looked around helplessly, trying to figure out exactly where to stand when the device went off again.

0:00:00:23

A roar came from above and the tyrannosaur stepped down directly in front of him.

Oh shit. Tim froze, silently urging the counter to speed up.

The tyrannosaur took two steps forward and opened wide. There was nowhere to go and no way Tim could outrun it.

The white truck barreled through the guardrail and slammed into the tyrannosaur. It knocked the giant off of its feet. Tim stumbled down the bike path, trying to get far enough away before the device went off.

A woman pushing a jog stroller ran up in his direction, craning her neck to look at the dinosaur ahead. Tim shouted at the top of his lungs, *"Stay away! Get away from here!"* She turned around.

The ticking sound began again. Tim sat down and watched as the other Tim climbed out of the truck and stabbed the tyrannosaur in the eye. The final few seconds flashed by on the timer. The ticking stopped with a pop and Tim was transported ten minutes forward.

Upstream, the gutted carcass of the tyrannosaur lay next to the truck.

SIXTY-TWO

Where is Julie? What happened to her? He concentrated and the memories flashed in his mind. He saw her die. He saw her ripped to pieces. It had happened. He still remembered it.

A piercing pain ran through his head. Tim collapsed, lying back on the grass. The muscles around his fractured leg trembled. He had seen her die, but the memory felt foggy, dreamlike. There was something else. He began to remember something different. He remembered standing up in the café as the tyrannosaur stepped out of the building. Lisa put her hand on his shoulder. Callie had been there too, helping Helen, who had received yet another cut that would not stop bleeding.

They had all been together: Tim, Callie, Helen, and Lisa, soon to be dubbed "The Dinosaur Four" by the press. Buddy made five, of course, but they didn't count the dog. They all climbed out into the bright morning sunlight and watched the tyrannosaur lumber away. Buddy barked incessantly, but the dinosaur ignored him. Across the street, a man gaped from a white pickup truck on the sidewalk. In this memory, the dinosaur did not eat Julie.

Tim remembered feeling a vibration in his pocket. Had he answered the phone? He remembered the words. *"Take the shovel and grab the white truck."* Had he spoken those words or had he heard them? He wasn't sure. He remembered both. Thinking about it sent the sharp pain through his head again. He remembered taking the man's truck and not really understanding why.

Tim lay next to the slow burble of Cherry Creek, feeling cold and clammy. Sirens grew close. Above, at street level, an excited crowd gathered along the edge of the canal. Dozens of phones were out, snapping pictures of the dead dinosaur, the smoking pickup truck, and Tim MacGregor, exhausted and covered with gore.

He closed his eyes and tried again to sort out the images in his head. All of his memories from the prehistoric era were the same. Ten people had gone back, but only four had returned. The fuzziness began when the tyrannosaur lumbered out of the café. Two memories overlapped, one full of anger and despair and another full of confusion. Had the timelines actually merged? Both memories included him killing the tyrannosaur and cutting the device out of its gut. Was the football still here, lying beside him on the grass?

He opened his eyes to look for it, but before he could turn his head, he saw three familiar faces up in the crowd looking down at him. Helen had her arm around Lisa for support. Callie stood apart from them both. They had followed the commotion to find him.

Tears ran down Callie's cheeks. Tim had not been able to stop the café from going back in time. He had been unable to save Hank, Beth, and the others. Only the four of them had survived. But what about Julie?

A blue blur came running down the sidewalk. Tim's face broke into a wide smile as Julie knelt beside him. The blue pea coat. The blond hair resting on her shoulders. And the most beautiful eyes in the world.

ACKNOWLEDGEMENTS

My heartfelt thanks go out to those who read early drafts and provided feedback. You helped make this book better. Thank you especially Jacob Beucler, Cathy Bowen, Melissa Dixon, Poornima Farrar, Tara Giovenco, Ben Gomez, Ned Harding, Amy Holland, Jordan Itkowitz, Reed Knight, Steve Love, Sara Moeller, Michael Starks, Brandie Stephens, Jacob Stephens, Nate Stormzand, and the Louisville Writers Workshop.

I could not have written this book without the support of my wife Erin, my daughters Shannon and Sydney, my parents Bill and Lida, and my brothers Christopher and David. I love you all.

Thanks to Rachel Weaver for editorial services, David Kang for the cover art, and Michael Starks for design and marketing support.

Finally, I want to thank you the reader for coming along on this ride. I hope you had as much fun as I did. If so, please take a moment to post a review and tell a friend.

Geoff Jones
Broomfield, Colorado
May 2014

ROBYN SISMAN

Special Relationship

Mandarin

A Mandarin Paperback
SPECIAL RELATIONSHIP

First published in Great Britain 1995
by William Heinemann Ltd
This edition published 1996
by Mandarin Paperbacks
an imprint of Reed International Books Ltd
Michelin House, 81 Fulham Road, London SW3 6RB
and Auckland, Melbourne, Singapore and Toronto

Reprinted 1996

The lyrics from 'I Feel Like I'm Fixin' to Die Rag'
by Joe McDonald are reprinted by kind permission
of the publishers, Alkatraz Korner Music Co.,
and by Chrysalis Music Ltd. Those from
'I Wanna Go Back To Dixie' (1953 © Tom Lehrer)
are reprinted by kind permission of Thomas A. Lehrer.

A CIP catalogue record for this title
is available from the British Library
ISBN 0 7493 2488 0

Printed and bound in Great Britain
by Cox & Wyman Ltd, Reading, Berkshire

Acknowledgements

My thanks go to Carole Blake and her supremely efficient literary agency, Blake Friedmann; to Caroline Upcher for prompting new lines of thoughts; to my mother for her moral support; and to the following for practical help and information: Sean Magee, George and Marjorie Misiewicz, Lucy Sisman and Mickey Spillane of Magdalen College.

I owe two special debts. One is to Douglas Hawes, for his heartening faith in my writing ability; he has had to wait a long time for any evidence. The other, and greatest, is to my husband, Adam Sisman. Without his encouragement, inspiration, practical support, and constant constructive criticism, this book would not have been started, and certainly never finished.

1992

PROLOGUE
It was twenty years ago today

It was dark outside. Jordan sat at the kitchen table, kicking the leg the way his mother always told him not to. But she wasn't home. He was alone in the house. The only sound was the scurry of wind in the cottonwood trees. Suddenly the porch door opened. A tall figure stood in the doorway, wearing a uniform. His face was shaded by his army cap, but Jordan knew, with miraculous certainty, that this was his father. Joy flooded through him. His father stepped into the room, his polished shoes eerily silent on the wooden floor. He started to walk towards Jordan, with a tread so slow and measured that it became menacing. The visor still hid his face. Jordan began to feel frightened. 'It's me, your son!' he wanted to say, but no sound came from his throat.

Then the man stretched out his hand, and Jordan shrank back in terror. His father was holding a live rattlesnake. Jordan tried to get down from the table, but he couldn't move. The snake came nearer, its flat head weaving, searching. Despite his fear, Jordan felt a desperate curiosity to see his father's face. One more step would bring it into the beam of light from the kitchen lamp.

3

Then Jordan would *know*. Jordan looked up, but under the army cap there was only blackness. He could see the cold glitter of the snake's eyes, inches from his own. The rattle of its tail grew faster, louder. Inside, Jordan was screaming, 'You can't do this! I'm going to be President of the United States!' His father stepped into the light –

Jordan woke with a shout of terror, his heart stampeding. A low buzzing came from an alarm clock by the bed. He slammed it quiet and sat up, taking stock of the bland hotel furnishings, the pile of yesterday's ransacked newspapers, his empty suit hanging like a shadow on the closet door. Pale sunlight seeped through blinds closed tight against the snooping lenses of the world's press.

'Jesus!' Jordan blew out a great gust of breath, and pushed back his sweat-soaked hair. He wasn't back in Indian Bluffs. He wasn't a small, frightened boy. This was Dallas, Texas. He was forty-six years old, and running for President.

Jordan got out of bed and swung his arms, easing the tension in his shoulders. It was months since he had had this nightmare. He knew what had triggered it. The call had come late last night – a voice out of his past, the voice of a girl he had once loved, who now threatened to ruin his career.

No, girl was wrong. Jordan shook his head in self-reprimand, though there was no one to see him as he sprawled into the hotel armchair. His wife had drilled him thoroughly in the vocabulary of political correctness; besides, 'girl' could no longer be an appropriate term for a forty-two-year-old woman with a grown-up son. But when he thought of her, as he had once done fiercely, passionately, a hundred times a day, and did even now, especially after one of the painfully sensual dreams which still haunted him, he always thought of her as a girl. Her responsiveness and vitality, the quick-changing flush and pallor of her skin, the bouncing energy of her

4

long legs, the abandonment with which she laughed and cried and made love – once, he remembered, all three at once – could surely, without offence, be called girlish.

If it had been anyone other than this particular girl he would by now have talked the matter over with Ginny – coolly, sensibly, point by point, as he discussed everything with his wife nowadays. He would have called an immediate damage-limitation meeting, no matter how late the hour or how tired they all were after months on the campaign trail. If it had been anyone other than this particular girl, he would have suspected a dirty tricks operation which made pinpricks of all the innuendoes and FBI ferretings that he had suffered, and survived, up to now.

But the hours had ticked by while Jordan dozed fitfully, letting his wife sleep on undisturbed in the bedroom next door. Even now, when the first electronic whines from the outer room of the suite that served as his temporary campaign office told him that some eager beaver was stoking the fax machine, Jordan sat calmly sipping his Mountain Valley spring water, remembering.

Bare willow trees, warm beer, bicycles swishing through rain, the peppery smell of the Lower Reading Room, gas fires that lit with a *whump* and ran out of money. He had never been so cold in his life. Or so lost. It was as if he had passed into a looking-glass world that turned all his values upside-down and set at naught the very talents that had brought him to Oxford in the first place. His manner was wrong, his jokes were wrong, his ideas were wrong.

Until he met Annie. She was the rightest thing that had ever happened to him.

This wasn't a trick, he was sure of it. He couldn't have mistaken her voice. But *why now*? In 1970 she had disappeared from his life with a thoroughness that a retiring spy might have envied, and eventually he learned to file her away in the mental drawer marked 'Oxford', an

5

era in his life which privately, despite the powerful allies he had picked up there, was also labelled 'failure'. How dare she re-enter his life now, of all times, demurely laying this ticking bomb at his feet?

When breakfast came he had no appetite for it; nor for the jubilant congratulations that accompanied the morning's newspapers which conceded, with varying degrees of enthusiasm, that Jordan Hope was indeed, against all the odds, in with a chance. He played his part successfully enough – he had always been good at that – but with secret anxiety hammering at his heart. As he got ready for his speech, the intoxicating headlines spread over his work-table mocked him. There were only six more days to go, and the whole damned circus was riding on his shoulders. Nobody knew how hard he had worked for this, how long he had planned. Not Shelby, who went way back to Miss Purvis's class in that funny old schoolhouse that had been turned into a museum. Not Rick, who had seen him at his best and his worst and had always kept his mouth shut. Not even Ginny. The thought of Ginny made him twist his fingers viciously in his hair and groan softly. She wanted this as much he did. She had to, after what she'd sacrificed.

Jordan could pinpoint the exact moment when the mixture of emotions that had raged within him as a boy – tenderness, hate, resentment, yearning, guilt, fear – had coalesced into an adamantine spike of pure ambition. He could remember in hallucinatory detail the brilliant green of the lawn, so different from the yellow scrub of his own back yard. The heavy scent of the roses – imagine having a whole garden just for roses! The dampness of his palm, which he had anxiously wiped on the thigh of his Boys' Nation regulation trousers. The immaculate little triangle of handkerchief that peeked out of the President's breast pocket. Above all, the way those candid, forgiving eyes had seemed to look into his heart and see nothing unworthy of that sunburst smile of approval, almost of

6

complicit acknowledgement. Jordan had truly felt as though the hand of God were pointing straight out of a cloud, like those pictures back in Bible class, in a shaft of light that burned into his soul. *This is my beloved son, in whom I am well pleased.*

For the team, it was just a publicity gimmick. Jordan was to be packaged as Kennedy reincarnated – young, energetic, idealistic, with a gorgeous wife. Only no bad stuff. No Marilyn Monroes, you hear? And please, no Lee Harvey Oswalds, Rick had drawled. But for Jordan that moment nearly thirty years ago when he and JFK had clasped hands was sacred. He had a mission to carry on where Kennedy had been stopped dead in his tracks just three months later – but in his own style, on behalf of his own generation.

Now he was so close it hurt. If the people would only give him a chance, he knew that he could do it. He understood their problems. Hell, he had been there himself. Poverty, racism, alcoholism, unemployment, corruption – they had been part of his everyday world from his earliest memories. They had been the spurs that drove him to ever more spectacular heights of achievement. Which was more than could be said for those carping media-snobs who portrayed him as some down-home boy getting a mite uppity. He would show them. There were no prizes for losers. Adlai Stevenson, Barry Goldwater, Michael Dukakis and all the other almost- Presidents – what had they been able to achieve without the ultimate mandate of real power? Jordan Hope, President of the United States of America. From Indian Bluffs, Illinois, to Washington, DC. From clapboard shack to White House. That was what he wanted. That was what he was going to get.

Jordan wasn't sure that he could manage this crisis alone. It would help if he could take somebody into his confidence – but who? Ginny was out. Shelby had always idolised Jordan in his 'good ol' boy' way, without a trace of envy; on the other hand, he had the subtlety of a jack-rabbit in the mating season. Besides, he would be shocked. Jordan swept his hands through his hair and shook his head like a swimmer. Rick was much more suited to the role of go-between. At Oxford his parties had been legendary, and his First a foregone conclusion. He cruised the political shadows like a shark masquerading as a dolphin. He had pledged his allegiance to Jordan's cause, and proved to be a public relations genius. But something made Jordan hesitate.

The intercom crackled. *Five minutes*, sang a cheerful voice.

Shit. For a moment Jordan tuned in to the buzz of activity coming from the outer room of his suite: phones, faxes, TVs, urgent voices shouting across each other. 'Who's got the schedule?' 'Milwaukee wants to know, can we confirm Thursday?' 'I'm saying no to Johnny Carson and the saxophone show, OK?' 'Two points ahead in, wait for it, *New Hampshire*!' They were a great team. He loved every one of them. He couldn't let them down.

Five minutes. For a scary second he couldn't even remember what town he was in. For months he'd been carrying a whole raft of speeches in his head. Detroit meant Japanese car imports and gun laws. Florida meant pensions and immigration. Kentucky was GATT, God and horses. What the heck was Dallas? Up until now he hadn't put a foot wrong. The hand of God was on him. Like Elijah, when he opened his mouth to speak the right words just poured out.

She must have used every ounce of ingenuity to get hold of him. Even his mother had trouble getting through. Letters were opened, faxes scanned. All conversations were taped, all messages filed, every call-back telephone number logged in the computer. As well as screening out the weirdos – there had already been over a hundred assassination threats – a record had to be kept of promises

8

made, funds pledged, deals done. It was also, he knew, the team's way of keeping tabs on him.

Time to go, Jordan.

Time. It was a rarity to get even five minutes alone. How was he going to slip his leash for several hours? What would it be like to see Annie again?

'We have nothing to fear except fear itself.' This had been Jordan's mantra since the day he had got his college scholarship, and it had served him well. He repeated it now as he put on the pressed dark jacket and sober tie that had been chosen for his forthcoming speech, just as yesterday's jeans and corduroy had been judged appropriate for California. He flashed himself his heart-throb smile in the closet mirror while the surface of his mind automatically reshuffled the familiar phrases. Change. Hope. The economy. The deficit. Maybe his stetson joke, if the mood was right. Dallas meant oil, banking, the aerospace industry. Dallas meant Neiman Marcus and the Cowboys. Dallas meant Kennedy.

But while the autocue played in his head, the wheels of memory whirled and clicked on another loop. Oxford. The summer of 1970. Moonlight on the Cherwell, the throbbing rhythm of the Doors, and Annie silky and warm under his hands.

Annie. Of course it had been her voice, that actressy huskiness softening the crystalline consonants. Typically she had come straight to the point. The curious thing was that, amid the flood of disbelief and despair that engulfed him, Jordan had also felt an unmistakable surge of elation.

'Jordan, I have a son. He thinks you're his father, and he's coming to find you.'

1

Picture this

Oxford, England – two weeks earlier

Tom rested his arms on the broad stone windowsill and leaned into the misty air, chilly and sharp with woodsmoke. He was actually here. He had made it. For a moment he listened to the echoing off-beat chiming of many bells. Soon he would learn to distinguish the deep note which boomed from Sir Christopher Wren's gatehouse tower at the entrance to the college – his college – marking the quarter-hours for anyone in central Oxford, from scurrying shoppers in the tinselly malls of St Ebbe's to the most reclusive don toiling in a corner of Duke Humfrey. Now it was lost in a pleasing jumble, evoking a collage of hazy images in Tom's mind: mediaeval monks, Jude the Obscure, Sebastian Flyte with his teddy bear. Taking a final look at his view – a typical first year's allotment of lead roofs, twisting stone pinnacles and a triangle of grey sky – he pulled the casement window closed and turned to survey the eccentrically shaped room under the eaves that was to be his home for the next year.

His father had looked askance at the stained pseudo-Persian carpet and the worn leather chairs leaking stuffing at the elbows. Tom hoped that he hadn't noticed that someone had carved 'Oxbridge Sucks' into one of the desks. Dad could be incredibly high-minded. Perhaps he would have been more hearty in his approval of the modern block, but its boxy uniformity held no charm for Tom. There was more to life than showers that worked. Here he could feel the aura of history, of young lives lived to the full, even, perhaps, a very faint echo of Evelyn Waugh's county families baying for broken glass.

Or had he already fallen under the spell of Aldworth's tall stories? Aldworth was to be Tom's scout, an elderly man with burgundy cheeks and badger-striped hair, and the burr of rural Oxfordshire still strong in his speech. He had chanced upon Tom and his father taking a breather on Tom's trunk in the middle of Peckwater, and offered to show them the way. Any egalitarian squeamishness Tom might have had about servants evaporated when Aldworth gave Tom's sprawling baggage a glance of magnificent disdain and, like the family butler in some horror movie, led them to Tom's room, pausing ceremonially at each landing as Tom and his father breathlessly manhandled his trunk up the sharply angled stone stairs. At the sight of a whisky bottle which Tom's father unexpectedly produced as a room-warming present, Aldworth graciously accepted a generous measure in a mug and set out to live up to his reputation as a Character. Tom heard about the young gentleman who had thrown his bed into Mercury, the young gentleman who used to take Aldworth to the races having provided him with a hundred-pound betting stake, and the young gentleman who had been sent down after being found with not one, but two young ladies in his room. '*And* one of them of royal blood. But that would be going back a good bit now. Nobody cares what the undergraduates get up to nowadays, young gentlemen and females higgledy-piggledy all over the college.'

When Tom's father, with an amused lift of his eyebrow,

said he'd better be getting back to London – 'and don't forget to ring your mother tonight' – Aldworth accompanied him, leaving Tom with the clutter of trunks and cases, cardboard boxes, squash rackets, lamps and coats which now confronted him. Not all the stuff was his, of course. Tom would be sharing this room with Brian, a tall guy in a baseball cap who had dumped his baggage before going off to have tea with his parents. He had looked OK, though his belongings were a good deal more flash than Tom's. He had brought an elegant black halogen reading lamp and a set of matching olive suit-cases which easily outclassed the paint-stained Angle-poise and wooden-ribbed trunk that Tom had wrested from the cobwebbed corners of his parents' attic.

Tom dragged the trunk into his bedroom, an unheated cubicle with an iron bedstead, a chest of drawers and a basin scarred with limescale. Brian had its identical twin next door. Tom opened the trunk and stared gloomily at the jumble of his belongings. Inside the lid his mother's name was written in large, neat capitals which had later been elaborated into a swirling, psychedelic design bright with stylised flowers and eye motifs. She had done it herself, he supposed. It was funny to think of his mother being young, though she had been a student here herself, back when everyone had to wear gowns and all the col-leges were single-sex.

Tom yanked out his shiny new kettle, Walkman, tapes, umpteen books, and dumped them on the floor. In a nest of socks he found his Prague poster and unrolled it carefully. He had already decided to hang it above the little Victorian mantelpiece next door. Here were his photos, and he sat back on the heels of his trainers to riffle through them. There was a brilliant one of Rebecca, grinning at him through a tangle of dark hair. He couldn't help smiling back. His 'older woman', he called her – six months older, anyway, and already in her second year at Sussex – a wonderful and mysterious being whom he had

12

met just a few weeks ago. He hoped she wasn't going to fall for some Sussex stud. Then there was Mum and Dad, his sisters, him under the arch of the Brandenburg Gate, and all his other photos from last year. The trip to Eastern Europe had been his reward for getting into Christ Church, even if it was his second attempt. Maybe he'd find a more intelligent audience here than he had encountered at home, where his sister Cassie had dogged his footsteps, melodramatically intoning, 'It is an ancient brother and he stoppeth one in three.' She was studying the Romantics at school.

He was just finishing when he heard a knock on the door. Shouting, 'Come in!' he lifted out the last wadge of underpants and T-shirts. Clothes were easy. Apart from one decent jacket and shirt, he had operated on the brilliantly simple principle of packing nothing that would ever need ironing.

Aldworth appeared in the doorway. 'Dinner in Hall at seven-thirty. And if you want to get rid of that, there's a store-cupboard down the bottom. Give you a hand with it, shall I?'

'Great.' Tom flipped the trunk shut, not bothering to fasten it, and he and the old man took hold of the worn handles at each end. 'Have you always been at the House?' he asked as they manoeuvred through the door, somewhat self-conscious at using the college's nickname for the first time.

'Fifty years, man and boy. Apart from the war. I was in the desert, mending tanks. And bloomin' hot and thirsty work it was too. Still, we had them on the run in the end.'

Tom tried to work out how old that made Aldworth. Even if he'd started at Christ Church when he was fifteen he must be practically seventy now. Christ. They said scouts were a dying breed. From the way Aldworth was puffing Tom hoped he wasn't going to expire on the spot.

'I suppose the college has changed a lot in your time.'

'It has. We've had the young ladies now six years. And the new block, of course. Nice little cottages they knocked down — and for what? Load of bloomin' egg boxes. The last duel in the history of the university was fought there. Young gentleman shot his friend over a female.' Aldworth sighed heavily, as if the decline in the ritual slaughter of undergraduates were a matter for regret. Perhaps it was this which made him relax his hold on the trunk, for as they neared the top of the final landing Tom felt the whole weight of the empty trunk hanging from his hand, before the old leather strap snapped and the trunk catapulted head over heels down the steps, clouting Aldworth on the way.

Tom clattered anxiously down to him. 'Are you all right?'

Aldworth pointedly brushed down the sleeve of his jacket, then chuckled. 'Take more than that to do for me.'

Together they retrieved the battered trunk and stowed it in the cupboard. Tom waited politely while Aldworth locked it again with fussy solemnity. Then, apologising again, Tom took the stairs two at a time back to his room. He was just in time to witness the protracted goodbyes between Brian and his parents, a jovial golf-club sort of man in a blazer and his hair-and-teeth wife. Brian withstood the usual parentspeak about work, late nights, and the existence of launderettes before closing the door with a mighty exhalation of breath.

'Parents.' He hurled himself into one of the armchairs. Tom nodded in solidarity.

Over the next half-hour the two of them fenced around the groundrules of cohabitation. The Prague poster could stay as long as Brian was allowed to put Paul Merson on the other wall. (Bloody hell, Tom thought, an Arsenal fan.) They would use Brian's brand-new bicycle helmet, which he wouldn't be seen dead in, as the communal kitty for buying coffee and tea. They would both try out for the college football team and one of the rowing eights.

They would have a tremendous party as soon as they knew enough people.

They sealed their agreement with Tom's whisky, and he went into his bedroom to get changed while Brian put up his picture. Off with the jeans and checked workshirt; tonight the jacket and decent shirt would get their first airing. Through the open door he could hear voices. Aldworth was back again, engaged with Brian in a competitive discussion of cup finals. Tom wandered back into the living-room, shirt-tails trailing, and eavesdropped on a blow-by-blow account of England's legendary defeat of Germany in 1966, which Aldworth claimed to have witnessed in person. 'We had them bang to rights,' the old man said gleefully, 'just like in the war.' Catching sight of Tom, he gave him a wink. 'I've put your young lady on the mantelpiece', he said incomprehensibly. With a last word to Brian about the college team, he took himself off again.

'Mad old tortoise,' said Tom. 'What was he on about?'

'Dunno. Something about a photo falling out of your trunk. It's up there.'

Mad or no, there was a photo on the mantelpiece. Tom picked it up, frowning. It wasn't one of his. For a start, it was obviously old. The colour had faded. Nobody produced photos like this any more – small and square, with a white margin all the way round. Even more mystifying, it was not a picture of a girl by herself, as Aldworth had implied. There were two people in the photo, a laughing couple of Tom's age sitting on the grass with their arms around each other, squinting into the sun. The man had tousled coppery hair and a big cheesy grin. Cuddling into his chest, spilling golden hair across his shirtfront, was a girl in a white dress. Behind them was the corner of a redbrick building. With a shock Tom realised that the girl was his mother. The man he had never seen before.

'It is yours, then, is it?' asked Brian curiously.

'I suppose so.' Tom flapped it casually, and as he did

so he noticed that there was something written on the back. He took the photo into the privacy of his bedroom. There was something about it that was oddly unsettling. His mother looked so – well, so unlike his mother, or anyone's mother. Young, and wild. And incredibly happy.

The writing was bold and loopy, set at a diagonal across the blank back of the photograph. Tom read: *'For Annie, my two-times girl. Love always. J.'*

For a long while Tom sat on his bed, gazing into the faces and rereading the corny message, though neither needed much interpretation. Here was a young couple wildly, obviously in love. Abruptly, he shoved the photo in with the others in his rickety bedside table. He banged the drawer shut. Tucking in his shirt, he moved over to the basin to wash the grime of unpacking off his hands. As the water filled the basin, he looked absently into the mirror above it. His hair needed smoothing down. He flicked the drops of water from his hands, then stopped dead. He could feel his heart begin to pound. The trickle of water was suddenly loud in his ears.

The photo. Aldworth had confused him by saying it was a picture of Tom's girlfriend. Now he knew why. Aldworth had thought that the man in the photograph was *him*. The reason was staring him in the mirror. He and the man could have been brothers.

2

It's alright, ma (I'm only bleeding)

'*Benedictus benedicat. Per Jesum Christum dominum nostrum. Amen.*'

From the dais a bulky figure in black said grace with the casual disdain of a judge passing sentence, then turned his back with a flourish of scarlet lining. Tonight was the first official supper of Michaelmas Term. As the dons clustered around High Table, nodding and bobbing in their academic gowns of crimson and blue and lilac, they resembled a particularly prize collection of endangered fowl. Below them the undergraduates settled themselves noisily like so many common crows.

Tom forced himself to concentrate on details. Squat shaded lamps punctuated the polished length of two dozen or more refectory tables, lighting up the faces of his companions and sending a golden glow into the Great Hall. Wood panelling rose to a height of some thirty or forty feet, broken by vast fireplaces and soaring Gothic windows. Then stone took over, culminating in the spectacularly carved and studded hammerbeam ceiling. Christ Church was not academically the top college, nor were its History results the best in the university, but on his tour round Oxford Tom had fallen in love with it. This was the hall where Charles I had assembled his Parliament during the Civil War, where Dean Liddell had entertained the young mathematics lecturer who was to immortalise his daughter in *Alice's Adventures in Wonderland*. Portraits by Gainsborough, Reynolds, Millais, Orpen, Sutherland and lesser artists cluttered the walls in what was a very grand version indeed of family snaps on the kitchen pinboard. Tom recognised one or two – Anthony Eden, Gladstone, was it? – but of the dozens of faces that loomed out of the shadows most were just that. Faces. A stray line from Shakespeare wormed its way into his mind. 'There's no art to find the mind's construction in the face.' Faces could tell you things. Perhaps it didn't take an Old Master to do the trick. Perhaps even an old snapshot would do.

A plate of soup was put before him and automatically he began to eat. He wasn't hungry, but Brian had just assumed they would go in to supper together and Tom hadn't been able to think of a reason not to. The reason was there, though, sticking into his brain like a thorn. *Love always. J.*

Conversations ebbed and flowed around him. A group of men opposite had clearly been at school together. They were boisterously swapping stories of somebody called Charlie, a figure of legendary rebelliousness. Next to Tom two women students seemed to be having some impenetrable feminist discussion. He had been abroad for so long that he was out of touch. 'I agree that she shouldn't have to bake cookies,' one was saying, 'but then why does she feel she has to highlight her hair?' He tuned back in to Brian's story of his summer as a camp counsellor in Maine, a tangled account of waterskiing feats and forbidden encounters with female campers. Tom nodded and exclaimed at what seemed appropriate points. He felt completely removed from the scene, as if his head were encased in a glass bubble.

18

Loads of people looked like each other, he thought. How often had he mistaken a complete stranger for a friend, if only for a brief moment or at a distance? It would be madness to read anything into the fact some man in some crummy old photo looked rather like him. Except that it wasn't just 'some man'; it was someone whom his mother had known. Had known bloody well, in fact. *Annie, my two-times girl*. Whatever that meant.

There was something else too, the thing he privately called The Quarrel, though he had never discussed it with another living person. For as long as he could remember it had descended on the family without warning, like a black cloud. Conversations missed a beat, stories faltered. There were whispers in the hall, warning frowns across the dinner table. It had something to do with a bust-up between his mother and her family before he was born. To Tom, Grandma and Grandpa meant Dad's parents. For years he had spent a part of every summer at their house near Cuckmere Haven, roaming the cliffs and learning to sail.

But on his mother's side there was a black hole which had simply sucked in the sort of anecdotes and recollections that were common currency in most families. He didn't even know exactly how old his mother was. Her coyness about her age was a family joke. Whenever they travelled as a family she was guardian of the passports, and never allowed anyone to see what she called the Hammer Horror of the Photobooth. Her father had died before Tom was born. The last time he had asked about her mother – his grandmother – she had said flatly, 'I don't know where she is and I don't care.'

A hand removed Tom's soup bowl and replaced it with a plate of sole with baby vegetables. In response to Brian's questions, Tom embarked upon his party piece about the drunken soldiers he had encountered in Slovenia. At home he was accused of embellishing this story with new and ever more death-defying details each time he told it, but tonight he wasn't doing it justice. He couldn't concentrate.

Odd memories kept floating into his head. His little sister's bossy voice as she took a visitor through the family photograph album. 'And here's me again when I was a little baby. Wasn't I sweet? There are hardly any of Tom because Mummy and Daddy were too poor to have a camera.' And Cassie, the family drama queen, wailing, 'How come Tom gets the gorgeous curls and the rest of us have this mousy *string*? It's not fair.'

He remembered his tenth birthday, the best ever. Dad had taken him and five chosen friends to see *Raiders of the Lost Ark* the very week it opened. A ride into town on the top of a double-decker, hamburgers and chips for lunch, popcorn during the film and ice-cream after, and larking about on the way home. In the evening his friends' parents came to collect them, lingering interminably, talking of nothing. Somebody's mother, flushed and laughing, burst out: 'I feel such an idiot – thinking you were the nanny, I mean. It's only that you look so young compared to the rest of us. You must have been a child bride.' What Tom remembered particularly was the look his mother had given him – a split-second glance of such electric intensity that he could still feel the bubbly texture of the anaglypta wallpaper under his fingertips. At the time he could not fathom that look. It was simply catalogued with the many other inexplicably charged moments of childhood. Now he could decode it effortlessly. It was panic.

Tom was beginning to feel very peculiar. The heat of closely packed bodies had raised the temperature to an unpleasant level. His stomach was churning the way it did before an exam. He looked round for the jug of water, but it was out of reach. A college servant refilled his glass with wine; Tom swigged it down. Across the table another story of the infamous Charlie was reaching its rowdy climax. Over the roar of a hundred different conversations he heard the exuberant voice: 'Drunk? I tell you, Charlie wouldn't have recognised his own father – ' Tom felt sweat break out across his back. Muttering something to Brian, he climbed over the bench and ran out of the hall.

Cold air swept up the broad stone stairway to meet him. Idiotic fragments ran through his head. When did you last see your father? Honour thy father and thy mother. It's a wise child that knows his own father. He made himself count the steps down . . . thirteen, fourteen, fifteen. The clatter of plates and cutlery faded. At the turn of the landing he slumped against the newel post, cooling his cheek on the stone.

Who *was* that man, the mysterious 'J'? Ridiculously, Tom at once felt jealous of him and furious with his mother. He was frightened, too, as if a private terror that had stalked him for years had finally stepped out of the darkness.

At home he had a shoebox crammed with postcards from all over the world, each with a one-line message. *Wellington trounced Napoleon here. Ate a live shrimp today! The boy in this painting reminds me of you.* They were invariably signed 'All my love, Dad'. He had never missed, even if it was a short trip. The best thing was that they were always addressed to him alone – not the family, not his sisters. It was a special thing between him and his father, man to man. Father to son.

Impossible to question this bond. Impossible not to.

Tom walked slowly back towards his rooms through the frosty night. At the bank of phones at the foot of his staircase he paused. Why not? He had promised, after all.

She answered at the first ring, sounding brisk and busy. She was grilling steaks, she said, 'but I'm taking them out *this minute*, so we can talk. It's lovely to hear from you, darling, you must have a thousand more exciting things to do.' Hearing the warmth in her voice, picturing her wandering about the kitchen with a wooden spoon in her hand and no shoes on, Tom felt a sudden rush of love.

'Is Dad all right?' he asked.

'Of course he is. He's right here, reading the paper. Do you want a word?'

'No, I just – Mum, who's "J"?'

'Jay who?'

'No, the letter J. I found something in that old trunk of yours, signed "J".'

There was the smallest of pauses before she asked, 'What sort of something?'

'A photo.'

'Of who?'

'That's what I'm asking you.' Let her squirm a bit, Tom thought. If there was a mystery about this man he wanted to know.

'I don't know, Tom,' she said impatiently. 'Are we playing Twenty Questions? What makes you think I know him anyway?'

Him, she said. Tom hadn't said whether it was a man or a woman. She must know perfectly well who 'J' was.

'Because you're in the photo too. Looking rather pally with old "J".'

'It could be anybody. There was a boy I went out with in Malta once called Jonathan. Is there anything else written on it?'

' "For Annie, my two-times girl. Love always, J".'

Tom heard a catch of breath. Was it a gasp or a sigh?

'That sounds like him. Very romantic and very dull. And an awfully long time ago. Now, Tom: football boots. I don't know how you and your father managed to forget them, but they're still here, under the hall table. Shall I post them?'

And that was that. They talked inconsequentially until his pound ran out, and Tom put down the phone feeling outmanoeuvred. Back in his room, he took the photo out and looked at it again. Maybe the man didn't really look that much like him. It was just that they had similar hair. He couldn't even see the colour of the eyes.

Jonathan, a boy she had known in Malta. He supposed this was plausible. What, after all, did Tom know about his mother's life before he was born? She never talked much about herself, probably because no one ever asked. Putting together the little he did know — only child, a succession of boarding-schools, problems with her mother, an adored father who had died — it struck Tom that this might not have been an ideal childhood. Perhaps that was why she was so brilliant at planning special treats. He thought of the Easter egg hunts, the surprise outings to the zoo, on the river, to a restaurant; the longed-for gifts that appeared with a fanfare just as one had abandoned all hope. She *seemed* happy. Tom felt a clutch at his heart. He didn't want anything to change.

Damn Aldworth. Why had the old idiot had to drop the trunk? Why couldn't he have left the photograph where it lay? It must have been in the lining, or perhaps one of those poncey little elasticated pockets. There was probably no mystery, except in his own head.

That night, in his cold, narrow bed, Tom turned back and forth on the squeaky springs. There went the bells again, marking the passing of each quarter of an hour, jangling and clashing like the thoughts in his head. He was still awake when Brian came in, well after midnight, swearing at the furniture. Tom counted six more quarters, and at last fell asleep.

3

Tracks of my tears

Annie held her front door open with a slim, Ferragamo-shod foot, running a mental check. Note to cleaner – check. Chicken out of freezer – check. Bag, keys, Filofax, briefcase, spare tights for tonight's party. Check. Wallet? For heaven's sake, she wasn't a complete moron. Annie banged the door shut, hard enough to make the Georgian fanlight quiver, and at that precise moment remembered the football boots. With a growl of exasperation she unlocked the door again, retrieved the boots from the kitchen table where she had placed them ready in a plastic shopping bag, and started again. As she was double-locking the door she caught sight of her bus sailing down the hill towards her, and sprinted for the bus stop, bags banging at her legs. She took her place in the queue behind a man in an elegant camel coat who appeared to be carrying nothing but his travel pass. How did men manage it? The only woman she knew who passed serenely through life carrying nothing more than a shoulder bag the size of a piece of toast was Rose. But then she went everywhere by limousine.

Annie found a seat and unzipped her briefcase. She

took out a plastic folder and slid out a bundle of type-script. If she got paid for the hours of reading she put in every day commuting to and from work, she would be a rich woman. Today it was an outline for a book on arms-dealing, by one of her writers who had become a successful television presenter. Though prodigiously talented, he had the attention span of a setter puppy, and she feared that some new cause would claim his enthusiasm before the ink on the contract was dry. On the other hand, his last book had been a bestseller. It had also, she reminded herself, been a sizzling account of a royal scandal. Somehow armaments sales to the Gulf didn't have the same allure.

The word 'scandal' set up reverberations in Annie's head. Her concentration slipped. As the grey London buildings slid by, her hands tightened unconsciously around the plastic parcel of football boots. How could she have been so stupid as to leave that old photo in her trunk? The image of Tom blundering around Oxford with a photograph of her and Jordan made her want to sob out loud with anxiety. For years she had successfully impersonated a typical, middle-class professional woman. She had worked hard, checked her children's homework, kept the freezer stocked and the front hedge clipped just like a grown-up person. She had made every effort to bolt the door on the past, constructing a version of events so close to the truth, so fiercely defended, that she had begun to believe it impregnable. If memory and desire could not be so easily silenced, that was her problem. But for Tom it was different. He was an open-hearted boy, guileless and uncomplicated. As a baby he had been a charmer, chuckling at her with such innocent delight that even on her most suicidal days he had lifted her spirits. In his teenage years the reign of loutish pimple-dom had been mercifully brief. He would breeze through life happily enough – drawing friends to him, finding doors of opportunity swinging open as if to a magic password – as long as nothing damaged the core of his identity. But he was still young enough to be stampeded into doing something stupid.

Had he believed her story about the photograph? Like the best lies, it was partly true. When she was sixteen a boy called Jonathan had invited her to a tennis dance. Her mother had insisted on putting Annie's hair up into an elaborate arrangement stiff with hair lacquer, which drew Jonathan's wondering gaze. She had no idea how to behave with boys and veered between tongue-tied shyness and arch ripostes. On the dot of eleven he had brought her home, thanking her with a chill formality that could still curl her toes with mortification. But Tom was not to know that. She could only hope it would not strike him that the background was not very Mediterranean. For she remembered that photo. She remembered every detail of that day, and of the previous night, and of each moment she had spent with Jordan. Whenever she saw his picture in the papers – wholly familiar, yet unreal – she wondered whether he remembered too.

As the bus neared her usual stop, Annie guiltily gathered up the unread script and stowed it away. Everything would be all right, she told herself. Tom was a happy-go-lucky boy with all the temptations of Oxford at his feet. An old photograph would surely not be enough to distract him.

Annie took her usual route through the alleyways that joined Charing Cross Road to St Martin's Lane and led into Covent Garden. Smith & Robertson was one of the dwindling number of literary agencies still left in the old heartland of London publishing. Positioned halfway between the covered market and the Strand, its offices occupied the top three floors of a sturdy Victorian building of which old Mr Smith had had the foresight to buy the freehold. There was no lift and the décor was strictly 1950s grunge. Pigeons warbled maddeningly on the window ledges and occasionally fell down one of the disused chimneys in a shower of soot. Some people liked to complain about the area – too many tourists and tramps and overpriced boutiques, not enough ordinary shops where you could get milk or shampoo. Annie adored it. Where else could you buy a nineteenth-century edition of Gibbon and a Madonna-style bustier, eat ten different types of cuisine, take tap-dancing lessons and bump into Maggie Smith or Pavarotti on a rehearsal break – all within a half-mile radius? Besides, running up and down three flights of stairs kept her in shape. At the office door Annie tapped in the code on the electronic entry box and let herself in.

The reception area was still empty. Annie liked to get to work early, before the phones started, and nowadays only hired secretaries prepared to do the same. Sally was her latest, an Australian raised on a cattle-farm, whom no crisis or bizarre request could ruffle. Her personal reading material did not stretch beyond *Hello!*, but it was typical that she took Annie's request to post the football boots without a blink.

'Jack's in,' Sally said. 'He wants to see you at nine-thirty.'

'Oh,' Annie said flatly.

'And,' Sally smiled broadly, 'the GWH has delivered his last chunk.'

Annie whirled round. 'He has? Why didn't you say? Where is it? Did you read it? Is it good?'

Sally held up a hand like a traffic cop. 'It's on your desk. And I didn't even peek. Would I spoil it for you?'

Annie strode into her office, half out of her coat, and hurried round to the other side of her desk. As always, her post was in three piles. On top of the priority pile was a blue folder with a note pinned to it: 'Any good? – Sebastian.' Annie smiled. Sebastian Winter, her Great White Hope. What a nincompoop he was.

Two years ago she had suggested that he should try his hand at fiction. At thirty, he already had a column in a

27

prestigious newspaper and three non-fiction books to his name, but Annie had a hunch that he just might have the talent for a blockbuster. After a long silence, he had come up with a plot which put a wholly original spin on the Nazi thriller – an idea so powerful and so different that she had felt the pricklings of excitement which come an agent's way only once or twice in a lifetime. Over the months she had coaxed, cajoled, threatened, flattered and finally shamed him into producing the first hundred pages. Last July they had landed on her desk, accompanied by a diffident note in which Annie could read his terror of failure. In jitters herself, she had stayed up late that night, reading with rising jubilation. If she knew anything about anything, this was going to be a bestseller. She had called him at once. It was well after midnight, but she had long ago learned that there was no such thing as an inconvenient moment for telling an author good news. The next day they had met for lunch at Orso's and downed two bottles of champagne, hysterical with mutual congratulation. It was only as Annie was making her way tipsily back to the office that acid reality curdled the *crostini da basilica* in her stomach. She had better make a success of this – a spectacular mega-success, in fact – or she might as well start looking for another career.

Over the summer news of the book leaked out. By September she was besieged by requests for an early look at the manuscript. It was just at the time when editors were slinking back from their holidays in Umbria or the Dordogne, hungry to boost their reputations with a splashy buy. Annie took another gamble and while interest in London was raging, offered the unfinished script at auction. The auction stretched to four days, and was finally concluded at a figure exactly twice what Annie had dared to hope. Just as she had planned, the British companies had slipped the script to their American partners, and now they too were hot for it. Where New York led, Europe and Japan would follow. Maybe even Hollywood. With the right director it would make a sensational film. Earlier this month Annie attended the Frankfurt Book Fair, as usual. She had been showered with invitations to dinners and exclusive parties and tête-à-tête drinks. On her last night a gravel-voiced American publisher of legendary ego made her a pre-emptive bid of a quarter of a million dollars in the back of a taxi. Annie refused. The Fair wasn't the place to sell this particular project. She would wait until she had the full script and sell it in New York herself.

And now here it was, nestled innocently in its baby-blue folder. Annie's fingers itched to take it out and start reading, but she was due to see Jack shortly and he didn't like to be kept waiting. Besides, this deserved her absolute concentration. For the next twenty minutes she worked methodically through her post. At the bottom of the pile was one letter that hadn't been opened, a handwritten airmail envelope marked 'Personal – please forward'. Curious, Annie flipped it over and read the return address. Lee Spago, Sheridan Road, Chicago. It meant nothing to her. She placed the envelope in the middle of her desk where she couldn't miss it later, then took the linoleum-covered stairs up to the next floor.

At the landing she ducked into the Ladies. If Jack had changed his mind about the partnership, she ought at least to look the part. She examined herself critically in the mirror. Black skirt, black tights, silver-buttoned tartan jacket nipped in at the waist over a cream Lycra T-shirt. Thick tiger-striped hair blunt-cut to within an inch of her shoulders, assessing blue eyes, this morning's lipstick still in place. Good enough for Jack.

Nodding to Tabitha Twitchit, Annie's private name for Jack's fluttering secretary, she knocked on his door and went in. Memories assailed her, for she did not come in here much any more. The crowded shelves, the elegant pedestal table piled with new books and magazines, the brass reading lamp, even the square green glass paper-weight recalled the man whose portrait now hung above the mantlepiece. Bow-tied, grey-haired, with an ironic twist to his mouth, old Mr Robertson had been her boss, her mentor, finally her friend. It was Miss Kirk, of all unlikely people, who had recommended Annie for the job, explaining her delicate situation. If in business Mr Robertson had displayed all the canniness – sometimes the sheer pig-headedness – of a native Scotsman, in private he had been kind beyond expectation. In recent years he had taken things easy, popping in only occasionally after a good lunch at the Garrick, but there had never been any question of Jack's taking over his office until he had died, quite suddenly and peacefully, in his sleep.

That was nearly six months ago, but to Annie it still didn't look right to see Jack behind the familiar old part-ners' desk. To be fair, he had put in a decent apprentice-ship as an editor in various publishing houses, and he could lay on a show of boyish charm which went down well with the older, female writers. But Annie continued to see the bumptious schoolboy who used to fiddle with her papers and ogle her legs when he came to visit his father. She couldn't detect any backbone of real authority underneath a skimpy cloak of management jargon – not that it bothered her. Mr Robertson had long ago given her a free hand to manage her own affairs. She figured that as long as she was making money – and she was – Jack would leave her alone.

'With you in a moment, Annie,' Jack said, gesturing with a characteristic unfurling of his fingers towards the chair where faithful Tabitha spent hours encoding the let-ters and eternal memos which he dictated with the speed of a dripping ketchup bottle. Jack regarded the word-processor as a mystical, exclusively female tool, on a par with the spinning-wheel. To Annie, who composed her own complicated letters straight on to the PC and trained her secretaries to draft the routine ones, his old-fashioned methods seemed a shocking waste of resources.

After a good minute or more, Jack finished annotating the document he was working on, put down his pen and pushed back his ridiculously boyish forelock of dark hair.

'I've had a rather worrying letter,' he began, 'which I thought I should share with you.' He moistened the tip of a finger and leafed one by one through a pile of papers in front of him. At length he drew out what he wanted. Annie recognised the letterhead of one of the major publishing groups.

'Apparently you did not see fit to offer them Coburg's new book on Eastern Europe. Could you fill me in on that?'

Annie, who had come prepared to battle for her partnership, was momentarily wrong-footed. 'There was a good auction,' she said defensively. 'Four bidders, I think, and an advance of forty or forty-five thousand. Not bad for a heavyweight political book that's bound to have a lot of competition.'

'I think you're missing the point – if I may say so.' Jack gave her his more-in-sorrow-than-in-anger smile. 'The point is, why didn't you offer it to a powerful group that already has some of our best authors on their list?'

Annie sighed. 'I suppose Madame Guillotine is complaining,' she said, using *Private Eye*'s nickname for the group's publisher, a woman notorious for her staff purges. 'The reason I didn't offer it to them is that I couldn't think of an appropriate editor. Celia does schlock and showbiz, Simon likes his non-fiction with a more wacky edge to it, Sarah's drowning in a sea of admin. Bill would have been perfect, but she fired him last month.'

'You forgot Martin.'

'The Boy Wonder? You know, Jack, I sometimes wonder if his reputation isn't just PR. Whenever I offer him anything, all I get is a five-page report telling me what's wrong with the script and how brilliantly he'll edit it. I suppose I wouldn't mind that if he actually published effectively. But of the last two books I sold him, one came out nine months late and the other had half its photo captions the wrong way round and no proper index. And whenever you ring him up he is never, but never, in the office. I'm not saying Martin isn't bright, but – well, let's just say efficiency is not his middle name.'

Jack took his time carefully placing his fingertips together. 'That doesn't seem to be the general view. Just between you and me,' he added confidentially, 'Martin's name has already come up more than once in connection with the Nibbies.'

Annie looked at him blankly for a moment, then burst out laughing. The Nibbies were annual awards conferred by one of the trade magazines on writers, editors, designers, distributors, publicists and anyone else they could think of. It was a bit of fun that pierced the winter gloom every February, and Annie enjoyed the circus atmosphere of the awards ceremony, but it wasn't exactly the Nobel Prize. Even Jack, she was sure, didn't give a fig who won what. Any more, she suddenly realised, than he cared who had bought Coburg's book.

'What's this all about, Jack?' she asked directly. 'I came up here to discuss the partnership. Let's not waste time bickering about an auction that, in my view, was entirely successful.'

'In *your* view,' Jack repeated, with a quiet venom that startled her. 'That's what it always comes down to, doesn't it? Annie Hamilton's view is that we need a television specialist – and lo, my father appoints one. Annie Hamilton's view is that the office should be computerised. Bingo! Thousands of pounds' worth of equipment appears overnight. Annie Hamilton's view is that one of the world's major international publishers is not good enough for her author, and I'm the one' – Jack brandished the letter – 'who takes the flak.'

Wow, thought Annie. But it was her fault for laughing at him.

'I'm sorry about the letter, Jack,' she said soothingly. 'I'd be happy to answer it myself. I'll even show you my reply, if you like. But we did need a television expert – and Elizabeth's already done brilliantly, as you know. And the computerisation was years overdue. Your father only did what I suggested because he trusted me to know what I was talking about.'

'And I don't. Is that what you're saying?' With a furious shove Jack pushed himself away from the desk and stood up.

'Of course not – '

But Jack was now thoroughly angry. Bracing his hands against the desk he leaned across it and addressed her in a strangled shout. 'Smith & Robertson is my firm now, whether you like it or not. I decide how and with whom we do business. The way you're always chattering with the staff, sorting out their problems, setting up new systems, arranging foreign trips without a by-your-leave – I sometimes think you forget that. It was all very well in my father's day, running helpfully up and down in your miniskirt doing whatever job he wanted, but we're a modern business now and we should be following modern business practices.'

In her miniskirt? Up to now Annie hadn't been too bothered by Jack's display of adolescent temper. Tantrum management was a vital skill when you had teenage children. But this remark was so outrageous that she felt her mouth fall open. In a sudden flash she remembered the humiliating scene that had taken place in this very room, years ago, at some Christmas party. Was that what this was all about? Surely Jack wasn't going to use his newly inherited position to make her pay for that?

Regaining control of himself, Jack sat down. 'I've said I'll consider the partnership, and I will – when I judge that you have understood the financial and management controls necessary in a modern business. To take a current example, we can't have everyone running off to New York every five minutes. You know perfectly well that I have for some time been planning an American trip in December. Yet I gather that you have unilaterally decided to go yourself shortly. That's a quite unnecessary duplication, and I have decided to postpone your trip until next year.'

'But what about Sebastian? I've got the whole script now. You know the Americans are desperate to buy it. We need to strike while the iron is hot.'

'I shall handle the sale of Sebastian Winter myself,' Jack said pompously.

Annie gasped. 'But he's *my* author.'

'You see, there you go again, Annie.' Jack stabbed a finger at her. 'Winter is not my author or your author. He is a Smith & Robertson property, which we shall exploit as effectively as we can.'

'But I've always sold American rights in the big books myself. People will be expecting me.'

'Then they'll just have to make do with the head of the agency,' said Jack with a smugness that made Annie long to slap his ferrety face.

'But in the past – '

'I've made my decision, and I'm afraid you'll just have to accept it.' Jack's mouth tightened into a spiteful line. 'Better not go into the past, don't you think?' he said, with a subtle emphasis that made Annie tense with wariness.

'I've been sorting out some of my father's private papers,' he continued casually. 'Fascinating stuff. Letters from famous authors that I should think are really rather valuable. But also some unfortunate personal stories which are probably better destroyed.'

'Like what?' Annie asked steadily.

'Just little human dramas.' Jack gave a tight smile. 'Past history, nothing that need concern us here, I'm sure. For the time being, I would be grateful if you would draft a reply to this – ' he handed her the offending letter – 'as from me. This afternoon will do.'

Annie stood up and stalked out of the room, leaving the door wide open. Rose was right, she thought, she should have set up her own agency years ago. But it hadn't seemed necessary when old Mr Robertson was alive. She had an office she liked, colleagues for company, specialist departments for foreign and television rights, and as much freedom as she wanted. It had always seemed too difficult to disentangle her own personal deals from those of the firm.

That wasn't the whole story, though, and she knew it. It was sheer cowardice, the little Miss Mouse syndrome, that had kept her from striking out boldly on her own. Boldness had not rewarded her in the past. Once she had followed her instincts, and they had led to unhappiness and muddle. It had taken years to regain her equilibrium. If she sometimes dreamed of a different life, she had learned to value what was solid and dependable.

Stupid, cowardly, blind – Annie heaped every insult on herself that she could think of. Jack had been waiting in the wings for years. It was obvious that one day he would take over. How could she not have guessed that he might abuse his position?

Annie was seething when she got back to her office. The first thing she saw was the strange letter from America. Without premonition she ripped it open.

Dear Annie,

That seems a pretty familiar way to start, so I guess I'd better explain right away that your mother and I have been married twelve years now. Marie always said that you two didn't get along, and up to now I have minded my own business. Marie is very precious to me and I would never upset her.

Annie stiffened in her chair, and reread the paragraph in disbelief. *Married?* Annie had not seen or heard from her

mother for over twenty years. Memory had warped her
mother's image into a monstrous icon that bore no
relation to a real woman. It had not occurred to Annie
that anyone might want to marry her mother, any more
than that someone would propose to Bette Davis if she
stepped from the screen of *Whatever Happened to Baby
Jane?*

Anyway, just who the hell was 'Marie'? The last Annie
had heard, her mother was plain Mary Paxford, born
Mary Hoggett. An old, familiar rage made her whole body
flush with heat. How utterly typical of her mother to have
upgraded her name, as she had always tried to refine her
family. 'No tie, Charles?' she used to say in that poisonous, fault-finding voice, as she dolled up for yet another
cocktail party, and obediently Annie's father would
return to his wardrobe like a dog fetching its toy.

Annie nearly crumpled up the letter there and then.
But her eyes had already jumped to the next words. With
a sick feeling she read on.

*Now she is in the hospital and they don't give her much
more than a month. The thing is, she has started talking
about you. I think there is something on her mind which
she wants to settle. It's a lot to ask, but if you could come
see her I truly believe it would help. If it is a question of
money, I have plenty. Let me know if I can take care of your
ticket and hotel – though we have a nice little condo-
minium by the lake where you would be welcome.*

*Please think about it at least. I have made a lot of mis-
takes in my life, and I know there are some you can never
fix. Whatever happened in the past, Marie needs you now.*
Yours respectfully,
Lee Spago

Well, the part about the money made sense, Annie
thought viciously. It wouldn't be like her mother to pick
anyone poor. She slapped the letter face-down on the
desk. There was a postscript on the back.

PS. I hope this letter reaches you. I got your business address from an article Marie clipped in the New York Times. *I found it in her jewellery box.*

Annie remembered that article. One of her authors had been tipped to help Margaret Thatcher write her memoirs. In the end, he didn't get the job, but for a few short weeks both he and Annie had received a measure of useful publicity. There had even been a photograph of her.

How strange to think of her mother reading that article. In fact, now that Annie thought about it, it was more than strange. For the article must have appeared well over a year ago. Which meant that her mother had not only taken the trouble to cut it out; she had also kept it, all this time, in the place where most women keep their very special treasures.

Annie bowed her head and rested it on her desk, cradled in her folded arms. Jordan. Tom. Her mother. Would the memories never leave her? Would the lies ever stop? When would it be her turn for happiness? She didn't even notice that she was leaning on Sebastian's precious script, darkening its pale blue folder to navy with her tears.

4

I heard it through the grapevine

It was a perfect autumn day, the sky as fresh and blue as if it had never heard of the ozone layer. Tom decided to walk, having been given detailed directions of the scenic route by Aldworth. It took him up Catte Street, past the Pitt Rivers Museum and into the University Parks. On this quiet Sunday morning – only the second of term – there were few people about, a sprinkling of old ladies with their dogs and mothers with prams, enjoying the bright bursts of autumn crocuses and the way the sun set the copper beeches on fire. Just as the duckpond came into sight Tom took the narrow brick-walled path that led to the bottom of Norham Gardens.

Lady Margaret Hall had not escaped the brutalist additions of the 1970s, but its central quad, rosy-bricked with a clock-tower and cupola, had a cosy domestic charm appropriate for a college built to house women. Tom followed the gravel path around the square of green, peering furtively into the windows. One side of the quad was taken up by a library, traditionally divided into bays, empty at this hour. On the other side were student rooms, most with their curtains still drawn, though Tom could hear the thump of music and caught sight of one man shrugging himself into his sweater.

Which had been his mother's room? he wondered.

Opposite the library was an archway linking two buildings. Tom passed through it into the gardens. Though not as grand as those of the older, originally male colleges, they were surprisingly extensive, sweeping down to the Cherwell. He took the willow-shaded path along the river, past the boathouse and grass tennis courts, then turned off to explore a small garden, hedged with yew, where grey stubs of lavender encroached on mossy paths and wind-blown chrysanthemums shrouded the broad, shallow steps of old brick.

'Good morning, young man. I take it you are not a member of the college.'

Startled, Tom turned to find a bulldog of a woman, stoutly encased in tweed, outlined in one of the entrances to the garden. She was wearing gardening gloves and carrying a pair of secateurs. Before Tom could answer, she went on, in the same well-spoken boom, 'Otherwise, you would no doubt be aware that this is the Fellows' Garden, and out of bounds to junior members.'

'I'm terribly sorry,' Tom stammered politely. 'I was just having a look round. My mother was an undergraduate here.'

'Indeed?' The woman stood her ground for a moment, legs well braced, then stripped off a glove and advanced towards him. 'That puts a different complexion on the matter. I am Miss Reeves, Dean of the college. How do you do?'

Tom shook her hand. 'Tom Hamilton. I've just come up to Christ Church.'

'Oh, well done,' said the Dean heartily. 'I approve of continuity in the University. The great-granddaughter of one of our founder members has just come up to the college. Charming girl, could have had her pick of any of the colleges – but no. LMH or nothing, she said. Most gratifying. We're not as popular as we used to be when we were a women-only college.' Grunting, she bent down to lop off a cluster of rosehips with the secateurs. 'I was against integration, of course, but what chance has a lone voice against the baying of the herd for progress?' She allowed Tom no chance to respond to this rhetorical question, but shot him a penetrating glance. 'So, young Mr Tom Hamilton, who was your mother? Dare say I might remember her, I'm quite a fixture here.'

'Paxford was her maiden name. Ann Paxford.'

The Dean's lumpen features softened into an unexpectedly sweet smile that gave Tom a glimpse of the young girl she had once been. 'Good heavens, Annie Paxford. Read English, had rooms in Lodge and – was it Wordsworth? Very quiet at first, just seeing how the land lay, you know, but then she quite blossomed, found herself some chums. There was one particular friend, a real "live wire", as they say. Rose something. Carlton? Kennedy?'

'Rose Cassidy? She's my godmother.'

'Is she? Splendid. And what has become of her?'

'She's something very grand in New York, editor of *The Magazine*. You must have read about her, she's always in the gossip columns.'

'But do I read them?' the Dean asked drily. 'I am afraid one becomes shamefully insular. And your mother, what does she do with herself?'

'She's a literary agent, with Smith & Robertson.'

'Good for her. It is dispiriting when our old girls simply turn bovine with domesticity and motherhood. And your mother was clever. I believe Miss Kirk had hopes of a First.' Snip went the secateurs, and another thorny plume fell to the ground as Miss Reeves added, 'We were all very disappointed when she didn't stay to take her degree.'

Tom tried to hide his astonishment, but the old lady was sharp. 'Didn't tell you, eh? I expect she had her reasons. Difficult home life, as I recall. We do our best, but we never really know what goes on inside their pretty little heads.'

Tom rummaged in his back pocket. 'I've got an old photograph of her. Would you like to see it?'

The Dean, long-sighted with age, held the photo at arm's length. 'Well, well, Annie Paxford.' She shook her head, smiling. 'To think that she has a grown-up son. And who is the young man with her? He looks familiar.'

'I don't – I can't remember. Why, do you recognise him?'

Miss Reeves gave a barking laugh. 'If I were to try and keep track of all the boyfriends that come and go in this college I'd have my work cut out.' She handed back the photo. 'They've filled in that flowerbed now. Pity. We used to have splendid black tulips in the spring, but one simply can't get the gardeners these days.'

Tom was confused. 'Do you mean to say that the photo was taken *here*?' he asked.

'Yes, by the archway where you probably came in. The girls like to sunbathe there in the summer; that slope catches the sun beautifully.'

Tom stood for a moment, digesting this. The Dean looked on kindly, but with a gathering frown that threatened awkward questions if he didn't take himself off quickly. 'Well, thanks,' he said, waving the picture. 'I'll just have a look, if you don't mind, on my way out. I'm sorry to have trespassed.'

The Dean held out her hand, 'Not at all. A pleasure to have met Annie Paxford's son.'

As he turned to go, Tom remembered something. 'You mentioned another lady, Miss somebody. Is she a tutor here?'

'Miss Kirk? She retired a good many years ago. I'm afraid there has been something of a decline, although she still dines occasionally.'

'Is she still in Oxford? Perhaps she wouldn't mind if I dropped in on her one day.'

41

'What a kind thought. Honeysuckle Cottage, Wytham. It's a charming little village. Though you may find her somewhat... frail. There's a pub, I believe, the White Hart.' She flourished the secateurs encouragingly. 'You could make it a real outing.'

Tom thanked her again, and headed back the way he had come. He wondered what reminiscences his mother might have about the old battleaxe. But the thought of his mother brought the old anxiety flooding back. At the porchway into the quad, he checked the photograph again. The Dean was right. The flowerbed might have gone, but here was the same climbing rose, the same strip of gravel, the same criss-cross shutters over the ground-floor window.

So why had his mother told him that the photo was taken in Malta?

5

She's not there

Leaving the untidy sprawl of Wolvercote behind him, Tom raced his bicycle over the hump-backed bridge by the Trout, passed the flat reaches of Port Meadow, and arrived at a string of vine-clad cottages hugging the twisting road. This must be Wytham. The village was indeed charming, dominated by a spectacular mediaeval abbey. As in most English villages, the pub was conveniently placed next to the church, and easy to find. The White Hart was panelled inside, whitewashed on the outside, with rustic benches and tables in the sun and a dovecote loud with cooing. It was already crowded and, judging from the accents around him, firmly established on the tourist map, but the long ride up Woodstock Road had taken its toll of Tom's calf muscles, and it was with considerable relief that he leaned his bike against the low stone wall, bought himself a pint and took it into the garden. Brian had muttered something about a picnic on the college lawn today, but it was just too bad if he missed it. After LMH Tom had gone straight back to college to pick up his bicycle. Never put off till tomorrow what you can do today, as his mother always said. Well, he would take her advice.

For the moment, however, beer and sunshine made a seductive combination. Downing his pint thirstily, Tom went indoors to queue up for sausages and beans and another half, and settled himself in a little rose-covered bower vacated by a family of enthusiastic Germans. It was astonishingly warm for the time of year, and the bees were buzzing round the roses as if a whole lifetime lay ahead of them, instead of a few short days before the autumn chill froze them dead. It must be odd, Tom thought, to live your life with no premonition of what was to come.

Having asked directions from the publican, Tom walked a few yards back the way he had come and on to a rough track until he reached a white picket fence with a gate marked Honeysuckle Cottage. The front garden had an untended look, without a twig of honeysuckle to be seen, just daisy-studded grass and a few blowsy holly-hocks. There was a sagging trellis round the door and a brass knocker shaped like a sleeping cat. He let it drop noisily, and waited. Eventually, he heard a faint shuffling, so slow and erratic that he began to fear that his journey would be wasted, that he would be met by the blank gaze of senility. But when the door at last opened, he found himself looking into a pair of faded blue eyes in which intelligence still glimmered. Miss Kirk was tiny, her face as wizened as a monkey's under a frizz of grey hair, kept tidy with a fine net. She cut an elegant figure in her dark skirt and pink silk blouse caught at the throat with a cameo brooch, though Tom noticed a splash of foodstain on the sleeve. A shawl of muted colours was draped across her shoulders, and she breathed audibly, leaning on a brass-headed stick.

'Good afternoon,' she said, politely enough, but with an upward inflection of enquiry. It must be an anxious business, Tom realised, living alone in a world of conmen, muggers and rapists. Carefully he offered his credentials, conscious that he too, in his own way, was here under false pretences. But the old lady seemed delighted.

'How very kind. Come in, come in. I always enjoy hearing of my old pupils. May I offer you a cup of coffee? Or perhaps lemonade might be more fitting for such a splendid day.'

Picturing the slow and painful arrangements this might entail, Tom convinced her that his pub lunch had left him wholly satisfied. Besides, a peculiar smell, which he identified as cat, made him feel queasy about the state of her kitchen. Tap-tapping with her stick, she led him into one of the most extraordinary rooms he had ever seen.

It was a typical cottage parlour – beamed ceiling, diamond-paned casement windows, stone fireplace – but transformed into an Aladdin's cave crammed with antique treasures. Through a gap in the heavy curtains sunlight gleamed on delicate Georgian side-tables, a pigeonhole desk inlaid with ivory, a long-case clock, bronze busts, a Regency *chaise-longue* with yellow silk bolsters, leather-bound books scrolled with gold. In fact, books were everywhere, spilling out of the shelves that lined one wall and filled the fireplace alcoves, piled on tables and windowsills, balanced on chair arms and rising like giant anthills from the jewelled Persian carpets on the floor. Above the fireplace, where most people would nail their horse-brasses, hung a striking print of the expulsion from Eden, a beautiful naked Eve and a protective Adam quailing at the sight of the corrupt world that awaited them. Everything was of an austere classical elegance; there was nothing feminine about the room. A wing chair flanking the fire marked itself out as her familiar work-station: kidney-shaped writing-board to balance on her lap, tartan rug for her knees, scatter of cushions for her back. The only incongruous element was a modern trolley holding a kettle and assorted tins, a large bottle of ink standing on a pad of blotting paper and a sheaf of papers covered in handwriting as tiny as a doll's. On the lower shelf of the trolley a vast ginger cat lay splayed in sleep.

Tom picked his way round the teetering plinths of books to the magnificent carved chair that she indicated, its polished arms ending in lions' heads, and removed a bulging file from the seat. It was, he noticed, marked 'God'.

'It is untidy,' Miss Kirk agreed crisply to Tom's unspoken thoughts, as she settled herself in her chair. She spoke a beautiful, precise English of the sort Tom had only ever heard from the BBC radio archives. 'Hodge does *not* approve, do you pusskins?' – she ran a fragile hand over the cat's pale, spreading stomach – 'but I need my books about me. I am too old to be leaping up and down like a jack-in-the-box. My work is nearly complete, but I must keep at it, you know, before I am Called.'

'You're writing a book?' Tom hazarded.

'*The* book, dear boy, *the* book. My *magnum opus*. The definitive concordance to the works of Milton. Oh yes,' she said, as if Tom had voiced some objection, 'there have been attempts at it. American scholars, with their computers and research students.' Her tone was dismissive. 'I have no aides but my memory and my brain. And the good Lord to guide me. Tell me,' she asked with an almost coquettish turn of the head, 'do you read Milton?'

'Er, I'm afraid Pepys is more my line.'

'Pepys!' she cried enthusiastically. 'Nothing to be ashamed of there. A most lovable man, though not perhaps of scrupulous morals.

'Certainly I remember Ann Paxford,' she continued without a pause. 'Nineteen sixty-eight is a year I could hardly forget. That was the last time the old syllabus was taught, before it was decided that young minds were too impatient and too sensitive to endure the rigours of proper study. The whole of the Michaelmas and Hilary terms were spent in preparation for the Preliminary

Examinations. *Beowulf* – complete, and in the original, naturally; Latin – *The Aeneid*; Old English and morphology; and of course Milton.' She clasped a hand to her thin chest. 'The sublime Milton. He was always my particular love. *Paradise Lost*, "Lycidas", *Areopagitica, Comus* . . .' Her eyes closed for a moment and her lips moved, as if recalling some fragment of verse.

She reopened them with a snap. 'It gave one a grounding, don't you see?' she said fervently. 'What is one to make of literature without the basics of language and classical allusion? They tell me that critical theory has supplanted a study of the text, that it is no longer thought necessary to read literature.

'But *this* is where the precious life blood of the master spirit resides.' She patted a pile of books at her knee – all, Tom saw, volumes of Milton. 'The blind can be very perceptive. The poor man had to keep all his verse in his head, you know, waiting for someone to come and write it down for him. Like a cow waiting to be milked, he said.'

A silence fell. Miss Kirk leaned forward courteously. 'Who did you say you were, dear boy?'

'Tom Hamilton. Ann Paxford's son.' She was like a doll, Tom thought, a macabre clockwork doll whose essential mechanism had received some fatal injury. Parts still moved, but in a grotesque and unpredictable way.

'Yes, of course, forgive me. One gets so tired these days. Do tell me about her. Is she well? Does she flourish?'

Tom told her about his mother's job, realising as he spoke how little he knew, had never bothered to ask. Miss Kirk questioned him about his sisters and the likelihood of their coming up to LMH one day. Nil, in Tom's opinion, though he was too polite to say so. All the while, something niggled in his brain. He would pin it down later if he could, but for the moment he needed to keep her talking.

'You must have been disappointed when she gave up her studies,' he prompted.

47

'It was a blow. I enjoyed teaching your mother. She had an instinctive response to the sounds and rhythms of language. I did hope that, with proper study and guidance in her final year, she might do very well indeed. But alas – '

Her eyes strayed to the picture above the fireplace, and she began to quote, in a passionate low warble. ' "These two/ Imparadised in one another's arms,/The happier Eden, shall enjoy their fill/Of bliss on bliss." ' Then, eerily, still on a note of reverie, Miss Kirk continued, 'Annie Paxford. I wonder what happened to her.'

Tom's hands tightened over the lions' faces on his chair, willing her to continue. Somewhere in her memory, he was sure, was a piece of information he wanted, though if the condition of her brain were anything like that of her room, he had little hope that she could lay her hands on it even if she wanted to. A snowstorm of dust, spotlit by the sun, floated down on to files and papers and piles of indexers' slips that would surely, one day soon, prove to be no more than an indecipherable muddle, fit only for carting away in black plastic sacks.

Miss Kirk spoke again, in the disengaged drone of a medium. 'I tracked her down, you know. Oh yes, I found her in that filthy hole. But it was too late. I did what I could, a word in the right place. It was my Christian duty.'

'Where?' Tom demanded, abandoning any pretence of polite chatter. 'Why did she leave Oxford? Tell me. Please.'

But the old lady was deaf to his questions, following her own mazy track. 'No doubt it was easier for our generation. We had no distractions from our academic calling. All our young men were killed in the Great War. Young men like you. All gone.' She looked at Tom reproachfully. 'No one visits any more, you know. One might as well be dead.' Her voice deepened again as she declaimed, ' "Oh, dark, dark, dark, amid the blaze of noon".'

With an air of finality she closed her eyes and leaned

into her chair's familiar embrace. She was silent for some long seconds. In the shadowy room the clock ticked loudly. The seconds stretched into one minute, two minutes. The old lady's face slackened, and she began to snore gently. She was asleep.

Tom didn't know what to do. It would be rude to leave, but worse to stay until she awoke. Besides, he was unlikely to get more from her pitifully scrambled brain. Eventually he rose carefully from his chair and tiptoed his way round the furniture. At the door he looked back and saw, with a thrill of horror, that her eyes were open, fixed on him with the wide, vacant gaze of a sleepwalker. She gave him a smile, as if inviting him to share a delightful joke.

'She left because of you, dear boy, didn't she?'

Then her lizard lids fell, and she slumped into instant, slack-jawed sleep.

It was on his way back along the towpath, his mind floating free, that something which the old lady had said hit Tom so hard that he nearly wobbled into the river. 'Nineteen sixty-eight is a year I could hardly forget.' So his mother had gone up to Oxford in 1968. That meant she had left at the end of her second year, which would have been the summer of 1970.

One thing Tom did know was his own birthday. It was the seventeenth of March, 1971.

In Jericho Tom passed a corner newsagent's and remembered that Brian had asked him to bring back a Sunday paper – any of the qualities, he wasn't bothered. Tom's eyes slid listlessly over the headlines. On the masthead of the *Sunday Times* the word 'Oxford' caught his eye. He paid for the paper, stuffed it into his bicycle basket and rode home.

6

Daydream

A truth universally acknowledged by women's magazines is that the departure from home of her children plunges every mother into soul-searing depression. Bunkum, balderdash and baloney, thought Annie, as she wriggled deeper into her warm nest of pillows. Tosh, tripe, poppy-cock, piffle and pure applesauce. With Tom in Oxford, and Cassie and Emma staying with friends following last night's rave, the house exuded a deep Sunday morning calm that was as palpable and relaxing as a blanket. It was not so much the actual noise the children made, now that they were slouching towards adulthood; it was the continual expectation, day in, day out, of some epic eruption that was so wearing.

Edward, thank God, had never been the erupting type. An inveterate early riser who complained that breakfast-ing in bed got scratchy crumbs in his pyjamas, he would be downstairs tranquilly working through his legal papers and a fearsomely strong pot of tea. Annie luxuriated in the knowledge that some batsqueak communication perfected over the years would shortly impel him up the stairs with a tray of coffee, freshly squeezed orange juice, a croissant flanked by an indecent amount of unsalted butter and apricot jam, and a slab of newspapers. Today there would be no Sunday lunch to cook, no squabbles to resolve, nobody to ferry to a party, swimming pool, football game or film. She was nobody's mother and nobody's employee. Just for one day she would not worry about Tom or her job or the letter from Chicago, which she had hidden in her knicker drawer, knowing that Edward would say she should go. Today was hers.

Still languorous with sleep, she hadn't the energy even to turn her head towards the bedside clock, but she could tell that the morning was well advanced. Sun blazed through the yellow chintz curtains, and a warm breeze sent them fluttering like circus pennants. She could sense an energy in the air outside that promised a delicious Indian summer's day. Later they might walk across Hampstead Heath and have lunch in a pub garden. They could even try to get a court and play tennis. Or if Edward were busy, she might dead-head the roses and give the lavender a good haircut. Or . . . . Or what?

Annie felt a spurt of unfocused longing. What had she done on this kind of day when she was young? Sleep, said a cynical voice. Her children's capacity for sleep was astounding, and Annie knew that she had once been the same, though she could not recapture that teenage sense of limitless time. But as she stretched out on her back, feeling her body still lithe and responsive, another answer whispered to her. Make love. That's how people used to spend their mornings – and their nights and afternoons – when she was young. Then it had all seemed so innocent, so natural, so all-embracing, as if sex conferred some kind of universal benediction on the planet.

Nowadays it was easy to poke fun at sixties philosophy – the rhetoric of peace and love, handing out flowers, the earnestly argued views that everyone was bisexual and that rock music could shatter barriers of class and colour. With hindsight one could see how women had allowed

51

men to abuse them in the name of sexual liberation. Mysticism had become tainted with materialism. Few rock musicians had survived their fortieth birthdays with their bodies or their brains intact. But there had been a joy, a sense of expectation, that was shockingly absent among today's knowing, anxious teenagers. Did nobody know how to have fun any more?

'Breakfast is served.' Like a shimmering Jeeves, Edward appeared at the bedroom door carrying a loaded tray. Compared to most men she had known, and certainly to Tom, who sounded like a cavalry regiment on the stairs, Edward moved like a cat. He had the lean, wiry frame of the sort of Englishman she used to see in the old wartime films shown every Saturday in the army film club, typically dispatching a croquet opponent's ball into the shrubbery, or giving a jubilant thumbs-up through the windscreen of a Spitfire. Often there would be a brash Yank who blundered through English etiquette, calling the gardener 'Mr' or scoffing a week's rations at a sitting. Sometimes he got the girl; other times he heroically sacrificed his life for his Limey chum. Those Saturday afternoons, sitting with her father in a darkened Nissen hut, cocooned in a world of adventure and romance, had been some of the happiest moments of her childhood.

Edward put the tray on the bed, and dropped a slithering mass of newspapers beside her. Annie studied him as he went over to pull the curtains open. Clothes always looked good on him, even today's old sweater and pale cotton trousers that had shrunk above his ankle bones.

'Good sleep?' he asked.

'Heaven.' Annie sat up and stretched her arms wide. For a moment her cream silk pyjamas pulled open across her breasts. Edward was fiddling with the window catch, his back to her. 'Isn't it bliss to be alone, just the two of us? Or am I a shockingly unnatural mother?'

'Definitely a case for the Social Services,' Edward said absently, still busy at the window.

Annie pulled the crisp tail off her croissant and munched it thoughtfully. 'Have you got a lot on today?'

'I've a meeting this week with the Union of Democratic Mineworkers, poor buggers. There's a fair amount of homework to do if I'm to be of any use to them.' He left the window and leaned on the brass rail at the foot of the bed, considering his wife. 'Why? Was there something special you wanted to do?'

'Not really. I just feel like doing something frivolous, like – oh, I don't know, having a lazy lunch in Julie's Wine Bar or watching some wonderful old Truffaut film. Just *being*, for a change, instead of always doing.'

'Julie's Wine Bar! That's a blast from the past. We can go out for lunch, if you like,' Edward said amiably. 'But the parking's impossible round Julie's, and I've got a colleague phoning around three. He's giving me some advice with the case, and it would be rude if I wasn't here. What about that Thai place you like in Islington?'

Annie shrugged. 'Never mind. I've got hundreds of things I should be doing too. I just thought it might be fun to forget the real world and do something spontaneous, for a change.'

Edward came round and sat next to her on the edge of the bed, steadying the tray with one hand. He put his other arm around Annie and drew her head to his. 'What a disappointment I am to you,' he said. 'I'd love to whisk you off to some romantic paradise. How about if I make you a special little alfresco lunch later and whisk you into the garden instead? We could have some champagne, if you like.'

Annie put her arm around his warm, familiar body and hugged him fiercely. 'You're never a disappointment. You're my favourite husband, and the work you're doing is important.' Tilting her head up she gave him a kiss and rubbed her hand against his stubbly cheek. 'It's all right. Really. Now bugger off. I'm going to have a lovely wallow in the soft porn that passes for today's journalism.'

'Oh yes, I meant to tell you,' said Edward, pausing in the doorway, 'there's a piece that may amuse you about your old friend Hope.'

'Amuse me?', Annie queried sharply, her heart beginning to thud. 'In what way "amuse"?'

Edward raised his eyebrows. 'And I thought I was supposed to be the QC. It's just some story about Hope when he was at Oxford. Looked a lot of nonsense to me, I didn't read it. But you might know some of the people quoted.'

'He wasn't *my* friend, anyway,' Annie said. 'You know me and politics. It was Rose who was always having earnest discussions with him about the means of production or positive discrimination.'

'Mmm. It's funny to think of Rose as a feminist revolutionary. Nowadays I suppose she'd only be interested in trying to get him into some beefcake pose on the cover of her magazine.'

Annie giggled, and threw a bit of *Observer* at him, which Edward neatly sidestepped. 'We can't all be as lofty as you, Mr Lawyer-with-a-social-conscience.'

When Edward had gone, the smile faded from Annie's face. She listened to his light padding down the stairs and waited tensely for the thunk of the study door as it closed safely behind him. Then she put the breakfast tray aside, threw back the duvet and sat up cross-legged. Urgently she started sifting through the mass of newspapers, discarding each unwanted section on to the floor. Fashion, Books, Appointments, comics, magazines. Please don't let me be in it, she begged. Style, Review, Travel, Business. Ever since the story of Jordan's draft-dodging had become an election issue, the media searchlight had been trained on Oxford. Annie had spent over twenty years disengaging from her past and keeping her profile at snail height. But when journalists were in a feeding frenzy, who knew where and when they might attack?

The picture caught her eye first – a grainy blow-up of

Jordan, centre stage in a group of Rhodes Scholars. Fresh-faced in their dinner jackets and gleaming Beatle haircuts, they were as adorable as choirboys. She had never seen the photo before and couldn't help lingering, just for a moment, over the details of Jordan's broad shoulders and blazing smile. This was just as she had seen him for the very last time, right down to the tuxedo. On the next page there was another picture, an informal little snapshot of him in his Afghan coat, so familiar that a wave of memories washed over her. The angry, staccato chanting. The red nostrils and rolling eyeballs of terrified horses. The pub which she had never been able to find again.

A YANK AT OXFORD, ran the headline. Annie saw that no fewer than twelve people had researched it. She reached for her orange juice, poured its contents down her dry throat in a single slug, and settled down to read every word.

7

Love child

The south end of Kingsway is dominated by Bush House, home of the BBC World Service. From above its yellow stone porch a statue of two men grasping a flaming torch leans perilously into the Aldwych traffic. At their feet the rubric reads, 'To the friendship of English-speaking peoples.' You can't miss it, the commissionaire at Somerset House had told Tom. Stand under the statue, look right, and St Catherine's House will be staring you in the face.

Tom crossed the road to the grey building with its ugly sixties frontage. Could this really be the Public Search Room? Dog-eared census posters and hand-drawn arrows indicating the entrance were sellotaped on to the blank windows, projecting a crushing image of bankrupt state bureaucracy. Inside, however, it was surprisingly efficient. A colour-coded plan at the entrance explained the layout. It was not so much a room as a warren of rooms, each crowded with gunmetal bookcases holding leather-bound ledgers, two foot by one, stiffened with a brass spine. Red for birth, green for marriage, black for death. There was an enquiries desk, a counter where one could apply for copies of certificates, and a collection point. Between each pair of bookshelves an extended wooden lectern provided a place to prop open the heavy ledgers. Tom had been expecting something like the British Library. This was much scruffier, but also more relaxed, with an air of bustling, companionable activity. Teenagers swarmed in the Births section; older people seemed more attracted by the Deaths. Several couples were working in tandem, one calling out names and dates while the other heaved books in and out of the shelves. Here were the personal records of every man, woman and child born in England and Wales since 1837, wide open to public scrutiny, waiting to yield up their secrets.

No point in hanging around now he was here. In the Births section Tom found the volume for January, February and March 1971, E–K, and hauled it out by its black strap. He carried it to a space on the nearest lectern and propped the ledger open. His heart quickened as he reached 'H' and looked for his name. Hamid, Hamilford, Hamilton. HAMILTON, Thomas Stanley. There he was, in black and white, sandwiched between Sylvia Mamie and Tracey Monique. Mother's maiden name, Paxford.

Thank God for that. At least there was one fixed point in the spiral of doubt which had begun to engulf him. His birth had been registered in Chelsea. That sounded right. His mother had often mentioned the little flat in Battersea Park Road, where she had been forced to carry Tom and his pram up and down two flights of stairs, and the landlord banged on his ceiling with a broom handle whenever the baby cried. 'We would have been out on the street if you hadn't been such a good little thing.'

There was a final column of numbers: 0372 06 J74. A notice explained how to obtain a copy of a birth certificate by quoting this reference. A sample taped to the wall showed Tom that the information offered in a full certificate was extensive. Name, place of birth and occupation of father; maiden name of mother, or surname at marriage if different from maiden name. He took one of the forms, but didn't fill it in yet. There was something else he wanted to check.

He wandered deeper into the network of rooms, noting the gold-blocked spines: Consular Births, Service Department Births, Overseas Marriages, War Deaths. Two vast black tomes caught his eye, and he was moved to see that they listed the dead from the First World War, divided into Officers and Other Ranks – as if it mattered after you were dead. Passing through a lino-covered corridor, he came to a room that was wall-to-wall green. Marriages.

Half an hour later he was hot, frustrated and his arms were aching from the weight of the ledgers. No wonder the regulars came in their shirtsleeves. Starting from the date of his birth he had worked backwards for five years, looking in both the E–K and P–S sections for every quarter. A lot of men called Hamilton had got married, including two called Edward Hamilton, but none of them had married Ann Paxford. Only one female Paxford had married, but she was called Marissa, and came from Pontypridd.

But Tom had seen pictures of the wedding, his mother long-haired and laughing with flowers in her hair, his father in a suit with hilariously wide lapels and a rather dashing silk scarf round his neck. His godmother Rose had been there too, exotic in a kaftan and headband. Tom was sure that it had taken place in London, a small, informal register office wedding. Neither of his parents was religious.

He decided to work forwards instead. 1972 – nothing. 1973 – nothing. January–March 1974 – nothing. Tom thought of all those doomed Catholics trapped by marriage in the novels of Graham Greene and Evelyn Waugh, of poor Mr Rochester with his wife cackling in the attic. Could it possibly be that his father had already been married, to a woman who wouldn't divorce him? He heaved down the next volume. He would just keep looking, even if it meant going right up to 1992.

But he never got that far. There it was – HAMILTON, Edward C., married Paxford, Chelsea, 16 June 1974. Tom considered for a moment, then checked the spine to make sure of the date, then double-checked in the P–S volume. PAXFORD, Ann M., married Hamilton, Chelsea, 16 June 1974. No doubt about it. He had been alive for over three years before his parents got married.

Tom suddenly craved fresh air. He retraced his steps past the Births and out into the cold. Mean little crosscurrents of wind sent litter skittering about his feet, and he started walking.

So his parents weren't married when he was born. Was that the big secret? Tom opened his mind to the idea, taking stock of his emotions. It didn't seem too terrible. Hadn't he read a statistic recently that a third of all children nowadays were conceived out of wedlock? There was even, perhaps, something rather buccaneering about being illegitimate. For a moment he felt quite buoyant. Then he remembered the photograph, and his mother's reaction to it, and all the doubts and anxieties about his parentage which they had set off. It was one thing to be illegitimate. But exactly whose illegitimate son was he?

As he trudged along High Holborn, hands thrust deep into the pockets of his football jacket, another inconsistency struck him. If he had been born when his mother was still Ann Paxford, how come his birth had been registered under the name of Hamilton? Tom quickened his step around the block and re-entered St Catherine's House.

Back to Births, January to March 1971, but this time the P–S volume. Here he was again. PAXFORD, Thomas Stanley. Ignoring the sign telling him not to remove more than one volume at a time, he got out E–K to cross-check the details. They were identical except for the reference number.

Tom joined the queue at the enquiries desk, where a large lady in a floral dress was patiently answering questions. When his turn came he showed her the two entries he had copied out.

'This is the same person,' he explained. 'Paxford is the name of the mother and Hamilton the father. I was just wondering, is it normal to register somebody under both names?'

'It's probably a case of re-registration. Let's have a look.' She picked up the spectacles that dangled from a cord around her neck and peered through them at the page in Tom's notebook.

'Yes, you see, the reference numbers are different. Do you know when this person was born?'

Tom felt himself flush under her assessing gaze. 'March 1971, I think.' *I think.* What an idiot he was. Why should she suspect, or care, that he was enquiring about himself?

'Well, look at the reference number in the Paxford entry – 0371. That means the birth was registered in March 1971 under that name. That would be the compulsory registration within six weeks of birth. But this column, in the Hamilton entry, has a different code – J74. That means June 1974. So for some reason this person was re-registered three years after his birth.'

'Why would that be?'

The woman took off her glasses. Her eyes flicked down the queue. 'That I couldn't say. We're only trained to explain the registration system. You'd have to look at the documentation to understand why.'

'Supposing – well, supposing the parents weren't married when the baby was born, but then they got married three years later. Would that explain it?'

'That's one possible reason.'

The woman was not going to make this easy for him. Tom tried to work out what other explanation there might be. She had mentioned documentation. 'So would both birth certificates say the same thing? I mean, assuming the mother is definitely the mother, would both certificates show the same father?'

'Not necessarily.'

'Why not?'

'Sometimes the person registering a birth leaves the space for the father's name blank. They may not know who the father is, or they may choose not to name him, or he may refuse to be named. You can't put just anyone's name down, you know,' she added reprovingly. 'The man has to agree that he is the father.'

'Do you mean to say that the first certificate, the 1971 one, might have no name for the father, or a different one from the Hamilton one?'

'There could be no name, certainly. And it is possible that the names would be different, though it's not very common. As I said, you have to get the man's permission to put his name down, and if you then want to register a different father's name you would have to persuade the registrar that the second man was the real father, and explain why his name hadn't been given in the first place.'

Tom became conscious of the queue shifting impatiently behind him.

'So even if the second man, er, Hamilton, agreed that he wanted to be named as the father, it wouldn't just automatically happen?'

The woman's eyebrows rose in disapproval. 'Certainly not. He could legally adopt the child, of course, but he couldn't register himself as the birth father.'

Adopt. Christ!

Tom wrenched his mind back on to the track. 'So if I wanted to check that the two entries married up, I could apply for copies of both certificates.'

'Wouldn't do you much good. The most recent

registration supersedes all previous registrations. Either way you would get the 1974 document.'

'Even if I gave the reference number of the 1971 entry?'

'That's right.'

'So what you're saying is that I can't look at the 1971 certificate.'

'That's right.'

'Not ever? Not anywhere?'

'Not here, anyway. If you apply on one of the pink forms you will be sent the re-registration details, which-ever reference you give.'

'So – ' So nothing. Dead end. Impasse. Tom stared into the woman's doggy brown eyes.

'Look,' she said finally, 'you can write to this address, if you like, and explain why you want to see the earlier certificate. They might show it to you. But you need a very good reason.'

Tom took the piece of paper from her and moved away from the crowded desk. In a quiet corner he read the printed slip, which gave a Merseyside address for the Office of Population Censuses and Surveys. Tom folded the slip and put it in his jeans pocket. What now? Bang in front of him a bookcase of yellow-backed ledgers caught his eye. 'Adoptions From 1927,' said the label.

No harm in making sure. He did the job thoroughly, checking every year from 1971 to the present. But there were no Thomas Stanleys, whether of the Paxford or the Hamilton variety.

Tom left the building and walked up Kingsway until he came to a café tucked away behind the archway lead-ing into Sicilian Avenue. It was still only half-past eleven, and apart from the cheerful Israeli owner he had the place to himself. He ordered a cappuccino and carried it to a corner table. For a while he just stared into the speckled froth, trying to make sense of the facts he had discovered. Then he drew out his notebook and pencil and a bundle of papers from his rucksack. The whole point of education was to train your mind to assess facts logically and draw a conclusion. So what exactly did he know?

One, he was illegitimate. Two, there was no accessible documentation that proved who his father was. Three, his mother had lied to him consistently. The photograph he had found hadn't been taken in Malta, but in the gardens of LMH some time between 1968 and 1970. Nor, he now knew, was it a picture of some half-forgotten teenage admirer called Jonathan. Tom unfolded the News Review section from yesterday's *Sunday Times* and smoothed it out on the table. Again he felt a jolt of familiarity as he studied the confident young face. How carelessly he had joined in the laughter as Hugh had read out extracts from the Jordan Hope profile. The scene that had taken place in the Christ Church gardens – was it really only yesterday? – replayed in his mind with a retrospective irony that made him squirm.

On his return from Wytham, he had only just padlocked his bike and was walking across the quad to his rooms, preoccupied by his thoughts, when he heard someone shouting his name. Brian and a group of other first-years were sprawled on the grass in the sun, surrounded by the remains of a picnic. 'Eat, drink, and be merry,' Brian gestured expansively, 'for tomorrow ye may have to write an essay.' It showed how drunk they all were that everyone laughed as if Brian had just coined an aphorism of exquisite Wildean wit.

Suddenly, getting drunk seemed the perfect thing to do. Tom dumped the hefty newspaper on the grass and Brian divided it up among the group. As in the miracle of the loaves and fishes, there was a section for everyone. Tom poured himself a glass of Chardonnay, drained it thirstily and refilled it. He lay down on his back, balancing the drink on his stomach and lazily watching cotton-ball clouds chase each other across the sky. He was thinking about Miss Kirk – her frail body confined to that bizarre room, her brain locked in perpetual, pointless motion like an old rat in a familiar maze – when one of the blokes suddenly let out a howl of laughter. It was Hugh, a tall Wykehamist with flowing locks and a braying laugh, who had already taken on the role of class comic.

'Listen to this, chaps,' he said, brandishing the paper, ' "A Yank at Oxford" – the rise of Jordan Hope, from his humble beginnings as a mere Rhodes Scholar to potential President of the Yoo-nited States.' He started to read aloud a profile of the presidential candidate, Jordan Hope, imitating the clipped voiceover from old film newsreels.

' "As the USS *United States* slipped its New York berth, bound for Southampton, Jordan Hope marvelled at the sight of Manhattan slipping away. Leaning on the rail alongside him were some of America's most favoured sons, Rhodes Scholars bound for Oxford, England." ' A raucous cheer went up, and Tom raised his glass in a mock toast.

' "Hope, a small-time boy from the wrong side of the tracks, knew this was a special moment in his life; a romantic departure from the country of his birth and the start of an adventure in – " God, I don't believe this – "in 'swinging' Britain, land of the *Beatles*"!' Howls and groans greeted this masterpiece of painting-by-numbers prose, interspersed with cries for 'More!' Hugh was a good mimic. Encouraged by his audience, he read out highlights in a range of voices, from schmaltzy American soap-opera – ' " 'The moment I met Jordan I knew that some day he was gonna be President,' said fellow Scholar Donald Custard Flugelbaum" ' – to drawling Blanche du Bois Southern. ' "Merrilee Meriwether, a former Miss Mississippi, invited Hope to his first British anti-war march. 'Y'all, I want to go, I've never been to a demonstration.' And Jordan said, 'Gosh, can I come too?' " '

By the time Hugh reached the last, finely delivered line – ' "It was the start of his climb to the White House" ' – his audience was hysterical. Tom felt quite sick with drink and sun and laughter. Gradually the mood of hilarity quietened and the afternoon began to cool. People started to drift away, muttering about strong coffee and overdue essays.

Tom was helping Brian to gather up the scattered newspaper when he caught sight of the picture accompanying the article. All subtlety deserted him. 'Just remembered something,' he said, grabbing the paper and running. The first place he came to was the cathedral. Evensong was not for another half-hour, and it was empty. Tom tucked himself away in the side chapel, pulled out the photo of his mother and 'Jonathan', and compared it to the newspaper photos. There was no doubt about it. It was the same man.

That night, wild fantasies chased round his head like a jumble of Hollywood film trailers. In one Tom sold the photo of Hope and his mother to a hard-faced tabloid hack for a million pounds and disappeared to a new life in Australia. In another, evading Secret Service men with the panache of 007, he confronted Hope on the tarmac as he ran down the steps of his campaign plane. Another had Tom's mother sobbing at his feet begging for his forgiveness. When he finally did get to sleep he had a terrifying nightmare in which he dreamed he had killed his father.

It was barely light when Tom woke. He walked round to the twenty-four-hour cash till in the High and took out his limit of fifty pounds. On the way back he stopped to buy a handful of chocolate bars and a newspaper. A middle-aged, phonily coiffed Hope – unrecognisable from his Oxford self except for the cocky smile – had once again made the front page. Tom packed everything he needed into his rucksack. It didn't amount to much. Then he left a note to Brian outside his door, weighed down by an empty wine bottle, and drove down to London.

And here he was. Tom drained his coffee. He wished there was someone to talk to. He thought of his two oldest friends, one at Cambridge, one studying law at the City

University here in London, virtually round the corner. There was Rebecca, in Sussex. But what exactly was he going to say? Hi, guys, I've just found out I'm illegitimate and I think my father might be the next President of the United States. Just thinking the words made Tom wonder again if he weren't going mad. But why had his mother made such a mystery of everything? Why had she tried so hard to hide the fact that she had once known Jordan Hope?

As the catalogue of his mother's lies and evasions mounted up, so did Tom's anger. It was his life. He wasn't a child any more. He deserved to know the truth.

8

Get off of my cloud

'Right, I've got that,' Annie said, scribbling furiously. 'Presumably those royalties would apply to European sales too?'

Pen poised, she listened intently to the voice on the other end of the phone. 'Good. Now, what about the movie escalator? Remember, you'd probably be getting a second bite at the paperback and a tie-in cover ... *Fifty*?' Very gently Annie laid the receiver down on a soft pile of papers. She reached for her pocket calculator and, swivelling her chair out of earshot of the phone, stabbed out a calculation. Eighty thousand, it said. The receiver was squawking. Annie picked it up quietly, frowned, listened, waited some more, and finally laughed. 'Hard bargain? Me?' she said. 'Come on, Mike, this is the Freddie Forsyth *de nos jours*, and you know it. A hundred thousand ought to do it.'

As soon as she put down the phone Annie shot her arms into the air like a Wimbledon champion. The scribbles in front of her represented a major new deal for Sebastian Winter's next novel. His publishers had now read the last section of the first book which they already had under contract. Evidently, they liked it. They were so confident of having a winner on their hands that they wanted to make sure that he couldn't be lured away to another stable. By offering a temptingly large sum for another book they had bound him to them with chains of gold and tied up his time for at least two years. If she said so herself, Annie had just done a terrific deal. She spared a moment to offer up a prayer to a fellow-agent who had taught Annie the art of the silence. When you don't like an offer, Julia Barnes used to say, just go dead on them. Nine times out of ten, the other party will crack. Once they start blustering, you know you've got them cold.

Annie checked her watch. Noon. In half an hour she was meeting Sebastian. They had set up the meeting in order to discuss some minor changes to his book, but this new offer would be a perfect opening for the other proposition which had been buzzing round her head all week.

She looked round her funny, familiar cubbyhole of an office. Packed into her shelves were just some of the books she had worked on. There had been failures, of course, and plenty of promising books which had nevertheless sunk without trace. But there were others which needed an entire shelf to encompass the history of their success: translations into every language from Czech to Korean to Urdu, bookclub and large print editions, paperbacks, educational abridgements, comic strips, even tapes and videos. Framed photographs of authors, book posters and prize certificates crowded the walls, and some of the postcards and cartoons stuck to her pinboard went back ten years and more. The geraniums on the windowsill had unfurled their green leaves, blossomed and dropped their petals in a drift of pink and white, year in and year out. Soon it would be time to take them home again, to overwinter in her tiny conservatory. Whether she would be bringing them back next March, as usual, was another question.

None of her contemporaries had stayed with the same company for the whole of their working life, as she had done. Everyone moved. That was the way to get on. But for Annie the company had been her family and her home when she had no other. She could still remember the precise figure of her starting salary as a filing clerk — £937.80. It had been a particularly miserable December during the miners' strike when she joined. The three-day week meant that she had to wear her overcoat and fingerless gloves and work by the light of a hissing camping lamp. The office manager, horrified to hear that Annie had no Christmas plans, had invited her to spend the day at her flat with her eighty-five-year-old mother. The mother turned out to have a wooden leg, which provided an embarrassing source of fascination to two-year-old Tom. They had drunk sweet sherry and worn paper hats, and stood up for the Queen's speech.

Eventually Annie had become Mr Robertson's secretary. Then he had started deploying her in other departments. Step by step, she had achieved her current position. Whatever that was. With Jack in charge, she no longer knew where she stood. Ever since their meeting last week Jack had been remote and nit-picking, checking up on minor details and burdening her with unnecessary administration. Annie suspected that his ambitious wife had been nagging him to exercise his authority. She thought that he probably would agree to a partnership, in the end. Even he would see that it was in his interests. But she dreaded the grudging negotiating process. Besides, in the last week the vista of a much larger and more frightening ambition had opened before her: the Annie Hamilton Literary Agency.

She knew exactly how to do it. It would be a two-pronged attack. Sebastian Winter, potentially her most lucrative author, was one prong. The other was the grand old man of English letters, Trelawny Grey. His recent books had proved too oblique and whimsical to be very successful commercially, but the string of novels he had written from the 1930s into the 1970s had made him a household name. He had retired to Ireland with his severe Swedish 'housekeeper' and a brace of Burmese cats. Annie had once been deputed to go over to Tipperary and coax his latest book from him – 'he likes clever blondes,' Mr Robertson had said. Fortunately Annie had always loved his books and knew them inside out. She had weathered a cantankerous grilling about his work, a roisterous trip to the races and a four-hour whiskey marathon in a Dublin bar. 'I like your Annie,' Grey had written to Mr Robertson afterwards, adding cryptically, 'she reminds me of Salsabil, the only filly to win the Irish Derby this century.' Thereafter Grey had insisted that no one but she – not even his editor – be allowed to tamper with even a semicolon of his prose. Grey was currently threatening to write his memoirs. If he ever got down to it, the book would be a sensational literary event, for his youth had been politically adventurous and sexually exotic. But just having his name on her list would be enough. With both Winter and Grey in the bag, surely other authors would follow.

Sebastian Winter's new deal would bankroll the setting up of her own agency and give her breathing space to build her list. But she had to grab it now. The minute Jack found out about the offer, the new book would become the property of Smith & Robertson. Not tomorrow or next week or next month but today, in ten minutes' time, she had an opportunity to take a decisive step in her life. Here was her chance to be her own boss, financially independent, free to choose the course of the rest of her life. The prize lay before her; all she had to do was step forward and pick it up. Yet fear of the unknown and a guilty sense of disloyalty held her like the bars of a cage.

The sudden buzz of her phone made her jump. Annie

just had time to hear Sally begin, 'I'm sorry, Annie, but your son – ' when Tom walked into her office and slammed the door behind him. He looked so pale and unhappy that Annie dropped the phone at once and ran round her desk to him.

'What's happened?' she cried, fearing some terrible accident to Edward or the girls. She put her arms around him, but Tom stiffened and turned his head away, as he used to do as a sulky child.

'What is it?' she asked again, tightening her hold protectively. 'Tom, don't frighten me like this. What's the matter?'

'What's the matter?' he said, stepping out of her embrace. 'Oh, nothing much,' he spat out bitterly. 'I'd just be grateful if you would enlighten me on the small matter of who my father is.'

Annie gasped and took a step backwards. 'Your *what*?'

'Come on, Mum, you heard.' He stared hard into her face. Annie was shocked by the bruised look about his eyes.

'I don't understand what this is about,' she said. 'Your father is who he has always been. Edward, Daddy, Dad. Your father.'

'Then why didn't you marry him until I was *three years old*?'

'Who told you that?' Annie whispered.

'Nobody told me. I looked it up in the Public Search Office – as anyone else could. Half the world could know I'm illegitimate. It's only me that has to be kept in the dark.'

Tom's voice wavered, and he turned to hide his hurt. Above the rim of his T-shirt Annie could see the delicate, boyish furrow at the back of his neck. Her heart went out to him even as her brain raced like a fox before the hounds. This moment had haunted her for twenty years, but she was still unprepared for its sudden, savage arrival. 'Tom – darling,' she pleaded, 'I know it's been a shock,

71

but there were reasons. Do stop glowering and sit down for a minute.' She gestured towards a chair.

Tom thumped his rucksack on the floor. 'For God's sake, I'm not one of your bloody clients,' he said angrily.

Annie suddenly remembered Sebastian. Was he already sitting in the restaurant, waiting for her? Sebastian Winter, her ticket to freedom. Without thinking, she checked her watch with a quick flick of her wrist. The gesture infuriated Tom.

'Stop looking at your watch!' he shouted. 'What sort of a mother are you? You lie to me about my birth. You lie to me about my father. You lie to me about that photograph of "Jonathan" in Malta. God, you must think I'm stupid not to recognise a man who's got his picture in every newspaper in the world.'

'What do you mean?' said Annie. 'And keep your voice down,' she added angrily. 'Why we have to discuss this in my office rather than somewhere private I don't know. As it happens I do have an appointment. You might at least give me half a minute to cancel it and make other arrangements.' Annie moved towards the door. She could get Sally to ring the restaurant. A moment alone might calm Tom down and give her time to think.

Tom reached out and grabbed her arm, hard enough to hurt. 'I don't give a stuff about your stupid appointments,' he said. 'I want to know about Jordan Hope. Some people think that I look like him. Is he my father?'

'Don't be ridiculous.' Annie yanked her arm out of his grip.

'Then why did you make up that lie about the photograph? Hope is front-page news. How come you never bothered to mention that you even knew him?'

'I should have thought that was obvious.' Annie realised that she was shouting too, and tried to control her voice. 'The press has been hounding everybody who even went to the same Oxford party as Jordan. You might like to wake up to a gaggle of prurient newsmen on your doorstep, but I don't fancy it.'

'So you did know him?'

'He was a friend of Rose's. They were both interested in politics. I used to see him around.'

'What about all that "two-times girl" stuff? "Love always, J".'

'For heaven's sake, Tom, he was an American,' Annie said. 'A big, gee-whizz American who wanted to be President even then. He was always hugging people and signing books or photos for them. That's how politicians work.'

'So you never went out with him?'

'We might have turned up at the same party. I don't remember.'

'You don't remember?' Tom was nearly crying with frustration. 'When are you going to start telling me the truth? You'd better be careful, Mother, I've been doing some checking up. That photograph was taken in the LMH gardens. I've been to the very spot. I know all about how you didn't take your degree, how disappointed Miss Kirk was, and Miss Reeves – they send their best wishes, by the way.'

Annie felt panic overwhelm her. The walls she had built round her past were crumbling on every side. 'How dare you go around prying and spying into my private life?'

Tom's face twisted as he tried to squeeze the tears back into his eyes. 'How else can I find out the truth?' he asked. 'Can't you see, it matters to me what happened back then. It matters to me who my father is. Do you want me to check with Jordan Hope and see what he says?'

Annie rounded on him like a tigress. 'Don't you dare contact Jordan. Grow up, Tom. Do you realise the damage you could do to him if you even suggested he had an

73

illegitimate son? And all because you've built up some utterly absurd fantasy based on an old snapshot.'

Tom's face closed against her. He picked up his rucksack by the strap and moved towards the door. Annie took a deep breath, fighting to regain a tone of reason. 'Tom. Edward is your father. We fell in love, then we . . . parted. That was a mistake, and we put it right. I can explain – we'll both explain. But not here. Why don't you go home – please. I'll come as soon as I can. We can all talk this evening.'

Tom didn't even look at her. He opened the door and walked into the corridor, where Sally sat nervously in her glass box. Annie followed him. 'Tom . . .?'

He carried on, quickening his pace. Annie ran after him. At the angle of the corridor she nearly bumped into Jack by a bank of filing cabinets. As Annie brushed past she caught a glimpse of his face, inscrutable as a mask. Now they were at the stairs. Tom, sure-footed in his trainers, bounced down them ahead of her.

'Wait!' Annie yelled. 'Where are you going?'

Annie caught only two words from his angry, muffled shout – 'my father'.

'*No*!' she screamed. 'Tom, if you upset Edward I'll never forgive you.'

Tom whirled around on the landing below, and looked up at her with a face she hardly recognised.

'Who said anything about Edward?' he asked coldly.

Annie moved towards him, but it was too late. She heard his urgent tread continuing down the stairs, the jingle of his rucksack buckle and the thud of the heavy front door. He was gone.

9

Bridge over troubled water

From its niche above the shelves of cookbooks the Victorian clock struck eleven. Annie sat alone in her kitchen, elbows propped on the scrubbed pine table, staring into the fruit bowl. She was wearing one of Edward's old shirts over her T-shirt and leggings, clutching the too-long cuffs tightly in her fists. Hair tumbled from a knot on the crown of her head, roughly secured with a tortoise-shell clip. On the principle of the watched pot, she kept her back to the telephone, which had remained obstinately silent all evening. At the sound of a footstep in the hall Annie looked up eagerly. But it was only Edward.

'Come to bed,' he said. 'There's nothing you can do now. It won't do you any good to be tired on top of everything else.'

Annie raked her fingers into her hair and clenched them tight, until her scalp ached. 'Where is he?' she asked fiercely.

'Probably kipping on somebody's floor,' said Edward. 'He's a sensible boy. He got himself through Eastern Europe. He'll manage a night on his own, wherever he is.'

'I handled it all so badly, Edward.' Annie turned to him a face pale and dark-eyed with tiredness. 'I shouted at him. I told him to mind his own business. I did the exact opposite of everything I should have done – everything we planned to do if he ever found out. But after all this time, I thought we were safe. I still can't believe he just went and looked up those records himself.'

'Stop blaming yourself. We always knew this might happen. Tom needs time to think about it. He'll come to us when he's ready.'

'But what's he doing?' she growled. 'Why can't he at least ring? How can you be so bloody calm?'

'Because I know our son.'

'You wouldn't have this afternoon,' she said bitterly. 'I couldn't even tell you some of the horrible things he said. And this ridiculous bee in his bonnet he's got about Jordan Hope.'

'Yes,' Edward frowned for a moment. 'That does seem perverse. It's not as though you even knew him particularly well.'

'I told you about the photograph, didn't I?' Annie snapped. 'Tom's had a shock, and he's gone off the deep end. Didn't you use to imagine that you were adopted, or swapped at birth in the hospital?'

'When I was about seven or eight,' Edward said dubiously.

'God, I used to long for my real mother to come and reclaim me. I imagined her just like Mother in *The Railway Children* – brave and loving, with a kind face and sensible clothes and home-made cakes in the oven. And that was without any lies or mystery about my birth. Tom's entitled to indulge in a few wild fantasies, I suppose.' Annie rocked impatiently in her chair. 'I just wish he'd come home.'

Edward came round behind her, and squeezed her shoulders. 'Leave it alone, darling. It's late. He'd be here by now if he were coming.'

Annie pressed her cheek against his hand. 'You go on up. I'd only thrash about in the bed and drive you mad. I might have a whisky, that always makes me sleepy.' Edward sighed, and let her go. 'Don't be too long. You know I can never sleep properly when you're not there.'

When he had left, Annie poured herself a small whisky, and filled up the tumbler with water. Drink in hand, she wandered restlessly around the room, pausing to look at the postcards and invitations propped up on the dresser shelf, pulling dead leaves off her plants, straightening the chairs around the table. She loved this room. She had colourwashed the walls herself, long before the 'distressed' look had become fashionable, experimenting to reproduce the kind of pure colour she'd grown up with in the Mediterranean. She'd designed everything, too, from the shape of the arch above the cooker to the slate-topped worktops made specially high so that she didn't get backache. In the mornings sunshine filled the room; at night the pulley-lamp which she and Edward had bought years ago in the Paris flea market gave it an intimate, friendly glow. This is where she liked to work in the evenings, laying out her scripts on the big table or reading in the cushion-filled wicker chair by the window.

She and Edward had committed their last penny to buying this house and had invested years of their life in doing it up. Midway in an elegant Georgian terrace, separated from the road by a phalanx of magnificent horse chestnut trees, it exuded a calm English confidence. It was the only place Annie had lived that felt truly hers. After her own haphazard childhood, she had been determined that her own children should never be in any doubt where 'home' was.

Annie's thoughts circled back to Tom. Her stomach lurched as she tried to envisage where he might be or what he might be doing. It was perfectly possible for him to have flown two thousand miles across the Atlantic by now. Nobody could be more supportive than Edward, but there were certain things he couldn't fully appreciate. Suddenly Annie was struck by a thought of such blinding obviousness that she choked on her whisky. America! It was too late for anything to be happening in stuffy old London, maybe. But it was barely cocktail time in New York. Annie grabbed the phone and punched in a familiar pattern of digits.

'Rose Cassidy's office,' said a sugary voice. 'How may I help you?'

'Is Rose there?'

'I'm sorry, she's in conference right now. May I have her call you?'

Annie nearly groaned aloud. 'Is it an important meeting? I mean, could you interrupt it? I need to speak to her very urgently.'

There was a pause, then the same singsong inflection. 'Whom may I say is calling?'

Annie spelled out her name letter by letter, rolling her eyes in frustration. Why did American 'assistants' always sound as if they'd had their personalities surgically removed, like graduates of some Stepford Wife training school?

Annie was treated to a few bars of Vivaldi's 'Winter', then there was a series of clicks and, miraculously, Rose came on the line. 'Darling, I rushed straight out of my meeting. You've never said "urgent" before. What's happened?'

At the sound of Rose's voice, pukka English with a subtle American slur, Annie's eyes brimmed with tears. She took a deep breath, wondering where to begin. The problems that had been crowding in on her seemed overwhelming, insoluble. 'Oh, Rose,' she moaned, 'my whole life is falling apart. I don't know what to do.'

'Hang on a minute,' Rose said briskly. 'This sounds serious.' Annie waited, hunting for a tissue in a drawer of the oak dresser. Rose came back on the line. 'All done. Now, tell me everything.'

Many yards of newsprint had been devoted to profiles of Rose Cassidy. Annie had seen her described as a genius and a witch; as dictatorial, calculating, capricious, and snobbish; as Queen of the Brit Pack and even – in one notorious American headline – 'Killer WASP'. But Annie had no secrets from Rose. Too much had happened between them. She poured out her story, and with it every emotion good and bad. Rose grasped instantly the implications of Tom's disappearance.

'My God, Annie, you really think he might get in touch with Jordan?'

'I don't know,' was Annie's anguished reply. 'He seems completely obsessed by this father thing. I had to ring Edward and warn him, in case Tom burst in on him as well. But he never turned up at Edward's chambers, and he hasn't come home either. By nine o'clock I couldn't stand it any longer. I drove up to Oxford like a lunatic, and found out that his room-mate hadn't seen him since last night. But he showed me a note from Tom. Can you believe it, Rose? Tom told him that his father was seriously ill in hospital and he'd be away from Oxford for *several days*. The room-mate was stunned to see me, as you can imagine. I had to pretend I'd come up to get some of Tom's clothes for him.'

'His passport!' Rose said excitedly. 'Did you think of looking for that?'

'Of course I did. It's not in his room at Christ Church, and I can't find it here either.'

'Annie,' breathed Rose, 'this is seriously terrible. The election's next *week*. Everyone with half a brain wants Jordan to win. I hate to think what might hit the fan if Tom turned up claiming to be his illegitimate son.'

'Don't,' Annie groaned. Tethered by the long telephone wire, she paced round the kitchen in her bare feet. 'But what can I do? I can't exactly ring up Jordan and explain. I suppose it's preposterous to think that Tom could even get to him. But he's in a dangerous mood – all wired up and unstable, like a package of Semtex. He might have gone to stay with a friend, which is what Edward thinks. But he might be throwing himself off Beachy Head. He might be getting on a plane. Wherever he is, he's unhappy and mixed up, and I'm terrified he could just explode and start talking. God knows whether Jack overheard us shouting in the office today. He was only yards away. As if I haven't got enough trouble with Jack as it is. . . . Rose? Are you still there?'

'I'm thinking. Go on. What's all this about Jack?'

Annie explained.

'But that's brilliant! Tell the silly prat to stuff his partnership, and do your own thing. This isn't a problem, Annie, it's your big chance.'

Annie snorted. 'You sound like some ghastly Victorian sampler. "Man's extremity is God's opportunity." You don't understand. I'd have to do it now, like tomorrow, before Jack gets his mitts on Sebastian. I can't possibly think about that with Tom on the loose. Besides, I – well, there's a chance I might have to leave the country for a few days.'

'Whatever for?'

Annie fiddled with the curly telephone wire. 'It's my mother,' she confessed. 'Apparently she's dying and wants to see me.'

Rose was astounded. 'But you've always hated the old dragon. I felt like carving her up myself once.'

'I know, I know. I've tried not to think about it. I've tried to say, Go on then, die, you old bitch. But I can't. She's dying, Rose. She wants to see me. I suppose I'm curious, if nothing else.'

Rose was silent – disapproving or sympathetic, Annie couldn't tell. 'I probably won't go,' Annie sighed. 'Not with Tom and everything else. Anyway, she could be dead already. I got the letter about her over a week ago, and – '

Rose interrupted, sounding incredibly portentous. 'On the contrary, you positively must go.'

'I must?'

'*Eppur si muove*,' Rose said enigmatically.

'Rose, stop being mysterious. What are you talking about?'

'It's what Galileo said about the earth moving round the sun, you oick. Annie,' Rose lowered her voice to a conspirator's whisper, 'I have just had a truly awesome brainwave. It would solve everything – Jordan, mother, job, the lot. Listen. Here's what you do.'

After thirty seconds Annie burst out, 'I can't!' After a minute she protested, 'I couldn't possibly.' At the end of three minutes she sagged against the wall, completely silenced. Maybe Rose was a witch after all.

'Admit,' Rose said smugly, 'it does have a kind of fearful symmetry to it.'

'Fearful is the word. I don't think I'm brave enough.'

'Rubbish. Is this the Annie Paxford who brought Oxford to its knees with her incandescent Rosalind?'

'But that was – '

'. . . who smoked joints through Helen Gardner's Shakespeare lectures?'

'Only once,' Annie protested.

'The Annie Paxford,' Rose continued remorselessly, 'who jumped fully clothed into the river at the Eights Week Ball and danced the rest of the night away wearing only a rugby shirt?'

'No it isn't,' Annie said sadly. 'It's boring old Mrs Hamilton, aged forty-two and a quarter, with her career on the line, a dying mother and a missing son.'

'Don't be feeble. I didn't like to tell you, but while we've been talking I've had to leave John Updike and Stephen Spender kicking their heels next door, with only Cindy and some iced water for company. Imagine, two literary lions with their tails positively twitching. If I can risk alienating those two for you, *darling* Annie, you

81

could at least consider my fiendishly cunning masterplan. I'm volunteering to do the tricky bit, after all.'

'But – '

'Got to go now. I'll call you back when I've got the information. Don't worry. Everything will be fine.'

Rose smacked a kiss down the phone, and the line went dead. Annie hung up. She felt buffeted, wiped out, drained – and starving. She rummaged in the food cupboard until she found half a chocolate biscuit at the bottom of a packet. Munching hungrily, she pushed open the double doors from the kitchen and went into the back living-room that gave on to the garden. She lay down in the dark on the big, comfortable Chesterfield and wrapped herself up in a worn quilt that was always kept folded over one arm.

Now she knew how Rose managed to get celebrities to do impossible things. Hadn't there been a sensational cover showing a naked filmstar astride a rearing stallion? And a portrait of the Princess of Wales in the style of Gainsborough? She had probably already lined up Ginny Hope for a full-colour, centre-spread make-over.

Still, the Rose treatment was kind of exhilarating, once you got used to it. No doubt people felt much the same about whitewater rafting or bungee-jumping. Annie thought her way carefully through Rose's outrageous plan, combing it for flaws. There weren't any. Unless you counted one or two tiny deceptions.

Annie tried to imagine what it would be like to see Jordan again. How would he play it? Embarrassed, businesslike, angry? Would he try to smother her in professional charm like one of his prospective voters? A smile tugged at her mouth. Let him try.

She yawned. It was all such a long time ago. What were those lines she used to quote to herself when it was all over?

Shake hands for ever, cancel all our vows
And when we meet at any time again,

82

> Be it not seen in either of our brows
> That we one jot of former love retain.

Well, maybe. But one thing you found out as you got older was that the important things didn't change. Perhaps Rose was right. Somewhere inside sensible Mrs Hamilton, Annie Paxford still lurked – a secretive nineteen-year-old with her head stuffed full of literature and a passion to prise life open like an oyster.

Annie yawned again. A glorious drowsiness invaded her body. She loosened her hair and dropped the clip on the floor. As her eyes closed, the years curled back and floated away like the pages of a burning book.

OXFORD

1969–70

Michaelmas Term 1969

10

Wild honey

Annie leaned out of the train window, watching the stoutly mackintoshed figure recede to a square of navy blue and fluttering white. She returned a final wave, drew in her head, and pulled the window shut. Alone at last. Squatting on the floor of the corridor, she rummaged in her Greek bag and extracted a packet striped in purple and azure blue. With two forefingers she flipped her heavy, honey-coloured hair over her shoulders, letting it trail down her back. Then she lit a cigarette in relief and celebration. Soon she would be back at Oxford, in a world she loved and understood, where she could do her own thing, without muddle and rows.

Aunt Betty meant well. For ten years her Kensington mansion flat had been Annie's staging-post between boarding-school and wherever home then happened to be. Annie knew every creaky floorboard, and the proper position of each piece of Staffordshire pottery. She had long ago lost her terror of the clanking cage of the lift, which rose and descended at a dowager's pace, and learned the knack of making the lavatory chain work first time. From this flat she and her aunt had sallied forth to Fortnum's for lunch and Gorringe's for school uniforms, to museums and art galleries, walks in Kensington

Gardens and the occasional 'suitable' film. When she was old enough to be allowed out on her own, she had spent hours wandering down the King's Road or foraging through stalls in Portobello Market. Sometimes she met schoolfriends whose parents lived in London. They would doll themselves up in high heels, pale lipstick and thick mascara, and backchat their way into 'X'-rated films like *Tom Jones*. Once they had taken the train to Surrey and walked for miles to stand outside the high walls of George Harrison's house, fantasising about how he might invite them in to meet the other Beatles. Later they had discovered that the Fab Four had been meditating with the Maharishi at the time.

Annie enjoyed her aunt's schoolgirlish zeal for treats, usually edible ones involving a great deal of cream. But three days with Aunt Betty, when Annie desperately needed to sort out her thoughts, was long enough. Aunt Betty was an unworldly spinster of fifty-something, married to her secretarial job at the BBC. The guiding principles of her life were doing her duty, being kind to animals and wearing wool next to the skin. Her idea of excitement was watching *The Forsyte Saga* on Sunday nights. She was not the sort of person one could talk to about sex.

Annie took a last, determined drag of her cigarette. Her aunt disapproved of smoking. After a period of polite abstention the cigarette tasted of burning rubbish tips and made Annie's head spin. So what? She was free, female and nineteen. She was officially an adult. She could do as she liked. She blew out the smoke with a loud sigh, wishing she could as easily expel the memory of that ghastly last day in Malta.

Annie swayed down the corridor, nearly tripping over her fashionably long purple scarf, and slid open the door of the second-class compartment where she had bagged a corner seat with her coat. An elderly couple sitting by the door drew back their legs, as if the terrifying word 'student' were branded across her forehead. Annie glanced at her other travelling companions: a bossy-looking woman who reminded Annie of her old piano teacher and a furtive man with a gingery halo of hair, reading T.S. Eliot. A postgraduate student, Annie diag- nosed, the quintessential Oxford gnome who haunted the upper reading room of the Bodleian by day and spent the evening crouched over cocoa in some damp bedsit off the Cowley Road. Annie shook out her hair to form a curtain between her and the rest of the compartment, turning to look out of the window. Grimy London terraces gave way to privet-screened suburban semis and finally to the open countryside. England looked misty and mel-ancholic, just as it should. Ponies huddled in the corners of fields, ears back, tails clamped tight against the October wind. Leaves of amber and bronze sagged under the weight of rain. Annie felt restless, excited, and nervous all at once.

Over the Long Vac she had relived every moment she and Edward had spent together. She had first seen him last April. *As You Like It* was to be put on in the sixth week of Trinity term in St Hilda's meadow. In First Week the cast had gathered for a read-through in a bleak college seminar room furnished with moulded plastic chairs. Annie was to play Rosalind. It was her first big part at Oxford, and she was nervous. The director was an intense second-year with John Lennon glasses and a corduroy cap, bent on making theatrical history. This was to be a landmark production, he proclaimed, making a break with the trendy, modern-dress approach to Shakespeare which had become such a cliché. No Peter Brook or Charles Marowitz for him, thank you very much. This *As You Like It* would be as Shakespeare himself would have liked it. It would emphasise the roots of the play in masque and romance. It would be pastoral, poetic and perfect. The verse would be beautifully spoken and the songs sung properly – to the strains of a lute, if obtainable.

He was in discussion with a local farmer about borrowing a sheep for the bucolic scenes. Instead of the traditional strawberries and wine, mead and syllabub would be served in the interval. In the final act Hymen, god of marriage, would waft magically across the Cherwell, a *coup de théâtre* to be effected by means of a punt and underwater ropes.

In the middle of this visionary speech a tall, dark-haired student had strolled in, casually apologetic. Seating himself at the front, he had stretched out long legs encased in tight, bright red trousers tucked pirate-like into black boots. From the row behind, Annie studied his profile – sloping forehead and narrow, disdainful nose – as he listened to the remainder of the speech. He appeared quite unruffled by the director's grandiose expectations. Annie knew at once that he must be monstrously arrogant. He would make a perfect Jaques.

As it turned out, she was right. There was an amused detachment about Edward Hamilton that suited the part of Shakespeare's self-dramatising old cynic. He was in his second year at Trinity, reading Law. His natural theatricality expressed itself in black shirts and a succession of outrageous waistcoats. As Jaques he was to wear a long black cloak and broad-brimmed hat, with which he made much dramatic play. Along with the rest of the cast, Annie teased him about his clothes and the stuffiness of his chosen career. But she was intrigued. There was a calmness about him that was attractive.

One gloriously hot afternoon they were rehearsing in St Hilda's meadow. Hymen had smuggled a bottle of Pimm's past the director and Annie was feeling giggly. Egged on by the rest of the cast, she tried to put Edward off his 'All the world's a stage' speech by acting it out behind the director's back, hamming up each part from the mewling, puking baby to the old codger 'sans teeth, sans eyes' etcetera. Edward never blinked an eyelash. At the end of his scene he beckoned Annie over to the river's edge, looking serious. Annie followed, half nervous and half defiant. Surely he could take a joke. As she approached his eyes narrowed with concentration.

'Is that a new dress?' he asked.

As a matter of fact it was. Annie thought she looked rather wonderful in it. She looked down, brushing the skirt dismissively.

'What, this old thing?'

'Good,' he said, picking her up, and dropped her, squealing and kicking, into the river. The cast applauded.

After that Annie was aware of a certain *frisson* of complicity between them, but they had few scenes together and were never alone. Anyway, there was no shortage of men asking her out, a fact she made no special effort to conceal. She wondered if Edward had a girlfriend, and discovered that the very idea made her feel savage. On the night of the dress rehearsal she was waiting to go on, dressed in her Ganymede outfit of breeches, boots, shirt and jerkin. A pall of gloom hung over the cast. The weather had turned cold. Touchstone still hadn't learned his lines. The lights kept fusing. In the darkness and confusion someone had stepped on the lute. Annie could already feel the sarcastic bite of the reviews.

She was waiting in the dark, hunched with cold and anxiety, when Edward suddenly appeared beside her, opened his cloak and enfolded her in it. For a moment Annie was shocked into stillness, then she slid her arm round his warm body. They stood in the shadows, still as statues, not speaking, hardly breathing.

Afterwards she found him waiting for her outside the changing tent. He took her to the Bear and bought her a schooner of sherry, looking at her with those grave, grey eyes as if every idiotic thing she said and every nervous gesture she made was a miracle. When last orders were called, she watched him carry their glasses to the bar, boots scuffing across the bare floorboards, eyes half closed against the smoke twisting up from his cigarette. She saw the way his body moved as he fished for coins in the back pocket of his tight jeans. As if he could feel her eyes on him, he turned round and gave her a slow-burn look across the crowded room. At closing time he walked her back to Lady Margaret Hall, a distance of about half a mile, but they stopped to kiss so often that it took an hour. When at last Edward let her go, Annie stumbled through the brightly lit corridors to her room, her lips on fire, her cheeks sore from his rough stubble.

It was Annie's first intoxicating taste of an Oxford summer term. Suddenly the Cherwell, which had been the wintertime preserve of ducks and willows, sprouted punts full of exhibitionist young men in striped blazers and barefoot girls in hats. Trees she had never even noticed exploded into blossom, of every shade from palest vanilla to raspberry pink. By day the lanes were loud with bicycle bells and the anguished protestations of third-years that they would never be ready for Finals. At night the Beach Boys and the Stones and Pink Floyd blared out of open casement windows. The air smelled of wistaria and roses and newly mown grass. There were tea parties, tennis parties, garden parties, beer-cellar parties, river-barge parties, Edwardian parties, twenties parties. Annie fell headlong in love with Oxford and summer and Edward all at once.

The day after the dress rehearsal Annie went to lunch with Edward at Trinity. The sun had reappeared, and they carried their plates of salmon mayonnaise and bowls of strawberries and cream on to the lawn. Edward's room-mate, Anthony, brought over a bottle of cold white wine. He was an Old Etonian with a Roman nose, who looked Annie over with frank admiration, stamping his foot like a stallion. 'What a heavenly girl. Can I have one?' After lunch they wandered down to Christ Church Meadow, idling along the broad elm-shaded path to the Isis to watch the boat races. By chance it was the day that Trinity bumped Oriel. The college boathouse was raucous with celebration. Everyone seemed to know Edward and to think it quite natural that he and Annie belonged together.

The few remaining weeks of term passed in a blur of new enchantments. Annie had to work at night. The days were too exciting. They bicycled out to the Perch and the White Hart for drinks, returning in the late midsummer twilight. They held hands through *Un Homme et une femme* and sighed over Terence Stamp and Julie Christie in *Far From the Madding Crowd*. One rainy afternoon they played darts for champagne stakes with Edward's friends, consuming three bottles in Trinity beer cellar. In the evenings Edward took her for a curry at the Taj Mahal or cannelloni at La Cantina.

Every night there was the adrenalin rush of another performance – making up, horseplay in the changing tent, and that shivery moment in the second half when darkness stole across the meadow and Shakespeare's verse, even indifferently recited, worked its magic. On the third night a gust of wind caught the punt sideways on, depositing Hymen in the undergrowth five feet from his target. Instead of gliding ethereally on-stage, he spoke his lines invisibly from a hawthorn thicket, to the sounds of his costume ripping and muffled hiccups of laughter from the other players.

Fortunately the reviewers had already pronounced. If no one hailed it as a landmark production, the seats were filled almost every night. One morning Rose burst into Annie's room to show her the *Cherwell* review which rated the production beta-query-plus, but called Annie's Rosalind 'enchanting'. It was enough to guarantee an all-night cast party, awash with booze and sentiment, in the director's digs in the Iffley Road. Annie flirted with most of the men and danced with all of them. She hugged everybody and drank everything in sight. She wished that the party could go on for ever and ever, and called Edward an old bore when he tried to take her home. Only when the director passed out and had to be put to bed did Annie concede that it was time to leave.

It was already light when they crossed Magdalen Bridge. A thin layer of mist hovered above the river. Before them the High curved gracefully away, looking much as it must have done two hundred years ago. Oxford was utterly still, apart from the electric whine of a milk van and the chatter of the dawn chorus. Edward and Annie walked up the middle of the empty road, hip to hip in an easy rhythm, their arms around each other. Annie still felt full of energy. She wanted to do something. But Edward was silent, his thoughts apparently far away. She pinched him in the ribs.

'Say something.'

He stopped and turned to look at her, dropping his arms to his sides. 'OK,' he said slowly. He took her face in her hands. 'Come back with me. I want to make love to you.'

'Edward . . .'

'Anthony's gone to London for a party,' Edward urged. 'He won't be back until tonight.' He moved his hands to the sensitive skin under her hair, then down her back, pulling her hard against him. He pressed his forehead against hers, staring into her eyes. She felt their eyelashes brush. 'I love you, Annie. Come back with me. Please.'

Annie leaned into him. 'All right,' she smiled.

His attic bedroom was high and secret. Annie lay tangled with Edward in the narrow bed, eyes shut, mind floating. How was it possible for her body to feel like this – at once as tight as a drum and as limp as a rag doll's? The sweep of skin and muscle down Edward's back was delicious. Her fingers found two little hollows at the bottom of his spine and tickled them gently. Edward moaned. He must like that. She did it again. On the inside of her eyelids she could see zigzag patterns from the sunlight that glimmered through the curtains. 'Busy old fool, unruly sun – ' how did that poem go? Was it the

94

same one that went on 'Licence my roving hands and let them go/ Before, behind, between, above, below'? Edward must have read it. His hands were warm and inquisitive. Annie did a bit of exploring herself. Heavens, how extraordinary! – she had always imagined that it would stick straight out like an old-fashioned car indicator, not *up* like this. At Edward's persuasive touch on the inside of her knee Annie stretched her legs out languorously, sinking deeper into a narcotic trance. In a distant corner of her brain a voice was saying, 'My God, I'm really going to do it. Please don't let him realise this is my first time.' But it didn't really matter. Nothing mattered except the amazing sensations in her body and Edward's breath urgent on her neck.

Annie crossed her legs as the train shuddered through a culvert and out into the flat plain around Didcot. They must have passed through Reading without her noticing. The piano woman had gone, and ginger hair was eyeing her interestedly over *The Four Quartets*. She gave him a cool stare, noting his brothel-creeper shoes and baggy trousers. He must be nearly thirty! A creature like this could be her fate if she followed her mother's advice and waited until she was a hundred and twelve for Mr Right to appear. All the beautiful men like Edward Hamilton would have been snapped up.

On her last night in Malta she had gone with her parents, as usual, to the club for her farewell treat, driving the long way round to see the castle at sunset. At the bar of the officers' mess there was the usual heavy gallantry about her father's 'harem'. 'Hard to tell which is the mother and which the daughter, what?' The colonel teased Annie about the number of suitors awaiting her in Oxford, and congratulated her on returning to 'civilisation'. Each expatriate community she had lived in was the same – Aden, Cyprus, Malta. Everyone acted as if they were perilously marooned among a remote tribe of cannibals. They were scathing about the locals and talked of 'ukay' as of some lost paradise. Annie believed most of them wouldn't last five minutes in rainy Guildford, with no clubhouse or tennis courts or the much-reviled 'girls' who did all the work. Privately, she saved up a few choice phrases for Rose, who loved her to 'do' Malta.

But publicly she smiled and charmed, and in due course they had moved on to the dining-room to eat prawn cocktail, well-done beef with Yorkshire pudding, followed by baked apples and custard. Afterwards there had been more banter at the bar. As usual her mother had collected a circle of eager admirers and drank too many brandies. But she had seemed in a good mood. Annie had no inkling of what was to come.

Her father drove them back to the villa through the darkening countryside. Annie wound down her window and relaxed in the back seat, enjoying the warm wind on her face. Tomorrow she would be leaving.

'This young man who keeps writing you letters,' her mother suddenly began.

Annie stiffened. 'I've told you, Mummy, his name's Edward.'

'This "Edward", then,' she said, enunciating carefully as if it were some outlandish name, 'I hope you aren't sleeping with him.'

Annie said nothing. I'm nineteen, she thought. It's none of your business.

Her mother twisted round from the front seat to peer at Annie. Her earrings glinted in the headlamps of a passing car.

'Well?' she insisted.

Annie stared at the blonde nimbus of her mother's bouffant hair.

In the lengthening silence her father cleared his throat. 'Mary dear, I don't think we really – '

'Shut up, Charles. Anyway, it's no good her pretending she isn't, because I found some contraceptive pills in her room this afternoon.'

'You were snooping!' Annie was shocked. What if her mother had read Edward's letters too? The idea made her feel sick.

'I do not call it snooping to be concerned about my daughter. Are you sleeping with him or aren't you?'

'Yes, I am. And I'm not ashamed of it.'

'I knew it,' shrieked her mother, clasping her temples. 'You stupid, stupid girl. Don't you know anything about men? This Edward, he's just using you for sex.'

'He's not! Edward loves me. And – and I love him,' she added defiantly.

'My darling child.' Her mother threw out a dismissive arm, bracelets jangling. 'You're barely nineteen. What could you possibly know about love? You wait. You'll get back to your precious Oxford and find he doesn't even give you the time of day – let alone a proposal of marriage.'

Annie gasped. 'Marriage! I don't want to marry him,' she said scornfully.

'The way you're carrying on you may have to,' her mother said grimly. 'I've read about all this student non-sense – pop concerts and sit-ins and not wearing bras – but I never thought you would lower yourself to that kind of behaviour.'

'It's not like that,' Annie protested. 'You're just jealous because I'm having a good time. People in your day didn't have sex before marriage because they didn't dare to. It wasn't anything to do with morality.'

'Well, actually – ' began her father.

'Stop the car, Charles!' shouted her mother. 'I will not be spoken to like this.'

Far from slowing down, Annie's father gunned the car forwards. 'You're drunk,' he stated coldly. 'If you ever thought before you spoke, you would realise that what you're saying is both cruel and unfair.'

'At least I do speak,' her mother retaliated. 'All you

ever do is read the bloody paper and play chess with yourself.'

'And why do you think that is?'

Annie put her hands over her ears. 'Shut up, both of you,' she begged, tears squeezing under her eyelids.

She felt the car turning into the villa gates, and was out of the door even before it stopped. She ran inside and up to her room, slamming the door. Bicker, bicker, bicker. Why did they do it? Even on her last night they couldn't stop themselves.

When she was a little girl, she used to get right down under the bedclothes and pour out her heart to an imaginary sister, a twin rather improbably named Rita. The great thing about Rita was her total fearlessness. She thought up brilliant things for Annie to say to people who were nasty to her, and she made up fantastic stories, usually about running away, of which Annie was always the heroine. But Rita had faded away when Annie went to boarding-school. The real brothers and sisters she had longed for never appeared. When it came to dealing with her parents, she was on her own.

She undressed, put on her nightshirt and locked herself in the bathroom. She washed her face in cold water, rubbed Vaseline into her eyelashes, and swallowed one of her pills. The next time she took one she would be in England. Where Edward lived.

As she went back down the hall she could hear a familiar pattern of sounds downstairs: her mother's voice loud and petulant, heels tapping on marble as she crossed and re-crossed the room, and the conciliatory murmur of her father's replies. Were they talking about her? She paused by the balustrade, listening.

'. . . do as they bloody well like?' Her mother's voice rose to a crescendo. 'Thank God I never let you persuade me to have any more. Nine months of feeling sick and fat and ugly, and then all that terrible pain. And for what?'

There was the chink of bottle against glass, and the

gurgle of liquid. 'So that my own daughter can tell me to leave her alone so she can "do her own thing".'

There was a pause. Her father's reply was inaudible.

'Oh yes, throw my past in my face.'

Annie heard the rustle of a newspaper.

'That's right, Charles, ignore me. Bury your head in the paper. Go off and cure some bloody patient. Just don't expect me to help when she gets herself into a mess. Thank God it's her last night.'

'I imagine she feels the same way.'

'And don't expect me to get up to see her off. I'm taking a sleeping pill.'

This time, even as she was sidling back to her room, Annie heard her father's weary reply. 'Take as many as you like.'

In the morning she found him at the kitchen table in front of yesterday's *Times*. His face looked thin and grey. He had missed a patch of stubble under his jaw. Annie went over to him and put her hands on his shoulders. She breathed on the bald spot on the top of his head and made as if to polish it with her sleeve: an old joke. He reached up to pat her hand.

'Ready to go, monkey?'

They bumped along the pot-holed airport road, between rows of scrubby oleanders. A young man on foot, seeing their British army licence plates, shook a fist at them. Right on, Annie cheered silently. The British were in retreat everywhere from their old Empire – and about time too.

'You mustn't mind what your mother says,' her father began hesitantly. 'Life hasn't been quite as she expected. Always living abroad. Moving on every few years.'

'She hates me.' To her horror, Annie felt her eyes fill with tears. 'My own mother. That's why she never had any more children, isn't it?'

Her father negotiated carefully round a mule, almost invisible beneath a load of firewood.

'*Isn't it*?' Annie sniffed, rummaging for a tissue. He handed her his handkerchief.

'What was so awful about me?' Annie blew her nose loudly. 'I adored her when I was little. I remember hanging on to her knees and begging her not to leave me with Yasmin or Concepcion or whoever it was. Just sometimes she stayed home with me. She'd put on the radio and try to teach me to dance – jitterbug, she called it. Such a funny word – like a beetle. She loved that music. It made her happy.

'But she was always on her way out somewhere. And then you sent me away. I used to keep her photo on my chest of drawers – even at that awful first school where we were only allowed to have one personal item showing. The other girls said how lucky I was to live abroad and have such a glamorous-looking mother. But I always wondered . . . I think . . . she just wanted to get rid of me.'

Her father pulled up at the low airport building, and switched off the engine. In the distance the Mediterranean looked grey and choppy. The windsock strained at its pole. It would be a rocky take-off.

'It's not you who's disappointed her,' he said finally, staring ahead. 'It's me.

'When we first met your mother seemed to, well, admire me. She was a very young nurse just down from Lancashire, and I'm afraid she thought of me as an experienced older man who was going to sweep her into a glamorous new life. The National Health was only just beginning then. Doctors were still thought of as rather grand. Big houses in the country, pillars of the community, perhaps a knighthood one day. And I'd been to university, and not done too badly in the war.' He grimaced diffidently. 'All that nonsense.

'The fact was, I hadn't even qualified yet. I soon saw that she would never be happy while I struggled my way up to becoming a surgeon. So I found myself a medical officer's job instead. It meant more money, travel abroad, all sorts of perks. Rather dull work, of course, but I didn't mind that if Mary was happy.'

But she isn't. The unspoken words hung awkwardly between them. Annie didn't know how to respond. She had never heard her father say so much.

'Heigh-ho.' He tapped the steering wheel, breaking the mood. 'What about those cases, then?'

They checked Annie in, then sat on high stools at the bar and ordered coffee. It came in little glasses, thick and syrupy.

'So – why did you marry her?' Annie asked abruptly.

Her father stared back in surprise. 'I loved her. I worshipped her.' He laughed almost joyously. 'She was like a firework lighting up the sky. Everyone was after her – all the doctors, and half the patients too. But ... well, she chose me.'

He set his glass on the aluminium-topped bar with a click. 'Say not the struggle naught availeth. You stick with your young man, if you think he's worth it.'

'Yes,' said Annie thoughtfully.

'No need to be in too much of a hurry, eh?'

'No.'

'That's the ticket.'

Annie's face softened with affection as she remembered her last sight of him as she crossed the tarmac to the plane, an upright, emphatically English figure in checked shirt and heavy shoes, glossy as conkers.

The train squeaked to a halt. Jolted out of her reverie, Annie looked up to see a little graveyard chequered with afternoon shadows and tumbled about with leaves. She exchanged a smug, conspiratorial look with ginger hair. This was a familiar trick of the Oxford train, designed to confound outsiders who hustled to collect their bags when the train slowed and were then left stranded among their luggage in the corridor. She could still recall the anxiety that had gripped her, at exactly this spot, twelve months ago. 'I'm afraid there's been a mistake,' she had

101

imagined them saying at Lady Margaret Hall, with that chilly Oxford courtesy, perusing a leather-bound ledger. 'Paxford, did you say? We have no record of that name here.' She had actually brought with her the telegram offering her a place at the college, in anticipation of such a scene. The memory of her insecurity made her blush now, but the early days had not been easy. No one had told her that LMH was the 'posh' college, attracting shriekingly well-bred girls with double-barrelled names, and high-caste Indians in saris. Annie's achievement in getting into Oxford had been unusual enough, at her school, to merit a half-holiday and a new line on the wooden scroll of honour in the assembly hall, and she had come up – one always went 'up' to Oxford – knowing no one.

She found soon enough that her unusual background did not mean she was more stupid than others. It took even less time to discover that, in this university of twenty-odd male colleges and only five female, she was socially in high demand. Fresh from a girls' boarding-school, Annie had said yes to every man who asked her out, until a few evenings of crippling boredom and gauche gropes had made her more discriminating. By the end of the first term she had begun to make friends within the college and had landed a non-speaking part in an Oriel production of *Twelfth Night*. By the second term – Hilary, they called it – she had dumped Aunt Betty's idea of a suitable college wardrobe at the Oxfam shop, exchanging her Jaeger skirts and 'nice' dresses for groovier gear. Her minuscule Oxford University diary, printed on India paper and furnished with a tiny wooden pencil, into which she had dutifully copied the times of lectures and worthy-sounding society meetings, filled up with parties, lunches, films, auditions. Annie had had no idea that anyone could have so much fun.

Oxford was, she had found, a place of secret pleasures, closely guarded. The best pubs were invariably hidden in courtyards and down unpromising alleyways; the most breathtaking buildings behind walls black with car fumes. A chance turning in the monastic gloom of a Gothic archway could lead equally well to enchanting cloistered gardens or the Fellows' car park. There was an entirely new language to learn, too. The head of a college might be a dean, provost, warden, rector, president, master or principal. Exams, depending on their nature and timing, might be called collections, prelims, mods or schools, and when you took them you had to dress entirely in black and white, known as 'subfusc'. New College was 'New', University College 'Univ', Brasenose College 'BNC', St Edmund Hall 'Teddy Hall'. 'Matriculation' was the Latin ceremony which formally admitted students to membership of the University. If you were going *on* the river, that meant punting on the Cherwell – from the 'Oxford' end of the boat, naturally. Going *down to* the river meant rowing, or watching the boat races, on the Thames, which in Oxford was called the Isis.

Like all first-years, Annie had initially found this new vocabulary strange, even pretentious. Now she wouldn't think twice about referring to one of the world's greatest libraries as 'the Bod'. She was a cool second-year, with friends and a lover waiting. Annie stretched out her legs, admiring the boots which she had bought yesterday from a new shop called Biba. They were ravishing pink suede, tightly laced to follow the curve of her calves from ankle to knee. She was sure Edward would like them. Even Rose might concede that they were cool.

Everyone knew Rose Cassidy. It was impossible not to. She had distinguished herself in her very first term by being dragged away from a demo outside the Union, hair-first, by the police, then lodging a complaint for excessive violence. She argued with her tutors, played Frank Zappa at top volume and smoked French cigarettes. Dressed almost exclusively in purple, with lots of jangly silver jewellery, her dark hair long and loose with a fringe cut dramatically just above her extraordinary green eyes, she looked quite unlike the other LMH girls. Although Annie had overheard some disparaging remarks about Rose – too bossy, too outspoken, too politically extreme – she had rather admired Rose from afar. But their rooms were in different buildings. It wasn't until their second term that they had become friends.

All first-years reading English were bound together by their terror of Prelims, an exam designed to get all the really boring bits over with in one huge gulp of mindless learning. As well as literature tutorials, which they attended in pairs, there were classes in the history of the English language, in which they all struggled together to grasp the significance of sound-changes and the Great Vowel Shift. It was dreary work. One gloomy February day, in the middle of such a class, Rose had flipped up her fringe in a characteristic gesture and exclaimed in exasperation, 'This is all bullshit, isn't it?' The teacher, an Irish woman not much older than her students, froze in front of the blackboard. The rest of the class had sat in stunned, well-bred silence, broken by Annie's quip, 'The Great Bowel Shift'. Even the teacher had laughed.

After that, Rose had taken Annie up. Annie's room was near their tutor's quarters, and Rose often banged on the door to borrow Annie's gown when she was late for tutorials and couldn't be bothered to get her own. On the rare occasions when they both ate in Hall, they sat together. Last summer, they had played tennis before breakfast a few times, until the novelty wore off. Rose seemed to find Annie's life abroad glamorous, and Annie let her think so. For her part, she loved to hear about Rose's large, noisy family, the bizarre patients who frequented her parents' consulting rooms, and the succession of lame ducks, refugees and revolutionaries who inhabited the basement flat of their London house. When the time came to choose where she wanted to live the following year, Annie was flattered to be recruited for what Rose called 'my' corridor. Whatever happened with Edward, life with Rose would not be dull.

Suddenly the train lurched into movement. In a couple of minutes it would be drawing into the station whose rusting Victorian ironwork and crumbling wooden structure testified to Oxford's carefully cultivated air of shabbiness. Stuffing *Lord of the Rings* into her bag, Annie pulled down her case from the overhead shelf and dragged it through the compartment door into the corridor. It was heavy with books, for there had been little else to do but read during the interminable Long Vacation. She couldn't possibly lug it from the bus stop to LMH; she would have to fork out five shillings for a taxi.

Her spirits rose as she counted the landmarks out of the car window. Behind this grimy wall was Worcester, where a shy boy called Colin had taught her to ice-skate when the lake froze over last winter. Here was the Playhouse, where she and Rose had once hung out in the coffee bar hoping to be spotted. Instead they had found an all-male posse of egomaniacs admiring each other's bone structure. At the top of Beaumont Street, where the taxi turned into the extravagantly wide avenue of St Giles, Annie was reassured to see that no amount of scrubbing had been able to obliterate the famous graffito on the walls of the Taylorian: 'Matriculation makes you blind.' Almost next door was the pub where she had often met Edward: the Eagle and Child, known to initiates as the Bird and Babe – and to a few would-be wits as the Fowl and Foetus.

At St Giles' Church the taxi forked right into North Oxford, the far-reaching Victorian suburb colonised by dons, almost a century ago, when they were at last allowed to marry. Annie felt a squeeze of excitement as they turned into a gloomy street lined with monstrous houses of neo-Gothic patterned brickwork, each gabled and crenellated like an ogre's castle. This was Norham Gardens, at the bottom of which lay Lady Margaret Hall.

She leaned forward as her taxi rounded the final curve. There at last was its undistinguished but friendly redbrick façade, shaded by lime trees and cluttered with the usual ramshackle array of bicycles.

Annie paid off the taxi and stepped through the arched gateway, checking the blackboard for any phone messages; there were none. Leaving her case, she went down the steps into the porter's lodge to look in her pigeonhole. As always at the beginning of term, it was stuffed with flyers. A Chinese restaurant was offering a free bottle of Mateus Rosé with every meal for two during the next fortnight. The Oxford Revolutionary Socialist Students were staging a demo next week. 'We will make your parties go with a bang!' promised a pop group called Climax Far. Annie discarded them impatiently and riffled through a pile of college bumf, identifiable by the LMH crest on the envelopes. From Edward there was nothing.

'You've been somewhere warm,' said the porter brightly. 'Good Vac, was it?'

'Great,' Annie lied. She felt bitterly disappointed. She looked through her post again, wondering if her mother could be right. Had last term just been a casual interlude for Edward, easily forgotten over the long summer months?

Retrieving her case, she crunched along the gravel path round the quad and pushed open the door to Wordsworth, the pretty nineteenth-century building where she had chosen to live this year. As she climbed the stone staircase, she could hear laughter and doors banging. Someone's record player was on, blasting out a song about revolution.

Her new room was at the far end of the corridor. Outside it she could see her old school trunk which she had left in store over the Long Vac. But there was something else as well. Annie dropped her case, and ran down the hall.

Propped against her door was a bunch of tightly furled,

dark red roses, encased in cellophane and tied with an extravagant bow. A small, stiff envelope was attached, addressed to Miss Ann Paxford.

Annie drew out a card and read: *Welcome back, darling. Dinner tomorrow at seven? Can't wait. All my love, Edward.*

11

Keep on runnin'

Jordan rested his elbows on the parapet of the little hump-backed bridge by the Trout Inn, catching his breath. He was out of condition after a long summer back home and too much of his mother's home-fried cooking. This run from his new place off Walton Street – 'digs', they said here – took him across Port Meadow to the Trout, then back down the other side of the river. It was a distance of only five or six miles, but hard going over the waterlogged ground. The English thought he was crazy, of course. Mackintoshed dog-walkers tended to avert their gaze from his U of Illinois sweatshirt and fraying cut-off jeans, as if he were practising a bizarre foreign ritual. But he needed an escape valve for the energy that drove him to fill every waking hour. Today, after Mrs Dickson's letter, he wanted to run until he dropped, until sheer physical exhaustion numbed his emotions and his heartbeat hammered thought into silence.

In the grey October twilight the river looked like lead. The ruins of Godstow Abbey seemed to float above the cow-cropped grass. Jordan could almost fancy that he saw a ghostly shrouded figure at one of the broken Gothic arches. A desolate wail pierced the silence, startling him with its piteous appeal until he remembered where he was. Not a child, not a ghost: only a peacock, one of the ornamental features which made the Trout such a popular pub. Jordan shook his head as if to clear it, crossed the bridge and opened the gate on to the towpath. Then he was running again, past dark copses and tilting willows, past staring piebald cows and stumpy ponies already showing the fuzzy outlines of their winter coats. He could hear his breath and the slap of his sneakers on the mud. In time with them the words beat in his head: dead, dead, dead. Eldridge was dead. He had been flown home from Saigon in a body bag. Mrs Dickson had copied out the letter from the captain of Eldridge's company for Jordan. Eldridge had been shot down on a reconnaissance mission. He had been a fine soldier. The officer had nominated him for a citation. He was very sorry.

Jordan vaulted a stile between two pastures and pounded on, the past scrolling out of his memory like a reel of film. He could picture the exact moment when he had first seen Eldridge. Jordan was nine years old. He had been kept home that day because of an outbreak of mumps at school. He was pleased, because it meant his mother had to take him with her to the fancy college where she worked as the Dean's secretary. 'Up the hill', they called it. Indian Bluffs itself, a straggle of sagging clapboard homes punctuated by the schoolhouse, the inn and the church, was known simply as 'the village'. Ever since the river trade had moved down the Mississippi to the next town, with its superior wharf, most village people who were not farmers or bums worked for the exclusive private college set high on the bluffs overlooking the river. Jordan loved going up there. With its white-steepled chapel and creeper-covered dormitories, tennis courts and landscaped gardens, it was like a fairytale playground. The students were godlike beings, the men in pressed flannels and two-tone saddle shoes, the girls deliciously perfumed and draped in cashmere, hugging their books. Sometimes Jordan earned a few nickels as a ball boy. Once he had been given a quarter just to deliver a note to a girl on the other side of the lawn. Mostly, though, he obeyed his mother's fierce instruction to stay out of sight and out of trouble. It had cost her every dime she had, and late nights struggling with her correspondence course, to land this job. She could not afford to lose it.

The day he met Eldridge, Jordan had gone into the wild land behind the chapel. He had a favourite spot, high on the bluffs, overlooking the great brown river. If he lay on his stomach along the grassy clifftop, his nose just over the edge, he could look a thousand feet straight down to the derelict roof of the old mill, where they used to make lime from stone quarried from the bluffs. Further along were crumbling warehouses and a tall chimney, all that remained of the distillery that had burned down long before he was born. Behind them, hugging the shore, was the barred line of the old railway track, soon to be dismantled to make way for a new highway. Each of these had its own fascination, but what Jordan liked best was watching the river. Here it was almost a mile wide. It was always different, sometimes as smooth and empty as a brand-new road, sometimes frothing white as powerful currents swept around the tree-tangled islands where Jordan went in spring to look for turtle eggs. You never knew what kind of a boat you might see: fishing boats drifting along the shore, patrol launches with their flags fluttering importantly, paddle steamers churning past carrying tourists. The most exciting were the huge, flat barges carrying logs from the north or bringing cotton up from the south, and the police launches cruising for bodies. Everyone in Indian Bluffs learned to respect the river. It was not a place for pleasure-boats or swimming. One fierce winter, when the river froze, a party of students from 'up the hill' had gone skating on it and drowned.

You couldn't see the village from here; that's why Jordan liked it. There was just the river, and beyond it the Missouri flatlands stretching south to the horizon.

It was one of those summer afternoons when the mosquitoes drew blood and the air was like steam. Jordan was looking for Indian arrowheads. Instead, he found the biggest snake he had ever seen, lying quite still in thick, black coils in the sun. He had been staring at it for some time when an awed voice behind him said, 'He's a big one.' Jordan turned to see a skinny-legged coloured boy in shorts. Together they admired the magnificent and fearful beast.

'I reckon he's dead,' Jordan said eventually.

'Let's poke him and see,' suggested the boy, looking round for a stick. Jordan wasn't too sure about this. He didn't like snakes, even though his mother had told him that the black ones were harmless, unlike the rattlesnakes that infested the caves in the bluffs and regularly had to be gassed. In the village it was rumoured that Sy-boy Carson kept a sack of live rattlesnakes under his bed. No one knew why, but Jordan could well believe it. He always checked the ground when he walked by Sy-boy's porch, just in case.

The snake wasn't dead. Jordan let the other boy do the prodding. The snake unwound to an awesome length and slid away while the boys watched. Afterwards, bonded by this adventure, they shook hands solemnly and exchanged names. Then they had a contest to see who could throw a stone furthest into the Mississippi. Eldridge won every time.

'You can come to my house and see my cowboy outfit, if you want,' Jordan offered. 'There's a short cut through the woods.'

His new friend hesitated, then explained that his mother, who worked in the kitchens, had told him not to go far. She always had to leave work right on time, Eldridge said, so that they were home before dark.

'Scaredycat,' Jordan jeered.

'I ain't scared of the dark,' Eldridge shot back. 'Negroes have to get out of the county by nightfall. It's the law.'

Jordan couldn't make sense of this, but that night over dinner he asked his mother what Eldridge had meant. She loved explaining things to Jordan, getting down the atlas or the encyclopedia, or drawing pictures and diagrams for him while the dishes soaked in the sink. She read the *St Louis Dispatch* every day; there was always a story which fired her up, like the Rosenberg execution or the McCarthy hearings. Tonight she tried to explain about segregation. A law had been passed the previous year, 1954, outlawing segregation, but there was a lot of resistance, particularly in the South. Had Jordan never wondered why there were no coloured children at his school? Why did he think that the coloured men going to the fields in the back of pick-up trucks, or helping out in the village store, or manoeuvring barges down the river, went home to the next county at night? That's why her friend Minnie, who worked as a cleaner 'up the hill', could only visit with them on weekends, never for dinner. 'A lot of white folks don't want to mix with Negroes or have them living next door,' she concluded.

'Why not?'

'They're frightened of them, I guess.'

Jordan considered this. Eldridge hadn't seemed very frightening.

'Are you frightened of them?' he asked his mother.

She laughed. 'I'm a lot more frightened of Sy-boy when he's all liquored up. I had to take a shotgun to him once, when he came sniffing around after your father died.' She took Jordan's hand. 'Honey, you play with Eldridge all you want. He's welcome in our house. Don't pay any mind to what other people say.'

Jordan didn't. And once Eldridge had passed the initiation test of being held head down over the disused well in the woods, he was accepted by Shelby and the gang, too. They played touch football and Capture the Flag, and shot baskets against Shelby's dad's garage doors. They fooled around in skiffs down by the old wharf. Eldridge was smart, with a quick, mocking humour that at first threw Jordan off balance, then formed a special communication between them. When Jordan discovered that Eldridge loved reading, as he did, Jordan lent him books. Sometimes they would go off along the river, just the two of them, acting out adventures from *Tom Sawyer*. In the summer, when school was out, Jordan's mother used to let him stay overnight at the Dicksons'. After a huge dinner of fried chicken, cornbread and gravy, the boys would set out a timber and cane bed-frame on the porch, talking and watching the fireflies until they fell asleep.

Things got more complicated as they got older. Jordan went off to high school across the river, in St Louis, and then to college. Eldridge finished school early and took a series of casual jobs. The Civil Rights movement brought them together again; they spent hours in passionate, sometimes fierce discussion.

When the draft was instituted, there was no student deferral for Eldridge as there had been for Jordan. He had come back from his first Vietnam tour physically tough but mentally distant. The last time they had met, Jordan was about to take up his Rhodes Scholarship and Eldridge, now a sergeant, to return to Vietnam. Jordan had gone over to his house to say goodbye but there had been no chance to talk. Now there never would be. At twenty-two, Eldridge's life was over.

It began to drizzle. Jordan slicked back his hair and wiped the moisture from his eyes. Before him were the blurred outlines of Oxford's spires against a watery sky, grey on grey. Sometimes the mystery and exotic beauty of Oxford overwhelmed him with delight, but not today. This endless, terrible war bit into his soul. He loved his country, and was ashamed of it. Every day he gave thanks that he was not in Vietnam, yet felt guilty nevertheless. They all did. The Americans stuck together in Oxford not just for the familiar companionship or because the Brits were so snooty, but out of a compulsive need to examine and probe and pick at this perpetual sore. They had all grown up as patriots, believing in America the Beautiful, pledging daily allegiance to the flag, hands on hearts. The growing awareness that this was a bad war, which bombed civilians and propped up a corrupt government, was bewildering and hurtful. Inside, most of them were a mess. It was the war that had turned Bruce into a recluse; that drove Rick to play dangerous games with drugs and sex; that made Eliot retreat into the patrician haughtiness of his Boston Brahmin family.

Jordan had supported the war at first. JFK himself had initiated the first moves to protect South Vietnam from the aggression of the communist North. It had seemed as noble a cause as fighting the Nazis. The accidental napalming by the US of twenty of its own servicemen, four years back, had brought home the barbarity of America's war technology. Reports of gruesome civilian massacres had become commonplace. When Shelby had come home on leave last year, Jordan had been shaken by his account of the fear, the drugs, the racism, the degradation, the shame and the cynicism. Afterwards, he had read everything about the war that he could lay his hands on. Intellectually he was now convinced that this was a bad, brutal, pointless war, conducted under the false colours of ideology and patriotism. He wanted no part in it. But from a personal angle, the situation looked different. For every American who ducked the draft, as Jordan had, another American died, as Eldridge had.

At Medley's Boatyard Jordan crossed the river and stumbled over the railway bridge. His sweatshirt was soaked, his mud-spattered legs ached. He was panting as he crossed the final bridge over the canal and trudged up Walton Well, past Lucy's Eagle Ironworks into Jericho, once the working-man's part of Oxford, where Jude the Obscure had lived and died. He reached a three-storey Victorian house and pushed open the squeaky gate.

Hearing the door slam, Eliot shouted out from the kitchen to ask Jordan what time he was setting off tonight. Getting no answer, Eliot appeared in the hall at his usual elegant lope, a steaming cup in his hand, and took stock of Jordan's arrested stance halfway up the stairs.

'Don't tell me you forgot,' Eliot chided, eyebrows raised under a thatch of black hair. 'Rick's party? In *Magdalen*? With the *Viscount*?' His ironic emphasis made Jordan smile. They both knew Rick's little weaknesses. Magdalen, pronounced maudlin, was probably the most seductively beautiful of all the Oxford colleges. Bordering the river, it had its own elm-shaded deer park, an ancient stone pulpit where Newman had preached, and a fifteenth-century bell-tower from which choristers sang at dawn on the first of May each year. Its grounds covered more than a hundred acres; its buildings were of golden stone, arranged around precise quadrangles of emerald grass. Joseph Addison had given his name to the riverside walk where rare lilies grew in spring. C.S. Lewis and Tolkien had read their work to each other here; Edward Gibbon and Oscar Wilde had been undergraduates. Magdalen admirably fulfilled Rick's social pretensions and his taste for theatricality. His party had been billed as a reunion of old friends after the Long Vac. It would also give Rick an opportunity to show off the magnificent suite of rooms which he was sharing this year with a titled undergraduate of fabled degeneracy.

Of course Jordan would be going. Everyone knew he never missed a party. Rick had a genius for attracting interesting and influential people. Only something as devastating as Eldridge's death could have driven it from Jordan's mind.

'I remember,' he said lightly. 'You want a ride?' Last summer Jordan had squandered a chunk of his Rhodes allowance on the smallest, cheapest convertible he had ever seen, a soft-topped Morris Minor the size and shape of a small elephant. His compatriots bellyached about the leg room, but rarely passed up the chance to keep out of the cold and rain.

'Thanks. And let's try to get, you know – ' Eliot pointed a finger upwards, indicating the room where their other housemate Bruce sat for hours closeted with Leonard Cohen and a dwindling stock of cannabis. Bruce should have gone back to the States last summer, in answer to the draft. Instead he had bummed around Europe and North Africa, ignoring the summons. Now he was an official draft dodger. Ignominy and a five-year prison sentence awaited him if he ever went home. Both Eliot and Jordan had been shocked by Bruce's bloated appearance and depressed mental state. It was an unspoken agreement between them that they should get Bruce out of the house as much as possible.

'I'll see what I can do,' Jordan promised.

Upstairs he turned on the hot-water geyser and fed a shilling into the meter for the gas fire in his bedroom. After a meagre bath that made him homesick for real showers, he towelled his hair roughly and dressed for the party, adding an old sweater on top to keep warm. He switched on the goose-neck lamp on the rickety table that served as his desk, and sat down. A sheet of writing paper lay in front of him. 'Dear Mrs Dickson,' it read. That was all.

What could he say to comfort her? It didn't seem enough that Eldridge had been his friend, or that he had triggered Jordan's earliest awareness of social injustice – not that his nine-year-old self had thought in terms any more sophisticated than a schoolboy cry, 'It's not fair.' Besides, a calculating part of his mind which Jordan could not silence whispered that Mrs Dickson would be pleased by anything he wrote. He was a Rhodes Scholar, one of America's elite, studying at the world-famous University of Oxford. His letter would be passed around the neighbours and kept with other treasured documents in the family Bible. He must choose his words carefully.

Half an hour later, with a growl of frustration, Jordan scrunched up yet another piece of paper and threw it into the waste-paper basket to join its predecessors. There was no way of hiding from Mrs Dickson – or himself – the brutal truth that he had avoided the summons to war, and Eldridge had not. Eldridge had gone to boot camp while Jordan was still in college. Later, Jordan had benefited by the rule that graduate students could defer the draft. When that had been revoked in July 1968 he had protected himself once again by joining the Reserve Officers' Training Corps. This committed him to the army but deferred active service, buying him time which he had privately sworn to commit to the anti-war movement. This had seemed an inspired solution; today, it look like a shabby compromise. How could expressions of affection for Eldridge, or of sympathy with Eldridge's mother, be worth anything while Jordan spent his days dipping into Hobbes and Locke in the hush of ancient vaulted libraries, or talking over a beer in the Turf Tavern – or going to parties?

The problem spun round and round his brain, tying his conscience in knots. He could not get the picture of that body bag out of his mind. How had Eldridge died? Had he been shot, or burned, or blown up? Jordan was assailed with vile images of spongy, mouldering flesh, which corrupted his memories of Eldridge's springy hair, his slow smile, his loose-limbed body full of strength and energy. Eventually he tossed down his pen and gave up the struggle. He replaced his heavy sweater with a dark jacket, combed back his hair and methodically filled his pockets with wallet, keys, his tiny University Diary and its miniature pencil for jotting down useful names and numbers. Experience of frosty undergraduettes to the contrary, he still dreamed of meeting a beautiful, intelligent girl willing to find him a romantic prospect. Sometimes he yearned for a distraction from conscientious study, and from all the Vietnam discussions and activism that swallowed his time and made him question his own motives. Was that too much to ask?

In the hallway Jordan caught sight of himself in the full-length mirror, a tall, broad-shouldered guy with no glaring deformities. Maybe this would be his lucky night.

12

Eight miles high

Rose lay submerged in sandalwood bubblebath contemplating her red-varnished toenails. Perhaps tonight would be her lucky night. There were bound to be some useful men at Rick's party – men with power and contacts, not least Rick himself. Men were gloriously simple. They would do anything for you if you handled them right. And she wanted a favour.

Rick Goodman was a New Yorker, a Rhodes Scholar. He was older than the usual undergraduate and infinitely more sophisticated. When he wasn't giving parties, he wrote a gossip column for *Cherwell*. Last year Rose had been the subject of one of his scurrilous 'Ox Vox' pieces when she was 'gated' after attending an all-night vigil for Jan Palach in one of the men's colleges. Outraged at the antiquated university rule that forbade her to leave LMH for two whole weeks, she had organised a constant stream of visitors to her room. Someone – well, Rose herself actually – had daubed 'Free Cassidy Now!' on the college walls. Her plight had been taken up by 'Ox Vox' under the headline 'Red Rose'. She had been interviewed by Rick in her bedroom. It had been the sensation of the week, but to her fury she had still not managed to prise open the door to Oxford journalism. Men wrote everything, even the fashion and make-up pages. Anyone female was automatically allocated the backroom drudgery. Rose was sick of her role as little helper, typing up other people's listless copy. She wanted Rick to get her a proper job.

From the bath cubicle she could hear girls doing the usual girlish stuff – getting ready for Hall, moaning about essays, swapping stories about their holidays. Rose stirred impatiently in the cooling water and pulled the plug. None of them seemed to see further than the next essay crisis, the next tea-party, the next boyfriend. Even Annie was not immune to such bourgeois distractions.

Rose Cassidy had been brought up in London, 'the Smoke', competing with two older brothers and a younger sister in a chilly Victorian house with dog-pee carpets and anti-Apartheid stickers in the windows. Her parents were both psychiatrists and left-wing activists. 'Cause' was their middle name. Once they had spawned the great Cassidy tribe, they were too busy saving the world to take much notice of their children, beyond insisting on a sound education. Rose had been sent to one of London's best schools for girls, where she had always been among the top two or three in her class – though that had not stopped her from carving 'Fuck the public school system' on the headmistress's door. Many of her friends had elected to go to the newer universities, Sussex or Warwick, scorning the elitism of Oxford and Cambridge, but Rose had been determined to follow her elder brother to Oxford. An Oxbridge degree still carried more cachet. Even so, she had been shocked to discover how provincial and conservative Oxford was. As soon as she got her First she would be straight back to London and the real world.

Gathering up her belongings Rose unlocked the cubicle door and ran across the corridor to Annie's room. She found her sprawled bare-legged on the floor unpacking her trunk, wearing an outsize T-shirt. She smiled dreamily at Rose through her Joni Mitchell hair.

'Buck up and get changed, or I'm not taking you,' Rose said.

Annie unfolded her legs and stood up. 'I like your gownless evening strap,' she said, nodding at the damp towel wrapped tight above Rose's breasts. 'Whose party is it anyway – one of your boyfriends'?'

Rose made a face. 'What a horrible word. It's being given by an American, a real smoothie. You must tell him how brilliant I am. I want him to persuade *Cherwell* to let me write something for them, maybe a piece about the demo.'

'What demo?' Annie asked, taking off her clothes and rummaging in her wardrobe.

Rose was shocked. '*The* demo. Vietnam, remember? Even in Malta they must have heard about the Moratorium. In the States it's going to be like this incredible, massive protest strike against the war. Millions of people are going to stay home from work. In Washington they're going to march on the White House and read out the names of the dead. Only the Americans, of course,' she added disapprovingly, hitching up her towel. 'Nobody cares about a few hundred thousand slitty-eyed peasants. Anyway, next Sunday we're going to march to Grosvenor Square with a petition. We're hoping to get Vanessa Redgrave to deliver it.'

'It sounds amazing.'

'It will be. Everybody's going. You should come.'

Annie hesitated. Rose read her mind effortlessly. 'You want to spend a cosy day with Mr Red Roses,' she said accusingly. 'You could keep a Biafran family for a week on what they cost.'

'You're just jealous,' Annie retaliated calmly, taking a white button-up skirt out of her wardrobe.

Rose felt stung for a moment. Then she laughed. 'I don't

give anyone a chance to send me red roses. Fuck 'em and chuck 'em, that's my motto.' She watched Annie button up her skirt, then undo the bottom two and slide her knee forward to see how much leg showed. 'One more,' Rose commanded.

'Really? You don't think it's too . . .'

'Of course it is. That's the whole point.' Rose shook her head. 'Isn't it funny, how we're so different? Like chalk and cheese.'

'Yin and yang,' Annie countered.

'Kama and sutra.' Rose joined in the game.

'Jekyll and Hyde.'

'Rowan and Martin.'

'Pride and Prejudice.'

'Sense and Sensibility. And bags I be Sensibility,' Rose added.

'Pearls and swine.' Annie gave a piggy snort. 'Now get out so I can concentrate on my eyeliner.'

Back in her room, Rose put *Surrealistic Pillow* on her record player, then covered herself in skin cream. While she waited for it to sink in she lit a Gauloise and practised narrowing her eyes seductively as she inhaled, then blowing the smoke down her nose, like Jeanne Moreau. Her eyes watered.

'Plastic fantastic lov-errr . . .' she sang to herself into the mirror. She modelled herself on Grace Slick: creamy skin, dramatic green eyes beneath a dark fringe, silver rings crammed on to her fingers, short, tight dresses. If you were small, you had to do something to get noticed.

She stubbed out the cigarette in her Chairman Mao ashtray and started to pull on her purple tights. The thought of Annie's long, tanned legs made her wonder if it had been such a good idea to invite her along. But the two of them did make a wonderful picture, one statuesque and blonde, one petite and dark. They were bound to cause a stir.

Jordan stood in the doorway, surveying the scene. The party glittered, as Eliot had predicted. Black candles in ornate candelabra cast a dramatic light on wood-panelled walls and frayed brocade curtains. White-coated college servants proffered champagne cocktails on silver salvers. Under the ripple of conversation Fats Waller sang about his very good friend the milkman. The company was a daring mix of dons, students, theatrical types, LSE radicals, left-wing journalists, and a pack of the Viscount's aristocratic cronies with London dollybirds in tow. Over it all presided Rick, a charismatic guru in black Nehru jacket and white collarless shirt buttoned to the neck. Only his snapping brown eyes betrayed his excitement as he pointed out his prize catches to Jordan: several heavyweight dons including two heads of college; the theatre director who was having a wildly successful season at the Playhouse; a notoriously radical ex-President of the Union; a snake-hipped character in purple velvet trousers whose underground magazine had been the subject of a scandalous obscenity trial. In a far corner brooded the pocket-sized son of a famous novelist, cocky in snakeskin boots and patterned shirt.

Jordan stood in awe of Rick's social panache, as he did of Rick's Choate/Yale education, his summers in the Hamptons, his winters in Aspen, even the dubious glamour of his multiple stepmothers.

'I'm impressed,' he admitted.

'Well, you know, we try.' Rick looked satisfied. 'Did you bring Bruce?'

Jordan and Eliot exchanged glances.

'He said none of his clothes fit him any more.'

'Shit.' Rick reached up to put his arms around his friends. For a moment they stood together, three young Americans, heads bowed as if in grim silent prayer. Then Rick straightened.

'The show must go on. Eliot, come and be witty. I've been telling my room-mate's sister *all* about you.' He waved a hand at Jordan. 'I know you can take care of yourself. Enjoy.'

Though Jordan didn't much like champagne, he took a glass for camouflage and cruised the party. He flirted mildly with the third wife of a famously uxorious philosopher, and was rewarded by an invitation to Sunday lunch later in the term. Taking pity on a lonely-looking Nigerian, he made a date with him for a drink in the King's Arms. A likeably bumptious Conservative candidate called Jeffrey introduced himself as Britain's youngest MP-in-waiting, and promised to show Jordan around the House of Commons when he got there.

Jordan had one unsettling encounter, with a bow-tied senior member of the college, to whom he had made some polite remark about Magdalen's rich historical associations.

'Ah yes, history,' the don enthused. 'Very important for you Americans. I understand that in your country you believe that the Second World War started in 1941.' He chuckled mischievously.

Jordan gave a stiff smile. He had discovered that the English, particularly the older generation, were obsessed by the war, constantly harking back to rationing and Dunkirk. It seemed to rile them that they had not managed to win it single-handed.

'Well, 1941 *is* when the war started for us,' he said mildly.

'Better late than never, eh?' suggested old Bowtie with a malicious twinkle.

'I think so,' Jordan said evenly. 'I guess the Russians would have defeated Germany in the end, but without the Americans the map of Europe might look very different today.'

The old man frowned at this, then changed tack. 'Bloodthirsty lot, aren't you? First Korea, now Vietnam. Still,' he nodded at Jordan's champagne glass, 'I suppose you wouldn't know about that, all tucked up and cosy at

Oxford. Must be a cushy billet, being a Rhodes Scholar, what with your fares paid and a salary and all that.'

What was it with these dons? Sometimes the most frosty turned out to be extraordinarily generous with their time and knowledge; others seemed riddled with spite.

'Yup, it's almost as good as being a don,' Jordan agreed blandly. 'Except we miss out on the free port.' Before politeness failed him utterly, he reached forward and shook the other man's hand. 'It's been a real pleasure.'

Jordan moved quickly away, angry with himself for losing his cool, stung by the man's words. He looked around, wondering whether to try to break into one of the knots of men that signalled the presence of a pretty girl. The party was hotting up. Fats Waller had been succeeded by the Stones and T. Rex, and dancing had started up in the next room. The older contingent were collecting their coats, off to dine elsewhere. Jordan's gaze rested idly on Rick's room-mate, the Viscount, who was leaning on the mantelpiece, staring hungrily at a waif-like girl with kohl-rimmed eyes. She looked stoned. While Jordan watched, the man reached over, put his hand down the girl's dress, and squeezed one of her breasts. Jordan could see his knuckles moving under the thin material. Involuntarily he remembered Eldridge, for whom there would be no more fleshly pleasures, to give or to receive. Suddenly he felt sickened by the noise and the smoke and the press of warm bodies.

He looked round for Rick, wondering if it was too early to go home. Finally he caught sight of him, talking to a dark-haired girl whom Jordan was sure he'd seen demonstrating outside the Union last summer. He gave her a big smile, just in case, and mimed his intention to leave. Rick just shrugged. By the time Jordan had retrieved his coat and scarf, Rick was holding the hand of a tall girl with her back to him. Great legs, he noticed, and a sheet of blonde hair to her waist. For a moment Jordan was

125

tempted. But his mood had soured. He was eager to be alone with his thoughts.

'But don't you see, that kind of materialism is just another manifestation of the sick society?'

Rose was trying to persuade the President of St John's that he should sell all the college property and distribute the proceeds to the needy of the Third World, when she felt a warm hand caress her back.

'How's my favourite little Marxist?' asked Rick, drawing her away from the affronted-looking don.

Little yourself, Rose thought, with a flicker of irritation. Rick's dark, knowing eyes were only a few inches above her own. She always felt he was laughing at her. But at least he had sought her out. She flashed him one of her best smiles.

'About *Cherwell*,' he drawled. 'I hear they need some help on the advertising side. I'll see what I can do for you.'

Advertising! Rose bit her lip with disappointment. How could she get Rick to take her seriously? He seemed to have lost interest in her already, and was signalling to someone over her shoulder.

'Someone I know?' she asked, determined not to be ignored.

'Just one of my compatriots – Jordan Hope, the man most likely to.'

From across the room a tall man with a suntan and that sheen of health all Americans seemed to possess gave her a blazing smile.

'Wow,' murmured Rose. 'Is he for real?'

Rick frowned. It was the first time Rose had ever seen him at a loss for words. 'Good question,' he said at last. 'On the boat coming over I got seasick – vilely, abominably seasick. Jordan used to come and read to me. I couldn't believe it – this Southern hick from the boon-docks, reading Dylan Thomas!'

'But is he worth knowing? Is he interesting?'

Rick made a see-saw gesture with his palm. 'As long as you stay off politics. He once lectured me for so long on the economic and social significance of the watermelon crop that I almost prayed for us to hit an iceberg.'

Jordan Hope. Rose stored the name in her mind, while her eyes moved on. Suddenly she clutched Rick's arm. 'I don't believe it! Isn't that Don Jago over there?'

'Probably. You want to meet him? Foxy lady he's got there.'

Rose clicked her tongue. 'That's no lady, that's my best friend.'

Annie had been dancing with an Australian called John, or possibly Don or Ron – it was too noisy to hear any-thing. It didn't matter. He was a good dancer, and she had drunk enough champagne cocktails to send her float-ing. The stroboscobe twirled. 'Let's Spend the Night Together' throbbed through the floorboards. She smiled into the middle distance, shook out her long hair and undulated her body to the beat. It would have been even better if Edward were here, but a party was a party. At least Rose had saved her from a dull evening of solitary unpacking. When the track ended the Australian grabbed Annie's hand and pulled her towards the drinks table shouting, 'Drink! Drink! I'm gasping.' In the light she saw that he was quite old, late twenties probably. He poured two glasses of wine and handed her one with a sly wink.

'I've got some grass you might like to try. Interested?'

Annie had never actually taken any drugs, though it seemed uncool to say so. Before she could reply she heard a familiar voice saying, 'I am.'

There was Rose, flipping up her fringe the way she did

when she was excited about something. 'Aren't you Don Jago?'

'I could be. Depends who I'm talking to.' He bared his teeth, slid an arm around Annie, and pushed her towards the man following in Rose's wake. 'Hey, Ricky baby, have you met this fabulous creature?'

Rick clasped Annie's hand in both of his and gave her a piercing look of concentrated charm. 'Annie,' he said solemnly, 'hello and goodbye.' He withdrew his hands with a slow, regretful stroke across her palm that made her shiver. 'Do me a favour, guys,' he added coolly. 'If you want to smoke dope, go outside.'

'Great!' said Don. 'We can get high, and look at the moon.'

'Only if you've got X-ray vision,' Rose laughed. 'It's pouring. What do you say, Annie?'

Annie looked at her friend. Rose was fizzing like a firework. This mad Australian she had picked up must be some kind of star.

'Why not?' she said.

The staircase was littered with people leaning against the banisters or sprawled on the steps, nursing their glasses and tapping ash down the stairwell. Don led the way down to the shelter of the long colonnaded porch. Checking to make sure that no one was looking, he drew a little packet from his jacket. Annie watched carefully. Although everyone talked about pot parties, she had never seen anyone roll a joint.

Lighting the twisted end, Don took the first drag, then passed the joint to Rose. When it was her turn, Annie copied their way of sucking in the smoke with a hiss, then slowly exhaling. She waited for her brain to melt or some mystic revelation to appear. Nothing happened. Feeling relieved, she leaned back against a pillar, taking her turn with the circulating joint. Above the whisper of rain, she could hear 'Marrakesh Express'. Don told them all about the trial. The worst bit, he said, had been the compulsory prison haircut. England was ruled by a bunch of blinkered, geriatric old farts. Still, London was the scene; he was never going back to Australia.

'You know the difference between Australia and yoghurt?' he asked.

'Yoghurt has a live culture,' Rose answered, blowing smoke down her nose.

'Yah. Spoilsport.' He pinched her knee. 'Listen, chicks, I'm freezing my balls off here. Why don't we go back to your place, get warm, have some fun?'

'College, you mean?' Rose asked dubiously.

Don jumped up excitedly, as if he had seen a vision. 'Wow, yeah, a whole college full of beautiful pink and white girls. I can start with you two, and gradually work my way through. Let's split!'

Annie giggled. He was rather attractive, despite being so old. Perhaps the joint was having some effect after all. She felt pleasantly dopey; the stuffy, conventional world of home was slipping blissfully away. Besides, she had a feeling that Rose wanted something from him.

'You can drive us home, if you like,' she heard herself say.

As they went back in to collect their coats, they heard a strange grunting noise from the trees behind them.

'Jesus! What was that?' Don asked, clutching both girls to him.

'Rutting deer,' Annie said distinctly. For some reason they all found this hilarious.

In the High, Don stopped beside a mini painted in a psychedelic pattern of hearts and flowers and exploding suns.

'Here it is, the pash wagon.'

Annie climbed into the back. The seat was covered in a sheepskin and embroidered cushions. Strips of Indian tasselled silk hung above the windows. The car had a strange, musky smell.

They shot into the road with a squeal of tyres.

'Which way, lovelies?' Don shouted. Annie could tell that he was drunk, but who cared? So was she. She lay back across the seat with her legs braced against the far window, feeling her head spin.

'Red light!' Rose yelled.

A horn honked furiously. The car braked and lurched off again. Something rolled thunderously along the ledge behind Annie's head, and she reached up to grab a bottle of vodka. She could hear Rose in the front seat, swearing at Don.

'Was that really a red light?' he asked in amazement. 'I thought it was some wonderful, phantasmagoric great *strawberry* in the sky.' He made an expansive gesture, and the car wobbled again.

He started singing, drumming out the beat on the steering wheel. Annie and Rose joined in, as they zoomed up St Giles.

'And it's one, two, three, what are we fighting for?
Don't ask me, I don't give a damn
Next stop is Vietnam
And it's five, six, seven, open up the pearly gates
Ain't no time to wonder why
Whoopee! We're all going to die.'

'Not Woodstock Road,' Annie shouted as the car wavered at a fork in the road, 'the other way!'

'Woodstock! That's beautiful!' Don gave an ecstatic shiver. 'I wish I'd been there. All those people wandering hand in hand, just like the Garden of Eden. Can you imagine how mind-blowing it must have been, lying on the grass, listening to music and making love? That's what the future will be like. No one's going to get married and imprison themselves in boring little boxes. We'll all live in communes, surrounded by fields and animals, with barefoot children running free in the sunshine.'

What sunshine? wondered Annie.

'Monogamy's dead, that's for sure,' Rose agreed. 'It's so *bourgeois*. What a drag to be stuck with the same person all the time.'

'What if you love them?' Annie asked from the back, but no one heard her.

The gates were just closing when the car screeched to a halt outside LMH.

'Oh, no,' Don complained, jumping out. 'I only just got here. Couldn't you hide me in a cupboard – or in your bed? I promise to be good.'

Rose stroked a consoling hand down the sleeve of his velvet jacket. 'Another time, maybe.' She shot him a sparkling look from under her lashes. 'If you asked me to write something for your magazine, I could come up to London and . . . discuss it with you.'

'You're a little witch,' he grinned, patting her bottom. 'You want to watch out for her,' he said to Annie, 'she'll lead you astray.'

He took out a felt-tipped pen, pushed up Rose's sleeve and wrote his telephone number on her bare arm. Then he sighed and kissed each of them enthusiastically on the lips. 'You're both gorgeous, and I love you. See you, girls.'

Annie and Rose watched him prance back to the car in his high-heeled boots.

'Bet you he has a water bed,' Annie giggled.

'He's got a magazine,' Rose answered repressively. 'You must learn to concentrate on the essentials.'

'Oh, but I do.' Arching her eyebrows at Rose, Annie pulled something from under her coat and flourished it.

Rose yelped with laughter. 'Annie!'

'Don't "Annie" me.' She handed Rose the bottle and threw an affectionate arm around her shoulders. 'Come on, let's go finish his vodka.'

*

Jordan ran to the car, jumping puddles, and drove slowly home, thinking about Eldridge. Even now, it was not too late to change his mind. One phone call to the States, and his name would go back into the draft pool. Maybe this was one time when he should let the great diceman in the sky roll for him. But he wanted his life. He did not want to die. The Morris's windscreen wipers clacked back and forth. Yes, no. Yes, no.

Jordan stopped in Walton Street and picked up a couple of birianis and some poppadoms. The house was dark and silent. Alarm washed over him. With the warm, aromatic bags still in his arms, he took the stairs two at a time and knocked on Bruce's door. There was no answer. He turned the handle, releasing a gust of stale smoke and rancid body smell.

'Bruce?' he called anxiously.

There was the squeak of springs and a tired voice. 'For Christ's sakes, Jord, I keep telling you guys, I am not going to kill myself.' Bruce sniffed loudly. 'Do I smell curry?'

They ate in the kitchen, straight from the tinfoil cartons, with the oven door open to warm the room. Jordan tried to turn Rick's party into a string of anecdotes, while trying to imply that Bruce had not missed much. Afterwards Bruce said he felt like a walk. He didn't care about the rain. He liked it. Jordan watched him shamble off, unwashed hair hanging in clumps down the back of his plaid lumberjack's shirt. There was no point in saying that he would be soaked to the skin in minutes.

He took a cup of instant coffee up to his room and switched on the light. His eyes went straight to the white square of writing-paper. *Dear Mrs Dickson* . . . . Jordan hung up his jacket, pulled off his tie and sat down heavily, banging the teetery desk. A pile of books collapsed. Carefully he restacked Jouvenel's *Sovereignty* on top of Beloff's *Europe and the Europeans* and Theodore H. White's *The Making of a President*. Amid the clutter on his desk was a Perspex cube with a photograph on every facet. They were all the rage in the States. This one had been a going-away present from his mother. Jordan picked it up and rotated it idly. His whole life, it seemed, was contained in this little box. Here was a little boy, posing on the porch steps one Hallowe'en in his pirate's outfit; and here, an absurdly clean-cut sixteen-year-old, shaking hands with President Kennedy in the Rose Garden of the White House. Here was a picture of Miss Purvis, his teacher from the two-room schoolhouse in Indian Bluffs, who had encouraged Jordan to believe that he could achieve anything he wanted. Here was a picture of his mother, triumphantly holding up a fistful of dollar bills after a day at the racetrack. The final photograph was a black and white studio portrait of his father, handsome and serious in his army uniform – the father he had never known.

It was not the Second World War that had claimed Jordan's father, but a car accident just weeks before Jordan was born. Jordan couldn't have been much more than three years old the first time his mother had shown him his father's presidential citation for war service. Every year thereafter, on the anniversary of his father's death, she had made a point of bringing out the citation and talking to Jordan about the man she had admired and loved. Jordan sometimes dreamed of his father. In the dreams his father was always dressed like this, in uniform, and always seemed on the verge of imparting a momentous secret. For hours after Jordan woke, he would feel infused with a nameless, bittersweet emotion composed of loss and longing.

How would his father judge him now? Was it nobler to fight in a bad war – or against it? While his coffee grew cold Jordan stared into the clear, light eyes, searching for some message. At last he picked up his pen and started to write, hesitantly at first, then with ease, almost with pleasure, as he took control. He would mail the letter at once, tonight, slotting it into the red pillarbox at the corner of the street before he could change his mind. He would make Mrs Dickson guardian of his conscience; whatever he wrote now would commit him for ever.

The words flowed on. Eldridge was vivid in his mind, alive and whole. He was the key to everything.

13
Satisfaction

'So where are we going?' Annie asked as they passed through the LMH porch, arms wrapped tightly about each other. It was early evening, just twenty-four hours after Rick Goodman's party.

'Dudley's, I thought,' Edward said.

Annie looked at him in surprise. 'Dudley's' was the colloquial name for the Lamb and Flag, a country pub run by a canny father and son team, known as Old Dudley and Young Dudley. Its cheap food and lively atmosphere meant it was always packed with undergraduates. The only trouble was, it was at least ten miles from Oxford, in the village of Kingston Bagpuize. Annie's heart sank at the idea of getting a lift from someone. She wanted Edward to herself.

'And just how are you proposing we get there?' she asked. 'The Tardis?'

'I thought a car would be more convenient.' He pointed theatrically to a bright blue sports car parked at a rakish angle under the street lamp. 'Da-dah!

'Present from Dad for my twenty-first,' he explained, watching her face. 'I wanted it to be a surprise.'

Annie circled round it. 'Edward, you lucky thing. It's fabulous. Can we have the top down?'

He looked at her as if she'd said something marvellous. 'You'll freeze.'

Annie gave him a sexy, sideways look from behind her hair. 'No, I won't. Not after what we've been doing.'

Edward unsnapped the roof fastenings, and pushed back the hood, then held the passenger door open for Annie. She slid down in the low-slung seat until she was practically horizontal, aware of Edward's gaze as her coat fell open, exposing her legs and a tiny fringe of skirt high on her thighs. As he came round the other side to get in, she smiled lazily at him and dropped one hand provocatively on to the knob of the gear lever.

'Don't do that,' Edward groaned, climbing in. He leaned over to pull Annie into a lingering kiss, sliding his hand under her coat.

'God, I've missed you,' he said at last in a voice furry with lust. 'Are you absolutely, totally, one hundred per cent sure you want to go to dinner?'

'Yes,' she laughed, then raised her eyebrows mischievously. 'There's always later.'

Edward sighed good-humouredly, and started the car. He raced through Oxford with a lot of showy revving and gear-changing, then sped up Hinksey Hill.

'What do you think of her?' he shouted.

Annie just smiled, shutting her eyes against the cold wind, listening to the trees whoosh past. She thought she had never been so happy.

Edward had come at seven as promised, looking more beautiful than ever. At first they had been slightly self-conscious, making small talk. Edward had been on a walking holiday through the Sierra Nevada in Spain. He had brought her a hand-painted coffee mug as a present, and also a small leather-bound edition of Elizabeth Barrett Browning's *Sonnets from the Portuguese*, which he had inscribed to her in his spiky hand. Annie thought this was desperately romantic. Their awkwardness with each other dropped away. Soon they were kissing. Then Edward had got up to lock her door, and had made love to her on her narrow college bed. Nothing had changed. If anything, it was better, more natural and intimate than before. Afterwards they lay pressed together, Annie's leg thrown across his body, talking quietly. At length they had got up and dressed slowly, smiling at each other as they did up buttons and zips. This is how it will be, Annie had thought, a whole year of loving each other and being together.

She found she was smiling, and opened her eyes to look over at Edward. He looked wonderfully serious as he drove, his hair tangling behind him, the collar of his leather jacket turned up. A bubble of happiness rose within her until she thought she would burst. She started to belt out a Rolling Stones song, head back, hands clapping out the beat, until Edward joined in exuberantly.

Annie arrived at the restaurant with her cheeks glowing, so pleased with herself and the world that when Young Dudley recognised her from last summer, she kissed him. He found them a place at the end of one of the long candlelit trestle tables. 'I know what I want already,' she confided. 'Chicken casserole, honey and brandy ice-cream and lots of lovely wine.'

The restaurant was warm and noisy and jumping with life. Annie looked happily around the familiar barn-like room, with its brick walls and criss-cross roof timbers. Their wine came almost at once. Edward lit two cigarettes, and passed her one.

'So what play are we going to try out for this term?' Annie asked him. 'Wouldn't it be great if we could get parts together, like Beatrice and Benedick, or Eliza and Professor Higgins?'

Edward sighed regretfully. 'I'd love to, but I can't. Not this year. It takes up too much time.'

Annie laughed incredulously. 'But Finals aren't until June!'

'You make it sound like the year 2000. I've got to get a good degree if I want to get into a decent chambers.'

Annie drank her wine. She felt sharply disappointed. 'Well, I think it's very dull of you,' she pouted. 'I hope you're not expecting me to sit around mopping your brow and making you cups of coffee.'

'Don't be silly.'

'I've seen it happen. There are some girls at LMH who meet some boy in their very first term, and afterwards spend their entire time cooking them Vesta curries in the pantry. It's true,' she protested when Edward laughed at her disdainful tone. 'I've knocked on their doors to borrow milk or something, and there they are in arm-chairs by the fire, with a drying-rack of socks and horrible grey Y-fronts between them. They might as well be married.' She shook back her hair. 'Monogamy is so *bourgeois*,' she pronounced.

Edward raised his eyebrows, amused. 'Who said that?'

'I did.' Annie bristled.

While they ate, Edward told her more about his holiday. After the Sierra Nevada, he had gone down to the sea to a village called Cadaques, which sounded very cool, full of hippies and jazz bars.

'And beautiful girls?' Annie asked.

'Crawling with them. But none as pretty as you.' Edward took her hand and kissed it. 'Anyway, I had to come home early to be an usher at my cousin's wedding. Talk about a family palaver! Cakes and flowers and bloody bridesmaids' dresses – and the bride swanning up the aisle in white, three months' preggers.'

'Oh dear,' Annie giggled.

'Yeah.' Edward rolled his eyes. 'My ma was very tight-lipped about it all.'

'And what about your cousin?'

Edward shrugged. 'It was OK once we took him into

138

the vestry and poured a hipflask of whisky down him. Poor bugger, he's only a year older than me. Still, he'd been going out with the girl for years. I suppose one has to do the honourable thing.'

Annie began to tell Edward about last night's party. Feeling jealous of the beautiful girls in Spain, she set out to impress him, telling him about all the cool people who had been there and quoting Don's funny stories.

'You mean you went off with him?' Edward looked hurt.

'Nothing happened. I was with Rose. Anyway he was old – even older than you,' she teased. 'And he did have the most amazing grass. It was just fun,' she added defiantly.

'Ah, Rose,' Edward said suspiciously.

One afternoon last term Rose had come punting with them. It had not been a success. Rose and Edward had done everything they could to present themselves to each other in the worst possible light. What should have been an idle afternoon turned into a heated argument about whether students could legitimately claim solidarity with workers. Of course, Rose had insisted. Idealistic claptrap, Edward had argued, citing the Paris *événements* of '68. Annie had ended up exasperated with them both.

'Well, I like Rose,' she said now. 'I'm going on a demo with her next week. We're going to march to the American Embassy.' Until that moment Annie hadn't made up her mind.

'Since when have you been interested in Vietnam?'

'It's important,' Annie flushed. 'A supposedly civilised Western nation is perpetrating a terrible crime against humanity. They're bombing civilians, and burning little children to death and devastating the landscape. If enough people stand up against it, we might actually stop it. Isn't that worth doing?'

'What's going to end that war is the realisation that it

139

can't be won, plus Nixon's desire to get himself re-elected in three years' time.'

'How can you be so cynical?' Annie asked hotly. 'Even if you're right, shouldn't we do everything we can to shorten the war? For every person who makes a protest, a life could be saved. Hundreds of thousands of people could be killed in three years. It's oppression of a poor nation by a rich one. It should be stopped. If you can't be bothered to go because of your stupid work, that doesn't mean I can't.'

Edward sat back. 'Well, well.' His mouth tightened. 'You've turned into a proper little Lady Margaret Hall revolutionary.'

Annie was stung. 'You think it's a waste of time, do you?'

'I think you must do as you choose. Not accept what Rose or anyone else tells you to.'

'Including you.'

'Including me,' Edward agreed. But he looked annoyed.

Perhaps in an attempt to restore their good humour, he ordered two 'rusty nails', a Dudley's speciality that was half whisky and half Drambuie. The drink scorched down Annie's throat, but the alcohol only made her more defiant. She was still smarting when they went outside. Edward put his arm around her.

'So what shall we sing on the way back?'

'Nothing. It's too cold. I don't want the top down again.'

They drove home in silence. Annie had eaten and drunk too much. She felt sick as the car wound round the corners. She shut her eyes, pretending to be asleep.

The car slowed as they approached Oxford. 'Wake up, little Suzie,' Edward sang in her ear, when he stopped at a traffic light. 'Back to my place?' he asked lightly.

'Not tonight, Edward. I haven't even finished my unpacking, and I've got Collections on Monday. As you say, work is very important,' she added pointedly.

He drove her back without comment, but the atmosphere inside the car was charged. As LMH came into sight, Edward put his hand on her knee.

'Don't change', he begged. 'I love you just the way you are.'

'Everyone changes,' Annie answered, feeling depressed. If he thought she had changed, did that mean he didn't love her any more?

As soon as Edward stopped the car, Annie clicked open her door. 'Thanks for a super dinner,' she said stiffly, starting to climb out. Edward reached out to grasp her elbow. 'What about lunch tomorrow? The King's Arms at one?'

Annie turned to him with a rush of relief. 'OK,' she smiled.

The first thing she saw when she switched on the light in her room was her bouquet of roses. Annie felt her heart twist. She did love Edward. Perhaps she would just have to accept that things could not be the same as last term. She bent down to sniff the flowers, but could smell nothing. The petals were already browning at the edges.

14

Something in the air

Annie sat with her face turned to the watery sun, hugging her knees with excitement. Perched high on a plinth with the giant paw of one of Landseer's bronze lions at her back, she had a clear view across the thronged northern half of Trafalgar Square. Immediately below her was a crude platform of planks and scaffolding for the speakers and other dignitaries. If she tipped her head right back she could just see a foreshortened Nelson at the top of his column, today wearing a US Marine's cap on top of his admiral's hat.

Ten of them had travelled down to London in a clapped-out van. Annie had grumbled when Rose had woken her up at seven to a damp, grey dawn, but things improved once they had stopped for breakfast, at a transport café somewhere outside Henley. Afterwards one of the girls got out her guitar. Sprawled in the back on cushions Annie had sung along with the others. They had started quietly with protest stuff like 'We shall overcome' and 'Where have all the flowers gone?' By the time they reached London they were yelling 'We all live in a yellow submarine', banging out the rhythm on the metal sides of the van. They had left the van near Hyde Park, where the march was due to end, and walked arm in arm through the quiet Sunday morning streets, which gradually filled as they approached Trafalgar Square.

When they arrived the crowd was already sizeable. Now it seemed impossible that the square could accommodate the people who still converged on it from all directions. Some burst from the tube in rowdy student groups, carrying placards which proclaimed the distance they had travelled: Durham, Brighton, Leicester, even Berlin and Amsterdam. Others were disgorged from the coaches, vans and cars that crept into the square in a slow line of traffic and drew up in front of the formal pillared façade of the National Gallery. Couples ambled from the side-streets, amorously entwined, as if this were a normal sunny Sunday, making Annie wish for a moment that Edward had come too. On the steps of the church of St Martin's in the Field six tramps sat in a row, passing a cider bottle back and forth, waiting as if for a play to begin. High above the crowds, lining roofs and pediments and windowsills, hunched several hundred displaced and disgruntled pigeons. There would be no peanuts from the tourists today.

Vietnamese flags poked defiantly out of the crowd. There were hundreds of placards with angry slogans – 'Better Red than Dead', 'Hands Off Vietnam'. Annie even saw a WANTED poster with a photograph of Nixon's furrowed, jowly face. A group of students, presumably Americans, carried a US flag daubed with a black cross. She could hear their hoarse chant: 'Hell no, we won't go.' Around the edges of the square dark blue clumps betrayed the presence of the police in discreet, watchful huddles, the silver stars on their helmets glinting in the sunlight.

Rose gave a deep sigh of satisfaction, as if she had personally conjured the crowd out of the ether. 'Far out, man. There must be at least eight thousand people – maybe ten.'

143

Annie put her rolled-up demo leaflet to her eye like Nelson's telescope. She squinted at the multicoloured sea of denim and tweed, embroidered coats and military jackets, headbands and hats. 'How on earth can you tell?'

Rose pulled on her Gauloise, blowing the smoke out through her nostrils in a way Annie had tried to copy but which always left her out of breath. 'It's in the blood. Not for nothing am I named after Rosa Luxemburg. I've told you, my parents are demo freaks – CND, Anti-Apartheid, Labour rallies. I was only ten when they took me on the Aldermaston March.'

When Annie was ten her parents had put her on the P & O liner back to England and boarding-school. How much more exciting to share the warmth and solidarity of a crowd like this one, perhaps carried high on her father's shoulders. 'What was it like?'

'Spam sandwiches and blisters from my school sandals.' Rose scowled. 'I sometimes think that what would really please my parents is if I wound up dead in a canal like old Rosa, martyr to some noble socialist cause.'

'Don't be silly.' Annie gave Rose a friendly nudge. 'My mother dreams of marrying me off to somebody frightfully rich and pompous, giving candlelit dinners so she can flirt and give her awful tinkly laugh. You know, a stockbroker or an advertising executive or a – ' Annie paused, trying to think of something truly terrible.

'Chartered accountant,' supplied Rose in a doom-laden voice.

'Yeuch!' they groaned, clutching each other in horror. Annie remembered uncomfortably that Edward was going to be a lawyer.

I'm never going to be a parent,' Rose swore fiercely.

'God, no,' Annie agreed. 'At least, not until I'm too old for anything else.'

'Shh!' Rose put a hand on Annie's knee. 'It's her!'

The speeches were nearly over. First had been a man in a dog-collar, next a trade union leader in donkey jacket and corduroy cap, then a bearded American who turned out to be a draft dodger. Now the last speaker, a woman. There was a ripple of excitement from the crowd.

'Look!' cried Rose. 'There she is.'

Annie scrambled to her knees and balanced herself against Rose's shoulders, feeling the sharp edge of the plinth bite through her jeans. A tall woman was climbing on to the speakers' platform. She was wearing a long man's overcoat with a black band around one arm.

The crowd fell still as the unmistakable voice began a passionate denunciation of America's misbegotten and brutal war on the Vietnamese people. Annie unfurled the leaflet which she had been fooling around with earlier. She felt ashamed of her levity as she scanned the grim statistics – forty thousand Americans killed, billions of dollars wasted on killing-machines, more bombs dropped than in the whole of the Second World War, hundreds of square miles of Vietnamese forest devastated by Agent Orange. The pictures were the worst, even these muzzy photocopies. A man winced at the gun pressed to his head, frozen in the split second before the bullet entered his brain. A woman holding her dead baby, dark with blood, opened her mouth in a scream of anguished denial. Annie had seen such pictures before, on television and in the newspapers, but for the first time they entered her heart. This was real. She was involved. She could do something about it. It was an incredible feeling to be part of this vast crowd, to march with them, shout, make a fuss. Perhaps it was good that Edward was not here after all.

The speaker was now reading aloud the letter of protest to the American ambassador that was the focus of this demonstration, then raised a fist in a kind of Black Power salute. The crowd began to sway and rumble, ready to start the march. A girl on the lion opposite Annie's stood up on its broad back and pulled her poncho over her head. She had nothing on underneath. 'Peace and Love!'

she shouted, arms stretched wide, bare breasts bobbing. Annie and Rose whooped their appreciation, laughing as a pair of policemen hustled the girl away, wrapped in one of their jackets – as if nakedness were a crime.

'Quick,' called Rose, sliding down to the ground. 'If we go round this way we can be near the front.' They linked arms, pushing and dodging through the crowd until they found themselves moving steadily up Charing Cross Road in a controlled stream. Annie strode out in her boots, an Indian scarf tied warrior-like about her head, chanting 'Peace Now!' She could feel the energy from the thousands of people flooding through her. Quite suddenly a door swung open in her mind. I've cracked Wordsworth, she thought with elation. 'Bliss was it in that dawn to be alive/But to be young was very heaven!' The exhilaration she was feeling, this extraordinary combination of intellectual purpose and thrilling human solidarity – that's what Wordsworth must have felt about the French Revolution. How simple it all was! She resolved to tackle *The Prelude* again.

At Tottenham Court Road tube station the crowd turned left into Oxford Street, bunching up quite suddenly and frighteningly as people fought to keep their place. Annie was swept away from Rose like a piece of flotsam and pushed into a steel barrier, so hard that she cried out. By the time she had found her feet, Rose had disappeared. Annie jumped in the air, hoping for a glance of Rose's crazy hat, but it was no good. She had lost her. She moved up along the outside of the crowd, squeezing past the bright windows of the Oxford Street shops. But as she neared the front the crowd closed tight about her, changing direction once again. The pressure tightened until Annie could see nothing but the bright blue Chairman Mao jacket of the man in front of her. Her elation was gone. She felt shaken. Something had gone wrong.

An aggrieved murmur rose to an angry buzz as the word was passed back. 'They won't let us in . . . fascist traitors. They won't bloody well let us in!' Annie weaseled her way forward. Her heart began to race as she realised what was happening. The police were trying to stop them getting from Oxford Street into Grosvenor Square. They were spread out in a cordon right across North Audley Street, arms linked, maybe fifty of them and – Jesus! – horses. Annie had felt anxious about horses ever since she had been flung on to the sand by a nasty seaside pony and broken her collarbone. These were no ponies, but great slabs of muscled flesh, with iron soup-plates for feet and massive hindquarters swivelling un-predictably at eye level. For a moment the crowd was stopped, seething and shouting but not yet advancing. A rhythmic chanting started up, growing louder and faster as it passed down the crowd. 'Let us through. Let us through. *Let us through*!' People stamped their feet in time, and banged placard-staves on the road. Annie could feel the pressure building up behind her as more and more of the thousands of demonstrators moved inexor-ably forward, oblivious of the problem. The press of bodies was stifling. She heard a girl's voice screaming, 'Let me out!' But it was too late.

There was a sudden, explosive bang. One of the horses reared into the air, then plunged down again, whirling and snorting. Somebody must have thrown a firecracker. After that everything happened very fast. First, the nasal boom of a megaphone, urgent but unintelligible. Then two more loud bangs and the high whinny of a horse. The chanting dissolved into a sustained baying roar. Without warning the crowd surged forward, and Annie was swept with it, slipping, lurching, grabbing hold of people to keep her balance. In front of her a man tripped over the pole of the Red Flag he was carrying and crashed to the ground. In seconds the bright folds were trampled. No one helped him up; it was impossible to stop. Through a gap in the crowd Annie caught a split-second glimpse of Rose running, her mouth open and her eyes wide. She

147

looked scared. Then the bodies closed in again, jostling and shouting.

With a cry of triumph they burst out of the tunnel of North Audley Street into the open space of Grosvenor Square. It was huge – a garden the size of two cricket pitches, with trees and statues and a fountain, enclosed by dignified old buildings. Annie filled her lungs with fresh air and ran faster, trying to escape from the crowd at her heels. But almost at once she was brought to a halt. Breathless and disoriented, she found herself pummelled by the crowd into a ragged line no more than fifty paces from the American Embassy.

It was a huge building, stretching right across one end of the square, a modern statement in pale stone and plate glass. With its high metal palisade and protective moat, it had the air of a fortress. People said that there was a secret underground link in its vast basement, so that key personnel could be whisked to safety in the event of a nuclear attack. High above the entrance was set an enormous golden eagle with a wingspan of perhaps thirty feet. Below the eagle hung a limp Stars and Stripes. Underneath the American flag, hundreds of English policemen formed a slash of dark blue across the Embassy's broad, polished steps. They did not look friendly.

A police officer walked into the no man's land between demonstrators and police and raised a megaphone to his mouth. 'In the interest of your own safety, please clear the square,' he enunciated in booming suburban vowels. The crowd giggled. He repeated the instruction.

'Go home, fatty!' a voice shouted back. The laughter swelled. Annie could feel the crowd flexing its collective muscle. She looked behind her at the thousands of people milling round the square, snapping branches off the trees and hedges for makeshift weapons. They must outnumber the police by ten to one. The pack instinct was strong.

A figure burst out of the crowd and hurled something into the air. Red paint spilled out in an arc, splashing like blood across the rump of a police horse. The can landed on the Embassy's pristine steps, just short of the police line, and clanked down to the bottom, spilling more paint as it went. Two policemen sprinted from nowhere and brought the figure down in a flying rugby tackle. Then they yanked him up and dragged him, shoes scraping across the tarmac, towards a police van – except, Annie suddenly saw, it wasn't a he but a she, a girl, with blood pouring down her face.

The crowd roared its disapproval. One of the policemen had lost his helmet struggling with the paint-thrower. A figure darted into no man's land and scooped it up. He tossed his trophy into the crowd. Delighted, they threw it back and forth with whoops and squeals, like bridesmaids catching a wedding bouquet. More paint cans sailed through the air and clunked on to the tarmac. The megaphone man stepped forward again, and was met with a barrage of stones. Retreating fast, arms raised defensively, he slipped in a pool of paint and fell. The crowd surged forward hungrily. 'Let's get the pigs,' growled a voice. Then the front section of the crowd ran forward, yelling, pointing their placards and branches like battering rams. They were going to charge the police line! Policemen thundered forward to intercept them. They met in an ugly, scrabbling fight.

Annie saw a policeman gasp with pain as the edge of a placard jabbed him in the stomach. His companions fell on the attacker, kicking him as he slumped to the ground. Somehow he wriggled out of their grasp, leaving his jumper behind. A policeman raced after him and thwacked him across the back with his truncheon. Stones rained down on demonstrators and police alike. More police on horseback cantered on to the scene. A girl screamed. The megaphone boomed again. '*Clear the square.*'

Stop it! Annie pleaded silently, digging her nails into her palms. She turned to look for a way out, but the crowd was now in pandemonium, some trying to get into the fight, others desperate to get away. The effect was to push Annie nearer and nearer to the fighting and the horses as if she were in the grasp of a huge wave. A firecracker exploded almost under her feet. She heard a squeal. A horse reared terrifyingly over her, then plunged back to the ground, its hooves slicing within inches of her face. She could smell its warm barleysugar breath and see the tiny red veins pulsing in its nostrils. Panicking, she ducked under its neck and ran. There were steps in front of her and a smooth wall. Somehow, she scrambled up it. The next thing she knew she was crouched, panting, on top of one of the pillars that flanked the Embassy steps. It was, she realised, just about the most dangerous place she could have chosen. Immediately behind her was the police cordon, arms linked, heads cocked defensively downward to ward off the rain of makeshift missiles. On the steps below, more police were fighting off the demonstrators. Annie was marooned between them, in the firing line. Beyond them, the police horses were now charging at the crowd, scattering them to the far corners of the square. Annie was completely cut off.

Through the din Annie heard a man's voice shouting, 'Jump!' She looked around wildly. She couldn't jump. It was too far. She would hit the steps, crack her head, break a leg. She tried to see who was shouting at her, but there were only police, a tangle of arms and legs and flying truncheons.

'C'mon. Over here. *Jump!*' urged the voice. Fighting panic, Annie crawled to the other edge of the pillar and peered down. She had a blurred impression of long hair swept back from a man's anxious face, a tan jacket, arms stretched forward. It was a hell of a way down. She would never manage it. As she hesitated, stones thunked around her feet. Something hit her stingingly on the temple. Annie took a deep breath and jumped.

15

Hello, I love you, won't you tell me your name?

Annie felt the wind lift her hair, then the slam of her body into hard muscle. She had an impression of strong arms at her waist and soft material against her cheek, as her feet slid to the ground. Before she could say anything, a hand grabbed hers and raced her across the empty ground, into the skirmishing crowd.

Head down, she barged through the crush of yelling, fighting bodies. The ground was littered with debris. Annie stumbled over broken branches and stones, paint cans and the splintered remains of placards, even a discarded man's shoe. The noise was horrible: megaphones, police whistles, the scrabble of horses' hooves on tarmac, and over it all the din of a furious, frustrated crowd. At one point Annie's hair snagged painfully on somebody's coat button, but the hand clasped about hers dragged her forward. Her eyes watered as she felt the hairs torn out of her scalp. Two ambulancemen carrying a stretcher shouted for people to clear the way. Annie caught a glimpse of a white-faced policeman lying still. Without his helmet, he didn't look any older than she was.

Suddenly the crowd thinned. Annie slithered to a halt

as she felt the hand around hers tighten warningly. Angled across the road, blocking the way, were two police vans. A group of officers were standing outside, some murmuring into their walkie-talkies, others interrogating mulish-looking demonstrators.

'Shit,' breathed her companion.

Behind the vans Annie could see an empty street with a huddle of spectators at the far end. Beyond them, a line of trees marked the boundary of Hyde Park – and freedom. They were so close she could have wept. She turned to look at the ugly crowd behind her and quailed at the thought of fighting her way back through it.

The hand tightened on hers again. 'OK,' he said. 'We're going to walk between those trucks – nice and easy. If anyone looks at you, smile like they're your long-lost brother.'

Smile, indeed. He doesn't want much, Annie thought. Then they were moving casually forwards, a couple out for a Sunday stroll. As they reached the vans, one policeman looked up from his notebook and frowned at Annie. She beamed back at him. He shot an uncertain look at his colleagues, but they were busy. His eyes darted back to Annie, mesmerised by her fixed grin. Just as they reached the narrow gap between the vans, there was an alarmed shout.

Annie felt herself yanked forward. 'Go!' yelled her companion. Annie stretched out her long legs and ran. There was a blur of iron railings, then the knot of gawping spectators at the end of the street came into focus. Their shocked faces and staid Sunday clothes made her want to laugh. There was even a dachshund wearing a daft coat. In unspoken agreement, they pushed through the crowd and ran straight across Park Lane, leaping the central barrier, until they reached the quiet green expanse of Hyde Park. Then he swung her round to face him and let her hand drop.

'Are you all right?' he asked.

'Yes,' she laughed in amazement. 'No.' She ran a hand over her head, feeling the loose tumble of her hair. 'I've lost my scarf.'

'Then I guess,' he said slowly, 'I'll just have to go back and get it.'

Hearing the teasing note in his voice, Annie looked at him properly for the first time. He was tall – she had to tip her head back to see into his face – with thick chestnut hair, streaked to gold by the sun, that waved to his shoulders like a lion's mane. His blue eyes slanted in amusement. Underneath his Afghan coat he was wearing jeans, and a tartan shirt with little buttons on the collar-tips. Annie remembered the odd way he spoke, and her brain suddenly clicked back into gear.

'You're American,' she said.

'Yes, ma'am,' he agreed, and held out his hand. 'Jordan Hope, from Indian Bluffs, Illinois.'

She shook it, smiling at his formality. 'Annie Paxford. You were fantastic. If it weren't for you, I'd probably still be clinging to that pillar, like patience on a monument.'

Jordan just grinned at her, rocking on his toes with his fists pushed deep into his coat pockets. Was he waiting for her to say goodbye? Maybe he had friends to get back to. Annie suddenly remembered Rose, and looked back anxiously towards Grosvenor Square. Jordan gave a startled exclamation and put out a hand to her chin, turning her cheek towards him.

'You've cut your head,' he frowned.

Annie rubbed at the stickiness on her temple. 'Something hit me. It doesn't hurt.'

But he had already taken a handkerchief from his pocket. 'Here, let me fix that.' He smoothed her hair away, and dabbed her face gently. He smelled of leather and shaving soap.

'There. Good as new. That was a pretty wild scene back there. Just as well your policemen don't carry guns.'

'Unlike yours. They shoot students, don't they?' Annie

153

tried to sound composed. Now that the danger was past, she felt an odd exhilaration that left her breathless and jittery. She could still hear the distant roar of the demonstration.

'Well, I'm not going back there. No way,' Jordan said. 'I think we deserve a rest. There's a great little pub not too far away – if I can find it. What do you say to a Bloody Mary?'

'I don't think I've ever had one,' she said happily.

Jordan clapped a hand to his heart and staggered as if he had been shot. Annie burst out laughing, startling a pair of disapproving Mayfair matrons in headscarves.

Jordan shook his head at her. 'The trouble with you English,' he drawled, 'is that you just ain't educated.'

'I'm at Oxford,' Annie replied haughtily.

'You're kidding.'

'Certainly not. Do I look frightfully dim?'

'You look fabulous,' he said frankly. 'All is mean is, I'm at Oxford too.' His smile broadened. 'I knew I'd seen you before. You were in that Shakespeare play in the garden.'

'*As You Like It*?' Annie was amazed. 'And did you like it?'

'I liked you.'

'Oh.' Annie scuffed the leaves at her feet.

Together they strolled south across the park, towards Knightsbridge. Sunshine warmed their faces and made the trees flame into colour. Londoners were out in force, taking their pleasure with an urban lack of reserve. Jordan and Annie pointed out to each other a dedicated sun-worshipper lying on grass stripped to the waist, and an old woman with her life's belongings tied on to a shopping trolley, feeding pigeons from a plastic bag. There were lovers everywhere. As they walked they talked of Oxford. Annie learned that he was at Corpus, doing a graduate degree in PPE – philosophy, politics, and economics. Jordan seemed to find the whole place beautiful but weird, a sort of cross between *Tom Brown's Schooldays* and *Alice in Wonderland*. He told her about the two college tortoises, one called Corpus and the other Christi, and of the ceremonial race held between them each year; and how until 1963 it was the rule of the college that no living woman could be named at High Table. 'I guess it was open season on the dead ones,' he commented drily. One of his tutors liked to sit cross-legged on the floor trying to convert Jordan to Marxism. Another had offered to dedicate his next book to Jordan if Jordan went to bed with him.

Annie giggled. 'What did you say?'

'I said I wasn't sleepy. Yeah, he laughed too, but it makes me mad the way these guys don't take their subject seriously. They treat politics like some intellectual game. It's not. Politics is about everyday stuff, like jobs and homes and having enough to eat. Fooling around with ideas in isolation is exactly what leads to craziness like Vietnam.'

They reached Rotten Row, waited for a rider in tweeds and black velvet cap to canter past, and crunched through the yellow sand.

'This way,' Jordan urged, leading her across Knightsbridge and into a quiet side-street.

'The trouble is,' Annie explained seriously, 'all these tutors and politicians and generals – and parents, of course – are *old*. They think everything's the way it was in the Second World War. They can't understand that the world is different now, that we don't care about all those stuffy things like class and money and religion and – oh, I don't know, marriage and proper jobs and singing "God Save the Queen".'

'Wow.' Jordan grinned at her. 'That's quite a list.'

'But don't you agree?'

'Sure. Though I don't think that dropping out is the answer either. You can't expect a better world to materialise out of thin air. You have to do something to create it.'

155

'What about today – the demonstration? That was doing something.' When Jordan didn't answer Annie stopped and turned to face him. He looked sober and distracted.

'Well, wasn't it?' she insisted.

Under her earnest gaze his expression softenened. 'Yes,' he reassured her, 'it was doing something.'

The sounds of the traffic died away. They could hear the echo of their own footsteps as they walked through a calm square. Then they entered a cobbled mews lined with garages.

'Eureka!' Jordan cried, as they turned a corner. At the end of the mews was a whitewashed pub garlanded with ivy. Jordan led the way up the steps and held open the door for Annie. It was dark and warm inside. Immediately in front of her was a bar, with cosy, crowded rooms adjoining. Almost at once Jordan found them a table next to a crackling log fire. Annie pulled off her coat and sat down, while Jordan ordered the drinks. The barman had a large handlebar moustache, and wore a white jacket like a ship's steward. Annie watched as he began to mix ingredients in a cocktail shaker with military precision. The drinks arrived, frothy and coral coloured, in outsize wineglasses. Annie took a sip of hers. It was delicious.

Jordan sat down opposite her. 'Have you got plans for this afternoon?' he asked.

'Not really,' Annie lied. She was due back at the van by four. But she was not going to pass up the chance of spending a day with this intriguing man. Edward didn't own her, after all.

'Good,' Jordan smiled. 'It's a beautiful day. I thought we might take a walk in the park, maybe catch a movie later. I'm heading back to Oxford tonight. I could give you a ride, if you want.'

'You have a car?'

'You know us Americans. We don't move without our cars, our cameras, our Bermuda shorts and a refrigerator as big as a bus.'

Annie heard the barbed undertone. 'Don't you like the English?'

'Yes, I do — at least I probably would if I could get to know them. I'm sorry if that sounded impolite. Just sometimes I get tired of fighting the same old American stereotype: too rich, too loud, too stupid. And with "frightfully amusing" names.'

'I think Jordan's a great name,' Annie said truthfully. 'If it makes you feel any better, there's a girl in my college called Arabella Farquharson Tennant. Anyway, there's no need to apologise to me. I've lived abroad most of my life. I don't belong either — especially at LMH.'

'Lady Margaret Hall? Why, what's wrong with it?'

'Nothing. I love it. I mean that thing about it being the *ladies'* college. You must know the old joke.'

'No, I don't.' Jordan leaned towards her, elbows on the table, eyes alight. 'Tell me.'

Annie hid her face in her hands. 'Oh, God, now I won't be able to remember it.' She swept back her hair, took a slug of her Bloody Mary and licked the froth from her lips. 'Let's see . . . . There are five girls having tea together, each from a different college. Suddenly one of them spots a divine-looking man crossing the quad, and they all rush to the window to have a look.'

She stopped in confusion, flushing under his concentrated gaze.

'Yeah?' Jordan prompted.

'So the girl from St Hugh's says, "What does he play?" The girl from Somerville asks, "What's he reading?" The LMH girl says, "Who are his people?" The St Hilda's girl says, "I want him." And the St Anne's girl' — she finished triumphantly — 'says, "He's mine." '

Jordan rocked back in his chair with a big, easy laugh that made the people around them look up and smile in sympathy. Annie, feeling incredibly witty, drained her glass with a flourish.

'That's terrific,' Jordan said. 'I must write it down.'

Annie thought he was joking until he drew out a tiny notebook from his inside pocket. She felt almost embarrassed as he committed her silly little story to paper.

'I know you think I'm crazy,' Jordan said in a resigned tone, 'and you wouldn't be the first. It's a habit. I like being able to remember.'

Annie watched him write. 'You're left-handed,' she remarked.

'Is that bad too?' He looked up at her teasingly.

'It's a sign of extreme intelligence,' Annie replied, 'meaning that I'm left-handed as well. In fact,' she confided, 'I'm a left-handed Leo, which is the best thing of all. Not that I believe in astrology really, but Leo has all the best things, like fire and gold and power and – '

'And having a birthday in the summer.'

'How did you know?'

'Because, smartypants,' he tapped the back of her hand with his finger, 'I'm a left-handed Leo too.'

They grinned at each other, as if they'd made a secret pact.

After one more drink they left the pub, and crossed back into the park. A mellow, golden light shimmered through the trees. Annie laughed aloud at the beauty of it all.

'Isn't it lovely?' She threw out her arms, and twirled round, her coat flying open.

'It certainly is,' he said, watching her.

'Race you to that tree,' she challenged, and set off across the grass.

Jordan overtook her easily, clowning around. Panting with laughter, they leaned back against the broad beech trunk.

'This morning seems like a hundred years ago,' Annie said. 'It's so awful that we never even delivered the petition. Do you think they'll have another demo?'

'I hope so. I sure hope something happens before next summer, anyway.'

158

'Why next summer?'

Jordan reached over and gently pulled a leaf from her hair. He took a breath. 'Last week I decided to put my name back in the draft pool. Yesterday I got a letter. I've been rated 1-A. Unless something happens by the time I leave Oxford in June – ' he pointed two fingers at her like a gun, making a joke of it – ' "Look out, gooks, here I come." '

Annie looked at him in horror. 'I don't believe you. They can't make you go. You're a student.'

'Oh, but they can. That's what it's all about. I'm twenty-three, Annie. Some boys didn't even make it to nineteen.'

Images of the war flooded into Annie's head – a weary Marine smoking a cigarette against a backdrop of skeletal trees cobwebbed with black, blindfolded prisoners roped together, Vietnamese women crouching over their babies while American bombs rained down. A year from now Jordan could be in Vietnam. He could be dead. He could have killed someone. And from what he said, this was his own choice. It was the bravest thing she had ever heard. She held on to his arm as they walked on, feeling its reassuring muscle, while he told her about his friend Eldridge and the crisis of conscience which had precipitated his decision.

They reached the Serpentine. Annie watched people going about the ordinary business of enjoying themselves – reading newspapers on sunny benches, scattering bread for the ducks, throwing sticks for their dogs. Two school-boys in grey flannel shorts and sagging knee-socks had got into difficulties with their model boat. Jordan left her for a moment to help them retrieve it, showing them how to manoeuvre the boat so it didn't capsize. Annie watched him squatting by the water, chatting easily, the boys utterly captivated. He looked up, caught her glance and winked. Annie turned away, hugging her coat around her. It just could not be right for someone like Jordan to risk his life for that criminal, stupid war.

'Couldn't you just stay here – or go to Canada?' she asked when he rejoined her.

Jordan shook his head. 'That's not the kind of revolutionary I want to be,' he said simply. 'I don't think this war is right. It's not consistent with the democratic principles of America. But I can't just run away. We need to get back to our roots, to that *real* revolutionary spirit that drove America to independence in the first place – "the preservation of life, and liberty, and the pursuit of happiness".' He smiled sadly at her. 'I don't want to kill anyone. I want to change things.'

They walked on in silence, crunching through the dying leaves. The days were getting shorter now. There was already a chill in the air. In the Bayswater Road, a few hopeful artists and traders had laid out their wares against the park railings.

'There's quite a decent cinema up here, at Notting Hill Gate,' Annie said. 'We could see what's on. What's the matter?'

For Jordan had stopped suddenly, as if struck with an idea. He marched Annie back the way they had come, hands on her shoulders, then swung her to face a tiny makeshift stall. It was crowded with beads, embroidered belts and headbands, silver jewellery, packets of joss sticks – and silk scarves.

'Choose one,' Jordan said.

'I couldn't!'

'Sure you could. What about this one?' He leaned forward to pick one out. She felt his chin graze her hair. Just for a second she let herself lean back against his chest. He felt big and solid – a man, not a boy. Then Jordan moved away and held the scarf up to her face. 'See, it matches your eyes.'

Eventually they settled on one in turquoise and indigo paisley. Annie wound it round her neck, watching Jordan count out the money. She touched his elbow.

'Thank you very much. It's beautiful.'

He just laughed and jingled his change. 'Come on, let's go see a movie. I don't care what it is as long as we can sit down. That was one hell of a walk you took me on.'

'I took you – !' Annie protested.

At the Gate Cinema they joined the queue for *Easy Rider* and listened to a busker mangling Beatles songs. Jordan put half a crown into his hat, to Annie's disgust.

'That's far too much. He can't even sing.'

'Me neither.' Jordan shrugged. 'He's got to live, like everyone else.'

When they came out of the cinema it was dark. They wandered around looking for somewhere to eat, and at last found a little restaurant with bare wooden tables and candles stuck into Chianti bottles. There were sepia photographs on the wall; Françoise Hardy sang softly on a record player.

'I think I'll just have a salad,' Annie said, looking at the prices. She had only about seven and six in her pocket.

Jordan's eyebrows flew up. 'You're not going to tell me you're on a diet. That I won't believe. Come on, I'm going to have steak, and French fries, and the whole shebang. Let me treat you.'

'But I'm making you spend all your money.'

'What the heck else is it for? Listen, Annie, they give us a salary as Rhodes Scholars. It's worth about five times your student grant. That's how come I have a car. At home I had to work summers and wait tables to get through college, but here I'm rich.' He spread his hands, drawling extravagantly, 'As we'all say down South, I'm living high on the hog.'

Annie gave in. They ordered their food and a carafe of red wine. Then she leaned forward into the candlelight.

'Wasn't that film fabulous?'

'I guess. The music was good. I liked the guy playing the hobo. Otherwise, it seemed pretty dumb to me, just riding motorbikes and smoking joints.'

'Well, I loved it.' Annie took a sip of her wine. 'It's my dream to go to America.'

His eyes slanted in amusement. 'Anywhere in particular?'

'Everywhere. It all sounds amazing. New York, San Francisco, Woodstock, the Grand Canyon, Big Sur.' Annie intoned the names like a chant, making Jordan laugh. 'Memphis, Tennessee,' she went on. 'Phoenix, Arizona. Route 66.' She leaned across the table and stretched her eyes wide. 'Badlands,' she whispered.

'And what about Indian Bluffs?'

'Is that an invitation?'

'You bet. My mom would love you.'

'And your father?'

While they ate Jordan told her about his family and his little town on the huge brown river, about the steamy summers and the winters when he and his friends had built snow forts and attacked each other with snowballs.

'And what about you?' he asked. 'Do you have brothers and sisters?'

'No.'

'Kind of lonely, isn't it?'

'Yes,' she said, surprised. She had never admitted it so easily before.

She found herself telling him all about her odd peripatetic life, her exile to boarding-school, even her bickering parents. The restaurant filled up and emptied again as they found more things to tell one another, to discuss, argue over. Annie felt she had known him for weeks, not hours.

In the end, the waiter pointedly brought their bill. They realised it was late. Reluctantly, they left the restaurant and took a taxi back to Jordan's car, a snub-nosed Morris Minor with red upholstery. It was chilly. Jordan flicked the switch that controlled the heater. Soon Annie could feel warm air blowing up her legs and lulling her into comforting drowsiness. She watched as the ugly old fac-

162

tories and harsh street lamps at the edge of London gave way to dark fields.

'If you don't have to go to Vietnam, what will you do?'

Jordan glanced at her. 'Law school, maybe, then some kind of public service. There are so many things that need to be done, especially where I come from.'

'You mean politics?' Annie said in amazement. She pictured Nixon's brutal face, Harold Wilson with his pipe and horrid belted mackintosh, looking shifty. They didn't fit at all with her heroic image of Jordan.

He laughed. 'You say that as if I wanted to boil little babies in oil. There are good politicians, you know.'

'Yes, and you kill them,' Annie responded tartly. 'Kennedy, Bobby Kennedy, Martin Luther King – even Abraham Lincoln.'

'I guess I'd sooner be shot because I'd achieved something, than be blown to pieces in Vietman before I had a chance to do anything. Anyway, it's good to have a goal. Don't you have ambitions?'

'Of course.' But when Annie thought of them, they seemed vague and frivolous in comparison – holidays in Greece; her own flat in some groovy corner of London; a car to drive whenever and wherever she liked; perhaps a year in Nepal; a stab at drama school; lovers, parties, fun.

'I suppose you want to be President,' she said, more aggressively than she intended.

'Why not?' he said mildly. 'Somebody has to be. Wouldn't you rather it was me than some racist bigot like George Wallace?'

A fragment of a Tom Lehrer song floated into Annie's head. Without pausing to think, she started singing.

'I wanna talk with Southern gentlemen,
And put my white sheet on again,
I ain't seen one good lynchin' in years . . .'

Jordan shouted with laughter. 'You're crazy, Annie Paxford, you know that? Are all Oxford girls like you?'

'You should know,' she said provocatively.

'Should I? I've only met one girl at Oxford I really liked.'

'Really?' Annie felt faintly piqued. 'And who was that?'

'You,' he said calmly.

Annie relaxed deeper into her seat as the dark road twisted through sleepy villages, watching Jordan's hands on the steering wheel. When at length they drove into Oxford, the clock at Carfax said half-past one. The college gates had closed long ago. She would have to climb in.

Outside LMH Jordan stopped the car and snapped off its lights. The fan-heater died into silence. They sat in the dark, listening to the tick of the cooling engine.

'So,' Jordan turned to her, 'when do I get to see you again?'

Annie bent her head, hiding behind her hair.

'Jordan,' she began.

'Mnnh?'

'I have to tell you something.'

He tensed, then flopped back into his seat with a sigh. 'I know,' he said flatly. 'You're very sorry but you already have a boyfriend. He's brilliant, and handsome as hell — and probably English — and you don't want to hurt him. Etcetera.'

Annie looked at him in surprise. 'How did you know?'

Jordan let his head drop on to the backrest with something between a laugh and a groan. 'How did I know?' he asked himself. 'I know because there are about forty guys to every girl in Oxford, which means that anything in skirts is already attached. I know because nine out of ten Oxford girls are either Marion-the-Librarian types, or act like the Queen; whereas you' — he cocked his head at her — 'are pretty and smart and funny and just the kind of girl I only ever seem to see on some other guy's arm. I know because nothing has gone right for me ever since I arrived in Oxford, so why should it change now?'

'I'm sorry, Jordan.'

'Me too, believe me. Though I guess I wouldn't like you so much if you cheated on your boyfriend. Still,' he propped his elbow on the back of Annie's seat and smiled down at her wolfishly, 'I'll give you one more chance.'

Annie twisted her hands in her lap. 'I can't.

'We could just be friends,' she offered at last, raising her head to meet his eyes. Jordan looked at her searchingly. Annie's heart began to thump.

'Could we?' he asked.

Annie dropped her eyes and fumbled for her bag. 'I'd better go.'

'I'll come and help you.' Jordan clicked open his door. 'I haven't broken into a women's dorm since the panty raid in my freshman year. This will be something to tell my grandchildren.'

It was cold and windy outside, full of night noises. Annie shivered, then felt Jordan put his arm casually across her shoulders. She left it there.

'This is the best way,' Annie whispered, taking him down a narrow path flanked by a high brick wall. 'If you can help me over this, there's a girl on the ground floor who will let me in.'

'I can see you're an expert.'

Annie could hear the smile in his voice. She thought how much she liked his accent – the slow trickle of words with an upward inflection at the end, as if everything were a question, but not a very urgent one. She stopped at a certain point in the wall where a broken brick provided a foothold. 'Here.'

'Hey,' Jordan pulled her gently round to face him. 'Thanks for a great day. I had a ball.'

Annie steadied her hands against his chest. 'Me, too,' she said, feeling miserable. 'I'm sorry.'

'Yeah. Well, if you change your mind, you know where to find me.'

For a moment she thought he was going to kiss her. She decided she would let him – just once. Instead he gave her an encouraging shake. 'Up you go.'

Annie set her foot in the wall. Jordan lifted her high, as if she weighed nothing. In a moment she was sitting astride the wall. She looked down. A faint light from the street lamps shone on his handsome, already familiar face. All she had to do, she told herself, was jump back down into his arms. She hesitated.

'Jordan, you're not really going to Vietnam, are you?'

When at last he replied, his tone was weary. 'Oh, no. I'll get out of it somehow.'

They stared at each other for a long moment. Then Jordan patted her leg. 'Now get inside where it's warm. Scoot!'

Annie swung over the wall and dropped to the ground. She waited for the crunch of his slow tread back to the car. Not until she heard the Morris fire into life did she move, making her way through the trees to the curtained windows.

Trinity Term 1970

16
Walk on by

June sunshine streamed into the lofty room, glowing on its elaborate Gothic panelling and the spines of thousands of books. For almost the first time in his two years at Oxford, Jordan was positively hot. His tutor must be melting underneath his heavy gown and the same pea-green tweed suit he had worn all term. But the casement windows were resolutely closed against the seductive assault of birdsong and mellow bells and the clack of croquet being played in Chapel Quad below. A fly buzzed tetchily, searching for a way out. Jordan knew just how it felt.

He took a breath and turned the page of his essay. It was beginning to sound turgid, even to his own ears. He glanced at his tutor. Cecil Quelch, Reader in Russian and Slavonic History, rested in his usual fireside chair, eyes closed, tortoise neck extended, chin balanced on fingertips pressed precisely together. He looked like a gargoyle popped off a college parapet. Sunlight cruelly highlighted the liver spots on his bald head and a trail of toast crumbs down the front of his gown. He seemed very absorbed indeed in Jordan's views on the Russian Revolution. Unless he was asleep.

Jordan and the imprisoned fly droned on in a monotonous

duet until Jordan at last reached the conclusion of his essay and fell silent. His tutor gave a melancholy sigh.

'Interesting.' Opening his eyes, Quelch nodded briskly seven or eight times in succession. 'You perhaps overstate the *inevitability* of Lenin's rise to power. History is a great deal more accidental than one thinks. What, after all, if the Archduke's chauffeur had not taken the wrong turning in the backstreets of Sarajevo? No assassination, no war. No war, no Revolution.' He cocked his head, as if assessing Jordan's ability to appreciate this piece of donnish whimsy.

'And of course you will hedge your bets. The Revolution was a Good Thing in that it overthrew a corrupt aristocracy; a Bad Thing in that it got people killed. Naïve twaddle,' he sniffed. 'Read your Cicero, my dear fellow. *Salus populi suprema est lex*. However: you're sound on the economics. Your grasp of political imperatives is not unpromising. What shall we say: alpha beta? Next term we shall be able to tackle – '

Jordan interrupted gently. 'Sir, if you remember, I won't be here next term. I'm going back to the States.'

Quelch gaped like a fish. 'Bless my soul, so you are. What a pity. Another year, and I believe we might have made something of you. Ah well.' He raised his arm in a gesture of helplessness and allowed it to fall theatrically on to the worn arm of his wing chair. 'It's been a pleasure, Mr, ah – '

'Hope.'

'To be sure. A glass of sherry, Mr Hope, to cheer you on your way?'

'Thank you, but I have an appointment.'

Jordan stood up. He folded his essay and pushed it into the back pocket of his jeans, then bent to retrieve his belongings from behind the *chaise-longue*. There were a couple of books to return to the college library, the camera that went everywhere with him, his saxophone in its hard black case. He had a rehearsal for a gig in thirty minutes in Queen's, and he wanted to walk the long way round through the Meadow and maybe take a couple of pictures. It could be his last chance.

He straightened up to find his tutor peering over his half-moon spectacles in extravagant alarm, a hand pressed to his heart.

'Great heavens, what is that contraption?'

Two could play at this game. Jordan decided to have some fun. 'This?' Jordan dangled his saxophone by the strap. He looked his tutor solemnly in the eye.

'This, sir, is an 007 automatic double-action repeating machine-gun.' He smiled engagingly. 'You know us Americans, we just don't feel comfortable without a real good gun at our sides.'

Reaching out, he shook the astonished tutor by the hand. 'Goodbye, sir, and thank you. It's been an education.'

Jordan clattered down the staircase and out into the fresh air. He felt like turning cartwheels, or giving old Quelch a blast of Charlie Parker. He felt like goosing the girl in the short dress, whom he saw bending provocatively over her croquet mallet. But he didn't. This was England. It had been his choice to take special tutorials with Quelch, outside his own college. Quelch was *the* man on modern Soviet history. No one had warned Jordan that Quelch had become unreachable behind his barricade of self-parody and intellectual gamesmanship. Jordan had been made to find out for himself. That was the Oxford way.

Jordan sighed. Another failure. He stood watching the croquet players, thinking that it would be fun to join their game. He took a last look at the graceful buildings. Pembroke was not one of the grand colleges, but it had its own charm. Samuel Johnson had played draughts in a summerhouse once situated on this very lawn. William Fulbright had been a Rhodes Scholar here some forty years ago. One of the first things Jordan had done on arriving in Oxford was to send the Senator a postcard of Pembroke, on which he had written, 'I'm here!' He winced at the memory.

Turning into the cool entrance archway, Jordan stopped to say goodbye to his friend the porter, then emerged into the bustle of St Aldate's. In front of him a coach was loading up a trail of dispirited-looking tourists. Jordan could guess the itinerary. Oxford in the morning, Blenheim and Warwick Castle in the afternoon, a play at Stratford in the evening. Throw in Bath and London, and that was England done. What would they make of it? There was a trash can on the lamp-post next to him – what the British prissily called a litter bin. Jordan reached for his essay on 'Power and the Economy in Revolutionary Russia 1917–20', and stuffed it in. Seeing a gap in the traffic, he ran across the road and into Christ Church Meadow.

It was a day of soft, delicious beauty. The roses in the War Memorial garden were in full bloom. A faint breeze rustled the elms in Broad Walk and wafted the sweet, tickly smell of cow parsley from the meadow proper, where cattle still grazed. 'Schools weather', they called it. Except that Jordan wasn't doing Schools. He felt a perverse pang of envy for the undergraduates scribbling away in the vast examination rooms. It was a tremendous ordeal, a blitz of written papers morning and afternoon for a week, covering three, sometimes four years of study. But at least they would leave Oxford with a degree. They would have something to frame and hang on the wall. Something to show their children.

Jordan paused to take a picture of the poplar-shaded walk that led down to the Isis, then turned the other way, towards Merton. He could have completed his postgraduate degree in two years, he chided himself. He could easily have extended his Rhodes Scholarship for a third year, and taken his B. Phil. Bachelor of Philosophy (Oxon): it sounded fine. But the sense of time drifting away in this dreamy, elusive place filled him with anxiety, especially since the threat of the draft had at last been lifted.

Last November Nixon had instituted a lottery system whereby all potential draftees were randomly issued with a number. Low numbers were bad news; high ones virtually guaranteed that one would not be drafted until the war was over. For there seemed no question now that Nixon would yield to overwhelming public pressure, and honour his election pledge to end the war. Last December Jordan had received his lottery number. It was a high one, in the three-hundreds. That day he had gone into the Corpus Chapel, and thanked God for his deliverance. He took it as a vindication of his belief that he had never been meant to fight.

But from then on Jordan's impatience with Oxford had sharpened. This year he would be twenty-four years old. He needed to get started on his career. Last winter, without telling anyone – 'hedging his bets', as Quelch would say – he had applied to Harvard Law School, and been accepted. A part of him yearned to get back to a regular campus with a regular syllabus, grades he could understand, targets he could achieve to mark his progress. Hamburgers, for crying out loud, frisbee games, cold beer, people who didn't look affronted when he said 'Hi' to them. And yet . . .

Jordan turned into Dead Man's Walk, following the line of the mediaeval city wall. The sun reflected hot off the stone. Bees buzzed in the cascading wistaria. Here, in the heart of this swarming city, it was as peaceful and unpopulated as Gloucestershire. Jordan found that he had slowed to a stroll, then to a standstill by one of the temptingly placed benches. He shook himself and walked on. Maybe that was what was wrong with Oxford – the weather, either enervatingly grey or bewitchingly beautiful. Maybe that's why no one seemed wholly serious, as if lacking the energy to see anything through.

His generation was living through one of the most stirring periods in Western history. Prague – Paris – Vietnam; the police in Chicago, the Colonels in Greece; assassination and terrorism everywhere. You'd never know it here. Jordan had read a poll in *Cherwell* claiming that ten per cent of the Oxford faculty were Marxist-Leninist, Trotskyist, or some other kind of communist. The percentage of self-styled 'communist' students must be double or triple that. But what were they *doing*, apart from grouching about Harold Wilson, or leafleting the Oxford car factory workers with incomprehensible socialist propaganda? Jordan bet that ninety per cent of the student body had never seen inside a factory. *Cherwell* itself seemed less interested in the poll than in its 'Seduce a queer peer in Christ Church' competition.

Last May Day a group of students had drowned out the traditional choristers' singing from Magdalen Tower by playing the 'Internationale' over loudspeakers from an adjacent room. When apprehended, they were found drunk as skunks, knee deep in bottles of Bollinger. While students in the States and elsewhere in Europe were actually being killed in violent protests, Oxford didn't even have a proper student union. 'The Union', so called, was really a political club, and an archaic and elitist one at that. Sure, it drew an impressive calibre of guest speaker. But Jordan and the other Americans had been dumbstruck to find that its members wore formal dress and hadn't even admitted women until 1963!

He stepped up his pace. If Oxford was the home of lost causes, it was no place for him. He would shake its decadent dust from his good old US of A sneakers. Nevertheless, he was aware that he had missed something. What, after all, had he achieved here? He had travelled, joined a jazz band, learned to play rugby, failed to grasp the rules of cricket. He had read a lot of books, and opened his mind to new ideas. He had made a couple of good friends, and had collected the names of hundreds of people who could one day be useful to him. But deep in his soul, he was disappointed in himself. He wished he had shone at something. When he left Oxford, he wanted to be missed. He wished he had met more English people. He wished he had met more girls.

He had been more successful than many Americans in that department, given that there were no mixers or any dating structure he could recognise. At least he had been invited for tea in a couple of women's colleges. For a few short weeks last year he had shared his bed with a good-time girl from the Oxford and County secretarial college – known locally as the Ox and Cow. But the one girl who had really fired his soul – and his body – was unavailable.

Annie Paxford was unlike any girl he had ever met. Her brand of Englishness seemed unique – a matter of spiky humour and challenging intelligence without the chilliness or adolescent bumptiousness of other English girls. She was open, inviting, with a sense of fun that he envied. Also – and this was the most arousing thing of all – he knew she had liked him too.

He had thought of her often, and seen her twice: once speeding by in a sports car with her hair flying – with another man, of course; and once in a New College production of *The Importance of Being Earnest*. He had been invited by a St Hugh's girl who thought he needed educating. Their relationship was strictly platonic. She wore granny glasses and droopy flowered dresses, and had a forehead as wide as Nebraska. She claimed to be a lesbian anyway. But she had seemed annoyed by Jordan's fascination with the blonde girl playing Gwendolen, giving him a whispered lecture on the oppression of women in male society when all he wanted to do was admire Annie's breasts. That evening Jordan had actually started a letter to Annie, ostensibly congratulating her on her performance, but the words eluded him. It was not about words. It was about feeling, mystery, excitement. But she already had a boyfriend. He was going home. And anyway – had anyone ever made it to President with a foreign wife?

Jordan reached the iron gates which led out of the Meadow into Rose Lane. Here was the famous notice-board, rotting with age, that had made him laugh out loud when he first read it.

Christ Church Meadow

The Meadow Keepers and Constables are hereby instructed to prevent the entrance into the Meadow of all beggars, all persons in ragged or very dirty clothes, persons of improper character or who are not decent in appearance and behaviour; and to prevent indecent, rude or disorderly conduct of every description.

To allow no handcarts, wheelbarrows, bathchairs or perambulators (unless they have previous permission from the Very Reverend the Dean): no hawkers or persons carrying parcels or bundles so as to obstruct the walks.

To prevent the flying of kites, throwing stones, throwing balls, bowling hoops, shooting arrows, firing guns or pistols or playing games attended with danger or inconvenience to passers-by: also fishing in the waters, catching birds, or bird-nesting.

To prevent all persons cutting names on, breaking or injuring the seats, shrubs, plants, trees or turf.

To prevent the fastening of boats or rafts to the iron palisading or river wall, and to prevent encroachments of every kind by the river-side.

Jordan decided to take a picture of the notice. His mother would enjoy it. As he did so, a crocodile of Magdalen College School boys in grass-stained cricket flannels filed past him, nudging each other and giggling. A Yank, they signalled to each other, taking in his shoes, his camera and the white T-shirt showing at his unbuttoned collar. Jordan grinned back.

'Good game?' he called.

'It was only batting practice, you know,' patronised a piping voice.

'Can't win 'em all.' Jordan smiled at his own foolishness.

They trotted past, proper little English gentlemen in the making. Jordan wondered whether, in twenty or thirty years' time, he might find himself confronting one of them across some international conference table. If so, he thought he would have the edge.

He snapped his camera back into its case and loped after them, crossing the High and turning back towards Queen's. Across the road, outside Schools, a crowd of undergraduates awaited the release of their friends. Standing slightly apart, with her back to him, was a girl with long blonde hair. Jordan caught his breath, and stopped short. It was Annie.

The roar of the traffic between them faded. Time slowed. Jordan heard the blood pounding in his ears. He could feel the hot sun on his head. He stepped to the edge of the pavement. As if she had heard a voice calling her, Annie began to turn slowly in his direction. Her head twisted. He saw the curve of her cheek, the gleaming slither of hair down her back. Jordan already had his hand half raised, when he became aware of a gathering noise, a rustling and chattering like the approach of migrating birds. To his dismay, Annie turned away again. Jordan looked to see why.

A black and white crowd of undergraduates was pouring out of the Schools entrance, giddy and raucous with relief. Girls clutched each other, covering their eyes at the memory of their imperfect answers. Men stumbled down the stairs, shouting like football supporters, tugging at their white bow-ties. Annie moved forward, scanning the crowd, and Jordan now saw that she had a bottle of champagne in one hand, and two glasses held loosely by their stems in the other. Suddenly her face lit up. She waved the glasses high in the air. A man with dark hair ran lightly down the steps towards her, pulling the white carnation out of his buttonhole. He presented it to Annie in a gesture so tender and self-mocking that Jordan bit his lip. Annie laughed and held her arms wide, signalling 'No hands!' The man bent to fix the flower behind her ear, then kissed her possessively on the lips.

At that moment a rowdy group swept across the road and engulfed Jordan, blocking his view. Schools over, they were deliriously in love with the whole world. They offered Jordan a swig of their champagne and he accepted, infected by their mood. He clapped the men on the shoulders. One of the girls kissed him. Then they moved on. By the time Jordan looked back, Annie was standing among a large, laughing circle of friends, clinking glasses. The strange man had his arm around her. She looked happy.

Jordan felt a savage sense of loss. He wished he could have said goodbye, that he could have let her know how he felt, that he could leave her something to remember him by.

Hitching his saxophone back on to his shoulder, he ran up the steps of Queen's and into the lodge, blind in the sudden dark.

17

Where do you go to, my lovely?

Annie lay naked in Edward's bed, her back to him, eyes open. Through the doorway she could see plates of chicken bones and strawberry stalks on the sitting-room floor – the remains of their celebration lunch. An empty wine bottle lay on its side among a muddle of album sleeves and discarded clothes. It all looked terribly sordid. Without meaning to, she sighed heavily.

Edward stirred beside her. She could feel his breath on her back as he nuzzled close.

'I'm sorry, darling,' he mumbled. 'I was too quick for you.'

Annie didn't move. 'It doesn't matter.'

'Yes, it does. I can tell.' She felt his hand on the curve of her waist. 'It's just that I've been cramming my brain with so many dates and cases and precedents, that I can't get rid of them. You know how uptight I've been about Schools. But it's all over now, thank God.'

All over now. What dreary words, Annie thought.

'Hey,' Edward rocked her gently, 'come here.'

After a second or two Annie turned towards him,

hearing the bedsprings grate. She settled her head in the hollow of his shoulder.

'I thought you'd fallen asleep,' she said. 'You must be exhausted.'

He squeezed her to him. 'You're the most important thing in the world to me – much more important than exams or sleeping or anything else. I admit I could do with one mammoth sleep to get me back on form. But I want this last week together to be special. I want to take you on the river, and out to Dudley's, and to do the things I've been dreaming of all term. I want to go to parties and get drunk and dance with you all night.'

'It's all right for you,' Annie grumbled. 'I've still got two essays to write.'

'Stop being sensible. Nobody does any work in their second year. Besides, we need to get into training for next week.'

For a moment Annie wondered what he was talking about. Then she remembered the Magdalen Commem, and how thrilled she had been when Edward had asked if she wanted to go. The commemoration balls operated on some kind of rota system, so that each college held one every few years. But the word was that this year's Magdalen Commem was going to be out of sight – the most fabulous ever, and the most fabulously expensive. Top of the bill were the Doors, who would be playing in a huge dancing marquee to be erected in front of New Buildings. There would be five or six support groups, a jazz band, and a discothèque in the Hall. The cost of the ticket included dinner with wine and a champagne breakfast. There were to be dodgems in St Swithun's Quad, fireworks over the river at midnight, madrigals sung in the cloisters at dawn. Rumours seeped out of extraordinary precautions against gatecrashers – of some kind of hand-stamp that would show up only in ultra-violet light, and special bouncers imported from London who would be posted along the river and even at the entrances to the city sewers. The Magdalen Commem was the talk of the term. Everyone wanted to go, though many undergraduates were just too poor. A double ticket cost a colossal eleven guineas. You could fly to Athens for that.

Annie had dug into her father's legacy to buy an amazing dress from Annabelinda. She knew that when she got to the ball, she would have a fantastic time. It would be incredible to see Jim Morrison in the flesh. But right now she wasn't in the mood to think about it.

Edward put his mouth to her ear. 'How would you like,' he whispered, 'to have dinner beforehand at the Elizabeth?'

'Edward! You'll go broke.' The Elizabeth was the grandest restaurant in Oxford. Only dons and rich parents went there. It cost at least two pounds a head.

'So what?' he said recklessly. 'Soon I'll be stuck in an office all day – chambers, anyway – with a load of geriatrics. I want to have fun before the prison walls close in.' He pumped his arm into the air, singing 'Born to be wi-i-ild' until Annie giggled and dug him in the ribs.

'Stop it! You sound like a wolf howling at the moon.'

'I'll have you know there's a very fine Blues singer called Howlin' Wolf,' Edward replied with dignity. He rolled eagerly on top of her. 'So how about it, darlin'?' he said in mock-cockney. 'Fancy an evening out at the Elizabeth?'

Annie put her hands to his chest, holding him at bay. She looked at him seriously. 'It would be lovely – if you're sure. But Edward, I may not be around the whole time.'

Edward frowned. 'Why not?'

'These essays for a start. In fact,' she struggled to get up, 'I really should go to the Camera and put in a few hours.'

'You can't go now.' Edward sat back on his heels among

the rumpled bedding, watching in dismay as Annie swung out of bed and started to put on her clothes.

'I might as well. You know you're longing to go to this college piss-up with all the other lawyers tonight. I'd only be a terrible drag while you make in-jokes about torts and party-wall disputes.'

'You're never a drag.'

'This way, I can do my work while you catch up on your sleep.'

'But when will I see you?'

Annie couldn't keep the impatience out of her voice. 'I don't know. Soon.' She hesitated, then added casually, 'I won't be around tomorrow anyway, and possibly not Friday either. God, my hair!' she rushed on. 'Can I borrow your brush?'

'What do you mean, you won't be around? Where are you going? I thought you said you had to work.'

Annie pulled her stripy T-shirt dress over her head. 'I do. But there are other things in my life. I don't belong to you, you know.'

'Of course you don't belong to me. I don't belong to you either. It doesn't mean we have to have secrets.'

With an angry gesture, Edward reached for his cigarettes. He lit one moodily, hunched on the edge of the bed. 'I hate it when you're like this.'

Annie stared into Edward's mirror, silently brushing, hating herself too. At length she put down the brush and walked over to Edward.

'Can I have a puff?'

He passed her the cigarette without looking up. She took a drag and handed it back. Then she dropped her arms loosely on to Edward's bare shoulders.

'The thing is, Eddie, there's something I have to do, but I can't tell you what it is. It's not my secret to tell. I don't want to spoil your celebrations. Just give me a couple of days, and everything will be back to normal.'

Edward grunted, and leaned away from her embrace to

stub out the cigarette in the bottom of a coffee mug. Then he got up, and started pulling clothes out of his drawers. Annie watched from the doorway as he slid on his jeans and a white Indian-style shirt, then pushed past her, barefoot, to his sitting-room. She followed him in, thinking how beautiful he was. She loved his long slim legs and his aloof profile.

She cleared her throat. 'So . . . I'll come round on Friday evening, if I'm back. OK?'

'Yeah. Whatever.'

Edward was crouched by the record player, flicking through his albums. Annie hesitated, half wanting to go back to bed and make it up with him, waiting to see if he would look at her. When he didn't, she turned and let herself out of his room. As she clumped down the stairs she heard the record come on. It was Otis Redding singing 'Dock of the Bay'. She felt like crying.

When she reached Trinity gates, she remembered that she'd left her bicycle outside Schools. She couldn't be bothered to get it now. And she had no intention of working in the Radcliffe Camera. She was going back to LMH to make sure everything was OK for tomorrow. She turned left into the Broad, deciding to walk through the Parks.

The air was absolutely still, and oppressively hot. The freshness of the morning had gone. Her skin itched and her head ached. In the late afternoon glare Oxford had a tawdry, hang-dog air. The buildings looked dirty. Even the stone heads outside the Sheldonian Theatre – the Emperors – looked miserable. Nothing could more clearly have signalled the end of term than the windows of Blackwell's bookshop, full of tourist maps and student guides to 'Abroad' – Greece, Kathmandu, America. Annie stopped to stare at a photograph of the Statue of Liberty on one of the book jackets. She knew one reason for her depression. It was that American, Jordan Hope.

Today, when she was celebrating with Edward outside

Schools, she had suddenly caught sight of Jordan on the other side of the road and felt her heart leap like a fish. He was quite unmistakable, almost a full head taller than anyone else, with that clean American look, smiling his wonderful smile. He looked on top of the world, surrounded by a great group of laughing people. Then she had seen a girl kiss him, and felt a spasm of such terrible jealousy that she'd had to hide her face in Edward's shoulder. Annie shook herself and walked on. It was ridiculous to feel so intensely about a man she hardly knew. Eight months ago, she had spent a few hours alone with him. That was it. She hadn't seen him since – though she had looked for him often enough. She had not forgotten the magic of that day, the excitement of meeting someone so different, so exuberant, so . . . sexy, she whispered to herself, feeling guilty.

Reaching the entrance into the Parks, Annie paused to take off her sticky sandals. The sky was a strange colour, almost white. There was a distant thwack and a ripple of clapping. Shading her eyes, she made out the bleached figures of cricket players. Edward played cricket.

Annie struck out across the grass towards LMH, feeling it dry and prickly under her feet. Why had she not taken her chance with Jordan? It wasn't just her feeling for Edward, or a sense of fair play. The very things that seemed most romantic about Jordan – his Americanness, his political passion, his ambition, the threat of the draft – also warned her off. Well, it was too late now. By asking around, Annie had discovered that Rhodes Scholarships lasted for two years. That meant Jordan would be going down this term. It was just as well, she told herself. She had already hurt Edward enough by being so secretive. Thinking of what she had to do tomorrow, Annie's misery deepened.

She might never have noticed that anything was wrong with Rose if they hadn't been tutorial partners this term. It had started off by being quite fun, and rather revealing.

Although Rose liked to project a devil-may-care image, Annie had discovered that she was actually very serious about her studies and intended to get a First. Her essays were invariably well researched, well written and on time. So it was surprising when, two weeks ago, Annie had gone as usual to collect Rose on the way to Miss Kirk's tutorial and found her still in bed, saying she was too ill to go. Annie had conveyed Rose's apologies to Miss Kirk. Afterwards she had gone back to bring Rose a cup of tea, and was extremely pissed off to find that she had gone out. Later, when she asked Rose for an explanation, Rose was irritatingly offhand: she was bored with her studies, Oxford was an elitist anachronism out of touch with the real world. It was all a waste of time.

Rose's behaviour became increasingly strange. Often she would still be in bed at midday, with the curtains drawn and her room stale with smoke. Sometimes she had the electric fire on, even though the temperature outside was soaring. Annie began to suspect that Rose had been dumped by some man. She sensed that men didn't always treat Rose well – though who could blame them? When it came to the opposite sex Rose was like a professional card player, discarding that one, picking up this one, constantly reshuffling the pack. She never talked about love, just of 'getting' someone, although she seemed to lose interest as soon as they were got. Annie had once spent an entire evening cheering up some poor boy from Balliol whom she'd found waiting pathetically outside Rose's room, unable to believe that he had been stood up. If Rose had at last met her match, it might be no bad thing. Nevertheless, Annie couldn't help watching out for her friend. She had started bringing Rose cups of coffee to coax her out of bed in the morning, and had offered to bring her books from the library or food from Hall.

Yesterday Rose had casually mentioned that she was going to miss their tutorial again. Annie had lost her temper, complaining that it wasn't fair to make her invent yet another excuse. But late last night, hearing music from her room, she had knocked on Rose's door to apologise. Rose was lying flat on the floor in the flickering light of a candle stuck on to a saucer, listening to *Nashville Skyline*. She raised her head.

'Oh, it's you. Come in.'

As Annie dropped cross-legged on the floor next to her, Rose spoke solemnly to the ceiling.

'I have had a revelation. Lying here, listening to this music, I have realised that the sixties are really and truly over.' She propped herself up on an elbow to look at Annie. 'Can you imagine, a whole album without a single protest song? Just drippy ballads about lurve and the simple country life. Dylan's given up the fight. It's all over – peace and love and a better world. The sixties haven't been the beginning of something new, just a romantic little hiccup in history. My prediction is that the world is going to get meaner and greedier and slicker.' She flung herself back on to the carpet. 'In ten years' time we'll all be working in advertising.'

'I won't.' Annie shook back her hair. 'You're just depressed. I wish you'd tell me why.'

' "Depressed",' Rose enunciated thoughtfully. 'Our parents banned us from using that word. According to them, depression is a serious clinical condition, which we were not entitled to suffer until we'd made at least one suicide attempt.'

Annie was shocked. Rose had always given the impression that the Cassidys were one great big happy family. She put her hand on Rose's ankle and waggled it gently.

'I'm sorry I was annoyed with you earlier. It's only that Miss Kirk keeps ticking me off for not bringing you to tutes. I don't mind, I just wish I knew what was wrong. I do think it would do you good to get out of your room, even if you haven't done your essay. Why don't you at least come with me on Thursday and – '

'Stop sounding like the God Squad,' Rose snapped, sitting up to scowl at Annie. 'Once and for all, I am not coming to our stupid tutorial. I'm not even going to be in Oxford.' She pushed her fringe up furiously with the palm of her hand. 'If you must know, I'll be in London. In a clinic.' She gave Annie a defiant stare. Then her face crumpled. 'Having an abortion.'

They had stayed up until dawn, talking. Annie had insisted on going with her to the clinic. She was appalled at the idea of anyone going through such an ordeal alone. She couldn't get that horrifying scene in *Alfie* out of her head where Vivien Merchant, alone and in agony, had expelled her aborted foetus into a tin bucket. Of course, abortion was legal now. There were anaesthetics and clean sheets and proper hygiene. But the whole idea made Annie squeamish.

Perhaps Rose felt the same way. It was hard to tell. She agreed to Annie's company, but would say very little else except that being pregnant was 'ghastly', and that the father was 'irrelevant'. Annie had no idea who it was or what he felt about the baby – if he even knew about it. This made her faintly uneasy. If she became pregnant, she would tell Edward – wouldn't she?

The thought of Edward reminded her of their unsatisfactory parting. But there was no help for it. Rose was Annie's friend. Rose needed her. For the next couple of days, Rose must come first. Besides, she knew that Edward would forgive her, attributing any moodiness to the loss of her father.

Annie's father had died quite suddenly, of a heart attack. It was the last day of the previous term. Carrying her suitcase through the lodge to her taxi, Annie had seen her name on the blackboard, and had gone to look in her pigeonhole for the telephone message. *Ring your mother urgently.*

By the time she had reached Malta, her father's body was in the hospital mortuary. The funeral had taken place the next day.

Infusing her shock and grief was a terrible anger that her father had not waited just twenty-four hours so that she could have seen him one last time. Logic said that it would have made no difference. Her father had died almost instantly. But Annie felt an illogical, desperate regret that she had not had the chance to see him, even in death, in his hospital bed. People said that the bodies of the dead looked shockingly empty and alien. Annie knew this must be true, but she still wished that she could have seen for herself. She could not rid herself of the fantasy that her father was still alive, and would appear around the next corner, smiling his diffident smile, saying, 'All right, monkey?'

The sky had been steadily darkening. As Annie neared the path that led out of the Parks to LMH, she heard a rush of wind in the beech trees. A fat drop of rain landed on her arm, then another, and another. She began to run, wincing at the sharp stones underfoot. From far away came a long growl of thunder. Annie could not suppress the superstitious thought that the gods were angry.

18

With a little help from my friends

Rose stood in front of her open wardrobe, naked apart from a scrupulously clean pair of pants. Exactly what did one wear to an abortion? Should she dress like a bishop's wife to quell comment, or like the tart without a heart they would be expecting? Forget respectable, she decided. There was no need to add hypocrisy to her other vices.

She reached for a long, wraparound skirt in bright cotton paisley, then rummaged in her chest of drawers for something to go with it. A skinny black T-shirt – that would do. She pulled it on, then wound the skirt about her waist and tightened the sash viciously. According to a book she had sneaked a look at in the public library – a horrorama of photographs and disgusting cross-sections – the 'thing' was only about the size of a kidney bean. But Rose could feel it – she knew she could – low in her belly, smugly swelling by the minute. She loathed the sensation, as she loathed the way her whole body had suddenly gone into overdrive. Lie down, it urged, flooding her with a horrible, unfamiliar lassitude. Let's pump up those breasts! it ordered, like a gung-ho games mistress, as if she were going to start breast-feeding tomorrow. Rose curled her hand into a fist and punched herself hard in the abdomen. *Get out!* she whispered to the incubus within her. *Go away. I don't want you.*

How did anyone stand this for nine whole months? Ever since that electrifying moment when the doctor had told her that the test was positive, the streets of Oxford seemed to have sprouted pregnant women. Rose saw them behind serving counters, hauling shopping on to buses, even working in the Bod, as if their monstrous, swollen condition were perfectly normal. Their stoicism stunned her. All Rose wanted to do was lie down, nibbling water biscuits to mask the perpetual faintly metallic taste in her mouth. She had even gone off alcohol.

And all because of a missed pill and a few minutes of sex – be honest, Cassidy, a few *seconds*. Rose shoved her feet into shoes and pulled open the curtains. Last night's thunderstorm had cleared the air. A disgustingly perky blackbird was hopping across the sparkly grass, looking for worms. The sky was pearly blue. It was going to be another beautiful day. Everyone would be enjoying it except her. She leaned her forehead against the cool glass of the window and closed her eyes against a prickle of self-pity.

She had never meant to go that far. She had run into him in First Week, at a damp squib of a party in St Hilda's. It had always faintly nettled her the way he regarded her as a useful organiser, a political sparring partner, never as a woman. When she saw him lolling against the wall, paper cup in hand, oozing that easy American charm, she had set out deliberately to alter his perception. Somehow the conversation had got round to Jimi Hendrix. They were both fans. The next thing she knew they had skipped out of the party and were sitting in his room listening to *Electric Ladyland*. He had a bottle of whisky and some good grass. They got completely wasted; later Rose suspected that he had slipped something into her drink. She couldn't remember much, although one memory mercilessly persisted – of herself, dressed only in tights and his tie, strumming along with Jimi on a tennis racket. It had seemed funny at the time. Then suddenly – wham! – he was on top of her doing his electric woodpecker impersonation. You couldn't call it lovemaking. The whole thing was fast, impersonal, brutal. Rose was still trying to catch up with him when he gave a loud moan and slumped on top of her, as if he had been shot in the back. Almost immediately he started snoring.

Rose had lain still on the hairy carpet, her head cricked against a sofa leg, feeling the warm trickle between her legs. He was very heavy, but she daren't move him. She didn't fancy looking him in the eye just yet. After a while she started to get cold, and rather depressed. She felt bruised and used. Eventually she rolled the inert body off her. Even zonked out, he looked wickedly sexy: not a bad conquest to notch up. She tiptoed about the room retrieving her scattered clothes and walked back to college, uncomfortable in soggy knickers. She ran a bath, not caring if the noise woke anyone up. She lay in the cooling water, recasting the evening's events. It had been a wild time with a wild man. She had really turned him on, but sadly not vice versa. What was it her Yorkshire grandmother used to say? 'All mouth and no trousers': that was a good line.

Rose usually slept naked, but she had an old flannelette nightie which she sometimes wore if she was cold or ill. That night she put it on and climbed into her narrow bed, pulling the blankets tight around her body. Outside some damned owl or something was hooting away. Perhaps it was the mating season. She didn't know and didn't care. She was clean and warm and sleepy. She was alone. Everything was cool.

Except it had all turned out to be extremely uncool. The truth had smitten her, bizarrely enough, in the middle of a tutorial on John Donne. Miss Kirk was talking in her prim way about Donne's having 'anticipated the marriage

189

ceremony'. It was obvious from his poems that Donne was terrifically sexy. He had made his boss's niece pregnant, then married her secretly. His wife had died, aged thirty-three, after giving birth to their *twelfth* child. Rose was pondering the life-saving benefits of contraception when the word 'pregnant' lit a firework in her brain. The odd symptoms she had noticed only subliminally – nausea, tiredness, the pain in her breasts when she turned over in bed, the way she had gone off sex – crystallised into an immediate, awful certainty. She tried to remember the date of her last period. For the rest of the tutorial she had sat in a trance, hands hidden in the folds of her gown, counting days on her fingers.

She couldn't bear to confess her stupidity to anyone she knew, including the college doctor. There had been an article about abortion in *Cherwell* not too long ago. Rose looked it up and found the telephone number of a clinic in London. The next day she went up for a test. A week later she returned to London for the result. The doctor was a supercilious Scottish cow. 'Abortion is a very serious matter, Miss Cassidy. You can't just walk in and ask for one like a packet of soap.' Two doctors needed to sign a certificate saying that Rose was physically or mentally unfit to complete the pregnancy. Rose had been dragged through her family background, financial circumstances, feelings about the pregnancy. She even had a lecture on adoption. Rose held her ground. She wanted the thing out. Now. Finally she was referred to a Harley Street clinic. There were more questions, tests, forms, examinations. She never wanted to see a pair of rubber gloves again.

Now the waiting was over. By this afternoon she would be herself, single again. The moment she had longed for had arrived. And she was petrified.

Rose banged her head against the window, trying not to think of sharp instruments in tender, private places, of fat prying fingers, of the anaesthetic that would dull her will and suck out her spirit until she was just a slab of flesh to be prised open and sliced. Anaesthetics could go wrong. She had read that sometimes the patient heard every word in the operating theatre and felt every agonising pain without being able to move a muscle. 'Don't be silly,' her mother used to say briskly when Rose had nightmares before school injections. 'In Africa you'd be dying without them.' Right now Rose didn't care about Africa. When it came to doctors and hospitals, she was a first-class coward.

A door slammed. Rose opened her eyes with a start. She could hear the shuffle of slippers in the corridor, the flush of a lavatory. The college was beginning to stir. From the window she could see two first-years scampering down the gravel path to the tennis courts, rackets swinging. She looked at her watch: past eight already. Annie would be collecting her any minute, and she hadn't even done her packing.

Rose had been determined to go through the abortion on her own. It was her mistake, and she would have to rectify it. There was no point in turning to her family. Her parents were too busy saving lost souls to bother with their own daughter; it would be different if she were a homeless teenager or a drug addict. As for her brothers, of course they would have helped if she had asked, but asking them would mean losing face. All her life it had been a point of honour with Rose to be as clever and as tough as the boys. When her brothers joked about paternity suits and buns in ovens, she had joined in their cavalier, laddish talk. It was unthinkable to be on the receiving end of their pity.

Nevertheless, the experience of being pregnant had been strangely disturbing. As the day of the abortion neared, Rose had begun to suffer bouts of real panic. It had occurred to her to confide in Annie, but she didn't know how to do it. Once Annie's insistent, gentle, maddening questioning had broken through her stubbornness,

191

the relief was overwhelming. Annie had not judged her or laughed at her. She was just sympathetic and practical. Though Rose had still not managed to say so, it made all the difference to know that Annie would be coming too.

Rose was still frowning over the contents of her carpet bag when there was a knock on her door and Annie entered, wearing her mauve Laura Ashley dress. On her shoulder was the inevitable overstuffed Greek bag. She looked ridiculously pretty and healthy, as if she were going to a garden party. Trapped in her own alien, treacherous body, Rose felt a spurt of envy.

'Tell me what I've forgotten.' Rose waved towards her bed. 'It somehow doesn't look like enough.'

Annie dumped her bag on a chair, and considered the collection of items Rose had laid out. A nightgown, neatly folded. A spare pair of pants. A new box of sanitary towels for the bleeding afterwards. Rose watched Annie's face grow sober.

'Gruesome, isn't it?'

Annie caught her hand. 'Oh, Rose. It's not wicked, you know, or immoral. You mustn't think that. It's not a baby yet, just a tiny little, um – '

'Yeah, yeah, I know – thing.' Rose answered flatly. It seemed impossible to explain to Annie that she didn't give a damn about the baby – it was the operation she was worried about.

'OK,' Annie put a forefinger to her temple like a gun. 'Think, Paxford . . . . Soap and towel,' she said after a moment. 'You might want a bath. Slippers and dressing-gown. And your mouth will feel like an armpit after the anaesthetic. Mine did when I had my appendix out. Where's your toothbrush?'

Rose handed her things, watching Annie pack them neatly away. Then Annie stooped over her own bag. 'I've brought you some treats,' she said.

First she held up a little bottle. 'Chanel No. 5, only half full – sorry about that – to make you feel nice.' Next she drew out a book whose tattered jacket showed the haunted face of a girl against the backdrop of a Roman bridge. 'One slushy novel, slightly foxed. Total bilge. I loved every minute of it. And finally – ' she flourished a chocolate bar.

'My favourite!' Rose made a grab for it. 'Do you know, I'm not supposed to eat or drink for twelve whole hours before the – the grisly deed. I'm starving.'

'Afterwards,' Annie said firmly, packing it away. 'The anaesthetic will make you sick otherwise.'

She zipped up Rose's bag, and picked it up. 'Ready? We'd better go, or we'll miss the train.'

In the doorway Rose paused to take a last look at her familiar things: her Che Guevara poster, and the Indian bedspread which she'd hung on the wall, her psychedelic tea tray set out with glasses and sherry and a tin of Chocolate Olivers, Oxford's smartest biscuit. The next time she saw this room, everything would be over. If she saw it . . . .

From outside the room came Annie's voice. 'What is it? Have you forgotten something?'

Rose stepped into the corridor, pulled the door shut and locked it. 'Too late now.'

Annie and Rose travelled to London in silence, intimidated by the presence in their compartment of two middle-aged women in silk print dresses, nose to nose in a discussion of wedding hats. Annie was reading *Tom Jones*, making notes in her cramped, left-handed way. Rose held Annie's slushy novel on her lap, but her eyes kept skittering across the print. She could already predict that the man with the cynical twist to his mouth would turn out not to be a murderer, after all. On the final page he would claim the ninny-brained heroine with a fierce, possessive kiss on her heart-shaped face. True love. Yuk. No one ever said what happened afterwards – whether Jane Eyre itched to tell Mr Rochester that he had spilled food down his frock coat yet again, or whether Elizabeth

Bennett threatened to ban Darcy from her bed if he invited Lady Catherine de Bourgh for Christmas. Rose did not want to be married; she wanted to be famous. In only five years' time she would be as old as Keats was when he *died*. She would not, not, *not* be boxed in by domestic trivialities, even if it meant being carved up by some cold-eyed surgeon.

Fear washed over her again. She sucked in her stomach as tight as it would go, feeling the 'thing' lodged within her. Looking out at the flash of sun on the Thames, she saw only the chill glitter of instruments. At least the days of coat-hangers and death by septicaemia were over, she told herself. This would be a Rolls-Royce of abortions – 120 guineas' worth. Rose had hated asking him, but there was no one else. He seemed as embarrassed as she was by the memory of the Jimi Hendrix night. He hadn't even challenged her statement that the baby was his, just asked what she needed and given her the money, glad to be rid of her. Rose had taken it in silence, feeling cheap. It was like hush money.

From Paddington they took the tube to Baker Street, and emerged into the hot, acid air of central London. Annie insisted on carrying Rose's bag. 'I'm not an invalid,' Rose protested, but she was grateful. Annie stopped by a newspaper seller who shouted directions over the rumble of buses. They passed a long queue of wilting tourists outside Madame Tussaud's, then crossed Marylebone Road. There was a big church with an ornate clock. Rose wished she believed in God.

Halfway down Harley Street Annie stopped outside a black door with a posh brass doorbell. Rose felt sick.

'You ring,' she said to Annie.

A woman in a lime-coloured suit and silvery hair teased back from a broad hairband opened the door. She led the way down a marble-floored hallway, high heels echoing, into an ultra-modern reception area. There was a glass coffee table scattered with magazines, and pop art prints on the wall. Two long-legged girls who looked like models were giggling together on a leather sofa. Rose suddenly felt scruffy and schoolgirlish. She curled her bitten nails into her palms.

Indicating two chairs, the woman sat herself on the other side of a futuristically curved desk and picked up a pen. She gave a professional smile. 'Which of you is Mrs Cassidy?'

'Me. *Miss* Cassidy,' Rose added defiantly.

The woman's smile remained in place. 'We find it easier to call all our ladies "Mrs". Now, we'll just sort out the paperwork and then pop you upstairs to see Doctor.'

'She can come too, can't she?' Rose nodded at Annie.

The woman frowned.

'Please,' Annie said. 'I won't be any trouble. I'll go away when you say.'

Rose laid a hand on Annie's arm. 'I *need* her.' It sounded melodramatic. But it was true.

The woman shrugged. 'Just for a bit, then, to settle you in.'

It was all eerily businesslike. Rose handed over the forms with all her medical history and wrote the biggest cheque in her life. She was given a form which seemed to entitle the doctor to perform any further surgery on her he thought necessary. Rose read only halfway, then signed it.

A nurse came down to collect them and led them up the broad, curving staircase to the next landing. Here the character of the building changed. Heavy swing doors opened on to a polished expanse of pale linoleum. Trolleys and wheelchairs were stacked down one side, beneath reproductions of famous paintings. The other was lined with a series of cubicles screened by flowered curtains. At the far end was another pair of swing doors. Bright lights gleamed ominously through two frosted panes set at eye level. Rose flared her nostrils at the sweet hospital smell.

195

The nurse showed them into one of the cubicles and told Rose to undress, put on the folded gown and get into bed.

'Not like that, you idiot,' Annie giggled. 'The ties go at the back.' She fiddled for a bit, then patted Rose on the shoulder. 'There you go. And very kinky, too.'

'Huh,' Rose said grumpily, climbing into the high bed. She bounced nervously on the mattress, eyeing the pristine walls and Van Gogh's sunflowers. 'At least it's not a dump,' she conceded. 'Thank God for rich Americans.'

At that moment the nurse came back, pushing a trolley piled with alarming-looking objects. On top was an enamel bowl and a syringe. The nurse whisked the curtains shut behind her.

'Right,' she said brightly. 'Visiting time's over.'

Rose's heart accelerated. This was it.

Annie slid off the bed, and touched Rose's hand. 'Will you be all right?'

Rose nodded. But her face must have given her away, for Annie suddenly bent down and hugged her fiercely. Without meaning to, Rose whispered the words that were in her head.

'I'm frightened.'

Annie held her shoulders. 'It will be fine,' she said with calm authority. 'I absolutely promise.' She walked over to the curtain, looked back to blow Rose a kiss, and ducked out of sight.

The nurse picked something off her trolley and gave it an experimental buzz.

'What's that?' Rose asked suspiciously.

'We need to shave you first, don't we?'

Rose lay staring at the ceiling, her gown pulled up around her waist, legs splayed. She felt hot with humiliation. Never again, she vowed.

The nurse took her blood pressure, checked through her notes, and then swabbed a little patch of skin on Rose's arm and reached for the syringe. 'This is the premed,' she explained. 'It will help to make you feel more relaxed.'

Rose looked away as the needle went in. Almost immediately she felt the drug take hold, flooding through her body. For a moment she fought the loss of control, then subsided beneath a tide of lazy well-being. The feeling was not altogether unpleasant. It was a little bit like being stoned.

The next thing she knew, a West Indian man was pushing her bed down the corridor and into the bright room at the end. Rose had an impression of white walls and shiny metal. The doctor's face surged into view. He had purple cheeks, and smelled of mints and cigar smoke. He touched her arm.

'Mrs Cassidy, is it?'

Rose nodded. Who the hell did he think she was? She hoped he knew which operation he was supposed to be performing.

'Splendid. Do you think you can open and close your fist a few times for me?'

Rose tried it. Miraculously her muscles obeyed.

'Good girl. Now, just a little prick to put you to sleep. I want you to count to ten for me. Can you manage that?'

Of course I can, you moron, Rose thought. She saw the flash of a syringe in his hand and felt a sting in the crook of her elbow. Aloud she said, 'One, two, three, f . . . .'

Downstairs in the reception area, the model girls had gone, leaving an ashtray full of pink-tipped cigarette butts. Annie flipped the pages of *Punch*, seeing instead Rose's pale face, remembering her casual words, 'Thank God for rich Americans.' Which particular American? she wondered.

'Your friend won't be able to see you for at least an hour,' the receptionist said finally. 'Why don't you enjoy

197

this lovely sunshine? Regent's Park is just across the road.'

Annie practically ran into the park, clearing her lungs of exhaust fumes from Marylebone Road. She walked up the broad path between gaudy municipal flowerbeds, so different from Oxford gardens. The scene was like a Victorian painting, full of incident. There were office workers eating sandwiches on the grass, old men on benches with their newspapers, solitary women feeding buns to the birds, children everywhere. She even saw a proper old-fashioned nursemaid, bowling along a pram like a miniature carriage.

She walked as far as the zoo, where a couple of deer-like creatures stood dejectedly in their dirt allotment. Further on she could see Lord Snowdon's famous new aviary poking into the sky, but it was time to go back. Rose might need her. As she turned, a shiny red ball rolled into her path. Annie stopped, looking round to see whose it was. From a couple of feet away a small boy stared solemnly into her face. Annie picked up the ball and held it out to him, smiling. He put his thumb in his mouth. She stepped closer. She could see the fresh perfection of his skin, the lustrous lashes fringing clear, shining eyes. He still wouldn't budge. Annie rolled the ball gently to his feet. He bent his fat knees, lifted the ball with a grunt and carried it off like a trophy to his mother.

Annie walked back slowly, her thoughts returning to Rose, hoping she was all right. Though she knew that Rose would never ask, Annie couldn't help wondering if Rose's baby had been a boy or a girl.

19

Band of gold

The Elizabeth boasted not only the best cuisine of any Oxford restaurant, but also the most spectacular view. Situated in a small, oak-panelled room above Alice's Shop, where the old sheep had sold Alice an egg in *Through the Looking-Glass*, it looked due east across St Aldate's to Christ Church. Edward had booked them a window table. While they ate they watched high pennants of cloud flush apricot and pink in the sunset. When dusk approached, a sudden spotlight magically illuminated the soaring Gothic pinnacles of Christ Church Cathedral.

Annie ran her spoon round and round the earthenware dish in front of her, and swallowed the last mouthful of *crème brûlée* with a regretful sigh.

'That was the most delicious pudding I have ever eaten,' she pronounced. 'In fact, the most delicious dinner. I hope all these buttons can take the strain.'

She gestured at her dress, a shimmer of white taffeta with a row of tiny buttons running from the deep V-neckline to below her waist. There were more buttons on the long sleeves, beginning almost at her elbows and extending down to tight cuffs, which ended in points low on her wrists. She wore no jewellery, just a white velvet ribbon fastened around her throat. Her hair fell loose, apart from two slim gold plaits which held it away from her face.

'You look like a mediaeval princess,' said Edward, smiling at her over his wineglass.

'And you look like Byron.' Annie leaned forward and kissed him on the lips, unembarrassed by the other diners. Edward did look ravishingly romantic, she thought. Under his dinner jacket he wore a ruffled white shirt with a bottle-green velvet bow-tie and matching cummerbund. Dinner jackets could make men look like either smug Tory MPs or dissolute dandies. Annie was pleased to discover that Edward fell into the latter category.

There was only one other couple dressed, as they were, for a Commem. Everyone else was old. Full Term was over now, and most undergraduates had gone down the previous weekend. For days the streets of Oxford had afforded the painful sight of overdressed mothers beaming at their insouciant offspring from a respectful distance, and fathers grumpily loading cardboard boxes into car boots. LMH was unnervingly quiet. The libraries were empty. Every day there were more tourists, and fewer students. It was this valedictory, slightly wistful air about the very end of Trinity Term which the Commems were designed to counteract in as noisy and hedonistic a fashion as possible.

Annie had mended her fences with Edward on her return from London. The whole Rose affair was over so quickly, she need never have been so secretive. Annie had imagined days of looking after Rose in college, perhaps even escorting her home to her parents. But as soon as the operation was over, Rose had bounced back to normal with almost shocking swiftness. She had insisted on returning to Oxford on the evening of her abortion, her only concessions being to allow Annie to pay for a taxi from the station and bring her supper in bed of baked beans on toast. She seemed to regard the whole episode as a humiliating failure, a blot on her breezy reputation. If Annie didn't wholly understand her reaction, she was pleased to see her friend back in good spirits. Tomorrow night Rose was going to the Keble Ball with a group of friends. Next week she would be flying to Boston for a coast-to-coast trip across America by Greyhound bus.

Edward had hardly let Annie out of his sight. Now that his Finals were over, the realisation had struck that he was leaving Oxford for good. Together they revisited all their favourite places, as if Edward had to put his stamp on them before he left. He had been in a strange mood, veering between exuberance and nostalgia. Although he had never questioned her further about her mysterious disappearance, Annie would catch him looking at her thoughtfully, as if making up his mind about something. He was doing it now. She hoped that he wasn't going to go all sentimental on her. Tonight she just wanted him to be wild and witty and dance with her until dawn.

But all he said was, 'Coffee? Brandy?'

'Both,' she said extravagantly. 'Tonight I'm not going to say no to anything.'

Edward gave her a smile she couldn't quite interpret. 'Good.'

As they sipped their brandies, the waiter set up a glass coffee-maker in the middle of the table, and lit a spirit lamp underneath. Annie watched dreamily while the water heated and began to bubble up through the coffee.

'I'm glad we finally made it here before I go down,' Edward said in a melancholy way.

'Me, too. It was a sumptuous dinner. Thank you.'

'I wish I wasn't leaving.'

'You'll be back again next month if you get a viva,' Annie said cheerfully. She knew that Edward was hoping for a First, in which case he would probably be called

201

back for an oral examination to determine which class of degree he merited.

'Yes, but you won't be here. And next year I'll be stuck in London.'

Annie laughed. 'You sound as if it's Outer Mongolia. London's only an hour away on the train. You can come up for weekends.'

'It's not the same. In fact – '

Some emotional undertone in his voice made her suddenly alert. Annie saw that Edward was looking at her solemnly while he reached into his jacket pocket. All at once Annie knew what was coming. Every nerve in her body protested: *No! Not now!*

Edward placed a small, square jeweller's box in front of her. Annie stared at it, searching for words. Then she looked at Edward. His face was quite impassive. He had looked like this when she had escorted him to his first Finals exam. She picked up the box. In the front panel was a small metal button, which she pressed. The lid flipped up. Fixed in a bed of pale velvet was a gold ring with a dark blue stone. There could be no mistaking what kind of ring it was: not a present; an engagement ring.

The silence between them seemed to go on for ever. Annie became aware of the clank of heavy silverware, and a burst of laughter from another table.

'We can exchange it if you don't like it,' Edward said.

'It's lovely,' Annie said, her eyes welling with tears. 'Just what I would like if – if I wanted to get married.' She touched the blue stone gently with one finger, then pressed the lid down slowly. The box snapped shut with a click.

'But I don't,' she whispered. 'I mean, it's too soon.'

'We don't have to do it right now,' Edward said defensively. 'Just . . . one day.'

Annie shook her head. 'It doesn't feel right. I've got another year here. You're the first proper boyfriend I've ever had. I'm not even twenty yet.'

'I know.' Edward made a despairing gesture. 'I'm too young to get married, too,' he said almost angrily. 'I never thought I'd want to. But I can't bear to lose you. Every time I think I know you, you ... evade me. It's that damned upbringing of yours.' His voice softened as he reached for her hand. 'Don't you love me?'

'I think so.' She squeezed his hand. 'But *marriage* ....' Her voice trailed away. Like any other girl, she had sometimes daydreamed about a candlelit proposal by a handsome man in romantic surroundings. But it had always been something immeasurably distant, in the realms of pleasant, foolish fantasy. The reality was uncomfortable. Although she was ashamed of herself for feeling this way, Annie felt angry with Edward for laying such a heavy trip on her just now, before the ball that was intended to be so much fun.

'So it's "no", then,' Edward said flatly.

Annie stared miserably at the tablecloth. 'It is for now, if you don't mind. I'm sorry.' She wiped her nose surreptitiously on her napkin.

With a sudden, swooping gesture, Edward reached across for the box, and pocketed it. 'No sweat. Forget it.' He tried to smile. 'I may try again one day; I may not. Who knows?' He raised his hand and summoned the waiter with an imperious gesture.

'Two more brandies, and a large cigar for me, please.'

Annie didn't think she could manage another brandy, but she said nothing. Two more balloon glasses arrived with an inch of deep amber liquid at the bottom. Edward swigged almost all of his in jittery gulps. The waiter brought a large, polished box and displayed its contents to Edward, who selected an important-looking cigar. Deferentially, the waiter sliced off one end with some kind of implement Annie had never seen before, and lit the cigar for Edward with a long match. Edward took an experimental puff, and coolly blew out the smoke, head turned to admire the view. Annie's eyes lingered on his haughty profile. He looked self-contained and unreach-able. She feared she had hurt him horribly.

'Nothing like a real Havana.' Edward lounged back in his chair, giving Annie a narrow-eyed smile. 'Rolled on the thighs of luscious Cuban virgins, you know.'

'Do you still want to go to the ball?' Annie asked gently. 'I won't mind if you don't. Honestly.'

'Of course we're going to the ball.' Edward's eyes glit-tered. 'I may not be allowed to marry you, but I can at least dance with you, can't I?'

'Of course. I'm really looking forward to it.'

Edward nodded curtly, and continued to puff away at his cigar. Annie thought it looked rather hard work.

'So, how's your ma?' he asked conversationally.

'All right. Now that the initial shock is over, and she knows she's got a decent pension to live on, I think she's quite enjoying herself. She's on a sort of royal tour round her friends, supposedly to decide which part of the country to settle in. But I don't think she can face setting up on her own yet. And of course, now she's finally back in England, she does nothing but complain about everything.'

They continued to make small talk about their families and holidays. Annie was heading for the Greek Islands with some friends from the cast of *The Importance of Being Earnest*. Edward was going to Mallorca with his parents in August. By the time he asked for the bill, they were talking normally. Only a certain tightness in his face, and the amount he was drinking, betrayed Edward's emotional turmoil. He signed a cheque with a flourish.

They walked across the Meadow, hand in hand, with-out speaking, enjoying the great sweep of trees and shadowed grass. The sky had paled to opal. There was a white semicircle of moon on the horizon. As they approached Rose Lane, they could hear the thump of music from the ball.

Suddenly Edward threw back his head and laughed theatrically. He was drunk, Annie realised.

'You're quite right, my darling – as always.' He threw an arm around her, staggering slightly. 'Marriage is a *terrible* idea. I was just thinking about Oliver – remember, my cousin who had to get married last summer? He wanted to be a songwriter. You know what he's doing now? Selling vacuum cleaners on commission. Every night he goes home to a squalid little flat in Fulham that smells of nappies and baby sick. So, thank you.' Edward planted a wet kiss on her cheek. 'You have saved me from a ghastly fate.'

They had now reached the far side of the Meadow. Just here a branch of the Cherwell divided from the main river to enclose St Hilda's Meadow, where Edward had pushed her into the water almost exactly a year ago. Before Annie realised what he was doing, Edward had taken the jeweller's box out of his pocket and was moving towards the river with the curious, tight run of a slow bowler.

'Edward. No!' Annie shouted.

But it was too late. Suddenly he stopped, leaned back, and sent the box arching through the air. Annie heard a small splash, and the grumbling of disturbed ducks. Edward brushed off his palms and walked back to her, looking pleased with himself. He grabbed her hand. 'Come on,' he said, dragging her down the lane at a run. 'We're going to have *fun*!'

Despite everything, Annie felt a thrill of excitement as they walked through the archway into Magdalen. There was a tremendous burst of music and laughter and the hurdy-gurdy sound of the dodgems. While Edward showed their tickets to a posse of Ball officers and received a fistful of vouchers and a programme of events in return, Annie peeked into the first quad. Chinese lanterns had been strung around the high walls, giving out a fairytale glow. Right in front of them two men in

205

harlequin costumes and masks were juggling with phosphorescent balls. In the middle of the quad a twenties band in striped blazers were playing 'Has Anybody Seen My Girl?' There were high banks of flowers everywhere. Couples in DJs and long dresses streamed past, swinging champagne bottles by the neck. Over the rooftops the sky was stained with the flashing colours of a giant stroboscope. Annie tugged impatiently at Edward's hand.

'Come on, let's dance.'

Annie rather fancied herself at the Charleston, and Edward was brilliant at it. She hoped that the bouncy music might restore his confidence and good humour. He certainly threw himself into it, laughing when he bumped into the other dancers. He sang along to the music and smiled, but not at her. When they left the dance floor the first thing he said was, 'Let's go get our free wine.'

They walked under a tower and through into the cloisters, where tables and chairs had been set out on the lawn and a string quartet played. Under one of the covered walkways they found a trestle table covered in bottles. Edward traded in the appropriate voucher and poured them a glass each. They sat in one of the stone arches for a while, watching the spectacle, until the pounding disco beat drew them upstairs to the dining hall. Here it was all heat and sweat and flailing hair. Heliotrope lights swirled over the linenfold panelling and across the impassive portraits of Elizabeth I and Cardinal Wolsey. In the centre of the packed bodies a peroxide blonde in bare feet and a short chainmail dress, with apparently nothing underneath, had all the males goggling, including Edward. Men were so simple, Annie thought. All they wanted was for you to say yes to everything, and take off as many clothes as possible. She tossed her hair and spun round, giving herself to the music.

They danced to Mungo Jerry and Smokey Robinson, Creedence Clearwater and Procul Harum, until it was too hot to breathe. Edward retrieved their wine bottle from a high ledge and led the way back outside. It was quite dark now. The air felt marvellous. They slipped through a narrow passage and into the last, and largest, open quadrangle, where a huge marquee striped red and white like a circus tent had been set up in front of New Buildings. It was here, Annie remembered, that she had smoked her very first joint. It seemed a lifetime ago. She wondered what the deer were making of the extraordinary noise.

Inside the marquee a group called Audience was playing the sort of druggy music you couldn't dance to.

'When are the Doors coming on?' Annie asked.

Edward consulted the programme, then looked at his watch. 'They should be on now. Punctuality probably isn't their strong point. Let's see if we can find the dodgems.'

They pushed their way back through the jostling crowds until the clank and crash drew them into Longwall Quad. Here they joined the queue for a car. While they waited Edward drank steadily, and kept topping up Annie's glass. Her head was beginning to feel numb. When they finally got into the car, Edward drove like a maniac, crashing into everybody.

'I thought "dodgems" meant we were supposed to dodge the other cars, not hit them,' Annie complained. Edward just laughed and spun the wheel. Annie was beginning to feel sick. Every few seconds, another car banged into them from some unexpected direction, making her head snap. Suddenly she half rose in her seat.

'I feel sick,' she shouted into Edward's ear. 'I have to get off.'

As soon as they were near enough to the edge, she jumped out of the car and ran into the darkness, a hand clamped to her mouth. There was a herbaceous border at the edge of the quad. Annie made it just in time to retch behind a large shrub. Tears of effort and shame squeezed under her closed eyelids as she heaved up the Elizabeth's legendary *haute cuisine. De haut en bas*, she thought inanely.

She felt a hand stroke her back. 'Poor baby,' Edward said. These were the first tender words he had spoken to her since they had left the restaurant.

At last the nausea subsided. Annie stood up, trembling slightly. Edward handed her a paper napkin, and she wiped her mouth. 'How disgusting,' she said. 'I'm sorry.'

Edward took her arm. 'It doesn't matter. You need to lie down. Hang on – ' he reached into his breast pocket – 'they've allocated us a room somewhere. Let's see if we can find it.'

Eventually they found themselves in a small college bedroom. Stripped of all personal belongings, it had a depressing air. Annie washed out her mouth at the basin, then bathed her face in cold water. Now that she had actually been sick, she felt almost as good as new. Waiting for the water to dry on her skin, she checked herself in the mirror. She looked quite normal – pretty, even. She tucked a strand of hair back into her plait, and turned to Edward. He had taken off his jacket and was lying zonked out on the bed, not looking too good himself.

He opened one eye, and shut it again. 'Come here,' he commanded, stretching out his arm.

Annie hesitated, then went over and let him pull her down beside him. He gave her a squishy kiss. 'That's better,' he murmured, stroking his hand over her body. He knew what she liked. Soon she began to respond. She was just wondering whether they should lock the door, when Edward rolled on to his back with a sigh and settled her head on his shoulder.

'Isn't this nice?' he yawned.

Annie lay there silently, wondering what he was up to. Was this a punishment? She could hear distant whoops, and the cacophony of the different bands. It seemed terrible to miss out on all the fun. Then another, much closer noise intruded. Edward was snoring.

'Edward?' Annie shook him. He felt like a giant lump of dough. She prodded him in the ribs. He groaned protestingly and settled his head deeper into the pillow.

Annie slipped out of his embrace and got off the bed, watching him. He was definitely asleep. She picked up his arm, and lowered it again. It was as heavy as lead. By the look of him, he would not wake until well after the ball had finished. There was a sudden crackle from outside. Annie went to the window. Bright green stars were falling out of the sky. She opened the window and leaned out. Another firework streaked up through the darkness and exploded into scarlet and gold lilies. She turned from the window, making up her mind. First she took off Edward's shoes, and covered him as well as she could with the bedspread. Then she filled the plastic toothmug with water and put it next to the bed. Edward was bound to wake up with a dry mouth and a hideous hangover. As her hand hovered over the light switch an idea occurred to her, and she fished the ball vouchers out of Edward's jacket. With one last look at his sleeping figure, she switched off the light, and closed the door quietly.

In no time she was outside again, hurrying down to the crowded riverbank to watch the fireworks. It was the most spectacular display she had ever seen; not a simple matter of rockets and Catherine wheels, but multiple explosions of stars that drew shrieks and sighs of pleasure, cascading fountains that gushed one out of another, pillars of flame that lit up the sky and left a smoky trail. At the very end a fixed display on the other side of the Cherwell spelled out the words, 'Magdalen Commemoration Ball 1970' in letters three feet high.

When the crowd began to disperse into couples and groups, Annie felt faintly self-conscious about being on her own. But it was all so beautiful, with the river and the lights and the music. Everyone was happy, or drunk – or both. It was a relief to be on her own, free of Edward's reproachful presence. She thought it was just as well that

209

they were both going down the next day. They needed some space. For the moment it was fantastic just wandering at will, observing the other people, slipping among them like a white ghost. Underneath the kitchen walls, she came to a table laden with bowls of strawberries. They looked delicious.

'Got your voucher?' said a voice.

Annie held out her sheaf of vouchers and let the man take one. She strolled on towards the big marquee, spooning fruit into her mouth. At the entrance was a group of dishevelled undergraduates, swaying gently.

'Have the Doors been on yet?' she asked.

'There's been a hiccup backstage,' one said, and then hiccupped loudly himself. His companions clutched each other, finding this excruciatingly witty.

'Eh-oop, trouble at t'mill,' quipped the first clown, setting his friends off again. Then he squinted down his nose at Annie and said in his normal voice, 'I say, do you want to dance?'

'No, thanks,' she laughed.

She strolled back through the cloisters and into the first quad, where a steel band was now playing. In one corner of the quadrangle was a stone pulpit with a canopy over it. Annie sat on the curving stone staircase, and finished her strawberries. She was turning to go back, when an intriguing little archway caught her eye. She set down her strawberry bowl and walked down it. A network of fairy lights stretched over the vaulted ceiling like a spider's web. The tink-tonk noise of the steel band receded, and was replaced by a lazier, more seductive rhythm. She could hear the slow, upward slide of some instrument that was exhilarating and melancholy at the same time. Her nerve endings tingled. The music drew her like an enchantment.

Annie stepped through the arch, and caught her breath at the scene. She was in a small, triangular courtyard, enclosed by high monastic walls on one side, and a chapel with stained-glass windows on the other. On a swath of perfect grass couples sat or lay as if in a delicious trance. In the far corner, lit only by an Edwardian standard lamp with a tassled shade, a jazz band was playing. The black pianist was singing, 'Is you is or is you ain't my baby?' in a low, heart-breaking voice.

It was with no surprise at all that Annie saw that the saxophone player was Jordan Hope.

20

Love me two times, girl

Annie stepped on to the lawn, feeling as if she were in a play and had just heard her cue. When she was a few feet from the band, she sank down on to the soft grass, her eyes on Jordan. He was wearing a white jacket and a black bow-tie. Golden sparks flashed from his saxophone. Behind him Magdalen tower rose out of the shadows like a fairytale castle. Annie wasn't sure if he had noticed her until he took the saxophone from his mouth. An incredulous smile spread over his face, revealing almost every one of those perfect American teeth. Annie leaned back on her hands, slid off her shoes and wriggled her toes in the velvet lawn.

The music he was playing was unfamiliar and bewitching. This band had none of the frenzied peacocking of pop groups. It was spontaneous and intimate. They all seemed to be enjoying themselves. She liked the way they gave each other a chance at a solo, and consulted each other between songs, communicating in a secret language of raised eyebrows and casual gestures. In one such break, Jordan whispered something to the pianist, unlooped his saxophone from around his neck, and walked out of the pool of light, over to Annie.

'Hi,' he said, squatting beside her.

'Hello.' She felt herself beaming back helplessly, and tried to sound cool. 'Shouldn't you be playing?'

'I'm sitting this one out.' He lowered himself to the ground and clasped his hands around his knees. 'My friend the piano-player is going to sing something for you.'

'For me!'

The pianist was rippling up and down the notes in an introductory way. Suddenly he swung into a lilting rhythm and started singing, 'When somebody thinks you're wonderful . . . .'

Annie hid her face in her hands. They both laughed.

Jordan plucked a blade of grass from the turf and started to chew it.

'What are you doing here by yourself?'

'My partner passed out.'

'Uh-oh.'

'What about you? Haven't you brought someone?'

Jordan held up a disclaiming hand. 'Hey, I'm working.'

For a while they watched the band in silence. Annie couldn't stop smiling.

'You never told me you played the saxophone.'

'You never asked. . . . Listen, I'll be through at two. Maybe we could talk, have a drink, check out the ball – I don't know.' He laughed almost shyly.

'I'll wait,' Annie said.

At the end of the song he stood up, then turned slowly back to her, as if he had remembered something. His handsome face was serious, regretful.

'I'm going home tomorrow, back to the States.'

'It doesn't matter.' Only when the words were out of her mouth did it strike Annie that this was an odd answer.

When he rejoined the band, Annie understood that Jordan was now playing for her. She felt his awareness of her in the way he stood, bending low over his

213

instrument to coax forth moody sounds as husky as his own voice, or throwing back his head to release a triumphant blast of pure energy. Annie had never realised what a wonderful instrument the saxophone was. Whatever Jordan did, her eyes followed him. A current flowed between them. It was a new and exquisitely exciting form of flirting. The other spectators seemed to sense that there was something going on between the big sax player and the solitary girl in the white dress. Annie could tell from their indulgent glances that they found the situation intriguingly romantic. A beautiful boy with a public school forelock loped over the grass towards her.

'We thought you needed this,' he said, gracefully setting down an almost full bottle of champagne and two glasses in front of her. 'We're all pissed as newts anyway.'

Annie stared at him speechlessly. By the time she had recovered, he was back with his friends. She poured herself some champagne, and raised her glass to them. They nodded encouragingly.

Just before two, Jordan announced the last number. Right on cue, the bells in Magdalen Tower pealed out their chimes and struck the hour, drowning out the applause. Jordan stepped forward, scowling humorously at the bells while he waited for them to finish. Then he bent to the microphone, and spoke in his slow drawl.

'Everyone in the band tonight is from the United States. I guess you all know that Christopher Columbus discovered America in 1492, which was the year they started building this old tower behind me. If all that bell-ringing is Oxford's way of telling us colonials to shut up, well, we can take a hint. Goodnight, and thanks for being a wonderful audience.'

There were enthusiastic whoops amid the applause that followed, and a ripple of laughter. People began to climb to their feet and drift away. Jordan beckoned Annie over. She went shyly, taking the champagne, and let him introduce her to the rest of the band. They were friendly and relaxed, admitting her to their circle. Retrieving the drinks they had stashed around the small stage, they stood around chatting, winding down. Here, in this intimate corner, it was hard to believe there was a whole ball going on around them. Annie sat on the piano stool, watching Jordan unscrew his saxophone, clean it out and fit the pieces into the case. He arranged for one of the other players to take care of it for him, then picked up the champagne bottle and glasses and turned to Annie.

'Ready?' he smiled. 'Let's go find somewhere to talk.'

They walked through into the cloisters and found an empty table where they could sit down. Jordan poured their drinks. Annie leaned forward into the candlelight and asked the question that had been in her mind ever since the day she had met Jordan.

'You said you were going back to America. That doesn't mean you've been drafted, does it?'

'No, thank the Lord.' Seeing the anxiety in her face, he explained about the lottery system. 'It looks as though I'm off the hook,' he concluded, 'and I owe it to Richard Milhous Nixon, of all people. Still, it's kind of nice to know you were worrying about me.'

'Well, I was,' Annie flushed. 'I read in *Cherwell* about a Rhodes Scholar – a draft dodger – who committed suicide, and I thought of you.'

Jordan looked down at the table. 'Yeah, that was Bruce. He lived in our house.'

'Jordan, no! How awful,' Annie whispered.

'He got this letter from his dad saying it would be better for Bruce to be dead than to disgrace his family through cowardice. Can you believe it? What kind of a father would say such a thing? That was in April, just about the time Nixon started the attacks on Cambodia. We all knew that Bruce was pretty rocky, mentally. I guess the two things together just flipped him over the edge. We tried to keep an eye on him. But – we failed.'

'What happened?'

'One night he slipped out of the house and went down to the canal. He put some stones in his pocket and jumped off the bridge. At the inquest they said his body was chock-a-block with alcohol and drugs. He probably passed out pretty quickly. But, Jesus, what a waste. He had the courage to say no to the war, and he had the courage to take his own life.' Jordan gave a harsh laugh, as if admitting something painful. 'Bruce was braver than me.'

Annie laid her hand impulsively on his sleeve. 'Don't say that.'

Jordan's face softened. In a sudden, swift gesture, he picked up her hand and kissed it. Annie's body jolted at the touch of his warm lips. Their eyes met.

'What's that for?' she asked.

'For being a nice girl. For thinking about me. For being here on my last night in Oxford.' Jordan grinned. 'What the hell?'

He was flying back to St Louis the next day. Most of his things had already been packed up and sent home. He had stayed this long only because of his commitment to play at the ball. Annie listened to Jordan's plans for a summer job in Washington, then law school in the fall. First he would go see his mother, and maybe take her on a trip over to the Ozarks lakes. As before, Jordan conjured up an exotic and alien world. Annie envied his positive sense of his future, when hers was so cloudy. She didn't even have a home to go to any more. When she told Jordan about the death of her father, he was sympathetic in a way that was easy to accept. Most people didn't know what to say. Annie had found it was usually simpler to avoid the subject.

'Isn't it sad?' Jordan said thoughtfully. 'Here you and I are, without fathers, and there's Bruce's father, without a son. People are too alone these days. I tell you, Annie, when I get married I want to have a great big family. I want lots of daughters I can give away at weddings and make sentimental speeches about; sons I can teach to

216

play baseball and take duck-shooting. One day, when I've achieved everything I can, I'd like to be one of those white-haired old men who sit rocking on the front porch, telling the same tall stories, and who can count their grandchildren in dozens.'

Jordan radiated so much energy that Annie found it hard to imagine him sitting anywhere for long. Still, he made marriage and family life sound like an adventure, not a trap. Annie felt a pang of envy for the girl he would one day marry.

They talked on, one subject leading to another, as if they would never run out, until they became aware of a commotion around them. People were streaming through the cloisters, all headed in the same direction.

'Listen!' Annie sat up excitedly. 'It's the Doors.'

'What doors?'

'The Doors, you idiot – the group. They're finally playing. Only three hours late,' she laughed happily. 'I bet they're stoned out of their tiny minds by now.'

Jordan saw the light in her face, and jumped to his feet. 'Well, come on, what are we waiting for? This could be my last great cultural experience in England.'

They began to make their way towards the big marquee. Every one of the hundreds of people at the ball had the same idea. Now that the group they had waited for – and paid for – was finally playing, the narrow passageways between the quads were clogged. People pushed impatiently. Jordan put his arm around Annie, keeping her close. It seemed the most natural thing in the world to put her arm around his waist, too. She could feel the breadth of his back and the pressure of his thigh against hers. Above the noise of the crowd rose the scream of an electric guitar. Annie shivered with excitement. Jordan felt the movement and looked down at her with his smiling, seductive eyes. Her stomach somersaulted. He bent his head to her ear.

'Did I tell you that you look sensational in that dress?'

217

'No.' She smiled mischievously into his face.

'Or that you're the prettiest girl at the ball?'

Annie shook her head, eyes sparkling.

Jordan lowered his head further. 'Or that I want to kiss you?'

Annie turned her face into his shoulder, hiding her smile. Later, she thought, her body fizzing.

Finally they burst out on to the lawn of New Buildings. Everyone ran towards the music. It was such a warm night that the flaps of the marquee had been raised. Behind the stage loomed a giant screen. Coloured lights flashed across it like the rays of the sun in some drug-induced vision, converging on a fiery ball. In front of it, outlined against the lights, was the brooding figure of Jim Morrison, singing 'When You're Strange' in his hypnotic wail. The marquee was packed. Every last chair was taken. People were standing on the tables, sitting shoulder to shoulder on the dance floor. Some had even shinned up the tent-poles for a better view. Jordan took Annie's hand and threaded his way through the crowd until he found a tiny space and folded himself into it, pulling her down between his knees.

At first they just sat and listened reverently. But at the first screaming guitar slide of 'Two Times Girl', the audience exploded. People rose to their feet, clapping their hands over their heads and jumping up and down until the dance floor bounced like a trampoline. They stood on tables, twirling dangerously. They spread out on to the lawn and started dancing. The mood was intoxicating. Jordan tapped Annie's shoulder.

'Come on,' he said, 'dance with me.'

They pushed their way out on to the lawn and joined the whirling bodies. Annie took off her shoes and leapt into the beat. The lights flashed across their faces, turning them different colours. They could see the marquee swaying. A man on one of the punts got so carried away that he jumped into the river, fully dressed, with a jubilant scream. One song rocketed into another. Annie and Jordan showed off shamelessly, laughing at themselves and at each other. Annie felt as if her body was an instrument tuned to perfection.

When the music slowed, Jordan reached out and drew her into his arms. They swayed together across the grass. Annie slid her arms up around his neck and leaned her face into his shirt. He smelled delicious. They danced like that for a long time, learning the feel of each other's bodies. Then she felt his mouth against her ear.

'I have a dream,' he murmured. 'I have a dream about punting a beautiful girl down the river in the moonlight.' His arms tightened around her.

There was a punt station under Magdalen Bridge. Normally it would be closed by now. But the ball organisers had made a special arrangement to lease a few punts for the night. When she saw the crowds of people waiting for punts, Annie almost cried out with disappointment. Jordan steered her to a quiet spot on the riverbank. He took off his jacket and wrapped it around her shoulders. 'Wait here,' he said.

'But the queue,' she pointed. 'You'll never get one.'

Jordan pivoted on one toe, and spread his hands cockily. 'Watch me.'

Annie didn't need the jacket, but she hugged it to her. It smelled of Jordan. While she waited for him, she gazed across the silken river to a line of trees hung with fairy lights. This was Addison's Walk, where she had often strolled with Edward. Ruthlessly she closed her mind to him. Edward wasn't here. Jordan was. Tomorrow he would be gone. Once before, she and Jordan had been thrown together, and she had resisted. This time, it seemed like fate.

Five minutes later a punt glided towards her out of the darkness. She saw the gleam of a white shirt. Jordan was standing at the sloping end of the flat-bottomed boat in bare feet, trousers rolled above his ankles. He had removed his bow-tie and loosened his shirt. He swung the long pole through the water and brought the boat to the bank.

'Jordan!' Annie laughed with delight. 'How did you do that?'

'Ah-ha.'

'You didn't steal it, did you?'

'Of course not. I was raised a Baptist. I know the punt guy. He eats lunch in George's, in the Market. Now get in.'

Annie took his hand and stepped in carefully. She began to settle herself among the cushions.

'Contacts, you see, Annie,' Jordan sighed in a worldly way, 'that's what life is all about. Also,' he added, 'I gave the guy a pound.'

'A pound!' Annie shot up in the boat, sending it rocking.

'Jesus!' Jordan dropped to a crouch, trying to keep his balance.

They punted upriver, past Magdalen Grove towards the Parks. Annie stretched out her legs and leaned back luxuriously against the headrest, watching Jordan drop the pole into the water and bend down to propel the boat forward. It was a soothing rhythm – the rumble of wood on wood as the pole slid down the side of the boat, the crunch of gravel as its metal tip hit the riverbed, then the sudden hiss of water as the boat shot forward, fading to a gentle ripple. They passed one or two other punts. Then there was nothing but trees and river and sky. The noise of the ball faded. The darkness deepened. Annie draped her arms over the sides of boat, trailing her finger-tips in the warm water. Behind Jordan's head she could see a million stars and the pale glow of a half-moon. Then she felt leaves brush her hair as the boat nosed towards the bank, under an arching willow tree. Jordan ducked down to avoid the branches.

'The trouble with punting a beautiful girl down the

river,' he complained, 'is that you can see her, but you can't touch her.'

He thrust the pole deep into the mud to secure the boat alongside the bank. Annie shifted to one side of the cushions to make room for him.

'Be careful,' she said, as Jordan stepped over the far headrest and walked down the boat towards her, 'the boat's rather wonky.'

Jordan slid down beside her. ' "Wonky"?' he said disbelievingly. He pulled her close to him, laughing into her eyes. 'What kind of a crazy English word is that?'

'Wobbly. Unstable. Liable to capsize.' At the first touch of his hands Annie felt a kind of delirium sweep through her. 'Unsteady. Shaky. Prone to collapse. Not – '

'Stop talking,' Jordan said, and kissed her.

For a long time there was silence, as his lips, then his tongue, explored hers. When at last they drew apart, Jordan let out a long sigh. His eyes wandered over her face in delight and astonishment.

'You know, this is like a miracle. I saw you in the street the other day, and I thought it was for the last time.'

'I saw you, too,' Annie said dreamily, then frowned. 'You were kissing a girl.'

'I was not!'

'You were. Outside Queen's. A girl in subfusc.'

'Oh, her. She was just someone who'd finished her exams. I'd never seen her before. She'd have kissed Joe Stalin if he'd been standing where I was.' He smiled exultantly at Annie. 'Don't tell me you were jealous?'

'Madly.'

'Anyway,' Jordan carefully stroked a strand of her hair from her cheek, 'that wasn't kissing. *This* is what I call kissing. . . .'

'These buttons,' he mused after a while, fingering the neckline of her dress. 'Are they just for show, or do they do something?' He undid the top one, answering his own question. Annie watched languorously as he unfastened

221

her dress. She was wearing nothing underneath. Her breasts fell into his hands like warm fruit.

Under the touch of his fingers and his lips Annie began to tremble. Jordan peeled her dress down her shoulders and leaned over her. He swept back her hair, and put his face to hers.

'Are you sure?' he asked fiercely. She could feel the effort it cost him to ask the question.

'I'm sure.' Annie mouthed the words. She had no breath left to make them audible. For answer, she tried to put her arms around Jordan, but they were imprisoned in the folded-back sleeves of her dress.

'Wait,' Jordan said. 'Let's do this right.'

He freed Annie's arms from her sleeves, then slid her dress down her body, hooking off her pants as he went. Annie gasped as she felt the soft air on her skin. All she wore now was the ribbon round her neck. Jordan put his hand low on her stomach, and they both felt the deep muscles contract.

'Now you,' she whispered.

Kneeling in the bottom of the boat, Jordan stripped off his shirt. Then he stood up carefully, catching hold of a willow branch to steady himself. His body was dappled with moonlight. Annie could see smooth curves of muscle and the taut hollow under his ribcage. He loosened his trousers and kicked them off, to stand naked above her. Annie reached out, suddenly wild with impatience, and ran her hand up the inside of his thigh. His skin was hot, as smooth as silk. Jordan let go of the branch and gently fitted his body on top of hers. The sheer weight of him brought tears of desire to her eyes. Water lapped at the boat as it began to rock, cradling the two of them in their willow cave. Annie felt pierced with joy. She heard a low, crooning sound that might have been Jordan's saxophone, and realised that it was her own voice. She closed her eyes, thinking, *I am going to remember this for the rest of my life.*

1992

21

Honky tonk woman

Rose Cassidy stood at her living-room window, flushed from her shower, wearing the monogrammed robe she had stolen years ago from the George V in Paris. One hand rested on her hip, elbow cocked assertively. In the other was a Styrofoam cup of freshly squeezed orange juice which she had picked up on her way back from the gym. She sipped impatiently as she looked across Central Park at the skyline of Fifth Avenue. It was a stupendous view, one that normally made her spirits soar. On clear winter mornings, when the bold pinnacles reared up against a fiery sunrise, she felt like Mistress of the Universe. But today the buildings seemed tawdry and diminished under a blanket of dark cloud. The park was a dripping expanse of stunted trees. Eight floors down Rose could see the jostle of umbrellas and a snarl of yellow cabs along Central Park West. She suddenly remembered the bright red umbrella inscribed with '*Merde, il pleut*', which she used to think so dashing in her *Harpers & Queen* days, and felt the faintest twinge of nostalgia for shabby old England.

There was still no message from Chris. Where was the

bastard? Last night Rose had left messages on his work number and with his answering service. She had tried his mobile dozens of times, crashing down her receiver when she found it switched off. That corn-fed wife of his had promised to make him call back urgently, but it had probably slipped her brain cell. Ten to one Chris was right this minute snoring off a bender, or hustling pillow-talk from some ball-breaker in the White Office press corps. Rose rattled her polished nails across the window pane. Chris was Chris. She would simply have to wait. Exasperating as he might be, he was still her best route to Jordan Hope's inner circle.

Rose herself had been up for over two hours. Her alarm was always set for 5.45, though today she hadn't needed it. She had slept badly, her thoughts whirling round Annie and the thunderbolt she had delivered yesterday afternoon. Thank God Annie had possessed the wit to phone her. Best and oldest friend though she was, Annie was not sophisticated enough to see past her own anxiety about Tom and her absurdly romantic desire to shield Jordan from disaster. British elections were like a children's tea-party compared to an American presidential race. Annie would not be able to conceive of the millions of dollars – not to mention careers, ambitions, businesses and vested interests – staked on a Hope victory; nor of the vindictive rage if, at this late stage, he ruined everything with another sex scandal.

No one must learn about Tom. The damage must be contained. That was Rose's mission. Schemes, alternatives, contingency plans chased each other round her head. And somewhere, in the midst of the crisis, she caught the sweet scent of opportunity.

Rose drained her juice and crossed the expanse of immaculate grey carpet to deposit her cup in the kitchen trash can. Naturally she had a perfectly good kitchen of her own, stocked with the expected gadgets, doubtless including an orange juice squeezer. There was a frighteningly authentic-looking butcher's block whose virgin surface reproached her every time she slunk past it to get her wheatgerm and vitamins out of the giant refrigerator. But it was pointless to stock up with food when she was always out, easier to buy what she wanted when she wanted it. That was the Manhattan way. No one cooked for themselves here, even the minuscule fraction of the population that wasn't permanently on a diet. This was not a city where people stayed in. New Yorkers did not have friends to 'supper' in the cosy way they did in London – pasta slopped on to plates straight from the stove and handed casually round the kitchen table, followed by cheese remnants from the fridge and pickings from the fruit bowl. This was partly a question of space, but overridingly a matter of style. Manhattan was a stage – the most fabulous, glitzy, intimidating stage in the world with every player fighting for the spotlight. You didn't so much live here as perform with a capital P.

The evidence that Rose had performed her socks off surrounded her in gratifying profusion. Success was conspicuous in the lofty grandeur of her apartment and its fabulous view, in the Hockneys and Stellas on her walls, in the elegant lines of the Eames reclining chair and Italian floor lamps, in the walk-in closets lined with dress-bags full of Chanel and Versace and topped by precise ranks of labelled shoe boxes. The apartment was stylish, precise, severely modernist – the exact opposite of her childhood home, with its mismatched furnishings and lurking squalors. In a city that disdained nobodies, Rose was undeniably a somebody.

She took it for granted now. Shrugging off her robe, bare feet padding across the polished parquet and Persian silk rugs, Rose returned to her bedroom to dress. She had laid out her clothes the night before. It had become a habit. She put on the black silk underwear, slid her stockings up smoothly waxed legs, then sat down at the Biedermeier dressing table. Tilting the swivel mirror to catch the light, she shaded her eyes and rubbed colour into her lips and cheeks. As she leaned close to darken her eyelashes she caught sight of her furrowed forehead, and winced.

Abruptly she stood up. Still in her underwear, she went over to the full-length art deco mirror, taking stock. Her glossy dark hair was cut precisely at earlobe level in a style that was both elegant and gamine. No grey hairs, thanks to her hairdresser. Her neck was holding up pretty well, her green eyes clear. Her body, petite but curvy, was in better shape than when she was twenty. There was nothing wrong with her legs – apart from being about twelve inches too short. She still looked thirtysomething. Didn't she?

Rose felt a clutch of panic. In February she would be forty-three. Middle-aged. Decaying. Heading for the menopause and the dreaded o-word. The ageing process for women seemed to progress in quantum leaps. They could go on looking twenty-three until they were thirty-five. Then, almost overnight, they started looking thirty-five and could go on doing so until they were fifty. After that there was nothing to do but get the telephone number of the best plastic surgeon in town. Or retire from public view. That gave her another, what, ten years?

Rose stepped into her skirt and zipped it snug around her waist, allowing her mind to wander in a familiar groove. Her supremacy in the magazine world would not last for ever. The honeymoon between America and the 'Briterati' was over. It was important to have an alternative fantasy up one's sleeve. Rose had determined that she would never wait to be eased out. If the crunch came, she would throw the best 'fuck you' party of all time, then disappear. She had always fancied the Suffolk coast, some whitewashed cottage tucked behind a honeysuckle hedge. In summer she would go to concerts at Aldeburgh and learn to sail and tie up her lupins – whatever lupins were. Winters she would spend by a crackling fire, a cat draped across the back of her armchair, catching up on the books she had only pretended to read for so long. Long walks on the beach would take the place of blusher and the stairmaster. She would become a regular at some atmospheric local pub. She would –

A screech from the fax machine cut across her thoughts. Automatically Rose started down the hall towards her study, adrenalin flowing. Could it be Chris? Had Annie found Tom? Maybe John Updike had changed his mind about the '*Couples* '90s style' piece. The fantasy of the Suffolk cottage evaporated. Who was she kidding? Cat hairs – yuk! Rain – double-yuk! Who wanted to sit in the pub listening to conversations about the royal family and dog-breeding until some overweight, opinionated publican turfed her out into the rain with an insincere 'Mind how you go'? Rose shuddered, smoothing her jacket into place.

She tore the fax out of the machine, but it was only a confirmation of her booking at the Golden Valley Spa over Thanksgiving weekend. It still amazed her the way Americans, otherwise so hard-nosed, turned to marshmallow every November and willingly incarcerated themselves with the very families that had driven them crazy the other fifty-one weeks of the year. Rose had crossed Thanksgiving off her social calendar after one memorable experience of non-stop schmaltz and brown food. The whole thing was a frightful waste of good working hours at one of the busiest times of year. Now, while others overdosed on turkey and pumpkin pie, she grew sleek on lemon water and mud baths and ten-hour sleeps, and dreamed up killer ideas for the magazine.

Rose tidied the fax away, picked up the neat piles of last night's work and began slotting them into her briefcase. Her entryphone buzzed twice, the signal that her car had arrived. Right, Chris, she thought, your time's up. To think she'd nearly married that scumbag! For a few weeks they had thought they were made for each other –

two maverick Brits flaming with talent and ambition, out to conquer America. They had talked and argued and made love with a ferocity that Rose had never experienced before or since. Fortunately they had recovered their sanity in time. Now Chris had cute, compliant Kimmie and a brace of tow-headed children with weird American names she could never remember. And Rose had . . . her freedom. Sometimes she thought it would almost be worth being married just to silence the gossip columnists, or to have someone to wake up and say 'Look, it's snowing!' On the other hand, a husband might not let her go out to black-tie dinners five nights a week, or slob out in front of old Hollywood weepies, spooning frozen yoghurt straight from the tub. Come to think of it, he probably wouldn't let her sleep with other men either.

It was a pity that society had not yet evolved to a point where women could have wives too. What Rose really needed was a male version of Kimmie, someone who would make dental appointments, put clean sheets on the bed when Rose was ill and otherwise keep a low profile. But the sexes didn't work that way. It would be a long time before Penelope came home from her adventures to find faithful Odysseus by his spinning-wheel.

Rose stiffened like a bird-dog. She sensed an article in this. Dropping her briefcase she switched on her computer and brought up her 'Ideas' file, fingers flying over the keys as she made notes. There was that new Hollywood star whose husband took the kids to school and checked her contracts: that would give it a glamour angle and an excuse for pictures. Maybe she could persuade that classy English woman who wrote about myth and madonnas to write a little commentary, supplying a gloss of intellectual cred. It would need a good shout line: 'The Little Man' or 'Chain Male' or – oh well, it would come to her later. Hurriedly, Rose saved the file and shut down the computer.

Feeling more cheerful, she carried her briefcase into the hall and set it on a chair. She took her Vivienne Westwood raincoat out of the closet and put it on, assessing the effect in the mirror on the back of the door. Stylish but slightly wacky – just right. That was the fine line Rose trod in this rigidly conformist city. She had learned that if you played by most of the rules, you could bend the rest. It was OK to live on the West Side as long as you lived in a 'named' building. You could confess to liking alcohol if it was something eccentric like manzanilla sherry. You could get away with mixing designers, but only if it was done with panache.

Rose picked up her briefcase, scooped a pile of clothes off the hall chair and slammed the apartment door behind her. She pressed the polished elevator button and did a few pelvic floor exercises while she waited. Although she loved the kitsch grandeur of the Dakota, with its sentrybox and moat and Wild West adornments, its elevator system retained the habits of a more leisured age. When the doors opened again on to the lobby, she came out like a bullet from a pistol, firing instructions at the hovering doorman.

'Morning, Carl. Ida says the vacuum cleaner's started growling again – could you be an angel and take a look? Here are my shoes for polishing, and this stuff needs to get over to Louie's pronto.' She handed him an armful of clothes without breaking stride. 'Tell him I need the green dress back by five tomorrow or I'll be looking for a new cleaner's.'

Coat billowing behind her, she sailed through the door and across the sidewalk straight into the back seat of her waiting car. The driver shut the door after her and got in behind the wheel.

'Office,' Rose said succinctly.

She took her latest gadget out of her briefcase, an electronic notepad that had been a present from Japanese advertising clients. As the car wound its way across

Central Park, she tapped in a code and brought up her agenda for the day.

There was that new photographer to see at eleven, then lunch with Mitzi Meyerhof, whom Rose was thinking of appointing as a contributing editor. A former chat show hostess now married to a phenomenally successful plastic surgeon, Mitzi was a total airhead, but she had great contacts. At three o'clock Rose had a strategy meeting with Walt. After that she had planned to sneak out of the office to see an English girl she secretly wanted to replace Barney as Art Director. Barney had acquired a fatal habit of thinking he was right about everything. If the entire art department walked out – tough. Walt would forgive her when she told him about the December advertising pages. At five-thirty John was coming to the apartment to blow out her hair ready for tonight's dinner at the Metropolitan – the Temple of Dendur *again*. Really, the place was becoming so popular it might as well be called Club Met.

Rose reached for the carphone and postponed her meeting with the English girl. She had enough problems for one day. Then she pulled out the folder she had been working on last night. The Lagerfeld piece was good – plenty of insider gossip and a sassy style that was just right for *The Magazine*. Steven had sneaked some fabulous backstage pictures at the Collections. Together they would make a great story. And yet – wasn't there something a little banal about the copy line? Rose closed her eyes, trying to summon up one particular tranny that had stuck in her memory, a terrific black and white shot that had caught Karl's sly, sideways smile and the impish thrust of his ponytail against a background blur of half-dressed models. She imagined how it would look fully bled opposite the text. Fabulous – with the right headline. Rose considered for a moment, then crossed out 'King Karl' and in bold capitals wrote 'Moi?' That was more like it.

A sudden outbreak of honking horns and furious shouts made her look up. A delivery truck had jumped the lights on the 50th Street intersection and was now imprisoned in a gridlock of cars. Two cab drivers with their torsos thrust halfway out their car windows, like latterday jousters, yelled abuse at each other. 'You wanna drive a car, get a licence!' 'What's your problem, asshole?'

Rose felt a spurt of pride for her adopted city, like a mother for her wayward child. New York was a cesspit, but it was *her* cesspit, and she loved every unique and fabulous inch of it – from Castle Clinton, where the poor and huddled masses had awaited entry to the promised land, right up to the spooky Cloisters.

She had arrived in the city ten years ago with a thousand pounds, some good magazine contacts and a frizzed hairstyle she didn't now like to think about. It was August. An editor on *Ms* magazine, whom Rose had met in her *Spare Rib* days, offered Rose the use of her place on the edge of Chinatown while she was on vacation. It had seemed a truly sisterly gesture until Rose discovered that the air conditioner emitted nothing more than a rhythmic clanking, and that she would be sharing the apartment with several families of cockroaches. At night, sweating on to the futon with every muscle tensed for the click of insect legs on the wooden floor, she felt like Alec Guinness in his hot-box in *Bridge on the River Kwai*.

New York had been dead. Everybody was on 'the Island' or 'the Cape'. Rose gritted her teeth and spent the month acquainting herself with the city she was determined to conquer. She read all the magazines and papers, standing at bookstalls until her calves ached or burrowing in the Public Library. She lived on salad and bagels and lost ten pounds in two weeks. Just before Labor Day, her friend came back from vacation early, lured by a rumour that Walt Kernitz wanted someone to revamp *A La Mode*. It certainly needed it. Rose said nothing, but laid her plans. Walt was famous for starting work at four in the morning. Rose got hold of his number and called him at four-thirty the next day. Ratcheting up her English accent a few social notches, she apologised for disturbing him; she knew he was an early riser, and so was she. She knew about the job and she knew she was the person to do it. She had already prepared a ten-page editorial and business plan. He would regret it if he didn't see her. There had been a long silence, then, 'OK, breakfast tomorrow. Is five too early for you?' 'Five is perfect.' That day Rose had spent her last five hundred pounds on a new outfit, shoes and a haircut. She had felt a teensy pang, but her old friend already had a job. Rose hadn't. Besides, she knew she'd do it better.

The rest had passed into magazine legend. Walt gave her the job. Rose fired thirty per cent of the staff, imported a stable of British talent, wormed her way into high-life parties, cajoled the advertisers. Amid howls of outrage and hopeful predictions of failure, Rose had brought the magazine into profit within six months and eventually established it as the Bible of America's well-heeled woman. As a reward Walt had given her the chance to start another magazine for a younger, hipper readership. With supreme confidence she had named it, simply, *The Magazine*. Now it was threatening to outsell its elder sister, and New York had bowed its head in homage to her success – though waiting, Rose knew, to sink its teeth into her ankles at the first opportunity. She wasn't really worried. Annie's phone call had given her an idea.

The car dropped her outside the Kernitz Building. Rose took the elevator to her office. Catching sight of Cindy already at her work-station, Rose checked off her mental list as she strode towards her office.

'Did you remember to send those flowers to the Plaza?'
'Yes, Miss Cassidy.'
'Has anyone called Chris rung?'
'Not yet.'
'The Whatsernames have had their baby – you remem-

234

ber the TV star we profiled who set up a birthing pool with a dolphin in her basement? Can you buy it a present in your lunch hour? A hundred dollars max.'

'Boy or girl?'

'It's bound to be one or the other,' Rose threw over her shoulder as she walked into her office and shut the door.

Hanging up her coat, she worked through her messages and mail, then checked the editorial line-up for the December issue. There was an article about the gravitation of stars to Ireland, provisionally called 'The Irishtocracy'. Jeremy Irons and Daniel Day Lewis had places there. So did Ken and Emma, Nicole and Tom, Mick and Jerry of course. Rose gave it a tick. An attack on supermodels by that new backlash feminist sounded a lark, but it would have to be toned down or the advertisers would kill her.

The centrepiece of the whole issue was a photo essay on Ginny Hope, including a revolutionary double-page spread of photographs without a single line of text. The pictures spoke for themselves: Ginny as a little girl with gappy teeth and pigtails, Ginny as high-school class president, virginal college girl, peacenik, Civil Rights campaigner, bride, children's case-worker, electioneer and finally – via an astonishing number of hairstyles – potential First Lady.

The article had already cost a bomb in researchers, travel and outright bribery. Even Walt had warned her about putting all her eggs in one basket. Now Rose wished she hadn't been quite so adamant. All the mags would have a presidential story in the post-election issue. The question was, which President? Until yesterday Rose had been betting on Hope. And now? Rose had flamboyantly nailed her professional colours to the mast. She didn't fancy going down with the ship. *The Magazine* prided itself on being first with the buzz. If Jordan lost, Ginny would be about as hot a topic as the bubble skirt.

Rose's glance roamed around her trophy office, noting

235

the two-way view across and down Madison Avenue, the fresh flowers delivered daily, the famous slate table that was kept scrupulously empty except when she was working at it, the handmade bookshelves stacked with contemporary novels and social registers, heavyweight political diaries and Hollywood biographies. Hanging on one wall was the framed cover of the first issue of *The Magazine*, which had sold out by noon, and a calculatedly modest selection of *de rigueur* celeb shots of herself with Jack Nicholson, Ed Koch, Henry Kissinger, Diane Sawyer. It would hurt to lose all this. On the other hand . . .

The telephone buzzed. It was Cindy, sounding puzzled. 'I've got a Robert Maxwell for you? He says he's sure you want to speak with him. I thought – I mean, isn't Robert Maxwell dead?'

Rose couldn't help grinning. This must be Chris's interpretation of 'discreet'. She could just picture his foxy face. 'Put him on,' she commanded. Unclipping an earring from her telephone ear, she prepared to charm him into submission.

'Darling,' she cried, 'how are you? That was a very naughty piece you wrote about La Harrington. I hope you've got your balls well insured . . . . *Is she*? How riveting.' Rose's eyes narrowed to crafty green slits as she reached for her notepad and pen. 'Of course not,' she cooed reproachfully, scribbling fast. 'Not beyond these four walls, I promise.

'Listen,' she went on briskly, 'I need a favour. I've been asked to set up a telephone call to Jordan Hope. It's a purely personal matter – nothing to do with the election – but it's very private and very confidential and extremely urgent. I can't call the campaign office, obviously. You know what it's like with everyone on top of each other, gossiping like mad. "My Lord, it's that uppity Rose Cassidy from *The Magazine*",' Rose drawled in a very bad imitation of a Southern accent. ' "Now what in tarnation

236

does she want?" What I need is a middleman, someone really close to Jordan who can contact him right away and will fix the whole thing up without asking questions. And naturally, darling, I thought that of all the people in the entire world you would know who's the best person.'

As she listened to his familiar voice, clotted with south London vowels even after a decade in America, Rose's face grew stony.

'I'm not up to anything,' she protested. 'Honestly, darling, I hardly know what's going on myself, I'm just trying to help someone out. You always used to complain that I didn't need you,' she wheedled. 'Well, now I do. I admit it.'

It was no good. Chris knew her too well. He was firing questions like the bloody Gestapo. Who was she doing this 'favour' for? If this was some cretinous media stunt, she could stuff it. Was there another financial scandal brewing, or was it something more juicy? Was it – ouch! – anything to do with Hope's Oxford days?

Rose's brain whizzed through alternative strategies. She could invent some cover story, but Chris would be sharp enough to spot the flaws. She could promise to tell him the whole story the next time he was in New York – from the downy depths of her double bed, if he liked. But as she had no intention of telling him anything, that would be lying. Rose was well aware of her reputation for dressing facts up or down, depending on the angle of a story. She realised, to her surprise, that she didn't really want to lie. Not to Chris.

A silence fell between them. 'All right,' Rose conceded, 'I do know what it's about. But I can't tell you. I can promise you that it's nothing that you would truly regard as being in the public interest, but that's it. There's no *quid pro quo* here. Sorry. I only asked because there's no one else I can trust and I'll probably make a balls-up of it on my own.' She sighed. 'You've got your rules, and

I respect them. So – change of subject – are you coming to my election party? Everyone else is.'

But mysteriously she seemed to have pressed the right button. Chris's voice came back at her brisk and business-like. 'I know the bloke you want. Smarmy bugger, but bloody fast on his feet. Hope thinks the sun shines out of his arse. Hang about, I'll give you his private line.'

'Who is he?' Rose asked, writing down the number.

'Some sort of glorified PR goon, can't remember his title. Checks the speeches, holds Hope's hand, takes the tricky phone calls – that sort of thing.'

'No, what's his *name*, dumbo?' Rose held her pen poised. She had a horrid feeling she knew the answer.

'Christ, didn't I say? That bloody bourbon. Zaps the brain cells. His name's Rick Goodman. You must have seen him on TV.'

'Yes, I have,' Rose said slowly. She wrote the name down and drew a bold, black box around it, like a funeral card. 'I suppose it has to be him. . . . I mean, that's terrific, Chris. I really appreciate it. Thank you.'

'Always a pleasure, Madame Mystery. Don't worry, I'll tickle your secrets out of you soon enough.'

'I can't wait. Love to Kimmie. And, um, Drew and Tyler, of course.'

Rose put down the phone. Her smile faded. Rick Good-man. That made things awkward. Or did it? There was a nasty little skeleton in his cupboard which she could rattle if he didn't cooperate.

Rose looked at her watch. Missouri was an hour behind. It would be just nine o'clock. Perfect. She sat quite still for a minute, collecting her thoughts. She had been in touch with Rick once or twice since Hope had won the Democratic nomination and enlisted the help of his old Oxford friend as PR supremo for the campaign. There had been times when Jordan had needed all the media support he could get – and Rose had given it willingly. Rose hesitated, thinking of all the possible

238

consequences of what she was about to do, then straightened her shoulders and tapped in the number.

Rick himself answered at the first ring.

'Rose, how delightful to hear from you,' he said with that dangerous, mocking charm. 'What can I do for you?'

Trying to sound matter-of-fact, Rose stated her request. A friend of hers needed to get in touch with Jordan personally, as a matter of urgency. Could Rick help?

'What friend?'

'An old friend from England. Nothing political.'

'Has he got a name?'

'She.' Rose hesitated. 'Her name's Annie. Jordan will know who it is.'

There was a calculating pause. Then Rick said, 'I'm not absolutely sure I like the sound of this.'

'I think Jordan will,' Rose countered steadily. 'I think he will consider it extremely important.'

'Really.' Rose could almost hear his brain clicking. 'Well, it's no big secret,' he said at last in a casual tone. 'Jordan will be in Dallas tonight. Here's the number. He's a busy man, though. The best time to catch him is between midnight and six.'

'Thanks,' Rose said coolly. 'I'd be happy to return the favour with something on Jordan in *The Magazine* when he wins – as I'm sure he will.'

'That's thoughtful of you, Rose, but I think we'd probably want an American on board for that kind of thing.'

Rose flushed at the snub. It was true: Brit-bashing was the latest blood sport. Aloud all she said was, 'Call me when you need me', and put down the phone.

She let out her breath in relief. She had the number Annie needed. But she still felt uneasy. Rick would move heaven, earth and probably hell to find out what was going on, and turn it to his advantage – not that she altogether blamed him. She too felt the temptation of holding such a bombshell of a secret in her hands. Imagine, what a scoop! Jordan Hope's illegitimate son!

No one knew the inside story as she did – and what a story! Sex and drugs and rock 'n' roll, with Oxford and Vietnam thrown in. Move over, Woodward and Bernstein.

Rose was seized by an irresistible urge. Before she knew it she was sitting at the computer, her fingers itching. She pulled up the list of directories and scooted the cursor up and down until she found 'Liabilities'. Perfect. No one ever looked in there. She created a new file and gave it the dullest name she could think of: 'Storage'. If she blocked the file off with a password, no one would ever be able to read it anyway. So what was the password? Operation President – too obvious. No, she had it: 'Special Relationship'. The *double entendre* amused her.

Placing her Tiffany bangles on the desk, Rose began to type.

22

I gotta get a message to you

Annie pushed open the heavy front door, shook the rain-drops from her umbrella and climbed the stairs wearily. It was so early that the central heating hadn't come on yet, and the office was cold. But it was empty: that was the main thing. At this hour, she could be sure that no one could observe what she was about to do.

She hoisted her bulging briefcase on to her desk and slumped for a moment into her chair, keeping her coat on against the chill. It was just like the old days, during the miners' strike, when there had been no heating two days a week. But then Harry Robertson had been her boss, and she an eager, loyal employee. Now she felt as guilty as a sneak thief.

She took the telltale blue files from her case, then fished out the computer disc that contained hours of work done late at night in her tiny study at home. Encoded here were letters to her authors, explaining her new plans; faxes to the American publishers involved in the Sebastian Winter auction; and, most difficult of all to write, her letter of resignation to Jack. She had burned her boats now. Sebastian had leapt at the idea of becoming the first client of the Annie Hamilton Literary Agency. His faith in her was touching, but terrifying too. What if she wasn't as smart as she thought? What if she had miscalculated her ability to sell his novels? If she bungled the auction, she could kiss her career goodbye. No other agency would employ her. The authors who might otherwise follow her to the new agency would politely, regretfully, melt away. Annie jumped up from her desk and pulled off her coat, trying to banish her fears. She had a fierce need to make this work. Tom's disappearance had made her see what was truly important. It was time to grab hold of her life and dictate its direction.

Switching on her computer, she slotted in the disc and set up the printer. The machines began to hum and click, processing her future. With luck the letters would be signed and in their envelopes, the faxes ready to send, before anyone arrived. But first she had something else to do. Now, quickly, before anyone came in. With an accelerating heartbeat Annie reached for her Filofax. Her palms filmed with sweat, her fingers fumbled over the pages. For a moment she couldn't find what she was looking for. Panic rose in her throat. No, it was all right. Two pages had stuck together. She pinched them apart. There it was, the telephone number Rose had given her. Annie had copied it down in tiny writing, as if to mini-mise its significance. But it was everything – her past, perhaps her future. Annie smoothed out the page. Thank God for Rose. At least there was one person she could trust.

Annie frowned at the figures, trying to focus her thoughts. Dallas, Texas. It would be about two in the morning there. Jordan would be asleep, perhaps dreaming of the glorious future that now seemed to be within his grasp. There had been times when she had longed for an excuse to contact him. Here it was, and she could hardly force her hand to the telephone.

'Yeah?' A male voice, not sleepy at all. Alert, expectant, eager for news.

'Jordan?'

'Who is this?'

There it was, that husky twang she remembered. Annie's toes curled.

'It's Annie Paxford.'

Silence.

'We met at Oxford years ago. Remember?'

'Of course I remember you, Annie. It's been a hell of a long time. What can I do for you?'

His tone was distinctly cool. He must think she was ringing to claim an old friendship with him, now that he had become famous.

'Nothing,' she said quickly. 'At least, there's something you need to know.' Annie cleared her throat. 'I have a son. His name is Tom.'

'Uh . . . congratulations,' Jordan replied, polite but mystified. 'When was he born?'

Annie closed her eyes. He thought she'd just had the baby!

'No, you don't understand. He's grown up. Sort of,' she added, recalling Tom's recent behaviour. *Get to the point.* Her tongue felt swollen and clumsy. 'The thing is,' she took a breath, 'he thinks you're his father.'

There was an audible gasp. 'He *what*?'

'It's not my fault,' Annie protested. 'I never told him – that is, I've never mentioned that we . . . knew each other.' She rushed on. 'Jordan, this is too difficult on the phone. I'd like to explain in person. I happen to be coming to the States this weekend, on business – Chicago and New York, but I could meet you anywhere that fits in with your schedule. Any town you say. Day or night. A bar, hotel, park – it doesn't matter. But I need to see you.'

She could feel his resistance in the long silence. 'Couldn't this wait until after the election?'

Annie flushed with impatience. 'There won't *be* an

243

election – not with the result you want, anyway. Tom's in shock. He's gone missing. Don't you understand? *He's coming to find you.*'

'Coming *here* – to the States?' Jordan sounded appalled.

'It's possible,' Annie back-pedalled. 'To be honest, I don't know where he is or who he's talking to, but it wouldn't take much to get a rumour into the papers.'

'But it isn't true!' he shouted indignantly.

Annie hesitated only for a second. 'Of course it isn't,' she agreed. 'I just wanted to warn you – in case.' Her voice softened. 'I'm thinking of *you*, Jordan. The election. Your wife.'

There was a long pause. Then, 'It *is* you,' he said unexpectedly. 'Annie Paxford. You sound just the same. . . . Are you?'

Annie thought of the laugh-lines round her eyes, the traces of childbirth on her body, of all that she had been through since they last met. 'Hardly,' she said tartly. 'Are you?'

'I guess not. Listen, Annie, this all sounds crazy to me. I don't understand how you can have gotten me into this mess. Still . . .' she heard the crackle of paper, 'Chicago's on my schedule for, let's see, Saturday night. Tell me where you're staying.'

Annie gave him the name of her hotel.

'I can't promise anything,' he warned.

'I understand.'

'Even if I could get away, it would be late – maybe the middle of the night.'

'It doesn't matter.'

'You're sure this isn't some kind of hoax?'

'Oh, Jordan . . . I haven't changed that much.'

'You still say things like "wonky" and "actually"?'

'Probably.' She could hear the smile in his voice. 'You'll find out on Saturday. Goodbye.'

Annie carefully put the receiver in place. She felt as though she had just run a race. At least he hadn't said,

'Annie who?' The printer was beeping at her. It had run out of paper. Automatically Annie rose and went to the stationery cupboard, feeling a wonderful calmness take control. Rose's masterplan was falling into place. Under the cover of an emergency trip to America to visit her dying mother, Annie was going to auction Sebastian Winter from under Jack's nose. She was going to sneak a meeting with her old lover. She was going to lie to Edward. Annie closed her heart to the clamourings of conscience. She deserved her own business. She needed – wanted – to see Jordan. Taking a fresh supply of paper, she squared the sheets with a determined rap on the desk. She had been good long enough. Now she was going to be bad.

23

It's my life

'I don't believe it!'

Tom looked up accusingly from the paper in his hand. He felt winded by disappointment.

Across the small conference table the senior officer met his eyes sympathetically. 'I tried to warn you, lad. We're only an information service. We're not God.'

'But it's completely blank,' Tom protested, stabbing a finger at the document. 'I've spent three days persuading you to let me see this, and now – ' He broke off, not trusting his voice to stay steady. His throat ached with the effort of keeping back tears of frustration.

'Take your time,' the older man said gently.

Trying to collect himself, Tom turned away and let his gaze travel round this small room, buried deep in the Office of Population Censuses and Surveys. But there was no comfort to be found in its bare walls and government-issue furnishings. He swallowed painfully and looked back at the treacherous document.

It was his birth certificate, his *real* birth certificate. The one they wouldn't let him see in London. The one he had been so sure would silence his doubts. For this he had driven hundreds of miles north, practically as far as Scotland. For this he had wasted days mooching around the Southport seafront, waiting for the Population Office people to find his file and check his bona fides. For this he had spent wakeful nights on Mrs Pritchard's slithery nylon sheets. Tom could feel a tide of self-pity welling inside him. Shut up and concentrate, he told himself.

The document in front of him was dated 27 March 1971, ten days after his birth. It had been issued in the name of Thomas Paxford. OK, so his parents weren't married at the time. He could cope with that. But surely, if Dad was truly his father, his details ought to be here. Three lines were allocated for information about the father. All three spaces were empty. No Edward Hamilton, no Jordan Hope – nothing.

Tom reached into his jacket pocket and pulled out his copy of the later certificate, issued after his parents' marriage in the name of Hamilton. This one had been easy to get. He had picked it up on his very first day in Southport simply by filling in a form and writing a cheque. Now he unfolded the paper and read again the details under 'Father'. *Name: Edward Hamilton. Place of birth: Lewes, Sussex. Occupation – lawyer.* There might be other differences between the two documents. He laid them down side by side and began to cross-check.

'We do offer a counselling service,' suggested the senior officer, sliding a leaflet across the table. 'People often find it helpful.'

'What?' Tom said absently. A name at the bottom of the original certificate caught his eye. That was odd. 'Is this my copy?' he asked. 'Can I take it away?'

'Of course. Found something helpful after all, have you?'

'Well . . . interesting, perhaps.' Tom folded the papers and stuffed them back into his pocket. 'Thank you,' he said, getting to his feet. 'I'm sorry if I've been a nuisance.'

The man shook his hand quite warmly. 'I've seen worse. Good luck, lad. You'll be able to find your own way now.'

Tom followed the zigzag corridor out through Reception and hurried across the car park. Cold air, clammy from the sea, seeped through his thin football jacket. He ducked into the Morris and fitted the key into the ignition. Now what?

He had come up here on impulse, furious with his mother, burning to find evidence of her deception. He had been so sure of finding a definitive answer in this bizarre repository of documentation that looked like a First World War nursing home. Now he was even worse off than before. *Name of father* – blank! A thought suddenly occurred to him. Did Jordan Hope have any children? He couldn't remember. What would it be like to meet this man and say, 'Hello, I'm your son'? It was impossible to imagine. Tom dismissed the thought and started the car. At least he didn't need to spend another night in that grungy Bed and Breakfast.

He drove back into Southport and parked outside Mrs Pritchard's house. 'You might have given me a bit more notice,' she sniffed, wrapping her cardigan tight. Upstairs, Tom collected his few belongings and threw them into his rucksack: notebook, sweater, passport for identification purposes, toothbrush and other stuff he had hastily picked up at a chemist's. He looked at his watch. Eleven-thirty on – what was it today, Wednesday? He ought to be in mid-tutorial now, delivering his essay on Metternich. Oxford seemed like another universe. He wasn't ready to go back.

Tom zipped up his bag, slung it over one shoulder and slammed the door shut on his dismal room with a suddenly lifting heart. He knew what he would do. He would go to Rebecca after all – beautiful, calm Rebecca. He needn't tell her anything; he would just drop in for some tender loving care. Tom studied the road map. Sussex University was just outside Brighton, at least three

hundred miles away. He found his way on to the motorway and headed south, holding Rebecca in his mind like
the holy grail, remembering the warm September evening
when they had met.

There was a pub in Hampstead which had become a
hang-out for kids from the local schools. Every Friday
night in the summer months the broad pavement outside
would be thronged with groups of hair-tossing girls and
lounging boys. Tom had outgrown the scene, but shortly
after his return from Europe his sister Cassie had wheedled him into taking her and two girlfriends. As soon as
he had bought them drinks – this was his key function,
since they were under age – they had dumped him without ceremony, and he had found himself propping up the
pub wall, observing the ritual of teenage flirtation with a
superior eye. He had noticed Rebecca almost at once,
a tall girl with dark, waving hair, wearing white jeans
and a man's chalk-striped waistcoat with nothing underneath. Slim almost to the point of boniness, she had a
quality of stillness that was both intriguing and intimidating. It had taken him half an hour to manoeuvre his way
casually to her side and deliver his suave chat-up line:
'Hello, aren't you at Camden School?' She had looked
back at him with amused grey eyes and replied drily,
'South Hampstead, actually, and I left a year ago. But nice
try.'

Tom had bought her a drink, then persuaded her to
have a hamburger with him. While they sat outside, sharing a plate of french fries, Tom had learned that she
was in her second year at Sussex, studying Biology. She
wanted to be a geneticist. Her air of self-possession was
explained by the fact that her parents were divorced, and
she and her younger brother lived with their father, a
political journalist of great brilliance and zero domestic
skills. Rebecca had come home from school more than
once to find the fridge empty, or the gas cut off for non-
payment of bills. In her year out between A levels and

university, she had worked at a health centre in northern Kenya. She played the viola, and adored Guns n' Roses.

Tom went home that night, thinking he might be in love. The next day he cruised round Rebecca's neighbourhood in the open-topped Morris, nearly running out of petrol before he spotted her and casually offered her a lift. She wasn't deceived, but she liked the attention. In fact, it seemed that she liked him. Over the next few weeks they went to open-air concerts on the Heath, wandered round Camden Market, listened to bands at the Town and Country Club. Just before Rebecca went off to Sussex, they had borrowed her mother's remote Welsh cottage for a long weekend, walking miles over the heather-topped hills by day and making love in front of the fire by night. Tom had planned to invite her up to Oxford once he felt secure enough to show her round. He had fantasised about holding a party in some grand, panelled room, where he would introduce her to the sophisticated Oxford life. Now all he wanted to do was see her and breathe in her calm air of sanity.

The drive seemed interminable. His car had not been built for modern motorways. At anything over fifty-five miles an hour it swayed alarmingly, buffeted by overtaking lorries. Tom had to stop regularly to top it up with water and oil and give it a breather. He grew sick of the sight and smell of motorway cafés. At the ring road around London he got caught in commuter traffic, which advanced in ten-yard bursts. It was nearly nine o'clock by the time he turned on to the Sussex campus. Stained concrete buildings gleamed depressingly in the harsh flare of blobby lamps. The ornamental ponds were empty, apart from a sludge of dead leaves. It was hard to believe that this had been the brave-new-world university of the 1960s and, according to Rebecca's dad, a hotbed of revolution.

Tom drove on until he found a couple of students who gave him directions to Rebecca's hall of residence. At long last he stopped the car. His eyes felt gritty, his skin stiff. Too tired to get out, he bowed his head on to the steering wheel and whispered, 'Rebecca.' It was like a prayer.

When he found her room, the door was locked. Tom rattled it savagely. How could she be out? What could she be doing? He slid his back down the wall and slumped furiously outside her door. He would simply wait – all night if need be – until she returned from whatever irresistible student entertainment might be detaining her. He must have fallen asleep, for the next thing he knew Rebecca was standing over him, eyes shining with delight.

'Tom! Why didn't you tell me you were coming?'

Tom peered blearily up at her. 'Where have you been?'

'In the library,' she said, with a provocative lift of her eyebrows, 'having an unbelievably wild time with the reproductive system of invertebrates.' She unlocked her door and pushed it open, then reached down a hand to pull Tom up. She wrapped her arms around him. 'It's wonderful to see you. I can't believe it.'

Tom staggered out of her embrace and collapsed into the only comfortable chair in the room with a monumental sigh. He knew he was behaving boorishly, but something about Rebecca's very cheerfulness irritated him. She obviously had no idea what he had been going through. He pressed a hand to his forehead. 'Have you got any coffee?'

Rebecca's smile faltered. 'Of course.' She switched on the kettle and started laying out mugs and spoons in her precise way. Tom watched the curve of her back and the swell of her hips under tight jeans as she bent down to reach into a cupboard.

'Oh, come here,' he said impatiently. 'Stop fiddling about and give me a kiss.'

She turned at once and folded herself into his lap. Her lips were warm and soft. Tom gripped her hard, thrusting

251

his tongue deep into her mouth. He could feel her surprise at his roughness, but tightened his hold, desperate to crush all his worries under an avalanche of pure sensation.

He broke off abruptly. 'Let's go to bed,' he said.

Rebecca pulled away with an incredulous look. 'What?'

'Let's go to bed,' he repeated. 'You haven't gone off me already, have you?'

Rebecca stood up, her face flushing. 'Of course I haven't. But, Tom – you arrive here without any warning, like a bear with a sore head, and after one second expect us to make love. What's going on?'

'I don't want to talk about it.' He grabbed at her. 'Let's just go to bed.'

Rebecca stepped out of reach. 'No,' she insisted. 'Not while I get the feeling you want to just . . . fuck something. Someone. Anyone. Besides, I haven't – I'm not fixed up.'

Tom's whole body cramped with exasperation. 'That's bloody brilliant, that is. Why not?'

'Because,' Rebecca enunciated carefully, 'I didn't know you were coming and I hadn't planned on sleeping with anyone else.'

Tom couldn't believe how unsympathetic she was being. 'Come on, Becca, it won't matter just this once. I'll be careful.'

'Tom,' Rebecca protested, half laughing, 'you sound like a contraception ad. Of course it might matter "just this once".'

Tom glowered at her, then jumped furiously to his feet. 'Right. I might as well be off, then.'

'Don't be silly.' Rebecca reached out to stroke his arm. 'I'd like you to stay. Tell me what's wrong. I can't help if I don't know.'

Tom stood his ground, unyielding. Rebecca eyed him thoughtfully.

'This isn't anything to do with your mother, is it? She

252

phoned me this week – to see how I was getting on, she said. She asked if I'd seen you. I thought it was a bit odd.'

Tom felt as if he had been plunged into a well of icy water. His mother and Rebecca – *his* girlfriend – colluding behind his back, discussing him, tut-tutting as if he were a child. He felt utterly betrayed.

Throwing off Rebecca's arm, he stalked to the door and yanked it open, then turned to look into her shocked eyes, wanting to hurt her.

'Well, you have seen me now,' he said coldly. 'You'll be able to make a full report.'

Tom bounced the car over the campus traffic bumps and revved on to the main road towards Brighton. He needed a drink. Several drinks. Brighton was supposed to be a ravey town. Flooded with a pure, cold energy, he flung the car around bends, king of the road. As he neared an intersection he felt tempted to drive straight across and take his chances. At the last minute he braked. It was just as well. A huge lorry thundered by. Its headlights lit up a sign pointing back in the direction Tom had come: *Gatwick Airport, 23 miles.*

Tom drove around Brighton until he found somewhere he liked the look of, a glowing timbered pub tucked among the back lanes. It turned out to be disappointingly quiet. The few men clumped around their pints looked up when he came in as if he were a novelty. Tom took his drink and a fistful of crisp packets to a corner seat. He was starving. At the next table an elderly man dressed like a racing tout in tweed jacket and flamboyant cravat said good evening. Tom nodded back politely, his thoughts elsewhere.

A plan was forming in his mind. It had first occurred to him days ago, but only as a fantasy. Now it was taking concrete shape. The name he had seen this morning on his birth certificate had opened up an entirely new possibility. He drank his pint quickly and bought another one, the alcohol making him bold. Ought he to let anyone know what he was doing? No, why should he? No one ever told him anything. Let them worry. He sat there, wholly absorbed, until the landlord's noisy stacking of chairs and dimming of lights indicated that it was closing time. Tom went out into the street and fumbled at the car door, trying to get the key in the lock.

At his elbow a soft voice said, 'You're a nice-looking boy. Want to come back to my flat for a bit of fun?'

It was the man from the pub, smiling in an ingratiating way which made Tom's flesh creep. Tom backed against the car. His horrified reaction must have been plain, for the man's face tightened with spitefulness.

'Just came in for a little thrill, did you, dear? See how the other half lives?' His eyes lingered on Tom, eloquent with longing and disappointment. Tom was uneasily reminded of Rebecca.

'Suit yourself.' The man shrugged. He flounced away down the hill, cravat fluttering.

Tom leapt into his car and flipped up the catch to lock the door. His heart was thudding. Right, that was it. He was getting out of here. Everything he had tried to do had gone wrong. Rebecca had let him down. His mother had lied to him. He would be thrown out of Oxford for missing tutorials. His father – Tom could hardly bear it – might not even be his father. There was no one left. Except, maybe, a complete stranger who was running for President of the United States.

Tom negotiated his way out of the town, following the signs to Gatwick Airport. For weeks Virgin Atlantic had been advertising standby tickets to America for only ninety-nine pounds. What had he got to lose?

24

Spirit in the sky

Jordan bounded up the aeroplane steps. At the top he turned to face the crowd from Billings, Montana, who had followed him out to the airport. Straining hands, grinning mouths, a ripple of red, white and blue: it was a routine sight that stirred his soul every time. A few steps below him the new Secret Service man froze into position, scanning the crowd through dark glasses, an attaché case clutched to his chest. Jordan raised a hand to his supporters, extending five fingers in a now-familiar mime. 'Five more days!' they chanted back joyously. A fusillade of camera shutters erupted from the tarmac below. Jordan held his pose for a count of ten, then ducked into the plane.

Immediately he pulled off his jacket and tie, and started unbuttoning his shirt. It was soaked with sweat. Someone handed him a new one. 'Way to go, boy,' bawled Shelby, saluting him with a can of beer. Others called out their congratulations as Jordan passed down the aisle, though they were careful not to touch him. Wherever he went strangers fought to shake Jordan's hand, clap him on the back, pat his arms, his shoulders, even his head. These days his body looked as though he had gone five rounds with a champion boxer.

Bare-chested, Jordan made his way towards the one person whose opinion really counted. He stood over her as he thrust his arms into his shirt. The starched sleeves made a noise like ripping paper.

'Go OK?' he asked huskily.

'You know it did.' His wife smiled up reassuringly. 'You were incredible – *are* incredible. Stop worrying.'

'But the polls – '

'The people will decide, not the polls,' Ginny interrupted firmly. 'Sit down and save your voice.' She laid her head back against the seat and closed her eyes.

Jordan watched her for a moment, wanting more, then obeyed. On his wide armrest was a scatter of personal items: bottles, papers, a paperback thriller, a couple of cigars. Jordan unscrewed the lid from a brown bottle and took a gulp, then washed the sticky medicine down with some Ozark Mountain Spring Water. He could feel the pressure in his ears as he swallowed. Soon he would be back in the sky, cocooned in that strange no man's land above the clouds where he now seemed to spend half his life. Rapid City was next, then Cheyenne, then on to tonight's rally in Denver. Tomorrow he would criss-cross the corn states on his way to another huge rally in Chicago. His mind shied away from the other, more intimate meeting that awaited him there – if he chose to go.

One of the girls brought him a folder of the latest clippings. Jordan put on his reading glasses, skimming the passages marked with yellow highlighter. But his mind wouldn't focus. The engines roared, preparing for take-off. Jordan raised the window shutter and peered out. The media pack that followed them everywhere, cameras and pencils poised to record the tiniest lapse, were still straggling aboard their separate plane. A litter of discarded 'Hope' banners gusted across the runway. Jordan prayed that it wasn't an omen.

He didn't feel himself: that was the truth. The last couple of nights he had woken, dry-mouthed and disoriented, from wild, piercing dreams. He felt jittery and distracted. He had started to suffer lapses of concentration. Take yesterday. They had touched down in Idaho for an informal lunchtime meeting with a farmers' group. Hot dog in hand, Jordan had worked the crowd, shaking hands, signing autographs, kissing babies, patting dogs, listening to problems, promising to fix them. One of his aides discreetly handed him a napkin to wipe a blob of ketchup from his chin. Jordan signed it.

They all laughed about it afterwards, but it was one more thing that made Jordan feel out of control. This morning he had blanked out in the middle of a simple answer about beef imports. It was only for a few seconds, but it shook him, particularly now he understood the reason. *He had been looking for his son.*

Ever since Annie's shattering phone call Jordan had been obsessed by the thought of his unknown son. He found himself scanning the crowd for a face he might recognise – a face like his own. Every time he stepped on to a stage the subconscious thought was there, that he was performing not just for this particular audience in this particular city, but for his son – a young man who might be proud of his father.

It was a perverse fantasy. Jordan didn't need an adviser to tell him that the emergence of an illegitimate child would kill his chances of the presidency stone dead. 'Hope is a four-letter word.' That was one of his opponents' catchier slogans in what the media had labelled the dirtiest election campaign in America's history. His own guys didn't exactly wear kid gloves, but at least they tried to stick to the issues. The Republicans, on the other hand, had scoured the waterfront for every scuzzy rumour. They had already done their best to portray Oxford as a foul sink of un-American activities, crawling with commies and acid-heads. Throw in sex, a foreign mystery woman and a long-lost love child, and they would think they had died and gone to heaven.

It must not happen. Unconsciously Jordan balled one hand into a fist. He would not – could not – allow the American people to suffer another four years of that corrupt, self-satisfied regime. He wanted to change things, to make them better. It was his God-given mission.

Jordan had learned a lot of things, profound and trivial, since deciding to run. He had learned that the Secret Service men's briefcases weren't briefcases, but bulletproof shields; that to survive the campaign trail you needed an iron stomach and a bladder like a steel-trap; that after exhaustion came an energy so exhilarating it was addictive. He had learned not to look at his opponents during television debates, but to woo the camera. He had learned that a small meeting in a local diner could have more impact than the glitziest, ritziest rally, and that audiences liked soundbites better than policy. He had learned that he was his own best asset, and the more he gave of himself the more people liked him. Conversely, he had learned that his biggest liability was his wife.

Jordan looked over at Ginny, asleep, hair falling across her calm, wide brow. He kind of liked her blonde. It made her look sexier, though he would never dare tell her so. He had never seen her so angry as when Rick suggested she needed a new image. Jackie Kennedy was right when she said 'First Lady' sounded like a saddle horse, she shouted. She was damned if she was going to get all prinked up like an exhibit in the Easter Parade. But in the end she had – and for one reason. Because she loved Jordan and believed in him.

He sure wouldn't be here without her. There wasn't a single issue they hadn't debated or a plan of campaign they hadn't discussed. She was an ever-present reminder of the ideals they had cherished back in the days when 'liberal' and 'radical' weren't dirty words. She told him when he hit a false note and pulled him up when he started believing his own publicity. 'Man smart, woman smarter', as the old blues song went. This was the quality that had attracted him to her all those years ago. It had never been sex. For that he had gone elsewhere.

He had met her in his first year at grad school: Ms Virginia 'no cracks please' Lake, valedictorian and *summa cum laude* from Smith. Mousy in a cute kind of a way, she was outspoken, indecently bright, a mover and shaker with a smile that could light up Boston Harbor. Jordan had liked her at once, but that was it. Oxford had thrown him off balance. Harvard marked a new beginning. Jordan's game plan was to study hard and extend his political connections on the East Coast. Romance was not on his agenda.

But Ginny kept popping up – on student committees, in Law School debates, in the library. During the summer of 1972 Jordan found himself working with her on the McGovern campaign. Late one night after too many beers he had revealed the full extent of his political ambitions. Ginny hadn't laughed. The following winter she surprised Jordan by inviting him for Christmas in Minnesota with her folks. Jordan had told everyone that he was too broke to make the trip home that year, though that wasn't the whole story.

The fact was, home had never been the same since his mother had remarried. Sy-boy Carson had worn her down at last. Jordan never knew whether he would find his stepfather drunkenly abusive, drunkenly charming or just plain absent, off on one of the 'business trips' from which he invariably returned penniless and remorseful. Jordan had tried not to blame his mother. She must have been lonely. Sy-boy took her out dancing, to restaurants and the racetrack. Maybe she thought she could 'save' him. If she regretted her decision, she never admitted it to Jordan. But there were no more late-night talks, no more bursting into each other's bedrooms to brandish the latest headline. That special communion between mother and son was broken.

Ginny's parents lived on the outskirts of Minneapolis-St Paul in a large neo-colonial home picturesquely dusted with snow. Her family was as large and supportive as Jordan's seemed small and beleaguered. Sixteen people sat down to Christmas lunch, ranging from Ginny's grand-parents to a rabble of small nephews and nieces. The Lakes were welcoming, argumentative, noisy and obviously devoted to one another. In their company Ginny relaxed into girlishness. Jordan achieved hero status after fixing a broken toy train for the children. He dried dishes while arguing with Ginny's mother over Nixon's intentions in Vietnam. Ginny's kid brother taught him to play chess. Quite suddenly a new vista opened to Jordan of a life of hard work and political commitment, shared with a like-minded partner and anchored in a secure, loving home. The following summer he and Ginny were married.

At first, everything worked out better than he had dared to hope. After graduation, he and Ginny kept leap-frogging each other with better and better jobs. When Jordan said he wanted to try for Governor of Missouri, Ginny supported him, even though it meant passing up a job offer in Washington. Everyone said Jordan was too young, too brash, too inexperienced for Governor. He won anyway. That autumn they moved into the Governor's mansion in Jefferson City. It was an occasion that still glowed in his memory. He would never be so purely happy again.

It was a gorgeous fall day. Maples and dogwood flamed in the front yard. Ginny supervised the move with her customary efficiency. He could picture her now standing on the colonnaded porch in her lumber-jacket, brown hair scragged into a ponytail, glasses slipping down her nose as she consulted a clip-board. She kept yelling at Jordan to stop distracting the movers. 'The campaign's over. You won. Remember?' In the evening friends dropped by for beer and chilli-dogs and a tour of the house. Spilling over with excitement, Jordan and Ginny shared their vision of a new kind of political life. As well as introducing reform programmes, they planned to revolutionise the usual Governor's lifestyle of stiff, hierarchical functions with barbecues and Little League games and swings on the lawn. Jordan unearthed the stereo and played all eight albums of *Motown Chartbusters*, turning the evening into an impromptu party. Everyone felt the same. The dream was happening. A new generation was on its way to creating a new society.

After their friends had gone home, Jordan and Ginny stayed up. This day had a special, private meaning for them. Alone, they walked hand in hand through their new home, allocating rooms: the den here, a study for Ginny there, and at the top bedrooms for the family they now planned to have. At least two children, thought Ginny. Four, Jordan insisted, thinking of his solitary childhood, dreaming of all the things he would do and be as a father. He had steered her towards the bedroom, eager to begin right away. He could still remember the way their laughter had echoed round the huge, half-furnished house as they invented ever more outlandish names for their children.

But of course there had been no children.

Ginny suddenly opened her eyes, as if sensitive to Jordan's thoughts even in her sleep, and caught his wistful look. She reached for him across the aisle. 'Something the matter?'

He took her hand and stroked his thumb across her fingers, feeling the hard metal of her wedding ring. 'You look tired,' was all he said.

Ginny goggled at him. 'No kidding. I've heard the earth is round, too.'

Jordan laughed. 'Dumb comment,' he agreed. 'I was just thinking of this tour of yours. Will you be all right by yourself? It's a hell of a schedule.'

It had been decided that Ginny would split off at Denver for another mini-campaign of her own, something she had done more and more in the run-up to the election. Ginny pulled her hand free.

'Of course I'll be all right.'

'It isn't the way I wanted things to be,' Jordan persisted. 'We're a team, you and me. But the guys thought it was better for you to, you know – '

' – stay in the background looking pretty? Keep a low profile on my own little circuit of schools and mothers' groups and welfare clinics? We've been over this, Jordan.'

'It will be different in the White House, I promise – if I make it.'

'Yeah,' Ginny smiled wearily.

The plane was bustling. There were people perched on the edge of seats and draped over the backs – talking, arguing, laughing. Jordan hated not knowing what was going on. He got up and pushed past the coat rack that offered him and Ginny some measure of privacy at the back of the plane. On the other side of it the Service boys were playing poker. Some nights, when Jordan was too wired up to sleep, he'd invite them up to his hotel suite for a few rounds of hearts – better for his image than poker. Individually they were good guys, but as a breed they made him nervous. Their muscle-bound physiques and tick-tock eyes reminded him of Arnold Schwarzenegger – and everyone knew where *he* stood politically.

Every day the plane got more cluttered. Miniature Stars and Stripes hung above the seats along each side. In between them, taped to the luggage lockers, were signed celebrity photographs, favourite cartoons, good-luck cards from Secret Service men who'd completed their duty tours, campaign slogans, random memorabilia. Every spare inch of floor space was covered with cardboard boxes crammed with campaign buttons, banners, posters, pennants, photographs. Sometimes Jordan got off a plane and wondered: who is this guy Hope? He would look at his own name repeated a hundredfold, a thousandfold, and it wasn't a word he even recognised.

Jordan felt a hand on his elbow. It was one of his speech-writers, wanting him to approve a couple of new paragraphs he'd added to the Denver speech, rebutting the latest attack on Jordan's defence policy. Jordan skimmed the material. Suddenly his eyebrows snapped together. He hit the paper with the back of his hand.

'What's this war record crap?' he growled. 'Did you clear that with Rick?'

'Actually, no. It just sort of came to me.'

'Well, take it the fuck out!' Jordan exploded. 'Don't you read the goddamn signs around here?' He put his hand on the speech-writer's head and forced it round to face the slogan that read, 'A Clean Fight!' 'That's what it says, and that's what it means.' Jordan tossed the speech into the man's lap. 'The rest is OK.' He patted his shoulder. 'Thanks.'

The first galley doubled as a kind of technical control centre. Dozens of mobile phones, each with a name tag, hung from a makeshift peg-board. There was a printer, a fax machine that doubled as a photocopier, some spare lap-tops. Two guys were fiddling with tape machines. Jordan got a sudden blast of an old Fleetwood Mac song that he used to like.

'This for tonight?'

'No, sir. Denver's done. This is for Chicago.'

Chicago. It was racing towards him full tilt, and he still didn't know what to do. His mouth felt dry with anxiety. Collecting his notes on Rapid City, Jordan headed for the next galley to get himself a ginger ale. He found Bonnie there, among the piles of cardboard lunchboxes and crates of soft drinks, munching a cupcake. She eyed him critically.

'Uh-oh. Emergency repair time. What exactly is it you do to your hair?'

'I don't know,' Jordan grinned, automatically ruffling it up from the back.

'We're landing in fifteen minutes.' Calmly she brushed the crumbs from her fingers. 'How about we make it look like you travelled *inside* the plane.'

Bonnie was one of the assistants in charge of Jordan's personal appearance, and his favourite. Short and plump, with a smile like Bugs Bunny, she had magic hands and a fund of lurid stories about her extended Italian-American family. She settled Jordan down on a stool and wedged a mirror into position – a makeshift arrangement they had perfected. She started massaging Jordan's neck and shoulders. He shuffled the pages of his notes, but found his thoughts drifting back to Ginny.

It had taken them three years of trying before Jordan had agreed to visit a fertility specialist. He dreaded the possibility that the fault might lie with him. In fact it was Ginny who could not conceive normally. They had tried temperature charts, fertility drugs, surgery, even a faith healer. Nothing had worked. Eventually Jordan was prepared to settle for adoption. Ginny refused. She said it must be God's will.

Jordan had reacted badly. Cheated out of the dream of fatherhood which he had nursed since childhood, he blamed Ginny for the cruellest disappointment of his life. The realisation that they were not to be part of a family, just two striving individuals yoked together, sent him a little crazy. The future seemed empty. Recklessly Jordan set out to fill the void. Without consulting Ginny he started gambling their money on speculative business schemes. He became obsessed by sex and started affairs with a string of women, the dumber the better. He didn't even feel guilty. Ginny complained, threatened, cried. Jordan heard, but he wouldn't listen.

One day, quietly, over the lamb chops, Ginny told him she wanted a divorce. She had packed her bags for a visit with her parents. Jordan had two weeks to clean up his act; otherwise she was leaving him for good. Jordan had raged through the empty house, knowing he didn't really have a choice. He visualised gossip and scandal spreading like a stain across his record. Deep down, it hurt him that he had lost Ginny's good opinion.

That all seemed a long time ago now. It had been a slow road back to a new kind of partnership, but the dream of the presidency had brought them together and driven them on. They had worked together like one perfectly oiled machine until the nomination – at which point Jordan's 'two for the price of one' slogan had backfired disastrously. Ginny wasn't cute. She wasn't a beauty. She wasn't a housewife or a mother. Middle America didn't know what to make of her, but feared that it was she who might be wearing the pants in the White House. Hence the softening of Ginny's image, the separate tours, the insistence that Jordan mention her as little as possible. The situation made him squirm. It was as if he had an unmentionable social disease. He longed to find a means of making people understand her quality without alienating them. He wished he could explain just why she wasn't a mother. But Ginny wouldn't let him.

It was one of the few secrets they had kept from the American people. Not even Rick or Shelby knew for sure. Let them call me pushy and tough, Ginny had insisted. Let them say I'm too selfish to have a baby, or too feminist. Just let me keep my dignity. And what if it became known that Jordan had fathered a son by someone else? What would that do to her dignity?

Annie and Ginny: they were so different, one exotic and unexplored, the other domestic and familiar. Whenever he pictured Annie it was out of doors, against trees and grass and soft summer skies. Ginny belonged in a room – at a podium or a conference table, managing things.

'Tell me I'm a genius.' Bonnie slapped down her comb and peered over Jordan's shoulder at his reflection. 'You sit down looking like a cockatoo, and you leave looking like Richard Gere.'

For a wild moment Jordan wondered if Bonnie could help get him into Annie's hotel. Everyone said she had a crush on him. He met her guileless gaze in the mirror and felt ashamed. He stood up and gave her a sudden hug.

'Thanks, kiddo. You're a doll.'

Head bent, Bonnie helped him into his jacket and whisked him furiously with a clothes brush.

Jordan made his way back to his seat. That dumb song was still buzzing in his head. *Yesterday's gone, yesterday's gone ... Can't stop thinking about tomorrow.* He could feel the plane bank as it began its descent towards Rapid City. Another crowd, another speech, another milestone towards the magic 270 – the number of electoral votes he needed to win. His skin prickled with anticipation. He could almost feel the hot blaze of lights, see the clouds of campaign balloons, hear the screams and brassy oompah-pah renditions of 'Happy Days are Here Again'. Out of the corner of his eye he saw swift hands gathering up the poker cards and felt as if a lightbulb had been switched on in his head. Suddenly he knew exactly how he could sneak out to meet Annie.

It would be madness to risk being caught in a hotel room with a strange woman. He had everything to lose – his wife, his career, his future. But reason melted to nothing in the heat of his desire to see Annie again, and to find out about his son. After all those barren years – *a son*. Jordan's heart speeded. He knew he had to go.

25

In the midnight hour

After four rings the answer machine kicked in with its terse announcement. *Rose Cassidy. Leave me a message.* Tom put down the receiver and looked about him in rising desperation. Gum wrappers, cigarette butts and old bus tickets littered the floor. A drunk lay passed out on one of the benches. The telephone booths were sprayed with graffiti. A man in a hooded tracksuit patrolled one end of the waiting area, quartering his territory with precise, ritualistic steps, talking to himself and snapping his fingers. This was New York's Port Authority bus terminal. Tom didn't like it one bit.

Outside didn't look much better, the streets dark and ominously empty. This menacing, midnight city was not the New York Tom remembered. Two years ago, at May half-term, his mother had brought him on one of her business trips. They had stayed in a suite with a mini-bar and a television *each*. Tom remembered how he used to get up late, and order pancakes or Eggs Benedict from room service. During the day, while his mother went to meetings, he wandered around the Village and hung out in Washington Square Park, watching the roller-skaters.

That's where he had met some students from NYU, who had told him to check out the range of music at Tower Records. One incredible evening at sunset he had taken an elevator ride to the top of the Empire State Building. At night his mother took him to movies, and to restaurants that served enormous steaks and amazing ice-cream. Afterwards, while his mother slept or worked next door, he sprawled on his king-size bed, blissfully channel-surfing.

It was different being alone. First of all, he had landed at a strange airport called Newark, which turned out to be in New Jersey. The immigration officer was huge and unfriendly.

'Business or pleasure?' he had asked curtly, scrutinising Tom's still-valid visa.

When Tom, with a weak grin, said he wasn't quite sure, the officer had expanded his massive chest and growled, 'Which is it to be, Mac?'

The bus had taken him through unfamiliar territory, into a long tunnel and out again along a desolate highway. Tom had pressed his forehead against the dirty windows, desperate to recognise a landmark in this alien wasteland, seeing only the reflection of his own anxious face. The biggest disaster of all was finding that Rose wasn't at home. She was crucial to his plans. He had always known that she would be surprised to see him – in fact, he had felt unexpectedly awkward just dialling her number. But it had never occurred to him that she wouldn't be there when he wanted her.

Tom looked at the big clock on the wall. It was one in the morning. Perhaps Rose had gone to bed, and switched on her machine so that she wouldn't be disturbed. The more Tom thought about it, the more likely this explanation seemed. If he turned up at her apartment she might be rather cross, but that was preferable to walking the streets all night. He couldn't afford a hotel. In the long hours he had spent at Gatwick waiting for his standby ticket Tom had changed all his remaining pounds into dollars — fifty dollars to be precise. It had seemed a princely sum; but nearly ten had gone already on the bus fare and phone calls. He would have to be careful with the rest.

Not liking the look of anyone inside the terminal, Tom went back out to where the buses were parked and asked a driver how to get to Central Park West. Amazingly, he was already on the right street, except it was called Eighth Avenue here. He learned that about twenty blocks north it would turn into Central Park West. The bus driver told him to take a bus or the subway, but twenty blocks didn't sound too bad. Tom went back through the terminal and out into the street, standing for a moment in the brisk cross-town wind while he got his bearings. From the shadows he heard a low, aggressive voice.

'Hey, you buying, man?'

'Sorry?' Automatically Tom moved towards the voice. A tall figure stepped from a doorway tossing something casually in his hand. Tom could see a big, bulbous hat and eyes glittering above a scarf wound tight. The thing in his hand was a tiny plastic bag. Christ, a drug dealer!

'No thanks,' Tom said politely, backing off. He turned up his palms and added cunningly, 'No money, I'm afraid.'

The man let out a derisive giggle and turned back to the doorway. Two more men lurched into the street light, punching each other with exaggerated hilarity. 'Neo money I'm afride,' they mimicked to each other. The three of them moved towards Tom in a jostling, menacing group. Tom turned and ran. He could hear them shouting, but they didn't bother to chase him. Too stoned, probably.

Tom walked purposefully north, giving a wide berth to the figures who scrabbled in trash cans or swayed at street corners. Gradually the neighbourhood improved, though the blocks were much longer than he remembered. Taxis bounced past, but Tom refused even to turn his head to check if their roof lights were on. He was determined to make it alone. At length the glittering black canyon opened out into the southern end of Central Park. There were still a couple of carriages waiting for lovers or insomniac tourists. The horses slept between the shafts, each with one back hoof cocked restfully. Tom was daunted to see that the numbers on the buildings started again at one. How much further could it be?

He was waiting for the lights to turn at the next cross-street when he saw a woman in shorts and a singlet jogging towards him. Perhaps she would know. He stepped forward to intercept her with a polite 'Excuse me.'

'Outta my way, creep!' she yelled, putting a hand to her waist. 'I've got a knife.'

Tom leapt out of her path, his heart hammering. The woman ran on, skinny arms pumping, ponytail swinging.

Tom began to hug the buildings, hurrying from one pool of light to the next, aware of figures across the street skulking in and out of the park. Finally, on the corner of 72nd Street he reached number 120. It was an extraordinary building, like a giant's castle out of Grimms' fairytales. There were iron railings outside, decorated with gods and dragons, and a guard in the sentry-box.

'May I help you, sir?'

'I'm looking for Rose Cassidy.'

'Out of town.'

'Are you sure?'

'One hundred and ten per cent.'

'Do you know when she's coming back?'

'It's against house rules to say. She expecting you?'

Tom explained who he was. He tried to imply that Rose would be thrilled to see him, and shocked to hear that he had been turned away from her door.

'I've known her all my life. I'm sure she wouldn't mind if I slept on her floor – just for one night,' he pleaded.

The doorman's eyebrows beetled down to nose level. 'You English?'

'Yes, as a matter of fact.'

'How about that?' The man's face cleared. 'My wife's crazy about *Upstairs, Downstairs*. Watches all the re-runs. Drives me nuts telling me about Sir James this and Lady that. I say to her, Edna: don't bother me with that stuff.' He shrugged. 'Women.'

Tom nodded politely.

'I'm sorry, son, but I can't let you into Miss Cassidy's apartment without her say-so. Why don't you just check into a hotel?' His eyes skimmed Tom's jeans and football jacket. 'Or a hostel. I think there's one a few blocks away. Wait here and I'll check.'

Armed with an address and a sketch map, Tom trudged back the way he had come. He must have walked over forty blocks now. His feet were stinging. When he reached the cross-street where the hostel was supposed to be, he turned into it cautiously. This was where he had met the jogger. He had gone only a few steps when he saw a figure straightening from a crouch. Tom froze. Then he saw that it was an elegantly dressed man with a poodle on a leash, who had been bending down to scrape its steaming droppings into a plastic bag. The two of them minced past Tom. The poodle's hair had been clipped into pom-poms around each paw and at the tip of its tail. The man swung his little trophy bag like an Elizabethan courtier with his pomander. Suddenly Tom wanted to laugh. This was a seriously weird town.

The hostel was a brownstone, guarded by a taciturn Pole with more creases in his face than W. H. Auden. The price of the cheapest room, sharing with five others, was nineteen dollars, and Tom had to pay another nineteen dollars for a youth hostel card. They didn't take credit cards. Tom counted the bills on to the desk, one by one, as fatalistic as a gambler placing his last stake in the pot. He now had precisely four dollars and fifty cents left.

271

The man unlocked a cupboard and wordlessly piled two blankets and a towel into Tom's arms. He escorted him up the stairs and swung open a door. The light from the corridor showed a dormitory-style room with six beds, the bedclothes humped over five of them. There were backpacks spilt open on the floor, and a strong smell of socks.

'Swedes.' The man jerked a thumb. 'From Sweden.'

Tom crept to his bed among the sleeping strangers. He stripped to his underwear in the dark and slid under the covers. After a few seconds he jumped out again, retrieved his wallet from his jeans pocket and stowed it under the thin pillow. He lay tensely on the iron bedstead, his brain jumbled with questions. The night porter at Rose's building had given him a meaningful look at the last moment and told him to try again the next evening. Was that a hint? What if Rose didn't return? Would anyone accept his British credit card? Did they serve breakfast in this place? What was he doing here anyway?

With difficulty Tom brought his thoughts under control. It was really very simple. Problem one: he needed money. Problem two: he needed to find out where Jordan Hope was. Both could be solved with one visit to a newspaper office. The *New York Times* was supposed to be a decent rag. He didn't even need Rose.

One of the Swedes was snoring like a pig. Tom pulled up the blankets and held them over his ear. Gradually his muscles relaxed and his eyes closed. The man at Rose's apartment building had been quite nice in the end, he thought, stretching his feet down to a cool part of the sheet. Just before his mind finally drifted free, it snagged on one tiny, puzzling detail. What on earth, he wondered, was *Upstairs, Downstairs*?

26

Let it be

'Hope for President – President for hope.' Jordan's face was the first thing Annie saw at O'Hare airport, smiling out at her from an election poster ten feet high. Coming closer, she saw that somebody had crossed out the 'h's and substituted 'd's. Exhausted as she was, she couldn't help smiling. The kerfuffle about whether Jordan had, or had not, smoked pot at Oxford was absurd – as if every institution on both sides of the Atlantic wasn't stuffed with respectable fortysomethings who had got high in their youth. Annie could have told anyone who asked that the stuff made him sick.

She took a taxi into Chicago, dazed by the headlights speeding round huge looping highways. Her body told her it was way past bedtime, but here it was only ten-thirty on a busy Friday night. The traffic thickened as they neared the heart of the city. Outside movie theatres and jazz clubs people stood in line on the sidewalks, loosing trickles of cloudy breath into the cold air. Everywhere she looked there were flags and banners and election posters.

'Have you decided who you're voting for?' Annie asked her cab driver.

He pressed his beefy shoulders against the seat and turned his head to shout through the grille. 'Listen, lady, you know what Jordan Hope did last time he was in Chicago? After his speeches and stuff he went out to the stadium to watch the Bears play. He was eating popcorn and cheering like one of the guys. So what if he's fooled around – who wouldn't with that uptight wife of his? Sure, he gets my vote.

'He's going to be in town tomorrow for some big shindig in the Hilton. That's right by your hotel. Look out your window, you might get to see his motorcade.'

'Really,' Annie said faintly. She subsided in her seat, feeling her stomach knot. Don't think about it, she told herself. First things first.

There were no messages at her hotel, which meant no news of Tom. It was the fifth day. Hiding her anxiety, Annie followed the bell-hop to her room. It was large and old-fashioned, with big windows looking across Grant Park to Lake Michigan. Annie thought of Jordan, sure that he too would remember this park as the scene of a notorious riot between police and anti-Vietnam protesters during another Democratic Convention, in 1968. On one of the side tables was a huge display of flowers, which she at first assumed was courtesy of the hotel. Then she saw the card. 'Welcome to Chicago – Lee Spago.'

He sounded like a nice man. They had spoken several times on the telephone to arrange Annie's visit. She had felt churlish resisting his repeated offers of invitations to stay at his home, but of course it was out of the question. Instead he was picking her up at the hospital at noon tomorrow and taking her to lunch. Annie was curious to see her mother's second choice of marriage partner. She imagined someone dashing and slightly shady. This was Al Capone's home town, after all.

After she had unpacked, Annie undressed and took a

long shower. She was so tired her legs trembled. The last few days she had worked feverishly in the office trying to clear her desk, then gone home and stayed up late, toiling over her own secret plans. It was a kind of therapy: she was too worried about Tom to sleep much anyway. Each night, when she finally crept into bed, her mind was like a boiling sea that took a long time to subside. Each morning, she would wake early and steal out to the bathroom to listen to the radio, counting the minutes until the news came on, waiting for a matter-of-fact voice to announce: 'Democratic candidate Jordan Hope's chances of the US Presidency look slim today, following rumours of an illegitimate son fathered when he was a Rhodes Scholar at Oxford. . . .' It hadn't happened yet. Meanwhile she tried to present a normal front to the girls, to whom she and Edward had decided to say nothing about Tom's disappearance. It was fortunate that there was no creature so self-absorbed as a teenage girl. Emma and Cassie remained as dreamy, unreasonable and casually charming as always.

Annie dried her skin and hair slowly, savouring her privacy, profligate with the thick hotel towels. Then she tied her robe around her waist and returned to the bedroom. She longed for sleep, but there was one more job to finish. At Heathrow she had managed to buy a cheap photo album of the sort used for holiday snaps. She tore off its plastic wrapping, then tipped the contents of a large brown envelope on to the bed. Photographs cascaded out: babies, birthday parties, holidays, her wedding – twenty years' worth of simple, domestic memories. It had been Edward's idea to raid the family albums and present Annie's mother with a record of their lives. At the time, safely in London, Annie had agreed that this would be a generous gesture. Now, as she began to sort the pictures, her good intentions faltered. She lingered over one photo of Tom as a beaming six-month-old, spherical and featureless as an egg, that made her want to laugh out loud with love. Instead, her face tightened as an old, resentful fury flamed through her. If she had followed her mother's advice, Tom would never have existed.

Annie slumped on the bed, and closed her eyes, wondering whether she had the courage to face her mother tomorrow. Was there anything to be said between them? For her part there was no way of forgetting a single detail of their last meeting, or of forgiving the careless cruelty of her mother's words: *You'll have to get yourself seen to* — as if she were a tomcat.

It had taken a long time for Annie to discover that she was pregnant. After the climactic events of what was to prove her last term at Oxford she was in an unsettled, reckless state. As planned, she had joined a group of friends who were backpacking across Europe. When the group had split up, Annie stayed on in the Greek islands, sleeping on beaches, waitressing in bars and tavernas. She put her loss of appetite down to the heat and a monotonous diet of kebabs. In early September she had returned to London, driven home by the relentless seasonal wind which was said to incite murder and madness. Aunt Betty had taken one look at her and insisted on a medical check-up. The doctor had asked her a few questions, given her a brief examination and pronounced her ten weeks pregnant. At first Annie had felt literally nothing, not even surprise. It was as if the world had dissolved under her feet. Wandering through the London streets, she remembered the television images of last summer's moon-walkers. She too felt like an eerie faceless blob drifting in slow motion through space. Then a horrible panic gripped her. Rose was still in America. Not knowing where else to turn, Annie had gone to her mother.

Her mother was in Kent, staying with a legendary family figure known as 'my friend Gloria', an old schoolmate who had married well. Annie had arrived at the rose-covered house on a blazing September afternoon. Gloria's daughter Camilla was to be married the next day, and the hall was full of wedding clutter. The talk was all of lace-edged pillowcases and buttonholes and reception lines. Skinny and sickly, still wearing the Greek sandals that wound halfway up her calves, Annie had felt like a ghost at the feast. While the others took tea on the terrace she managed to get her mother alone in the drawing-room. It was cool out of the sun. Annie remembered how she had shivered among the brocaded sofas and expensive knick-knacks while she waited for her mother to settle herself in an armchair.

There were no histrionics when Annie blurted out the bald, still unbelievable fact of her pregnancy. Her mother's face had simply closed down into its harsh, discontented lines. When at last she spoke, it was with a familiar, wounding undercurrent of sarcasm.

'Am I to assume that there is no young man prepared to make an honest woman of you?'

Annie thought of Jordan in his faraway American town; of Edward, whom she had treated so badly. She couldn't admit that she didn't even know which man was the father.

'No. I mean, yes, there's nobody I would want to ask.'

'Well, then, you'll just have to have yourself seen to. Believe me, Annie, I know what I'm talking about. You see,' she paused delicately, 'I was once in the same position.'

Her mother rose and walked over to the mantelpiece. She had started smoking again since Annie's father had died. Annie watched, mesmerised, as she picked a cigarette out of a silver box and clicked her lighter.

'I've never told you this before because your father insisted that I didn't, but I think the time has come. It might stop you making a stupid mistake that could ruin your life.'

Annie could hardly breathe. 'What?'

Her mother pulled hard on her cigarette, head tilted back, one arm along the mantelpiece, then released the smoke in a fretful burst. 'The truth is, darling, that when I married your father I was already pregnant.'

Through the open window Annie could hear wood-pigeons and the sound of workmen hammering in pegs for the marquee.

'With me?' she ventured.

'Of course with you. What do you take me for? I'll have you know that your father was the first man I ever went to bed with – and only then after we were engaged. Unfortunately, he scored a direct hit first time. Rather uncharacteristic, wouldn't you say?'

Annie just stared.

'In those days, one simply got married. There was no question of having an illegitimate baby. Abortion was a nasty backstreet affair. And of course,' she added, 'your father and I were in love.'

Annie sat on the sofa as still as a stone.

'Darling, you have no idea what it's like to have a baby. They may look rather sweet as they gurgle past in their prams, but when you have to look after them day in, day out, night after sleepless night, it's a very different affair. They don't even look you in the eye for weeks, just scream and shit and demand to be fed. The whole thing's so *boring*. I was already feeling ghastly at our wedding – though I didn't show,' she added proudly. 'The next thing I knew I was knee-deep in nappies. It wasn't the way to begin a marriage, and it certainly isn't the way for you to start your life.'

'Is that what you felt like, having me? Boredom? Disgust? Regret that you couldn't go out on the town every night?' Annie's voice trembled.

'It's only like that at the beginning. Don't be cross, darling. Of course it was more fun when you got older. One could dress you up and take you about. You were much prettier than most people's children, you know.'

278

'And then, as soon as you could, you sent me off to school.'

Her mother stubbed out her cigarette. 'Annie, I do find this holier-than-thou attitude rather tiresome. It doesn't suit you – especially in your present situation. It is not my idea of fun to have you turning up like this the day before Camilla's wedding. I'm sorry that you've got yourself into a pickle. But I'm telling you, you are not ready to be a mother.' She looked unselfconsciously into the mirror over the mantelpiece and smoothed back a sickle of blonde hair. 'And I am far too young to be a grandmother. Tell you what,' she spun round girlishly, 'I'll pay for the operation, and afterwards we'll go away somewhere nice for a couple of weeks. I could do with a little holiday.'

Annie stood up. 'I hate you!' she shouted, backing away. Tears spouted from her eyes. 'You must be the worst mother in the whole world.'

'Keep your voice down.' Her mother eyed the door. 'Think what you must. I'm only trying to help you.'

'Bullshit! The only person you've ever wanted to help is yourself. You couldn't even be bothered with Daddy. I think he *died* of disappointment. Don't worry, you needn't bother about me any more either.'

'Annie!'

Annie saw, with an ignoble thrill, that she had shaken her mother. Power surged through her.

'I never want to see you again. I hope you have a horrible, lonely life.'

'Wait! Where are you going?'

'Away. Anywhere.' Annie fumbled for the door handle. Tears spilled over her mouth and ran into her neck.

Her mother's angry hiss followed her into the hall. 'What shall I tell Gloria?'

Annie found herself shaking at the memory. She stood up abruptly and crossed her hotel room to the mini-bar. She pulled open the door and stared at the bottles.

Whisky – that's what she needed. Picking out a miniature, she wrestled off the cap and slopped some liquid into a glass; then drank the whole lot neat, her eyes watering. Her mother had been vile, unforgivable. It was no excuse that Annie had been born too soon for her liking – or born at all. Life dealt you the cards and you bloody well played them.

Annie poured the rest of the bottle into her glass, and this time topped it up with water and ice. She returned to the bed and sipped slowly, spreading the photographs across the bed. Here was Emma, dwarfed by her first school uniform; Cassie playing the innkeeper with a tea towel on her head in the Christmas play; Edward in a panama hat on the Spanish Steps. This was *her* family, *her* life. She owed none of it – not a single possession, not a second's thrill of achievement, not one jot of happiness – to her mother. Annie's mouth set in a harsh line. What Edward had intended as a gift might easily be twisted into a punishment.

Annie put down her glass and began to slot the pictures into the plastic envelopes, scribbling brief captions underneath. Yes, she thought vengefully, let the old horror see what she had missed. Her hands moved swiftly, mechanically, the way forward clear. She had almost finished when a recent photo of Tom, snapped in a mock-macho pose with his hair ruffled, caught her attention. She paused, then withdrew it from the album and popped it into the drawer of her bedside table. In a few minutes she had completed her task and laid out the album ready for tomorrow. At last she climbed between the stiff, clean sheets, switched off the light and fell instantly asleep.

27

Rescue me

In Times Square the giant Calvin Klein girl posed in her underpants above a swirl of people and cars. Steam rose from the subway shafts into the night sky. Horns blared. Music thumped. Neon signs in a dozen different colours winked and flashed and glittered on rain puddles. Then the lights changed, and the car sped up town between looming towers to Columbus Circle. Huddled below the statue of the great explorer slept one of New York's home-less, wrapped in what looked like sheets of bubble paper that flapped in the vicious wind. Couples in evening dress swept into the Circle from Lincoln Center, clutching their minks and cashmere coats about them, desperate for a cab.

Rose watched this familiar Friday night spectacle through the window of her car, and let out a deep sigh of happiness. If there was one thing even better than escaping the city, it was returning to its brutish charms. Though she was supposed to have stayed through the long weekend, twenty-four hours in the country had been enough for her, and she had caught a train home, pleading pressure of work. No one could question the lavishness of Blaine and Dexter's hospitality. Their position in New York's society was such that their invitation to see their refurbished mansion on the Hudson could absolutely not be ignored. But admiring curtain fabrics and chandeliers and imported French stoves was not Rose's idea of entertainment. At lunch she had been pinned to her seat by the trainer of their new steeplechaser, a bore of the first water. She never wanted to hear another word about blood lines or bone chips or linseed poultices. All that way out into the sticks, and all the way back to Penn Station: was it worth it, just so she could get first rights to publish the photographs of Blaine's baby, due on New Year's Day?

You bet. The Blaine–Dexter romance was a real-life soap opera, of which the American public showed no sign of tiring. Did Blaine get pregnant on purpose? Would Dexter marry her? Would she sign a pre-nuptial agreement? A gooey picture *à trois* on the front of *The Magazine* would boost sales by twenty thousand minimum.

Rose's car whispered to the kerb, precisely level with the entrance to her apartment block. The doorman hurried to open her door.

'Good trip, Miss Cassidy?'

'Fabulous. Can you get the bags out of the trunk?'

'Brad says a young man came asking for you last night.'

'How exciting. Who was it?'

'I don't know. He said he'd left you a phone message.'

Probably that photographer who kept bugging her, Rose thought, a pushy amateur who thought he was the new Herb Ritts. Any more harassment, and she would set the cops on him. She let the doorman bring her bags up in the elevator and deposit them in the hall of her apartment. Shutting the door behind him, she hung up her coat and slid off the phoney riding boots which had been slowly strangling her feet to death. If anyone needed a linseed poultice, it was her. There was a pile of mail waiting. Rose limped through to her study, shuffling the usual mix of bills and invitations. She zapped the 'play' button of her answer machine and stretched out on the couch with her letter-opener to hand.

Beep, click.

Hi, this is Cindy. I thought you'd like to know that some great new pictures of Ginny Hope just came in. They're from an old schoolfriend who's gone cold on her. You'll just die when you see Ginny in her Senior Prom dress. I've put them in an envelope on your desk in case you want to come in and look at them over the weekend. See you Monday.

Hurray. That meant she hadn't lied when she told Blaine that she couldn't stay for the weekend after all. Rose laid aside her florist's bill, her credit card bill, and a begging letter from the Bodleian Library.

Beep, click.

Hello, Rose. Rick Goodman. We need to talk. Call me.

Rose shivered. Not for nothing had one of the scandal sheets dubbed him Jordan Hope's *Gauleiter*. She was going to have to handle Rick very carefully indeed. Rose slit open her phone bill.

Beep, click.

Rose, this is Tom. . . .

Rose leapt up so quickly she stabbed her thigh with the letter-opener. Hopping across the floor, she turned up the volume on her machine.

. . . I'm at the airport. I know it's rather short notice, but I was hoping I might be able to stay with you for a night or two. Er . . . Tom Hamilton, your godson. I suppose you must be out. I'll try you again when I get into New York.

Beep, click.

Sorry, it's me again. Don't tell Mum I'm here. I'll explain later. Goodbye.

Rose fast-forwarded through the remaining messages. Altogether there were six from Tom, unfolding like a radio drama. He was at such and such a hostel. He had left the hostel. He was at a phone booth downtown. He was in a coffee shop. He was in a music store. He was running out of money, but she wasn't to worry. The silly boy never told her the time he was calling, but fortunately her machine did. He had made the last call half an hour ago from an eating spot in the East Village, shouting above the clash of plates. Rose grabbed a pencil and wrote down the name, gloating with excitement.

Walk into my parlour, said the spider to the fly. Tom Hamilton, the boy who thought Jordan Hope might be his father; the boy who could turn the election upside down; the boy whom every single journalist in the world would kill to interview. Everyone was looking for Tom Hamilton. And he had come to *her*. Why, she had no idea. But she intended to find out. Rose called down to the lobby for a cab, then ran to her bedroom for some comfortable shoes, grabbed her wallet and a coat, and raced out of the apartment.

The cab driver didn't know where he was going, which made two of them. 'Just off St Mark's Place,' Tom had said. 'I think.' They cruised the blocks until Rose finally shouted to the driver to pull up outside a low-life eaterie with 'Ribs!' scrolled on its façade in blinking lights. There was a row of motorbikes outside. Through the glass Rose could see that the joint was jumping. She climbed out of the car, cutting short the driver's protests.

'If you want to get paid – wait here,' she ordered.

A blast of salsa music and the smell of greasy meat hit her in the stomach as soon as she opened the restaurant door. Rose picked her way through the rabble like a princess in a pigsty. She saw Tom before he saw her. He's grown up, she thought. Far from the forlorn figure she had expected, he was sitting at a table crowded with beer bottles, apparently at ease, holding forth to a trio of highly unprepossessing characters. Then he looked up and caught sight of her. Rose read relief on his young face. But he kept his cool.

'Hello Rose,' he said smoothly, kissing her cheek. 'Let me introduce you: Mickey, Ramon, and Buck.'

'Hi, boys,' Rose nodded, keeping her hands in her pockets. Needless to say, Buck was the leering giant in the sleeveless leather jerkin with a tiger's head tattooed on his biceps.

'Would you like a drink?' Tom asked politely. 'I'm afraid you'd have to pay for it yourself, though – I've run out of cash. Or some barbecued ribs?'

At that moment a sweating waiter pushed past Rose with a giant platter, bearing what looked to her like an entire cow's carcass lying in its own blood.

'That's very sweet of you, Tom, but I think we should get back. Can I settle up here?'

As she went to pull out her wallet, an arm gripped hers. Rose looked down into pair of hot, dark eyes. This must be Ramon, a skinny street-kid with a baseball cap on backwards.

'We gotta deal here, lady. We buy him one beer. When we come to London he's gonna take us to some fancy place for tea and scones – hey, Tom?'

'Absolutely.' Tom flashed a grin at Rose. 'I've been telling them about London.'

'So I see.' Rose raised her eyebrows. Some charm, she thought, to make these guys turn down hard cash. 'Tom, shouldn't you have some luggage somewhere?'

'This is it.' Tom held up a loathsome object of shiny nylon to Rose's wondering gaze. She had taken three cases to the country. Tom's rucksack wasn't even full.

She shepherded him out to the taxi, and directed the driver back to the apartment. Side by side with Tom in the back seat, Rose could feel his awkwardness gather as the obvious question loomed between them. What was Tom doing here? She made herself relax against the seat, and gave him a teasing smile.

'Of all the joints in all the towns in all the world, you

285

have to walk into this one. Good grief, Tom, I've never seen such a creepy bunch of hoods.'

'*Casablanca*,' Tom smiled delightedly. 'Ace film. Oh, they were all right. Except that they kept telling me where I could buy crack, when what I really wanted was something to eat. I'm starving. I've only had two of those bagel-things off a street-cart all day.'

'Oh.' Rose was disconcerted. No one in her world ever admitted to being hungry. 'Well, we'll have to see what we can find for you.'

'You mustn't go to any trouble. Just an omelette would be fine.'

Rose made small talk for the rest of the journey, pointing out landmarks. Under his polite public schoolboy veneer Tom seemed keyed up. Rose's instincts told her to go slow. She would find out everything in time.

It had been a long while since Rose had had a house-guest, as opposed to a bed-partner. She felt almost shy as she let Tom in and showed him around. He could sleep on the fold-out living-room couch, she decided. She would need her study, officially the second bedroom, to work in. But first she suggested that he might like to take a shower, while she prepared a little supper for him. He seemed to have only the clothes he stood up in. Rose had the distinct impression that he had been wearing them for longer than was strictly desirable. She led him to the guest bathroom and was amused to see his reaction to the array of shaving equipment and other male toiletries. There was nothing worse than bringing home a lover for the night and then finding that he'd borrowed her leg-razor and left a tidemark of stubble in her basin.

The moment she heard the bathroom door lock, Rose raced to the telephone. Then she paused. Was it really a good idea to let Annie know where Tom was? Emotionally, she was in a critical state: if she did her hysterical mother bit on Tom, he would probably walk straight out and into the arms of some drug dealer or pederast or −

ghastly thought! – tabloid reporter. It would be much better to calm him down, ascertain how much he knew and what he was up to. If Annie insisted on flying to New York to talk to Tom, she might miss her secret rendezvous with Jordan – the dazzling pinnacle of Rose's whole brilliant masterplan. It was unthinkable. Anyway, Tom had specifically asked her not to tell his mother. Her conscience clear, Rose gave the telephone a dismissive little pat and went into the kitchen. The poor boy was starving.

She pulled open the door of the refrigerator and took a rapid inventory of its contents. One bottle of vitamin pills, three lemons, two rolls of fast film, eight bottles of mineral water, two half-bottles of pink champagne and an eye-pack. Didn't you need eggs to make an omelette?

Rose considered. She could always get Sfuzzi to deliver something yummy, but Tom was obviously used to his mother rustling up a little supper for him. If Annie could manage it, so could she. Rose started opening cupboards and drawers she hadn't touched in months. The only edible things seemed to be teeny jars of luxury items flounced with ribbon. In one drawer she found an apron. What a good idea. She put it on and got to work. She was still surveying her efforts critically when Tom re-appeared, looking faintly sheepish in a towelling robe, wet hair slicked back.

'Gosh, this looks fantastic.'

Rose smiled like a sphinx. She had laid a small table for two by the window overlooking the park. Candlelight flickered on silver dishes of macadamia nuts and California olives. There was a cut-glass bowl of caviare flanked by lemon wedges and a fan-shaped arrangement of crackers – the limp remnants of some forgotten diet which she had crisped up in the oven. Both bottles of champagne stood chilling in an ice bucket. Rose had even found time to change into black velvet leggings and a cream sweater loosely belted with a gold chain. On her feet were little gold ballet slippers to match. She eased out the champagne cork and poured pink bubbles into two antique glass flutes. Handing one to Tom, she held the other aloft.

'Welcome to New York.'

Tom clinked her glass. 'Cheers.'

They sat down opposite each other in the glow of candlelight. Rose sipped her champagne for a while, watching Tom make short work of the nuts and olives. Then she put down her glass. She leaned her elbows on the table, chin propped on her hands, eyes alight.

'So. Do tell, Tom. I'm dying of curiosity. Have you run away?'

Tom frowned. 'Sort of. I'm – I'm on a quest.'

'How thrilling. And you want me to help you?'

Rose slid the caviare towards him. Tom piled a mound on to a cracker and took a bite. Rose waited while he chewed noisily and swallowed. He looked up.

'You know Jordan Hope, don't you?'

Sonofabitch. He was on the right track, after all. Rose stretched her eyes wide.

'Jordan Hope! Well, I used to. Our paths have somewhat diverged in recent years.'

'I want to meet him,' Tom said doggedly. 'I want you to arrange it. Mum always says you know everybody and can fix anything.'

'Everyone has their limitations.' Rose's eyebrows curved ironically. 'Why on earth do you want to meet him?'

Tom reached for another cracker. 'That's my business.'

'Tom,' Rose purred reproachfully. 'You know I'd do anything for you. But how can I help if I don't know what's going on?'

There was a ping from the kitchen. Rose excused herself, and reappeared shortly with the Crab Supreme she had found at the back of the freezer. Transferred from its tinfoil container to a grand Wedgwood platter, it looked surprisingly impressive. Rose placed it temptingly in front of Tom, refilled his glass and sat down again, waiting.

'Something funny is going on,' Tom began.

Gradually she coaxed the story out of him. It was much as Annie had feared – the photograph, Tom's search for his birth certificate, his growing anxiety that his real father might not be the man who had brought him up, but some strange American whom his mother professed not even to know. Rose murmured sympathetically, making no judgements. She could see that Tom was genuinely troubled. At the same time, she had the impression that he had driven himself into a corner and didn't know how to get out.

'I even got as far as looking up the address of the *New York Times*,' he admitted, too self-absorbed to notice Rose choking on her champagne. 'But I lost my nerve. I don't really know anything for certain.'

'What does Annie say?' Rose asked.

'She's too busy with her work,' he said witheringly. 'She won't even listen to me.'

'And she thinks you're in Oxford, does she?'

'I suppose so.' Tom shrugged it aside. 'The thing is, I know now that Mum and Dad weren't married when I was born. But I'm not sure they were even living together.' He lifted his chin challengingly at Rose. 'Well, were they?'

'Goodness, it's all so long ago. To tell you the truth, I lost touch with Annie for a bit when she left Oxford. She was certainly going out with Edward then. The next I knew, they were married with a baby.'

Tom banged his knife on to the plate with a clank. 'You know that's not true,' he attacked hotly, blue eyes wide. 'Why does everyone lie to me? *I* know isn't true because I've seen my birth certificate. The person who registered my birth is you. "Rose Cassidy, Lady Margaret Hall, Oxford. Occupation: student. Relationship: friend." I've got a copy in my rucksack. Do you want to see it?'

This time Rose was truly shaken. 'I'd forgotten,' she said softly. Suddenly she remembered Annie in hospital among the neat rows of mothers, with nurses starchily ferrying babies to and fro according to some mysterious timetable. Neither she nor Annie had a clue what to do with a baby.

'What is it you're all protecting me from?' Tom asked. 'No one will tell me the truth. Mum won't. You won't. I can't ask ... "Dad".' His face twisted. 'Maybe Jordan Hope will.'

'Hmm. Tom, you don't you think it would be a bit awkward to confront Jordan with this four days before the election?'

'I don't give a stuff if it's awkward. What do you think it's like for me, not even knowing who my father is?'

Tom's voice broke embarrassingly. He looked terribly young and serious. His hair had dried, and stood up at the back, where he kept ruffling it, like a woodpecker's crest.

'I'm sorry,' Rose said contritely. 'You're quite right, of course. Ice-cream?'

'What? Oh, yes please.'

Rose brought him a large bowl of loganberry sorbet. It was crystallised with age, but Tom seemed too absorbed with his own thoughts to notice. When he had finished, he set down his spoon. His shoulders sagged.

'No, I'm not right,' he said heavily. 'I've made a hash of everything. I've made everyone hate me. I've spent all my money. They'll probably expel me from Oxford.' He looked beseechingly across at Rose. 'What do you think? Honestly.'

Rose reached over and squeezed his arm. 'I think you've had an absolutely beastly time,' she said solemnly. 'And I think you've been incredibly brave and resourceful, if perhaps a little ... confused? What I honestly think is that you should go to bed right now and get a good night's sleep. And don't worry.' She smiled bewitchingly. 'I have a plan.'

28

Have mercy

In the morning Annie dressed carefully, choosing one of the power suits she had brought for her business in New York the following week. She put up her hair in the severe style she adopted when she wanted to look especially competent – what Edward disparagingly called her 'Fräulein' look. There was to be no mistake that she was now an adult in full command of her life. She looked approvingly in the mirror at her unsmiling, immaculate self. Only as she entered the hospital and caught that telltale smell of sickness and hygiene, did she remember Edward's last words to her on the subject of her mother: 'Be generous.'

In the event she had no need of his reminder. When the nurse showed her to the glass cubicle labelled 'Marie Spago', Annie's heart flooded with dismay. A woman lay flat on her back, so thin that she scarcely rippled the bedclothes. She seemed to be sleeping. Her hair had been cut short and clung to her head in yellowish grey clumps, the same colour as her skin. Her arms had been neatly arranged outside the sheet, stiff and pale as a doll's. They were taped with tubes carrying the drugs and nourishment that kept her just this side of death. Annie stood watching for a long moment. Last night's raging fire of resentment went out like a snuffed candle. This was not the monster who cruised her dreams, just an old woman in pain.

She pushed open the door and sat down quietly in the chair by her mother's head. Suddenly she felt strong.

'Mummy?' she said gently. 'It's Annie.'

The woman's eyes opened. Very slowly she turned her head on the pillow, and now, for the first time, Annie could recognise the outlines of her mother's face, like the strokes of a half-erased drawing. Her lips moved. As Annie bent forward to catch the words, she could see a pale crust of dried saliva on her mouth.

'I look a fright,' her mother said.

It was so honest that Annie's heart went out to her.

'Never mind. Lee wrote to me. He sounds very nice.'

Her mother just gazed, her eyes travelling slowly over Annie's face and hair and clothes.

'He said you might like to know about my life – what I've been doing – my children.'

Annie saw a slow fire kindle deep in her eyes. 'Tell me.'

So Annie told her. About Edward and Tom, about Cassie and Emma, about the house they lived in and the lives they led. As she listened to herself she realised how lucky she had been. She talked for a long time. Often her mother's eyes closed. Once or twice Annie lifted her carefully to take tiny sips of water. Her body felt like a huddle of twigs. After she stopped talking, there was a long silence. Annie could hear her mother's breath move painfully in and out of her body.

'I'd like to have seen your children.'

The admission turned a knife in Annie's heart. She held up the album, trying to smile. 'I've brought some pictures. You can look at them when you feel stronger.'

'Ohhh.' It was a sigh of pure joy.

Annie put the album on the bedside table. When she turned back she found her mother staring.

'You look very important,' she said with a trace of her old waspishness.

'I know. I'm sorry. It was a mistake.'

Her mother closed her eyes. Her fingers twitched. 'I was a lousy mother.'

Annie's eyes filled with tears. 'Yes, you were,' she said truthfully. But I'm not,' she added, struck by a new thought. 'I've had fun with my children. You didn't spoil it for me. Perhaps you were better than we both remember.'

'Lee has improved me . . . I think. Kind man. . . . Hate to leave him alone.'

'Oh, Mummy . . .' Annie leaned forward and touched the stiff hair. 'I'll stay in touch, if that would help. Perhaps Lee would like to come and visit us in London.'

Her mother moved her head in approval. Annie could see she was past speech.

'You should rest now. I'll come again tomorrow.' She stroked her mother softly on the hand. The skin of her wrists was like old cloth stretched between two pegs of bone. 'I'm glad I came. Goodbye.'

Annie went out into the hall and stood for a moment, fighting for control of her emotions.

'Annie?'

She looked up blankly. In front of her was a thickset man of about seventy, with a face like a boxer's and a slick of improbably black hair. Annie saw that his navy blazer was too tight, the cloth straining at bright anchor-stamped buttons. He didn't look like a doctor. He touched her gently on the elbow, as if waking a sleepwalker.

'I'm Lee,' he said.

Lee took her to lunch in a skyscraper restaurant famed for its panorama of Chicago, apologising for the fog which had rolled in overnight from the lake, eclipsing the view. He was desperate to talk, so Annie let him. He told her how he had met 'Marie' on a cruise. It was the first vacation he had ever taken, a celebration of the sale of his bathroom fixture business, which he had started from scratch – the first of many successes, Annie deduced.

'She was the classiest woman I'd ever met. All the men were after her – and all their wives were mad as fire.' He chuckled. 'My advantage was, I didn't have a wife. Never had time.'

As if he could hear Annie's private thoughts, he added, 'I guess it didn't hurt that I had plenty of money, but we clicked just like that. Boy, did she know how to have fun. She made everything an adventure. My whole life had been work, work, work. I guess I overdid it. My father blew his brains out in the Depression, did you know that? When I was a kid I promised myself I was never, ever going to kow-tow to somebody else for a job. So, Marie and me, we were kind of like Beauty and the Beast. When the cruise was over, I flew back with her to England, packed up her stuff and brought her home. We got married a week later.'

It had clearly been a very happy marriage. For some years after Lee retired, they had owned a house in Florida, joining the 'snowbirds' who flocked there every winter. They played golf and swam. In Chicago they went to the opera and the theatre. They belonged to some kind of country club and drove out there every Sunday for lunch. Marie had become interested in historic houses and went on guided tours round the old mansions. She took cordon bleu lessons and gave dinner parties. Annie listened intently, waiting for some trace of the discontented, selfish person she remembered. When Lee asked if she'd like to see their apartment Annie said yes, hoping to find some key to the mystery. They lived in a lavish block overlooking the lake, some twenty minutes' drive out of the city. Annie had been in hundreds of American apartments like it: pale carpets, dark reproduction furniture, neat to the point of anonymity. It told her nothing.

Lee gave her coffee, fussing with silver spoons. Finally he got to the point.

'So what happened between you and your mom? She never even told me she'd been married and had a kid, until a couple of years ago, when she saw that article about you. That's when she knew she was starting to get sick.'

Annie hesitated. 'What did she tell you?'

'Just that her husband had died and her daughter didn't like her. I couldn't get any more out of her. She'd kind of laugh it off, saying, "Think of me as a woman of mystery." '

Annie looked into his baffled tough-guy face, seeing the dread in his eyes. He didn't want to know the whole truth.

'I got pregnant when I was very young. I wasn't married, and Mummy was terribly shocked. I was . . . rather pig-headed. We both were, I suppose.'

'I see,' Lee said doubtfully.

'It was my fault,' Annie added quickly. 'I sort of ran away. I didn't tell her where I was. It came at a very bad time for her. My father had died recently. He was an army doctor, so when she lost him she lost her home as well. I don't think she was emotionally capable of any more demands. She needed to be free to find her feet as a woman on her own. Which she seems to have done – very successfully and happily.'

Lee nodded slowly. 'I just couldn't understand why Marie would turn her back on her own daughter. Or how anyone wouldn't love Marie. You sounded OK on the phone but, well, I wondered if you were going to turn out to be some kind of monster.'

'I thought you might be a gangster,' Annie confessed.

Lee laughed delightedly. 'That's my nose. If you grow up on the South Side you learn to be a pretty good street-fighter.'

It was time to go. At Annie's insistence, Lee called a

cab to take her back to the hotel. As they waited for the elevator to take them down to the lobby, Lee gripped her hand.

'I can't tell you how much I appreciate your coming – and not just for Marie. For me, too. It's been like going back twenty years.'

Annie was puzzled. 'In what way?'

'Well, you know, the way you look just like Marie. Same eyes, same skin, same wonderful legs – if I may be personal.'

Annie felt the hair rise on her neck. Her mouth opened, but no words came out.

'Wait here,' Lee commanded, turning back towards the apartment.

Annie waited, watching the empty elevator come and go. She couldn't have moved if she had wanted to. She heard the apartment door slam. Lee hurried towards her with a photograph in his hand.

'That's Marie on the cruise ship in 1974. Now,' he challenged, 'tell me that isn't where you got your looks. You two could be sisters.'

Annie stared at the picture in astonishment. It was true. She grabbed the photo and held it close, tracing familiar features.

'Could I keep this?' she asked.

Lee hesitated for a second, then pressed it into her hands.

'She'll be happy to know you wanted it.'

Annie travelled back to her hotel along the shrouded lake road, oblivious to anything but her own thoughts. *She looked like her mother.* People had told her that when she was a girl. How could she have forgotten? Her appearance had sometimes pleased her, more often disappointed her, but she had always thought of it as *hers.* She felt suddenly awed by the potency of genetic inheritance. How precise it was, and how utterly impersonal. Human beings were always so eager to read messages into coincidence or accident. It was hard to accept that physical resemblance had nothing to do with love and everything to do with the random encounter of this particular egg and that particular sperm. Annie thought of the way Lee had looked at the photograph one last time, clenching his teeth against any show of emotion. She had seen how much he would miss this elusive woman whom Annie had never dreamed existed. She had missed her mother all her life. Now it was too late.

For the first time it occurred to Annie that her father, for all his qualities, had simply not been the right man for her mother. Perhaps nothing else marked one's life so strongly as one's choice of marriage partner – not parents, not schools, not even love affairs. Marriage was never the simple sum of one plus one. It had the potential to enhance or to diminish out of all recognition the individuals it bound so tightly together.

As soon as she was back in her room Annie rang home. She could have cried when she heard the click of the answer machine and Edward's remote, recorded voice. She started to dial Rose's number, then remembered that she was away in the country for the weekend. Instead, she ordered tea from room service, and huddled in an armchair by the window, staring out at the fog which held her blindly in mid-air. But the hot drink could not warm her. At length she unpinned her hair and took off her ridiculous suit. She climbed into bed in her underwear and lay there shivering, longing for someone to hold her close.

29

Jumping Jack Flash

The lobby of the Savoy Hotel was thronged with Japanese tourists. Jack Robertson waited for his wife in the shelter of a palm-frond, his tongue furtively probing his back teeth to dislodge a nugget of wedding cake. He was feeling disgruntled.

It was bad enough to be dragged away from the golf course to waste his precious Saturday at a wedding reception. He never enjoyed these occasions – all daft hats and chit-chat and Jane digging him in the ribs to be polite to people he didn't recognise. Worse, in this case he had never even met the parties involved. He had been invited only because Jane edited the schlockbusters of the bride's mother, a terrifying harridan spiked with teeth and false eyelashes. Knowing no one, Jack had been in the humiliating position of wandering around in his wife's wake. Consequently, he had drunk too much champagne, and his head hurt. Worse still, halfway through the reception he realised that on Friday evening he had forgotten to bring home the advance copies of Molly McFiddick's latest Inspector Giles mystery. He would have to go past the office now to pick them up. Jane would not be pleased.

Jack transferred the weight of his wife's fake leopard-skin coat to the other arm with a gingerly air, as if it might bite him. He would simply have to insist. He needed those books to get him out of an awkward hole. First thing on Monday morning he was driving to Molly's cottage in some godforsaken corner of Norfolk. There had been a certain unpleasantness about Smith & Robertson's failure to forward royalties from her publishers. It was intensely irritating that she should find fault with the firm which had handled her books for thirty years and made her a fortune – 'made a fortune out of me, more like,' she had cackled rudely. Nevertheless Jack had eventually agreed to visit the old bat in person. He had been dreading it for days. When copies of her new book had arrived at the office yesterday, providing the peace offering he needed, it had seemed like a miracle. Then he had forgotten the damned things.

At last Jane emerged from the Ladies. Jack watched her bustle towards him, fresh lipstick gleaming. It was difficult to believe that she once had the reputation of a vamp in publishing circles. Though never exactly pretty, there had been something inexplicably arousing about her plump-breasted, head-girl looks which Jack was by no means the first man to notice. He had felt rather honoured when Jane had swivelled her guns on him. Her ambition was as voracious as her other appetites, and she had swiftly soared – no one quite knew how – from copy-editing drone to Queen Bee of commercial fiction. But three children and a regime of publishing lunches had left a trail of fat from jaw-line to hip. If Jack did not, on the whole, regret his graceful surrender six years ago, he had to acknowledge that the figure now advancing on him was unequivocally matronly.

Jane smiled approvingly as he helped her into her coat. 'Wasn't that fun?' she chirped over her shoulder. 'Famous faces practically wall to wall. Did you see the photographers? We might get our pictures in *Harpers*!'

Jack grunted.

'It's good publicity,' she urged. ' "Jack Robertson of Smith & Robertson, accompanied by his successful wife and mega-successful author, etcetera". Wake up, Jack. You could do with some new clients.'

Jack cleared his throat. 'Speaking of clients . . .' he began.

Jane's lecture on modern managerial principles lasted all the way up the Strand. She illustrated it with several examples of her husband's shortcomings which she had at her fingertips. After a while Jack tuned out. His wife's advice was always horribly sensible, but the truth was that he didn't like running a company. Every day since his father's death he had felt less like the beneficiary of his inheritance, and more like its victim. Of course clients were disapppointed in him; he would never be his father. No matter how often Jane pumped him up with ambition, he deflated of his own accord. He would have been quite happy trundling along as a dependable, middle-ranking editor publishing rather nice, rather old-fashioned books on golf and gardening and natural history. But such figures were redundant these days. Sometimes he felt like the Prince Charles of the publishing world.

This glimmer of self-knowledge did nothing to improve Jack's temper. He swore at the door-locks and thumped up the stairs to stand glowering in the empty, echoing offices. Where had his bloody secretary put those bloody books?

While Jack searched the outer office, Jane unashamedly riffled through his in-tray, picking up papers and opening folders, her spirits restored. She adored poking round other people's offices.

'What's this?' he heard her say from next door.

'What's what? I wish you'd leave my things alone.'

Thank God, there were the books, neatly labelled. Jack

picked up the parcel and hurried back. His wife was sitting at his desk, hefting a thick envelope.

'I smell trouble,' she said, tossing it over to him.

Jack recognised the writing at once. 'It's from Annie,' he said in surprise. He put down his parcel and picked up the envelope. His wife was right. There was something ominous about its weight and the firm underlining of the word 'Personal'. As he searched for his letter-opener and slit open the envelope, Jack felt a nudge of conscience. Perhaps he had been a little hard on Annie recently, but he had his reasons. Besides, it was essential that she appreciated the new management structure. Jane had told him so.

Jack unfolded the thick wadge and began to read. At first he couldn't make sense of it – some apologetic waffle about loyalty and his father. Eventually its message reached his brain.

'*The bitch*!' he shouted.

'What is it?' Jane rushed round the desk to read over his shoulder.

Together they skimmed the paragraphs over which Annie had agonised. She was sorry to end her long partnership with Smith & Robertson in this abrupt way – 'partnership,' snorted Jane – but circumstances had forced her to act quickly. Believing that there was no future for her at the agency she had decided to set up her own company. Sebastian Winter wanted to come with her, and had asked her to conclude the American sale of his novels on his behalf. That's what she would be doing in New York early next week. Details were enclosed. Naturally, Annie went on, Smith & Robertson would retain its share of revenue from their contract for the first book. She had carefully documented all recent business and would consider herself available for consultation for one month. Meanwhile, she hoped that by the time Jack read this letter she would have concluded a deal for

301

Sebastian Winter which would be extremely profitable for all parties.

'She knew I was going to spend Monday in Norfolk.' Jack's voice was shrill with injury. 'She was banking on the fact that I wouldn't find her letter until Tuesday. The devious little two-faced bitch.'

Jack slunk about the room. His eyes narrowed menacingly. 'By God, there's going to be a hell of a stink when she gets back from New York.'

'Don't be stupid, Jack.' Jane snatched the letter from his hand. 'We're not going to wait for her to come back.'

She stalked into the secretary's office and sat down at the computer, leopardskin folds trailing on to the floor. 'How do I get into your files?'

'I don't know. What are you doing?'

'*You don't know*? Aren't you networked?'

When Jack was a boy, his father had delighted in reading P. G. Wodehouse stories aloud on family holidays. Jack's memory flashed up the image of Lord Emsworth frozen in the headlamps of Aunt Agatha's imperious gaze. 'Er . . .' he floundered.

But Jane had already switched on the machine and was tapping away with an authoritative hand. 'You'd better ring home and tell Nanny she's got to look after the kids until we get back. And can't you at least make some tea? It's freezing in here.'

Jack hovered. 'What are you going to do?'

'*You* are going to fax all the American publishers and warn them what Annie is up to. You are also going to send a press release to all the trade magazines. Snotty cow – she never even offered me Sebastian Winter, she said it was too "upmarket" for my list. We can't stop her leaving, but we can bloody well ruin her career before it's even started.'

Jack's heart swelled with gratitude for that 'we'. His wife was a remarkable woman. Her watched her read

302

through the enclosures in Annie's letter, frowning as if something puzzled her.

'I always said Annie must have had an affair with your father,' she mused. 'It's a jolly good way of making yourself indispensable.' Jane gave a secret smile and smoothed her sensible, red-gold bob.

For a moment Jack said nothing. He was remembering the affectionate letters he had found between his father and Annie, and their baffling references to a baby. It was hard to believe that there had been an affair, but what was he to make of that outburst in the office the other day, when Annie's son had been shouting about his father? There was definitely something odd about the boy's birth. Jack had worked out that when Annie had rejected his advances at that drunken party, years ago, she must have been an unmarried mother. And she had acted like the Virgin Mary!

'It can't have been brains that gave her such a key position in this agency,' Jane went on.

'Why do you say that?'

Jane clicked her tongue impatiently. 'Just look at all this stuff.'

Jack looked. Annie had included a copy of her submission letter to all the American publishers and a list of the editors included in the auction. As far as he could see, everything was immaculately detailed – telephone numbers, bidding rules, marketing expectations. Secretly Jack was impressed. He couldn't accuse Annie of not playing fair.

Jane's scathing voice slashed across his thoughts. 'God, what a ninny,' she said. 'She's handed you her head on a plate.'

30

Downtown

Tom drifted slowly up from sleep. The room he was
in glowed with strong sunshine filtered through heavy
curtains. He felt a tingle of expectation, as if this were
the first day of the summer holidays at Grandpa's house,
with the sea and the beach waiting. Idly he watched
stripes of light shimmer on a geometric painting that
reminded him of a stained-glass window – or was it a
butterfly? Tom sat up suddenly. His grandparents didn't
have paintings like this. And their house had low ceilings, with beams. Where was he?

His eyes swept the room, taking in the curving furniture, the sofa-bed he was lying on, his rucksack on the
floor. Of course – Rose's apartment. The events of the past
few days rushed back: Oxford, his mother, Rebecca,
Jordan Hope. Suddenly he was wide awake, a familiar
anxiety knotting his stomach. He threw back the bed-
covers and walked across the soft carpet to open the
curtains. Christ! What had looked, last night, like the glitter of a thousand stars, turned out to be a line of magnificent buildings, windows glinting, flags flying, drawn up
on the other side of the park like an invading army. Below

him was a sparkling blue lake, dotted with boats, and the canopies of trees in brilliant fairground colours. He could hear the howl of sirens, and car horns honking impatiently. Wake up, they urged, time to get going.

He looked around for his watch, and saw that it had been used as a paperweight, to secure an envelope laid prominently in the middle of the floor. He opened the flap and pulled out a sheet of thick writing paper. *Tom – I've gone to the office for a couple of hours. Grab a cab and meet me for lunch at one o'clock. Coffee and rolls etc. in kitchen. Please double-lock door. Love, Rose. PS. Phone is switched on to machine – no need to answer.* She had written down her office telephone number for him, and the address of the restaurant. Enclosed in the envelope, along with a set of keys, was a wad of folded dollar bills. Tom counted them out: five crisp twenties – a hundred dollars! He slid them reverently into his thin wallet. Rose had never done things by halves. He thought of the presents she used to send him on his birthday – a Superman outfit, a skateboard, an Instamatic camera, an American football helmet – when she remembered. Her visits to London were like brief but spectacular volcanic eruptions. Sometimes she had been too busy to do more than zoom in and out of the house, leaving a vapour trail of distinctive perfume. When there had been time for treats, they had always been on an extravagant scale. He would never forget going with her to the men's final at Wimbledon, the year Boris Becker won for the first time. Once, she had managed to get them tickets to a Michael Jackson concert that had sold out months beforehand. He would rather have died than gone with his mother; somehow Rose was different. But recently Tom had seen less of her. The last gift had been a cheque, on his eighteenth birthday. It was as if she didn't quite know what to do with him now he was no longer a boy.

Tom strapped on his watch: half-past eleven. He put on the towelling robe, and wandered barefoot into the kitchen, where everything had been neatly laid out on the counter. He made coffee, piled his breakfast on to a tray, and carried it back to the table by the window where they had eaten last night. Spotting a pile of newspapers on a side table, he hauled over the *New York Times*. On the front page was a photograph of Jordan Hope, caught in mid-sashay across a spotlit stage. HOPE PROMISES A FAIRER DEAL, read the caption. Tom peered close. Behind Hope, he could see television cameras and pennants and row upon row of upturned, rapturous faces. They looked more like fans than voters.

He read the article as he ate, showering the paper with flakes of croissant. Hope was on the last lap of the most punishing campaign tour in election history. It struck Tom that, even if Jordan Hope wanted to see him, he might be too busy. Nevertheless Tom clung doggedly to his belief that Rose could fix a meeting for him if she wanted. More than anything else, he was curious. What kind of a man was this Hope? Would he be pleased or horrified to know he had an unknown son? Was Tom the sort of son he would like? The problem was like an itch he had to scratch, knowing it might bleed.

Tom dumped his dishes in the sink, and went into the bathroom to wash. He stared at himself for a long time in the mirror, wondering, who are you? Did he want to find out? Would it make any difference? Hope was hardly going to adopt him. Finally Tom turned away, impatient with himself, and went to put on yesterday's clothes. As he passed the open door of Rose's study, he peeked in curiously. Like the rest of the apartment, it was immaculate and stylish, with an array of high-tech office machinery and an extraordinary red sofa in the shape of lips. Tom went to take a closer look. The phone on the desk next to him began to trill. Despite what Rose had said about the machine, it seemed churlish not to answer it. He picked up the receiver.

'Hello?'

There was a surprised pause, then a man's voice said, 'Is this Rose Cassidy's apartment?'

'Yes it is, but I'm afraid she's out at the moment. She's at her office, actually, if you have the number.'

'Thanks.' The man didn't ask for the number. Tom had the odd impression that he was making some rapid calculation. There was the tiniest hesitation as he asked his next question.

'Tell me, is . . . Annie there?'

Tom felt a flutter of surprise. 'My mother, do you mean?' Immediately he could have bitten his tongue. Of course the man could not mean her.

'I'm sorry, I don't seem to have her last name,' the voice said smoothly. 'I understood that a friend of Rose's called Annie might be staying with her. I need to talk to her.'

'Well, she's not here,' Tom said, beginning to feel frightened. 'I mean, no one's here but me.'

'I see. Thank you for being so helpful. . . . Who am I talking to, by the way?'

'Tom – ' At the last moment, Tom bit back his surname. He had heard that burglars sometimes rang up places they had their eye on, casing the joint – not that he really believed that this man was a burglar. He sounded like one of those smoothie American lawyer types that Michael Douglas played in films. A cunning idea occurred to Tom.

'When I see Rose, who shall I say phoned?' he asked.

'She'll know,' the voice said coolly. 'Goodbye, Tom, it's been nice talking to you.' He hung up.

Tom put the receiver down, feeling unsettled. Then he shrugged. Perhaps Rose would be able to make sense of it.

On his way out of the apartment he caught sight of his reflection in the long hall mirror, and paused. He was definitely the least stylish object in this whole apartment. He tried zipping his jacket up to the neck to hide his grubby T-shirt. Now he looked like a mugger. Tom returned the zipper to its half-mast postion, hoping that the restaurant – an Italian-sounding place – wasn't smart.

But of course it was. Tom could tell he was in deep Trendsville by the offhand charm of the waiters and the way heads swivelled to check out each new arrival. Rose was already there, looking dead cool in sunglasses. She poured him a glass of white wine, and smiled conspiratorially across the table.

'Guess what I've been doing this morning? Choosing pictures of Jordan Hope's wife for a feature in the magazine. It's going to be sensational.'

His wife! Here was yet another element which Tom had not fully taken into account. In his fantasised meetings with Jordan Hope, he had never envisaged the presence of a third person.

'Is she interesting?' Tom asked.

Rose considered. 'People's reactions to her are. She's exactly the sort of role model women are always clamouring for – smart, successful, in charge of her own life, good marriage, blah-de-blah. But now they've got her, women say she's cold and calculating. It's as if she represents some kind of threat to their femininity.' Rose cocked her head, thinking aloud. 'I suppose one could say she has put a new spin on the old story. Bedroom or boardroom? Kitchen and kids – or limos and lovers? Do "real" women run families, or companies? Or the presidency, for that matter?'

Suddenly Rose pulled off her sunglasses, and subsided in her chair with a gurgle of laughter. 'For God's sake, Tom, tell me to shut up. Tell me I'm not just a walking repository of crass copy lines.'

'No, it's fascinating,' Tom insisted, half-truthfully. There was something he wanted to know. 'Do they have children, Hope and his wife?'

'N – O,' Rose said emphatically. 'People who don't like Ginny say that she was so busy with her career, and helping Jordan with his, that she couldn't face the hassle.' Rose sipped her wine. 'I don't know, though. . . .'

'What?' prompted Tom.

'Well, there are couples who can't have children. There could be a physical problem with her,' Rose paused delicately, '. . . or with him. Shall we order?'

Tom looked at his menu. *Bruschetta*, arugula, angel hair – the unfamiliar words blurred, as his mind veered off on a new tack. If Jordan Hope couldn't have children, then he couldn't be Tom's father. Or perhaps the fact that Hope didn't have children meant he didn't want children. In which case . . . Caught in the confusion of his thoughts, Tom heard the waiter acting out the day's specials, and Rose explaining precisely how she wanted something cooked. There was an expectant pause.

'I'll have the same,' Tom said, handing back his menu.

The food was delicious. While he ate, Rose told him one scandalous story after another about the private lives of Hollywood film stars. Tom forgot all about Jordan Hope. Rose persuaded Tom to have a dessert, then recklessly ordered one for herself. Afterwards they had some kind of fiery liqueur which you were supposed to drink while holding a coffee bean between your teeth. By the time they managed to empty the small glasses, they were both helpless with laughter.

'Tom, thank you,' Rose said, dabbing her eyes with her napkin. 'You don't know how much fun this is for me. Usually I get to eat lunch with fat men, or stick-insect women who shriek if they spy a blob of dressing on their lettuce leaf.' She shook her hair into place and sighed happily. 'I've probably gained five pounds – and I feel marvellous.'

Tom was feeling pretty marvellous himself as he stepped out on to the sunny sidewalk. They had not gone more than a few paces before Rose stopped at the entrance to some kind of department store. She slid her sunglasses up her forehead.

'Oh, look,' she said wonderingly, as if the building had been set down overnight by Martians. 'Barneys. Let's go in.'

309

Tom followed slowly, stopping to admire a pair of dead-black Ray-Bans with gold rims. When he saw the price, he nearly dropped them on the counter in fright. Rose beckoned him over. There was something about her small, imperious figure, looking dashing in high-heeled ankle boots and a sleek leather jacket, that made him smile. She was frowning at the floor-by-floor list of the store's contents.

'What do you think, Tom? Kenzo? No, too gimmicky. Armani? Calvin?'

'Don't ask me,' Tom laughed. 'I don't know anything about women's clothes.'

'Ah, but we're not talking about women's clothes.' Rose tapped him playfully on the chest, 'We're talking about *you*.'

One hour later Tom was gazing at a vision: himself. At his feet knelt a salesman, reverently adjusting the length of Tom's new trousers. Behind him he could hear Rose quizzing another salesman about the cotton-weights of shirts. Her hand rested proprietorially on a pile of jackets, trousers, sweaters, and a rainbow selection of shirts and T-shirts: all his. Inwardly exulting, Tom gave himself an implacable Clint Eastwood stare in the mirror. Goodbye grungy student, hello film star. He wished Rebecca could see him.

Tom had always loathed shopping, especially for clothes. To wake up one morning and set out deliberately to make yourself as tired and as cross as possible, and pay for the privilege, had always struck him as an exquisite torture. This was different. There had been none of that aimless trailing from shop to shop; no hopeless sorting through racks of identically dreary suits; no frustrated searching for your size in teetering piles of shirts that cascaded to the floor; no queuing up for a sweaty changing-room so small that when you bent down to take off your shoes you banged your bum. All Tom had been required to do was to sit in a potentate's chair while Rose commanded things to be shown to him. Those that he liked, he tried on. Those that he tried on looked wonderful. For there was something different about the clothes, too. Tom didn't quite know what it was, but they felt and looked nicer than any he had ever owned. He wondered if it could have anything to do with money.

The best thing of all was the speed with which everything was accomplished. Before he had tired of this new game of make-believe, Rose was snapping a card on to the sales desk. 'OK, I want these things sent over to this address this afternoon. The usual discount, naturally.'

'And what shall we do with these?' someone asked.

A salesman was emerging from the changing-room, holding Tom's old clothes at arm's length. His disdainful tone made Tom feel like a schoolboy.

'Pack them up with the other things, of course,' Rose shot back, without batting an eye. Tom could have kissed her.

'Now,' Rose rapped on the counter, 'where can I get my friend a tux?'

'What on earth's a tux?' Wandering over to her, Tom smiled at the unfamiliar word.

'Tuxedo. Dinner-jacket.' Rose's eyes widened teasingly. 'They won't let you into the party without one, you know.'

'What party?'

Rose waggled her eyebrows. 'Wait and see.'

31

Tired of waiting

It was already dark when Annie woke. She lay still for
several tranquil moments, as warm and lazy as a cat in
the sun, assembling her thoughts. Something mysterious
had happened while she slept. The emotional turbulence
of this morning's meeting with her mother, and the memories it provoked, had been magically soothed away, and
with it the lump of resentment Annie had carried for
half her life. She had regained a part of herself, some
wellspring of confidence that her mother's opinion no
longer had the power to block. There was something else,
too, a distant fluttering that was both alarming and
pleasurable. What was it? Annie sat bolt upright in bed.
Jordan!

She switched on the light and blinked at her watch.
Eight o'clock. Her heartbeat slowed. There was plenty of
time. Jordan had told her on the telephone that he could
not possibly make it until late at night – possibly not at
all. Annie sank back on the pillows, admitting to herself
how bitterly disappointed she would be if he didn't come.
Jordan had streaked through her private emotional universe like a shooting star, blazing one moment, gone the

next. Over the years she had held hundreds of imaginary conversations with him. She had fantasised scores of improbable meetings. Even though he could not possibly know her married name, she had daydreamed about him opening a book by one of her authors and reading, 'Last but not least, my thanks to my heroically patient agent Annie Hamilton, without whom . . . .'

She liked to think that Jordan had not forgotten her. She could never have forgotten him, even if every detail of his life had not been ferreted out by the media. Annie had read far more than she wanted about his wife, haircuts, and girlfriends; his devotion to jogging and his fondness for playing pool. Through countless pictures and yards of film footage she had witnessed his transformation into a public figure, handsomely packaged in slick suits. But she wanted to see him for herself. In the flesh. Was this disloyal to Edward? Annie didn't want to think about that. Squirming down into the warm nest of bedclothes, she tried to hold on to that floating sense of well-being with which she had awoken. Soon enough she would get up. The practicalities of her life, its urgent demands, would resume. But for a little while longer she held them at bay, allowing herself to drift back to the very last time she had seen Jordan, remembering how it was.

On that bright midsummer morning twenty-two years and four months ago, Jordan had punted her back to the boatyard under Magdalen Bridge. Annie could see him now, trousers rolled up over bare feet, water glistening on his forearms, smiling down at her. She had lain among the cushions, thinking, *He's leaving today. I'll never see him again.*

He had taken her to breakfast at George's in the covered market. She remembered the smell of freshly roasted coffee wafting out of Cardew's and the solid feel of Jordan's body next to hers as he steered her through the warren of cool, dimly lit alleys. There had been cherries and strawberries piled high on the fruit stalls, silver salmon laid out on slabs of ice, hams and salamis hanging outside Palm's Delicatessen. Annie had been conscious of her crumpled ball dress and tangled hair, but no one took much notice. It was always the same at the end of the summer term. Students were students. Soon they would be gone.

George's was an Oxford institution, a working man's café accustomed to reviving the occasional hungover undergraduate with milky tea and a fry-up. Jordan couldn't believe that she had never been inside before. He ate there practically every day. They had climbed narrow wooden stairs to a crowded room where the windows ran with steam. Jordan had led her from table to table, greeting van drivers and building-site lads like old friends.

Too lovesick to eat, Annie had leaned her elbows on the Formica table-top and watched dreamily as Jordan worked his way through a plateful of eggs, bacon, tomatoes, mushrooms, sausages and fried bread. She followed the movements of his hands as he cut up his food in that odd American way, laying down his knife and switching over his fork at every mouthful. Faint hollows appeared under his cheekbones as he chewed. She saw how his hair curled over his collar and ears, how his eyelids curved to give him that perpetual lazy smile she found so seductive. Every few seconds he forgot his food and looked up at her. Underneath the table his legs had clasped hers tight.

They had driven back to LMH with the top down. Oxford had never looked more beautiful. Some kind of academic ceremony delayed them in the Broad. They had waited in traffic to allow a crocodile of dons and dignitaries to cross to the Sheldonian Theatre, splendid in their velvets and silks and ermine-edged hoods. Annie remembered how Jordan had jumped out of the car to fetch his camera from the boot, while she slid down out of sight, feigning embarrassment at his crass American behaviour. As he stood on the driver's seat to take pictures – still in a DJ, bow-tie dangling from his pocket, the sun on his hair – he had looked quite glorious, a golden boy among the golden towers.

In Parks Road the acacias were in flower. Speeding under their cool canopy, Jordan banged the steering wheel angrily.

'Why did you have to wait until now? We could have done so much together. Everything would have been different.'

'Not everything,' she replied. 'You'd still be going home.'

As soon as they reached her room, she burst into tears. Jordan held her in his arms. 'It's OK, baby. Don't cry.'

She had left the room to wash her eyes. When she returned Rose was sitting in her armchair, chatting to Jordan like an old friend. A terrible thought had struck her.

'You know each other?'

'Sure.' Jordan grinned easily. 'We've had some gritty sessions in the Union bar.'

'Oh, *politics*.' Annie breathed again.

Jordan asked Rose to take a picture of him with Annie in the garden. The two of them sat on a slope of bright green lawn where pink rambler roses climbed up to Annie's window.

'Don't look so tragic,' Rose had shouted, and Annie had leaned into Jordan's shoulder and laughed.

Jordan had promised to send her the picture care of LMH. Annie's last memory was of standing by his car under the big lime tree, mute with misery. She was rubbing her finger back and forth on the jaunty red upholstery, summoning the courage to say goodbye, when Jordan reached into his pocket.

'So what do you think of my little car?'

'I love it.'

'Good.'

He had taken her hand and folded her fingers over the key.

'You keep it.'

He laid his jacket and camera on the dusty bonnet and kissed her until she could hardly stand. Finally they pulled apart. He smoothed her hair tenderly over each shoulder and smiled into her face.

'Two-times girl,' he had murmured, almost to himself.

Then he had slung his jacket over his shoulder and walked out of her life.

Annie shivered with nostalgia. Was there anything on earth as exciting as the beginning of a romance, when one was nothing but a bundle of emotions and nerve endings? No wonder people had affairs. She wondered what Jordan would remember – *if* he would remember. Their lives were so different. For all these years she had carried him round in her heart like a secret. But for Jordan it might have been no more than a one-night stand in a faraway country which he had never, as far as she knew, revisited. Perhaps the idea that he might have fathered a son would fill him with revulsion. Or would it excite him?

Feeling restless, Annie jumped out of bed and stepped to the window. She drew back the heavy drapes, and caught her breath. The fog had cleared. The city glittered before her, an urban fairyland full of promise. Suddenly she felt capable of anything.

She decided to celebrate her new self by dining in the hotel. Like most women she knew, she usually hated eating alone in formal restaurants. Men always seemed to feel honour bound to enquire after her *cotelettes d'agneau*, or to send over a glass of champagne and toast her exaggeratedly, drawing every eye in the room to her solitary female plight. It was normally preferable to sneak out to some anonymous coffee shop to eat tuna salad behind a propped-up book. But just occasionally, maybe once every five years, there was nothing more sublime than striding alone into a grand dining-room and eating a full three-course meal entirely on her own, with no need to make conversation or consult others. Tonight, Annie decided, was one of those nights.

First she showered, taking time afterwards to smooth cream into her body. She slipped on her underwear and carefully drew on sheer black stockings, fastening them high on her thighs. Then she put on her make-up – not too much. Stepping into black high-heeled shoes, she sucked in her stomach and cheeks, and studied the effect in the full-length mirror. Not bad. She turned her attention to the contents of her closet. She wanted to look marvellous for Jordan, without appearing to have made any particular effort.

Twenty minutes later she was still scowling at herself in the full-length mirror. No, no, no. The black trousers and cream silk shirt were all wrong. Just when she wanted to present an image of mysterious, unfathomable experience, here she was looking exactly like Mary Tyler Moore. Annie turned away from her dispiriting image and stripped again to her underwear, adding the latest discards to a growing pile on the bed. Her second-hand Armani suit was heaven, but too formal. The leggings she always wore on the plane were too sloppy. Her pink Chanel copy made her feel as if she were about to conduct an interview. So what was left? It would have to be her Slinky Black, a knee-length dress in fluid jersey that crossed over her breasts and fastened at the waist with two diamanté buttons. It was a little dressy, but the minute she put it on she felt better. She put her hair up and took it down again, pinned it back from her forehead and unpinned it. Eventually she brushed it until it gleamed and let it fall where it would. A generous dab of perfume in all the key places, and she was ready.

She went down to dinner, daring the *maître d'* to seat her invisibly by the kitchen doors. He didn't. The dining-room was a homage to turn-of-the century ostentation, an extravaganza of marble columns and chandeliers, gilt mirrors, tropical plants and white napery. A pianist in the corner tinkled out George Gershwin. 'You like potayto and I like potahto . . . .' Thoroughly enjoying the tender attentions of a dark-eyed waiter young enough to be her son, Annie took her time. She ordered an expensive Beaujolais, and somewhat to her suprise, an hour or so later, found that she had drunk the entire bottle.

After coffee she fetched her coat and took a walk round the block, relishing the sting of chilly air on her flushed cheeks. She saw the banks of police cars and limousines outside the Hilton and imagined Jordan inside, doing his stuff. It struck her that there was an extraordinary number of people out on the streets. Surely they couldn't all be Democrats. It was only when a party of teenagers in devil masks came shrieking round a corner that the truth dawned on her. Of course! It was Hallowe'en. That explained the festive atmosphere in her hotel. When she returned to the lobby she could still hear the piano: 'Thanks for the memory . . . .' Annie lingered, browsing through the little shop that sold magazines and toiletries and cheap souvenirs. As she looked to see whether there was anything to take home for the girls, she hummed along with the music. There was nothing suitable for Cassie or Emma. Nevertheless, she made one small purchase.

By the time she returned upstairs, it was getting on for midnight. But she still had time to kill. She turned her attention to the room itself, closing the bathroom door and tidying away her clothes and make-up bottles. Then she dragged the two armchairs across the carpet to make a kind of conversation group with the huge Empire-style sofa under the window. She switched off the overhead light and moved a table lamp over to the sofa. This hotel had been built on a grand scale, at the height of Chicago's prosperity. Though now slightly fusty, the high ceilings and heavy mahogany doors with gilt fixtures gave her room the air of a *fin-de-siècle salon*. She might have been an Edith Wharton heroine awaiting an illicit beau. What else? Jordan might be thirsty after all that speechifying. She checked that the mini-bar was fully stocked: it had everything. She brushed her hair smooth and touched up her make-up. Now she was ready for him. The question was, would he come?

32

Mama told me not to come

The Temple of Dendur was on the ground floor of the
Metropolitan Museum, a short drive across the Park from
Rose's apartment. It was early evening when Rose's
limousine drew up in front of an imposing turn-of-the-
century building, supported by massive columns and
flanked by spotlit fountains. Tom peered out at the people
streaming up the vast flight of steps and fingered his bow-
tie self-consciously. Never had he been to such a classy
party. The men were dressed as he was. The women
glittered with jewels.

'Do people really do this every week?' he asked Rose,
as he helped her out of the car.

She laughed, smoothing down the short black coat that
stood out around her knees like a ballerina's skirt. 'Every
week? Some people do this practically every *night*.' She
caught Tom's bemused expression and shook her head.
'You still don't get it, do you? Look, Manhattan is a tiny
island with some very rich people, and thousands more
people who would like to be very rich. These parties are
all about connections, society, money. Who's in, who's
out? Who's together, who's not? Remember, everyone

lives in minute apartments. American television is terrible. What else is there to do?' She took his arm. 'It may not be Ascot, but these affairs do raise a lot of money for good causes, and you can make them fun.' She lifted her chin at him. 'Actually, that is my speciality.'

They moved across the grand hall and through to a lofty gallery. Tables had been laid for dinner around a stunning, subtly lit Egyptian temple, but no one was sitting down yet. A few conscientious guests peered perfunctorily at the exhibits, but most stood in chattering groups with their backs to the pictures, hoping to be photographed by the paparazzi. Waiters circulated with trays of champagne and mineral water. Tom chose champagne. He sipped it appreciatively as he cruised the room with Rose, head bent to her running commentary.

'See the one with the amazing boobs?' Tom saw all right. 'Seventy-five per cent silicone. They say she went from a 32A to a 36D overnight. The redhead she's talking to is the latest weather girl: where she needs an implant is in her brain. . . . See the man with the ponytail and the earring? He makes sculptures out of chocolate. People are being very nice to him at the moment because Milton Vanderpump bought one of his pieces. Plus he's Mexican, and that makes everybody feel better about exploiting their Mexican maids. . . . Darling, how are you?' Rose proffered her cheek to a pretty woman with huge, dark eyes, who kept fingering her necklace nervously. 'She's rather sweet,' said Rose, after they had moved on. 'She just gave a million dollars to the Met, hoping to crack Manhattan society. But her husband made his money in something embarrassing like manhole covers or funeral parlours, and they're both Jewish. People are waiting to see.'

Tom was scandalised. 'Surely no one cares about people being Jewish any more. I thought there were supposed to be more Jews in New York than in Israel – or is it Tel Aviv?'

Rose gave him an old-fashioned look. 'Check out some of the exclusive golf club registers. I can tell you now you're not going to find too many Goldbergs or Rabino-vitches. Look, over there, the bimbette with the hair next to the tubby old man with the suntan – she's his fifth wife. The rumour is that she once posed for a *Playboy* centrefold, but no one's been able to track down the pictures yet.'

They circled the room slowly. Rose pointed out pub-lishers, playboys, bond-dealers, heiresses, politicians, journalists, interior decorators, even a hairdresser. She seemed to know most of them. Each time she introduced Tom as her godson. He got some funny looks.

'I had no idea it would be so exciting coming with you,' Rose whispered in amusement. 'Everyone's wondering who you are. Let's keep them guessing. And stop fiddling with your tie. You look great. . . . Uh-oh,' her hand tight-ened warningly on his arm. 'Here she comes, Muffin Grondquist, the *grande dame* of the Benefit circuit. Her parents must have thought Muffin was a cute nickname back in nineteen-oh-something. Don't worry if she doesn't smile at you. She's had so many facelifts she can't.'

A silver-haired woman in a long black dress glided towards them as smoothly as if she were on castors. Her face was a parcel of bones glued together with make-up. Tom watched as the two women leaned towards each other and kissed the air.

'And who is this lovely young man?' The woman swiv-elled her body towards Tom.

'This is Tom Hamilton.' Rose's eyes sparkled with mis-chief. 'My godson.'

'Ohhh.' It was a swooping note of innuendo, as if 'godson' were a code word for some new kind of sexual relationship, probably deviant.

The dinner began. Rose had warned Tom that the people at their table were her guests, and that she would have to leave him to his own devices while she gave them her full attention. She seated him opposite her, next to a sculptress with short streaked hair called Sidney. Tom quickly learned that Sidney was Sagittarius, never touched meat, and was very concerned with the issue of Tibetan independence. She was extremely attractive, but it took Tom a little time to hit on a subject they could both talk about. Eventually, they discovered that she had exhibited her work in Berlin. While they ate, Tom told her about his months in Eastern Europe. She watched him raptly, in fact so unblinkingly that he began to wonder if her eyes were glazing over in boredom. But when he broke off, she laid an insistent hand on his arm.

'Don't stop,' she breathed. 'I love listening to your voice. It's just like *Masterpiece Theater*.'

Tom was enjoying himself. Everyone was being very nice to him, and he realised that this was because of his special status as Rose's partner. He had not appreciated how famous she was. He glanced across the table, tuning into her provocative announcement that Oliver North would be elected President in '96. Tom caught her expression of satisfaction as a chorus of disagreement broke out around her. She was wearing a dress in some kind of shiny sea-green material with criss-cross straps over her bare back. A slim necklace sparkled at her throat. Matching earrings peeped from her glossy hair. Her lipstick was scarlet. She possessed an aura of power that was not just to do with looking glamorous. There was something about the way she sat, straight-backed and poised, that gave her distinction. She never fidgeted, he realised, never simpered or fiddled with her hair. She looked utterly concentrated, controlling her guests as expertly as, earlier, she had tied his bow-tie for him. Formidable: that was the word. Suddenly Rose looked across the table and caught him staring at her. She gave him a secret smile.

Sidney must have been following his gaze. 'Isn't Rose Cassidy a little old for you?' she smiled insinuatingly.

Tom looked at her pearly little teeth. 'I don't think so,' he said shortly.

During coffee there was some kind of award presentation, accompanied by fulsome speeches and applause. Afterwards people got up to leave or table-hop. Rose disappeared. A man at their table launched into an involved story of a leveraged buyout, of which he was evidently the hero. Tom began to feel bored. Sidney was just asking in a meaningful way if Tom were interested in primitive sculpture when Rose reappeared at his side.

'I'm frightfully sorry, Sidney,' she said smoothly. 'I'm afraid we have to leave early tonight.'

Tom made his goodbyes and accompanied Rose downstairs.

'This is so wicked,' she moaned, as they emerged out on to the steps of the museum. 'I never behave like this. But I thought it was time to get you away from Sidney. She would have eaten you for breakfast.'

Tom shook his head in innocent wonder. 'And she told me she was a vegetarian.'

'Ha ha. Get into the car. There's some place I want to show you.'

They rode down town, chatting about the party.

'You certainly seem to know a lot of people,' Tom commented.

Rose flipped off her spiky-heeled shoes and exercised her toes. 'That's one way of putting it.'

'You mean, they all want to know you?'

'Attaboy. I'm glad they still go for brains at Oxford.'

Oxford. Rose had a trick of bringing him back to earth with a bump. Remembering that he had never told her about the curious telephone call at her apartment this morning, Tom did so now. Rose quizzed him sharply, but offered no explanation. She swore she had told no one where he was. The car dropped them off at the glitzy entrance to a skyscraper. An elevator shot them up to the sixty-fifth floor. RAINBOW ROOM, read the control panel.

When the doors opened Tom stepped out and exclaimed in wonder at a dizzying, wraparound view of the whole city. Looking smug, Rose took him on a tour of the floor. It was divided into different sections – a restaurant, bars and a revolving dance floor where couples swayed to old-fashioned music. They walked slowly round the periphery of the room, then they found a dimly lit table on the south side, looking down town. Rose ordered them both something called a Perfect Manhattan. The drink was delicious and very strong, clinking with ice.

'God, I love this view,' Rose burst out passionately. 'It always makes me feel as if I'm king of the castle and a nobody, both at the same time.'

They stared at the winking panorama in silence. Then Tom put down his glass and turned to Rose.

'It's wonderful. So were the clothes, and the lunch, and the party. Why do I get the feeling that you've planned all this to distract me from thinking about Jordan Hope?'

Rose let out her breath as if she had been expecting this. 'Because I have,' she said seriously. She set her elbows on the table and leaned towards him intently. 'Listen to me, Tom. It's time you dropped this whole Jordan Hope thing. One, it's impractical. You know it's out of the question for you to meet Jordan right now. Two, if you go around saying Jordan is your father – without a shred of evidence, remember – you'll make trouble for yourself and everyone else. The man you talked to this morning is a very smart and very powerful slime-ball called Rick Goodman. He's been helping Jordan Hope to run his campaign, and if Jordan wins he'll expect to be rewarded with a key government position. Before the election he would do literally anything to shut you up. Afterwards, he wouldn't hesitate to use you as a threat to dangle over Jordan's head. I can deal with him, because that's the world I move in. But it's not your world and it's not Annie's.'

'Yes, but – '

'Thirdly,' Rose continued, 'there's your family to think

about – a nice, happy family where everyone cares about one another.'

Tom made a face.

'Yes, it sounds schmaltzy, but it's not common. I know.' Rose took a sip of her drink. 'My parents never really cared about us at all, though it took me years to figure it out. They always seemed so proud of the great Cassidy tribe: "all for one and one for all".' Rose gave a brittle laugh. 'They think what I do is terribly trivial and rather amusing. They pride themselves on never having had the time, or the frivolity, to look at a single issue of *The Magazine*.' Rose stared out of the window, holding herself stiffly. Then she shook back her hair and turned to Tom. 'Your parents will always love you, whatever you do. But you can wound them irretrievably. You can make them sad. Why? Don't do it.'

'But there *is* something about Jordan Hope,' Tom persisted. 'Otherwise why would Mum be so cagey about it? Why would this Goodman person be interested in me?'

Rose looked at him thoughtfully, as if making a decision. 'Tom,' she began portentously, 'promise you'll never tell Annie I told you this, but I think she may have had a one-night stand with Jordan. They met at a demo when they were students. Something happened, though she was always very secretive about it.'

'A demo?'

'Demonstration. Protest. You know, Vietnam and all that.' She put a hand to her forehead and groaned softly. 'God, I suppose you don't know. Anyway, it was one of the violent ones – riot shields and charging police horses and so on.'

'*Mum*?!'

'Yes, "Mum". I know this will come as a terrible shock to you, Tom, but she was once even younger than you are now. Anyway, there was some trouble, and Jordan rescued her – just like a knight on a white charger. I don't think she's ever quite got over it.'

326

Tom's mind clicked slowly. 'And when was that?' he asked casually. 'Roughly.'

Rose looked at the ceiling. 'Let's see, that must have been about . . . October 1969.'

Tom worked it out. He couldn't have been conceived then.

'Look,' Rose smiled persuasively, 'you're a mature adult. If Annie has some adolescent fixation about Hope, you're just going to have to forgive her. Everyone has a streak of silliness. It's not as if she and Edward aren't happy together. Even back in Oxford, everyone could see that they were made for each other.'

'Then why did they wait so long to get married?'

'I don't know. But the responsible thing to do would be to go home and ask them. Get the story straight before you blow Hope's chance of the presidency, and make yourself and your family miserable.' Rose sat back and slapped her hands lightly on the table. 'OK. End of lecture.' She stood up. 'I'm going to the Ladies' Room.'

While she was gone, Tom stared out across the alien city. Everything Rose had said made sense. He wished his mother spoke to him like this, as an equal. He tried to imagine his mother, 'younger than you are now', fighting the police and falling for a handsome American called Jordan Hope. Deep down Tom had always known that it would be difficult to meet Hope. Coming to America had been an act of defiance, to make everyone aware that he was upset. But if anything, his curiosity was intensified. He vowed that one day they would meet. And in the mean time, he had enjoyed his stolen weekend in New York. Turning from the window, Tom looked across the glittering room. He watched Rose approach with her quick step, flashing him a smile, and saw how people turned their heads as she passed, then checked to see who her partner was. Tom felt a surge of pride.

Rose settled back in her chair, waiting for him to speak.

'I've been thinking,' he began hesitantly. 'I've had a

great time being with you, and I'd love to stay on. But I've decided that tomorrow morning I should go out to Newark and see if I can get a standby to London.'

Rose eyed him consideringly. He couldn't tell if she were pleased or not. She reached for something in her bag, and placed it before him: an airline ticket.

'I've ordered the car for 7 a.m. tomorrow,' she said calmly. 'Your plane leaves at nine.'

Tom opened his mouth. He didn't know whether to protest or to thank her. The expression on Rose's face, half smiling, half defiant, touched him unexpectedly. Before he could say anything, Rose stretched out her hand and pressed two fingers gently to his lips. Tom felt his face flush scarlet. More as a distraction than anything else, he heard himself say, 'Do you want to dance?'

Tom didn't really know how to dance, but Rose seemed happy to be steered around the floor under the giant chandelier. She felt surprisingly fragile under his hands. Her skin was warm and smooth. Tom's spirits rose. Now that he had made his decision, he was determined to wring the last drop of pleasure from his New York escapade. Rose seemed to have relaxed too. When the number ended, she held on to him lightly, waiting for the music to begin again. 'I haven't done this in years,' she laughed. Tom became bolder, trying a couple of twirls. Rose sang under her breath, 'You're the top, you're the tower of Pisa, You're the top, you're the Mona Lisa . . .' When they eventually left the dance floor she gave a little pirouette. The sash of her dress flew out beguilingly. Her cheeks glowed.

'Tell me,' she asked, 'am I pissed, or am I having a good time?'

Tom looked her over carefully, from her gleaming cap of hair to her foot-fetishist shoes. 'Pissed,' he pronounced.

'Tom!'

They left soon afterwards. Alone with Rose in the elevator, Tom experienced a piercing moment of nostalgia, and traced its source to Rose's perfume, the same one she'd worn ever since he could remember. He shut his eyes for a second, inhaling the familiar fragrance. When he opened them again he found Rose looking at him intently. He stared back.

'What?' she laughed, sounding embarrassed. 'Tom, you're staring.'

'You've got green eyes,' Tom said wonderingly, bending close. 'Really and truly green.'

'But they've always been this colour.'

Tom's gaze slipped lower. Her coat had fallen open. He could see the swell of her breasts.

'Perhaps.' He stepped back. 'I've never noticed before.'

Outside, they waited in silence for Rose's car to draw up. The heater was on in the car. It was very warm. Tom sank into the cushioned seat next to Rose, feeling suddenly awkward. Here he was in the most glamorous city in the world – in a limo, wearing a tuxedo, with a beautiful woman – and he couldn't think of a thing to say. To tell the truth, his body was behaving rather disturbingly. The thoughts in his mind were not the sort you were supposed to have about your godmother.

He was struggling to construct some remark about New York traffic when he felt Rose place her hand unambiguously on his thigh. His body contracted with shock.

'To-om?' she asked, stroking absent-mindedly.

Tom summoned his entire store of oxygen. 'Yes?' he answered. The pitch was a little high, but it would do.

'What do you think?' Rose looked up at him, eyes glinting in that mischievous way she had, as if everything were a game. Her head barely came up to his shoulder. 'Is it incest if a woman goes to bed with her godson?'

Tom laughed out loud, too loud. He raised his arm and pulled her close. There was nothing to her. Suddenly he felt supremely confident.

'Definitely not.'

Rose slid her hand upwards. 'Hallelujah,' she breathed.

33

You can't always get what you want

Annie sat down in the armchair, then sprang up again. It was too quiet. She tensed every time she heard the rumble of the elevator doors. She turned on the television, and quickly switched it off. Then she noticed a radio built into the wall by her bed. After some experimentation she tuned into a golden-oldie music station: an inexplicable string of initials that sounded like the last line of an eye chart. But the music was good. Annie opened her briefcase, and laid out her papers on the desk, making herself look busy. There was a business plan to prepare for her bank manager. Annie stared at her cashflow chart, pencil poised, pretending to concentrate.

It was just after two when she heard a soft knock on her door.

She leapt up to turn off the radio with fumbling fingers, then peered through the spyhole. All she could make out was a figure in a dark overcoat, head lowered. She unlocked the door.

'Jordan?'

The door swung open. A tall man in a hurry stepped inside. It was him.

'Annie, hi. It's wonderful to see you again.'

Jordan reached for her hand and shook it, clasping his other hand warmly to her elbow.

'You look terrific,' he said huskily, though his eyes skipped quickly over her to scan the dim room.

He unbuttoned his coat, and raked a hand through his hair.

'I'm real sorry it's so late, but it was tricky to get away.'

Annie took his coat for him, and laid it on a chair. She felt as stiff as a marionette.

'What's wrong with your voice?' she asked.

'Too many speeches, I guess. You got anything to drink here?'

Annie silently poured him a beer, and decided to add a whisky for herself. He hadn't even looked at her properly. She watched him roaming about the room, glass in hand, circling the ornate furniture, twitching back the curtain, peering at the gloomy reproductions on the wall. He was so wired up she thought he might strike sparks. His face was squarer than she remembered, and his body had filled out. The rich chestnut of his hair had faded. But it was still thick and wavy. The streaks of grey suited him.

'So,' he turned, 'tell me what's going on?'

'Why don't you sit down?' Annie waved at the sofa.

Jordan sat down on the extreme edge, leaning his elbows on his knees. He was wearing dark trousers and a blue shirt that matched his eyes. Light from the table lamp glinted on the fair hairs on the back of his hands.

Annie remained standing. Holding on to the back of a chair, she began the speech she had rehearsed.

'First of all, I want to say that I'm really sorry to make trouble for you. I hope it wasn't a terrible shock when I telephoned. I wanted to warn you, but also to explain.'

Jordan nodded. 'OK. Shoot.'

'I, er, got pregnant at the end of my second year at Oxford – the summer of 1970. At the time I was going

331

out with someone, but we broke up that term. Anyway, I had the baby – he's called Tom – and eventually I met up again with my old boyfriend and we got married. As far as we're all concerned Tom is Edward's – my husband's – son. But just recently Tom has taken it into his head that Edward isn't his real father and that ... well, that you might be.'

Jordan jiggled his glass, swirling the beer. 'How come?'

Annie felt that she was talking to a wall. She took a sip of whisky and sat down in the armchair opposite Jordan.

'Do you remember a photograph you sent me? You and me on the lawn at LMH the day after – the day you left Oxford?'

Jordan blinked. Then, for the first time, he looked her in the eye. She thought his expression softened, but he was holding himself on a very tight rein.

'You still have it?' he asked.

'Tom has it.'

'Jesus.'

'He found it in my old trunk. It seems to have affected him very powerfully. He thinks that you might be his father. I tried to tell him it wasn't true, but I didn't do it very well. We quarrelled. He's been missing for nearly a week now. Nobody knows where he's gone. I just thought I should tell you. Tom hasn't got a sophisticated bone in his body. He could blurt out his worries to anyone. A rumour might get into the papers. Something he said made me think that he might even try to get in touch with you.'

Jordan was frowning. 'Is that it? Is that the evidence? Some kid finds an old photograph of his mother with a guy he doesn't recognise, and decides the man must be his father?'

Annie's lips tightened. How could he be so cold about this? 'No, that isn't the "evidence", as you call it. I obviously haven't made myself clear about this meeting. This isn't a scam, Jordan. This isn't blackmail. It isn't some ludicrous attempt to stop you being elected President. I am trying to help you.'

Jordan bowed his head. 'I apologise. Right now I'm living in a crazy world. There's no one I can talk to about this.' He smiled, in a way that transformed his face. 'Forgive me.'

'Don't mention it.'

Annie straightened herself in her chair and crossed her legs.

'No,' she continued, 'the "evidence", such as it is, is that Tom decided to look up his birth certificate, and discovered that Edward and I weren't married when he was born. Naturally, he was upset and confused. Plus the fact . . .' Annie hesitated. 'Well, I think somebody must have said to him that he looked like you. Like you used to look. Like you looked in that picture.'

For a long moment Jordan sat utterly still.

'This boy looks like me?' he said slowly, looking up at Annie from under his eyebrows. Something inside her jumped. His eyes, she thought, those lazy-lidded smiling eyes were exactly as she had remembered.

'Actually, most people say Tom looks like me.'

Jordan shook his head in confusion. 'Annie, let me get this straight. Are you telling me this isn't just some cocka-mamie idea of your son's? You mean he really could be mine? When was he born?'

Was it her imagination, or did he actually looked pleased by the idea? More than pleased – triumphant?

'We all consider him to be Edward's,' Annie said stiffly. 'Tom is a lovely, uncomplicated boy. I'd like him to stay that way. I also have two other children to consider, and my husband. You have your wife, and your position. All I want to do is find him, and straighten him out. Then we can all get on with our lives.' She smoothed her dress over her thigh, adding quickly, 'He was born on March the seventeenth, 1971.'

'I see.' Jordan was silent for a moment. Anne could

practically hear him counting out the months in his head. Changing tack, he asked, 'How did you know where to call me?'

'Don't worry, I was very discreet. I got my friend Rose to help me. You must remember – '

'Rose Cassidy?' Jordan interrupted, horrified. 'Queen of the Schmooze? Motormouth of the magazines? Jesus, Annie, why didn't you just go on *Larry King Live* and have done with it?'

'Rose would never say anything,' Annie protested. 'She's my best friend.'

'Hmm. And does she know why you wanted to get in touch with me?'

'Of course not,' Annie lied.

'How did she know how to reach me?'

'She didn't. She asked one of your henchmen.'

'My *henchmen*?' Jordan's mouth quivered just the way it used to when he was amused by some ridiculously English phrase.

'Your campaign people – ' Annie flapped her hand – 'whatever you call them. Rick somebody. She knew him at Oxford.'

'*Rick Goodman*?' Jordan's eyebrows snapped together.

'I think so. Is something wrong?'

Jordan didn't answer. She glimpsed an expression of intense calculation, quickly smoothed away. He leaned forward.

'Tell me about Tom.'

Annie tried to sketch Tom's character without sounding too much like a proud mother. She told Jordan about Tom's determination to go to Oxford – how he had failed the entrance examinations once and had the grit to wait a year and try again. Jordan prompted her with typically male questions that made her smile inwardly. Was Tom good at sport? Did he have a girlfriend? What had he made of the former Soviet Bloc? Jordan seemed fascinated by every detail of her answers. Annie remembered the speculation that he and his wife had been unable to have children, and wondered.

'He sounds like a great kid.' Jordan sighed wistfully. 'But Jesus, Annie, pregnant at nineteen! I wish I could have done something.'

'Well, you did, you know.' She smiled. 'I admit it wasn't all that easy at the beginning. I had no money, a tiny baby, and a grim little flat – just a couple of rooms, really, with a stove on the landing and a shared bathroom two flights down. I was working in the day, and studying at night to try to complete my degree. But I had one marvellous, liberating luxury.' She cocked her head at Jordan. 'Your car. Remember?'

Jordan nodded slowly. The memory of their parting outside LMH rose between them. For a moment, Annie forgot what she was saying. Then she continued.

'Every Sunday I used to put his carrycot in the back seat and drive out to Richmond Park or into the country. I'd park Tom on a blanket, and lie in the grass reading the Sunday papers. I can't tell you what it meant to me. It was the best part of my week. Even now, when I look at the car, I often remember those times.'

'You mean you still have it?'

'Tom has it. I gave it to him as a present to take to Oxford.'

'No kidding!' Jordan laughed incredulously, shaking his head. He leaned back against the sofa, visibly relaxing. 'It's so peaceful here,' he said, clasping his hands behind his head, and stretching out his legs with the easy physical charm that seemed the birthright of every American male. 'I don't know when I was last away from people and telephones and newspapers.'

'Was it easy to get away tonight?'

'I went to play cards with the Secret Service men. I do that sometimes, when I need to wind down. Usually they come to my suite, but tonight they were having a Hallowe'en party. I played a few hands and then said I was going to bed. Then I kind of snuck out. They were having too good a time to notice much. I stole one of their masks and pulled a hat over my head. Even my mother wouldn't have recognised me.'

'What's it like, campaigning? I can't imagine it.'

Jordan tilted back his head and laughed. 'Like riding the Coney Island Cyclone. Unpredictable. Exhilarating. Scary. Funny, too, sometimes.'

'Why funny?'

'Oh . . . people – what they want, the things they say. The other day I was in New Jersey someplace, taking questions from the floor, and this old lady asks me about health care. She's kind of specific and this is a speech, so I just answer in general terms. But I say, why doesn't she come up and talk to me afterwards? So up she comes, a nice little old lady all dressed up, with her friend egging her on. Go on, go on, he won't bite. Anyway, I listen to her problems and I try to answer her concerns, then I have to shake her hand and go. But just as I'm going, I hear her turn to her friend. "What a *mensch*," she says. "He shows more interest than my son. Are you sure he isn't Jewish?" '

Annie laughed with him. 'You love it, don't you?'

'I guess I do. Sometimes it's like winning the World Series and opening on Broadway and having sex all at the same time.'

He turned his head to look at her. 'But you know something about that. It's not so different from acting.' His warm gaze slid over her. 'I remember you in that play in the garden, wearing those great boots.'

Annie shifted. 'That was a long time ago.'

'Was it?' Jordan's eyes lingered. 'You look the same. I'm glad you kept your hair long. I've thought about you so many times.'

'Me too,' Annie said softly.

The silence lengthened, as they stared into one another's eyes.

Jordan put out his hand to her. 'Annie,' he said gently, 'tell me the truth. Tom is my son, isn't he?'

'I don't know.' Annie could feel her face betray her.

Jordan sat up. 'But you think he's mine.' He leaned towards her, searching her face.

Annie suddenly felt breathless. She stood up and moved towards the mini-bar. 'Do you want another drink?'

Jordan followed her.

'You think he's mine,' he repeated exultantly. He grabbed her hand and pulled her round to face him. 'Don't you?'

Annie had forgotten how big he was. Her mouth was level with the triangle of flesh at his open shirt collar. She could see the rise and fall of his chest as he breathed. She looked away.

'Maybe.' Annie tugged her hand free. 'I've said all I know for certain. Tom could be your son. He could be Edward's. If . . . If I've sometimes thought he was yours, it's only because we were so – because it was so – ' She cleared her throat. 'I mean, you may not remember – '

'Remember?' Jordan clutched her shoulders. 'Are you kidding?' he asked hoarsely. 'The river and the willow trees? And your face when we said goodbye? You never even wrote back to me!'

'I couldn't! I wasn't even at Oxford any more. The college only had a temporary address that summer; afterwards they didn't know where I was.' Annie twisted away, pushing back the hair from her face. 'Anyway, what would have been the point? What could I have said? "I'm having your baby"?'

The silence vibrated between them. Jordan's face softened into a slow, intimate smile that made Annie's heart turn over.

'Maybe, huh?' he said teasingly, his eyes flickering up and down her body. 'Maybe you and I made a baby.' He took a step towards her. 'Is that a definite maybe? . . .

Or a maybe maybe?' Another step. 'Or an "I hope so" maybe?'

Annie backed away. She could feel herself flushing. She shouldn't have drunk that whisky. She couldn't think properly. She wished she'd left more lights on. Suddenly the wall was at her back. Jordan stepped close. Slowly, seductively, he rested his hands on the wall on either side of her head, imprisoning her. He leaned over her, rocking gently, smiling his lazy smile. His breath was warm on her cheeks. Annie could smell his sweat.

'Stop it, Jordan,' she said.

'You stop it,' he whispered, and bent his head to kiss her.

Annie opened her mouth to protest and instead drew his warm tongue inside her. Sensation detonated through her body, leaping from one nerve ending to the next. Every thought evaporated except how good he felt – his thighs hard against hers, the breadth of his back warm under her hands, his tongue sliding and tugging and coiling, heating her up like a furnace. Jordan swept back her hair with both hands, tilting her head, pulling her to him. He kissed her eyes, her cheeks. He licked the corners of her mouth, and ran his tongue wantonly round and round her lips until she had to reach up and plunge her fingers into his hair to draw him back to her.

You shouldn't be doing this, nagged a distant voice. But her hunger for him left no room for pretence or withdrawal. Just once, she pleaded. She slid her hands round to the back of Jordan's neck, feeling his warm, soft skin and the taut muscles beneath. She pulled the tail of his shirt out of his trousers so that she could slip her hands up his bare back and over his ribcage. When she let him step away, it was only so that he could lay her down on the bed.

His weight came down on her. Annie closed her eyes, stretching herself out for his pleasure. He was kissing her throat, her ears, the tender spots behind her earlobes. She could feel his hair brush across her cheek. His breath on her neck spread ripples of excitement down her body. Jordan drew back his head, his expression dreamy and absorbed. Their eyes locked as he undid her dress and spread it open. His hand slid down to her breast. Her skin was slick with sweat. She felt him scoop the fullness of her breast into his palm and roll the ball of his thumb over her nipple.

There were too many clothes, Annie raged, craving the feeling of his flesh against hers. All these hooks and buttons and belts. She clawed at Jordan's collar and forced his shirt off one shoulder so that she could rub her teeth across his skin. Jordan lowered his head and lazily ran his tongue down the groove of her ribcage. Annie arched her back and moaned. She felt him licking her navel until it was too tantalising to bear. Reaching down, she flipped the tongue of his belt out of the buckle.

When the telephone rang they both yelled with fury, then fell into a panic-stricken silence. They could hear themselves panting. Jordan bowed his head agonisingly on to Annie's breasts. His eyes squeezed tight with frustration.

'*Shit.*'

The telephone went on ringing. Annie suddenly remembered who they were, and where they were, and all the reasons why she must – *must!* – answer it. She rolled Jordan aside and clambered over him, trailing her dress from one bare arm. Her hand nudged the bedside table and set it rocking. She could hear the thump of her handbag falling to the floor, and the rattle of its contents spilling across the carpet. Trying to concentrate, she huddled on the edge of the bed with her back to Jordan, and steadied her feet on the carpet. She picked up the receiver, and took a deep, calming breath.

'Annie Hamilton. Hello?'

'Annie, my darling girl, what grand news!' boomed a voice. 'You should have taken the plunge years ago, didn't

I always say so? Of course you must represent my work. You wouldn't leave me with Harry Robertson's mimsy milksop of a son, would you now?'

Annie breathed out a shiver of silent laughter. Trelawny Grey, sounding more cod-Irish than ever. How utterly typical of him to have no concept of transatlantic time changes! It was one of his famous eccentricities that he never ventured beyond the borders of civilised Europe. She pictured him in his half-panelled Georgian study, slippered feet to the fire, morning paper at his elbow. It would be well past breakfast time in County Tipperary.

'I had your letter yesterday,' Trelawny was saying, 'but I've been away up to Naas for the November Handicap. I knew it was a sign when Robertson's Lad was pulled up at the five-furlong post.'

While she listened to him rattle on, Annie fished behind her for the other sleeve of her dress. She felt Jordan slide it over her shoulder, then the brief pressure of his hand laid gently on the back of her head. The mattress bounced as he got off the bed. She could hear him putting things back into her bag. She did not look round.

While she drew her dress around her, the significance of Trelawny's phone call trickled into her brain. He had got her letter. He wanted her to be his literary agent.

'I'm honoured, Trelawny – and very grateful. I intend to make a great deal of money for you. But I should warn you, Jack may take it hard.'

Trelawny Grey made a rude noise down the phone. 'One tiny fart out of that pipsqueak, and I'll put him in my book. I've got as far as '36, the year his father and I went up to Univ together. Harry Robertson nearly got sent down, you know, for painting a fig-leaf on the Shelley Memorial.'

Annie struggled to make sense of this. 'Do you mean to say that you're actually writing your memoirs at last?'

'Most enjoyable thing I've ever done, my dear. It's funny

the things you remember. Did I ever tell you the story of Willie Maugham and the oysters, the time he took a fancy to a waiter on the Blue Train?'

'No, Trelawny,' Annie said slowly, fastening her buttons. 'I don't think you ever did.'

By the time he had regaled her with several more anecdotes and was winding up to his last round of goodbyes, several things had become clear to Annie. First, Trelawny Grey's book would need the best libel reading that money could buy. Second, it was going to sell faster than any cakes, hot or otherwise, in the history of the world. Third, her percentage of the advance, as Trelawny's agent, would keep her new business going for at least a year. Fourth and last, she was not going to make love with Jordan.

While she laughed aloud at Trelawny's stories, even while she coolly assessed the likelihood of his book being ready for publication next Christmas, Annie remained acutely aware of Jordan's presence in the room, of his eyes on her back. After Trelawny had rung off, she held the receiver to her ear for a few more moments, taking time to collect herself. Then she replaced the handset carefully and stood up, adjusting her dress to cover her stockinged legs. She turned to face Jordan. He was sitting on the couch, shirt tucked in, hair smoothed, watching her.

She managed a shaky laugh. ' "Fate keeps on happening." Isn't that what the girl says in *Gentlemen Prefer Blondes*?' She located her shoes, and stepped into them. 'Honestly, Jordan, we must be mad. What came over us?'

Jordan waggled his eyebrows. 'Sex?' he hazarded.

Annie saw that he had her bag next to him. He took something out and held it up like Exhibit A. With anguished embarrassment Annie recognised the packet of condoms she had bought in the hotel lobby. Jordan was smiling wickedly, holding her gaze. He put the condoms down on the couch, then drew something out of his

341

trouser pocket. 'Snap!' he said, placing an identical packet on top of hers.

Their eyes met in a long, rueful look. Then Jordan swept up the incriminating evidence, and patted the seat beside him.

'Come over here, superwoman, and tell me about this scheme you're cooking up. Was that really *the* Trelawny Grey you were talking to?'

Annie sat down – not too close – and told him how she had decided to start her own agency. She allowed Jordan to draw her out on the details of the business – copyright, sub-agents, percentages. They both knew that what they were really trying to do was to turn down the heat that still simmered between them. And it worked. Annie's mind started racing ahead to the big auction that awaited her in New York. Jordan slipped into his professional role as listener.

'Go for it,' he said, with that infectious American enthusiasm. 'I believe you can do anything you set your heart on.'

Annie shook her head, recalling his own, infinitely grander ambitions. 'It all sounds so trivial compared to your job.'

'If I win.'

'Oh, you'll win. You have winner written all over you. I think that's what confused me back in Oxford. Everyone likes a winner, but not necessarily to live with all the time. Just in the last couple of days I've realised something about myself. *I* like to win, too, sometimes.'

'You sound just like Ginny.' Jordan sighed, and rubbed a hand over his face as if trying to soothe an ache. 'She's helped me so much to get this far. We both know I'd never have got close without her. But right at the most important moment I have to cut her out of the limelight. I'm not even supposed to mention her any more in case it loses me votes. I feel bad about that.'

'So you should,' Annie said tartly. 'Advisers aren't

always right, you know. If you're going to be a good President you'll have to follow your own instincts sometimes, no matter what anybody else says. Don't you think you owe it to her to acknowledge her help?'

'But how?' Jordan looked troubled. 'Every time I say how much I depend on her intelligence and her moral judgement, people think I'm going to let her run the country.'

Annie clicked her tongue in exasperation. 'Well, no wonder they're worried. They don't want to rely on her moral judgement. It's not her they're electing. The point is what *you* think of her.'

Jordan considered this. 'But what could I say?'

'Speak from your heart. Just say you love her, that you're proud of her. There's no need to go into detail.'

'Never apologise, never explain?'

'Exactly.'

'Speak from the heart,' Jordan repeated thoughtfully. 'Yeah, I like that,' he nodded. 'I can do that.' He leaned back against the arm of the couch and gave her a look that made her toes tingle. 'You know, you really are something.'

Annie smiled into his eyes. 'I know.'

She saw his face tighten hungrily. It was time to break the spell.

'Jordan, shouldn't you be getting back?'

Jordan looked at his watch. 'Jesus, five o'clock!' He leapt to his feet. 'The early editions will be out. I need to catch the news on TV.'

Annie followed as he crossed the room to pick up his coat. Thrusting one arm into the sleeve, Jordan looked down and fingered his shirt. He shot Annie a sly look. 'Uh-oh, I've lost a button. Now how in the world did that happen?'

Annie blushed.

'What do you think of my disguise?' he asked, pulling a Hallowe'en mask from his pocket.

343

Seeing what it was, Annie burst out laughing.

'Yeah, yeah, I know.' Jordan grinned. 'Let me tell you, Annie, Secret Service men are not subtle people. This is their idea of a joke – a Hallowe'en party where everyone comes dressed as a President.'

'You might at least have chosen Abraham Lincoln, or Roosevelt.' Annie put the mask to her face, intoning, ' "There can be no whitewash at the White House." '

'Hey, give me that.' Jordan snatched it back and looped the elastic over his wrist. 'I just picked up the first one that came to hand. At least it got me here. Let's hope it works for the return trip. And don't worry, I'll put it on in the hall.'

He stooped over the desk to scribble something on a piece of hotel stationery. 'Here's where you can reach me if Tom shows up. If you don't get me, leave a message – something like "Annie says everything's OK". If he contacts me, of course I'll let you know. Meanwhile, let's try not to worry,' he said, catching her anxious look. 'He sounds like a smart boy.'

Suddenly Annie remembered something. 'Wait!'

She went over to the bedside table and drew out the photograph of Tom which she had saved for Jordan. She had picked it out at random, she imagined. Now she admitted to herself that she had chosen it because in this particular photograph, above all others, Tom had a look of Jordan. Holding the photograph so Jordan couldn't see it, she lifted the flap of his coat pocket and slid it in.

'What – ?'

'A present. A good luck charm. Look at it later, when you're by yourself.'

Jordan pressed his hand tenderly to his pocket, speculation leaping in his eyes.

'I'd like to meet him one day,' he said seriously. 'Of course I'd never say anything to him. I have too much to lose. But it would mean a lot to me.' Jordan beat his fist

344

against the other palm as if trying to express the depth of his feeling. 'I sure would love to see him.'

'I know. I'll think about it.'

She watched him finish buttoning his coat. There was nothing to keep him now.

Jordan set his hands lightly on her shoulders. 'Well, Annie, I guess this is it.'

She nodded. She looked up into his face – his mouth, his eyes, the crisp wave of his hair above his ears, memorising his features. His eyes told her all that she had longed to know for twenty-two years.

Jordan bent forward gravely.

'This is for my son.' He kissed her cheek.

'And this is for you.' He kissed the other cheek.

'And this is for me.'

The touch of his lips on her mouth came without warning. Annie rocked back on her heels for an instant, feeling his grip tighten. Her eyelids flickered. Then Jordan released her and slipped into the corridor. The door clicked shut behind him.

Annie stood with her fingers held to her lips as if they burned. She couldn't even hear his footfall.

34

Sweet talkin' guy

'Rose? It's Rick. What the fuck is going on?'

'You tell me.'

'Quit fooling with me! This is serious.'

'What exactly?

'At 5 a.m. this morning the Secret Service guys called to tell me they'd "lost" Jordan.'

'Careless.'

'He turned up. Said he'd been for a walk.'

'Hmm. Original.'

'Why do I get the feeling that this has to do with your friend, "Annie", who wanted so badly to talk to Jordan?'

'Pass.'

'And what about the English boy, Annie's son? He was in your apartment yesterday. What have you done with him?'

'Darling, what an indelicate question!'

'I thought you were on our side, Rose. I cannot have my candidate going AWOL. You want him to win. So what's going on? Who is Annie? I need to know.'

'Annie is my friend.'

'Oh, please. People like us, we have contacts, we pull strings, we do deals. We don't have friends.'

'Isn't Jordan your friend?'

'Yes he is! And that's why I hope you're not about to run some scummy story. No one wants to hear any more scandal. I would really, really hate to see anyone as smart and talented as you just pull the plug on your career. That's what would happen, believe me.'

'So what's the deal?'

'I'm not asking you to betray any confidences. Just tell me Annie's last name. Whisper it. I can do the rest.'

'How grateful would you be?'

'Very, very grateful. Humble. Positively prostrate.'

'And what's in it for you? Your choice of desks at the White House?'

'Rose, you shock me.'

'That's a first. Tell you what, I'll think about it.'

'Think fast. We're running out of time. Two more days.'

'You always were a bit of a speedy Gonzalez, weren't you, darling? Personally, I like to take my time. Goodbye, Rick.'

'Rose – ?'

35

Good vibrations

Annie's first inkling of disaster was an early telephone call to her room at the Algonquin Hotel. She had just returned from breakfast in the dining-room downstairs, galvanised by the sight of immaculately dressed New Yorkers doing business at seven o'clock on a Monday morning. She had a good feeling about the Sebastian Winter auction. On her arrival from Chicago yesterday afternoon there had been a pile of faxes and messages waiting for her. Although the deadline wasn't until midday today, she already had notes from several publishers announcing their enthusiasm and their intention to bid. When the telephone rang, Annie picked up the receiver with a buoyant heart. 'Annie Hamilton?'

'Well, hello Annie Hamilton. And who's been a bad girl, then?' Annie at once recognised the sardonic, Martini-rich voice of Peggy Rostoff, one of a dwindling breed of red-blooded female editors who still smoked and drank and knew the difference between 'lie' and 'lay'. Peggy was also a world-class gossip.

Annie's heart went cold. This was it. The story of her romance with Jordan had finally broken. Someone had got hold of Tom. Her Chicago room had been bugged. She glanced wildly at the television, cursing herself for not having watched the morning news.

'Don't say that, Peggy,' she pleaded. 'I wouldn't call it exactly bad.'

'Jack seems to think so.'

'*Jack*?'

Peggy clicked her tongue reproachfully. 'I know they say publishing is just a crazy game of musical chairs these days, but don't tell me you've forgotten your old boss already.'

'No, of course not,' Annie replied, flustered. 'But what's Jack got to do with it?'

'Everything, I'd say, judging from this piece of toilet paper he sent me. He sounds pretty pissed at the way you've snitched Sebastian Winter from under his nose, and given him the finger at the same time. Quoting at random from his fax: "deep personal disappointment . . . irreconcilable conflict of interest . . . regrettable lapse of professional integrity". Gee, I wonder which thesaurus he uses.'

'His wife's, probably,' Annie muttered, her thoughts spinning. What had gone wrong? Jack was not supposed to have read her letter until tomorrow. And he would never have reacted in this aggressive way on his own initiative. Smothering panic, she forced her brain to work.

'Who else has received this fax, do you think?' she asked.

'Everyone who's considering the Winter books, I guess. You probably gave Jack a submission list, you upright little soul.'

Annie groaned. 'Peggy, I'm really sorry that you should have been troubled by this misunderstanding. There were circumstances that forced me to take a quick decision, and with Winter's books already under submission I just had to jump.'

'Don't apologise to me, sweetie. I think it's great that

349

you're setting up your own business. No one in this city gives a damn about Jack Robertson anyway. Right now all they care about is buying Sebastian Winter.' She paused. 'Winter really *is* your client, is he?'

'He most certainly is. If anyone doubts it they can phone him themselves. And he's by no means the only one,' Annie added with bravado. Everyone in publishing respected Peggy. It would make a difference if she put out the word that Annie Hamilton was OK. 'Several of the writers I've handled will be joining my new agency.'

'Good for you . . . Such as?'

Annie played her ace. 'Trelawny Grey, for starters. I'll be selling his autobiography next year.'

'Smart work!' Peggy was impressed. 'Listen, I'll get back to you with our bid, once I've had it signed in triplicate by the head honcho – you know how it is these days.'

Annie put down the receiver with a shaky sigh. At once the phone trilled again under her hand. It was a reporter for *Publishers Weekly*. Would Annie care to comment on a press release received from Smith & Robertson that morning? For a moment Annie was struck dumb.

'I'm in mid-auction at the moment,' she rallied, summoning her most businesslike tone. 'But I'd be happy to ring you back this afternoon and give you an interview about my new agency. You can have the scoop on who's bought Sebastian Winter, too.'

She hung up, feeling under siege. What had she done to deserve this torrent of nasty surprises? She had a mental picture of two loutish devils propping up a bar in hell, beer cans in hand. 'I'm bored,' one was saying. 'Me, too,' said the other. 'Let's do over Annie Hamilton.'

She wondered where Tom was now. A week of silence: it seemed like months. This must be her punishment for seeing Jordan. Remembering the way she had practically flung herself into bed with him, Annie's cheeks flamed. She forced herself to banish the images that crowded her mind, and to concentrate on the job in hand. She had failed as a mother, failed as a daughter, failed as a loyal wife. She could not allow herself to fail in her career, too. Now, where was her Filofax?

The phone went again. 'Hello, it's me. How did the reunion go?'

Annie rolled her eyes. This was all she needed.

'Rose, do you mind if we talk later? My big auction has just blown up in my face, and I'm desperately trying to salvage the wreckage.'

'OK.' Rose sounded hurt, 'I just wanted to tell you – '

'Not now, Rose, please. I need to keep the line clear. I'll see you at lunch. 'Bye.' Annie put down the phone, exasperated. How many times had Rose put Annie on 'Hold', or relayed a message through some secretary? Now that Annie was trying to launch her own career, all Rose was interested in was tittle-tattle. Sometimes Annie wondered whether Rose had a sensitive nerve in her body. Then she remembered the champagne which had been awaiting her at the Algonquin – without a card, but a typical Rose gesture – and felt a guilty pang.

She put Rose out of her mind, took a clean sheet of paper from the desk and wrote herself a nice, neat list of things to do. First she rang Sebastian in London, wishing she had more positive news. After his initial dismay, he rallied once she had explained the problem. As a former journalist, he adored emergencies. He promised to stand by for calls from doubting publishers, sounding positively excited by the prospect. Next, she rang every publisher on her list, reassuring them that Winter had now become her client and that she was therefore empowered to act on his behalf, and apologising for any confusion. The reaction was more curious than condemnatory; a couple of people even volunteered indiscreet anecdotes about Jack's judgement. Annie started to feel only ninety-five per cent suicidal.

Now there was nothing to do but wait. Annie paced

the small hotel room, biting her nails and staring at her 'view' until she had memorised every rust-spot on the water tank of the next door building. She rechecked her notes on royalties and paperback splits and payment stages. Haunted by all the things that could go wrong, she prepared defensive strategies. At eleven o'clock she got her first serious call. The editor loved the book, he adored it, he would kill to have Winter on his list. But his paperback colleagues would not support his bid, the illiterate skunks. Regretfully, he was out. Annie commiserated and thanked him politely for his response, feeling the San Andreas Fault quiver beneath her brilliant career. The phone rang again: another publisher. The editor loved the book, he adored it, he would kill to have it – and he was offering half a million dollars. Annie leapt for her pen.

By the time the midday deadline expired, six more offers had come in, and the bid had soared to three-quarters of a million. Annie called everyone back to tell them the figure they now had to beat, then rang Sebastian to give him a progress report.

'Jesus!' His laugh was squeaky with hysteria.

'And that's only the first round. With so many publishers bidding, you'll probably be a dollar millionaire by this afternoon.'

There was a long ruminative pause. 'I was looking at a sports car yesterday – you know, that new four-seater with the great big – '

'Buy it,' Annie said crisply.

Interestingly, not a single publisher had rung Sebastian. So far her reputation had carried the day. Annie thought she would have quite a lot to say to Jack when the time came. But now she deserved a treat: lunch.

The Royalton was staffed by the handsomest young men Annie had ever seen, coiffed to perfection. Loose, high-collared jackets gave them a look of oriental houseboys. Their smiles were pure Hollywood. 'Hi, I'm Scott,' said one, in such a friendly way that Annie felt bound to tell him her name too.

'I'm meeting a friend for lunch,' she confided, 'but she doesn't seem to be here yet.'

Annie found herself expertly whisked into a quiet corner from which she could observe the power lunch in action. She had heard about the Royalton's transformation from poor-man's Algonquin to chic media hang-out, but had never ventured inside its almost masonically discreet entrance. Its waterfalls and Philippe Starck styling proclaimed a quiet, studied arrogance. At one table an Australian chat-show star was being interviewed on camera, winking his famous currant bun eyes. At another she recognised the diminutive media tycoon who owned the publishing house that had offered the highest bid for Sebastian. He was fiddling nervously with his glass of water, avoiding eye contact with his sober-suited lunch partner: not his banker, Annie hoped.

Ten minutes later she was beginning to get cross. She had told Rose that she wouldn't have much time. Rose herself had suggested this place because it was right across the street from the Algonquin. Annie walked over to Scott and asked if there had been any message from Rose. The second she mentioned Rose's name, the *maître d'* went into overdrive. Apologising profusely, he swept Annie to a prominent banquette seat and begged for the privilege of bringing her a complimentary beverage. Torn between amusement and irritation at this charade, Annie agreed to a Virgin Mary. Now, of course, the whole restaurant was staring at her, wondering who she could be to command such deference. Annie lifted her chin and stared haughtily into the middle distance, trying to project the image of a fabulously exclusive literary agent accustomed to million-dollar deals. Oh yes, sneered an inner voice, so exclusive that you have only two clients.

At last Rose breezed in, wearing a drop-dead grey silk suit with white facings. She waved gaily to Annie and came over, though not before pausing to share a little joke with Scott and then to shake hands with the mini-mogul. She pressed her cheek to Annie's, enveloping her in a cloud of perfume.

'Sorry to be late, I got stuck haggling with some unspeakable Hollywood agent over a cover pic. Classic tinseltown machismo – don't you just hate it? How are you? You look divine.'

'Fine.' Annie smiled, feeling overwhelmed. It was always the same when they met after a long separation. 'At least, I've had a horrible morning but I think I've salvaged the situation. You see, this auction – '

Rose held up a hand. 'Sorry to interrupt, I'm dying to hear about your book thingie – and about everything else.' She raised her eyebrows meaningfully. 'But I have to tell you first: Tom is safe.'

Annie stared. The words literally didn't make sense to her. She could think of no means by which Rose could possibly know this when she didn't. 'What do you mean?'

'What I say.' Rose smiled triumphantly. 'I was dying to tell you on the phone, but you didn't give me a chance. Tom's been here, in New York, staying at my apartment. He was very muddled, poor lamb, but I think I straightened him out. He's given up the, you know, wild goose chase. I put him on a plane back to England yesterday.'

Annie felt her face flush with rage. 'Here?' she stammered. 'In your – ? You knew where he was?' She half rose from her seat. Tears of relief and shock sprang to her eyes. 'Why didn't you tell me?'

'I am telling you. Calm down, Annie. If you'd just listen, you'd understand that I've done you a favour.'

'Favour! You call it a favour not to let me know that my son isn't lost or dead or – ' Annie shook her head. Her throat was so tight she couldn't get out the words.

'Don't be upset,' Rose said coaxingly. 'Of course I

realised how worried you were, but you didn't see what Tom was like when he turned up. Honestly, Annie, hand on heart, I know I made the right decision.'

'Do you?' Annie flung her napkin on to the table. 'You may be God in your own office, Rose, or in your precious magazine world, but you do not control my personal life. Tom is *my* son.' She stabbed her chest with her finger. 'If you want to play about with someone's family, get your own.' Annie's voice rose aggressively. As she became aware of the eyes riveted to their table, her fury deepened. 'And how you could possibly think it appropriate to tell me about Tom in this idiotic, self-regarding goldfish bowl, I don't know. It isn't the kind of news you just drop into the conversation over the beef *carpaccio*.' Annie scraped her chair back and stood up. The sight of Rose's shuttered face made her say more calmly, 'I'm sorry, but I'm too angry to stay. I'll call you later.'

Annie strode out of the restaurant, stiff with emotion. One of the beautiful young men leapt to open the door. 'Have a nice day,' he chanted.

She ran across the street, oblivious to honking horns, avoiding the cars by instinct. When she reached her room, a winking light on the telephone indicated a message. Ignoring it, she dialled Edward at home, praying that he would be back from work. She almost burst into tears when she heard his voice, stumbling over her words as she told him the good news.

'Oh good, you've seen Rose, then,' he said in a matter-of-fact way. 'Isn't it a relief? I slept properly last night, for the first time in a week.'

Annie gasped. 'You mean you *knew*?'

'Rose phoned yesterday morning to say that Tom had turned up at her place. Darling, I was desperate to tell you, but Rose persuaded me to wait.'

'But surely – '

'You know what I think about Rose's high-handed ways, but this time I think she is on the side of the

355

angels. Apparently Tom has abandoned this Jordan Hope nonsense and is ready to go back to Oxford. We'll have to come clean with him about why we weren't married when he was born and all that – but it's high time, don't you think?'

Annie listened to his reasonable voice, wondering if she were on a different planet.

'It seemed the right decision to wait until Tom had left New York,' he went on. 'I thought you had enough to deal with, what with your mother and starting the new business, and the book auction. Besides – ' he hesitated.

'You didn't trust me!' Annie burst out. 'You thought I'd throw a wobbly, act like a hysterical woman. Didn't you?'

'I hope we'll always trust each other,' Edward answered after a cool pause. 'And yes, I thought it might be best to get Tom safely home, on familiar territory, before you two saw each other again. You've both been so wound up, I didn't want one of you to say something you didn't mean and spark the whole thing off again.'

'Well, thanks for the vote of confidence,' Annie spat sarcastically. She felt patronised beyond enduring. 'Tom is *my* son, don't forget. I looked after him on my own for nearly three whole years before you even knew he existed.'

The minute the words were out, Annie regretted them. But it was too late. Edward's voice came evenly down the line. 'Tom is *our* son. You know that's the way I have always thought of him. And I always will. You're going to have to sort yourself out, Annie – decide what you want, and what you're going to tell Tom. I have work to do now. I'll see you tomorrow.'

There was a click, then the disconnected tone. He had put the phone down on her!

Annie was aghast. Edward had never done such a thing before. She had hurt him horribly. He had sounded so distant, as if her life were not bound inextricably and for ever with his. It seemed that this whole trip – Rose's so-called 'masterplan', which was supposed to straighten out her life – had only enmeshed her deeper in lies.

Annie tried to calm herself. At least Tom was safe. She must let Jordan know. Quickly Annie found her bag and drew out the piece of paper on which Jordan had written the phone number where he could be reached. She smoothed it out gently and dialled, telling herself that he could not possibly be available to answer it. Nevertheless, she was unreasonably disappointed when she had to leave her cryptic message. She would have liked to speak to him one more time, to wish him luck.

The light was still winking on the telephone. The message was to ring back a publisher. Annie tapped in the number, her mind elsewhere. A gravelly voice growled in her ear. Suddenly her brain snapped into action. He was offering her a million dollars. After that the phone hardly stopped ringing. No auction in her experience had ever gone at such a rollercoaster pace. Eventually it dawned on her that Jack's petulant attempt at sabotage had produced the opposite effect to what he intended. This was New York. 'Buzz' was everything. The thrilling story of Annie's dramatic breakout from Smith & Robertson, Sebastian Winter's defection and Jack's vengefulness constituted the perfect antidote to post-Frankfurt blues. By four-thirty the bidding had risen to $1.7 million and there were two bidders left, neither showing signs of slackening. Annie was in mid-phone call when she heard a knock at her door. She flung it open, expecting to shoo away an over-zealous maid. There was Rose, offering an appeasing smile and a bottle of champagne.

Annie signalled her in. 'I'm sorry, Elaine,' she continued into the phone, 'but if your offer is to be truly comparable with the others I have on the table, you're going to have to put more up front. Let's go through the payment stages again.'

Rose tiptoed across the room and sat in an upright chair out of the way while Annie shuttled back and forth between the two remaining publishers, ratcheting up the advance each time. Annie maintained her icy control until one of them finally conceded. The deal was done.

Only then did Annie let out a whoop of triumph. 'Two *million*!'

Rose came over and hugged her. 'Well done. I had no idea you could be such a toughie. I'm impressed.'

'Don't be impressed, open the champagne!' Annie shouted hysterically. She threw herself backwards across the bed, arms outflung, beaming at the ceiling. Then she remembered. 'Christ! I'd better tell the poor author.'

Sebastian answered at the first ring. The news left him dazed. 'I suppose I'll have to write that second book now,' he said rather forlornly.

Next was Jack.

'*Two million*?' he gasped.

'Don't worry, you'll get your fair share. You can get Julia to ring me about the contracts tomorrow.' Annie paused. In the background she could hear the ten o'clock news. How could he just be sitting there, his conscience untroubled? 'Why did you do it, Jack?' she asked finally.

'I – I thought you were behaving unprofessionally.'

'No, *you* behaved unprofessionally, treating me as you did, forcing me to go behind your back. I hated it. Your father never – '

'My father's dead! I don't know what there was between you, or who is the father of your bastard son, but it's past history now. You have no claims on me or my business.'

Annie caught her breath. So that's what it had all been about. Listening to his shrill, little-boy voice, she was surprised by sudden pity.

'Listen, Jack. Your father and I were friends – good friends. But I did not have an affair with him, and Tom is certainly not his son, if that's what you're worrying about. Tom was at least a year old when I came to work for him. And yes –' she gathered her strength to say the word – 'Tom is illegitimate. He knows it. I don't see that it's anyone else's business.'

Jack had the grace to sound ashamed. 'I didn't really think . . . It's only, Janie said' – he stopped unhappily.

Annie's mouth tightened. Trust Jack's wife to judge other people by her own standards. She wondered if Jack knew that Jane had been nicknamed 'La Couchette', after her practice of speeding to promotion on her back. Her spurt of sympathy subsided. She put down the phone thinking that the pair of them deserved each other.

Rose handed her a glass. 'This is better than the movies,' she said. 'Who's next?'

Sprawled among the pillows, sipping champagne, Annie rang back *Publishers Weekly* and gave them a string of hugely optimistic half-truths about her agency. They made her promise to courier over a photograph of herself so that they could run a feature in the next issue. Annie put down the phone, extremely pleased with herself, and raised her glass to Rose.

'This is very nice of you. I haven't had a chance to drink the other one yet.'

'What other one?'

'There was a bottle of champagne waiting when I arrived here. I assumed it was from you.' A wild alternative seized her.

'Perhaps it was from Someone Else.' Rose raised her eyebrows insinuatingly, as she took off her suit jacket and hung it carefully over the back of a chair. Underneath she was wearing a flimsy silk top with spaghetti straps. Annie frowned as she watched her climb on to the foot of the bed.

'Why don't your arms wobble like mine?'

'Because I spend several hours a week and a fortune on a personal trainer to ensure they don't. You have a husband and a family; I have a perfectly toned body: the modern woman's dilemma in a nutshell. And stop changing the subject.' Rose bounced gently on the bed, eyes sparkling. 'I'm dying to know: did Jordan make the meeting?'

Annie nodded. 'He came to my hotel room.'

'No!' Rose clasped her hands with excitement. 'How did he manage it?'

'Oh . . . you know.'

'No, I don't know, Annie. Come on, just a few teensy crumbs.'

'Well, he came late, about two. We talked about Tom.'

'Uh-huh.' Rose nodded encouragingly.

'I told him I couldn't swear Tom was his, but he seemed to like the idea.'

'Uh-huh.'

'And he told me a bit about his wife.'

'Uh-huh.'

'And I told him about my job.'

'Uh-huh.'

'And, well, then he went back to his hotel.'

'And what time was that?'

'Oh, fiveish,' Annie shrugged.

Rose reached to the floor for the champagne bottle and filled Annie's glass, then her own. She gave Annie an appraising look. 'Let me get this straight. You talked about Tom and Ginny and your job *for three hours*?'

'Yes. No. Sort of. It took a while to get used to each other again. I hadn't seen him for twenty-odd years. I thought he'd probably completely forgotten about me.'

'But of course he hadn't.'

'No,' Annie said, remembering. She caught her friend's sly glance. 'Oh, Rose, I know you always thought he was just a crude Yankee-Doodle-Dandy who wouldn't know the difference between a . . . a crouton and a futon. But, well, there's something about him.' She started to smile, thinking of the feel of his big shoulders and that look he had, as if inviting the whole world to fall in love with him. Rose arched her eyebrows knowingly as Annie fumbled for the right words. 'He is sort of attractive, in his way. I always . . . I mean, he always – ' Annie hid her telltale face in her hands.

'Annie,' whispered Rose in an awed voice. 'You're not going to tell me that you actually fucked the next fucking President of the US of A?'

'Of course not!' Annie looked up and gave a little giggle. 'Although we – ' She sank back into the pillows and started to laugh. Egged on by Rose, her tongue loosened by champagne, Annie blushingly gave her an edited version of events leading up to the timely phone call from Trelawny Grey. By the time she had got to Trelawny's anecdote about the exceptionally hairy publishing grandee, whose nude sunbathing at Cap Ferrat had given rise to a local rumour of an escaped baboon, they were both rolling on the bed. Annie left out the bit about the condoms: best not to put temptation in Rose's way.

Rose wiped her eyes. 'God, Annie, I have to hand it to you. Here I am thinking I'm the centre of the bloody universe, when it's you that waltzes off into some loony escapade like this. I like to think of you doing reassuring things like tidying the linen cupboard or entering for the mothers' race on Sports Day.'

It was an apology of sorts. Annie looked at her friend with affection. 'I'm sorry about lunch,' she offered. 'Edward says you made the right decision about Tom. It was just such a shock.'

'Don't worry.' Rose flapped a hand. 'I'll pay for my lapse of tact. By tonight the news will be all over town that I've had a quarrel with my hitherto unsuspected lesbian lover. Incidentally, when did you say your plane left?'

Annie looked at her watch and shrieked. Rose reached for her mobile phone. 'You finish packing. I'll get my car to take you to the airport. You can drop me on the way.'

While they drove up town, Annie interrogated Rose about Tom, learning of his search for his birth certificate and his impulsive arrival in New York. He had shown surprising resourcefulness, she thought.

'So what did you think of Tom?' she fished.

'Adorable – polite, handsome, good company. If I'd known children could turn out like that, I might have had one myself.'

'Really?' Rose's long-ago abortion, and the identity of the American father, had always remained a taboo subject between them. Having herself made such a different decision, Annie had often wondered if Rose felt regret.

'Sweetheart,' Rose chided, 'can you really see me with sick on my Chanel? Tom is different. He has grown up.'

'Has he?' Annie asked dubiously.

'Yes, and at risk of having you jump out of the car, I suggest that if you treat him like an adult, he'll respond like one.'

'Oh,' Annie said, surprised.

Everything seemed suddenly to be changing. If Tom was grown up, what did that make her? With a shock she realised that when her mother died, she would become the 'older' generation. Annie told Rose about the meeting with her mother, sharing her thoughts.

'At least I don't have to worry about that,' Rose said briskly. 'When I'm gone, nothing will remain except a tacky plaque in some crematorium: "Rose Cassidy, RIP. Not very nice, but a bloody good magazine editor".'

'Rubbish!'

'It's true. You were always the nice one.'

'I don't feel very nice,' Annie muttered. 'I've neglected my mother until she's on her deathbed, done the dirty on Jack, lied to Tom and Edward. I'm not sure they're going to forgive me.'

'We all make our choices,' Rose said bracingly. 'You're going back to a husband who adores you. Jordan and Ginny Hope are off to Washington, God help them. And I – ' she gestured as the car drew up in front of her building – 'have my fax machine to go home to.'

Annie reached over to hug her. 'Thanks for everything, Rose. It was a brilliant masterplan. If there's anything I can do for you – '

'Well actually, I was wondering about serial rights in Trelawny Grey's memoirs. They sound very juicy.'

Annie laughed. 'Don't you ever stop?'

'I hope not.' Rose kissed her and climbed out of the car. She ducked her head back in. 'Love to Edward.' She looked Annie in the eye. 'He's been a patient man, you know. Don't blow it.'

With that she shut the door and the car took off. Annie swivelled round. Through the rear window she could see Rose standing on the sidewalk, a small, solitary figure, watching her go.

Queasily she wondered what Rose had meant. It would be a cruel irony if, in the process of squaring things with Jordan, she had lost Edward.

36

Let's work together

It was midnight when Tom drove up the hill towards
Hampstead Heath and parked the Morris outside his
home. He took his new suitcase of new clothes out of the
boot, locked the car and stood for a minute breathing in
the damp, bonfire-scented English air. It would be Guy
Fawkes' Night on Thursday. Remembering that he had
been invited to a fireworks party in Oxford, he felt a spark
of anticipation.

As he set the case down on the doorstep to search for
his house keys, the door opened. His father drew him
into the warm, lighted hall with a powerful hug.

'Tom – how marvellous!'

Tom patted his shoulder, feeling awkward. 'Didn't Rose
tell you I was coming?'

'Yes, but – I thought you'd be here earlier. I must have
misunderstood.'

This was exceptionally tactful, Tom thought. Usually,
it was the old line about punctuality being the politeness
of kings. 'I had to collect the car from Gatwick,' he
explained. 'Seeing I was so near, I decided to drop in on
Rebecca. Sorry, I probably should have phoned.'

'Probably,' his father agreed wryly. He picked up the case and carried it to the foot of the stairs. 'What can I get you? Tea, coffee, food? . . . Whisky?'

'Thanks,' Tom yawned, 'but all I really want to do is sleep.'

'Oh. Of course. Up you go, then.' His father hesitated. 'I've got to be off early tomorrow, so I probably won't see you. And the girls are away until tomorrow. But Annie should be back in the late morning. She's been in New York, you know, and Chicago.'

'New York?' Tom's drooping eyelids snapped open. Had his mother been following him? What if she had come to the apartment when he and Rose – ? His stomach curdled at the thought. 'What's she been doing there?' he asked suspiciously.

'Selling a book. She'll tell you all about it – unless . . . I suppose you wouldn't like to come with me tomorrow? I'm driving up to Nottingham for a meeting with the UDM – the mineworkers. I'd have you back by early afternoon. We could chat in the car.'

It was said lightly, but Tom detected an uncharacteristically diffident note. He glanced at his father's face. It looked strained and wary, as if he were uncertain of Tom. 'No. You're tired.' He shook his head dismissively. 'It's a stupid idea.'

Tom gave him a slow smile. 'Can I drive the BMW?'

His father's face cleared. 'Within the speed limit, yes,' he laughed. 'And you'll need to wear a suit and tie.'

Tom hefted his suitcase. 'Suits, we got 'em. I'll tell you all about it tomorrow.'

Tom went upstairs, pulled off his clothes and got straight into his familiar bed without even turning the light on. The sheets felt soft and cool on his bare skin, reminding him of his very satisfactory reunion with Rebecca, to whom he had confessed everything. Well, nearly everything. He would never tell anyone about Rose, or not until he was an old man of forty or so, when life would be so dull that he might have to fall back on his memories. Tom settled his hands behind his head, grinning into the darkness. He had been to bed with two women in two countries in two days – and he didn't even feel guilty! He bet his Oxford room-mate Brian had done nothing more exciting than go to the pub. For a while he watched the erratic flash of car headlights across the ceiling, recalling his adventures. Then his thoughts turned to tomorrow, and the questions he wanted to ask. But it was late and he was tired. In a few minutes he was asleep.

The next morning it was raining hard. Driving up the crowded motorway was not as much fun as Tom had expected, and required all his concentration. IIis father was still behaving oddly. He seemed reserved to the point of formality, and had precluded conversation by studying his papers for the meeting. There had been no recriminations about Tom's disappearance from Oxford, no lecture on irresponsible behaviour, no interrogation about what Tom had been doing and why. Tom had expected to have to defend himself; instead, his father had yielded him the ground without a fight. It was worrying.

'So what are we going to do in Nottingham – close down a pit?' Tom asked, trying to lighten the atmosphere.

'Hardly,' his father answered drily.

Tom learned that, on the contrary, it was the government that was planning to close several pits, to the special fury of these particular miners, part of a breakaway union which had refused to take part in the crippling miners' strike of '84. Eight years ago the government had praised them for sustaining the coal industry: this was their reward. With the aim of saving their jobs, they had commissioned a feasibility study of certain collieries, hoping that these might be bought privately, possibly by a foreign buyer. Tom's father was to going up to advise them about the implications of a private sale on their conditions of employment. He talked to Tom about pensions, safety regulations, wage negotiations. Tom grunted in reply, thinking that he was in for a dull morning.

In fact, it was a revelation. If Tom had half envisaged his father, the posh London barrister, dispensing gobble-dygook to a circle of coal-begrimed workers, he quickly discovered his error. For a start, the meeting was intensely emotional. The men were in shock – aggrieved, belliger-ent, frightened of the future. It was clear that they knew Edward well, and looked to him for rescue. Equally clearly, his father felt passionately about their plight. During a coffee break, one man almost broke down as he spoke to Tom of his father's support over the years, and how he had put in far more work than he ever charged for. There was no doubt that Edward held the meeting in control. As usual he was immaculate, dark hair swept back, charcoal suit spiced with an eccentric touch: today it was red socks, to match his tie. But he was receptive, sympathetic, anything but patronising. Tom's concept of the legal profession as a dull, more or less cynical manipulation of statutes and precedents, underwent a quiet revolution.

Afterwards they lunched companionably in a pub. Over their halves of bitter and microwaved shepherd's pie, Tom began to tell his father about his experiences of Manhattan high life with Rose, making him laugh about her mesmerising effect on the Barneys salesmen and her bizarre acquaintances at the Benefit. They were both marking time, waiting to come to the point. Tom under-stood that he would have to make the plunge first.

'Did Rose tell you where I was before that – I mean, about going up to Southport to look at my birth cer-tificate?'

'Yes.' His father frowned into his beer, then drained the glass. 'Come on, we'll talk about that in the car. I'll drive.'

It wasn't until they were back on the motorway that he

began to speak, with a quiet intensity that gripped Tom from his opening words.

'I loved your mother from the first moment I saw her,' he began. 'I know it's an old family story that we joke about, how I threw her into the river to get her attention. But before I even learned her name I thought: that is the woman for me. It does happen. At times it seemed more like a curse than a blessing. I was younger than you are now. I wanted to have a wild time, see the world, have adventures. I didn't want to settle down. But I wanted Annie.

'When you're young you tend to grab at things. We'd been going out the whole of my last year at Oxford. When the time came for me to leave, I panicked. She still had another year to go. I was frightened of losing her. Unfortunately, I messed things up, rushing my fences. In fact, I made a fool of myself. I then made things even worse by writing her what I expect was a fearfully stiff-necked note saying I thought it would be better if we didn't see each other for a while. I didn't mean it, of course. It was just hurt pride.'

His father broke off. 'I'm sorry if this all seems a bit personal, but it is leading somewhere.'

'No, go on.'

'Well, that was the end of my last term at Oxford. June 1970,' he glanced at Tom, 'a date you may care to remember. Of course I missed her horribly all summer and wished I had never written that stupid letter. But I had no address for her. I simply had to wait until the new term started. I drove up to LMH the first weekend of term, only to be told that she had abandoned her studies and left the college for good. I was stunned. I couldn't think what had happened. The college didn't have an address either, and couldn't give me any reason for her leaving.'

'Didn't Rose know where she was?'

His father gave a harsh laugh. 'She knew all right, but

368

she wouldn't tell me. Annie didn't want me to know, she said. Rose wouldn't even pass on a letter from me – not even a message. God, I hated her. I accused her of manipulating Annie, poisoning her mind with Women's Lib rubbish, hiding from me that Annie was ill or dying – everything I could think of. I simply could not believe that the Annie I knew could be so cruel. But you know Rose: she wouldn't budge.'

His father fell silent. For a time there was nothing but the hissing of tyres on the wet road and the faint squeak from the windscreen wipers. Tom waited. At last, perhaps, the missing pieces of the puzzle were coming together.

'Anyway,' his father continued, 'life carried on. I was accepted into chambers and managed to pass my Bar exams. I even met some nice girls. But they weren't Annie. I looked for her everywhere – from the top decks of buses, in restaurants and shops, in the park. I used to run after total strangers in the street, thinking they were her. It was the mystery of the whole thing that drove me mad. I'm afraid the truth never crossed my mind.'

Tom tried to picture his controlled, sophisticated father running after girls in the street. It was hard to imagine.

'One day at work, I answered the telephone and heard her voice. She had just started working at Smith & Robertson and was ringing one of the partners for some advice on libel. It was like a miracle. I begged her to meet me, but she refused. I remember she said, "My life has changed." I couldn't think what she meant, but of course I was determined to find out. Now I knew where she worked, it wasn't very difficult to invent some story and get hold of her address. The following Sunday I just turned up at her flat. She was living upstairs from a newsagent's in a grotty terrace in Battersea, with lorries roaring past and litter in the street. I parked the car and was just a few steps away when the front door opened and out came Annie, bumping a pushchair down the steps. In the

pushchair was this funny little person in a bobble hat.'
He smiled across at Tom. 'You.'

'What a horrible shock,' Tom scowled, trying to disguise an unexpected flood of emotion.

'A wonderful surprise,' his father corrected, 'to find I had a son. I just knew the minute I saw you. It made sense of everything – Annie's disappearance, her peculiar reaction to me, Rose's hostility. It was all so typical of your mother – her bravery, that fierce pride of hers, that streak of secrecy she's always had. And I was so pleased. I felt an incredible elation that everything had at last come right.

'Of course it took a lot longer than that. Annie was very defensive. She had been through a bad time. We're all used to single mothers now, but in those days they were "unmarried mothers", and much frowned upon. It was difficult to get a job or find anywhere to live. However, I'd learned my lesson by then. I took it slowly, inviting her out to a film, or pushing you round Battersea Park, until eventually it seemed the right thing to get married. That's when we went to the Registrar and got him to write out a new birth certificate, naming me as your father. Illegitimacy carried a stigma then, which we didn't want you to suffer. We thought we were doing our best for you. You were so young, we knew you'd never remember that I hadn't always been around.'

Tom shook his head. 'I don't remember. But I always knew there was something odd. Did I come to your wedding, then?'

'No. Annie said it wouldn't be right. But afterwards we had an informal reception in the garden. It was summer. I had a flat in Islington. We tried to make the party special for you. We had a huge chocolate concoction instead of the usual wedding cake, and that disgusting stripy ice-cream you liked and – '

A vivid image of bright clouds falling out of the sky

surged up from Tom's memory. 'The balloons!' he burst out.

'Good Lord, you remember that? Yes, we let them go out of the top window, twenty or more. I can still remember the look on your face.'

'And didn't I have some sort of scarf thing?' Tom frowned, in the grip now of some sweet, elusive recollection. 'I remember I got it wet when I wasn't supposed to, but nobody told me off.'

His father laughed aloud. 'The tie of your sailor suit! Heavens, I'd forgotten. You got it covered in food and drink and grass and dirt until it looked like some horrible old kitchen rag. Though you did look very sweet.'

His face grew sober. 'We made sure you weren't in any pictures. We were covering our tracks already. It was the beginning of the lie. I see now that it was a foolish course. Too many people knew the truth. Someone was bound to make a slip one day. And I'm sorry, Tom. I apologise for not having trusted you with the truth, and making you unhappy.' He reached out to grip Tom's knee briefly. 'I didn't mean to. Forgive me.'

Tom had been only half-listening. That distant memory had sparked off others: the birthday when his father had set up a climbing frame in the garden overnight that was the envy of his friends; the Christmas when they had gone shopping in Harrods to buy a present for Mum and eaten lunch at Wheeler's, sitting up at the marble-topped bar; the time his father had taken him night-fishing for shark in Cornwall. It was true that he could not remember a time without his father's presence.

'It's all right,' Tom mumbled inadequately. 'I mean, I wish you'd told me, but I suppose I can see why you didn't.'

His father let out his breath. 'Well, we'll try to do better in future. No more secrets. I'm afraid it's hard for parents to judge the moment when their children have grown up.'

Tom nodded, warmed by the compliment.

'And you have to bear in mind that we were very young. Annie was only nineteen when she got pregnant.'

Nineteen! Tom couldn't help remembering his boorish behaviour to Rebecca last week. If he had had his way, she could be pregnant now, and himself a prospective father.

'I'm sorry you had to find out this way,' his father went on. 'It clearly made you unhappy.' He hesitated. A note of puzzlement crept into his voice. 'I can understand that discovering your birth certificate was a shock and made you start wondering if I really was your father, but what I still can't quite grasp is why you fixed on Jordan Hope.'

Tom shifted in his seat, watching the sprawl of outer London flash past. 'I found this old photo of him in Mum's trunk. My scout thought it was a picture of me, and quite honestly it did look a bit like me. I thought it was weird that Mum had kept it all this time, and when I asked her about it she told me all sorts of daft lies.'

'I see,' his father said uncertainly. 'At least – I know Hope was at Oxford at the same time as us, but so were thousands of people. I'm sure Annie never mentioned him at the time. I wasn't aware she even knew him until his name started appearing in the papers. She told me that Rose had known him slightly.' He frowned. For the first time his fluency faltered. 'I mean . . . who exactly was in this photo? Do you still have it?'

I think she may have had a one-night stand with Jordan. Rose's words flashed a sudden, electrifying warning in Tom's brain. Here was something he knew, or had reason to suspect, that his father didn't. It would be like Rebecca finding out he'd gone to bed with Rose. The photograph was in his suitcase at home. Tom had pored over it so often that every detail was clear in his mind. He remembered its powerful aura of intimacy and happiness, and the inscription, '*For Annie, my two-times girl. Love always. J.*'

Tom looked at his father, reading doubt and confusion in his face. He had to protect him.

'I think it must have been a party,' he said casually. 'There was Jordan Hope and Mum and a whole group of people in some garden. I had the photo in Southport with me, but one day I got so angry that I tore it up. I threw the pieces into the sea.'

Tom looked his father innocently in the eye and shrugged. 'Sorry, Dad.'

37

All right now

As the taxi rumbled northwards through the heavy morning traffic, the anxiety which had kept Annie awake all through the flight renewed its grip on her imagination. What was she going to say to Tom – and to Edward? She had a nightmare vision of the two of them sitting at the kitchen table in judgement upon her, waiting for her explanation. When the taxi drew up outside the house, she thrust notes into the driver's hand, overtipping wildly, too strung up to wait for her change. The front door was double-locked. Inside, the house was silent. Annie picked up a piece of paper from the hall table.

I've taken Tom to my meeting in Nottingham. He should be back by mid-afternoon. – E.

Annie's heart lurched at his chilly brevity. Why had he taken Tom away? What were they telling each other? Edward didn't say when he would be home. On impulse she ran down the hall to her study, still wearing her coat, and tugged at the deep bottom drawer of her desk. It was crammed with notes and cards from Edward – birthdays, anniversaries, Valentines. There were no great love letters, just a steady accumulation of small messages of love which she had popped in this drawer, incapable of throwing them away. Annie picked one out at random: a Cartier Bresson photograph of a couple kissing passionately. 'Happy fifteenth anniversary – here's to the next fifty.' There were hundreds of them: foolish, funny, tender, self-mocking – a twenty-year reiteration of love.

And what had she given in return? Not enough, was the answer. A corner of her heart, small but lovingly tended, she had reserved for Jordan.

In a sudden revelation, Annie understood that it was not just for Tom's sake that she had kept the circumstances of his birth secret. She too had wanted to cling to the mystery of his conception, to the memory of that magical, marvellous night under the willow trees. It was shockingly unfair to Edward. No matter whose sperm had produced Tom, it was Edward who had taught him cricket, nursed him through measles, showed up on Parents' Day. Edward was his real father.

What were the two of them talking about, closeted in the car? Remembering her last sight of Tom, distraught and angry, Annie could imagine him disowning Edward and claiming Jordan as his father. He would show Edward the photograph as proof. Edward would recognise the dress she had worn to the Commem and guess the rest. He would never forgive her. The image of Edward hurling her engagement ring into the river rose in her mind like a warning.

Annie slammed the drawer shut. There was nothing to do but wait and see. She would unpack, change, buy something Edward especially liked for dinner – and hope. Fetching her suitcase, she heaved it up to her bedroom. Out of habit she switched on the radio, just in time to catch the tail end of a news bulletin. *As the American people awake to a day that will determine their future for the next four years, we go to our Washington correspondent* – Annie turned it off hastily. She would not allow herself to think about Jordan. She absolutely forbade it. Nevertheless, as she hung up her clothes and changed into trousers and a favourite old cashmere sweater, she kept finding that she had unconsciously crossed her fingers.

By mid-afternoon, she had done her shopping, eaten a late lunch of cheese on toast, and was peeling parsnips in the basement kitchen, when she heard the front door slam and Tom's heavy tread in the hall.

'I'm down here,' she shouted.

There was a muffled reply, then the sound of him bounding upstairs. Annie's stomach tightened. For no very good reason, she grabbed her hairbrush from her handbag and swept it vigorously across her scalp. She heard him coming down again. Instinctively, she put on the kettle, then rested her hands on the kitchen counter, twisting her wedding ring, waiting.

Her first, irrelevant thought as her son appeared in the doorway was how handsome he looked. He was wearing a subtly coloured grey suit and blue button-down shirt, with a patterned tie in vibrant yellows that should have set a new standard in vulgarity but somehow looked supremely sophisticated. I produced this, she thought with a sudden thrill of wonder and pride – this handsome, six-foot, alien male. She felt faintly in awe of him.

'You look marvellous!' she exclaimed, then laughed to hear the surprise in her voice.

'Present from Rose.' Tom ruffled his hair self-consciously. He lounged into the room. 'Pretty flash, eh?'

'I should say.' Annie felt a pang of something almost like jealousy. 'You've always screamed blue murder when I wanted to buy you a suit.'

'Mum', Tom reproved gently, 'this is Armani.'

Annie tried not to gape. Since when had Tom known the difference between Armani and army surplus? 'Gosh,' she said humbly.

Tom sat down at the kitchen table and reached casually for an apple from the fruit bowl. 'Good trip?' he asked.

'Very successful, thanks. I gather we were both in New York at the same time.' Annie's heart sank. This was sounding like a business dinner.

'Mmm.' Tom nodded through a mouthful of apple, not volunteering more. Annie was trying to gauge his mood. If she weren't certain that he must be very angry with her, she would have said that he was relaxed, even happy.

'Tea?' she asked, giving herself time.

'Yeah, OK.'

Annie poured it into mugs and carried them across to the table, seating herself opposite Tom. Treat him like an equal, not your son, Rose had advised. Well, she would try.

'It's lovely to have you back, darling. And before we go further, I'd like to apologise for not being straightforward with you about the circumstances of your birth, and not taking proper account of your feelings when you discovered the truth. It was very wrong of me. It was only because I was frightened that it would make you unhappy. I'm sorry.'

Tom was gazing at her in some astonishment, forgetting to chew his apple.

'It's all right,' he said awkwardly.

'No, it's not all right. I can see that you feel there's a mystery that we've never explained, Edward and I, and it's time to put that right.' Annie paused. She still hadn't decided what to tell Tom. She knew she owed him the truth. On the other hand, what was the truth? Did she have the right to make Tom and Edward unhappy by telling them about Jordan, when for all she knew Edward was Tom's true, biological father?

'It's all right, Mum,' Tom repeated. 'Dad's explained everything.'

'He has?' Annie tried to hide her bewilderment. How could Edward explain what he didn't know? 'Everything?' she asked.

Tom nodded. 'All about how you two quarrelled, and

how you ran off and Dad couldn't find you – and then he did. You could have told me before, you know. It's not nearly as bad as some of the things I've been imagining. I've already told Rebecca about being illegitimate. She thinks it's dead romantic.'

Tom grinned, taking Annie's breath away. Then he sobered.

'Except Dad made me see it wasn't very romantic from your point of view – I mean having a baby on your own when you were so young, without anyone to help.'

Annie felt a lump form in her throat. 'That was my fault,' she said. 'I didn't want Edward to feel that he had to look after you.'

'But he wanted to, he said.' Tom frowned. 'Didn't he?'

'Oh, he did.' Annie was quick to reassure him. 'He was thrilled when he found out about you. But I couldn't guess that he would react that way. Besides,' she sipped her tea, 'there was something else.'

Even from the other side of the table she felt Tom tense. 'What?' he asked warily.

Annie began to describe the day long ago when she had gone to tell her mother that she was pregnant, only to learn that she herself had been conceived out of wedlock.

'I don't think my mother wanted a baby – not at all. She couldn't understand why I wanted to keep you.' Annie leaned urgently towards Tom. 'That's what I want you to understand: it was my choice to have you and to keep you. That's another reason I kept the truth from you. I never wanted you to think that you had just been a – an annoying accident I had to put up with. It wasn't true. *I wanted you.*'

'Oh.' Tom was silent for a long time, staring into his tea. When at last he looked up there was gleam of amusement in his eyes. 'So does that mean you're sort of illegitimate too?'

Annie couldn't resist running around the table to hug

him. He took it quite well, patting her shoulder as if she were a nice old horse.

'And is that why you never talked about your mother?'

'Partly.' Annie told Tom about seeing her mother and meeting Lee, trying to convey her feelings of sorrow and joy and disappointment. 'That's also why I wanted to protect you, to make you feel just like any other boy. I didn't have much of a family life, and I missed it. I know it can be claustrophobic, but sometimes it's nice to have a family, if only as a sort of useful trampoline to bounce you back into the world.'

Tom nodded slowly. 'That's what Rose said.'

'Really? I must say I've never seen Rose as a champion of family values.'

'You were the one who chose her to be my moral guardian,' Tom said teasingly. 'Isn't that what a godmother is?' He fiddled with his mug. 'She said some sensible things.'

'Oh? Like what?'

Tom gave her a look she could not quite interpret. 'Like telling me that I should forgive you your wild past.'

'Ah.' Annie felt herself blushing. What on earth had Rose said to him? As she fumbled for a sensible reply, she heard the door slam again – did no one in her family realise that it was possible to close doors gently? – and a familiar double-thump as schoolbags hit the hall floor. The girls were home. She could hear them squabbling companionably as they slopped down the stairs.

Tom jumped up and thrust something into her hand. 'You'd better have this,' he mumbled.

It was a plain white envelope. Annie pushed it into a pocket as her daughters burst into the room in their blue and yellow uniforms. Emma, as always, looked as if she had been put through the spin cycle of the washing machine, while Cassie was as stylishly dishevelled as if each twist of her cardigan sleeves and each wantonly unfastened button had been arranged for the catwalk by a master designer. To Annie's eyes they both looked impossibly fresh and beautiful, two dark-haired, grave-eyed girls out of an early Italian painting.

'Tom!' Emma squeaked excitedly, rushing over to him. 'What are you doing here? Don't you look lovely?'

'Hi, girls,' Tom gave them a lordly wave. 'My godmother just flew me to New York for a long weekend,' he added, with stunning aplomb. 'Didn't you know?'

Annie went over to her daughters and hugged them vigorously. 'How wonderful to see you!' she exclaimed, her eyes moistening with emotion.

'Loosen up, Ma.' Cassie rolled her eyes at Emma. 'Anyone would think you'd been away a lifetime, not just a few days.' She turned back to Tom. 'That's a wicked suit. I suppose Rose bought it for you. It's not fair. When is she going to invite me to New York?'

Tom eyed her critically. 'Don't call us, we'll call you.'

Annie went back to her dinner preparations, chopping onions for the bread sauce, laying bacon over the pheasants, covering the vegetables with water, as she listened to her children chatter. Life was back to normal. She liked it that way. Soon the girls persuaded Tom upstairs to check out the rest of his new wardrobe; Annie was left alone. She began to assemble ingredients for a blackberry and apple crumble, and turned on the radio for company. This time, when the election report came on, she could not stop herself listening. According to the exit polls, Jordan was almost certain to carry most of the East Coast states, which had been the first to vote. Hurray! His opponent would probably win in Indiana, South Carolina, Virginia, Oklahoma –

'Oh, shut up!' Annie snapped at the radio, slicing apples viciously.

But the pundits gathered in the newsroom seemed to agree that a return of the Democrats to the White House after twelve years looked likely. That certainly was the verdict of Harry's Bar in Paris, where exiled Americans had traditionally conducted their own elections since 1924. In sixty-eight years they had been wrong only once.

Annie listened, wholly engrossed, while she laid the table and set out candles, until a time-check alerted her to how late it was. Edward would be home soon, and she was sticky and bedraggled from cooking. She shot the pheasants into the oven, grabbed her handbag and fled upstairs to run a bath. She had planned to be dressed up and immaculate when he returned. Instead, she was only just stepping into the water when she heard the front door bang. She nearly jumped out again, embarrassed as a schoolgirl, then forced herself to relax and wait. Edward had seen her naked before.

She heard his quick tread on the stairs, then the creak of the floorboards as he crossed the bedroom to the bathroom door. It swung open slowly. Edward stood in the doorway, hands in his coat pockets, looking at her across the room.

'You're back,' he said, with that impassive look she knew so well.

'Of course I'm back.' Even to her own ears, Annie sounded horribly sprightly. 'Can't you smell the pheasant?'

'Are we celebrating?'

'I hope so.' Annie smiled tentatively, sinking deeper into the water under his stern gaze. 'You've still got your coat on.'

'Have I?' Edward took it off and ducked out of sight for a moment to put it in the bedroom. Annie waited for him to reappear.

'Tom seems in a very good mood,' she offered. 'I don't know what you said to him, but he seems different – calm, sure of himself.'

'Good.' Edward sat down in the wicker chair at the foot of the bath.

'So what did you tell him?' Annie persisted.

He eyed her mildly. 'The truth, of course.'

Annie hesitated, then summoned her courage. 'Edward, I'm sorry we quarrelled on the phone. I'm sorry for what I said. It was unfair and unforgivable. You've been the best possible father to Tom. I realise now how cruel I was to cheat you out of the early years. I never thought so before. I thought I was being noble.'

'You're wrong.' Edward paused ominously. 'It isn't unforgivable,' he went on, 'because I forgive you. And I understand why you did it, and so does Tom now. The truth is, I don't mind what you do, as long as you love me.'

He gave her such a warm, sad smile that Annie could hardly bear it. She sat up in the bath, clasping her knees. 'Edward,' she began, 'there's something I should explain.'

'No!' Edward sprang from the chair, making an odd gesture with his hand as if warding off a blow. He paced to the other end of the room and turned back to her, gripping the towel rail. 'No more words. I don't want to hear anything I won't be able to forget.' He took a breath and said more calmly, 'It's enough that you're back and that there are no more secrets in the family, and that we're truly together.' Edward plucked at the bath towel under his hand and came over to her.

'Come on, you beautiful mermaid. I'm starving.'

Annie stood up, water running down her body, and stepped into the warm embrace of the towel. Edward wound it about her, pulling her possessively close. She rested there a moment, eyes closed, ear to his heartbeat. This was how their love affair had begun, on a chilly night in Oxford when Edward had stepped from the shadows and enfolded her in his cloak. She had always known that he was the man for her. She could feel the depth of his anxiety and his passion. Tonight she would find a way to obliterate the last of his doubts.

While Edward went down to see to the wine, Annie put on her clothes, dressing up her trousers with a shimmery silk blouse and earrings, and spent extra time on her make-up and hair – enough to make her children whistle at her as she came down the stairs into the kitchen.

'I basted the pheasants,' Emma announced with a pink face. 'Was that right?'

'Absolutely inspired.' Annie hugged her.

When everyone was ready, and the candles had been lit, Annie carried the platter of pheasants to the table. Edward produced a bottle of champagne, eased out the cork with a gentle pop, and poured everyone a glass.

'What's this for?' Emma asked, putting her finger in the bubbles and licking it.

'A toast,' Edward said solemnly, 'to your mother – '

'*Me*?' Annie looked at him in surprise.

' – who, Rose tells me, has pulled off a two-million-dollar book deal.'

There was silence for a millisecond before Cassie asked, 'Are we rich? Can I go to New York and buy Armani clothes?'

'When you're as wise and mature as your brother, perhaps,' Annie answered, smiling into Tom's blue eyes.

He held her gaze. 'Can we watch the election on TV after dinner?'

When the last spoonful of crumble had been consumed, Annie urged everyone upstairs to the drawing-room while she cleared away and made coffee. Now that the moment had come, she felt too nervous to watch the election. She didn't think she could bear to see Jordan's face if he lost. And if he won, she wasn't sure she wanted anyone to see hers. When she could delay no longer, she carried up the coffee tray. Edward and Tom were on the sofa, the girls sprawled on the floor in front of a coal fire. Nothing much seemed to be happening, just a screenful of talking heads.

'Why do they keep talking about a "young" generation taking over?' Cassie was complaining. 'Jordan Hope is forty-six. He's got grey hair!'

'Only round the edges,' Emma pointed out fairly. 'I

think he's rather dishy. And he's miles younger than the other one. He fought in the First World War.'

'Second, birdbrain.' Tom walloped her over the head with a cushion.

When the squabble had died down, Annie concentrated on the television.

Gradually it dawned on her that everyone was acting as if Jordan had already won.

'Yeah!' Tom bounced on the sofa. 'He's got another state. He's bound to win now.'

'You're for Hope, then, are you?' Edward asked. 'Why?'

'He's so energetic, so alive. He really wants to help people – like you, Dad.' Tom sipped his coffee, then added, 'Besides, he wears great suits.'

'I suppose Rose will be very well positioned, if he wins,' Edward commented.

Annie looked at him. 'In what way?'

'Well, isn't she a friend of his?'

'Yes, but – ' Annie fell silent. 'I mean, it was very long ago.' Edward was right, though, she realised. It had not occurred to her before that Rose might have a personal stake in all this.

Cassie uncurled herself elegantly from the floor. 'If the drama's over, I'm going to bed,' she announced with a yawn.

'Me, too.' Emma scrambled after her.

Annie waved them goodnight, her eyes fixed to the screen which was flashing up scenes of jubilation across the country. Two more states fell to Jordan. They were talking of a landslide. A statistician came on, standing in front of a bank of giant bar charts. Tom drained his coffee and said it was time to hit the pillow. He wanted to set off for Oxford early the next day. Edward thought he had seen enough too, but when Annie rose to follow, he shook his head at her.

'No you watch if you want to. I need to have a shower first. I'll see you upstairs.'

384

Annie reached her hand over the back of the sofa. 'I won't be long – promise. You won't go to bed without me?'

Edward took her hand and rubbed it gently. 'I'll come and carry you up if I have to.'

He was at the door, when something clicked in Annie's head. 'Edward . . . it was you who sent me champagne at the Algonquin, wasn't it?'

'Who else?' The door shut behind him.

When Annie turned back to the screen, it was showing pictures of a little American town, the crowded streets hung with flags. The camera panned across stone and clapboard houses, with deep porches and scraps of front lawn. Even before the reporter said the words 'Indian Bluffs' Annie knew that this was Jordan's home town. She leaned forward, transfixed with curiosity. Here it was, just as he had described, the old schoolhouse with the bell on top, the white Baptist chapel, the grocery store shaded by a maple with astonishing bright leaves. And here was Jordan's childhood house, small and ordinary-looking, and a view of the Mississippi River, so vast it took her breath away. The Cherwell must have seemed like a ditch in comparison.

Before she had taken it all in the scene changed. Another reporter was shouting into the microphone against the baying of an ecstatic crowd. This was a clip from Jordan's airport reception at Jefferson City, where he had returned to the Governor's mansion that morning. Drum-majorettes in high white boots and very little else twirled batons with red, white and blue streamers. There were men in cowboy hats with 'Hope' rosettes in the hatband, women in shorts and T-shirts that proclaimed 'I Love Hope'. And suddenly, there he was, dressed in jeans and a tan suede jacket, smiling like an Oscar winner and shaking the hands stretched out to him. Annie pressed her fingers to her mouth, gazing at his face. Then he moved aside, and Annie saw his wife. She peered closer, trying to read the character of this neat, smiling woman, looking smaller and more vulnerable than Annie had expected.

When the telephone rang Annie reached impatiently for the instrument next to the sofa, then realised that it was her work line that was ringing. Immediately she thought of Sebastian. Had something gone wrong with the American deal? Dragging her eyes from the screen, she ran into the small back room and picked up the receiver. It sounded like a party. There was a roar of conversation, and muffled squeals of excitement.

'Sebastian?' she asked doubtfully, when no one spoke.

The noise receded, as if a door had been closed. 'Are you alone?' said a voice.

'Jordan!' Annie gave an incredulous laugh. 'I've just been watching you on television. You were getting off a plane. I've seen your house, and your little town and the river.' She tugged at her hair, to stop herself babbling. '. . . Is anything wrong?'

'Nothing's wrong. I just called to say thank you.'

'For what?'

'For telling me about Tom,' he said, his voice low. 'It was kind of a turning-point for me. Last week I was almost beginning to lose faith in myself – wondering if I was just a smiling dummy with nothing inside, begging the world to love me. I'd even started writing my speech conceding victory. You changed that. You can't imagine what it was like seeing you again, remembering the old days, and knowing I had a son.'

'We don't *know* that,' Annie said gently. 'We'll never know for sure.'

She heard Jordan sigh. 'Maybe it isn't the biological truth, but for me it's a kind of moral truth. It feels right. It makes sense of all that doubt and turmoil at Oxford. It makes up for not having kids with Ginny. When I saw that picture of Tom, I suddenly felt as if I had a personal stake in the next generation. I was darned if I was going to let the other guy win. I think that knowing about Tom will make me a better President.'

'You'll be a brilliant President,' Annie said. Hot tears stung her eyes.

'It means that what we felt for each other all those years ago was real. It wasn't true what I said in Chicago, in that funny old hotel room. It wasn't just sex, was it?'

'No,' she whispered.

'Well, not *just* sex, anyway,' Jordan teased, trying to make her laugh. 'By the way, who's Sebastian?'

'One of my lovers, of course,' Annie said lightly. With a wave of anguish she realised that she would never see Jordan again. This would be the last time they spoke. She swallowed hard, determined not to cry.

'Annie, I wish – ' But she would never know what he wished. There was another burst of celebratory noise at Jordan's end, and a woman's voice yelling, 'Come *on!*'

'I have to go,' Jordan said urgently. 'I'm sorry. Thanks for everything. I won't forget.'

'Good luck!' Annie called, as the line went dead. She wondered if he had heard.

For a long moment she stood quietly in her study, staring into the garden. Then she took a tissue from her desk drawer, blew her nose firmly and went back into the living-room. She switched off the television. She had seen all she needed to. Jordan had won. Tom had not stopped him. It seemed, in fact, that he had helped him. And she had made the right decision, all those years ago. She was glad not to be the wife standing in the shadows. She was herself, Annie Hamilton. A new career awaited her and, upstairs, Edward's warm, familiar presence.

The fire was still burning brightly. Annie squatted down to scatter the coals, and felt something jab her thigh. She reached into her pocket and drew out the envelope Tom had given her earlier. She had forgotten all about it. Her heart jumped when she saw what was inside: the photograph that Rose had taken of her and Jordan the morning after the Magdalen ball. Annie knelt on the floor and peered closely at the faded image in the firelight. It was years since she had seen it. A flood of nostalgia washed over her. She couldn't help smiling. There was Jordan, young and carefree and irresistible, with his shirt unbuttoned and his laughing eyes creased against the sun. She rubbed a finger gently over his face and sighed, then turned the photograph over. Her heart melted at the sight of his sloping American handwriting. The old song ran through her head. *Love me two times, girl.* Oh, I did, she thought. I did.

She looked again at the image of the two of them, at Jordan's bare forearm clasping her tight, at the intimate curve of her body into his. Tom's instincts had been impeccable. She was filled with amazement and gratitude. Giving her back the photograph was a gesture of tact and grace worthy of Edward. On the other hand, the eyes that looked out at her from the faded old picture – those eyes, surely, were also the eyes of her son.

Annie roused herself. The picture had caused enough trouble. Her final glance was at herself – at the glowing face and tumbling hair of the girl she once was, that she was no longer. With a resolute gesture, she held the picture to the fire. The shiny surface blistered and blackened, and spurted into flame. She twisted it this way and that, then dropped the little square of burning paper into the grate and watched until the last corner was consumed.

EPILOGUE

Rose sat at the computer in her darkened study, still wearing the scarlet dress which had caused such a sensation at her Election Party. It was four in the morning, but sleep was out of the question. Entering the list of files she brought down the highlight bar over 'SPECIAL.REL' and tapped the 'Delete' key. Immediately the screen blinked at her: 'Delete SPECIAL.REL? No/Yes?' Rose's hand hovered over the keyboard: one tap of her forefinger and the whole thing would disappear.

Rose had promised herself that she would wipe the file if Jordan were elected President. She had no time for God, but she did have a shadowy concept of some giant ledger in the sky that balanced favours given with favours received. Jordan was on his way to the White House, where she wanted him; in return, she ought to consign the scandal of his illegitimate son to oblivion. But now that the moment had come, she hesitated.

She stood up and paced restlessly round the room, pausing at the window to raise the blind and look out at the city she had conquered. After tonight's spectacular success, there could be no doubt of that. It had been the kind of all-American party that only an English genius could have conceived and orchestrated. Rose had hired a vast loft space in SoHo that perfectly combined sixties casualness with the new nineties disdain for ostentation. *Le tout* New York had crammed into the industrial iron-meshed elevator, decorated with red, white and blue balloons, and pronounced it FUN: senators and anchor-women, millionaires and rock stars; society women in Versace and diamonds, who had hardly ever been further downtown than Lord and Taylor; busty *arrivistes* in leather miniskirts and peroxide crops, who had only ever gone uptown to neck in Central Park. The photographers and gossip columnists were in seventh heaven. In one corner the latest supermodel wilted anorectically before a famous American writer in his trademark white suit. In another, an Oscar winner flashed her horsy teeth at a handsome young Kennedy. On the dot of midnight that hot English novelist with a face like a bloodhound, who was covering the party for *Harpers*, had passed out dramatically in the arms of a famously camp painter.

Music from Jordan Hope's baby-boomer generation had played all night – the Supremes, the Rolling Stones, Joni Mitchell, Bob Dylan, the Doors. Rose had raided the model agencies for the prettiest boys and girls in town to act as waiters. Dressed in jeans and white T-shirts, they had served mini-hamburgers, oysters, Cajun delicacies, and the special brand of corn chips Jordan was known to favour. To drink, there was champagne, American beer in cans and Ozark Mountain Spring Water. All evening giant television screens relayed the election drama as it unfolded. After Jordan's acceptance speech, the waiters had poured more champagne and handed round slices of Mississippi mud pie.

The event had been original and hugely enjoyable. It would not be forgotten. The society pages would be plastered with photographs and reports. Rose's status would soar, transforming her from trivial magazine queen to an opinion-former, a broker between the worlds of politics and the media. Her network of friends and contacts included the man who was now President. Rose intended to be a frequent guest at the White House over the next four years. She would make sure that Jordan knew how much he owed her. Not only had she averted the scandal of Tom; she had neutralised someone much closer to home.

Rose had enjoyed her game of cat and mouse with Rick. He had been smart enough to guess at some scandal threatening Jordan, but without names he was nowhere. Rick was a control freak. He hated anyone knowing something he didn't. If she played him right, she might be able to keep him interested right through the presidency.

Rose had not forgotten the humiliation and pain she had endured in that Harley Street clinic twenty-two years ago. Yes, Rick had paid for the damned thing, but that had been the limit of his involvement. He had never shown the slightest sympathy, never asked afterwards if she was all right, never apologised. Now she could twitch his leash. Rose sighed with satisfaction. She had eaten her cake, and had it too. She had helped Annie, as she had promised. She had distracted Tom from his dangerous quest – that had been more fun than she expected. In return she had a foothold in the White House. She could persuade Rick to give her profiles when she wanted them, and she had a link to the President himself. One day she would find an opportunity to lure Jordan to a quiet corner of the Rose Garden and tell him, oh so regretfully, the truth about Rick Goodman. She was looking forward to it.

Rose had begun recording the story of Jordan, Annie and Tom as a form of insurance. It was not impossible that some reporter could have got on to Tom and leaked the scandal; Rose couldn't endure the notion that someone else might get the jump on her. Now the danger had passed; it would be foolhardy to preserve the evidence.

Still she hesitated. It was such a great story: the illegitimate son searching for his father, the ambitious politician, the pretty, sympathetic girl who falls from grace – even the scheming, go-between editrix, always calculating the angles, figuring the pitch. She could just see the movie – with Angelica Huston playing her part. At last she could be tall! With legs!

Rose turned back into the room eerily lit from the blue screen. That bloody cursor was still winking at her. 'Delete SPECIAL.REL? No/Yes?' Rose could not help feeling that it would be a terrible shame to waste it. One day, when her stock had peaked and some young whippersnapper threatened to cut her off at the knees as she had done to many a rival, she might need a good story. Re-election time was not that far away: who knew what skeletons might have popped out of Jordan and Ginny Hope's cupboard by then? Rose wouldn't want to forgo the chance of playing her trump card.

Rose waggled her head in a way that her close colleagues would recognise as the sign of a deliciously intriguing, slightly naughty, hugely saleable idea scorching its path through their editor's brain. She shook back her bangles with a defiant flourish, and with an immaculately buffed fingernail tapped 'No'.

A Selection of Fiction Available from Mandarin

While every effort is made to keep prices low, it is sometimes necessary to increase prices at sho
Mandarin Paperbacks reserves the right to show new retail prices on covers which may differ from
previously advertised in the text or elsewhere.

The prices shown below were correct at the time of going to press.

☐	7493 1313 7	**French Silk**	Sandra Brown	£4.99
☐	7493 1830 9	**Swan**	Naomi Campbell	£5.99
☐	7493 1709 4	**Unsentimental Journey**	Vera Cowie	£5.99
☐	7493 1836 8	**Suddenly**	Barbara Delinsky	£5.99
☐	7493 1597 0	**More Than Friends**	Barbara Delinsky	£5.99
☐	7493 1251 3	**The First Wives Club**	Olivia Goldsmith	£5.99
☐	7493 2055 9	**Summer Madness**	Susan Lewis	£5.99
☐	7493 1321 8	**Vengeance**	Susan Lewis	£4.99
☐	7493 1320 X	**Obsession**	Susan Lewis	£5.99
☐	7493 1813 9	**Charity**	Lesley Pearse	£5.99
☐	7493 1808 2	**Tara**	Lesley Pearse	£5.99
☐	7493 1470 2	**Georgia**	Lesley Pearse	£5.99
☐	7493 1798 1	**The Love of a Bad Woman**	Rose Shepherd	£5.99
☐	7493 1098 7	**Too Rich, Too Thin**	Rose Shepherd	£5.99
☐	7493 1356 0	**Happy Ever After**	Rose Shepherd	£5.99
☐	7493 1593 8	**Soft Focus**	Tess Stimson	£5.99

All these books are available at your bookshop or newsagent, or can be ordered direct from the address below. Just tick the titles you want and fill in the form below.

Cash Sales Department, PO Box 5, Rushden, Northants NN10 6YX.
Fax: 01933 414047 : Phone: 01933 414000.

Please send cheque, payable to 'Reed Book Services Ltd.', or postal order for purchase price quoted and allow the following for postage and packing:

£1.00 for the first book, 50p for the second; **FREE POSTAGE AND PACKING FOR THREE BOOKS OR MORE PER ORDER.**

NAME (Block letters) ....

ADDRESS ....

....

☐ I enclose my remittance for ....

☐ I wish to pay by Access/Visa Card Number

Expiry Date

Signature ....

Please quote our reference: MAND